Blood Feast

Blood Grace Book VIII

VELA ROTH

FIVE THORNS PRESS

Copyright © 2024 Vela Roth

All rights reserved. No part of this book may be reproduced in any form or by any electronic or mechanical means, including information storage and retrieval systems, without permission in writing from the publisher, except by reviewers, who may quote brief passages in a review. For more information, contact: velaroth@fivethorns.com

This is a work of fiction. Names, characters, places, and incidents either are the product of the author's imagination or are used fictitiously. Any resemblance to actual persons, living or dead, events, or locales is entirely coincidental.

ISBN 978-1-957040-24-0 (Ebook)
ISBN 978-1-957040-25-7 (Paperback)
ISBN 978-1-957040-26-4 (Hardcover)

Cover art by Patcas Illustration
www.instagram.com/patcas_illustration

Book design by Vela Roth

Maps by Vela Roth using Inkarnate
inkarnate.com

Published by Five Thorns Press
www.fivethorns.com

Visit www.velaroth.com

CONTENTS

Content Note ix
Maps x
22 Nights Until Winter Solstice 1
    A New Force of Nature 3
21 Nights Until Winter Solstice 13
    Reentering the World 15
    First Ritual 26
    The Next Duel 39
    A Most Personal Enemy 46
    The Complication 58
    An Old Nemesis 71
    Path of Destruction 76
20 Nights Until Winter Solstice 83
    A Future Dreamed 85
    A Worthy Artifact 94
10 Nights Until Winter Solstice 101
    Imperfect but Unbroken 103
    Eternal Oath 115
    Words in Blood 125
6 Nights Until Winter Solstice 133
    A Badge of Honor 135
    Reforged 142
    Fallen Immortals 151
    Nonnegotiable 157
Vigil of Mercy 167

Into the Unknown	169
Fugitives	181
How Negotiations End	189
Forgotten Rituals	194
Vigil of Union	**205**
Prey	207
The Burden of Violence	217
The Mourning Circle	224
The Sorceress's Duty	231
Vigil of the Gift	**239**
No Escape	241
A Spreading Fire	247
Winter Solstice	**257**
Salt and Bones	259
The Most Important Lesson	267
On Wing	274
Trial by Leaf	286
Trial by Claw	292
In Hespera's Honor	299
The Real Tower	309
10 Nights After Winter Solstice	**315**
Weapon Master	317
21 Nights After Winter Solstice	**327**
Call of Glass	329
Traitors' Grave	335
The Bargain	344
Heart Wounds	352
22 Nights After Winter Solstice	**357**
Her Only Protector	359
25 Nights After Winter Solstice	**363**
Peace Offering	365
26 Nights After Winter Solstice	**373**
Chasing Ghosts	375
Ritual Ground	386
Dangerous Experiments	396

40 Nights After Winter Solstice 407
Following Smoke 409
The Law of Loyalty 419
Atonement 433
41 Nights After Winter Solstice 445
Dame 447
44 Nights After Winter Solstice 449
The Real Goal 451
The Mage King's Fires 462
The Survivors 470
Three Times Three 477
The Contingency Plan 482
45 Nights After Winter Solstice 489
A Hesperine Heart 491
As A Circle 498
The Heart of the Lustra 505
46 Nights After Winter Solstice 517
The Final Sanctuary 519
Lio's Vow 531
The Barrow 542
The Relic Blade 552
The Wound 563
Justice 568
54 Nights After Winter Solstice 577
The Most Powerful Mage of this Epoch 579
Glossary 585

For USBP. Thank you for always empathizing, making me laugh, getting stabby in my defense, and encouraging me to see the mind healers. I couldn't ask for a better real-life errant circle.

CONTENT NOTE

For your self-care, content warnings can be found on the author's website at vroth.co/cw.

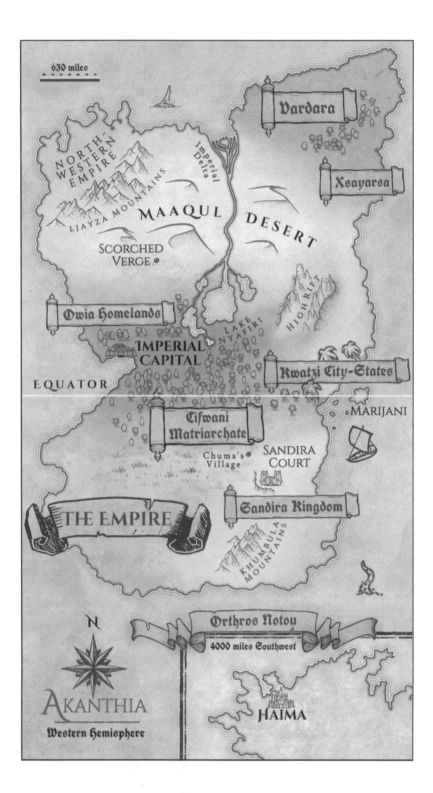

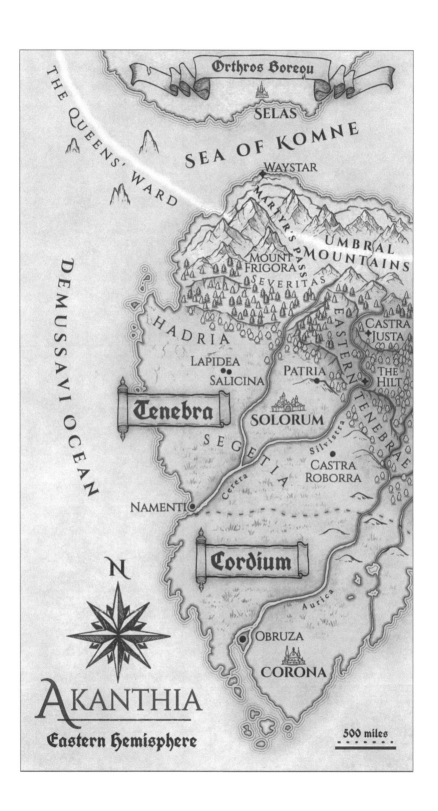

22
nights until
WINTER SOLSTICE

A NEW FORCE OF NATURE

MAGIC COURSED IN CASSIA'S veins, a thrill along her every nerve. Raw power throbbed up from beneath her feet and flowed through her as naturally as blood. Her heart pounded in time to her spell, and she heard her Grace's heart beating in unison.

Lio's voice sounded in her mind. *Now try one more time to channel your magic back to its source.*

She braced herself against the ultimate temptation—to pull him deeper into her spell. To get lost in this flow together. To pleasure him with it until she tasted his ecstasy in his blood.

She focused all her Will on her raging power and pushed it in the opposite direction. It only tangled tighter inside her, grasping, loving.

She bared her fangs. With a growl, she bent her magic and drove it back down into the ground. A shattering sound hurt her sensitive ears. The power of the Lustra, the wilds, retreated from her body and left her in her own skin.

Blinking to clear her vision, she beheld Lio's offered wrist. Her fangs shot farther out of her gums, and the spell lights in the tower room were suddenly bright to her dilated eyes. All her senses honed in on the delicate blue veins beneath his pale skin. But she made her parched tongue wait a moment longer, merely to prove she could.

"You need a sip after that much magical exertion," he said.

His voice undid her. She took his wrist in both her hands and sank her fangs into him. He gave a little hum of satisfaction and wrapped his other arm tightly around her.

She dragged in a mouthful of his blood and moaned in relief. Her world shrank to the Drink. The pressure of his flesh against her fangs. The warmth of his essence sliding down her throat. His magic cascading into her veins.

When he caressed her head, she remembered herself. She carefully withdrew her fangs but kept her mouth over the bite, licking gently at his torn wrist to heal him. As discreetly as she could, she lapped the remaining blood from his skin and her own lips. She was getting better at not making a mess. She was also greedy for every last smear of his blood. Lifting her head, she found him smiling down at her.

"Well done," he said. "You managed a channeling and a drink without losing control. Of course, you know I love it when you lose control, but this bodes well for our effort to leave our residence eventually."

"We've kept ourselves locked in here for a month. I have to learn faster if we ever want to see our family and friends again."

"They understand why we need this time in seclusion after your Gifting. They all faced the challenge of having powerful magic made even more powerful by the Gift of immortality."

"They mastered basic Hesperine skills like stepping and levitation in less than a month. I haven't even gotten to attempt those yet because I'm too busy trying not to cause explosions."

"They don't have your unique, never-before-seen duality of Lustra plant magic and Hesperine blood magic." He grinned, his own fangs unsheathed in response to her drink. "The amount of time a new Hesperine needs is always proportionate to their power. Therefore, you need a *lot* of time, and I will keep you in this tower until you've had plenty."

She licked her lips again. His black hair was windswept from her spell, his robe hanging half open over his bare chest. Their veil hours robes were the only things resembling clothes they had worn since the night of her transformation. She tended to lose control of her hunger at any given moment, upon any convenient surface, whether their bed, his desk, or the floor of the practice room.

But losing control of her magic wasn't nearly as enjoyable. They stood in the warded chamber where Lio had spent years mastering his volatile affinities for mind magic and light magic. The results of their experiments with her abilities surrounded them. Every test subject was in pieces, destroyed by the sheer amount of her power. A riot of rose vines in full bloom grew through the rubble.

Their latest victims lay at Cassia's feet. A scroll, now in shreds. A spare pane of glass from Lio's workshop, now in fragments. And a stone vase—miraculously undamaged, dangling from a branch of roses.

She nudged a fat bloom away with her toe. "I must do better than this."

"Be patient with yourself. We've scarcely begun to study your magic, and the results of our tests are unprecedented!"

That brought a smile to her face. At least her scrollworm was enjoying the research her magic required.

He waved a hand at the only intact furniture in the room, a warded chest, and the lid opened. His quill flew into his hand, and a scroll levitated before him. His eyes alight, he scrawled an addition to his notes. "This is progress! Resilient materials such as stone can now survive in proximity to your spells. With more practice, you'll be able to regulate your magic so you no longer break glass or shred paper, either."

Cassia sighed at the mess. "I'd ask you to teach me a cleaning spell if I wasn't afraid I'd disintegrate the entire tower trying to cast it."

Lio only chuckled. His amusement felt like a warm tickle in her own heart. To think, when she had been human, she had felt their empathic bond only in flashes. Now that her Gifting had fully awakened their Grace Union, she scarcely knew how she had existed without this constant connection to him. She sank a little deeper into their bond, and her frustration eased into contentment.

He turned to her, his notes forgotten, and placed a soft, slow kiss on her neck. Her new skin seemed to come alive under his lips. Her Hesperine senses weren't as unbearably raw as they had been right after her transformation, but she still wasn't accustomed to how sensitive she was everywhere. As much as she loved it when Lio grew a beard, for now she relished the smoothness of his clean-shaven face as he nuzzled her throat.

She tried to keep her wits about her. *Perhaps you should at least pay a visit to the main house to reassure everyone.*

I won't leave you alone with your magic and your Craving. You aren't ready for me to be out of arm's reach.

Her arms tightened around him instinctively. He was right.

Are you really in such a hurry to leave our tower? he asked.

She leaned into him. *No. I could stay here forever.*

Let me keep you to myself a little longer.

But worries from the world beyond intruded into her thoughts.

He gave her throat an adamant nip, and the sting of his teeth jolted her back to the here and now. *I know there's a war. I know people we love are in danger. But the warriors don't require diplomats like us right now. At this moment in eternity, your duty is to yourself, and mine is entirely to you.*

Her Grace instincts overtook her again, promising to banish her reason. She nuzzled his throat, her body melting against him of its own accord.

He slid his hand into her hair, tugging to give her the pressure her new senses liked. *Do I need to take you back to bed and make you forget the rest of the world? Or can you concentrate on your next magic lesson?* A wicked gleam filled his aura. *If you make it through one more lesson first, I'll keep you in bed twice as long, and we'll try something we haven't done with your Hesperine body yet.*

What a scandalous magic teacher you are.

Can you deny it's an effective way to motivate my student?

You know I can't deny you anything. She slid out of his arms and opened her arcane senses again.

The Lustra magic leapt up from below in answer. The letting site that her Gifting had created under the tower was a wild thing, always waiting for her to set it free. As miraculous as it was that she had opened a wellspring of nature magic for the first time in untold centuries, it made mastering her abilities much more complicated.

Lio sent his notes back into the safety of the chest. "Now I want you to practice resisting the letting site's pull."

Cassia mentally swatted away more tendrils of power trying to rise up into her. "For how long?"

"One minute longer than last time—while it's misbehaving." He lifted his hand to his mouth and bit into his palm.

"Oh, bleeding thorns," Cassia swore, realizing what he was about to do.

He made a libation of his blood on the flowers her power had brought to life. She felt the impact of those red droplets as a quake under her feet. Her letting site opened for her Grace's blood, and her mouth watered.

His light magic flared behind her eyelids, his thelemancy shadowing her mind. He was a part of the letting site, as much as he was a part of her, for they had made this magical phenomenon together the same night they had created her new Hesperine form.

The Lustra crashed up from the depths of the earth, drunk on his power. She wanted it. Needed to feel their combined magics feeding her veins.

No. Control. He had saved her life again and again with his magic. Now she finally had the strength to protect him in return. She must learn to use it.

She gritted her teeth and snapped her senses shut against the onslaught of magic. It filled the air and coiled around her, but she held it at bay, shaking with the effort not to channel it through her.

Lio gripped her hand, the physical contact anchoring her to the mundane world, even as her mind was swept up in the arcane. "That's it! You're doing so well. I knew you would."

After the ridicule she had faced throughout her human life, Lio's praise was always a balm. She squeezed his hand, grateful for his faith in her. The way he taught her magic made her feel as if she could do anything.

She stood fast against the force of her own power and made her Will known to it. *You do not control me. You belong to me.*

That's right, My Queen, Lio purred in her mind.

The Lustra coiled tight around her, but she centered herself, deep within her strong, new body where blood magic beat through her heart.

"One minute longer!" Lio said. "You're almost there."

He counted off the seconds in her mind. But the Lustra pushed against her mental defenses. And then, as if it had sprouted thorns, it sent sharp points of pain through her arcane senses. She gasped, feeling Lio's alarm in their Union.

Her letting site would never try to harm her. *This is a cry of pain. It's pleading for help, like the letting site at Paradum.*

That's impossible. Lio wrapped his arms around her. *At the Paradum site, the Lustra was damaged because the Collector stole your plant magic from you there. Your letting site is safe here in Orthros behind the Queens' ward, where the Collector cannot wound it—or you.*

But something is wrong. I have to listen.

Yes, he acquiesced. He couldn't hide his worry from her.

Cassia surrendered her control, and the Lustra magic overwhelmed her.

A vision took shape in her mind's eye. She raced along familiar halls—the secret passages inside Solorum Palace left behind by her ancestor, the Changing Queen, which still held her magical secrets.

The maze of corridors opened into a broad underground passage, too fast for Cassia to have any sense of direction. Ahead of her loomed a round portal sealed by a massive stone.

It's the door I saw in Miranda's thoughts, Lio said, *when I battled the Collector inside her mind so we could escape Paradum.*

In this vision, vines of Hespera's Roses grew along the passageway. As Cassia neared the door, the blooms wilted, and their leaves shriveled and died. Dread filled her the closer she came to that door. When she was close enough to reach out and touch it, she saw blood streaming down her hand.

The vision broke. Magic rushed out of her, and even her immortal body felt weak at the sudden depletion. She opened her eyes and found herself staring into Lio's dark blue gaze, which gleamed with magic. He held her on his lap on the floor. The flowers around them were still bright and fragrant, one tendril of roses growing against her cheek as if to make sure she was all right.

Lio caressed her other cheek, his distant gaze focusing on her again. "All is well with your letting site. I can feel that the magic is still pure. Kallikrates cannot attack us here." The Collector's true name left Lio's lips and puffed out of existence. The necromancer had no power in Hespera's Sanctuary.

But he was still at large in the human world.

Cassia swallowed. "We've certainly felt the Lustra's Will before, but… can our letting site…communicate?"

Lio hesitated. "According to what we know, it seems that all letting sites are connected to the Lustra as a whole. In theory, it is magically possible for one letting site to alert us of events near other sites in Tenebra."

"Then this was a warning." Her hand tightened on the front of his robe. "The Lustra is trying to tell us that Kallikrates hasn't given up on opening that door."

Lio's jaw clenched. "That can't be."

She shuddered at her hazy memories of their last battle with the Collector and his fanatical servant. The girl who had once been her dearest friend. "I thought you learned from Miranda's mind that his plan had two requirements."

"That's right. The first requirement was stealing your magic. Now that you're a Hesperine, he can never take it from you. His plan is ruined."

"He should have given up."

"Yes." Lio's fraught emotions felt like a gathering storm. "It should be over."

Cassia reached up and touched his face. "But it isn't."

Lio closed his eyes, leaning into her hand.

"We should have known," she said. "He wouldn't give up a conspiracy of centuries so easily."

"Of course. He has plans within plans."

What had Kallikrates done while she and Lio had been hidden away here? The last time they had seen her sister and their Trial brothers, they had been under siege.

Lio held her closer, tucking her head under his chin. "Don't you dare feel guilty for being unable to fight at their sides. Mak and Lyros will keep Solia, and each other, safe."

"What if...when we leave the tower...bad news is waiting for us?"

"It won't be. Trust Rudhira and the Charge to watch over them."

"You're right." Cassia let herself rest in Lio's arms a moment longer. If anyone could protect their people from Kallikrates, it was the First Prince of Orthros and his force of Hesperines errant.

She tried to think back to their last encounter with Rudhira at Paradum. "I have no memory of when he came to our rescue after the battle with Miranda. But you talked to him, didn't you? You had a chance to warn him what you learned from her mind?"

Lio was silent for an instant too long.

"No," he confessed at last. "I was so focused on getting you to safety. I didn't think to warn them about anything."

She could feel the possible consequences of that playing out in his emotions. His heart beat faster, and her own picked up pace to match.

"We left Miranda a captive at Paradum," Cassia reasoned. "She's most likely in Rudhira's dungeon now, and he found out everything he needs to know from interrogating her."

Lio gentled his tone. "I'm not sure he took any prisoners."

"Oh," Cassia murmured.

It was an unexpected blow. This was the result of her and Miranda's choices in life. Cassia had survived to become Rudhira's immortal Ritual daughter. Her one-time friend had gotten herself killed at the end of his sword.

No. Her friend had died a long time ago, when Miranda had willingly surrendered herself to the Collector's service.

There was no time now to mourn the girl she had once been. If her secrets had died with her, they were in deep trouble.

"I hate how much we don't know," Cassia said. "If Kallikrates is willing to go to such lengths to open the door, what could possibly be inside? And what harm will come to everyone if he accesses it?"

"I cannot bear to imagine," Lio replied.

"His second requirement is already met. He has the war he wanted—between Hesperines and the Mage Orders on Tenebran soil."

"We have to warn everyone," Lio said. "They need to know that the war they're fighting is exactly what Kallikrates wants."

Anger burned through Cassia. She didn't want to heed the letting site's call. She wasn't ready. How did the Lustra expect her to prevent whatever disaster lurked behind that door? She could barely control her own magic or survive a few hours without Lio's blood.

"I'm not ready, either," Lio confessed, his voice rough. "Almost losing you—again—changed everything. Gaining you forever changed everything. Even after we leave the tower, I won't be able to share you the way I did before your Gifting. Not with our duties, not even with people we love."

His rare possessiveness was the reassurance she needed. Somehow, when they left this enchanted world they had all to themselves, they wouldn't lose it. They would take the true depths of their Grace bond with them.

She wrapped her fingers around the braid of her hair he wore around his neck. "Remember what I told you when I first woke after my Gifting. I'm not capable of putting anything or anyone ahead of you now. That was another life. Another me. You are my everything now, and you always will be."

He wrapped his hand around his Grace braid on her ankle. "That's what I need, Cassia."

Her sweet, selfless Lio. He so rarely asked for anything for himself. For him to make such an appeal told her how necessary it was. She was ready to bleed to give him what he needed.

Her fears whispered to her. The world would not heed her promises. Allies would keep asking more of them, and enemies would keep trying to tear her away from him.

But she no longer relied on meager mortal strength to resist them.

She let Lio see her fangs. "Now I have the power to fight anyone who dares come between us. If they threaten you, I won't need control over my magic. All I'll need to do is let it loose."

"Goddess," he breathed. "You're so beautiful when you're making threats."

She pulled his mouth to hers, and their kiss was a rough, demanding promise to each other. Their shared fury pounded through their Grace Union, growing more powerful as it cycled between them, and yet somehow easier to bear.

They weren't ready to face the world, and yet they shared the same conviction. Their allies and their enemies were about to meet a new force of nature they could never have imagined.

The world was not ready for them.

21
nights until
WINTER SOLSTICE

REENTERING THE WORLD

"The pendant and our medallions can't be gone." Cassia stood in despair amid the masses of rose vines and moonflowers growing all over their bedchamber.

"They're not gone," Lio said. "They're simply…not evident at the moment."

Cassia put a hand to her chest. She was dressed to leave their residence, but without her two talismans, she felt like a piece of her was missing. "Oh, Goddess. What if my magic disintegrated them?"

"The Changing Queen's pendant is an artifact of Lustra magic, and our ambassador medallions are artifacts of blood magic. I doubt your power is harmful to them."

"Where was the last place you saw them?"

He scratched his head. "The floor, where I threw them while I was stripping us naked for your Gifting."

She peered between the flowers covering one of the carpets. "When you lost your medallion before, you were able to sense it with your magic and find it. Surely that will work now."

"I can't detect its resonance," he admitted. "Why don't you try?"

She flexed her senses amid the profusion of magics in the room. Within the Sanctuary ward that sheltered their bedchamber, blood magic and Lustra magic lay tangled up like wanton lovers. Light magic and thelemancy emanated from Lio's stained glass windows. The scent of his blood on the messy bedclothes threatened her focus until he cast a cleaning spell.

"I can't begin to separate a particular magical signature from all the spells in here," Cassia said. "Wait. Let me try one more idea."

She called out to the letting site, softly, so as not to provoke a raging channeling again. She sensed its mournful answer.

Where are our medallions and my pendant? She knew a force of nature didn't comprehend words or even images, so she focused on what the talismans felt like to her arcane senses. *They hold great power. I need them so I can protect the Lustra.*

A vine of roses and another of moonflowers snaked higher up one of the iron bed posts. When they were on Cassia's eye level, their leaves parted to reveal what dangled from their branches.

"No," Cassia cried. "How could this happen?"

Lio bent to study what remained of the artifacts, his aura bright with fascination.

Their two silver ambassador medallions had fused together with her ancestor's wooden pendant caught between them. The transformed artifact overflowed with their combined magics, just like everything else in the room.

Lio grinned. "I like this arcane pattern we've established, my Grace."

"What if I ruined them? This might have changed or broken the important enchantments that were already on them!"

"Your Gifting consecrated these artifacts. We can only wait and see what new magic they manifest." He reached out and gently took the melded talismans in hand.

When they broke apart in his hold, he gasped. The two halves fell onto his palms. The Changing Queen's pendant was still joined to Cassia's medallion, but it had not left Lio's untouched. Three wooden ivy leaves remained fused to the silver amid its celestial designs.

"What did I tell you?" he said in wonder. "You've left your mark on me. Thank you, Cassia. To be blessed by a Silvicultrix, by the Lustra…I appreciate how rare that is."

They untangled their ambassador cords and put on their medallions. The sight of him wearing her mark stirred a base sense of satisfaction in her. The letting site purred in response.

His own aura heated as a slow smile spread across his face. "Yes, I appreciate that very much."

Knowing he bore her mark, not only on his medallion but in his blood, she felt a little readier to leave the tower. They headed for the door, but she paused in front of the new window he had crafted during their seclusion. She touched the glass as if bidding this month farewell. And yet he had somehow captured it in the panes of blood red roses and pure white moonflowers.

He took her hand and ran her fingers over one of the flaws in the glass, which an unpredictable surge of her magic had created during his crafting process. "You know the imperfections are my favorite part of the design."

She wasn't sure how they dragged themselves down the stairs to the entrance hall. Lio's mood dimmed with every level they descended. She stood there before the front doors and started to take a deep breath to brace herself. Then she remembered she didn't need to breathe.

She didn't need a cloak, either. Lio, deprived of his ritual of bundling her up, kissed her forehead instead.

She smiled in the hopes of alleviating his somber mood. "I can finally dance naked in the snow without getting cold. Care to join me later?"

That got a laugh out of him. "Well, when you put it like that, there are advantages to leaving our residence after all."

She took his hands. "This isn't the end of anything, Lio. It's the beginning of our new lives together as Hesperines."

"I'm sorry. Of course it is. Don't think I'm not looking forward to this. I'm so proud of you. I can't wait for everyone to see the Hesperine you've become."

"You have nothing to apologize for. Of course you would rather keep me naked and locked in the tower with you for another month or eight."

"So very tempting." He adjusted the high collar of his red festival robe. "But I won't have you miss any of the traditions of Hesperine life. The family will want to hold your first Ritual tonight to welcome you into our bloodline. As soon as I sent our note ahead to the main house, I imagine my mother went into a whirlwind of preparation. She'll manage to make tonight special, war or no war."

Cassia smoothed the robe she had chosen for her presentation to the family, her black one embroidered with Hespera's Roses. "You'll have to help me remember the right words to say during the ceremony."

"I'll be with you every step of the way." He put on a smile for her.

She could still feel the specters lurking in his emotions. She would find a way to reassure him, she swore.

A plan came to her in that moment. It was the best way, perhaps the only way, to truly reassure Lio that their love was her first priority. But could she do it on such short notice in the middle of a war? With help from all the Hesperines who cared about them, it might just be possible.

"Go ahead, my Grace." He gestured to the double doors. "Your immortal future awaits."

The heavy iron panels felt light to her now. She opened their Sanctuary and, with her hand in his, reentered the world.

This time alone with him in the tower had become her reality, and setting foot outside felt like a dream. No shock of icy wind hit her in the lungs to jolt her awake. The cold of her beloved Orthros wrapped around her, familiar and safe. Fresh snow covered the terrace, and the starlight on that blanket of white was all the light she needed to see. Her swift eyes could track every snowflake that fluttered around them.

She let out a giddy laugh. She was impervious. She was free.

She lifted her face to Hespera's night sky and found herself riveted.

Lio stood at her back and wrapped his arms around her, looking up at their Goddess's domain with her. "You can feel it now, can't you?"

"I can *feel* the *sky*."

"How does it feel to you?" His aura stirred with curiosity. "Tell me everything."

As a bloodborn, her Grace had never been a new Hesperine. His mother's transformation had made him immortal in the womb. Cassia was happy he could experience this with her now.

"It feels vast," she said. "Deep. As if that vastness is inside my chest. The blood moon is running in my veins—I can feel its pulse. And the light moon is shining under my skin."

"And how does the garden feel?"

She stretched her senses and her gaze out over the grounds of House Komnena. The neglected gardens had always been a wild tangle of arctic plants that clung to life in Orthros's frozen soil.

But now they struck her nose with a thousand verdant scents. Despite the cloak of polar night, the bushes hung heavy with bearberries, and the dwarf willows were in full bloom. Vines of Hespera's sacred thorns had overflowed the arbor in front of the tower and formed a bastion around the terrace.

"I think they like your letting site," Lio concluded.

"Oh, my. Weeding will be even worse than I thought." She couldn't wait to get started.

But as they walked along the paths toward the main house, her delight faded.

"What is your greatest worry?" Lio asked. "Let us see if we can defeat it before we join everyone."

"Thank you, my champion, but I'm being foolish. The world is going up in flames, and the one I'm most worried about is..."

"Your dog."

Cassia nodded. "We can explain things to people. Animals don't understand."

"Knight is no ordinary animal. He will understand."

"What if he doesn't even recognize me?"

"You've been his entire world since he was a puppy. He'll be overjoyed to see you again."

"I'm his to protect, his *kaetlii*...or I was. Now the mortal he was bonded to is a Hesperine, a being he was bred to hunt. What if my Gifting severed our connection?"

"He already has a powerful bond with your Hesperine family. He will with you, as well."

"It might be worse for him if the bond didn't break." She swallowed the lump in her throat. "Liegehounds can't survive separation from their *kaetlii*. After a month without me, he might be gravely ill."

"But he recognizes Zoe as a *kaetlii* now, too. Staying with her this month will have kept him safe."

A frantic bark came from the distance, then another. Cassia's hand tightened on Lio's.

He smiled. "It sounds like Knight is waiting for you at the goat barn. I dare say Zoe is, too."

Cassia started running. The barking grew louder. The grounds swept past her in a blur, Lio keeping pace beside her. She slowed outside the low stone fence of the goat paddock.

A massive, dark form launched toward her with speed to rival her own. Lio made to move in front of her, but with a shake of her head, she stood her ground before the oncoming predator.

No matter how Knight reacted, she would face him.

His body struck her, knocking the air out of her lungs. Snow met her back. He pinned her under his weight.

And began to lick her face. His overexcited whines split her ears. His whole body shook with the force of his emotions and his wagging tail, all his training and discipline forgotten.

Cassia gasped a breath, tears flowing down her face. She rolled over, strong enough to push him off, only to wrap her arms around him. They half wrestled, half cuddled in the snow.

"I know, my dearest," she cooed. "That was the longest we've ever been apart in your whole life. It was so hard."

Sniffing her everywhere, he sneezed and shook his ears.

"Do I smell different?" she asked, her throat tight. "So do you. Did you know you smell terrible to Hesperines? Yes, you do, but I have never been happier to get a nose full of liegehound musk."

He licked her chin again. Laughing, she let him give her all the slobbery dog kisses.

She was still his *kaetlii*, fangs and all.

I told you so. Lio sat on the ground nearby, trying to hold his little sister's two goats out of the fray.

I should always trust your reassurances, Cassia said.

Then another, smaller form hit her, tumbling into the pile with her and Knight. Zoe squealed and squeezed the air out of Cassia a second time. "I missed you so much!"

Cassia sucked in a deep breath, learning her Grace-sister's scent. Betony flowers and syrup. Zoe was shaking harder than Knight. Cassia felt that tremble of emotion in her own bones. The child's old fears and new panic and very present joy made Cassia's heart speed up and a fresh wave of tears come to her eyes.

The Hesperines had taught her numb heart to feel, but this…this was the Blood Union. She, the lady of ice, would now live in visceral empathy with everyone who had blood flowing through their veins. Especially the people she loved, like this little girl who had suffered too much in her eight years of life.

Cassia held Zoe close. "I promised you that whenever Lio and I have to leave you, we'll always return. You'll never lose me now, Grace-sister. For I am as immortal as you."

Cassia let Zoe have a good cry while Lio stroked his little sister's hair. When the child's sobs of relief seemed wrung out, Cassia asked, "Do you want to see my new fangs?"

Sniffing, Zoe nodded. Cassia managed to sit up with Zoe against her and Knight sprawled across her lap. She beamed at the little girl, baring her teeth.

"Now you have fangs like me!" Zoe grinned back, revealing her own tiny canines and a missing bottom incisor.

Cassia gasped. "You lost another tooth! What did our Ritual father give you as a Tooth Gift this time?"

"Rudhira carved me a new toy goat. He says by the time I lose all my teeth, he'll complete a whole herd."

"I want to see the new addition to your collection."

"I'll show you later. Right now we have a surprise for you inside!"

Lio's brows rose. *Whatever excites Zoe more than a herd of goats carved by the First Prince must be marvelous indeed.*

Cassia tried flexing her new senses, probing Zoe's emotions in the Blood Union, but the child's aura gave her no hints.

Zoe giggled. "That tickles."

Cassia reached over and tickled Zoe's ribs as well, eliciting another peal of laughter. Zoe escaped with the speed of a Hesperine. Cassia looked forward to games of chase. They could play veil and step, too, if Cassia ever managed to learn essential Hesperine abilities.

She and Lio followed the suckling toward the house. Lio cast a quick cleaning spell over Cassia, only for Knight to start shedding and drooling on her anew. Her dog circled her every step, rubbing against her with his tail still wagging, nosing her for more reassuring pets.

House Komnena loomed before them, but it was not the magnificent white marble archways and buttresses or the brilliant stained glass windows that took Cassia's breath away.

It was the magic. The house of their bloodline was so bright to her arcane senses, filled to the brim and overflowing with warm, welcoming spells.

Lio and his family had always made sure she knew she belonged here. But she had never felt it as she did now. The magic in the stone foundations was the same magic in her blood. She was built into the house, and it into her.

"Welcome home, Cassia Komnena," Lio said with a smile of understanding.

They entered through the stained glass door of Komnena's study. But it was not Lio's mother who awaited them there. Cassia halted in her tracks, frozen by too many emotions.

"Surprise!" Zoe said.

Solia blazed before Cassia, the space around her crackling with the unseen force of her fire magic. Her face was hard, a warrior's mask of discipline, but her soul was bare in the Blood Union. Cassia was dizzied by the burning roil of Solia's anger and joy and grief and hope.

Immortality was not the future Solia had wanted for Cassia. Lio had reassured her that her sister had given them her blessing, but that had been when Cassia lay dying, the Gift all that could save her. Now, confronted with her new reality, what if Solia couldn't accept it?

Cassia would never regret her choices. But she could not deny that a piece of her childhood heart would break, as surely as her immortal one.

"You're alive," Solia said.

Cassia's throat ached. "So are you."

Her sister strode across the distance between them and pulled her into a fierce embrace. Solia hugged her as she had years ago, when she had been the only mother Cassia had ever known. As she had when they'd found each other again after half a lifetime apart. As if nothing had changed.

"Pup," Solia rasped.

"Soli." Cassia wrapped her arms around her sister. Her mortal sister. And yet somehow, even as a Hesperine, she still felt safe in Solia's arms.

"I thought I was going to lose you," Solia said. "After everything I did for you—I failed you, Cassia. You and your mother. I'm so sorry."

"How can you say that?" Cassia cried. "You sacrificed everything for me. None of it was your fault. Not my magical illness. Not Miranda capturing us. And not…" Cassia took a breath to steady her voice. "My Gifting was always inevitable, no matter what you did or didn't do to protect me."

"I know." Solia pulled back and looked into Cassia's eyes. "Did Lio tell you I gave you my blessing?"

"Yes." But Cassia wanted the reassurance of hearing it from Solia herself.

"I want you to be safe and happy." Solia took in the sight of her, rubbing Cassia's arms as if to test her new shape. "Are you? Happy?"

"I am whole. But I'll be even happier if you don't have regrets."

"None. This is who you are meant to be. I understand that now. I want to be here with you for your first Ritual…if that's all right."

Cassia could scarcely believe the powerful gesture of acceptance. Solia wanted to be part of this tradition with their Hesperine family. Cassia threw herself into Solia's arms again. "Of course I want you here for this. How did you manage it?"

"As soon as we got word you were ready to see everyone, Mak and Lyros stepped me here."

"What happened at the siege?"

"I am still the Queen of Tenebra," Solia said. "I'll tell you everything else later."

"Lio and I need to tell you something." Conscious of Zoe within earshot, Cassia didn't elaborate. "As soon as possible."

"We have a strategy session with the First Prince right after your Ritual. But for now, we're all alive, here, together. Let me forget about the war for an hour and celebrate with you."

For her sister's sake, Cassia could do that. "Of course."

Solia turned to Lio, who waited patiently with Zoe. "You've made sure Cassia will always be safe. I have no words… What do Hesperines call something even deeper than a bond of gratitude?"

He smiled. "Family."

"Agreed, Grace-brother."

Cassia watched her sister clasp her Grace's hands. Solia's fiery presence clashed with the sweet shadow of Lio's Hesperine aura, even as the Blood Union eased with their newfound affection for one another.

They continued into the Ritual hall together. Bright spell lights and echoing voices overwhelmed Cassia's senses. Lio rested a hand on her lower back while she stood and waited for her eyes and everything else to adjust. She was swimming in a room full of blazing stars. Their loved ones were moving balls of timeless power.

A crushing hug brought her to her senses. She would have known one of Mak's hugs anywhere, but now she could also smell his scent of warm clove and strong blackthorn. She could feel the dangerous, safe shadows under the friendly darkness of his warding magic.

"Be gentle with her new bones," Lio said in an aggrieved tone, punching his cousin in the shoulder.

"She's immortal now!" Mak replied. "It's officially impossible for me to squish the life out of her."

"You came home in one piece," Cassia sniffed. "Lyros—?"

She smelled mint and citrus, and another guardian shadow drew near. She felt Lyros's lean, strong hand on her shoulder. "Right here."

She breathed a sigh of relief. "Have you been on the front lines all this time?"

"We were summoned home to reinforce the Stewards," Lyros explained, "since we were relieved from duty as your bodyguards for the time being."

Mak snickered. "Since you and Lio's bodies were busy doing other things and not in need of guarding."

Kia's sharp, brilliant aura gleamed nearby, but her scent was surprisingly sweet…white crocus, Cassia thought. Xandra's cheerful mulberry aura gathered closer, then the lilting strains of cherry blossoms that were Nodora.

Cassia had seen them all before, but now, with her Hesperine senses, she felt she truly met them for the first time. People were so much more than their appearances. Impressions washed over her: the unique signatures of their auras, the sounds of their voices, and smells. So many smells that communicated more than just scent.

It's almost as if I can smell emotion, she commented to Lio.

You can, he replied. *Actually, you sense emotion in the Blood Union, but it can manifest as physical impressions.*

Everyone smells like a different kind of plant.

Fascinating. Your affinity for botanical magic must influence how you perceive their scents.

"Let's see those new fangs, then!" Kia demanded.

Cassia bared her canines to their Trial circle's admiring exclamations.

Someone else let out a whistle. "I'll have to promote your nickname from 'Freckles' to 'Fangs.'"

With an astonished smile, Cassia turned toward one of the most powerful auras in the room. "Tendo?"

FIRST RITUAL

TENDESO LIFTED ONE OF his black and tawny wings in greeting. Now she understood why Lio had thought him an enemy when they had first met. Even here, on the other side of the world from the land of Tendo's ancestral power, the shifter prince's magic was enough to make her rock on her feet.

She wrapped her arms around him, dangerous aura, sharp weapons, and all. He smelled of veld grasses and royal incense. "Thank you so much for coming."

His wings enfolded her. "Stop having close calls, *nyakimbi*. I went to a lot of trouble to save your life. I had to come in person to make sure your silkfoot rescued you properly."

Lio clasped Tendo's arm. "This silkfoot is glad you're here."

Tendo pulled Lio in to clap him on the back. "I might have to promote your nickname, too. I hear you fought your way out of a castle full of necromancers to carry her to safety. Not garden variety death mages, either—those Gift Collectors who assassinate Hesperines for a living. Well done."

"High praise from you, Monsoon."

Tendo shook his head at the mention of his fortune name, the epithet he had earned in his past as a mercenary. It must be a painful reminder of the happy years he and Solia had spent fighting with their mercenary band, the Ashes. He hadn't forgiven her for choosing her duties as a royal over their lives together.

"I'm nothing but the Ashes' messenger bird these days," Tendo said. "Karege, Tuura, and everyone in Ukocha's village said to tell you congratulations."

Solia put in, "Kella and Hoyefe send their love, as well. They're holding down the fort in Tenebra."

Solia and Tendo stood on opposite sides of the gathering, but they were in the same room for Cassia's sake. She didn't dare ask what truce the former lovers had agreed upon.

Her sister had now wrapped her bespelled golden scarf around her shoulders, concealing her aura from the Blood Union. Tendo must have similar magic at hand, for Cassia couldn't sense his emotions toward her sister, either.

But Cassia hadn't lost her touch for reading body language and expressions. The pair betrayed awareness of each other's every twitch and glare.

Lio sighed. *They're acting like two predators ready to fight.*

Or to mate. Cassia could feel the most natural form of magic sparking between the two simply because they breathed the same air.

With them, there isn't usually a difference, Lio pointed out.

Perhaps we can get them to do more than stare daggers at each other from across the room.

Time for one of our diplomatic schemes, he agreed, *of the matchmaking variety.*

But right now, the elders were beckoning Cassia toward the Ritual circle. Komnena opened her arms, her eyes shining with tears, and Cassia went into her Grace-mother's embrace. She would never be motherless again.

For a vivid instant, she recalled the spectral hold of her mortal mother's spirit. Now Thalia had a kind of immortality too—through Cassia.

"How do you feel?" Komnena asked in her bespelling, soothing voice. "If tonight becomes too overwhelming, tell me."

How like the mind healer to welcome Cassia into eternity with such a considerate question. "I will, but right now, I'm so happy to be with everyone."

Cassia turned to Apollon, surprised how quietly his presence had been dwelling at the heart of this gathering. "Papa, are you...veiling yourself?"

A chuckle rumbled out of Apollon's chest. "Yes. A room full of ancients can get a bit stuffy otherwise."

A kind jest at his own expense. He had always been so patient with her, even when she had cast her fears of her human father on him.

"You are one of the least stuffy elders in all of Orthros," Cassia protested. "Please don't feel the need for veils."

His dark blue eyes, so like Lio's, crinkled at the corners with amusement, and then his presence dawned on the room. She would never again understand why humans worshiped the solar god Anthros when the Goddess of Night's most ancient Hesperine was far more radiant.

Apollon's power was in the bedrock beneath their feet, In Komnena, Lio, and Zoe's heartbeats. In Cassia. His magic carried the current that flowed among their bloodline.

He searched her gaze, a silent question in his eyes. Could she accept this?

She couldn't find the words to explain how he eclipsed what fatherhood had once meant to her. So she simply hugged him, as Zoe would. The smile she sensed in his aura seemed to warm every hall and chamber of the house he had built.

By the time Uncle Argyros and Aunt Lyta finished handing her back and forth to congratulate her and reassure themselves, her new senses were dazed with their might and their love. Bosko peppered her with questions about her Gifting, for which she had no suckling-appropriate answers, until Javed stuck Thenie in the boy's arms and Kadi persuaded him to stand with them outside the Ritual circle. It took Cassia several attempts to convince Knight to stay there with Kadi and Solia.

Lio offered Cassia his hand. "Ready?"

"Yes, she is." Kassandra urged Cassia forward.

At this vote of confidence from Orthros's oracle, Cassia shot her a grateful look. Meeting Kassandra's gaze, Cassia bit back a gasp at the seer's fathomless aura. She was past and present, pain and joy existing in the same body and the same moment. How hard it must be to be her.

But Kassandra smiled. "All is well with me on nights such as these."

Together, Lio and Cassia joined Apollon upon the mosaic of Hespera's Rose within the Ritual circle. Zoe's slippers pattered on the tile as Komnena guided her to stand with them.

Kassandra, with one of her mysterious smiles, held out a long, rolled bundle across the sacred ring. "Weaving your Ritual tapestry was tricky. Your schemes aren't easy to follow through my visions, Cassia Komnena. But oh, what marvelous patterns they make."

Cassia put a hand to her heart. "Thank you."

She recalled the night when Kassandra had handed her the Mage King's banner, and she had thought that was her future. Now she took her Ritual tapestry from the Oracle with the certainty that this weaving represented her true destiny. Together, she and Lio unfurled it for everyone to see.

Cassia would have to look at this for centuries before she perceived every detail in the incredible weaving of rich blood reds, deep dark greens, and velvety black. Kassandra seemed to have captured all the wildness and beauty of the Lustra in a frame of celestial designs. Hespera's dark night sky encompassed all of Cassia's future, her moons and stars shining their light on her garden.

Plants danced in and out of one another in complicated knots that reminded her of the Changing Queen's pendant. She spotted Hespera's Roses and betony, Sanctuary Roses and cassia flowers, ivy and thorns. But there were animals too. A pack of liegehounds on the hunt made her smile. A hawk appeared at various points in the tangle, as if swooping in and out of her fate. Hidden among the flowers, was that elusive shape a woman's face, her lips parted as if to speak a spell?

Lio's aura honed with conviction. *The animals and the speaking woman must be symbols of beast magic and soothsaying. I was right, Cassia. It is your destiny for us to restore your other two affinities.*

You know how open to interpretation Kassandra's prophecies are. Perhaps the tapestry is merely a tribute to my Silvicultrix heritage. I'm happy with the Gift and my plant magic.

You must have all your power. This prophecy shows it's written in the stars. And if it weren't, I would make it so.

She knew that look in his eyes. He had made his choice about which path of destiny to fight for, and Goddess help anyone who resisted the new shape he would Will the world into.

I love you, my Grace, she said.

And I love you, my Silvicultrix.

When Rudhira and Nike set foot upon the stone petals of Hespera's Rose, the glorious magic around Cassia swelled so high she could drown in it. She handed her Ritual tapestry to them. "Ritual Father, Ritual Mother, you have my gratitude."

In Rudhira's complex scent, she picked out fresh-cut timber and the bold fragrance of Blood-Red Royal, his namesake rose in his family's greenhouses. But the rare smile he gave her was uncomplicated. He looked from her and Lio to Zoe. "I'm happy to be called upon for a third addition to Apollon's bloodline. Looking after the three of you for eternity is certain to be an adventure."

"Good thing you'll have my help with this one." Nike rested her hands on Cassia's shoulders. The evergreen scents of the dark forest where they'd first met seemed to have followed Nike home from her long quest in Tenebra. "I'm honored. When I first found you that night as a mortal child, I never could have imagined we would be standing here tonight. What a Hesperine you've become. I cannot wait to see what you do."

"I will cherish your words." Cassia could scarcely believe the Blood-Red Prince and the Victory Star were holding her tapestry for her during this momentous occasion.

A hush fell over the hall, pregnant with the question no one had yet asked Cassia and Lio.

They're too kind to ask if I've manifested any magic, Cassia said. *Shouldn't we warn them?*

Mischief sparkled in Lio's aura. *Why don't we let it be a surprise?*

Are you sure that's safe?

Father built this house. It's covered in so much magic, it can withstand anything.

Well, if you're certain...I'll do my best with a demonstration.

"Cassia Komnena," said Apollon. "Will you give of yourself for your bloodline, tonight and forever?"

My blood is your blood, Lio reminded her.

"My blood is your blood," Cassia responded.

She offered her wrist to Zoe. The smallest member of their family took Cassia's hand, and her little fangs stung Cassia's skin. Zoe tugged, and Cassia felt her life, her power, flow out of her to nourish the child.

She had always known she would spill every last drop of her blood for this little girl. But now, she would never bleed dry. She would always have the strength Zoe needed.

Zoe lifted her head, solemn with her effort not to make a mistake during the important ceremony. She managed not to spill and hastily accepted a handkerchief from her mother. Cassia bent and kissed Zoe's forehead, her wrist already sealing.

"Cassia Komnena," Apollon said, "we, your bloodline, will give of ourselves for you, tonight and forever."

My Grace. Lio gave her his wrist first, and the familiar taste of him steadied her. *You're doing beautifully. No urge to tear my clothes off in the middle of the Ritual circle?*

Sunbind you, you'll have to veil my blushing face if you keep on like this.

Then my goal is accomplished.

As she finished her drink from him, she felt a shiver of power go through the ground. *Not now,* she Willed the letting site.

Komnena held out her wrist. "Daughter."

Cassia focused on keeping her thoughts and her magic in line as she accepted her Grace-mother's offering. She tasted rich plum wine and sweet gardenia, and Komnena's magic poured into Cassia like rain. Cassia's own magic bloomed.

In a flash, she felt the shapes of the magic below them. In her mind's eye, she could trace the blood-infused Ritual circle, eight bright mosaic stars of the constellation Anastasios glowing with his enduring power. Deep below, strong roots ran, tracing back to the fertile nexus under the tower. The Lustra was everywhere.

Cassia turned to Apollon, visualizing every mental pattern she and Lio had devised to assist her self-control. She would not ruin her own first Ritual.

Apollon's blood hit her tongue. She couldn't taste anything but *power*. She braced herself and swallowed.

Magic blazed into her veins. Her jaw clenched, her heart ready to burst from her chest. The undiluted strength of her foregiver charged through her, and the Lustra tore out of her in answer.

You belong to me. She trembled where she stood, her ears roaring. *You do not control me. You are mine.*

But her power knew it belonged here. It rejoiced in her veins and flourished amid the centuries of her bloodline's spells.

Lio's mind drew deeper into to hers. *I'm here. Let's try to guide it together.*

With their combined force of Will, they took hold of the rampant power inside her. The chaos gained form as vines of magic they could grasp and guide, but still it fought them every inch of the way.

Komnena's power swept into the spell with the inexorable power of an ocean tide, taming the currents of the Lustra magic. Apollon joined her casting, sealing wayward power into the stone, building it into layer after layer of the ground. When Nike's magic charged into the fray, it was as if a master smith bent and shaped the raw magic with harsh artistry.

Rudhira joined the spell as gently as a winter breeze. If he hadn't been so careful, Cassia feared the infusion of royal Hesperine magic would have made her lose her grip on her magic all over again. His power made a battle cry rise in her blood.

With her Grace and the four ancient immortals bolstering her Will, Cassia sent the Lustra magic twining back down into its source.

She lifted her head from Apollon's wrist and opened her eyes. For an instant, she felt mighty, drunk on the power of their kind. Then she saw what she had done to the Ritual hall.

Roses had exploded everywhere. They had broken right through the marble to spill across the floor and climb the pillars. Cassia gaped up at a hole where the vines had collapsed the roof so they could turn their impossible dark blooms toward the moons. Their petals were as black as the night sky.

Cassia put her hands to her face, speechless. Lio held her steady, blanketing her in reassurance through their Union. But her cheeks burned.

Apollon's laughter split the silence, echoing through his wrecked masterpiece. "That's my daughter."

"Black roses." Nike touched a finger to one petal. "Hespera's sacred flower, taking on the color of her protection. A miraculous omen."

Solia stared at Cassia. "You have your plant magic. How?"

If Cassia must tell them the true horror of her past, this was how she wanted to do it, surrounded by Hespera's proof that she was whole now. "During my Gifting, I regained memories the Collector hid from me. We learned that my plant magic came to me when I was fourteen…and he took it."

The anger and grief of her loved ones raged up like her rampant roses. She thought the Blood Errant might charge out of the room that instant to hunt down the enemies who had made her suffer. She didn't want to cause them this pain, but oh, how grateful she was for such defenders.

Solia pulled Cassia into her arms, her skin hot. "I have many scores to settle with Lucis, but I will make him pay for this above all."

"It's all right now. They had to leave me a drop of my plant magic to keep me alive. The Gift took that last remnant and turned it into…" She gestured around them. "This. Thanks to Lio, I'm alive and well and, ah, rather powerful."

Lio smiled. "Don't be so modest. You opened a letting site under the tower."

Solia's eyes widened. "What does this mean for your other two affinities? Will your new letting site give you beast magic and soothsaying?"

"We're working on that," Lio said firmly. *See?* he added in her mind. *Your sister agrees with me.*

She decided this was not the time to debate it in front of their loved ones. "Right now I have enough magic and more than enough reasons to celebrate."

Solia swiped at her eyes. "I wish Thalia were here to see this, but I can speak for her. We are so proud of you, Cassia."

IN THE CENTURIES TO come, Cassia would never forget how cheerfully everyone moved the celebration into the library, as if her magical disaster were the greatest cause for celebration of all.

She hesitated in the doorway, where black roses threatened to invade the library from the Ritual hall. Leaning in to smell one bloom, she tested the texture of the dark petals between her fingers. Their fragrance held the aching beauty of Orthros's red roses, deepening into the indulgent sweetness of blood.

"I scarcely know what to make of this creation of mine—or Hespera's—or the Lustra's?"

"All three." Lio studied the flowers, a smile on his face, his magic sweeping over the nearest vine. "All the rosarians of Orthros will be clamoring to study these. They must be a magic-bred hybrid of some kind, don't you think?"

Cassia kept her hand in Knight's ruff. "The Winter Solstice festival starts in two weeks. I know how important it is for our tributaries to gather here and receive our gifts to them for the coming year. What will we do without a Ritual hall to put them in?"

"My dear," Komnena said with a laugh, "this is hardly the first spell that has gone awry in this house. You should see the repairs Apollon had to do when Lio's thelemancy first manifested. He had barely learned to walk, but he managed to shatter every window in the house."

Lio rubbed his face. "I suppose I can tolerate story hour about the embarrassing moments of my childhood if it will make Cassia feel better."

"It's dangerous to give your mother that kind of permission." Xandra's eyes sparkled. "We'll be here all night."

Komnena, never daunted as the Queens' Master Chamberlain, supervised the rearrangement of the festivities amid the half-empty shelves of their growing library. Friends and family brought the platters of food and wine, except for Apollon, who carried the sucklings on his shoulders. Rudhira and Nike levitated a dinner table in.

Uncle Argyros personally rescued his coffee service from the devastation and arranged it on the table in all its glory. With great ceremony, he poured Cassia a cup and offered it to her. "Now, an important rite of passage. Experiencing coffee with your Hesperine sense of taste."

"I shall need a bigger cup," Cassia predicted.

"Indeed, it is one of the greatest joys of immortality," Uncle Argyros said with a contented sigh. "You can drink as much coffee as you wish."

She took a deep whiff of the expertly crafted beverage. "Deukalion's Blend. My favorite."

"Of course." Their mentor's imposing gaze softened with good humor.

Cassia took a sip. Layer after layer of rich flavor warmed her mouth. She bit back a moan. "If I weren't immortal, I would be deceased."

"Do I have competition?" Lio asked with a teasing grin.

She met his gaze over the rim of the cup and blushed. "Coffee is the *second* best beverage known to Hesperine kind."

Uncle Argyros gave a wholehearted laugh, slipping his hand into Aunt Lyta's. "I couldn't agree more."

The diplomatic relations of the world were in upheaval, and yet the Queens' Master Ambassador had taken time to make Cassia's first cup of coffee. Solia and Tendo carried the weight of their kingdoms and heartbreak, but had pushed that aside to be here. Hesperines were at war with the Mage Orders for the first time in sixteen hundred years, and yet Rudhira had left the battlefield for her, his newest Ritual daughter.

Cassia might be immortal, but time was still precious, and none of them knew what tomorrow would bring. She held tight to the fragile, joyful moments they all snatched from the jaws of war.

Lio was the magic that imbued each cherished instant. Their Grace Union made him fully present in her every breath and glance as she experienced these familiar parts of their world with her new senses. She kept pulling him deeper into their connection, trying to hold him away from his own haunted thoughts.

When Tendo absorbed Lio in conversation for a few minutes, their laughter reassured Cassia somewhat. Now might be her only chance to put her secret plan into action without Lio plucking it from her thoughts and ruining the surprise.

She eased back from their Grace Union as subtly as she could. It felt like holding her breath. He was still within her, like that residual air in her lungs, and all her thoughts and emotions burned with the need to pull her next dose of him into her.

Before she lost her grip, she pulled Komnena aside. "I have a question. Could you veil our conversation, please?"

Komnena cast a glance at Lio as her magic enveloped them. "Of course, but if you intend to keep something from him, it will take far more than my veils now."

Cassia clenched her fists with effort. "Our Union makes romantic surprises terribly difficult."

Aunt Lyta joined their conspiratorial circle. The Guardian of Orthros gave off the fragrances of soothing meadowsweet and dangerous yarrow. "Do I sense a new Hesperine in need of mental defenses against a powerful thelemancer?"

"Do you mean that's possible?" Cassia asked.

"You must maintain *some* privacy to live with the same person for centuries. Especially when one's Grace is a mind mage."

"Can I learn how, even if I'm not a thelemancer myself?"

"Certainly. I may be a warder and a warrior, but over a thousand years with Argyros have honed my mind as well. I can teach you some tricks. Thelemancers like Lio and Argyros could certainly get through those defenses if they wished, but our conscientious diplomats would never."

"Of course not." Cassia grimaced. "I'm more concerned about how easily my own thoughts leak out of my mind for him to see."

"That I can help with. Here's a quick tactic to help you right away. Focusing on something else is more effective than trying to avoid a certain thought. If you fill your mind with words or images to distract him, he's less likely to notice the one you're trying to keep from him." Lyta added, "Have fun with that."

Cassia grinned. "Oh, that's a very good idea."

She started by focusing her thoughts on something that wouldn't draw his suspicion: a diagram of the greenhouse he, his father, and Mak were building for her. She ran through plant varieties and flower bed layouts, and Lio's light touch upon her mind didn't focus into full attention.

Once she got the answers she needed from Komnena, Cassia gathered her Trial circle around her. Before she had to ask, five layers of veils descended over them.

Xandra's aura was bright with interest. "I know that look in your eye. You're working on a scheme."

"It's clearly time for a strategy session," Lyros agreed.

Cassia sent her gratitude into the Blood Union, so glad to now have this way of communicating when words felt insufficient. "Kia, I need you to inconvenience your mother."

Her fangs flashed in a grin. "I thought you wanted *me* to do *you* a favor."

"Mak, Lyros, I would like to employ the Stewards' wards—not for battle, but romance."

Mak gallantly put a hand to his chest. "You know you can rely on us in matters of love or war."

"Nodora," Cassia asked, "could I ask for one more encore of Lio's and my favorite dance?"

She clasped her hands together. "Of course! It would be my pleasure."

By the time they had decided all the details, Cassia was running out of rose arrangements to envision to distract Lio.

"You look like you're about to strain a muscle," Lyros observed.

"Or hit someone," said Mak. "Give yourself some Grace, eh?"

"You all have my gratitude," Cassia said before returning to Lio and Tendo.

She stopped fighting the Grace Union. As Lio's thoughts and emotions flowed into hers again, she bit her tongue to keep from groaning with relief.

He slid his arm around her. *You've been trying to hide from me, Lady Circumspect. Tired of my company already?*

Did I seem tired of you when you fed me, right before we left the tower? She filled her thoughts with the sounds and sensations of their last, quick feast.

Lio rubbed his mouth. *Ah, there's only one explanation for those veiled conversations, then. You're conspiring.*

I was only talking with Mak about my greenhouses, she replied innocently.

That doesn't explain how my mother and aunt are involved. Should I be worried what you three are about to unleash upon the world?

Oh, I was only getting some advice about Graced life now that I'm a happily paired immortal. They've been keeping your father and uncle happy and out of trouble for years, after all. She thought of magical explosions.

Why do you have a tendency to get me deeper into trouble?

Have you ever considered that makes you happier than staying out of it?

Tendo snorted. "You two have that lovesick look on your faces again. Mak, Lyros, get over here and talk to me about violence."

Their Trial brothers joined them, Lyros raising his glass of wine to his Grace. "Mak isn't always much help with that. He's a hopeless romantic."

"I'm in a helpful mood," Mak said. "You'll spar with us tomorrow, won't you, Tendo?"

Didn't he already secure Solia's agreement to meet in the arena? Lio asked Cassia silently.

He certainly did, she replied. *Oh, clever Mak.*

Cassia put a hand on Tendo's arm. "Please stay that long. I'd love to come and watch."

"I'll even let you take me into the ring for a few beatings," Lio promised.

"We'll see," Tendo relented. That was far better than a no from the grumpy shifter.

No one breathed a word of war or politics as the night went on. Cassia managed to bring Zoe and Solia in on her plan with Lio none the wiser. But Cassia could feel everything left unsaid rising like a storm, until she could hardly bear the charge in the air.

The storm broke when a new aura slipped silently into the gathering. Cassia's magic rose in recognition, and she met the scout's startled green eyes across the now-hushed room.

"*Habuch joh bero*," Kalos breathed, an oath in the old garden tongue once spoken by their ancestors, the Lustri people, who had practiced nature magic in its most ancient and powerful forms. She sensed his beast magic prowling around the letting site, circling her. He bowed deeply to her.

She drew nearer to him. "Oh, Kalos, no need for that."

"*Silvicultrix*," he said reverently. "You made a Hesperine letting site."

"I'd love to talk with you about it. Later." Right now, she could tell their time was running short.

Kalos's gaze went to the First Prince, then Solia. The scout was veiling his emotions. For the sucklings' sake, Cassia thought. But she knew without a doubt that he was here to deliver the bad news she had feared.

THE NEXT DUEL

Lio allowed himself his anger. Cassia's Giftmoon was over.

He'd known it as soon as the letting site had issued its desperate warning. But he stood in denial for a moment longer, while Kadi and Javed helped Lio's parents herd the unsuspecting sucklings out of the room.

Zoe clung to Cassia and Lio, pleading to stay. He picked her up on his hip, while Cassia tucked one of her purple hair ribbons back into place.

"We'll go with you, Zoe," Nodora offered.

Kia nodded. "I'll read you a bedtime story."

Thank you, Lio mouthed to his Trial sisters over Zoe's head.

Nodora gave him one of her kind smiles. After a great deal of persuasion from her, Kia, and Xandra, Zoe let Lio hand her to their father. The look of disappointment on her face gave him a new level of hatred for the war.

On their way out, Xandra paused to give her brother a fierce hug. "You had better come home again soon, Rudhira. Don't make me drink your terrible hard cider alone."

"I'll join you for a bottle of your insufferably sweet mead as soon as I can," he promised. But their good-natured sibling rivalry about their brewing didn't make anyone laugh tonight.

Knight stood alert at Cassia's side. She gripped Lio's hand, and her reassurance pulsed along their bond, fueled by her new power. But neither of them could stop what was happening.

The Charge, the Stand, and the diplomats remained. Lio's minute of bitterness was up. His temper would simply have to come along for the ride.

Veil spells fell over the room, and Kalos announced, "Lord Lucis and the war mages are preparing to move."

Lord Lucis. Hearing that reminded Lio of their new reality, and his Grace's aura simmered with satisfaction at the words. Cassia and Solia's mortal sire was no longer the king by law. Even if he and his mage allies refused to accept it.

Kalos continued his rapid report. "They've received new ammunition from Cordium—arrows imbued with magefire. They plan to use them on Mederi Village."

Rudhira swore. "How much time do we have?"

"They'll attack at dusk," Kalos informed him.

"Again?" Solia demanded.

Rudhira shook his head. "They know their chances of victory would be higher during the day, yet they keep attacking when we're awake."

"They're baiting you," Solia returned.

"Yes," Rudhira confirmed. "Time to evacuate another target and evade their latest trap."

Solia's aura sparked. "We cannot keep evacuating my people forever. They need to know I'll fight for them, and I won't have the lords thinking a woman monarch is too reticent to face threats head on."

"You are the one who told me you must pick your battles," Rudhira replied. "And I don't think the first battle with magefire arrows is the one you want to pick."

"I won't spend this entire war retreating," Solia warned.

Rudhira's gray eyes gleamed, but his emotions were veiled. "Oh, I don't doubt that. But retreating to the most advantageous position in preparation is not cowardice. It is wisdom."

"I'll take that under advisement, First Prince, but they are my people. I will decide when it's time to make a stand for them."

To Lio's surprise, Tendo spoke up, his feathers ruffled. "The Empress—and the sister states who provide soldiers for her army—are ready to send reinforcements to Tenebra."

"Are you here in an official capacity?" Cassia asked hopefully.

"He's here to visit you." Solia looked directly at Tendo for the first time that night. "And tell me rumors from court that I already know. I can win this war without Imperial warriors coming to my aid. Except the Ashes, of course."

Tendo's jaw clenched, and Lio winced inwardly at Solia's pointed words. But Lio couldn't deny Tendo had squandered his chance to support Solia's bid for the throne—or talk her out of it for the sake of their love.

"What did I tell you?" Tendo snapped his wings. "I'm just a messenger bird. I'll leave you all to your official activities."

Lio caught up to him at the door, veiling their conversation. "Tendo, stay. Cassia would be so happy to spend more time with you."

"What did I tell you would happen with her sister and me under the same roof? It's a miracle House Komnena hasn't gone up in flames yet."

"You know you are welcome here in your own right. You won't leave Orthros before we've gone to the gymnasium, will you? You haven't even gotten to punch me yet."

Tendo let out a faint snort. "Fine. Karege is lending me his empty residence. You can find me there."

The door closed after him, harder than necessary. Solia wore her warrior face, as if they had not just had a former lovers' quarrel in front of half the family and leadership of Orthros. "Very well. We'll evacuate. For now."

Rudhira, unfazed, gave her a nod. "Kalos, keep watch for the mages. We'll be there shortly."

"Yes, My Prince." Kalos bowed with his fist over his heart.

"Be careful," Rudhira bade him.

"Not to worry," the Hesperine mumbled. "The mages may see through my veils, but not my Lustra tricks."

"I'll keep that in mind," Cassia said.

Kalos turned to her once more, hesitating. "Could I ask you a few questions later? About the letting site?"

"Of course." She smiled at him.

He inclined his head and stepped away.

Rudhira sighed. "I'm sorry, Cassia. Some Ritual father I am, leaving in the middle of your celebration. But with magefire arrows in play, I'm needed in the field."

Solia looked at Cassia with an apology in her eyes. "I can't send someone else, either. I must go myself this time."

"I understand." Cassia reached for Solia's hand. "I'm sorry we had to leave you all in the middle of the siege."

"I am not. Taking you to safety was exactly what Lio should have done," Solia replied, and he could not have been more in agreement. But he was not prepared for her next words. "And this is where I want you to stay."

"What?" Lio and Cassia said in unison.

"Your part is done." Solia spoke as if her word was already law. "I owe my throne to your diplomacy. Now we are at war, and your place is here. Help Argyros mediate between the Empire, Orthros, and my new Tenebra. Spend time with Zoe."

"You need us," Cassia protested.

"I've taken you away from your life here too many times. I won't stand between you and Orthros any longer. I want you to leave the fighting to the warriors now."

"Good luck with that," Mak muttered.

He was right. No matter how much Cassia longed to stay in their tower, Lio knew she felt compelled to finish what they had started. When she pulled him aside, he had no doubt what she would say.

She looked up into his eyes, resting her hands on his chest. *I will stay here with you, if that's what you want.*

Lio's mouth fell open. He put his hands over hers, speechless before his Grace for once.

I'll stay right here, Cassia repeated. *Not because Solia asked. Because you did.*

He found his words. *Could you really bear to do that?*

What I cannot bear is hurting you.

I don't want to hold you back from what you need to do.

What I need is to fulfill my Grace's need.

His conscience needled him. *I know I'm not the only person who needs you.*

They all need you just as much. But you've put me first so many times. I'll do the same for you in a heartbeat. I have Hesperine priorities now, my Grace.

Lio pulled her into his arms. At last, he hit the certainty that lay beneath all their anger and despair.

Her Gifting *had* changed everything—for her, too.

He had known she was his forever. But he hadn't believed it. Not until this moment, when she stood ready to turn the entire world away for his sake.

My beloved scholar, she said, *after all the times the world has tried to pull me away from you, I thought you might need a demonstration for the truth to sink in.*

Thank you, Cassia.

Seconds were slipping past, and the battle was looming closer, along with the choice they must make.

Neither of them spoke, but in their Grace Union, they both knew the truth.

Who would meet their enemies in the Changing Queen's forgotten halls? Who could possibly stand against a necromancer who was also a Mage of Dreams—a thelemancer with the power of the god of death?

No one could face the Collector as they could. She was the only Hesperine who wielded the power of the Lustra. He was the only immortal mind mage who had defeated Kallikrates before.

Their family needed them both. Not for their diplomacy, but for their power.

If you ask me to go with you, said Cassia, *I will do that too.*

We have to make this decision together, just like always.

Knowing we will put each other first, can we face what they need from us—together?

It would be too hard for you.

Just keep me fed, and I'll manage.

You know I'll never leave you hungry. But this is not what I want for you. You should have more time to come into your power.

I can come into my power right in the Collector's face. My fear is that it will be too hard for you.

It will be, he confessed. *But I think we must do it nonetheless.*

Then we'll make Kallikrates rue the night you gave me fangs.

He kissed her one more time, feeling the sharpness of her canines against his tongue, before he lowered his veil spell.

"We're coming with you," Lio announced.

They turned to find themselves facing a fearsome red-haired obstacle. Rudhira crossed his arms over his chest. "Have you forgotten you require my permission to join my forces?"

Uncle Argyros raised a brow, his dark gaze at its most intimidating. "And mine to resume your diplomatic mission to Tenebra."

"Orthros Abroad is no place for a new Hesperine," Rudhira said. "Even one who brings your experience and skill into immortality, Cassia. I suggest you develop your power before you and Lio go errant again."

A suggestion from their prince was not, in fact, a suggestion. Cassia's frustration rose in their Grace Union. One of the potted ferns in the library popped out a few new fronds in protest, and Rudhira gave her a pointed look.

"I would love nothing better than to keep Cassia here," Lio said, "but her magic, and mine, are necessary to stop the Collector. We have information about his plan that you need to know."

At the mention of the necromancer, the temperature in the room seemed to drop. Even Lio shivered at the elders' dangerous magic. The Collector had made enemies of the only beings as immortal as he.

Solia was the one nova of heat in the room. "This is what you needed to tell us? It sounds as if it can't wait much longer."

"No," Cassia said. "It's the reason Lucis and the mages are baiting Hesperines."

Rudhira and Uncle Argyros exchanged a look.

"Lio," his Ritual father said, "I will allow you to come with me—for now. While you assist me with the evacuation, you may tell me what you know and make your case for why you and Cassia should remain involved in the war."

"I will need to be informed as well," said his uncle. "Cassia should stay here with me and ensure the diplomatic service is prepared for what is to come."

The fern gave a threatening rustle, its pot nearly invisible under the outburst of new fronds. But Cassia's mind voice was controlled, matter-of-fact. *It's a sound plan.*

Lio's arms tightened around her new body. The form he had helped the Goddess make for her. Now he was not only her Grace but also her Gifter. The need to keep his new Hesperine safe turned his already fierce protective instincts into something feral. *I don't want to leave you.*

I'm not fond of the idea either. Panic edged her thoughts. *But we don't have much time, and we're needed in two places at once. It makes sense to split our forces and communicate with Grace Union.*

Everything within him resisted the very thought of being so far away from her.

"It's time to go," Solia said, almost gently. "Are you coming with us, Lio?"

Rudhira stood with her, ready to step. Nike clasped his arm, exchanging a veiled farewell with her Trial brother.

You are doing this for us, Cassia reminded Lio. *So we can get that necromancer out of our lives and go back to our tower in peace.*

For that, I can find the strength to leave you—briefly. He pressed a kiss to her forehead and made himself let her go.

"I'm with you," he said to Solia.

"I know there's no persuading you otherwise, when you've made up your minds." Solia held Cassia for a long moment.

"When will I see you again?" Cassia asked.

"Soon, I hope," her sister answered.

Mak saluted Aunt Lyta. "Requesting permission to return to our duties as protection for the Ambassadors for Tenebran Affairs."

She gripped his and Lyros's shoulders. "Yes. Both of you go with Lio for the time being. Cassia will be safe here with us."

"Don't worry, Cassia." Mak slung an arm around Lio's shoulder. "Lyros and I will keep these two out of trouble."

"And that's saying something." Lyros narrowed his eyes at Solia. "No familial magefire duels on our watch this time, all right?"

Solia held up her hands. "I wouldn't dream of it."

"No promises," Lio said.

Cassia smiled, but her deeper fears were almost enough to make Lio change his mind and stay.

He felt the letting site's magic running under Orthros and remembered the sight of that door in Miranda's mind. He recalled the Collector speaking through her to deliver a warning: *If you want that secret, you will have to duel me for it.*

Lio stepped away with the warriors to face the next duel.

A MOST PERSONAL ENEMY

Lio had never felt so vulnerable when stepping out of Orthros before. As the smells and emotions of mortals washed over him, he was not afraid for himself. He feared never making it home to Cassia. One magefire arrow could sentence her to death by Craving.

"I know." Lyros must have sensed Lio's emotions and guessed what he was thinking. "Going into battle is entirely different when someone else's life depends on yours."

Lio gave a tight nod. "You two understand."

"And we'll make sure you get home in one piece," Mak replied, "even if you are a squishy scrollworm."

"See here," Lio said, "I held my own against an army of Gift Collectors last time we were here."

"I seem to recall you had some help from us." Heedless of her fine dress, Solia crouched to peer out of their hiding place. They had arrived in one of the shallow gullies sheltered by brush that dotted the hilly landscape.

Rudhira appeared beside them an instant later. He must have made an extra stop at Hesperine speed, for his famous two-hander, Thorn, was now in a scabbard on his back. He tossed Solia her golden gladius and a cloak. She caught the sword and wrapped the cloak around herself to hide her Imperial finery.

"Have you used your blade before your people yet?" Lio asked.

"No," she grumbled. "Merely wearing it as a symbol. They still don't know I'm a warrior and a mage—or that I was ditching my duties in Orthros tonight, by the way."

"Your secrets are safe with the heretics," he assured her.

"Keep your veils tight," Rudhira ordered, "but use your magic with caution. The war mages are on constant alert, ready to catch Hesperines. Don't disregard the benefits of mundane stealth. If a war mage hits you with a revelatory spell and strips your veils, your chances of evading his fireball will be higher if you already have cover."

"Understood," Lio said.

Rudhira led them over the rim of the gully. Keeping low, they raced for the stone wall that surrounded the village.

Lio? came Cassia's voice, as clear as if she stood next to him. *Can you hear me?*

Mages with fire arrows might attack at any moment, but still he smiled. *Of course, my rose.*

What precisely is the range of Grace Union? she asked.

Hesperines have yet to find it. You could stand in the Empire and I here in Tenebra, and you wouldn't know we were on separate continents.

That's very reassuring.

But she did not feel reassured, judging by how his heart was pounding. *Feel how our hearts are still beating in time, even at this distance? That's how close I am to you right now.*

I'm sorry to inflict my racing pulse on you, but that makes me feel better.

Never apologize for how your power has changed me.

I wish I were there to protect you with my magic. What's the situation?

He scanned the familiar village with all his senses. It was a refuge for Solia's loyalists, and the former king knew it. The odors of sweat and fear were coming from here. *We're about to enter Mederi Village. It's well warded, but the spells won't hold against magefire arrows.*

Any sign of the enemy yet?

He turned his attention to the fortress on the horizon and the distant sounds of battle. Bright sparks of flame danced along the dark silhouette of the walls. "Who holds Castra Patria?"

"I do." Solia sounded smug. "*Lord* Lucis and the mages were so confident they could reduce the fortress to rubble with their enchanted trebuchets. But their 'three-day' siege has lasted more than thirty."

Rudhira seemed pleased with himself, too. "Once my Charge stepped into the enemy's camp under veils and disabled the siege engines, the enemy had to settle in for a long, old-fashioned siege. And with us smuggling supplies in for Solia's forces, we can hold out indefinitely."

"Looks as if Lucis is launching another assault," Lyros commented. "He's trying to distract us while the mages come for the village. But mundane attacks won't do much against the Hesperine wards we have on the fortress."

Queen Solia stands her ground, with Hesperine support, Lio reported to Cassia.

They shared a sense of triumph for an instant. Their victories had not been in vain—yet.

Lio leapt the village wall after the others. Rudhira beckoned for Lio to follow him and sent Mak and Lyros with Solia in the other direction.

"We'll gather everyone in the village square," Rudhira instructed, "then step them to safety in groups. Pray that no mages interrupt our spells while we're transporting mortals."

"So," Lio said, "this isn't your first evacuation."

"Lucis's forces have been launching surprise attacks on poorly-defended villages. He's bullying easy targets, the coward. We can't fortify them all, so we've been taking the residents to safety."

"But Mederi is one we fortified early on."

"Yes. He's getting more ambitious. But this strategy troubles me. It makes no sense for a warlord who needs to quash a rebellion as quickly as possible."

"No," Lio said with a grim shake of his head, "but it makes perfect sense for someone trying to make war on Hesperines. He knows we'll defend the innocent. Lucis and the Collector want to draw out the war as long as possible and engage Hesperines in open combat."

"Why?" Rudhira demanded.

Lio didn't have time to answer before they entered the first cottage. He braced himself, knowing it might take all his diplomacy to persuade prejudiced Tenebrans that he and Rudhira weren't here to steal their children and suck their blood dry.

At the sudden appearance of two immortals in her home, the weary young mother by the fire startled and went pale. But that was the extent of her reaction. She listened carefully to their instructions, then got her four little ones out of bed and half carried, half herded them toward the village square.

Lio held the image in his thoughts for Cassia. *Hesperines and Tenebran humans working together as allies. Who imagined we would live to see this?*

You did, Sir Diplomat. And you inspired me to believe in it, too.

They roused the young mother's neighbors next. The couple and their sons talked over each other, dashing every which way across the tiny hearth room to throw random belongings into sacks. Rudhira's calm leadership cut through their chaos, and he soon had them at the door with only what they truly needed.

From the loft above, a girl watched in silence until she asked Lio, "Can we bring our milk goat?"

Lio helped her down and took her out to the small garden to put a lead on the goat. He wished he could use his mind magic on the bleating nanny, but they couldn't risk drawing the mages' attention with too many spells. He settled for soothing her through the Blood Union. The girl led the now-quiet animal away.

Between that house and the next, Lio asked, "Did you take any of the Gift Collectors prisoner at Paradum?"

Rudhira paused to help a villager whose pack had spilled. Without hesitation, the First Prince knelt in the mud with Lio to pick up the old man's belongings at Hesperine speed.

Once the mortal was on his way, Rudhira sighed. "I know you've seen battle, but I still regret that you had to witness the…un-Hesperine level of violence that was necessary at Paradum."

Lio would never forget the sight of Rudhira's sword slicing through Skleros's neck before his eyes. "It won't give me day terrors, if that's what you're worried about. He almost took Cassia from me. I'll sleep better knowing you separated his head from his body. If I must pray for Hespera's forgiveness later, I will."

Rudhira rubbed his face and gave a hopeless laugh. "You have never sounded more like your father. There go our efforts to spare you from a life of violence."

"Diplomats can't always avoid violence, especially when we're trying to stop it."

"I don't disagree, for neither can healers."

Quiet weeping drew them to the next lane. A girl of about fourteen struggled to help up an older woman who had fallen. The grandmother grimaced in pain, even as she fought to regain her footing. The lightest touch of Rudhira's healing magic swept over the elder.

The girl's breath came in shallow pants. Her panicked mind fought to focus on the woman in her care. Lio shot Rudhira a beseeching glance, and his Ritual father gave a slight nod.

Lio infused his voice with thelemancy. "Everything will be all right."

As his subtle spell dampened her mind's fear response, her pulse calmed, and she regained her breath.

Rudhira eased the grandmother to her feet with strength and levitation. "Nothing is broken."

She didn't even limp as the girl led her onward toward the village square. The younger woman gave them a hesitant, but grateful smile over her shoulder.

Lio hurried onward after Rudhira to clear the next row of cottages. "I am the last to judge you if you destroyed every Gift Collector at Paradum that night. But I do need to know what befell the one we left for you. She was bound to a wall by Cassia's vines in one of the inner rooms of the castle."

"She?" Rudhira repeated. "You encountered a Gift Collector who's a woman?"

At his consternation, Lio's hopes sank. "Then you didn't find her."

"We searched every nook and cranny of the place and saw no sign of a woman necromancer. Who is she?"

"Miranda," Lio said. "The Collector's favorite. Paradum was her keep."

Rudhira shook his head. "Forgive me, Lio. It appears one Gift Collector escaped on my watch."

"It's not your fault." Lio's mind reeled. Hespera's Mercy, he had been such a fool not to tell Rudhira more that night.

Their most personal enemy was in the wind.

"How could she have escaped? I…I broke her mind," Lio confessed.

Rudhira looked at him sharply. "You destroyed a Gift Collector's dream wards?"

"I witnessed the Collector's plan in her thoughts. His endgame."

Rudhira hastened another group of villagers past, but his gaze searched Lio's. "What did you see?"

"He has been twisting minds, warping lives, setting off conflicts—all of this, for one reason. A sealed door beneath Solorum Palace. It's hidden deep within the Changing Queen's secret passageways."

"What's behind it?" Rudhira asked.

"We don't know. But whatever it is, he needs two things to gain access. One is a Silvicultrix of the royal line."

"Cassia," Rudhira said in realization. "That's why he targeted her."

The fury Lio still harbored made his magic rise, and he contained it with an effort. "Lucis used Thalia like an animal and *bred* Cassia so she would have his royal blood and her mother's magic. All so the Collector could steal Cassia's power."

"What does Lucis have to gain by aiding the Collector in his conspiracy?"

"I don't know. But he will regret it now that Cassia has taken control of her own destiny."

Rudhira gripped Lio's shoulders. "As a Hesperine, immune to displacement, she's of no further use to them. They will not want to take her alive. And they will not forgive you for freeing her from them. The Collector will be out for your blood."

Fear was Cassia's oldest enemy. She had battled it her entire mortal existence, each time she had faced Lucis. She'd thought she knew all its tactics and its every guise.

Until now, the first time in her Hesperine life when she must be apart from her Grace.

The walls of the library shrank in on her. Her heart pounded a warning that her immortal body was in mortal danger. There was a physical ache in her veins, as if his distance pulled on her blood.

She swallowed around the parched weight of her tongue. "Please tell me this gets easier."

"It will," Aunt Lyta said. "You don't see me wanting to hit something every time Argyros leaves the room."

He laughed. "But I fondly remember the violence you committed the first time we were apart after your Gifting."

The nearby fern pot cracked, and fronds twined around Cassia's ankle. She tried taking deep breaths, but her body cared nothing for air. It wanted Lio.

Are you all right? she asked. *You seem to be holding up much better than I am.*

I've had more time to develop a tolerance. But I understand precisely how you feel.

Her heart kicked even faster. *This is how you felt when you left me in Tenebra and we were apart for half a year?*

The way you comforted me upon our reunion was well worth the suffering. Just think of how good it will feel when we're together again.

If she thought about that in too much detail, her Craving would only make matters worse.

She must focus her thoughts on diplomatic calculations and hope that cold, clear political maneuvers would distract her from her hunger. "I'm ready when you are, Uncle."

"Allow me to step us." Uncle Argyros offered his arm.

He must have guessed she hadn't mastered that yet, given the state of her magic. Cassia beat back her frustration, lest the library turn into a fern forest. "By now I should already be able to step to your library without causing chaos."

"Ah, but we are not going to my library. Stay close and let me assist with any magical mishaps."

By the time she had blinked in surprise, House Komnena had slipped away. Cassia found herself and Knight standing in open air next to Uncle Argyros, Aunt Lyta, and Nike. Kadi joined them an instant later.

He had brought Cassia to a rocky precipice, where the wind stripped the snowdrifts away and sent them spinning out over the ravine below. The capital city of Selas was nowhere in sight.

The Queens' ward felt close enough to touch. Cassia stood speechless, dwarfed and cradled by the Sanctuary ward Queen Alea had cast over the entire border of Orthros. Queen Soteira's theramancy called to her from within the protection spell. Her Hesperine senses answered, her blood magic flaring toward the ward in a gesture of loyalty to their Queens.

"The ward knows you, the newest Hesperine under its protection," said Aunt Lyta.

Nike's aura told Cassia she was impressed. "And your magic is certainly determined to be known."

"Are we standing against the barrier?" Cassia asked.

Kadi nodded. "Right outside the node where the Queens first anchored it."

"Uncle Argyros and I are joining you on border patrol tonight?" At last, something Cassia could *do*.

"It's the only way we diplomats get to spend any family time with the warriors these days," Uncle Argyros said lightly, but she sensed the gravity in his aura.

"Alkaios and Nephalea send their regrets," Kadi told Cassia. "They offered to patrol the border during your Ritual so the rest of us could attend. We're heading to join them now."

"Give them my gratitude," Cassia said.

"Stay safe," Uncle Argyros fretted to his ancient, powerful Grace and daughters.

"We will," Aunt Lyta reassured him.

"And our enemies won't," Nike promised.

Her sister grinned at her as they stepped away.

Uncle Argyros's eyes darkened, and his immense thelemancy swept around them like a shadow wrapped in snow and wind. When his magic met the ward, the pressure on Cassia's arcane senses made her break out in gooseflesh. Knight put his ears back, but otherwise remained calm despite the flood of blood magic at work around them.

"You and Aunt Lyta are joining with the ward?" Cassia guessed.

Uncle Argyros nodded.

Cassia knew other Hesperines could connect with the Queens' magic to observe the entire border of Orthros, but she had never witnessed it before. "How can I help?"

"If the enemy attacks, try to channel what Lustra magic you can from here. It will be valuable to test what power you can access away from the letting site. I am also curious to see how your magic responds in proximity to the ward."

Trust Lio's uncle to turn this into a research opportunity. They were certainly far enough away from the tower for such a test, all the way across the Sea of Komne and in the Umbral Mountains.

"And Cassia…"

"Yes, Uncle?"

"If I tell you to retreat inside the ward, I trust you will do so." Silvertongue fixed her with his legendary stare.

She had to admit, her mentor could still intimidate her. "I will."

Cassia flexed her bare fingers, which would have been frostbitten by now if she hadn't been immortal. All she felt was a pleasing chill on her Hesperine skin. Knight pressed close to her, armored against the cold by his thick fur and hardy liegehound blood. Even though she didn't need his warmth, she gladly accepted his nearness. Would he ever stop protecting her as if she were human?

She opened and closed her hands again, trying to grasp any Lustra magic that might lay under the mountains. In theory, the magic of nature was everywhere and strongest in wild places. This was certainly wilderness, but what power would she find in barren terrain?

"Lio has taught you the foundational spell casting gestures, I see," Uncle Argyros commented.

"He explained that mages don't actually need these motions for the spell to work, but that they help us concentrate, and the right gestures are especially important with affinities that are difficult to control."

Uncle Argyros nodded. "Physical actions help you anchor your arcane power and focus your Will."

"He also said each mage must find which gestures work best for them as an individual. I've been experimenting to find what's compatible with my affinity." She didn't want to admit it was a work in progress. No amount of hand waving seemed to tame the Lustra.

She felt the faintest stirring of…something, like a vibration under her feet. Surely she would not have the opposite problem now and be unable to draw power when they might need it.

"How likely is an attack?" she asked. "The border patrols are cautionary, surely? All the fighting must be far away in Tenebra."

There came another flare of his mind magic, and the ward pulsed a response. "Organized warbands of heart hunters have been making surprise attacks directly on the ward."

Cassia's chest tightened. She scanned the ravine below with her keen Hesperine eyesight. It was only then that she realized where they were. She hadn't recognized it from this viewpoint, but she had once fallen to the very bottom of that chasm and been surrounded by possessed heart hunters.

"We're in Martyr's Pass," she said. "You're saying the Collector has more heart hunters under his control?"

"Yes. Nike and I have detected his presence in their minds, but he proves elusive. He avoids dueling with us and throws his pawns at the Stewards."

"Surely the worst the heart hunters can do is ambush Hesperines who step outside the barrier. The ward is too powerful for our enemies to penetrate."

"For all our enemies to date, yes. But we do not fully understand what the Collector is capable of. When he opened that portal inside Orthros during the Solstice Summit, he became the first enemy to violate Hespera's Sanctuary since the founding. We must not underestimate what sabotage he might attempt upon the ward."

The thought that Orthros's enduring defenses might actually be vulnerable made Cassia's stomach turn. "This isn't all the Collector has been up to for the past month. Of that I'm certain."

"This is merely the front where he is detectable," Uncle Argyros agreed.

"We promised that Orthros would keep the Empire safe from him too. Have our Imperial allies reported any signs that he's trying to infiltrate their shores?"

Uncle Argyros shook his head. "But as Tendeso said, they are ready to send the Imperial army, should Solia ask."

"Knowing the Tenebrans, her subjects would see military action by the Empire as a foreign invasion, not a heroic rescue."

"I fear so. Contact between the hemispheres after millennia of isolation is one volatile spell waiting to explode at the slightest provocation. Fortunately, Tendo is not here in an entirely unofficial capacity."

"Solia said he only came for a personal visit."

"He arrived on your Gift Night. Somehow, he received word of the danger you were in. He waited with us until Lio cast his spell light over your tower to signal that you had made it through."

Cassia wanted to give that prickly vulture another hug. "But he stayed after that?"

"He is still Prince Tendeso of the Sandira Kingdom, even when playing the mercenary. The sister states trust him to negotiate with Orthros to ensure their interests are not threatened by our growing alliance with Tenebra."

Cassia arched a brow. "Tendo is here as a diplomat?"

"Admittedly, he spends more time knocking about with Mak and Lyros in the gymnasium than drinking coffee in my library, but we are making progress allaying the Empire's concerns."

"I knew he had it in him," Cassia said. "He might have lost his throne, but he still thinks and acts like a king."

"The Queen Mothers of the Empire see the same in him."

"They're still trying to arrange a marriage for him with the Empress's daughter, aren't they?"

"The Imperial Court talks of nothing else."

Those must be the rumors Solia was bristling about. It was a promising sign that she was so upset by them.

If this war would allow her and Tendo a second chance. Tomorrow was not guaranteed for any of Cassia's mortal loved ones. Not even for Hesperines, in a time of conflict.

Uncle Argyros paused. "Another vote took place in the Firstblood Circle while you were in seclusion."

Cassia turned to him. "They can't have reversed their decision on the Departure. Tell me we are not about to withdraw from Tenebra, not now."

His ancient gaze rested on her. "When Lord Lucis and the Mage Orders declared war on Hesperines, we had to decide how to formally respond. The vote took place during the hours of your Gifting."

"Surely, after how hard Lio and I have fought for Orthros's new alliance with Tenebra, the Circle wouldn't vote for isolation. Not while we weren't even there to defend the treaty."

"It was your plight that decided the outcome. All of Orthros kept vigil, waiting to see if you would survive your transformation. Even your political opponents would not allow your sacrifice to be in vain. The vote was nearly unanimous. For the first time in Orthros's history, we will not withdraw to prevent violence. We will go to war and fight for Tenebra."

Lio, she cried. *Did you hear that?*

Yes. His own astonishment reverberated back to her. *I'm watching it happen, here and now.*

Cassia's thoughts spun. *We've always fought for peace. We didn't want Orthros to abandon Tenebra—but we didn't want a war, either.*

I know.

They had won the vote. But they had lost this round of the Collector's game. They had handed him the war he wanted, and there was no going back now.

"What have we done?" Cassia breathed.

"What this moment in history calls for," Uncle Argyros replied. "Sixteen hundred years ago, when Lyta and I halted the Aithourians' army in this pass so our people could escape Tenebra, I held the unwavering conviction that retreat was the only choice. Here and now, I stand by my vote that the time has come for Hesperines to act. We cannot in good conscience watch this unfold without using our great power to help."

Cassia knew what it meant for Orthros's greatest diplomat to say that. "I never imagined you would be in favor of war."

"I am never in favor of war."

His emotions cracked through his veils. For the first time, she felt Silvertongue's fury. He stood so still, but his protective anger seemed to fill the mountain passes where he and his Grace had halted an army to save their people. The force of his aura in the Blood Union made her new senses tremble, although she was not afraid.

"This is not what I wanted for you and Lio." Their mentor's voice resonated with mind magic. "After centuries of striving for peace, I wanted my successors to inherit a kinder era."

"This isn't what we wanted either. We thought our actions would lead to peace. Not play into the hands of an Old Master."

THE COMPLICATION

Lio stood his ground before the First Prince. "Cassia and I cannot think only of our own safety. This war was the Collector's plan all along. This is the second requirement: violence between Hesperines and the Mage Orders on Tenebran soil."

Rudhira shook his head. "You two will be the targets of his revenge. Step home to Cassia. Now."

"I can't, Rudhira. The visions I saw…Lucis and the Collector want a long bloodbath like the Last War."

Rudhira smiled. His fangs shot down, as threatening as the sword on his back. "Let them try."

Lio's eyes widened. "We cannot give them the violence they want."

"Oh, have no doubt. I will stand between them and everything they want."

"Let us stand with you."

"Listen to me. When I was a newblood, Orthros still lived in fear that the Last War would break out again. This is why I felt called to the battle arts. This is what I've prepared for since I first set foot in the arena. I always knew that when the next war came, it would be my duty to fight for my people. My duty. Not yours or Cassia's."

"And if the Queens had banned you from the arena then? If they called you home now? Would you obey their command?"

Rudhira's steely eyes narrowed. "You are not me, Deukalion of the Eighth Circle. Give me one reason besides your admirable devotion to our people why I should not order you home this instant to tend to your newgift."

"None of us are safe until we find out what's behind that door and how to stop the Collector from getting it."

"The Charge will hunt down a Gift Collector or two. They can answer our questions in my dungeon."

"And when they do? Who among your forces has dueled the Collector and freed souls from his possession?"

Rudhira's jaw tightened.

Lio pressed, "Where will you find a spare Silvicultrix to make sure the Changing Queen's secrets stay buried?"

A shout came from the center of the village. Rudhira muttered an oath, hesitating for an instant that seemed to last forever. Then he let go of Lio and headed toward the square. When Lio followed him, Rudhira did not order him to turn around and go home.

They had no chance for further debate as they joined the others in the square. Mak and Lyros were guiding the villagers into groups small enough for each Hesperine to step with.

"This is everyone," Solia announced. "I will stay until all the villagers are safely inside the keep."

"Two of us will stand guard while two others step," Rudhira said. "Mak, Lyros, you hold the wards here. Lio, with me."

Lio didn't miss the warning in Rudhira's tone. He was still here on probation.

Lio spotted two villagers he recognized and took charge of their group first. The last time he'd seen the older couple, the woman had wept tears of joy to discover that their beloved princess Solia was alive and had returned to deliver them from Lucis's tyranny.

The wizened woman clasped her hands. "Ambassador Deukalion. Have you and Princess Cassia heard from Lady Miranda since that night?"

"We fear the rumors," said her husband. "Is it true the three of you walked into a necromancer's trap at Castra Paradum?"

They still had no idea Miranda herself was the necromancer. The man on two strong legs, giving no sign the king's soldiers had once shattered his knee. The knee Miranda had mended with magic she had ripped out of the innocent healer Pakhne.

Had her love for these people been real? Miranda had claimed she felt a responsibility to them because she had once been their liege lady. Perhaps in her twisted mind, taking Pakhne's magic and using it to save this man was somehow justified. Or had her care for them been another deception to gain Lio and Cassia's trust?

Lio did not have the heart to rob these people of one of their few symbols of hope. "Lady Miranda escaped. I'm sure we'll see her again."

The couple breathed sighs of relief. "She has had to go into hiding before," the wife said, "but she always returns to us."

"Ready?" Rudhira asked Lio. "We're taking them to the great hall inside Castra Patria."

Lio nodded and gathered his magic around the eight villagers entrusted to him, layering veils over his spell. When Rudhira stepped, Lio followed his powerful aura, and together they slipped through the world bearing the weight of mortal beings.

In that split second between one step and the next, light seared Lio's vision. Fire tore him out of the fabric of reality. He landed hard on rocky ground that dug into his knees.

Lio! Cassia cried in his mind. *What's happening?*

I'm all right. He was on his feet again at immortal speed, tightening his veils around the mortals.

Was that a trammeling spell? The kind that halts a Hesperine mid-step?

Light flashed again, and his concealing spells shredded. *And a revelatory spell.*

"Get down!" he called aloud, remembering Rudhira's advice. He and the villagers threw themselves behind the only cover, a dip in the uneven ground.

A ball of fire sailed over their heads, sending a wave of heat over Lio's scalp.

Where is Rudhira? Cassia asked.

I don't know. Lio flared his senses around him.

Rudhira and his group were nowhere near. Lio was all that stood between that mage and the villagers.

The man in flame-colored robes rotated his hands, gathering another ball of his volatile magic.

Before the core of fire was fully formed, Lio drove his magic toward the mage's mind. Searing pain lit in his own head as he worked his thelemancy through the fiery battle wards surrounding the mage. He had broken through the dream wards in a Gift Collector's mind. He would not quail before a pyromagus's defenses.

The mage let out a grunt of effort. The fire grew brighter.

Lio unleashed more magic. White-gold light glared in his eyes, making the world disappear, and pain drove deeper into his skull. But through the fire, he caught hold of the mage's thoughts, disciplined structures built around a thirst for violence. Tonight, he would finally experience the thrill of killing a Hesperine.

Or so he thought. Lio, his skin burning, collapsed the mage's lifetime of training like a house of cards. It took one blow from his full power to reduce the man's intelligent mind to ruins.

The mage crumpled to the ground, the remnants of his fire fizzling out in the wet grass.

Lio had an instant of relief before alarm hit him in the chest. Cassia's emotions.

He sucked in a breath. *What's wrong?*

Her aura honed into determination. *Nothing Uncle Argyros and I cannot take care of.*

Where in the Goddess's name are you?

Martyr's Pass, she said with far too much grim delight. *Helping the Stand teach some possessed heart hunters just how well protected Orthros is.*

Lio swore. His blood boiled with the wrongness of it. His Grace was out of his reach and facing the Collector's pawns. But his rational mind knew he and the villagers were in a more precarious position.

He looked around him through the spots on his vision. They were only halfway to the fortress.

He reached for Rudhira's aura again, but all he felt were two fiery presences. Bleeding thorns. There were more war mages between them and Castra Patria.

"We must stay calm," he said to the eight frightened mortals looking to him for guidance. "We'll return to the village, where the Stewards' wards can protect us."

The elderly couple nodded, and their neighbors seemed to take their approval as reassurance. Lio made sure the fall hadn't harmed them, then stepped them all back toward the village.

His heart seemed to hammer a thousand times in that instant, waiting for a mage to trammel him again. When he set foot on solid ground and saw the village around them, he heaved a sigh of relief.

Until the volley of flaming arrows flew down from the sky. Twelve soldiers in Lucis's colors stood on the nearest hill, already drawing their bows again.

A dozen points of magefire struck the wards, and a dozen points of darkness flared where they landed. Mak and Lyros bared their fangs, their bleeding hands joined, as shadows rose from their auras to strengthen their spell.

Solia helped the elderly couple up, her aura dangerously warm. Lio feared that if the enemy broke through the defenses, she would draw her sword or even reveal her magic.

He swept out a veiled probe of thelemancy, testing the archers' minds. What he sensed sent a chill through him.

The Collector's rage whispered through their thoughts. *You've returned. I've been waiting.*

He's there too? Cassia called.

Throwing taunts through Lucis's soldiers, Lio said.

We'll send him our own message.

The Collector gave no sign he had sensed her in Lio's thoughts. Just like the first time they had dueled him together in a waking dream, their Grace Union was somehow shielded from his mental invasion. That sacred bond held true, beyond the Old Master's power.

Another wave of arrows rained down, and Lio shuddered at the pain he felt in Mak and Lyros's auras.

Miranda's visions rose again in his and Cassia's joined thoughts. Hesperines dying in flares of light. Mortals caught between them and the mages' flames. The odors of bloodshed and burning flesh.

Here, now, one of her visions could so easily became reality.

Pick our battles, Cassia said.

Retreat to better ground, Lio agreed. "We have to retreat!"

Still running from me, Deukalion? the Collector hissed. *You cannot run far enough. There is nowhere you can hide.*

Tell him we're not hiding, Cassia snarled. *We're coming for him.*

We always violate the rules of your game, Lio shouted at him. *We are the complication you fail to predict. Cassia and I will keep breaking your grand design—for eternity.*

Lio felt the moment when the certainty spread through the Collector's vast mind. His rage burst forth like a poison, and the archers he inhabited staggered.

It is done, the Collector hissed. *She is one of you now.*

A laugh tore out of Lio, rife with his and Cassia's triumph. *We won that round, Kallikrates.*

My most delicate instrument. You destroyed her. I will destroy you.

THE HEART HUNTERS, CLAD in white furs, blended into the snow below the precipice. But Cassia could easily track their movements with her Hesperine eyes. Her ears picked up four dozen distinct heartbeats.

They advanced through the brewing snowstorm, their white liegehounds baying at their sides. Knight let out a warning howl that echoed down into the ravine.

The men and their dogs looked like what they were: playing pieces on a great game board.

Cassia was watching the Collector advance upon the Queens' ward.

"His name is Kallikrates," Cassia said.

"Hespera's blood," Uncle Argyros murmured. "You have put a name to one of the Old Masters."

Cassia reached deeper into the mountains, searching for even a hint of the power that came to her so easily from the letting site. "There really are six of them, a hex of necromancers who have existed for thousands upon thousands of years. They were mortal men when the Diviner Queen opened her spirit gate in the Empire and traveled to this side of the world for the first time. When she taught the people here to use magic, the Old Masters began to abuse that power. She managed to protect the Empire by collapsing the gate, but this continent has been their tournament field ever since."

"Cassia...once again, what you and Lio have learned is turning our understanding of the past and present on its head. These are secrets of the ages. And yet you saw the shattered gate with your own eyes, and you have also beheld the Old Masters' game."

She watched the heart hunters reach the top of the pass, powerless to hold them off. Where was her Lustra now? "They control everything, Uncle Argyros. They're the puppet masters pulling the strings of every king and mage and peasant. It's all a sick contest to them. Their sport has killed entire civilizations. There are eras of history we never knew existed, because the Old Masters' past matches erased them."

"So this is what drives them. These are the inner workings we see when we peer into minds so powerful and ancient they have become inhuman. It is a wonder they have not destroyed each other yet. It seems they will preserve their own existence and the balance of power among them at any cost."

Cassia nodded. "They have rules. The game in our time is a match of subtlety and strategy. They are to keep their influence a secret from humankind. Kallikrates lives for conspiracy, so he thinks this is his opportunity to win a round."

"What are the criteria to win? What is the prize for the Old Master who emerges the victor?"

"We don't know, but the answer may well be hidden behind that sealed door. Lio and I need to find out what's inside."

A heart hunter's horn droned through the air, and Cassia shivered. The last time she'd heard that sound, the avalanche it conjured had nearly killed her. "We have to do something!"

Uncle Argyros held up a hand. "We must wait for the Stand's signal."

Down in the pass, five figures in black battle robes materialized out of the billowing snow. The Guardian of Orthros and the four Stewards moved in on the heart hunters.

Crossbow bolts ricocheted off Alkaios and Nephalea's wards. Kadi drew off the liegehounds with a trail of her blood, levitating and stepping with expert precision to dodge their leaps and bites.

Nike and Lyta swept through the warband in the blink of an eye. But now Cassia could perceive their every graceful blow. They moved in a tandem they must have practiced to perfection over their centuries in the arena. Crossbows broke in their grasp, then bones.

But the heart hunters kept fighting. They dodged the fleet immortals' attacks with eerie speed. When one of their fists landed on Nike's jaw, Cassia realized just how much preternatural strength the Collector could give his puppets.

The sight of the Collector laying a hand on Nike filled Cassia with anger.

Why must channeling be so much harder away from the letting site? she fumed.

It feels hard now because it's new, Lio reassured her, *but you will master it. Remember, it comes naturally to you.*

Her gaze darted to the few twisted pines that clung to the mountain slopes. *There is life in this soil. I will reach it!*

Dark shapes swooped over the ravine. Vultures, already circling in anticipation of death.

Cassia's anger rose higher. She threw her senses as far as she could with all her might, a silent yell into the chasm. It only rebounded back on her, making her sway on her feet.

Easy. Lio's voice steadied her. *Trust the Stand to hold them off. You have time to form your spell. Concentrate on your technique.*

She shut her eyes and tried to slow down, to focus.

Her concentration broke at the scratch of claws on stone. Knight growled. Her eyes flew open.

The six vultures had landed in a half circle in front of her and Uncle Argyros. Before Cassia's eyes, they transformed into men wearing white furs and armed with battle axes.

"Changers," she spat. *How dare he use Lustra magic against me!*

He'll never guess you still have yours. You have the advantage of surprise.

If I can use it!

Six clean strikes of thelemancy arced from Uncle Argyros's aura and slammed into the heart hunters.

Their heads snapped back, but they did not fall. Their lips parted, and with the same voice, they spoke in unison.

"Cassia," the Collector lamented. "I crafted you so perfectly. The Hesperines have ruined you."

"I'll ruin you," she snarled.

"Back up until you're inside the ward." Uncle Argyros's fangs showed. "He's fighting to hold these men. It will take time to drive him out."

She could see Uncle Argyros's battle for their Wills in their movements. The men raised their axes, their arms moving slowly, as if pushing against a great force.

Knight leapt for the heart hunter nearest to her. He clamped his jaws on the man's arm, and the axe dropped. The possessed hunter didn't even scream as Knight wrestled him to the ground.

The other five heart hunters lifted their leaden feet and managed one stride nearer.

"Cassia," Uncle Argyros shouted, "get behind the ward!"

She didn't obey. She didn't even think. In desperation, she tore her fangs across both her palms and held out her bleeding hands.

When her blood hit the stone at her feet, the power came roaring up to her. A shout of victory left her lips, and Lio echoed it in her mind.

She let the channeling overtake her. The Lustra tasted harsh here, frosty and sharp and determined to survive. She drew deeper. The power took on the metallic tang of blood.

Blood magic saturated these wilds. The Queens' ward had been anchored in this ground for countless seasons. Cassia drew Lustra magic up through the greatest masterpiece of Hesperine magic.

Stone cracked. Woody vines climbed out of the ground, their curved thorns hooking into the heart hunters' flesh. Everywhere they drew blood, dark buds sprouted. Magic pounded through Cassia, flowing into her creations, and the black roses unfurled.

"Impossible," the Collector cried with six voices. "I took your magic. I left you powerless."

Cassia smiled and ran her tongue over one fang, adding more blood to her spell. In that moment, she felt no fear at all. Her old nemesis was gone. Her new strength was in her veins.

She twisted her hands, and her rose vines twined tighter around the necromancer's pawns. Feathers drifted on the air as they shrank back into their beast forms, escaping her thorns and Knight's snapping teeth. The vultures hurled themselves from the precipice.

She curled her hands into fists, squeezing more blood onto the stone. The vines snapped outward over the ledge. One twisted around a vulture's wing, plucking it from the air.

He flapped madly, at last tearing himself away from the thorns. But on his ruined pinion, he plummeted into the ravine.

Cassia's heart seemed to stop. The missed beat left a gaping emptiness inside her. She clutched at her chest with her bleeding hands, but she couldn't hold it. Couldn't stop it. Life drained out of her grasp.

No. Lio's presence breathed into her. *Your heart is still beating with mine.*

At his reminder that she lived, her mind grasped what she had just experienced in the Blood Union. It was the heart hunter's blood that had stilled in his veins.

She crept forward to the edge of the precipice and looked down.

All through Martyr's Pass, tangles of black had burst through the white snow. Thickets of the dark roses now fortified the ward like rows of stakes below a castle under siege.

The dead vulture had landed at Nike's feet. Cassia watched the bird transform back into the remains of a man.

She tried to breathe, then regretted it. Death smelled so much worse as a Hesperine.

IN THE COLLECTOR'S MOMENT of distraction, Lio poured his thelemancy into the archers. Two of their minds sprang free from Kallikrates. With shouts of confusion, the pair dropped their bows and fled.

But the reprieve was over. The Collector's presence grew stronger in the ten remaining bowmen, and his full attention fixed on Lio.

They nocked two arrows to their bows and fired again at Mak and Lyros's ward.

His Trial brothers had made the most of the momentary advantage, too. Their spell felt more powerful, fortified against the next volley. As each arrowhead struck their barrier, the magefire hissed out.

Except one. The last bolt tore through the ward, hurtling at Lio's heart.

He leapt into the air, levitating out of the arrow's reach. It landed at the feet of the statues in the center of the square. Cassia's statue. Magefire licked at the offerings the villagers had left there, and the flowers began to burn.

Solia's hands were curled into fists, her knuckles white. How tempted she must be to put out that fire. Lio met her gaze and shook his head. This was not the moment to betray her secret.

Her eyes flashed, but she answered with a nod.

There was no time for Lio to duel the Collector for ten more minds, nor to wait for Rudhira. Lio had to get everyone out before the village burned—or Tenebra's new queen used her magic and got herself branded an apostate by her own people.

But with war mages waiting to intercept them, how?

His hand went to the medallion at his neck. *Cassia, do you think I can open the secret passageways into Patria now?*

The Lustra has accepted you as my mate. Try!

Lio focused his Will on his medallion. The villagers' fearful voices and Solia's calm commands faded from his awareness. He didn't hear the next volley of arrows hit Mak and Lyros's ward.

But no Lustra magic hummed at him from within his talisman, only blood enchantments.

Of course. He knew what the Lustra wanted of him. He bit his palm and clasped the medallion again in his bleeding hand.

The three ivy leaves warmed at his touch.

A flicker of his light magic shot from his hand. It winked out between two cottages. Then came another pulse, guiding him in the same direction.

"Mak, Lyros," he called out, "can you maintain the ward just a little longer?"

"If we can't," Mak shouted back, "I'll break the archers' hands myself."

Lio eyed the magefire charring the statues. "Watch out for the flames!"

"We'll ward those off as well, for as long as we can," Lyros said. "Can you get the villagers away from here?"

"Yes." Lio prayed that was true. "Everyone, follow me. There's a hidden passage that will take us to the keep."

The villagers looked to Solia. Without hesitation, she came to Lio's side and led her people after him. At last, their disastrous conflicts were behind them, and she trusted him in battle.

He followed his darting spell light through the village. It led him to a familiar gate at the very edge of Mederi. Just outside the village wall, his spell light struck the grass and traced out a symbol. A hawk drawn in the intricate knotwork of Lustri artists.

I found an entrance. He held the sight before him in his thoughts for Cassia to see.

The very spot where Miranda left her undead crow familiar as a taunt? That cannot be a coincidence.

The Collector must know the passages are here.

But the Lustra had deprived him of what it had given to Lio—the blessing of its Silvilcultrix. Lio made a libation of blood on the hawk symbol.

Grass and soil and roots pulled back, opening a portal into the ground. Rough-hewn steps led down into darkness.

It worked! he told Cassia.

Is the Collector trying to follow you inside?

Not a chance. He swept his power through every mind waiting to enter.

"Hurry," Solia bade the villagers. "Two at a time. Help those who come down behind you."

As she guided her people into the passage, Lio stood back. He felt the Collector nipping at the villagers' thoughts, seeking a way in. Lio pushed back, a declaration across the arcane plane. These people were under his protection.

When the last villager was safely inside, Lio scanned the flames engulfing the village. He couldn't see Mak and Lyros.

Can you sense their auras? Cassia cried.

I don't know. There's too much fire magic!

Fear seized him and Cassia together. He took one step forward, on the verge of dashing back into the flames to find them. But he had no wards to keep that fire from destroying him and Cassia's hope of survival.

Lio shouted their names until he was hoarse. No answer.

Then, at last, a whorl of shadow emerged from the smoke. Mak and Lyros ran toward him, wrapped in the last vestiges of their ward. More arrows arced over the village behind them, setting thatched roofs aflame.

"No harm done," Mak called over the sound of wooden beams collapsing.

Lyros pushed his sooty hair out of his eyes. "Except to the archers."

Thank the Goddess, Cassia breathed.

Lio echoed her prayer aloud and threw his arms around Mak and Lyros's shoulders, urging them into the passage. He levitated down behind them.

You cannot hide, came the Collector's final whisper, as the earth sealed behind Lio, shutting the necromancer out of the Changing Queen's hallowed halls.

AN OLD NEMESIS

*A*RE YOU ALL RIGHT? Lio asked Cassia in the sudden silence.

A heartbeat. *I don't know.*

He felt it in her blood. Death. He would never forget what it was like to experience that for the first time as a Hesperine.

Hold on, my Grace. We fall apart together, remember?

I refuse to fall apart while you're still in danger. Let me help you remember the route through the passages.

With her ever-present in his mind, he navigated the ivy-covered corridors, his spell light illuminating the way for the mortals. Along the twists and turns, her tension only grew. A burning thirst eclipsed the chill of death in her aura.

Lio's fangs dropped. *You need me.*

I can hold out. You must get everyone to safety.

Lio cursed the miles between them. He forged ahead, but with the villagers and their animals, they proceeded at a crawl. Cassia's pulse seemed to fill the passageways, her Craving needling deeper into Lio's own veins.

When he found the way out at last, it was through a portal into the great hall of Castra Patria. The exhausted villagers stumbled onto the dais behind the Hesperines and their queen.

The ceremonial chamber of the Lords of Tenebra was now crowded with bedrolls and worried mortals. Mages moved among Solia's subjects with food and bandages, while warriors stood around a table cluttered with maps. At Solia's appearance out of the wall, everyone leapt into action to assist her with the latest evacuees.

Gray-haired Lord Hadrian came to Solia's side. "Your Majesty, you went yourself, without your guards?"

"I was away from my people for fifteen years," she told him. "I won't spend this war out of sight inside the defenses."

"My Queen," her most loyal general growled, "will you not spend this war where I can make sure you survive it?"

"I do my best not to make your duties more difficult. Within reason."

"And I do my best not to hinder you, Your Majesty. Under protest."

"Your dissent is noted, my lord." Her eyes crinkled with affection. "I did have Hesperines with me."

"We'll always return her to you without a scratch, Lord Hadrian," Mak said, levitating a startled but grateful elder down off the dais.

"Stewards." The mortal warrior greeted them with a long-suffering sigh, but a chord of respect hummed between him and Lio's Trial brothers. "Take some steel with you next time, along with your"—he waved his hand in the air—"shadows and moondrizzle."

"Also noted," Lyros said with friendly salute, directing more of the villagers to descend.

Lio tossed their belongings down to them. "Alas, they only had a diplomat for reinforcements, but I assure you I brought my best moondrizzle tonight."

"Ambassador," Lord Hadrian said. "Well, this is a surprise. To the enemy as well, I take it."

"We have him to thank for our safe return," said Solia.

"And for Princess Cassia's life, I understand." Lord Hadrian's hard gaze rested on Lio.

He knew his Grace would always be Princess Cassia in Lord Hadrian's heart. "My lord, Orthros has bestowed on her all the power and honor she deserves. You have my vow that she will want for nothing—for as long as we both shall live."

Lord Hadrian clasped Lio's arm and pulled him near. "Well done," he murmured gruffly, before turning away to issue more orders.

Lio let out a breath. "I did not expect that."

"There is room in his definition of honor for resorting to Hesperine moondrizzle to keep Cassia and me safe." Solia gave Lio's arm a squeeze before joining her men at the table.

Lio looked around the chaotic great hall. How many souls in this room would they lose before the war was through? How many would they lose tonight?

He saw no sign of Rudhira and his group of villagers.

Stay until you know he's safe, Cassia insisted.

Can you manage?

He is in greater danger than I am right now.

Craving fever is no small matter, my Grace.

I can manage, she said again.

"Rudhira should be here by now," Lio said.

"I know." Mak's aura throbbed with worry. "But we have our orders, and it will not help him if we disobey."

"We're needed on the walls," Lyros told Lio. "We're going to reinforce the Charge's warders."

Lio nodded. "You two go. I'm heading back into the tunnels."

Lio plunged back through the wall. He sent his thelemancy deep into the tunnels, and strange impressions echoed back to him. Magic played by different rules here. The Lustra's rules.

But he managed to catch a hint of auras. Cursing the inability to step in here, he set off at a run.

He quickly came upon a group of eight humans. The villagers Rudhira had escorted out of Mederi were bedraggled but alive. His sudden arrival startled them, but then they breathed sighs of relief.

"Can you show us the way out?" the village miller pleaded.

Lio nodded. "Where is the Hesperine who stepped you out of the village?"

The man pointed back the way they had come. "He had to stay behind with the wounded one."

Lio's heart jolted.

Who is it? came Cassia's swift response.

I don't know.

Drawing blood from his hand again, Lio grasped his pendant and sent a spell light floating through the tunnels toward the portal. "Follow my light. It will take you to safety in the fortress."

The grateful villagers set off, and Lio raced deeper into the passages. Amid the bizarre magic that breathed around him, he caught a whisper, a certainty. The Lustra itself seemed to guide him.

He found Rudhira in the glow of another portal. The prince crouched over a fallen Hesperine. Lio showed Cassia the image before him.

Not Kalos! she cried.

Lio knelt by their unconscious friend. "What happened?"

"Someone put a magefire arrow in my best scout's chest," Rudhira growled. "And as soon as I heal the wound, I'll go find that archer and put Thorn in him."

Lio knew from his own experience with a magefire wound how much pain was burning through Kalos's veins as they spoke. "Will he make it?"

Rudhira's healing magic saturated Kalos's aura. "Yes. My spell is working faster than I could have hoped. I believe it's the strong Lustra magic here."

He's going to be all right, Lio relayed to Cassia, *thanks to the passages. The Lustra is helping Rudhira heal him.*

Her fear eased. *He's not the only Hesperine Lustra mage any longer. I hope this proves to him that I have his back.*

"How did you two get into the passages?" Lio asked. "No one could enter without Cassia escorting them until tonight, when we discovered I can now open them."

Rudhira raised his brows at Lio. "When the war mages intercepted our step, they pulled you and me out at different locations. I had just taken care of the one near me when Kalos found me. He said that glowing portals have appeared all over the countryside surrounding Castra Patria, and Hesperine blood will open and close them. When he led us to the entrance, I could sense your magic."

Astonished, Lio reached for Cassia's presence again. *I think we managed to open the passages for Kalos. Even the entire Charge.*

The Lustra has accepted not just my Grace, but all Hesperines?

At least in this network of tunnels. Orthros's Silvicultrix has given us quite a gift.

It's your Gift to me that did it. This wasn't possible before I was a Hesperine.

"The archers ambushed us as we were heading inside," Rudhira said.

"Kalos sent everyone else down first. The arrow caught him when he was sealing the portal behind us."

Kalos groaned and stirred.

"Lie still," Rudhira urged him.

He's awake, Lio reassured Cassia.

Tell him not to scare us like that.

Lio passed her words on to Kalos, who grinned faintly. "Tell her these tunnels saved my hide tonight."

"Yes, they did." Rudhira sat back from his patient at last.

"My Prince," Lio said, "tonight you've seen what Cassia and I can do."

Rudhira let out a heavy sigh. "I want you two safe at home. But I think the Goddess has other ideas."

"Let us use our power against Kallikrates."

At last, Rudhira nodded. "When Hespera creates new defenders for us, I will not dishonor her gift. I will inform Argyros and Lyta of my decision, and we will tell you when and where you, Cassia, Mak, and Lyros should report for duty."

"We'll be ready." Somehow.

Her newborn Craving was like a knife in his chest every time he drew breath.

"Now go," Rudhira said. "Dawn is coming, and you can't afford for the sun to catch you here."

He was right. Cassia couldn't withstand it if the Dawn Slumber trapped Lio in Tenebra.

PATH OF DESTRUCTION

I'M COMING, LIO SAID to her. *Where are you?*

They took me home. Her voice was faint under a cacophony of magic and Craving.

He loosened his collar. *Are you alone now?*

Yes.

He gave into Cassia's aura, letting their Union pull him out of the passages and back to Orthros. He looked around in surprise at where his step had brought him. This icebound thicket must be somewhere in the unkempt gardens of House Komnena.

Behind him, a trail of black roses and chaotic emotions marked his Grace's flight across the grounds. In front of him, a wall of thorns stood between him and her trembling presence.

"Cassia, what are you doing out here?"

Trying not to cause more destruction.

As he stood there, her bastion of thorns was growing and sprouting more black roses by the moment. He could feel the roots of her power spreading through the garden, feeding on the letting site's nourishment. Her thoughts were just as wild.

He caressed her beleaguered mind. *You're inundated. Won't you let me in so I can help?*

No! Your blood... He heard her swallow. *The magic will feed on it too.*

Let it, he said. *You need me.*

I don't want to hurt you.

He took a step nearer, almost gouging his hand on an icethorn bush. The black rose vines shot out and constricted around the other plant. He observed as they snapped off the branch that had threatened him and yanked the icethorn bush out of his way to clear his path to Cassia.

Your magic is having an overprotective response, not a threatening one.

But how do I stop it?

Lio thought fast. She was channeling a potentially unlimited quantity of magic out of the Lustra. None of the techniques he relied on when he suffered inundation would work for her. She needed somewhere to put all that magic until the Lustra's defensive instincts calmed.

Well, he knew of one place she could put it. Safely—perhaps.

I want you to try channeling all of this magic into me.

Lio, no! The wall of roses thickened with the force of her refusal. *I won't experiment on you.*

We've drawn on the letting site together before. You know how I enjoyed those experiments.

It was tame *then! It obeyed me. Right now it's...ready to kill.*

The image of the dead heart hunter flashed in their Union.

Let me come in, Lio pleaded. *Let me hold you.*

I have no control right now, she warned. *I can't promise what I'll do to you once you're within reach.*

I know that, and I'm choosing to come in.

Her lust coiled through him, and his fangs lengthened in readiness. He stripped out of everything but his medallion, dropping his clothes next to hers, where she appeared to have torn them off before the vines had closed around her. Cold air and the heat of her thirst sent a frisson over his skin. His own Craving stirred, tightening his body.

What if you need me to stop? she asked.

My magic can hold its own with yours, my Grace. I could stop you if I needed to. He ran his power deeper into her thoughts.

He heard the soft rasp of her tongue on her lips.

How would the Lustra's defenses like a taste of his blood? He reached out and tried pricking his finger on one thorn.

The roses shivered and stretched, parting to welcome him. As soon as he stepped inside, the thorn wall tangled tight again, enclosing him in roses on all sides. Through the barrier of vines overhead, a single moonbeam reached.

A shape darted through the shaft of light at immortal speed. He glimpsed her eyes, two glowing rings of green-gold around her dilated pupils.

Then she was upon him, her Hesperine strength carrying them both to the ground. He landed on his back with her nails digging into his chest. Vines caressed his arms and legs, coiling around his limbs.

The roses held him down for her as she struck his jugular. He felt the impact of her fangs all the way to his groin, suddenly, painfully hard. Oaths ran through his mind, but he was speechless. He threw his head back so she could dig her canines in deeper.

She ravished his throat, sucking and biting with desperate moans. Silken rose petals teased the inside of his thigh, but no thorns pricked him. Only her fangs pierced him, drawing pleasure-pain up out of his veins.

She ran a grasping hand down his body, finding his erection. Her firm grip made him hiss with pleasure. She put him where she wanted him, fitting them together with a rough stroke of her hand and a buck of her hips.

Her bite tightened and, anchored on his throat, she came down on him fast and hard. Wet heat closed over his shaft in the cold air. He arched against his bonds, pushing up into the grip of her new body's taut muscles.

Their breaths clouded in the air, and warm blood trailed down his neck for their bed of roses to feed on. Fragrance weighed heavy on his chest, and unbound Lustra magic saturated his arcane senses. He heard leaves sliding against each other and the snap of new vines spreading.

Bring all that magic into me, he said.

She let out another delirious moan, riding him at the same rough pace as she fed on his throat. Her magic stretched wantonly outward.

If it wouldn't obey her Will, he would have to make it recognize their bond.

His fangs straining, he wrapped himself closer in her mind. *Give it to me.*

Her thoughts tangled around his, possessive. She pulled his mouth to her neck.

Yes. He sank his fangs into her. As he dragged her blood into his mouth, he tugged her deeper into their Union, a silent demand for her magic.

The wild tendrils of Lustra magic around them suddenly flowed into a single, powerful current, as if finding their natural path.

Stop me now, she warned, *or I'll—*
I want every drop of you.

The full force of her channeling slammed into his chest.

Power. Limitless as his own. His to feast on for eternity.

Magic bloomed and prickled through his every nerve. Spasms of pleasure erupted deep in his muscles. He jerked under her, releasing inside her, and he could only ride the magic as it worked his body. When he was spent, the power kept pounding through him, driving him higher, harder, until he exploded again.

Her inundation ran its course in his veins, leaving his immortal frame scoured and exhilarated. He lay there at the mercy of his Silvicultrix and had never felt more indestructible.

At last, an arcane silence fell. Her aura was still. So were the roses overhead, which had eased apart to give him a glimpse of the moons. They had released his limbs at some point, but he didn't move.

Cassia pushed against his chest, raising herself up gingerly. Blinking down at him, she wiped the blood trailing from her lips.

Her eyes focused, and she gasped. "Are you all right?"

He let out a hoarse laugh. "You must be joking."

She ran her hands over him, as if checking for injuries, but her motions only reminded him how pleasing it was for his wrung-out body to still be inside of hers.

He caught her hand and began licking her stained fingers. She had bitten her tongue at some point. Their blood tasted so good together on her skin.

She rested her head on his chest and shut her eyes. "I cannot believe you did that—strode in here and faced the unbound Lustra, no matter the consequences."

"I had no cause to worry. Your magic loves me."

"We still didn't know what it would do to you! The risks you take for me…"

"I promised I would guide you, every step of the way."

"Thank you for helping me make sense of this," she said.

"You know making sense of your mysteries is one of my favorite pursuits," he replied.

"How did you even know what to do?"

"This kind of inundation has happened to me before because I have a dual affinity."

"Your light magic and mind magic cause this too? Not just my strange Lustra-blood magic?"

"Yes. Your magic is a unified duality, rather than a dual affinity, but it's the same principle. Remind me to add that to my notes."

She caressed his face. "When this happened to you, I wasn't here to help. How did you make it stop?"

"With decades of effort." He propped his head on his arm to look at her. "I walk through this world on eggshells, knowing I'm more powerful than most living things around me. You have no idea how good it feels to be confronted with your power."

"Oh," she exclaimed softly. "Now I understand. You need to feel magic as vast as yours." She frowned, tracing his lips with her fingers. "Did you feel alone before?"

"Of course."

"Even here in Orthros, where we're surrounded by powerful beings?"

"I think it must take its toll on every powerful Hesperine. It's that moment after a spell goes wrong and leaves you in pieces. You realize that in the place at your core, where only you and your magic dwell, you are truly alone."

She swallowed. "Yes. That's what I felt tonight."

"Not even the Blood Union reaches there." He swept his fingers into her hair. "But Grace Union does."

She touched her forehead to his. "Thank you for coming into that place with me."

"There is nowhere I would rather be."

"Sometimes I ask myself why Hespera yoked you to a half-mad Silvicultrix for eternity. But I suppose she knew you needed someone with as much magic as you. And plenty of unexplained abilities to keep that curious mind of yours from growing bored."

He laughed, but not without pain. "I thank her for giving me a Grace as strong as you. Do you know how much it means to me that no matter how powerful I am, I can never break you?"

She hid her face against his neck. "Yes."

Yes. She did know, for she had broken someone tonight.

He wrapped his arms around her, savoring the feeling of her mind resting with his. Her Will, beautiful and whole, protected forever by the mind ward he had cast for her. They had fused the spell to her mortal mind, but her Gifting had brought it into eternity with her, transforming it into something with roots that ran deep in their Grace Union.

Her presence was an antidote to his memories. He could still feel the mage's mind crumpling in his hold. A life, gone at his mere touch.

"I wonder if he had a child at home that he loved," Lio said, "like Dexion Chrysanthos. Or if he might have turned out like Eudias instead, if he hadn't been forced into the Aithourian Circle and taught to hate Hesperines."

Cassia nodded. "I was thinking the same thing about the heart hunter. Could he have become a Hesperine like Kalos, given the chance?"

Lio stroked her hair. "I'm so sorry, Cassia. I know how it feels to make your first kill. To experience death with a human through the Blood Union."

"I was so callous as a mortal. I considered assassinating my own sire. I never imagined I would take a life for the first time after becoming a Hesperine."

"You did what we all must do. Protect our people."

"I could have let him fly away."

"If you had, he would have been back tomorrow night to aim another axe at our family."

"I didn't think about that. I didn't use my judgment at all. I was consumed by this need to hurt him."

"Because he threatened the people you love."

"But I cannot afford to act on instinct." Her hand curled into a fist. "Self-control was always my greatest strength. My life depended on it. Why can't I manage that now, when other lives depend on me?"

"Cassia, you were never that self-controlled lady. You were always this powerful mage, locked inside your fear and pain and anger. Don't ever try to be that careful version of yourself again." He lifted her face toward his. "Break everything in your path."

20
nights until
WINTER SOLSTICE

A FUTURE DREAMED

Feeling safe in his arms, she let him carry her out of the tangle of thorns at midveil. Thank the Goddess no new black roses sprouted in their wake. He took her back to their tower, and when he laid her in their bed, the flowers on the bedposts merely turned toward them in welcome. Knight settled nearby on his favorite blanket, content to be back with his people.

Although there was no Slumber during polar night, she had learned that she and Lio could find a sort of rest together. They drifted in their Grace Union, a balm to each other's troubled thoughts, until the ringing of the city bells reached them within their Sanctuary.

Moon Hours had arrived in the world beyond, which meant nightfall in Tenebra.

"We'll see if there's any news of Kalos's condition," Lio said before she even voiced her concern.

She reached cautiously into her well of power. Still calm for the time being. "I think I'm fit to be in the company of others."

"Shame." Lio squeezed her backside.

Laughing, she pulled his hand away. "You may kidnap me back to our tower as soon as we keep our promise to Zoe to see her carved goats."

Lio gave a long-suffering sigh. "You have to promise me another round of magical experiments."

Despite his light tone, she sensed the need lurking within him, deeply possessive and barely reassured.

She kept hold of his hand, drawing one of his long, elegant fingers slowly between her teeth. "I will promise you more than that."

Both hunger and curiosity lit his jewel blue gaze. She quickly covered the plan in her thoughts with powerful imaginings of their next feast.

Lio groaned and dragged a pillow over his face, hiding his suddenly extended fangs. "Stop torturing me, my Grace, or *I* won't be fit company for others."

She asked him for a cleaning spell before they dressed, knowing that if they took a proper bath, they might not come out for hours.

When they arrived at the main house, Rudhira and Kalos's auras drew them to the library. They entered to find the scout slumped on a couch, a bandage visible in the vee of his loose robe. Knight trotted over to him with a whine, and Kalos rubbed her hound's ears with his good hand.

Cassia had never seen Kalos so haggard. "How are you feeling?"

"Terrible," Rudhira answered for him, standing over Kalos with his arms crossed.

"I'm fit for duty," Kalos protested.

"You're fit for duty when I say you are," Rudhira replied. "That arrow landed too close to your heart."

"You need me in the field, My Prince."

"I need you alive. When I told you you're temporarily relieved of duty, it wasn't a friendly offer of a holiday. With a magefire wound like that, you should be convalescing in the Healing Sanctuary."

Kalos shuddered. "If I'm cooped up in there, the cure will be worse than the kill. No disrespect to your esteemed mother, of course. You know I'm…not very Hesperine, when it comes down to it."

Rudhira's scowl deepened. "Don't ever say that about yourself again. That's an order. Taking that arrow for the rest of us is one of the most Hesperine things you've ever done."

A flush brought color to the scout's ashen face, and he ducked his head. "Very well, My Prince."

"Any progress finding the archer who did this?" Lio asked.

Rudhira scowled. "The only evidence he left behind was the arrow I took out of Kalos. All that tells me is that he favors apple wood for crafting his arrow shafts. But mark my words, I will bring him to justice. In the meantime, I'll see to it Kalos has the unique resources you need to fully recover. I hope you two can help me with this dilemma."

"Of course," Cassia said, already sensing Lio's agreement. "House Komnena must be the only place in Orthros where Kalos can properly convalesce, thanks to my letting site. He can stay here, and the healers can make house calls."

"I wouldn't want to impose," Kalos said.

"It's not an imposition," Lio hastened to assure him.

"No," said Rudhira, "it's your new assignment. Our Hesperine Silvicultrix is necessary to the war effort. Your task is to help Lio get her ready for action. Teach her everything you can about Lustra magic. You have until Winter Solstice to heal and train. The night after the festival ends, I—reluctantly, mind you—need all three of you back in the field."

Knight licked his hand and subjected him to a most pathetic gaze.

Rudhira sighed and ruffled the dog's ears. "Yes, I mean all four of you, you drooling monster."

Cassia hid a smile behind her hand.

But Lio was not smiling. His arm tightened protectively around her waist.

Is this plan acceptable to you? she asked.

Also reluctantly, he replied. "You can rely on us, My Prince. We'll ensure Cassia can hold her own Abroad."

"We'll be ready," she agreed. "Won't we, Kalos?"

Kalos hesitated, his brows knit, but then nodded. "I won't let you down."

At that moment, four more auras and the aroma of coffee filled the library. Uncle Argyros stepped in with Aunt Lyta, Mak, Lyros, and a very large, steaming pot.

Mak grinned at Cassia. "Those roses are wicked!"

She dusted red snow off his shoulder fretfully. "How wicked?"

"Wicked enough to make our duties easier, and Orthros safer," Lyros answered.

Aunt Lyta let down her long auburn hair down, her aura tired but relieved. "Your roses are so effective at protecting our border that I can spare these two to accompany you to Tenebra when you leave."

"Time for an adventure," Mak said with enthusiasm.

Lyros tucked his Grace braid behind Mak's ear. "A *defensive* adventure."

Mak's grin only widened. "I'm sure defensive maneuvers will require us to rough up the enemy a little."

Lio turned to his uncle, his brow furrowed. "It seems Cassia and I need to request a leave of absence from the diplomatic service."

Uncle Argyros shook his head. "No, my Ambassadors for Tenebran Affairs. I am sending you Abroad as diplomats errant with the Charge, empowered to represent Orthros on the front lines. Negotiate when you can. Fight when you must."

"Thank you for your trust." Cassia dropped her gaze. "I'm sorry I didn't obey when you told me to leave the battle."

"Never apologize for that," Aunt Lyta broke in.

A charge seemed to hum between her and Uncle Argyros, surely a silent exchange in their Grace Union.

"The protection of our border is my Grace's purview," Argyros said at last. "I must defer to her judgment on everyone's actions during the battle. Even when she corrupts my diplomats."

Lyta pointed at Cassia. "This diplomat just fortified our defenses along the entire length of the ward. We've found black roses growing all throughout the mountains. They're aggressive, too. One thicket already stopped another warband of heart hunters."

Cassia's heart seemed to miss a beat again. "Did they survive?"

"Those thorns made them wish they hadn't," Aunt Lyta answered, "but we turned them all over to the Charge with their hearts still beating."

"Fortress Master Baruti is working on them at a…secure location, shall we say," Rudhira explained. "This is a valuable opportunity for him to use his mind healing to study the Collector's influence."

"Do you need my assistance?" Lio asked.

"If he hasn't made progress by the time you join us in the field," Rudhira agreed. "Meanwhile, the Lustra passages you opened for us are making evacuations and sabotage much easier and safer. They also provide a refuge where Hesperines can pass the Slumber without being ambushed by mages. You two have given us a powerful reprieve, both at the border and the front lines. Use this time…and try to enjoy it, if you can."

Rudhira was taking his leave when Lio caught sight of Mak passing a note to Cassia. Where had that come from? Clearly, his Lady of Schemes was up to something. He knew it must be important when she abandoned an unfinished cup of her beloved coffee and drew him aside.

Instinctively, he cast a veil spell around their conversation. "Is your Craving all right?"

"It's not that." Powerful emotions infused her aura, projecting her thoughts into their Union. But all he heard in her mind was her reciting botany terms.

His brows rose. "Cassia, are you trying to conceal your thoughts? What's wrong?"

"Nothing." She blew out an exasperated breath. "I'm making an attempt to surprise you, if you must know. Please humor me."

He tucked his mind magic away, a smile coming to his face. If his Grace wanted to give him a gift, he certainly wouldn't dishonor it by ruining the surprise.

She bit her lip. "I hoped to do this differently…under better circumstances…but I suppose we've never aimed for perfection, have we?"

He brushed his thumb across her freckled cheek. "You know how I feel about perfection. It's that thing you rescued me from."

She broke one black bloom off the roses growing in the doorway. "Would you step us to the top of the Observatory tower?"

"Hypatia's Observatory? What can you have in mind?"

"No peeking into my thoughts," she reminded him, hugging her dog against her. "Please bring Knight, too."

He cast a glance back at the gathering, but Mak and Lyros had disappeared. His mother had entered and was talking with Kalos about the room she had prepared for him. She and Aunt Lyta made shooing motions, while Uncle Argyros sipped his coffee with an implacable veil over his thoughts.

Rudhira, on his way out the door, gave Lio a sly look and tossed him a plain wooden box. "Don't open it yet."

Lio caught the container and held it across his palms. He couldn't begin to guess at its veiled contents. "Is our entire family in on this?"

"Anyone who isn't soon will be," she said cryptically.

"You're wearing your kingdom-destroying look." He pulled her closer. "I know better than to resist."

Lio stepped them to the Observatory and was astonished to find they had it to themselves, even though it was usually crowded with Hypatia's colleagues and students. They surely had Kia to thank for this privacy.

No polar wind cut across the flat, open top of the tower. Mak and Lyros's wards enclosed the entire deck, protecting the soft flames of countless candles that Xandra must have arranged on the stone floor. Music began to drift up from somewhere below.

"It's our dance," he said. "The very first song we ever danced to back in Tenebra."

A smile finally relieved Cassia's expression, and she nodded. She murmured a command to Knight.

He trotted over to a purple basket filled with rimelace. That had to be Zoe's contribution. The hound picked up one of the delicate white flowers in his mighty jaws, reminding Lio of the night he and Cassia had smuggled the medicinal plants to Zoe and the other sick children. That had been when the canine member of Cassia's family had first granted Lio his approval.

Cassia set Rudhira's box down among the candles and took Lio's hand. "Come here."

She drew him to the very edge of the Observatory deck, and they stood without fear on the brink, where no railing separated them from the stunning view below. The city of Selas was spread out at their feet. Every stone their people had laid down over the last sixteen hundred years. Every fragile pane of glass they had spun into this unbreakable Sanctuary. Everything they were fighting for.

Cassia drew a deep breath, nervousness skittering through her aura. "This is where we were standing when you asked me to stay with you in Orthros forever. Where you offered me eternal night and spun dreams of the future we could have."

"How well I remember. This is where you admitted you wanted to stay."

She swallowed. "And then refused you. That's why I want to do this here."

He brushed her hair back from her face. "Do what, my rose?"

Her heart beat faster, making his own flutter in his chest. She turned the black rose in her hand. "That night, you offered me the white rose of Sanctuary. But you've always accepted my black roses, Lio. My thorns and my chaos and the long, difficult path it took for us to stand here, living the future we dreamed of all those moons ago."

He traced a finger along her lip and touched the tip of her fang. "It was worth it."

She blinked hard. "I promise you all of that is over. I want to prove to you here, now, that we won." She reached up and touched his neck. "You will not lose me. You cannot lose me. That's not possible anymore."

"Forgive me my fears, Cassia."

"No more fear, Lio. We are one. And it is time to say it." She held out the black rose, her aura aching, as if she held her heart in the palm of her hand. "Lio, will you avow me and profess before our people that our Grace bond is true?"

All his words and thoughts and expectations deserted him. He stood, stunned, his hand wrapping around hers and that flower.

"I know we don't have much time before we leave Orthros," she said in the voice that had rearranged the world for him so many times before. "I know we're at war. But that's why I am asking you now, my love. I want to call you Grace before every Hesperine. I want to wear your braid for all to see. And when we go errant, I want you to have our avowal oath to reassure you that no matter what the world throws at us, I am wholly yours."

He pulled her against him and kissed her lips, the sweet, dangerous lips that had brought down kingdoms—and just proposed to him. The refrain of their first dance drifted around them as he drank her in, his Grace, his newgift. His.

When he let her take a breath, she drew in a shaking one. "Oh, Lio. I *feel* your answer. But will you say it, too? No matter how deep our Grace Union grows, your words will always be important to me. That was our first promise to each other, after all."

"Cassia," he said, so aware of how easily he could crush her gift and her hopes. "You can feel how much I want to say yes. But you know what's required for an avowal. We would have to undergo our Ritual separation. Eight entire nights apart. That would be excruciating for you."

"I'm willing to face it."

"I cannot imagine putting you through that right now, a mere month after your Gifting, with your magic so hungry. I had thought to wait…"

"For how long, Lio? After all the waiting we've already had to endure?"

He caressed her face. "Until your Craving is more bearable for you."

"We don't know how long that could take. Or what could happen on the warfront in the meantime. But right now, everyone we love can be here. No matter what happens, we can make a memory that will last forever."

He brushed a single tear from her cheek. "I know. But my first concern is you."

"If you genuinely don't wish to do this right now, or it makes you unhappy to rush into it, I completely understand. I want it to be everything you've dreamed of. But know that I am ready whenever you are, whether that is now or in one hundred years."

He could not bear the thought of waiting another night, much less a century. But he had felt the agony of her Craving mere hours ago. He knew what eight nights would do to her. He had already seen the suffering he had caused her when she had been mortal.

Yes, and so had others.

A plan began to form in his mind. One worthy, he hoped, of the plan she had so lovingly enacted for him tonight.

She searched his gaze, her arcane senses probing their Union. "This is one of those moments when I need you to be honest with me about what you want and need, Lio. Don't answer the question of whether you want me to go through our Ritual separation right now. Answer my proposal."

He could answer, knowing there was hope of making this easier for her.

He lifted the black rose to his lips. "Yes, Cassia. I will avow you, and we will turn all our promises into an eternal oath under Hespera's Eyes."

She threw her arms around his neck, and he swung her around. The weight of the world seemed to disappear for that moment, and they both laughed.

He swept her into the familiar steps of their dance. Watching her move with Hesperine grace, he felt as they had never truly danced these steps until now.

"Why were you nervous when you brought me here?" he asked.

She brushed against him they turned together, and warmth echoed in their Grace Union at the intimate touch. "I was worried you would be disappointed."

He gripped her waist in one arm and lifted her. "Never. In fact, this is dangerously close to perfect."

A WORTHY ARTIFACT

After one dance, and not enough kisses for Lio's liking, their Trial circle joined them on the deck. Mak collared him and Cassia in a hug. "Thorns, congratulations, you two. It's about time."

"A triumph, Cassia." Kia tossed her turquoise silk mantle over her shoulder.

Nodora set her lute aside so she could embrace them, too. "Now we can start avowal planning!"

Released from his sit-stay, Knight bounded over to join the gathering. He came straight to Lio's side and sat on his feet, his tail wagging hard.

Lio gave Knight's back a scratch. "Thank you for welcoming me into your pack, old boy."

Xandra crossed her arms. "It's a good thing you said yes. We Trial sisters were prepared to take Cassia to my greenhouse with piles of handkerchiefs and chocolate, and possibly send an emergency message to Solia on the battlefield."

"And Mak and I were planning to take you drinking with Tendo," Lyros said.

Lio frowned down at Cassia. "You feared I would say no! Why in the Goddess's name would I do that?"

Cassia waved a hand. "Because it is objectively madness to try to hold the avowal ceremony of the century in less than three weeks. And because you are self-sacrificing and worried about my Craving. I thought I might need a great deal of consolation chocolate."

"I would never tell you no," Lio said. "Only, 'yes, later,' perhaps."

Her arm around his waist, Cassia leaned into him. "I'm so glad you said 'yes, now.'"

"So am I." He would have a clear conscience about it once he confirmed his plan would work.

Xandra pointed at her brother's gift. "Don't forget that. You can open it now."

Lio opened Rudhira's veiled box to find a cup, the traditional gift of congratulations to Hesperines upon finding Grace. Lio smiled, remembering the one he had given Rudhira when the prince had been doubting Kassandra's prophecies about his own Grace.

Rudhira had carved this goblet from a single piece of deep red wood. On its knots and flaws, he had engraved twining thorns, while exquisite roses adorned its smooth curves. A true symbol of the pain and joy of Grace. Lio sensed that Rudhira had imbued the cup with his blood, a promise to always lend them his strength.

"Our next destination is House Komnena," Kia announced.

"Zoe insisted on being the one to throw your congratulatory party," Nodora said.

Lio chuckled. "Of course she did."

They stepped to Zoe's spacious upstairs room and into a sea of purple flower petals and purpler ribbons. A collective sense of joy erupted in the Union like a cheer. Nearly everyone who had attended Cassia's Ritual was gathered in the light of the stained glass window depicting Zoe's goats and Knight.

Zoe threw her arms around Lio. "You said yes!"

He managed not to laugh at the riot of lavender and violet all around them, and said very seriously, "Thank you for hosting such a lovely party for us."

She whispered, "I'm so excited that I'll get to call Cassia Grace-sister in front of everyone."

"I'm glad you'll get to do that, too, Zoe flower." He turned to their mother. "But I know planning an avowal this quickly is a great deal to ask."

Instead of looking harried, his mother glowed. "That was Cassia's first concern when she hatched her plan. As I assured her, I decapitated a member of the Aithourian Circle in my kitchen while I was pregnant with you.

I am not daunted by throwing you an avowal worthy of eternity on the spur of the moment."

"Besides," Kassandra put in from nearby, "a certain Oracle gave her a few hints about what to have ready in advance."

Cassia's brows rose. "Does that mean I chose the moment of destiny to propose?"

Kassandra raised her glass to Cassia.

Lio's father held out a silk bundle in one war-honed hand. "I didn't know how many centuries might pass until I could give you this, Son. But even before you met Cassia, we crafted it, hoping you wouldn't wait as long as I did for your mother."

Lio unwrapped the gift. His parents' congratulatory cup was a chalice carved by his father's stone magic in an ancient style, masterful in its simplicity. It was engraved with calligraphy twisting among stars. The words, an ancient Hesperine blessing, emanated his mother's theramancy.

Cassia touched the stars, the constellation Anastasios. "It's beautiful."

"We'll treasure it." Lio placed it next to Rudhira's cup on the windowsill. "These will be the first we place on display in our residence."

"You'll need a room full of display cases once all of Orthros finishes congratulating Firstgift Komnenos," his mother predicted.

For the first time, Lio felt a hint of panic at their upcoming avowal.

He hadn't even started on his and Cassia's avowal cup.

The chalice they would drink from during the ceremony should be a powerful magical artifact and an eternal symbol of their love. An embodiment of Hespera's sacred cup, from which flowed her divine generosity, including Grace. And as the Hesperine welcoming Cassia into his bloodline, it was Lio's responsibility to craft it. How could he create something worthy in what little time they had?

As their loved ones presented them with a series of cups that were all exquisite masterpieces of craftsmanship and spellcasting, he tried not to despair.

Even worse, all of this celebration and the happiness shining in Cassia's aura would be for nothing, if he failed on another front.

His opportunity came when Konstantina floated into the gathering on a current of royal power. If anyone could advise him on his plan, it was the Queen's eldest daughter, Royal Master Magistrate and author of Orthros's legal scrolls. He only hoped such a traditionalist would not be thoroughly offended by what he was about to ask.

Twirling one of the black roses in her hand, Konsntantina paused to exchange a word with Xandra before coming over to Lio and Cassia. She lifted Cassia's chin. "Ah, my newest immortal rosarian. Let me look at you."

Cassia smiled, showing her fangs.

Konstantina gave her an arch smile in return. "Beautiful. Another bloom plucked from the mortal world to flourish in Hespera's garden. We will accomplish great things together, my dear."

"I think I have a new rose variety to present to the Circle of Rosarians," Cassia said.

"So I see." Konstantina held the black bloom to her nose. "These are the most fascinating conjuration. The concentration of blood magic in their petals is extraordinary. When I imagine how your Lustra magic will advance Hesperine botany in the centuries to come, the possibilities are thrilling." Her fingers tightened on the flower almost imperceptibly. "My brother had best return you to me in one piece."

Cassia's wince shot through their Grace Union. *I hate thinking that I'm the latest point of contention in Rudhira and Master Kona's relationship.*

If it wasn't you, Lio consoled her, *they would find something else to set off their epic sibling rivalry.*

I suppose it's inevitable, given how strong-Willed they both are—and how fiercely they love each other.

Cassia hesitated. "Thank you for your vote during my Gifting. You have my eternal gratitude."

"Don't make me regret endorsing the war."

Cassia reached out to touch Konstantina's hand with an air of beseeching her princess. "I hope Orthros will see our avowal ceremony as our promise not only to each other but to our people. We embrace our privileges and duties as the heirs of Blood Komnena. We will return to take our seats in the Firstblood Circle."

"See that you do. I look forward to the debates we shall have, as much as the gardening lessons."

Now, while Orthros's great politician was feeling charitable toward

Cassia, Lio took his opportunity. "Aunt Kona, I would be grateful for your advice on a legal question pertaining to our avowal."

"Gladly," she said. "I trust you and Cassia wish to have the full ceremony? No hasty, common-law admission of your bond before any convenient pair of ears outside the immediate family?"

"Of course not," he assured her. "We will have the full eight witnesses each who will swear before the Queens that they have beheld the symptoms of our Craving. There is only one modification I hope to make, not for my own sake, but for Cassia's. It regards our Ritual separation."

"An ambitious undertaking, so soon after her Gifting." For once, Konstantina gave Cassia a look devoid of subtext and full of genuine concern. "None of us doubt your fortitude, but we are worried for you."

"So am I," Lio said. "She already suffered so much as a mortal, as everyone who saw her illness can attest. If they were to bear witness to her Craving, would that satisfy the law and make a Ritual separation unnecessary?"

Surprise shot through Cassia's aura. *Lio, I don't want there to be any doubt. I will honor the requirements.*

Please, let me at least try to make this easier for you.

She squeezed his hand.

Konstantina pursed her lips. "That is a highly interesting legal question. The Ritual separation is defined as a period of eight nights in which the couple must abstain from one another's blood, and a different witness must hold vigil with them each night to observe their symptoms. It is understood this can only take place if the pair are both Hesperines, as mortals do not hunger for blood."

"But is that stated in the law?" Lio asked.

Konstantina shook her head. "No, but we have no precedent for what you are suggesting. The symptoms of Craving are not usually sufficiently evident in humans to prove the bond."

A muscle twitched in Solia's temple, the first sign she was less than supportive of the proceedings. "With respect, Second Princess, Cassia's need for Lio was tragically evident even when she was mortal. After their separation in the Maaqul Desert, I carried her back to him myself. She was dying in my arms."

"And Kella and I kept Cassia alive while they were apart," Tendo spoke up.

"For which Orthros is grateful," Konstantina said. "The question remains, however. How much of her symptoms were Craving and how much the result of her displaced magic?"

"I can attest to that." Rudhira stepped closer to his sister, despite the tension simmering between them. "Using my power as a healer, I studied how she absorbed his magic. It's true that her illness was caused not by Craving but by the Collector starving her of her magic. However, her aura would draw on no magic but Lio's as a surrogate for her missing power. The unbreakable channeling between them, the way his power kept her alive—that was only possible because of their bond."

Konstantina put a hand to her lips, considering. "That makes four witnesses to Cassia's symptoms."

Nike stepped forward. "I was there the night Rudhira and Annassa Soteira identified the arcane channeling occurring between Lio and Cassia."

"So were we." Lio's mother held his father's hand. "I was with her when she fell ill in the greenhouse, and Apollon helped her to Lio's side."

"That makes seven," Lio said, tense with hope.

"Eight," Kassandra interjected. "I trust the magistrates will take my word as the Oracle?"

The whole room seemed to hold their breaths, immortal and mortal alike, while Konstantina considered.

"As the Royal Master Magistrate," she said at last, "I say the separations Lio and Cassia endured are more than Orthros can ask of any pair of Hesperines, and their companions on their adventures are worthy witnesses to their Craving. As a friend of Blood Komnena, I say I am glad I can spare these two any further suffering."

Everyone let out exclamations of relief, then broke into applause. Cassia's hand slowly relaxed in Knight's ruff, the only outward sign that she had dreaded their separation more than she would ever admit. At that small, powerful betrayal of her relief, Lio felt an immense weight life off of him.

After this party, she swore, *I'm going to drag you into the nearest dark corner and devour every inch of you with the knowledge that I don't ever have to abstain from you again.*

Lio swallowed hard and tried not to show his fangs to everyone. "You have our gratitude, Aunt Kona."

The princess smiled. "I look forward to the ceremony. I expect a seat next to my mothers while they officiate."

Cassia's eyes widened. "The Queens are planning to officiate for us?"

"Of course," Konstantina replied. "They are the first Graces and seldom miss an opportunity to hear a couple's vows, especially a rare joining in Anastasios's bloodline. And as for your cupbearer, who will carry your avowal cup during the ceremony? That role is an honor even greater than witnessing."

Lio made an effort to shove his worries about the cup behind his veils. Through their Grace Union, he showed Cassia who he had in mind, and she sent him her emphatic agreement.

Lio turned to their mentor. "Uncle, I still regret how you found out about Cassia and me. I should have confided in you instead of letting you find out with the entire Firstblood Circle. Let me make amends now. Would you do us the honor of being our cupbearer?"

His uncle clasped his wrist and pulled him close. The full depth of Silvertongue's emotions escaped his veil spells and reminded Lio just how deeply his stoic uncle felt everything. "It would be my honor."

Now if only Lio could craft a suitable artifact in time. He must find a way to catch these memories in a cup before time ran on and they must face the inevitable course of the war.

nights until
WINTER SOLSTICE

IMPERFECT BUT UNBROKEN

CASSIA WAS OUT OF time for magic lessons. But she would tame her infernal roses to clear the way for the avowal ceremony if it was the last thing she did.

As if she could cow them with a gaze, she glared at the wild things still growing out of the broken floor. If she had learned anything from Kalos so far, though, it was that controlling her magic was more complicated than merely Willing the Lustra to obey her.

Tightening her grip on the sheaf of herbs she held, she swept her hand downward toward the ground in a forceful gesture. Magic puffed through the leaves. Promising. She felt an answering stir in the black roses.

One thorny vine, heavy with dark blooms, gave a creak. Ever so slowly, the rose branch slithered off a chunk of marble, receding back into the hole.

Then it stopped.

Cassia threw the herbs on the ground. "This isn't working!"

"It is." Kalos was out of his bandages but still moved carefully as he gestured around her. "Look how much progress you've made."

She surveyed the results of their painstaking magic lessons, which had demanded even more effort than avowal planning and rehearsals. She had managed to tame most of the roses and twine them artfully around the pillars. But the vines growing up from the heart of her spell still resisted her. Where the letting site had exploded through the floor, a riot of the flowers still spread every which way, holding the rubble in their clutches.

"You can't repair the floor like this, Papa," Cassia said in despair.

Apollon made a coaxing gesture at the one block of marble she had freed. The stone levitated out of the roses' reach. "Our guests can stand somewhere else."

"There won't be room for everyone." Cassia rubbed her temples.

"Then they can levitate," he said.

Aunt Lyta's laughter drifted down from the gallery. She adjusted a silk drape over the banister, then returned to conjuring wards over the hole in the roof. Flurries of fresh snow threatened to make their way in.

Cassia's magic pulsed in her veins like a panicked heartbeat. "Kalos, there must be something else we can try."

He rubbed his chin. "I was sure using the right plants in your casting would work for you. But we've tried all the incantations, gestures, and spell ingredients I've seen heart hunters use—or heard of Silvicultrixes using in the tales. I'm sorry, Cassia. So much knowledge of our magic has been lost."

"I'm sorry, too." Their sympathy for each other's plight twinged in the Blood Union.

"I'm afraid there may be only one solution," Kalos said.

She looked away from the roses to meet his grim gaze. "Whatever it is, I will try it."

"It's not that simple." He grimaced. "I think you need a triune focus."

"What is that?" she asked.

"Well, in the legends, a Silvicultrix would use artifacts in her rituals. A set of three that helped her focus the massive amounts of magic she could pull from the Lustra. Those were the most powerful Lustra artifacts, the ones the Silvicultrixes used to create letting sites."

Cassia's hand went to her pendant. "Do you think this could be one?"

Kalos nodded. "I think that used to be one of the Changing Queen's three foci. Now it has become yours."

Cassia's shoulders slumped. "How can I find two more artifacts this powerful?"

"Well, you can't. A focus has to be made. You give it life by using it during rituals." He pointed at the pendant. "Like your Gifting."

She stared down at the fused disc, half wood, half metal. Her bastardization of her ancient matriarch's artifact. "It's debatable whether I am even a Silvicultrix anymore."

He blinked at her in surprise. "Of course you're still a Silvicultrix."

"I only have the one Lustra affinity now, turned into something else altogether thanks to my blood magic."

"You are Orthros's Silvicultrix, regardless," Apollon said.

A smile came to her face. "Thank you, Papa."

He took her hand in both of his ancient, strong ones. "It's time for you to get ready for the ceremony."

"But the roses…" she protested.

"Leave the rest to me. This is your avowal. Lay all your worries in the hands of those who love you and Lio so you can fully enjoy this night."

It sank in anew, one of the quietest but most profound revelations of her new life. She could ask for help. She even had a father who would move mountains to ease her burdens. This heretical patriarch who was the antithesis of her mortal sire.

"You have my gratitude," Cassia said.

"You have my love," Apollon replied.

It was so hard to do, but she turned away from the roses. She let the latent magic drain out of her. Her years of survival and self-preservation were harder to fight than those wild flowers, but she relinquished control. Leaving her goal unfinished, she trusted her Grace-father to have her back.

CASSIA LOOKED INTO THE full-length mirrors and could scarcely believe the vision in the glass was her present life. It was so different from the future her past self had feared.

She wasn't looking at an empty husk dressed in a Tenebran wedding gown fit for a funeral. She wasn't dreading a march to Anthros's altar to be sacrificed to a man. And she wasn't alone.

The mirror showed her freckled self and her shaggy dog, the one constant at her side. But now her freckled self had fangs and wore a green silk veil hours robe, ready to be dressed for her very Hesperine avowal ceremony.

She was surrounded by people who wanted to make this night wonderful for her. Komnena smoothed her hair, and Solia pressed her cheek to Cassia's, looking into the mirror with her. Behind them, her Trial sisters were busy preparing her Grace-mother's lavish dressing room, where they would get Cassia ready.

She couldn't wait to walk through the Ritual hall to Lio's side.

A laugh bubbled out of her. No mortal wedding for her. She was about to drink her lover's blood in front of everyone in a circle consecrated to the profane goddess Hespera.

She had found her Grace, and tonight, she would finally get to say it to all of Orthros.

Komnena handed her a handkerchief. Cassia let out an exasperated groan at herself and wiped her eyes.

Solia patted her shoulder. "Let all the tears out now, before we get you dressed."

Cassia squeezed her eyes shut. "Bleeding thorns, I had planned to be triumphant tonight, not dissolve into tears."

"You've earned your tears, dear one," Komnena said.

"I will allow myself *one* cry. One." Cassia's shoulders shook.

"It's all right," her Grace-mother soothed. "We all wish Thalia were here tonight."

Cassia sobbed harder. "Yes, but... I also didn't think you and Solia and everyone else would be here. I thought tonight might never come. My life is so much better than I expected."

"That and missing your mother can be true at the same time." Solia wrapped her arms around Cassia. "I miss her too."

"And Iris," Cassia said through her tears.

Her sister's aura panged with shared grief. "Yes. We can't bring them back. But we can be here. All of us."

Solia released her, only to go and open the door. Cassia caught the scent of indigo plants just before Kella rode in on Tilili. They were dressed in white Azarqi finery, from Kella's flowing tunic to her cat's silver-bangled saddle.

"You were able to leave the siege," Cassia exclaimed in relief.

Kella's deep blue lips curved in a smile. "And I brought a friend from Tenebra."

When another mortal followed her inside, Cassia struggled not to start crying all over again. "Perita? You came to my Hesperine avowal?"

Her former handmaiden and oldest friend put her hands on her hips. "Of course, my lady. Did you think I would let anyone else dress you for such an important occasion?"

Cassia put her arms around Perita, careful not to jostle the infant her friend carried in a sling across her chest. Impressions of Perita's aura washed over her, new and yet so familiar. Pretty spring flowers and herbs with bite. "Thank you for coming all this way—with a new babe—and leaving your duties—"

"I'd like to see anyone try to stop me. I'm sorry you and your Hesperine owl won't get to have that Tenebran wedding you were planning on. But at least I can help with your avowal."

"Is Callen with you?"

"He wouldn't let me and little Callen out of his sight," Perita confirmed, patting their son. "He's with the other males, helping them make your Ambassador Fancy Soap even fancier for the ceremony."

Cassia laughed. "I missed you so much."

Perita sat Cassia down at the broad marble dressing table. "Where shall we start?"

"Can I help?" Zoe peeked out from under the table, where she was playing with her goats. Knight laid down on Cassia's feet, and Zoe put her arm around his neck.

"Of course we need your help." Solia smiled down at Zoe. "Cassia always helped me get dressed for important events when she was your age."

Kia pressed a goblet into Cassia's hands. "Here's something a little stronger than wine, guaranteed to relax Hesperines."

"Sit back and bask." Xandra draped a towel around Cassia's neck, the soft fabric deliciously warm.

While Perita laid out hairbrushes and ribbons, the Hesperines passed little Callen back and forth, cooing over the tiny mortal with fanged smiles.

Nodora, clearly the one in command of the entire endeavor, gestured to the dazzling array of cosmetics she had prepared. "I brought a complete color selection from the Kitharan Theater. Only Matsu's finest creations. This is the benefit of my Ritual mother being an icon of Hesperine fashion."

Nodora had told Cassia of Matsu's mortal life, when she had been born a man, only able to express her womanhood when she played feminine roles in the theater. As a Hesperine, Matsu could now live as her true self both on and off the stage, and she was renowned for beauty spells and alchemy that helped every immortal lady feel like her best self.

"Please give her my gratitude." Cassia clutched her hands together, hardly knowing which pot of feminine magic to pick up first.

She eyed a tiny, beautiful bottle of scent oil, wary of giving past fears an opportunity to intrude on this night. She picked it up slowly and popped the cork. All she felt were the loving auras around her. She took a deep whiff. All she smelled were roses.

Komnena smiled at her. "Well done, my brave girl."

Cassia squeezed her Grace-mother's hand, thankful for her and every other mind healer who had been an ally in her daily effort to heal from the memories of her past.

Solia took the bottle and dabbed rose oil on Cassia's wrists. "This is no Autumn Greeting, Pup. We're going to get you avowed to that faithful, adoring scrollworm of yours, and then we'll drink each other under the table like proper mercenaries."

Cassia's laughter was interrupted by the door swinging open again. Orthros's Oracle sailed in, directing a small army of her initiate weavers and seamstresses, who levitated Cassia's avowal robe in on a stand. Cassia had seen many of Kassandra's stunning creations, but clearly, she still had the ability to make Cassia's jaw drop.

The white silk robe looked like it had been woven from the Light Moon itself. The botanical patterns in the intricate brocade were exquisite, and Cassia could only imagine how long it had taken Kassandra to weave them. The embroidery gleamed, applied in thread of real gold.

Perita whistled. "Orthros white outshines Segetian gold, and that's the truth."

Kassandra straightened the hem, surveying her work. "When a Hesperine avows into a bloodline, they are the Whiteblood in the ceremony and wear this color as a symbol that they're bringing light to their new family. The Hesperine welcoming them in, the Redblood, will wear red to signify the giving of a new bloodline to their Grace."

"Like the two moons?" Perita guessed.

"Yes." Nodora let out a dreamy sigh. "It's such a beautiful tradition. The

Whiteblood's family wear white, too, and the Redblood's line all wear red to show that they're joining together along with the couple."

"Wait till I tell everyone back home about this!" Perita exclaimed. "They'll gossip about it for a decade, and every lady from Solorum to Corona will be green with envy."

The harpies of the court would hear about how the deposed king's bastard had risen from her past to wear a robe fit for an immortal. But that didn't matter to Cassia anymore.

She could see her future in this silk and gold. This night, when she and Lio would make their vows. The years to come, when a portrait of them in their avowal robes would hang in the home they made together. The centuries ahead, when they would wear these robes each time they brought a new Hesperine into their family. She would hold their children at first Ritual in this robe.

Cassia pressed Kassandra's hand. "I have no words."

Kassandra smiled. "The Oracle has made the Soothsayer speechless? High praise indeed."

Cassia looked into the seer's eternal gaze. Time flowed around Kassandra like light, past and future ever-present in her vision. Was she referring to the affinity that was lost to Cassia now? Or was she saying that Lio's quest to secure Cassia's other magics would come true?

When Cassia heard a staff tapping in the corridor, her heart lifted. The earthy fragrances of medicinal plants entered the room with Tuura. New lines creased her deep brown skin, and her round figure was less generous than before. But after her collapse in Tenebra, Cassia could only be grateful the Ashes' diviner was alive and on her feet again.

"Peanut!" Cassia helped her to a chair by the dressing table. "How are you feeling?"

"Much restored." Tuura waved her off. "No need to fuss over me, Shadow."

Solia slid a pillow behind Tuura's back. "You fuss over us every time we get a scratch in battle. It's our turn."

Tuura sighed. "You should know healers make terrible patients."

"Allow us to fuss," Kella said. "That's an order."

"If you insist, First Blade." Tuura leaned forward to peruse the cosmetics. "These are the work of a brilliant alchemist. Could they be Muse Matsu's famous creations that I've heard so much about?"

"Yes!" Nodora reached for a delicate ceramic jar that waited off to one side, offering it to Tuura. "She asked me to give this to you, a custom batch of her Eternal Silk Cream."

"Is this the one that magically dissolves beards?"

Nodora nodded. "It can be used anywhere you prefer not to shave."

"I'll have to thank her in person and chat about alchemy." Tuura was clearly delighted. She came from a kinder tradition in which no one questioned a diviner for rejecting manhood and embracing her spiritual nature as a woman, but her masculine features were still troublesome to her at times.

"I'll introduce you at the ceremony," Nodora promised. "I know she would love for you to come by her residence afterward."

Cassia bit her lip, hesitant to interrupt, but she could sense the deep exhaustion that lingered under Tuura's cheer. "How long can you stay? Lio and I would never forgive ourselves if coming to our avowal made you fall ill like you did in Tenebra."

"I believe I will be all right here in Orthros. I couldn't let the other Ashes witness at your ceremony without me."

Kella fixed Tuura with a gaze. "If you start to feel ill, don't try to hide it. Karege will take you straight back to the Empire to restore your connection to the ancestors."

"Don't fear, Standstill," Tuura reassured her. "I have no desire to repeat what happened last time."

The same worry clouded Solia's emotions. "Are you sure Orthros Boreou is safe for you? Our communication with the spirit phase is cut off in this entire hemisphere, isn't it?"

Cassia nodded. "The Diviner Queen cast a barrier to stop the Old Masters from traveling through the spirit phase to the Empire. Her spell affects Cordium, Tenebra, and Orthros Boreou as far as we know."

"That's what so interesting," Tuura said. "Being in Tenebra was certainly detrimental due to how it affected my ancestral magic. But Orthros feels different."

Kia's gaze sharpened with curiosity. "How so?"

"The barrier is less absolute here," Tuura mused. "I cannot speak to the ancestors, but they feel close to me."

The implications made Cassia's head spin.

Kia leaned forward. "Are you saying it might be easier to break through to the spirit phase here?"

Komnena shook her head. "It's not possible to make spirit gates in Orthros Boreou. We've tried. We can only open them in Orthros Notou, in the same hemisphere as the Empire."

"Even so," Tuura said, "the Diviner Queen's magic is weaker here. My theory is that the barrier is strongest near the site where she cast the spell to divide the phases. Orthros Boreou must be geographically farther from it."

Gooseflesh broke out on Cassia's skin. "That would have been where she collapsed her spirit gate between the shadowlands and the Empire." She thought back to the ruined city of Btana Ayal, deep in the Maaqul Desert, where she had seen the stone megaliths of the shattered gate. "Of course. The other side of the gate must still exist. Somewhere on this continent lies Btana Ayal's sister ruin."

"Somewhere far from Orthros," Xandra said, "where you don't need to worry about it."

Tuura nodded. "Don't let ancient mysteries trouble your mind tonight. Suffice it to say, I'm well enough to refuse Karege's invitations to carry me to your avowal."

Cassia tried to laugh, pushing her thoughts away. But they formed new specters to haunt the back of her mind.

If there was a sister gate, would the Old Masters try to use it somehow? If the barrier was weaker in Orthros, would they ever seek to exploit that to reach the Empire?

Cassia, what's wrong? Lio asked.

Will you believe me if I tell you it's nothing?

No.

Will you postpone getting a confession out of me, then, so we can enjoy tonight?

Hmm. That depends. I do enjoy seducing confessions out of you.

Tonight, I want all the seduction, no confessions necessary. Truly, Lio. I don't want to think about anything except us.

In that case, we will ignore whatever it is together, and I will seduce you to distraction.

With anticipation of their avowal night heating her veins, it was easier to forget about the necromancer lurking at the door.

THIS WAS LIO'S LAST chance not to ruin their avowal.

His final attempt at a glass masterpiece hovered between his hands. He levitated it deeper into the opening of his kiln. Just close enough to the heat but not too close.

"You're going to be late to your own ceremony." Tendo crossed his arms, perspiration trickling down his chest in the sweltering workshop.

"There won't be a ceremony if I don't finish this cup," Lio replied through gritted teeth.

He watched the glass soften, sensing how the resonance of the magic changed. Almost there. The sleeve of his work robe fell down, but he didn't dare shove it back up above his elbow.

Hoyefe folded it back for him. The Ashes' virtuoso swordsman somehow managed to look groomed and gallant while they were all covered in soot or sweat. "I can have you looking your best in minutes, but even I have my limits."

"Can we help with anything else?" Karege's legendary cloud of hair was frizzing around his head in the dry heat. The burly mercenary took a step closer, and glass crunched under his sandal.

Mak winced. "Not much we can do at this point. Lio's using the last of the glass he made from the ingredients everyone brought, and it took nights for that to reach the proper consistency."

Callen eyed the failed attempts that littered the floor. Perita's husband had abandoned his shirt too, his Tenebran constitution clearly unused to this heat. He picked up a chipped cup without a stem and carried it over to the worktable. "Anyone else need a drink?"

"I wouldn't use that one," Uncle Argryos advised. "It exudes unstable jinn magic."

Callen carefully set the vessel back down. Uncle Argyros poured him some coffee in a mundane copper cup, then added a generous splash of liquor.

Lio snatched his work in progress out of the heat, levitating it back to him. He took his tongs to the molten glass, shaping the rim of the chalice with the greatest care. To reveal the flower petals trapped within, he thinned the glass. But if he thinned it too much, all his effort to preserve the magic inside would be ruined.

"We should let the fellow concentrate on his art." Hoyefe shooed Tendo toward the stairs leading up into the tower.

"I'm not going anywhere," Tendo said. "I'll drag this silkfoot out of here myself before I let him leave Cassia at the Ritual circle."

"I would never do that to her!" Lio said. The glass panes in the shelves rattled. The chalice before him whined.

"I'd better stay too," Mak said.

Lyros nodded. "In case we need more wards."

"What this artist needs is inspiration." Tendo's eyes narrowed. "Threats are very inspiring. Work faster, or I'll break your toes. You don't need those to make glass."

"I need them to stand for the ceremony!" Lio protested.

Tendo waved a hand. "You heal fast."

Lio paused to bite his tongue and lick his tongs. He applied the bloodied metal to the cup again, painting the rim with his blood. More magic infused the glass. He prayed the fragile material wouldn't shatter this time. A scrap he had trimmed off the piece exploded at his feet.

Mak and Lyros trapped the flying glass in a warding spell, then shoved it out of the way into the pile.

Hoyefe strolled through the cleared path. "I shall work some magic of my own upstairs and be waiting with everything ready. The moment the cup is finished, I'll melt our wayward Redblood down and pour him into his avowal robes."

"That sounds painful," Lio muttered, "but thank you."

Hoyefe beckoned to Callen. "Come along, fellow warrior. It falls to us to save the day."

Callen grabbed the bottle of liquor and followed Hoyefe out. Their auras drifted upstairs while Lio kept his gaze on his work.

"It looks finished," Tendo said.

Lio shook his head.

Lyros peered over Lio's shoulder. "The magic isn't complete."

Tendo sighed and threw up his hands.

Lio gathered his thelemancy. Mak and Lyros conjured another shadow between the glass and everyone else.

"It is no easy feat to capture eternity in a single object," Uncle Argyros said. "The ceremony will wait."

As grateful as Lio was for the reassurance, he knew that if this cup broke, too, it would be too late to start over.

What's wrong? Now it was Cassia's turn to ask.

If I tell you it's nothing, I suppose you won't believe me, either.

Of course not.

I still haven't managed a perfect cup, he finally confessed. *Oh my Goddess, Cassia, I'm afraid I'm going to ruin this night.*

Her laughter sparkled through him, more beautiful than any glass. *Lio. It doesn't have to be perfect, remember? It only needs to be ours.*

Theirs. He could not possibly make this more theirs after everything he had poured into his unstable, powerful creation.

The flaws in the glass are my favorite part, too, she said.

Lio let the tension drain out of him, let his thelemancy flow as gently into the glass as into her mind every time he reached for her. He stopped trying to craft a precise spell and allowed his casting to flow according to natural laws he did not fully understand. The Lustra had taught him that.

His power took on the bizarre magical patterns he had wrought, against all odds, inside the material. Their disparate affinities, in Union, reacted with the forces that had brought him and his Grace together, retracing their painful, wondrous path to each other.

The glass hummed, hardening before his eyes. The enchantment came to life, sending a tremor through Lio's veins. He felt Cassia's ephemeral gasp.

A thousand shatters assaulted his ears. Shards of glass danced through the air around him. One nicked his face, and blood trickled into his mouth.

The chalice dropped into his hands, imperfect but unbroken.

ETERNAL OATH

Lio stepped into the antechamber with a comb still attached to his hair and Hoyefe holding the other end of it. All the congratulatory cups the guests had brought were arranged on an enormous table. In the center of the dazzling array, a velvet-draped pedestal waited for the avowal cup.

"Don't you dare drop it," Tendo threatened.

"The spell is complete," Lio breathed. "It's too powerful an artifact for a mere drop to break the glass now."

The weight of his uncle's hand rested on his shoulder. "This is a creation to be proud of."

Hoping Cassia would agree, Lio set their chalice on its stand. Reaching under his collar, he broke the seal on Cassia's braid, which had not left his neck since she had put it on him. He coiled her hair inside the cup, along with his own Grace braid, which she had entrusted to him earlier that night.

"Now hold still," Hoyefe commanded, reaching for the other side of Lio's head. "And be less tall."

Lio stooped to make his friend's work easier. Callen reached in with a rag to wipe the blood from Lio's forehead.

"Hespera's Mercy," Lio said, "did I get blood on my avowal robe?"

His uncle chuckled. "No, but it wouldn't be the first time an avowal robe was bloodstained before, during—or especially after—the ceremony."

Behind Uncle Argyros, Lyros gave Mak a sly look. Mak blushed.

Hoyefe motioned for Lio to turn.

Lio obeyed. "Do I meet the standards of Lord Hoyefe of the Owia, alumnus of Imperial University's School of Fine Arts, Theater Department?"

"You're not the only artist who did some of the finest work of his career tonight." Hoyefe dusted his nails across his shoulder. "You're too pretty to live."

"Thank you, my friend," Lio said.

"You may thank me by introducing Severin and me to every unavowed Hesperine guest at your ceremony. Since I dashingly rescued him in Tenebra, my shy darling has become quite the rebel. He's finally ready to invite someone to join our romantic adventures."

Lio grinned. "You won't be alone tonight, Lonesome. We'll ensure you two have the finest company."

Tendo, now in his own royal Sandira finery, looked Lio up and down.

"Well," Lio asked him, "do you deem me worthy to make my vows to one of the two most dangerous sisters ever to reach Orthros or the Empire's shores?"

Tendo's mouth tilted in a smile. "You're equal to her."

Lio considered the likelihood that Tendo would break his nose moments before the ceremony and deemed it low for Cassia's sake, if not his own. So he decided it was safe to speak his mind. If there was ever a time to do so, it was tonight.

Lio clasped Tendo's arm and pulled him in, saying in his ear, "Cassia and I may be first, but you and Solia are next. Don't think we'll ever give up hope of having you as a brother-in-law."

Tendo swore at him, but didn't punch him. And there was definitely a smile in his eyes.

The antechamber door opened, and Rudhira entered, dressed in his full formal red silks. But Lio glimpsed Tenebran riding boots hidden under the hem of the prince's robe, and there was still a whiff of adamas and castle stone about him.

"You made it," Lio said with relief.

Rudhira grinned, his fangs out. "I would never miss my Ritual son's avowal. The war mages will live another hour while we get you braided up."

"In truth, I wouldn't blame you if you preferred battle to avowals." How his Ritual father must struggle every time he watched another youngblood find their Grace, when he had been waiting sixteen hundred years for his.

Rudhira's aura gentled, and he shook his head. "Tonight, there is nowhere I would rather be."

"What about Nike?" Mak asked.

"Every Steward is here, too," Rudhira answered. "The Charge is holding down the border until after the ceremony."

"Then we're ready." Mak shoved Lio toward the door. "Let's get you to the Ritual circle!"

The truth sank in all at once. Everyone was here. Lio hadn't ruined the ceremony. No necromancers or war mages or deposed kings were going to prevent it.

"I'm avowing Cassia tonight. Goddess bless. *I'm avowing Cassia. Right now.*"

Lyros looked at his Grace, his gaze softening. "Here's our official advice. Enjoy every minute of it. The worst is about to get easier, and the best is yet to come."

Mak took Lyros's arm. "Don't you ever claim I'm the only romantic one."

As Lio Willed the door open and entered the Ritual hall, Cassia's anticipation simmered in their Union.

OUTSIDE THE MAIN ENTRANCE to the Ritual hall, Cassia stood alone, as was tradition.

Lio touched her mind. The entire wondrous night seemed to pause, and they held their breath together.

It's time, he said.

You're ready?

I've been ready since the moment I met you. Do you, Firstgrace Cassia, want this for yourself?

At that echo of his words from their first dance, from his first bite, she smiled. *More than I have ever wanted anything.*

Come to me, my Grace.

The double doors swung open to the splendor of the Ritual hall. White spell lights and roses in full bloom levitated in the air above her path. A chant in the Divine Tongue drifted down from the clerestory. That hymn had been sung for thousands of years in Hagia Boreia, the Great Temple of Hespera where Anastasios's bloodline had begun.

To demonstrate to all that she came to her Grace of her own free Will, Cassia walked forward on her own, escorted by no one but the Goddess in her blood.

Seeing the Whiteblood guests just inside, Cassia could scarcely believe how many were here as *her* family. Perita and Callen, her Tenebran confidants. Kella and the Ashes, her mercenary family, with their matriarch Ukocha, her daughter Chuma, and husband Mumba. And one winged prince Cassia would always consider her brother, no matter what his future held.

Her sister stood in front with Knight, a wreath of white silk and roses around his shaggy neck. With tears flowing freely down her cheeks, Solia was the first to stand aside and clear Cassia's path toward Lio. The others followed, a demonstration of support. Of surrender, giving Cassia over to her eternal bloodline.

They murmured a farewell blessing to her in half a dozen languages. "May the Eye of Light reveal your path to your Grace."

Cassia proceeded between them to meet the Redbloods. Her Hesperines. Relatives and tributaries of Blood Komnena had gathered under twinkling red spell lights and floating Roses of Hespera. Even solitary Kalos had braved the crowd, standing among the guests up in the gallery under her accidental skylight.

As she walked forward, the crowd of immortals parted like a crimson sea, their power washing over her. Their welcome blessing echoed through the hall in Divine in their eternal voices. "May the Eye of Blood sustain your journey with your Grace."

Between the shifting Hesperine guests, she caught sight of the black roses. The vines were as wild as she had left them. But now a new border circled them, built of marble she recognized as former chunks of the floor. Apollon had turned the damage into a flower bed, reshaping the stones not to hide her roses but to draw attention to them.

Their closest friends and family lined her final way. Alkaios murmured something to Bosko, while Nephalea's hands rested on Zoe's slim shoulders, reminding Cassia of how the two Hesperines errant had protected her as a child. Zoe looked like the most endearing little blood sorceress in her red robe, with an abundance of crimson ribbons in her hair. Cassia marched between the Graced pairs of Blood Argyros, then her Ritual parents, to be welcomed by her Grace-parents. Apollon and Komnena parted, clearing her last steps to Lio.

At last Cassia laid eyes on him. She felt as if all the spell lights in the hall took flight in her belly. The black waves of his hair were loose, ready for her braid. A ruby stud glittered on his earlobe. With his tall frame, he looked stately in his heavy crimson avowal robe, gleaming with gold.

He emanated power that called to her blood. Her Gifter. Her Grace. Could this magnificent immortal really be hers?

The look on his face left no doubt. He gazed upon her as if she were a goddess, and in that moment, she knew he would look at her this way forever.

He held out his open palm. Placing her hand in his, she joined him inside the Ritual circle.

Outside the mosaic, the first Graces were seated hand in hand. For the first time since her Gifting, Cassia beheld her Queens. Recognition sang deep in her veins. She felt the shared blood that ran from her to them, and from them back into a distant night when Hespera had touched the Ritual firstbloods and created their kind. Beside them, Princess Konstantina smiled in understanding. Together, Cassia and Lio made the heart bow to the royals, then faced each other across Hespera's Rose and the constellation Anastasios.

Queen Alea spoke, her aura shining. "Redblood Deukalion, for what reason have you called together our people?"

"To declare that through Cassia, I have experienced Hespera's abundance."

"Whiteblood Cassia." Queen Soteira's warm voice carried through the hall. "Do you join him in this declaration of your own free Will?"

"Under the Goddess's Eyes, I do."

Queen Alea lifted her pale hand. "Ritual Firstblood Anastasios watches from the stars. On his behalf, let those us of who still walk this world welcome Cassia's bloodline into his own."

The crowd shifted. The Redblood guests made room for her

Whitebloods to mingle among them, and all their loved ones stood together in one gathering.

Queen Alea squeezed Queen Soteira's hand. "Only Graces know the joys of their bond, and yet our pain is evident to all. Redblood Deukalion, can eight witnesses attest that without Whiteblood Cassia, you will have no eternity?"

"I call forth the eight who have seen my Craving for her," Lio answered.

"Whiteblood Cassia," Queen Soteira asked, "can eight witnesses attest that Redblood Deukalion offers you eternity?"

Cassia echoed, "I call forth the eight who have seen my Craving for him."

Their witnesses came forward from the crowd and proceeded down the central aisle, a festive procession despite the gravity of what they were about to describe. They stood in two half moons on either side of the Ritual circle.

Queen Alea addressed Lio's witnesses. "As the first Redblood to receive Grace, I will hear your testimony."

Mak made the heart bow. "Annassa, I have watched Lio make sacrifices to protect our people, and it is my honor to help him secure his happiness now. To prevent war, he returned from Tenebra without Cassia, no matter the cost to himself. He had been without her for half a year when my Grace and I saw him collapse in the gymnasium."

Lyros continued, "We recognized his symptoms, having experienced them ourselves. After minor sparring injuries, his body wouldn't heal. No blood, no matter how potent, could fully restore him."

Cassia's hand tightened on Lio's. She hated thinking of how close he had come to starvation. She listened as their Trial sisters described his collapse before the Firstblood Circle. Then Karege, Tuura, and Hoyefe related how his Craving had later endangered him in the Maaqul Desert.

I feel no more horror at those memories, he reassured her silently. *Let those wounds become part of our vows.*

"Eight times has the truth been spoken," Queen Alea concluded. "Let it be known for eternity that Deukalion's Craving for Cassia is the Goddess's Will."

You're right, Cassia said in his thoughts. *Somehow, those curses have turned into this blessing.*

Queen Soteira gestured to Cassia's witnesses. "As the first Whiteblood to bring Grace to our people, I will hear your testimony."

"Were my visions admissible as testimony," Kassandra began, "I would tell you of the first night I met Lio's Grace, when she was still a future dream. But I saw her in the flesh when she came to Orthros and, on the Vigil of Will, sought me out to ask for my wisdom. I helped her see the truth in herself: Craving is not merely a thirst for blood, but also a hunger in the soul. Without Lio, her spirit was dying."

It had been one of Cassia's darkest hours. But also the hour when she had found hope for this future that was now coming true before their eyes.

Tendo took up the story next, then Kella, relating how they had cared for Cassia during her illness when she'd been separated from Lio in the desert.

When it was Solia's turn, her aura was full of many things—but foremost, a sense of conviction. "In my fear for my sister, I was the greatest denier of her bond with Lio. Take my change of heart as powerful evidence that their love is true. I have seen him heal Cassia. Sacrifice for her. And most of all, make her happy, in ways I never imagined possible after what she suffered in her past."

After describing Cassia's near death before the Empress's Court, she gave over to Rudhira, who spoke from his experience as a healer. Cassia thought she caught a hint of tension in Tendo's aura then, but it was gone too quickly—and her senses were too full—for her to let it worry her at a moment like this.

Once Nike and Komnena had reinforced Rudhira's testimony, Apollon was the last to speak on Cassia's behalf. "I have seen Cassia face her Craving for my son with the same courage as she has withstood every challenge of her life. When she collapsed in her greenhouse, I helped her to her feet. Not because she lacked the strength to walk to Lio's side on her own. But because she deserves a father who will always lift her up, fight for her, and make her road easier whenever he can."

Cassia couldn't have spoken around the lump in her throat. But she didn't need to. She sent Apollon her gratitude in the Blood Union.

"Let my words seal Cassia's place in our bloodline," Apollon declared. "She is my Grace-daughter."

Queen Soteira nodded, the golden stars in her crown of dark braids clinking. "Eight times has the truth been spoken. Let it be known for eternity that Cassia's Craving for Deukalion is the Goddess's Will."

"Let your avowal chalice be brought forth," Queen Alea announced, "that you may drink from the Goddess's Cup together for all time."

Uncle Argyros proceeded up the aisle, his long silver braid and gleaming robes swishing softly in the breathless quiet. Holding the long-awaited cup aloft for all to admire, he joined them inside the Ritual circle.

Cassia's breath caught. *Lio, how could you have been worried about this masterpiece?*

You are happy with it?

It is...mesmerizing.

Blood and light flowed through the intricate botanical designs of the chalice, as if it were a living thing. Like their bond. Real rose petals, sealed inside the crystal clear glass, seemed to float. Not only the red roses that grew over their bed and the white roses of Sanctuary. But her black roses, too.

Silvertongue's harsh gaze was now quiet with joy as he held the cup out to them. "Bind yourselves together with immortal strands, that neither of you shall drift through eternity alone."

Lio lifted his braid from the cup, then Cassia took hers, their fingers brushing for a charged instant.

"Shed blood for each other," Uncle Argyros said, "that neither of you shall ever thirst."

They lifted their wrists to their fangs, and before the bites could heal, they joined hands. Lio held Cassia's gaze as he knit his fingers through hers, gripping her tightly so they bled into the chalice.

"Cassia," he began, "although I am known as Glasstongue, I struggle to find words worthy of what you mean to me. But I have always given you my truest words, however imperfect, ever since we first promised we would speak openly, honestly, without judgment. The trust you placed in me that night and every night since is the greatest gift of all. Let our first Oath to each other grow into this vow: I will always be honest with you. I will always be worthy of your trust. When you speak, I will make the world listen. When you fight, I will make your cause mine. And when you long for peace, I will be your Sanctuary. My love for you is as endless as eternity, and my vein will be your abundance for all time."

He dipped his fingertips in the chalice, then lifted his braid to her temple. The fragrance of his blood wrapped around her, and she felt his caress as he sealed the symbol of his vows to her hair.

"Lio," she said, savoring his cherished name on her tongue. "My soothsaying power may elude me, but know that I pour all my magic and all my Will into these words. When I was trapped in a life of silence, you heard me. You *listened* to me. And in the safety you offered me, I found my voice. From the night we made our Oath, you showered me with gifts: your patience, your kindness, your faith in who I could become. You held me through every transformation. Now I stand before you as my true self. With this power, I will keep you safe. I will hold you through your every ordeal. I will make all our promises come true. My love for you is as endless as eternity, and my vein will be your abundance for all time."

Their blood was warm on her fingers. She held her own braid to his hair, pouring a drop of her Will and magic and love into her touch. She felt the moment when the spell took hold, and a sense of completion filled her.

"Redblood Deukalion," Queen Alea said, "who is Whiteblood Cassia to you?"

"Cassia is my Grace," he said before their Queens, their family, and all their people.

"Whiteblood Cassia," said Queen Soteira, "who is Redblood Deukalion to you?"

"Deukalion is my Grace." The words felt so good, so powerful, their secret truth finally made into Ritual.

"Let it be known that your Grace bond is true," spoke Queen Alea.

"Drink before us in celebration of Hespera's blessing upon you," Queen Soteira declared.

Uncle Argyros placed the chalice in Lio's hand. Cassia's Grace lifted his creation to her lips. In their mingled blood, she tasted the hours of their lives, and she could name the sands he had halted forever to forge this glass. The crumbling stone of their shrine and its enduring Sanctuary magic. The sparkling black of Orthros's beaches, their home. The crimson slivers of his shattered window, remade. Even the treacherous sands of the Maaqul, each grain holding mysteries they had yet to discover.

She held the cup to his mouth in return and watched him drink her blood for all to see. Deep beneath the earth, the Lustra thrummed, as if a witness under some enduring, natural law.

Lio wrapped his hand around hers on the cup and leaned down close for the final tradition of the ceremony. His kiss on her neck was chaste and tender, and yet the intimate brush of his lips, a promise of his bite, made her fangs throb.

She pressed her kiss to his throat and felt his pulse in his vein, knowing it would always beat for her.

WORDS IN BLOOD

Lio watched Cassia dance. Her hair flew, and his braid twirled with her for all to see. She clapped her hands above her head, swaying her lithe body, now in red festival robes to show that she was no longer his Whiteblood.

She was Firstgrace Komnena.

The ceremony had begun in the Ritual hall, but the celebration had overflowed through the once-empty rooms of the house and out here into the wild gardens. The traditional chants had ended, and the new dances had begun. Their friends, drunk on wine or blood, danced around them while Nodora and her fellow musicians pushed their lutes and drums to the limit.

Lio lifted Cassia, and she threw her head back as they spun. Their Craving coiled tighter with each turn.

How long will the celebration last? she asked.

Until the last guest goes home.

She let out a laugh, bouncing away from him. *And when will that be?*

He chased her through the steps of the dance. *A house full of Hesperines during polar night, celebrating a once-in-an-eternal-lifetime event? They'll be here for nights on end.*

She let him catch her under a cloud of spell lights. *How long before the guests of honor can slip away for their avowal night?*

He pulled her back against him, moving with her body pressed to his. *It's tradition for us to try to sneak off under veils. If we're caught, everyone throws roses at us and chases us all the way to our residence. After that, we can come and go whenever we like.*

She let out a peal of laughter. *It's a good thing my Grace is such a powerful mind mage. I dare say we can escape without detection.*

He spun her around and lifted her so she could feel his heart pounding against hers. *Shall we try now?*

She whispered in his ear, her tongue darting out to tease his earring. "Yes. Your firstgrace is hungry."

The low rasp of her voice made his magic rise. He channeled all of it into a veil spell and pulled them deep into the shadows between the festival lights. They raced through the gardens with the music pounding after them. Their tower came into sight, and they darted along the final path.

A cloud of roses burst out of nowhere, and Cassia let out a shriek of surprise. Fat, soft blooms rained down on their heads

Lio almost didn't recognize the jovial laughter coming from the shadows. But he could think of only one mage who could defeat his veils.

"Uncle?" he sputtered.

Uncle Argyros emerged from his own concealments, his shoulders shaking with laughter, and flicked a rose at Lio's nose. Silvertongue's voice carried through the gardens. "Here they are!"

Hoofbeats sounded on the path behind them, and they turned to see the Blood Errant astride their war horses with saddlebags full of roses. Now breathless with their own laughter, Lio and Cassia fled, with Orthros's great warriors in pursuit, hurling flowers. The rest of their friends and family lined the path, enjoying the entire spectacle.

They made it to the steps of the tower. Lio snatched Cassia up in his arms and levitated the rest of the way. Applause chased them through the doors, which shut behind them to block out the final flurry of rose petals.

Cassia pulled his mouth to hers, kissing him in between her hiccuping laughter. Turning, he lifted her against the door, deepened their kiss. She raked her fingers through his hair, then gentled, caressing her braid. She let out a sigh.

He pulled his mouth back. "Do you still want the full ceremony? Including an avowal night in our very ceremonious bed where I Gifted you?"

She snatched a couple more kisses from his mouth, then nodded. "Oh, yes, we must do everything the official way first. We can feast against the door when we sneak off the next time."

"Mmm." He would take her up on that later, for certain. For now, he took them up to their bedchamber with one step, urging her toward the bed.

She halted him with her hands on his chest. "Wait. I have one more surprise for you."

She pushed him playfully away, and he staggered back, grinning. He came up against a pillar, and her roses slid affectionately about his shoulders.

"When we were in the Empire..." She lifted her hands to her collar and began to open her pretty festival robe. "...I visited a very secret tent in the Sun Market where they sell nothing but underlinens."

His fangs lengthened as he watched her. Bit by bit, she slowly revealed not her bare skin, but more silk. At last she pushed the robe off to fall at her feet in a pool of crimson.

She stood before him in an ephemeral creation of the sheerest white silk. Fastened at her bare shoulders with moonstones, the delicate garment wrapped around her figure and fluttered down to her ankles. Through the gossamer-thin fabric, he could see every line of her body. He wanted to devour every inch of her, from the flagrant impressions of her nipples, to the belly freckles peeking at him, to the dark invitation below.

A blush darkened her cheeks. "That's the second time you've given me that look tonight."

"What look?" He stalked toward her.

A little breath hitched in her throat. "Like I'm your goddess."

"You are, and now I shall kneel and worship you."

AT LIO'S WORDS, CASSIA realized her immortal knees could still go weak.

"Do you think you're ready for this?" he asked.

They had explored her new body in many ways so far, but this was a pleasure she had yet to know. With her heightened sense of touch, she hadn't felt prepared for the intensity of his mouth on her most sensitive places.

But she wanted that now, even if it overwhelmed her. Her body hummed with a Craving whetted by their sacred drink from the avowal chalice. She wanted him to inundate her.

"Yes," she said. "Let us make this a night to remember."

He went down on his knees in front of her. "This is a very important part of Hesperine avowal tradition. It's the Redblood's duty to make the Whiteblood scream."

She braced her hands on his shoulders. "No one mentioned that during avowal rehearsals."

"I declare it our private tradition, as of now."

He placed a tender, languid kiss on her stomach, his mouth and tongue warm through the cool silk. Her muscles twitched against his lips in anticipation. Slowly, he traced a path across her belly and over her hipbone.

She tangled her hands in his hair, cradling him closer, urging him on. He cupped her buttocks, and she eased her legs farther apart for him. The heat of his kisses trailed along the inside of her thighs, and she quivered.

How I've been looking forward to this, he said in her mind, his mouth busy in the groove of her hip and thigh. *I cannot wait to find out what you taste like now.*

Framing her apex with his hands, he smoothed out the silk that covered her. She realized he was not going to undress her.

Yet, he said. *If it becomes too much, tell me to stop.*

He pressed his mouth to her krana. A shock, even through fabric already warm and damp from her desire. She bit down hard on her lower lip, her own fangs pricking her.

Deepening his kiss, he gave her gentle pressure. A moan slid out of her, and on reflex, she arched against his mouth. His hands closed tighter around her buttocks, steadying.

When he laved her bud, the slide of his tongue against the smooth silk sent heat shimmering through all her senses. She melted in his hold, no longer breathing.

At her response, he licked her kalux again and again. Impossible pleasure sparked deep into her core and along her skin and to the tips of her toes. Shuddering in his hold, she could scarcely believe this part of her body was real.

You are a dream. His hands flexed on her. *And yet here you are, real in my hold. My immortal firstgrace.*

Her jaw dropped, her fangs throbbing with the sensations that pounded through her with every firm stroke of his tongue. She wrapped her arms closer around him for support. Their Grace Union bloomed, their intimate physical act spinning their thoughts and emotions deeper into each other.

The arcane paths inside her flooded with him. Her body sang, caught on the sharpest edge. At last she gasped a breath so she could speak, but all she managed was a desperate cry. She was either about to levitate right out of his hands or collapse.

Her knees buckled. His mouth left her on the cusp of release, and he caught her swiftly in his arm. The room spun, her senses full of stars, and then he was laying her down in the soft pile of the bedclothes.

He knelt between her knees. On reflex, she squeezed her thighs together against the delicious torture in her core.

"Too much?" he asked.

"Yes," she moaned.

"Ready for more?"

"Yes. I need you to—Goddess help me, I need—"

He parted her legs, and she nodded, giving up on speech. He swept his hands up her thighs, pushing the silk out of his way now. She dug her heels into the bed to brace herself.

With no buffer between them, he buried his face between her thighs and covered her with his mouth. She came up off the bed with an astonished outcry.

You taste incredible here, too, he informed her.

His hard kisses gave way to wicked, delicate flicks of his tongue. Her hands closed over the curving iron of the headboard, and she clung there while he held her legs down. Every heretical curse and prayer to Hespera that she knew flew from her lips.

That's my goddess, he said.

He took her bud in his mouth and began to suck. She felt as if she dissolved into a creature of pure sensation. Her immortal senses existed for one purpose. Pleasure, in its rawest form.

She still had a voice. That was her scream echoing around them. But it was distant compared to his palms on her skin, his fingers digging into her muscles. His mouth, a wet heat fused to her own, transforming her anew. Her body seemed to shatter and reform in his hold yet again.

Just when she couldn't bear to break anymore, he pulled his mouth away. He covered her in his weight, giving her shelter, stillness. She didn't breathe or move until her vision cleared, revealing his very satisfied smile and damp fangs.

He spoke softly. "Did that make a memory?"

"Bonded to my mind forever, like our ward," she said around her canines.

He stroked one of her fangs, making her moan again. "But now my goddess is hungry for blood. Let me feed you your avowal banquet."

He sat up, pulling her with him. She told herself she should slow down, make this moment last, but she tore open his collar with the ferocity of her Craving.

He let her. *There's no such thing as too slow or too fast in eternity. All our moments will last.*

Pain broke through her haze of revelry and pleasure. Did they really have unlimited time? They didn't know what would happen during this war.

Lio caught her hands, stilling her. "Yes, Cassia. We truly will be together for eternity, no matter what happens. We will live this life—or leave it—side by side. This, too, is the nature of Grace. There is no fear of loss. I will be with you, in this world or in Sanctuary."

He pulled his festival tunic the rest of the way off, and she saw the surprise he had for her. Divine script was tattooed across his skin like a vine. The glowing crimson letters trailed over his jugular, across his heart, and down into his trousers.

She traced her finger along the words. "It's our Oath."

"Every word I said to you that first night, and tonight. Feast on our vows, and once they're gone from my skin, know they're still in our veins."

She kissed his throat, tasting crushed rose petals and his blood. She took the words *I promise* into her mouth, his light magic sweet on her tongue.

I love you so much, she whispered in his mind.

I love you, my rose.

She pushed him onto his back. Framing the script with her canines, she slid their sharp tips lightly over his skin, drawing fresh blood. They gasped together at the well of pleasure in his aura. Blood trailed across his skin, tracing the contours of his chest. The infusion made the tattoo brighter, and she sucked the glowing swirl of script that circled his nipple.

Letter by letter, she licked the defining words of their lives from his body to savor each promise, each memory. She worshiped him in turn with her fangs. Her divine immortal, who had become sacred to her when she had believed in nothing.

The tattoo ended in a suggestive point above his groin. With a soft scrape, he dug his nails dug into the bedclothes while she pulled off his trousers. Freeing his straining erection, she realized her mouth was actually watering at the sight.

He lifted her chin, gazing at her mouth. "I'm ready for you to bring those beautiful fangs up here."

She slid up his body, baring her canines for him. He flashed his fangs back at her and flipped her over onto the pile of their pillows. His Craving sent a frisson through their Union and into her veins. Her pulse pounded faster, making her blood rush in preparation to sate her Grace.

But he hesitated, poised between her thighs. She sensed the flare of light magic. The air above them shimmered, then smoothed into a plane. Instead of the canopy bed overgrown with roses and moonflowers, she saw the two of them reflected back at her in a mirror spell. Her in a tangle of white silk. Him, pressing her down into the black silk sheets.

She ran her fingers along the brilliant red lines of the tattoo that continued on his back. His vows, written again in reverse like a never-ending promise.

He pressed his mouth to her ear. "Watch me avow you like this."

She saw his muscles play under the tattoo as he sank into her. He filled her, reshaping the inside of her body around him. With an appreciative groan, he pulled back, only to return with a heavy thrust that left her riveted to the sight of his buttocks in the mirror spell.

Her fangs gleamed at her in their reflection. *Give me your bite, now and every night.*

She remembered her first night in Orthros, when she had watched him feast on her in his glass mirrors. Now in his mirror spell, she saw her own fangs sink into his throat. She beheld her mouth, fastened onto his vein. And this vision changed her, just as that one had the night he had welcomed her into his world.

A shudder moved down his back, and his hips tensed. His reflexive response to her bite drove him deeper between her legs. Caressing his hair, she began to suckle his throat. As his pleasure-laden blood filled her mouth, she watched the rhythm of his body change, now pumping in time to her drink.

His blood spilled onto her from her bite. She caught the precious elixir and ran her hands over his shoulders and down his back. Making her own marks across his skin, she imprinted her vows next to his in bloody handprints.

"Cassia," he uttered, low and rough. Then his fangs clamped on her throat.

They overflowed into one another. She saw her body buck under his, saw him thrust down to meet her. They were so beautiful, feeding, undulating together, hard and slow. Then harder, faster. The flowers shook, scattering petals down over his rigid muscles.

Just as her vision began to haze, the spectacle above her fragmented. His shattered spell sent his magic flying into her. Her power, all hers, snapped out of her to entwine deep within him. They broke on each other, holding one another together through every spasm of release and rough groan against each other's throats.

Their Union only deepened to hold more pleasure. More time. Their vows could not break. No matter what was to come, Grace would remain.

nights until

WINTER SOLSTICE

A BADGE OF HONOR

Cassia and Lio wandered in and out of their avowal celebration as they pleased, joining in the dancing and laughter, then sneaking away again for more private gluttony. The hours flowed into nights, she knew not how many. Swept up in the current of emotions in the Blood Union, Cassia began to understand the immortal perception of time.

Eventually she found herself in one of the courtyards, sitting on Lio's lap with Knight at their feet, to watch the drinking contest Solia had promised. Her sister faced off with Tendo over a flask of ora, the finest spirits from the Sandira Kingdom, while their Trial circle and the Ashes looked on. Captain Ziara and First Mate Huru, the privateer queen and her beloved consort, took bets on the outcome with their favorite gambling partner, Kassandra.

Through an open archway came the fragrance of mangrove trees and reeds. Orthros's spymasters had joined the celebration as quietly as they glided in and out of enemy territory. Cassia and Lio stood to welcome the Queens' Master Envoys, clasping their wrists.

"Basir, Kumeta," Lio greeted them, "it's wonderful to see you."

"We weren't sure you would be able to make it home for this." Cassia could only imagine what dangerous corner of the Magelands the envoys had escaped from to be here.

"Of course we came," Kumeta replied. "We were there when you first met, after all."

A smile broke through Basir's usual dour expression. "On that journey to Tenebra, when Lio nearly destroyed our carefully laid plans by sneaking out for trysts with a certain mortal lady, I certainly failed to predict how this would end."

"He made a long list of possible disasters." Kumeta shook her head at him.

"This outcome is far better than anything I imagined," Basir said.

"You mean a best-case scenario came true?" Cassia covered her mouth in mock astonishment.

Lio widened his eyes at Basir. "Do I detect another shred of optimism?"

Basir frowned at them, but his aura smiled. "Optimism seems to befall me unusually often when you two are involved."

Solia and Tendo tossed back another shot, and the privateers clapped. But Mak and Lyros drifted away from the festivities to join Lio and Cassia near the envoys.

Basir hesitated, then a veil spell took form around them. "We have news for you from Cordium. We have debated how much to tell you. We would never want to tarnish this night."

"But we also understand that not knowing is seldom a comfort to you," Kumeta added.

Lio slid his arm around Cassia. *If you want to hear their findings, I will bear them with you.*

Cassia bit her lip. Once, she wouldn't have hesitated. Lady Circumspect would have gathered every secret to herself, no matter how painful, to use as a weapon. In this moment, though, Firstgrace Cassia wanted to forget about all of it.

What I want to do is dance with our friends until our heads spin. She glanced at their loved ones. *But for their sake, we cannot afford to squander a single weapon, can we?*

Lio sighed. *I don't disagree.*

"What did you learn?" Cassia asked.

Kumeta pursed her lips. "I take it you are already informed of the current political situation between the Order of Anthros and the Order of Hypnos?"

"Yes," Lio replied, "it's notable that the Order of Hypnos has yet to intervene in the war."

"Very odd," Lyros agreed, "considering their history of being both rivals and allies of the Order of Anthros. It is unlike the Order of Hypnos to let their brother mages in service to Anthros burn Hesperines without competing for our heads."

"I think the Collector is behind it," Cassia said. "We know the Old Masters are pulling the strings of all the mages, but especially the necromancers in the Order of Hypnos. Kallikrates must have called them off. He even holds the Gift Collectors back because a war between us and the war mages is part of his plan."

"Until now." Basir's aura was grave. "The Order of Hypnos has finally put out new bounties on Hesperines, and every Gift Collector from Corona to Martyr's Pass is racing to claim the reward."

"Who have they put bounties on?" Mak demanded. "Not the Blood Errant again?"

Basir shook his head. "Only two bounties—on Lio and Cassia."

"I suggest you take this as a badge of honor," said Kumeta.

Cassia's hands coiled into her fists. "Good. That means he feels threatened by us."

Lio's magic flashed in their Union, and his arm tightened around her. "I won't let anything happen to you."

She looked up at him. "I won't let anything happen to you, either. We'll face whatever comes—with our Trial brothers."

"That's right," Make said. "Your newgift has the best protection from Corona to Martyr's Pass, too."

"Thank you for the warning," Lyros told the envoys. "That will help us prepare."

Basir inclined his head. "We must report to our prince."

"And make time for a dance before we go." Kumeta slid her hand in his and accompanied him out of the courtyard.

His expression unusually grave, Mak looked to his Grace. Lyros paused, then gave a tight nod.

Mak didn't drop his veils. "We have one more avowal gift for you. Step to us at midveil, and we'll show it to you. Leave Knight with Zoe. You two should come alone."

THE MOONLESS SKY FELT heavy to Cassia when Lio stepped them to their Trial brothers later that night. Mak and Lyros awaited them on a cliff's edge overlooking the sea, shrouded in veils worthy of a secret council, not a party. She had never seen Mak so solemn.

Cassia glanced at the nearby sculpture of Nike. What were they doing out here on the grounds of House Komnena, holding a clandestine meeting near the Blood Errant's memorial statues?

Lio frowned. "The Vigil of Mercy isn't until tomorrow night. I thought that's when we were planning to pay our respects at Prometheus's memorial."

Cassia smiled at Mak. "No one keeps Vigil at your sister's statue anymore. Not when we can talk to the real Nike."

"That's why we're here," Lyros said. "No one will follow us."

"I take full responsibility for this gift—" Mak began.

"We've talked about this," Lyros cut in. "You know I wouldn't have helped you unless I was prepared to shoulder equal blame."

"Be that as it may, I started this." Mak took a deep breath. "Lio, Cassia, this is one time when you must not worry about dishonoring a gift. You deserve to know what I'm offering you, and you have the right to refuse."

"What are you talking about?" she asked. "Of course we would treasure any gift from you."

"This one is illegal," Mak said.

A moment of silence hung between them all.

He can't mean that the way it sounds, Cassia protested silently. *He would never break the law. He is too committed to the Stand.*

I don't know. Lio's worry throbbed between them. *Mak does rush into things without thinking them through.*

When no one spoke, Mak went on. "Only Nike, Lyros, and I know about this. Trust me when I say that as Stewards, whose sacred duty it is to uphold the law, we have not done this lightly. But sometimes we have to uphold the spirit of the law, rather than the letter of it—and our highest duty is protect our people."

Now I'm even more worried, Lio said.

Yes, Cassia agreed, *because he clearly has thought it through very carefully.*

There were a number of people they loved who orchestrated plots of dubious legality for the greater good. But Mak was the last person who would ever become a criminal mastermind. Wasn't he?

"Please explain," Lio said carefully.

"No." Mak spoke with calm confidence. "If you have any hesitations, it's safer for you if you don't know the details. That way, you can't be implicated if…things go wrong in the future."

"How can we make a decision without more information?" Cassia pressed.

"Here is all you need to know," Mak told them. "The gifts we have for you are against the Queens' laws but will never bring harm to the people we love. In fact, they could save lives. You would be among the few, but not the only Hesperines to possess them. And the Hesperines who have borne this burden before us have gotten away with it for centuries."

He gave his sister's statue a significant look.

Cassia stared at his warding spell, which hovered in the air before Nike's stone hand, an enchanted tribute to her legendary shield. Understanding dawned on Cassia.

Oh my goddess, Lio said.

Memories flicked between their minds, each of them recalling different hints. One night when Cassia had argued with the Tenebran lords about weapons, Mak had been strangely nervous throughout the debate. More recently, he had made allusions to a secret project with Nike, one that could help with the war effort.

Lio dragged a hand through his hair. *They have weapons. And if it's illegal, that means they're on this side of the border.*

And they have some for us, Cassia realized.

Lyros observed them and gave a nod. "Take a moment to make your decision. Once you're in, there's no going back."

How do we feel about this? Cassia asked.

I don't know, Lio answered.

We're diplomats. Joining the war effort pushes the boundaries of our role enough. But taking up arms?

If anyone found out, you and I would lose our medallions, and Mak and Lyros could never serve in the Stand again. We would all be arrested and tried for crimes against the Queens.

Cassia knew there was only one convicted criminal in Hesperine history: Phaedros, who had brutalized innocent mortals during the Last War. She should have been chilled by the thought. But they were not Phaedros. If they took this path, they would be following in very different ancient footsteps.

Yes. Determination began to form in Lio's emotions. *The Blood Errant have used weapons for hundreds of years.*

And they don't always lock them away at Waystar when they come home, as the Queens command.

Rudhira has brought Thorn into the heart of House Komnena and never been caught.

If Nike's brothers do the same…if Apollon's children follow in his footsteps… if the eighth bloodborn takes up arms, as did Methu, the first bloodborn…

It could be a disaster.

Or a triumph.

Lio looked into her eyes. *We must be of the same mind. We do this together, or not at all.*

She took his hand. *We are one. I will take up arms with you, my Grace, if you also feel called to.*

I will not shy away from anything that gives me more power to make sure everyone we love survives this war.

I feel the same.

Together, they turned to their Trial brothers.

"We're in," Lio announced.

Mak blew out a breath. "I was sure you would say no, Lio. And I wouldn't have blamed you."

"You're right, there was a time when I would never have considered this. But I'm not that person anymore."

"You weren't worried I would refuse?" Cassia asked.

"Not as worried," Mak replied. "You'll see why."

"Can we leave from here without detection?" Lio asked.

Lyros nodded. "The magic from Nike's statue will cover our departure."

Mak held out his hand. On his palm rested a charm of some kind, a four-pointed star the size of his thumbnail. The pearlescent metal caught the starlight, gleaming brighter than silver and steel.

"Is that crafted from adamas?" Lio asked.

"No more questions. Not here. Join hands." When the four of them linked their hands in a ring, Mak looked at each of them. "Ready?"

Cassia nodded. "Yes."

"Whatever happens," said Lio, "we have each other's backs. And no regrets. Agreed?"

"Agreed," they all echoed.

Cassia felt the pull of Mak's magic as he stepped. The cliffs seem to shift and split around them. A weight slammed into her chest, and she smelled blood. As a vice of power closed around her heart, she wondered what in Hespera's name they had just agreed to.

REFORGED

After the magic ground Cassia up, it spat her back out into the world.

She staggered, clutching at her chest, and caught herself on the edge of a wooden table. "Bleeding thorns. I see why we couldn't bring Knight."

A trail of red leaked from one of Lio's nostrils. "What did we just step through?"

Mak put a hand under Cassia's elbow. "Sorry. That was the best I could do to open Nike's wards. They aren't friendly, even to her own blood relatives."

"The first time is the hardest." Lyros steadied Lio and handed him a handkerchief. "Now that the protections approve of you, it will get easier."

Cassia looked around them, her chin dropping. The walls of the round stone chamber were lined with weapons of all kinds. More than she had seen anywhere in Orthros, except the Armory of Akofo, where they were to remain locked at all times.

A memory flashed in her mind of Lucis's solar, her personal torture chamber, where she had knelt before him in the shadow of armaments that had belonged to the kings of Tenebra.

She could not see any of that ugliness in the Hesperine creations around her. Perhaps she should. And yet how could she? These blades rang with the dark battle cry of blood magic. Like her roses, which had already killed for Orthros.

Lio walked over to study one sword. "It *is* adamas."

"The hardest metal in the world," Mak confirmed.

"But no one knows how to craft it," Lio protested. "It's well documented that the Blood Errant found their weapons in a Hesperite ruin with no evidence of how they were created."

Mak coughed. "Nike added that entirely fictional account to the annals herself, under the pseudonym of a dead historian."

"Your sister tampered with the historical record?" Lio seemed most scandalized by this above all, and Cassia almost laughed.

Lyros shook his head. "That's the crime you're most worried about, scrollworm?"

"Nike invented adamas," Mak explained. "She built this secret forge for the sole purpose of crafting the Blood Errant's weapons from her signature alloy. No one else has discovered it in eight hundred years."

"It's no wonder," Lio breathed. "The shadow wards and thelemantic veils she has over this place are a work of art in themselves. The Blood Errant could all set off master spells at once in here with no one the wiser."

"They probably have. Methu, Rudhira, and Uncle Apollon have all been here before." Mak beckoned them to the back of the deep chamber.

Geomagical heat bathed Cassia's skin as they approached the forge. Silver light and unseen, molten power emanated from the great crucible. A nearby pool of water let off such cold that it must have come straight out of Orthros's frozen mountains.

"Father never breathed a word of this," Lio said.

"Trying to spare your diplomatic career, no doubt," Cassia surmised.

"Nike brought you here?" Lio asked Mak.

"Actually, no." Mak held up the adamas star. "While she was missing in action, I discovered this in her abandoned residence and figured out how to get in."

"How did she react when she came home?" Cassia asked.

"She tried to kick me out. But I persuaded her to teach me instead." Mak gestured to the swords on display around them. "These are all practice pieces from our lessons."

Lyros crossed his arms, gazing into the forge. "When we came to the Empire—to bail you out of jinn prison, Lio—Mak felt his presence was more important than his blades. He gave up weapon smithing, and we asked for reassignment as your bodyguards."

Lio searched his cousin's face. "But you changed your mind?"

Mak strode back to the table and braced his hands on a black cloth that covered four mysterious shapes. "You know that what happened at Paradum changed everything. Lyros and I weren't there to protect you—again. And even when we made it there to help you fight your way out, we faced threats from the Collector that we've never seen before. I knew then that it had been a mistake to abandon the forge. We need weapons like the Blood Errant's."

Lio joined him at the table. "If Rudhira hadn't taken Skleros's head off with Thorn, Cassia and I would both be dead."

Cassia came to stand on the third side of the table. "Hesperine swords are not Tenebran swords. The Blood Errant have always used their weapons for good. Like them, we can wield these in Hespera's name without forgetting her tenets."

"Yes." Lio's gentle face was set in a hard expression. "Not in spite of being diplomats, but because we are diplomats, we will bear the burden of violence with you, so our people may know peace."

Lyros filled the empty space beside Mak, putting a hand over his Grace's.

A bittersweet smile came to Mak's face. "I'm sorry. But I'm also glad we're all in this together."

"Don't be sorry," Cassia said. "One night soon, a blade forged by your hands may destroy an enemy as evil as Skleros."

Mak took a deep breath and gave a nod. "Well, my errant circle. Meet your new weapons."

He swept back the black cloth.

Cassia had not thought she could ever find weapons beautiful, but these took her breath away. Four newborn artifacts of adamas, each adorned with a milky white moonstone the size of an eye.

A morning star, enduring as a light in the night sky. A spear befitting a sharp-minded general. The tall, elegant staff of a sorcerer.

But the one all her senses focused on was the dagger. Its blade was darker, less brilliant, but the wicked little thing called to her. She gasped and reached for it. As soon as her hand closed over the hilt, she knew.

"It's my spade."

Mak smiled at her. "I found the broken pieces inside Paradum. I couldn't bear for you to lose it. You can't replace an artifact like that, not when your battles have created it for you. So I reforged it—unbreakable this time."

She traced a finger over the moonstone embedded in the hilt, then the flat of the blade. The magic in the weapon rushed out to greet her like an old friend. "It's still imbued with Lustra magic and Hesperine blood magic, just as it was when it was a gardening tool."

"I was as careful as I could be, trying to preserve the original enchantments."

She held fast to it, her only weapon for so many years, now remade. Just like her. Tears pricked her eyes. "Thank you, Mak."

"You've wielded it with courage many times before. That's why I thought you would feel more comfortable taking up arms." He gave Lio a questioning glance.

Lio ran his fingers along the staff. "This one is for me?"

Mak nodded. "I hoped it would be acceptable to you, as a scholar and a mage."

Lio hefted the staff in his hand, then stood it on the ground before him. The pale metal was forged in a twisting design that reminded Cassia of vines, or perhaps molten glass just about to become a piece of art. Twists of adamas near the top of the rod caged the moonstone.

"At Paradum," Lio said, "in those moments before Rudhira arrived, I stood surrounded by Gift Collectors. I knew that by the time I broke through that many dream wards with my mind magic, Cassia would be…" He squeezed her hand and shook his head. "If I'd had a weapon like this, I would have had hope. I accept this gift with gratitude."

Mak picked up a sheaf of notes from a nearby shelf. He rolled the papers in his hands, hesitating, then held them out to Lio.

Lio took the papers, his gaze darting across the first page, and his eyes widened.

"You know I'm no politician…" Mak muttered.

Lio raised a brow at him over the papers. "Now you are. This is a proposal for the Firstblood Circle to allow the Stewards to use more than fists."

"If I can show on the battlefield that my weapons are of service to our people, I was hoping you would help me with the political part. You convinced the firstbloods to vote for the first Tenebran embassy to Orthros. If anyone can persuade them to approve armaments for the Stand, it's you."

"I don't think any diplomat can convince them of that," Lio said, "but a warrior like you can."

"At least critique the proposal for me. If it sits all right with your conscience, that is. Just read it and consider it. That's all I ask."

"Of course I will." Lio slid the papers into an inner pocket of his robes.

Lyros took up the spear. There was perfection in its smooth, clean form. "Mine turned out a masterpiece, my Grace. You've given these your greatest skill, strength, and magic. You should be proud."

"I will be—as soon as one of them saves a life." Mak picked up the morning star and gave it a few swings, then nodded as if satisfied. The spikes protruding from the ball looked deadly indeed.

Lio smiled. "If we hope for these weapons to become as legendary as the Blood Errant's, they'll need names."

"So will our errant circle," Cassia said. "What shall we call ourselves as we go on our quest in Hespera's name?"

Mak looked thoughtful. "Nike says it was Methu's idea to name the Blood Errant and their weapons."

"Don't let Lio choose any names," said Lyros. "We'll end up with a mouthful of specialized terms our enemies will need a glossary to understand, much less pronounce."

"You wound me." Lio put a hand to his chest. "As a bloodborn like Prometheus, I could think of suitably legendary epithets."

"Unlike him, you are not a poet," Mak teased.

"Lio appreciates poetry," Cassia defended him.

"If your idea of poetry is a six hundred page scholarly treatise," Mak said.

Lio held up a hand in surrender. "I'll only make a suggestion, then. The most meaningful names are gifts from those who truly see you. Each of us could name our Grace's weapon."

Lyros nodded. "That's fitting. Mak, you are their creator. Would you do the honors first?"

Mak ran his hand along the spear for a moment, thinking, or perhaps speaking silently with Lyros. "Night's Aim, for darkness is protection, and you are always true to that purpose."

Lyros's aura stirred with emotion. "Thank you."

"And mine?" Mak asked.

Lyros laid a hand on the shaft of the spiked club. "What could be more fitting for defending our homeland than a morning star?"

"Oh, that's right," Cassia murmured. "Orthros means 'morning,' the time when Hespera gives us rest."

Lyros nodded. "Let our smith's weapon be known as the Star of Orthros."

Mak met Lyros's gaze. "Thank you. Not just for the name. For supporting me in this mad endeavor."

"Always, my Grace."

Lio turned to Cassia with his staff. "And for an unlikely warrior's weapon?"

She arched a brow at him and smiled. "Yours should have a name fitting for a diplomat. 'Final Word,' for violence is always your last resort, and even in battle, you negotiate your victory on Hespera's terms."

He reached out and caressed her face. "Thank you for helping me keep sight of my true path."

She held out her dagger. "What will our bloodborn call my blade?"

He traced the place on her palm where the sharp edge of her gardening tool had once left a scar. Now smooth skin, thanks to her Gifting, but she felt as if those blood rituals had left an eternal, arcane mark on her.

"Rosethorn," he said simply. "There is no truer Rose of Hespera than our Hesperine Silvicultrix. And you know how I love your thorns."

Her cheeks warmed. "I told them you're a poet."

"Worthy names for soon-to-be-legendary artifacts," Mak approved. "Now you need a practical way to carry them."

He retrieved scabbards for them from another shelf. When he handed Cassia a dark metal dagger sheath attached to a matching belt chain, she was surprised to find how heavy they were.

"Are these forged of adamas as well?" she asked.

"There is some adamas in the alloy," Mak confirmed. "Nothing else would bear the weight. They'll dampen the weapons' magical auras, too, once we finish enchanting them."

"We?" Cassia asked.

"If you're willing, I'd be honored for all of you add your magic to our weapons." Mak set his morning star on the table in front of Cassia. "Starting with you."

"Me?" She took a step back from the spiked club. "You know how uncontrollable my magic is! What if I break the weapons?"

"They're made of adamas," Mak said cheerfully. "Nothing can break them. They're the perfect, indestructible artifacts for you to experiment with."

"What could my magic possibly add?"

"Think what happened when you channeled your Lustra magic at the Queens' ward. Your power has a defensive instinct, especially in combination with Hesperine protection spells."

Lyros put his spear on the table as well. "You've watched me enchant jewelry. You know the technique. You can imbue our weapons with your dual magic."

Cassia turned doubtfully to Lio.

He laid his staff before her. *You know I am always your willing test subject. And you did promise me another magical experiment. I cannot wait to test the results.*

You and your insatiable appetite for research.

For researching you, certainly.

She looked around at all three of them. "Do you think there will come a time when having my magic in our weapons could mean the different between victory and defeat? If I enchant them, could it save lives?"

"Yes," Lyros said. "Especially against the Collector. He told you himself that your magic is the most difficult of all paradigms for him to deal with."

If Mak or Lio had said it, she might have thought they were being too generous. But Lyros was their military strategist, who would never risk the outcome of the battle by mincing words.

She nodded to him. "Very well. I'll give them all the power I can. Let me try my dagger first, since it already has Lustra magic in it."

"Good idea," Lio agreed.

Cassia drew her finger along the sharp edge of the dagger. She gasped at the voracious Lustra magic that burst out of the artifact. The scent of roses filled the air. Vines coiled around her hand out of nowhere, their thorns raking her skin. Then they snaked out of existence, and she stood there watching her hand heal.

"Did it work?" she asked.

Lio rubbed her bloodstained knuckles. "It certainly did."

Lyros nodded. "There's a new enchantment on it that feels like Lustra and blood magic."

"But what does it do?" she asked.

Mak grinned. "We'll find out whenever the enchantment wakes up in battle."

"Are you certain you want me to cast an unknown enchantment on your weapons, too?"

"Mine first, please," Lio said without hesitation.

She examined the staff with her arcane senses. It reminded her of Lio and felt somehow connected to her, as he was. "All right, yes. I think I have a grasp on,,,I don't know the proper term. It's like an empty hole in the ground waiting for a plant. A place to root the enchantment."

"A potential enchantment anchor," Lio supplied. "Excellent analogy."

"Right." She held her spade-turned-dagger over her palm. "Brace yourselves."

As she had so many times in past hours of need, she used her blade to trace a line over her palm. The libation edged her dagger in crimson, and she felt the other three weapons respond to her blood.

Her artifact's Lustra magic flooded through her veins. She could channel out of the dagger itself, she realized. As the blade tapped the wilds, power spilled up through her feet.

The stones of Nike's Sanctuary shook with the might of the Lustra. She heard pebbles skitter and felt the magic in the forge bubble. But holding fast to the dagger, she could focus the chaos.

She tried to guide the magic into the weapons one at a time, only to wrestle with the unruly power. Acting on instinct, she grasped three tendrils of power at once. There. That felt right. She let the triune spell grow in the weapons.

She set her magic deep within the bed of Mak and Lyros and Lio's spells. She wasn't sure how long she stood there training her enchantment, building up her power around it so it would grow strong as a living part of the artifacts.

At last, vines sprouted right out of the metal, as if adamas were the richest soil and blood the most nourishing rain. Black roses coiled along the shafts of each weapon. Then the plants suddenly disappeared, leaving behind a flurry of black petals. The Lustra slipped back to sleep beneath their feet. But she could now feel the presence of her magic in the weapons.

A smile overtook her. "It worked! I think that was my first successful, controlled spell!"

"That's what we should call our errant circle," Lio said suddenly.

She looked up at him.

"The Black Roses." He wrapped his arms around her, looking to Mak and Lyros with a questioning brow. "What do you say?"

Lyros ran a hand down the front of Mak's battle robe. "Black for Orthros's protectors."

"Roses for our Goddess." Cassia's gaze fell to the petals laying across their weapons.

"The Black Roses." Mak gave a nod. "May the Goddess's Eyes light our path."

"And her darkness keep us in Sanctuary." Lyros finished the invocation.

Then Mak's gaze fixed on something over Cassia's shoulder. At the stark horror on his face, she froze.

Slowly, Cassia turned and saw who had crept up behind her with light steps and ancient veils.

In the doorway stood the Guardian of Orthros.

FALLEN IMMORTALS

Aunt Lyta stood very still, for once as unreadable as Uncle Argryos. Her eyes darted back and forth to take in the forge. The weapons on the table. The dagger in Cassia's hand.

Denial burned through Cassia's veins. This couldn't be happening.

But it was. In that split instant, calculations clicked in her mind. If there was ever a time for one of her schemes, it was now. Their fates were in her hands.

Lio, I need you to trust me.

Cassia—

There isn't time for debate. I have a plan. You and Lyros won't like it, but you must go along with it for all our sakes.

I will do anything to protect you.

"What is the meaning of this?" Aunt Lyta's voice was terribly calm.

"How did you find us?" Cassia responded with a question, although she thought she already knew the answer.

"It was rather hard to miss," Aunt Lyta snapped. "We're on the alert for responses from your roses so we can apprehend any enemies they snare. The magical disturbance here felt like the time they caught those heart hunters." Her voice rose slightly. "I thought the enemy was inside the ward, and your spell had spread to stop them. When I followed a trail of black roses into the mountains, I never imagined…this."

Cassia had been right. This was her fault. The horror in the pit of her stomach faded, and her thoughts grew colder, clearer. All that mattered now was protecting everyone she could from being implicated.

If only she could face this punishment alone. But it would take at least two of them to construct a tale Aunt Lyta would believe.

Mak took a step around the table, but Cassia held up a hand. "We owe your mother the truth. This is all my doing, and I will shoulder the full responsibility."

"Wait—" Lyros began to protest.

"None of you can protect me now," she interrupted him, Willing them to understand what she was up to. "Nor should you, after I dragged you all into this."

No. Lio's magic was a storm in his aura. *Don't you dare.*

If you trust me, my Grace, you will let me see this through.

"This was my idea," Cassia announced. "You know I've always been willing to do anything to protect Orthros. I thought bending the laws against weapons would be justified if it saved Hesperine lives." Her throat tightened. It was easy to spin this lie because it felt so true. "But I realize it was a very Tenebran thing to do. I suppose I am not as Hesperine as I should be, after all."

"Cassia." Emotion broke through Aunt Lyta's veils, and the hint of devastation there made Cassia's immortal blood ache. "That doesn't explain who crafted these weapons. You're no smith, and that forge is hot."

Aunt Lyta knew someone had been making weapons here. All Cassia could do was make it seem as if only one smith had been involved. She knew what Mak wanted. What they both had to do for their family and for Orthros.

"I found them," Cassia blurted, "some ancient adamas weapons in the Hesperite shrine back in Tenebra. I brought them to Orthros along with the glyph stone. I thought they must have been made by the same ancient smith who forged the ones the Blood Errant found." She turned to Mak. "Can you ever forgive me for showing them to you and asking your opinion?"

She waited, praying Mak would let her take this fall at his side so she could help him protect Nike. Cassia's bond of gratitude with her Ritual mother demanded this. If Nike hadn't saved Cassia's life all those years ago, she wouldn't have survived to stand here tonight, now an immortal.

Mak rounded the table and stood at her shoulder. "I don't blame you, Cassia. It was my decision to get involved."

"But if I had never brought them to you, you wouldn't have gotten the idea to study them and learn how to forge adamas. I even encouraged you when you decided to set up our research in this old forge of Nike's."

"To violate a Sanctuary of hers and craft weapons here…I know how deeply I've betrayed her."

Aunt Lyta's eyes narrowed. "That's why this place is covered in her wards, is it?"

Mak looked his mother in the eye. "I found this place while she was away. It's one of the First Circle's old bolt-holes, where she, Methu, and Rudhira used to escape their duties and work on their crafts. It makes her sad to come here now. So I borrowed it."

Cassia could have hugged honest, direct Mak for rising to the occasion. That was a masterful series of truths amounting to a lie of omission. "Mak and I have been sneaking out here for months. Then after I saw what my roses could do, I wanted to try adding their power to the weapons." She turned to Lio and Lyros. "We should have listened when you tried to stop us."

"They have nothing to do with this," Mak reinforced her.

"This is the first time they've set foot here," Cassia said fiercely. "They've been trying to talk us out of it all along, and they followed us here tonight to try one more time to stop us…before it was too late."

Mak was more composed than Cassia felt. "They only know about this because we couldn't hide it from our Graces. Under the laws of Orthros, Grace Union alone does not make a Hesperine an accessory to their partner's crimes. No Hesperine is required to testify against their Grace about something they learn through that private Union. Lyros and Lio committed no wrong, and we put them in the unforgivable position of being unable to report us for our crimes."

Cassia hadn't known any of that. Mak's dedication to the law was coming to Lyros and Lio's rescue, even as it sealed his and Cassia's fate.

She reached for Lio's hand and spoke the truth. "I'm so sorry Mak and I are putting you and Lyros through this."

His eyes blazed with anger. *She takes you and me together, or neither.*

It won't do me any good if you martyr yourself. Mak and I are counting on you and Lyros to stop Nike. Someone has to convince her not to tell Aunt Lyta the truth and get herself arrested.

You know it goes against everything in Nike to let you and Mak make this sacrifice for her.

Yes. She'll confess to exonerate us. We cannot let that happen.

She would sooner go to prison in your place.

She wouldn't allow anyone to imprison her. She would flee back to her quest to find Methu, never to return. You know losing her again will break Uncle Argyros's heart, and this time, he'll never heal.

She could feel Lio's heart breaking minute by minute. She sensed every new fracture spreading in their Union. She was asking him to choose between so many people he loved. To go against his deepest instinct to protect his Grace at any cost.

We agreed to put each other first. His protest rang through the mind ward.

This is my turn to put you first. Aunt Lyta witnessed me using my magic on the weapons. There's no way we can convince her I'm not involved. But we can still make you look innocent.

Or so Cassia hoped. Had her scheme allayed Aunt Lyta's suspicions?

The Guardian of Orthros pierced her palm, then curled it into a fist. Her power filled the air, pressing on Cassia's ears. The weapons levitated off the table. Then the scabbards rose and wrapped tightly around them, binding them in chains.

"Mak," she said. "My son. You know what I must do."

He faced his mother. "Yes, Guardian of Orthros. I'm sorry I have forced your hand."

"So am I." There came the briefest gleam of tears in the ancient warrior's eyes.

Then she cast her blood to the ground. Cassia felt warding magic close around her wrists. The Blood Shackles.

Mak's mother took hold of their arms with surprising gentleness. "Telemakhos Argyros and Cassia Komnena, you are under arrest for possession of weaponry within the borders of Orthros, failing to surrender your weapons at Waystar or the Armory of Akofo, forging the tools of war within the peace of the Queens' ward, and imbuing artifacts with enchantments designed to kill. These accusations and your defense will be heard by the magistrates of Orthros. May Hespera's Eyes see justice done."

Cassia's senses blurred, overwhelmed with the powerful magic in the room and the emotions inundating the Blood Union.

She had feared the Gifting would not find her worthy. She had never imagined she would succeed in becoming immortal only to fall so far.

Like Phaedros the Mad, she was now one of the few Hesperine criminals in the history of Orthros.

But she had always known she would do anything for her Hesperines.

Lio's power shook their Union. *You're asking me to stand here and watch you get arrested while I go free.*

Orthros needs one of the Collector's two worst enemies to not be in prison. Tonight, that has to be you.

Orthros can fight the Collector without me, then. I will fight for you.

You can't do anything to protect me if you're locked up with me. Take this opportunity I'm giving you. Work with Lyros to defend Mak and me.

That, at last, seemed to cut through his fury. *Yes. Of course. We'll fix this. I swear to you, Cassia, we'll get you out.*

Aunt Lyta addressed Lio and Lyros. "Inform your Elder Houses that members of your bloodlines are in the Stand's custody. It is the duty of your firstbloods to arrange their defense."

"As you command, Guardian of Orthros," Lyros said.

Lio said nothing. Cassia sensed that in this moment, Glasstongue did not trust what words would come out of his mouth.

She knew it was one of the most self-sacrificing things Lio had ever done when he silently watched her and Mak be taken away.

It took all of Lio's Will to hold back his power. The barrels and shelves around them rattled as his Grace's aura was torn from him. He felt like his heart was dragged through the forge's brutal wards with her.

"We can't linger here," Lyros said, "but I...can't face Argyros right now."

"Neither can I."

They stepped out of Nike's forge and back to her statue. Lio let out a howl of frustration over the cliffs, his magic crashing down to join with the choppy waves below.

Lyros sounded numb. "I don't know how I managed to misjudge so badly. I was never in favor of Mak's weapon smithing, but I'm his Grace. I supported him unconditionally. I thought, 'When this goes wrong, we go down together.'"

Lio was on the brink of falling into his own spiral of self blame. But how many times had Lyros been the one who pulled him back up again? Tonight, Lyros needed Lio to do the same for him.

"I know." Lio gripped his Trial brother's shoulder. "I am angrier at myself than anyone right now. But our regrets are of no use to Mak and Cassia. They need us to think clearly and act decisively."

"All my thoughts and decisions were wrong. I followed Mak down this path to try to protect him, and now look where he is. His parents trusted me to be a good influence, but my Grace-mother just had to arrest her own son, and I have to go speak with my Grace-father about his defense. Hespera's Mercy. Some kind of strategist I am."

"We can salvage this. Mak and Cassia made this sacrifice for us. We can't let it be in vain."

Lyros rubbed his face. "Goddess. That's true. I'm sorry."

Lio squeezed his shoulder. "No apologies."

"Right." Lyros drew himself up. "They made sure we went free, and we won't squander that. We need a plan."

They gave each other a long look.

"I have no interest in waiting on legal proceedings at an immortal pace," Lyros said.

"And I don't care if we are also wanted criminals by the time this is over," Lio told him.

Lyros held out his hand. "We do anything to save them. No matter what it takes."

Lio clasped his wrist. "I'm with you, Trial brother."

NONNEGOTIABLE

THE ROOM WAS BARE and lit by a single, dismal spell. Hard benches lined the gray stone walls. Cassia thought it must be the only place in Orthros devoid of comfort and beauty.

Worst of all, wards smothered the room. She felt deaf to the Blood Union. Especially when she tried to listen through the implacable veils over Aunt Lyta's emotions.

But the legendary warrior was not actually very good at hiding her feelings. There was care in her hands as she released Mak and Cassia's arms. Pain flickered in her eyes. Every tense line of her petite, muscular frame revealed her anger.

Cassia didn't blame her. She was so angry at herself for putting Aunt Lyta in this position.

"Mother," Mak said. "I'm sorry."

Aunt Lyta opened her mouth to speak, then shook her head. She closed her hands around the weapons hovering before her. She stepped away, the artifacts disappearing with her.

Mak sank down onto a bench and put his head in his hands.

Cassia paced the length of the chamber. She shook her wrists, hating the feeling of the Blood Shackles. They weighed on her veins, dragging at her every time her arcane senses twitched.

Some Lady of Schemes she was now. She had managed to slip out of the King of Tenebra's grasp every time, and yet she had just entangled her immortal family in a tragedy.

Hespera help her, how could she have made such a catastrophic mistake?

She pivoted and paced back the other way. She would think of how to make this right. She would.

"Where are we?" she asked.

Mak let out a humorless laugh. "The disenchantment chambers in Stewards' Ward. When rowdy youngbloods set off stupid spells, this is where we throw them so they don't blow themselves up. Do you know how many times I've been the one to toss someone in here for their magic to cool off?"

She winced. "That just adds insult to injury, doesn't it?"

"Well, this is better than Phaedros's prison under the midnight sun, I can tell you that. More darkness. Fewer polar bears."

Cassia gave a weak laugh. Trust Mak to find a jest, even now.

Lio hovered in their Union. *Are you all right?*

She had gotten them into this mess. The least she could do was be strong for her Grace. She mustered her composure. *We're perfectly fine. Aunt Lyta is being gentle with us.*

Nice try, my Grace. I know you're devastated. Where are you?

Panic stirred inside her. *Can't you tell?*

He hesitated. *No. Ah. That must mean you're in the disenchantment chambers. They're warded against stepping and all kinds of magic.*

She tried to reason with herself. At least the wards would prevent him from doing anything rash that would get him arrested next.

But her unruly heart began to race. He had been able to find her in the Maaqul Desert. Being taken from him right in their home city prodded all her instinctual fears of separation. And she had no hope of hiding it from him.

Nothing blocks Grace Union, he reminded her. His mind magic blanketed her thoughts.

Her heart began to slow, and she breathed.

Don't be afraid, he said. *Lyros and I have a plan.*

Lio, no—

He ignored her protests, although he didn't pull very far from their Grace Union. She couldn't help being grateful for his nearness.

She turned and paced past Mak again. "Are prisoners allowed veil spells?"

"Yes." Mak's magic wrapped around them. "The Stand isn't supposed to use magic to make us incriminate ourselves. That includes stripping our veils."

"I know how hard all of this is for you," she said in the hush of his spell.

"I accepted the possibility, when I asked Nike to teach me, but… Hespera's Mercy. This is all wrong. No one should be locked in here but me."

Cassia sank down onto the bench and put her arms around him. "I would have gotten myself arrested alone if there had been any way to convince Aunt Lyta I really had found all the weapons."

"There's too much evidence in the forge that they were crafted there." Mak hugged her close. "You had to implicate me to take suspicion off Nike. I'm glad you did."

"We saved her. That's what matters."

"But all you should be doing right now is celebrating. I never should have dragged you and Lio into this."

"We accepted the possibility, too. Admittedly, I didn't expect us to get caught five minutes afterward."

"I never dreamed Nike's wards and veils wouldn't hide your spells!"

"I should have known. Lustra magic is opposed to blood magic. Nike probably didn't account for anti-haimatic magic like mine."

"But your Lustra magic is in Union with your blood magic. No wonder you didn't suspect anything would go wrong."

"Regardless, it was my spell that got us caught."

Stop blaming yourself, Lio demanded.

Cassia held on to comforting visions in her mind, even if Lio didn't believe them. *Are you talking to Papa about my defense?*

He sent her a mental image of their smiling family sitting around the Ritual circle with mince pies and coffee. *Everything is fine here. Nothing to worry about at all.*

You made that up.

Two can play this game.

"Under Hesperine law," Cassia asked Mak, "what is the sentence for our crimes?"

He blew out a breath. "You always do ask the hard questions first. I wish I could tell you. But no one has ever been put on trial for this before.

There's no precedent. Our punishment would be at the discretion of the magistrates, unless the Queens stepped in to issue a verdict themselves… which they might, considering it's their ban on weapons."

"Do you think they would imprison us with Phaedros?"

"I hope not. We didn't actually use the weapons on anyone." He swallowed. "Perhaps exile Abroad, instead of with the polar bears. I think I'd prefer that over the alternative…house arrest in a silk-cushioned cell, knowing the whole city is right outside the door pitying us and our bloodlines."

She stared at the blank wall and made herself think through what lay ahead. "Conjugal visits?"

"Right. No one wants Lio and Lyros to die of Craving while their blood supplies serve out the sentence."

The people who loved them would be forced to put them on trial to uphold Hespera's tenets. Their families would be dragged through the legal process, surely a lengthy one, which would bring only grief and scandal. And their Graces would suffer the most.

All while the Collector got closer and closer to that door and whatever fate would befall the world if he opened it.

Cassia had knocked herself off the board. She had effectively removed herself from the game, and every life lost as a result would weigh on her conscience forever.

"What are our chances of escaping?" she asked.

Mak's shoulder slumped. "Considering Phaedros—an elder firstblood—hasn't managed it in sixteen hundred years, our odds aren't good."

Cassia contemplated the floor under their feet. "I wonder if your mother's wards can truly block Lustra magic…"

"Even if we could break out, the Blood Shackles will prevent us from stepping, levitating, or crossing the border. There's only one way we can escape."

"If Lio and Lyros rescue us." She gritted her teeth.

"And get themselves branded criminals in the process."

The blessing of Grace they had been celebrating earlier that night had already become a chain around Lio's neck.

"I won't do that to him," Cassia said. "I will keep my promise to put him first. I have to stay and face trial."

"I'm not going anywhere," Mak agreed. "I owe it to Lyros to make this up to him however I can."

"At least they'll still be considered innocent. They can keep their lives here."

"Yes."

Silence fell between them. What kind of lives would those be, carrying the shame of their Graces' crimes?

LIO CAUGHT THE SOUND of paws racing across the snow. He froze, tightening his veil spells alongside Lyros. But it was no use.

Knight headed straight for them, his nose to the ground. A cloaked figure forged a path behind him, leaving a trail of melted snow. He halted at the edge of their veils and wagged his tail.

"Good dog," came Solia's voice from within the hood. She lifted a hand toward the sky, and fire flickered in her palm.

That was when Lio noticed the dark silhouette crisscrossing overhead. Tendo dove down to land next to Solia.

Solia waved in Lio and Lyros's direction. "We know you're there."

"Open up," Tendo demanded.

"We signaled Nodora's ship, too," Solia warned. "Our reinforcements are already on the way."

Lio stood within arm's reach of them across the invisible layer of spells. "I don't want to involve them."

Lyros dragged his hands through his hair. "I know. If we implicate them, the consequences—"

He didn't have time to finish before their Trial sisters levitated over the cliff and landed on the edge.

Nodora's magic probed their veils. "We're here to help. We're your Trial circle. We take care of each other, even when one of us does something colossally stupid."

"Especially then," Kia agreed.

Xandra put her hands on her hips. "This is no time for idiotic, noble notions of keeping us out of this to protect us."

Solia's aura burned with outrage. "My sister has been arrested. Don't even think about trying to rescue her without me."

"Face it," said Tendo. "You need us. Especially me. After all, I'm the one who saved your soft hides the last time Cassia was a wanted criminal."

Lio and Lyros looked at each other.

"If any of them had been arrested," said Lio, "you and I would beat down their doors to help, even if it got all of us exiled under the midnight sun."

Lyros shook his head at Lio. "When did you become the person encouraging us all into a life of crime, instead of being the first one to confess our mischief to the elders?"

"The first time someone threatened a hair on my Grace's head."

"I know the feeling. But it goes against my grain as a Steward to make everyone else complicit in our crimes, and Mak would agree."

"They're making this choice. As much as I want to protect them, I have no right to tell them they can't take action to protect Mak and Cassia."

Lyros sighed. "You're right. It's a gift that they're willing to take this risk, and we shouldn't dishonor that."

Lio nodded. He and Lyros lowered their veils.

"It's about time!" Solia huffed.

Knight leapt to Lio's side. He hugged the dog's shaggy neck, looking down to meet his earnest eyes. "It's a good thing you're the only people in Orthros with a liegehound who can track us through our veils."

"I can make sure no one else finds us." Nodora beckoned them toward the cliff. "Hurry. My ship is waiting below."

It was an excellent plan. The ocean was rife with its own natural magical forces that few could control. It's powerful arcane currents would help disguise their spells and auras, especially with help from Nodora's water magic.

They stepped down to her ship, gathering under an awning bolted to the deck where there were warmth spells for the mortals. Nodora blew a few notes on her flute. The waves stirred around them, and her floating residence eased into motion. The large, graceful vessel sped away from the lights of Selas and out onto the dark Sea of Komne.

Lio reached for Cassia through their Union to see how she was feeling. There was a resigned confidence in her, and he hated it. He would not let her be the martyr tonight.

You're one to talk, she said. *You've attempting to martyr yourself for me on numerous occasions.*

That was different.

How so, pray tell?

That was me. Given the chance, I will always march to the gallows in your place.

Don't you dare.

You know I cannot see reason on this, my Grace.

Lio looked from their Trial sisters to Solia and Tendo. "Lyros and I are planning to break Cassia and Mak out of Stand custody and go errant, no matter the consequences."

Lyros gave a solemn nod. "Our elders are doing what they must for the integrity of this land they founded. We'll do what we must to protect our Graces."

"We have a higher duty, as well." Lio wasn't sure if he was justifying this decision to their friends or himself. "The Collector won't wait for Orthros's magistrates to reach a verdict. We must get to Tenebra and stop him from opening that door. But you all have duties to your kingdoms and your bloodlines, as well."

"Please," Lyros said, "if you have any hesitations about this plan, leave now. We don't want to hurt any of you."

Solia crossed her arms. "If you weren't planning to break Cassia and Mak out, I would do it myself."

Tendo narrowed his eyes at her. "Fortunately for you, I've infiltrated the Empress's secret prisons. I doubt the silkfoot version of high security will pose a challenge."

She looked away. "The Ashes are covering for us. Hoyefe is casting illusions at the celebration to give us all alibis while Karege helps Tuura and Kella smuggle out your packs and horses."

"I'm your escape transport," said Nodora.

Kia gestured at herself. "You'll need my methodological deconstruction abilities to get Mak and Cassia out of their Blood Shackles."

Lyros's eyes widened at her. "You can break Blood Shackles?"

"I can dismantle any spell, in theory, as long as I understand its structure. I'm afraid you and Mak will have to reveal some of the Stand's magical secrets if you want me to free him and Cassia."

Lyros grimaced. "To put this mathematically, that could dramatically increase your chances of getting arrested."

She lifted her chin. "I would consider it an honor."

Lyros gave her a sad smile. "Trust you to flout the laws for your principles without hesitation."

"When laws don't match our principles, the laws need to change." Kia touched his arm. "If that gets me exiled and imprisoned under the midnight sun with Phaedros, well, that just means I'll get to debate his latest treatise with him in person."

Lyros shook his head, putting his arms around her and Nodora's shoulders.

"We won't let anyone else get arrested tonight," Lio said firmly. Especially not the Blood Errant. "Who knows about the arrest so far?"

"Lyta has a council with my mothers in half an hour," Xandra replied. "That will be your chance to rescue Mak and Cassia while they're not guarded."

"That doesn't give us much time," Lio said. "Who else?"

"Argyros and Lyta have informed no one but your parents and Solia," Xandra explained. "Then Solia recruited the rest of us to help. Your families are keeping all of this very quiet for now. They haven't even stopped the avowal celebration."

Lio grimaced. "How did my father react?"

"He was so quiet," Xandra said. "Dangerously so. Then he went looking for you."

Lio muttered another curse. "What about Nike and Rudhira?"

Xandra shook her head. "Rudhira is in Tenebra, and Nike has been on patrol at the other end of the ward this entire time. I think your families are putting off breaking the news to them."

"We have to keep Nike distracted," Lio said. "Mak and Cassia made us promise we wouldn't let her do anything self-sacrificing."

Xandra's brow furrowed. "Is she more involved in this than you're letting on?"

Lio exchanged another glance with Lyros. Their friends only knew the version of the story Cassia and Mak had told Aunt Lyta.

"They have a right to know the truth," Lyros decided.

Lio nodded. "I agree. Nike needs their protection, too."

And so did his uncle. He had never thought of Uncle Argyros as a vulnerable person. And yet, in this moment, he was. They held his heart in their hands.

"Neither Nike nor Cassia ever found adamas weapons in an ancient ruin," Lio revealed. "Nike forged the Blood Errant's weapons and taught Mak how to make ours."

As soon as he and Lyros explained the true version of events, a flame sprang to life at Solia's temple. "Your elders welcomed Cassia with open arms, only to arrest her for something as natural as picking up a dagger!"

"I'm sorry, Solia," Lio replied. "You know I never meant for this to happen."

"I don't blame you." There was approval in her voice. "I'd be angrier if you tried to come between her and her blade."

Lio smiled. "I know better than that."

Xandra's aura flashed hotter. "It's not fair. The Blood Errant have never been punished like this. They'll be furious about Mak and Cassia's arrest. We should send word to Rudhira right away. He can advocate for them and talk Nike out of doing anything rash."

"No, Xandra," Lio said. "We can't do that to your family. Imagine what it would mean for the Queens—for all of Orthros—to know Rudhira has been disobeying their commands."

"At least stop hiding from your father, then!"

"I don't want him implicated, either. This will be hard enough for Zoe without our parents getting dragged into it."

"How about Alkaios and Nephalea?" Nodora suggested. "They're among the few Nike would listen to, and they know all her secrets."

Lyros shook his head. "Not them, either. They've just established their new lives here in Orthros. Mak would never want to ruin that."

"Neither would Cassia," Lio agreed, "not after everything they've done for her."

Lyros's expression grew bleak. "They'll be a comfort to Mak's parents now."

A look of determination came to Xandra's face. "Then I will protect Nike."

Kia opened her mouth to protest.

Xandra held up a hand. "Now isn't the time to shelter me like when we were children. I am a royal Hesperine, and I will see to this myself."

"What are you going to do?" Nodora asked her with concern.

Xandra's eyes narrowed. "Only one thing could possibly keep Nike from coming to rescue Mak and Cassia. An imminent threat to Orthros."

"Goddess," Lyros said, "we must pray there's no attack on the border while the Stand is falling apart like this."

"There won't be," Xandra said. "Just the appearance of one. I'll cast a few perfectly safe fire spells near the ward to make Nike think there's a rogue war mage in the mountains. And if an actual attack happens while I'm distracting her, I can turn around and fling real fireballs at the enemy. Orthros has never been safer."

"Xandra…" Lio shook his head. She didn't need him to tell her how many ways this could go horribly wrong. "Are you sure?"

"Yes. My Trial circle and my family are at stake. It's my turn to protect all of you. And if a Hesperine royal must be implicated, Orthros can bear it much easier if it's the wayward Eighth Princess rather than our beloved First Prince."

"May the Goddess's Eyes light your path," they all bade her.

"Her fire is about to light up the mountains." Xandra waved at them with flames dancing at her fingertips, then disappeared.

What's happening? Cassia's aura throbbed with worry.

Lio tamped down on his own worries and sent reassurance to her.

I see right through your sweetness and light, she replied. *I know you're on the warpath. Don't do anything that will land you and Lyros in Blood Shackles.*

We have no intention of getting arrested, Lio replied truthfully.

Give Mak and me more time to decide what to do before you and Lyros try anything rash.

This is nonnegotiable, he informed her. *We're coming to rescue you.*

VIGIL OF
MERCY

5 Nights Until Winter Solstice

INTO THE UNKNOWN

THE LOW, GRAY BUILDING cast a long shadow in the fresh snow, a shadow Lio deepened to conceal their rescue party. They slipped under the simple portico that sheltered the entrance to the disenchantment chambers.

The place was too covered in spells for Lio to sense who might be inside. They could only pray Xandra was right, and Lyta would be in council with the Queens for a long while.

Lyros paused at the door and looked at Lio in question. Lio nodded. His veils were ready.

Lyros eased the door open.

The central room was empty. The only guard was a battered practice dummy in the corner, with which a Steward usually whiled away the time while looking after initiates and their misbehaving magic.

The wards that steeped the walls did not feel so protective now. They stood between Lio and his Grace. Doors lined the walls, two of them shut tight and fortified with magic.

Cassia's presence stirred behind one of the closed doors. *Sunbind it, Lio, tell me you're here for an approved visit.*

I'm here to break things until you're safe.

Tendo peered through one of the open doorways. "Really? *This* is the only prison in Selas, and we can walk right in?"

"It's not a prison," said Lyros, "and the front door isn't the problem."

"I expected Hesperines to hold their captives in better comfort," Solia seethed.

"We don't hold captives," Lyros protested. "Any cushions we put in here would get destroyed the next time some youngblood's spell runs riot."

Solia stalked forward. "Let's see how this place holds up when *my* spells run riot. Which door shall I burn down first?"

Lio pointed to the one across from the entrance. *Stand back. Your sister is about to try magefire on the wards.*

Cassia's fury burned through their bond. *This is not the plan! We cannot risk Solia's alliance with Orthros! Mak and I have made up our minds, and we are not letting anyone else take the fall with us!*

Lio cast Lyros an amused glance. "If Mak is protesting this endeavor half as vocally as Cassia, your head must be a busy place at the moment."

Lyros half grinned, rubbing his temples. "Our Graces have tempers."

Unfortunately for Cassia, her ire seldom had the effect on Lio that she desired. He had too much of a taste for her anger to regret his actions. "She insists she won't set foot outside this cell, and if I try to carry her, she will tie me to the ground with rose vines before she lets me get myself arrested."

Tendo snickered. "Tell her I'll carry her off for you, then. But ask her not to step on my foot again."

Tell Tendo I'll aim for his wings this time!

Lio repeated this, and Tendo laughed harder.

Solia settled into a battle stance in front of the door and cupped her hands. "Ready?"

"Yes," Lio answered. "I've covered you in the best thelemantic veils I learned from Nike. Let us hope her experimental spells conceal fire magic."

Solia's aura crackled. In a flare of golden light, a ball of fire shot from her palms. It struck the warded door with an impact that reverberated through the stone.

The fireball rebounded back at Solia. She let out a filthy Imperial curse and held out her hands. Her flame returned to her, flitting up her arms. "I see why Aithouros had such a bad night when he tried to chase Lyta through Martyr's Pass. How much time do we have?"

"We're out of time," Lyros hissed, an instant before Lio sensed her, too.

Lyta's aura was approaching.

"How can their council be over already?" Lio glanced around them, then beckoned to the others. "In here."

They ducked inside one of the empty disenchantment chambers, and Lio eased the door almost shut. He slammed more power into his veils, wrapping them all in the gloom of the unlit room.

Your heart is pounding, Cassia said. *Oh, Goddess, she's coming?*

Lio gritted his teeth, unwilling to admit how close they were to getting caught by the Guardian of Orthros. Time to find out how the veils he had learned from her Grace and daughter held up against her.

Through the gap of the open door, he saw Aunt Lyta stalk in. She halted there, and Lio tensed. She stood for a long moment, pinching the bridge of her nose.

Then she sprang into motion all at once.

She hurled her fist at the practice dummy. Canvas ripped, and feathers tore through the air around her.

When another aura slipped into the room with her, Lio's heart leapt into his throat.

Uncle Argyros pulled her into his arms. "Talk to me."

She rested her fists and her tear-streaked face on his chest. "I remember how the pacifist Hesperites looked at me when I learned how to use my fists. Is that how I looked at Mak when I saw him with a weapon? Have I become them?"

"You could never be like them."

"No." Her voice fell to a whisper. "I don't want to tell the Queens. I didn't want to arrest our son."

"I know." He shut his eyes, pressing a kiss to the top of her head.

"I cannot make exceptions for our own blood. But I want to. Hold me, Argyros. Otherwise I will walk over to that door right now and open it so Mak and Cassia can slip away, as if I never saw a thing."

He held her tighter. "I'm afraid you'll have to hold me in return."

She wrapped her arms around him. He rested his face on her hair, and his eyes caught the low light, glowing dark gold.

Lio realized his uncle was looking directly at him.

Caught in Silvertongue's gaze, Lio could do nothing but hold his breath and his veils and pray.

"I wish you and I could open that door," said Uncle Argyros, "but we must not."

Perhaps Lio had lost his mind. Or perhaps he understood exactly what his uncle meant.

He gave his mentor a nod.

Was it his imagination, or was that minute motion of Uncle Argyros's head a nod in return?

"Let me take you home," Uncle Argyros said. "It's not necessary to guard them. Everyone in Orthros knows there is no possible way they could break out of this building."

She lifted her head suddenly, her brow furrowing.

He put a finger to her lips. "We should leave now. It is better for everyone that way."

The elders disappeared, their powerful presences fading from the room.

The rest of them stood in silence for an instant, then Solia said, "Is it safe to try again?"

"I'm fairly certain they won't be back," Lio replied.

She rushed to the sealed chamber and flattened her palms against it, the rest of them following. This time, her fire cascaded over the entire surface of the door. The stone gave a promising crack.

Then the glow faded. Solia smacked her hands against the door with a growl of frustration.

"You need either more time or more power," Tendo said, "and time isn't something we have."

She kept her back to him.

He snapped his wings. "Let me help."

Finally she looked over her shoulder, her jaw clenching. "Fine. But only for Cassia's sake, you understand?"

"Of course." His voice was hard.

But there was something gentle about how he approached her. She stood very still, letting him draw near to stand behind her. When he flattened his hands over hers on the door, a little start went through her body. His wings flared.

All the air in the room seemed to rush to them in one gust. Her fire flared again. Fed by his wind spell, her magic came alive in a conflagration. Lio and Lyros shrank back. Monsoon stood with nothing but her between him and the flames.

The door glowed molten orange. Then the fire reversed, slamming back into her. She staggered back into Tendo's arms. A chill wind swept through the room, cooling the door to gray. It fell in pieces at their feet.

Cassia stared at them through the rubble and dust, her aura spitting with anger. Her gaze shot past them. When her eyes locked with Lio's, he felt the quiver that went through her and knew, as angry as she was, it took all her Will not to throw herself over that threshold and into his arms.

Lyros levitated into the chamber first. Mak opened his mouth, his face flushed and brows drawn down in anger.

"Enough!" Lyros said. "You got us into this mess. Hush and let me get us out of it, will you?"

Lyros grasped Mak's face, preempting whatever protest he was about to make with a hard kiss.

When Lyros let him go, Mak put his arm around his Grace and exited the chamber with him in silence.

They left Lio and Cassia facing each other over the threshold. Her fists at her sides, she flashed her fangs at him.

Lio held out his hand to her.

She stood her ground. *I can't bear for you to lose our family. Our home. At least let me protect that for you.*

You are my family and my home.

He took a step toward her, gravel crunching under his shoe. She stood rooted, as if unwilling to walk forward but unable to pull back.

He reached out to touch his braid in her hair. *I will not let you take the fall alone. No matter what happens in our lives, we go through it as partners. What do you think our vows mean otherwise?*

She slipped her hand into his. He pulled her close, and for a moment, nothing else mattered. His Grace was back in his arms. Relief sank deep into their shared blood.

A boom sounded from the central room, jolting Lio back to reality. He had veil spells to maintain. Cassia hurried out of the chamber with him. Her eyes widened at the sight of her sister and Tendo working on the other sealed door.

"Leave the weapons in there," Mak said. "They're not worth it."

That image flashed in Lio's mind again: Thorn, cutting through the night, cutting down the Gift Collector. "We'll need them where we're going."

"I'm not letting you leave without your blades." Solia gritted her teeth.

Tendo pumped his wings, and more wind magic swept into her grasp. She hurled a jet of flame at the door. This time, their spell cleaved right through the stone, and it fell in two slabs at their feet.

I'm glad they're our family and not our enemies, Cassia marveled.

I can imagine how they carved their way across the Empire for eight years with the Ashes.

He simply needs to go carve his way across Tenebra with her, and then they'll both feel better.

Mak didn't move to retrieve his creations. So Lio took it upon himself. He found the weapons resting on the benches. Whatever spell Aunt Lyta had used to bind them must have worn off. Apparently she had thought the door would be secure enough.

Or had she suspected a fire mage bent on protecting her little sister could break it down?

Lio shook his head. No time to puzzle out the elders' motivations. He tossed Mak, Lyros, and Cassia their weapons and scabbards. He slung his chain across his chest, and the metal grips attached to it settled between his shoulder blades. He levitated his staff onto his back and felt it lock into the enchanted holder.

The magic in Final Word murmured to him like a friend. A temptation. It felt good to have it on his back, this aberration that had caused them so much grief already.

What did that make him?

"We'll get the Blood Shackles off you after we escape," Lyros said. "We'd better run."

Cassia cast a worried glance between her sister and Tendo, who now stood as far away from each other as the room allowed.

"Well, Sunburn," Tendo said, "do you want to take a slow, mortal stroll to our escape ship, or will you let me carry you so you can keep up with the Hesperines?"

She crossed her arms over her chest, her lips pressed together.

"The avowal celebration isn't over," he said, "which means our truce still holds. We agreed we wouldn't let our past affect Cassia."

"That's not all we agreed to. I will fly with you, but if you don't keep your hands to yourself, I'll burn them off."

Tendo smirked. "And if *you* break that part of our truce? Shall I give you a little distance from temptation? I'm sure dropping you over Orthros would cool you off."

"Say that again when I have time to answer in the arena," she snarled.

Laughing, Tendo scooped her up and marched out the door. In a rush of wind, his magic lifted them, and he spread his wings to carry her into the night sky.

Lio and Cassia took off running after their Trial brothers. They sped across the fields, and Stewards' Ward faded away in a blur of white. Then they darted through the back streets of the arts districts, where revelers were more interested in their own veiled trysts than prying into Lio's spells. All the way, Cassia kept pace with him, fleet and powerful at his side.

Soon they hit the beaches beyond House Kitharos, and they raced lightly across, the sand barely giving under their feet. Lio and Lyros led their Graces to the two boats waiting just above the tide.

"Our Trial sisters are in on this too?" Cassia demanded.

"And the Ashes," Lio said. "Lyros and I tried to keep everyone else out of it, but they wouldn't stand for it."

Cassia pressed her lips together in silent protest, but helped Lio push their boat out into the water alongside Mak and Lyros's. They leapt in, and the waves rippled with Nodora's magic, tugging them out to sea.

The beach had receded into the distance when her veiled ship emerged from the darkness ahead. Her flute trilled above them. The waves crested beneath them and lifted the boats gently onto the deck. Lio got out and reached to help Cassia, but she had already leapt nimbly out. Knight ambushed her, the water on her clothes soaking into his fur.

Tendo came in for a graceful landing on the starboard side. Solia jumped out of his hold as if she'd been burned, straightening with great dignity. Judging by his cocky smile, the flight had not been a waste.

"Thank the Goddess none of you got caught." Nodora ushered Cassia toward one of the benches under the awning.

Tuura was already waiting there with her medicine bag. "Who needs a poultice?"

Cassia sank down onto the seat. The anger drained from her aura, giving way to misery. "I'm so sorry I brought all of this on you."

"So am I," Mak said.

Kia hugged him tightly. "Stop it, you overprotective oaf. I, for one, am proud of you." She sat him down next to Cassia and took the seat across from them. "Can I hold one of these weapons that have the elders' underlinens in such a twist?"

Neither Mak nor Cassia hurried to display their weapons, and Lyros hesitated, too.

Metal whispered on metal as Lio levitated his staff out of its grips. He rested the end on the deck with a soft impact.

Kia circled it, her face bright with fascination. "May I?"

Lio offered the staff to her. "Cassia named it 'Final Word.'"

"Ha! You'll certainly have the last word when fighting with this." Kia lifted it, weighing it in her hands, her magic probing the artifact. "Mak, this is a marvel! It deserves to be studied, not outlawed!"

Mak slumped with his elbows on his knees. "Phaedros can write a treatise about it when we're all banished with him."

"No one is getting banished on my watch," Kia said. "Don't despair. Heretics never changed the world without breaking things."

Lyros interrupted, "Right now, we need to break these Blood Shackles off Mak and Cassia so we can make it over the border."

Kia handed Final Word back to Lio and rolled up her sleeves. "Show me how this spell works."

He joined her on the bench across from Mak and Cassia, and blood magic flared in the night as they went to work.

Lio hovered behind his Grace, longing to put a hand on her shoulder for comfort. But he sensed she wanted time to sort through her emotions. He had learned that when she was in this state, all he could do was give her the space she needed.

Lio sighed and retreated to the railing. He watched the lights of Selas give one last glitter in the darkness of polar night as home disappeared behind the horizon.

Kia had been working for hours when Cassia felt a snap in her blood. The Shackles finally gave way. The magical weight lifted from her, and she heaved a breath.

Kia flopped back on the bench, her face ashen and fangs out, but her aura was triumphant. Lyros rubbed his Grace's wrists, and Mak accepted this in silence.

Cassia's gaze drifted to Lio. He still stood at the railing, but now he was looking at her instead of the dark, empty sea. Her aura instinctively flowed toward him. She sensed him simply waiting, listening. He would be at her side in an instant if she asked.

He was too far away. And she had only herself to blame.

"All right," Kia said. "The shackles are off, and it will be twilight in Tenebra by now. Time for you all to go."

Nodora looked toward the southern horizon, although the border was too distant to be seen from here. "I wish we could wait for word from Xandra."

"So do I." Mak finally spoke. "We don't even know if her plan worked. If Nike turns herself in after all..."

Lyros shook his head. "It will be better if Xandra keeps her distracted until we're well over the border."

Mak gathered his composure. "Right."

"You all have our gratitude," Cassia said.

The Union was heavy with everyone's regrets. Lio sent reassurance to all of them, and selfishly, Cassia soaked it up like a thirsty scrub in the Maaqul.

"It's all right," he said. "This is how it must be. For now. We can worry about clearing our names after the war is over."

Nodora wiped her eyes. "We'll keep working to exonerate you. We will make it our cause in the Firstblood Circle."

There was a cold fire in Kia's gaze. "This will only inspire our partisans. The Eighth Circle, taking up arms like the First Circle, persecuted by those too afraid to rebel!"

"I'll write your first ballad myself," Nodora promised.

"Yes," Kia swore, "the name of the Black Roses will be in everyone's hearts."

Nodora swallowed hard. "And we'll visit Zoe every night."

Cassia covered her face with her hands. Lio's despair mingled with her own. Zoe. Their greatest regret of all.

Zoe's worst nightmare was that her loved ones would leave her, never to return. Cassia and Lio had promised her that would never happen to her again. But this time, it might not be in their power to come back.

They hadn't even said goodbye.

Strong arms, warm with fire magic, wrapped around Cassia.

"I will make sure Zoe is all right," Solia swore. "I'll have someone step me to Orthros to check on her every chance I get."

"She needs you," Cassia said, her throat tight. Solia was the only person who could fill the hole they were about to leave in Zoe's life.

"I haven't lost my touch at being an elder sister to a little girl. I couldn't be there for you when I was a fugitive. But I can be here for Zoe while you are on the run."

Cassia rested her face on her sister's shoulder. "I'm so glad you're in our lives now."

"Took me long enough, but I'm here to stay."

"And you, Tendo?" Lio asked, clasping his arm. "Will you go back to the Imperial court to make sure none of this affects the Empire's alliance with Orthros?"

"Eventually," he said, "but for now, I think I'll find out if Zoe likes flying with me as much as Chuma does."

Solia lifted her gaze to his. "So…you're staying in Orthros for the time being?"

"Someone has to clean up the damage these four left in their wake."

"If you grow tired of peaceful silkfoots," Solia said lightly, "there is a battle going on next door, you know. Helping me throw fireballs might be more entertaining, at least."

Tendo put his hand to his ear. "I'm sorry, I must have misheard you. Did the Queen of Tenebra, who insists she can win this war without any more Imperial warriors, just ask for my help?"

"I'm giving you an opportunity to escape that uncomfortable

chair a certain Imperial princess has in mind for you. You should be thanking me."

"And how does a certain Hesperine prince feel about me flying into his territory?"

Solia frowned. "He is unlikely to object to more Imperial support. And if he did, I would remind him my kingdom is not his territory."

There was an edge to Tendo's laugh. "Oh, I'm sure he'd object to the kind of support I gave you when you and I fought together. I don't get the impression he likes to share your sparring sessions, and neither do I."

Solia surged to her feet. "Is *that* what you think?"

Lio's eyes widened at the two of them, and Cassia couldn't help meeting his gaze.

Oh my Goddess, he said, *Tendo is jealous of Rudhira.*

Does he have a reason to be? Cassia asked in astonishment.

I have no idea. It never occurred to me. Our Ritual father and your sister? Did Solia say anything to you about it?

Not a word.

"I will not dignify your assumptions with an explanation," Solia said. "I am no one's 'territory,' and the only person entitled to an opinion on who I 'spar' with is me."

Tendo gave Solia a sardonic look. "There isn't room in your kingdom for two princes, Your Majesty. I'll be tending to Hesperine-Imperial relations on this side of the border, regardless of what sort of negotiations are going on between you and the First Prince."

He turned his back on a fuming Solia, flaring his wings. He paused only to look back at Lio and Cassia.

"Take care of yourselves," he said. "Don't make me come rescue you."

He vaulted off the railing and flew back toward Selas.

No one spoke for a long moment. Cassia's mind reeled with the implications, but she didn't dare ask her sister about it right now.

"I apologize for that display," Solia said at last.

Cassia stood and put an arm around her. "You have nothing to apologize for. You know you can talk to me about it when you're ready."

Solia's warrior face slid back into place. "Kella and Karege will meet us in Tenebra with your horses. You can use his aura as a stepping focus."

Tuura patted one of the packs she had brought. "We retrieved everything we thought you'd need from your residences. Quite easy, when your provisions are traveling with you. I packed food for Knight and plenty of poultices, though."

The diviner handed Cassia her hardy old gardening satchel, which had carried her prize possessions through many past travails. But leaving tonight felt harder than anything she had ever done, from walking into a war mage's assassination plot to trekking across the Maaqul.

They were out of time. These were her Trial sisters' last embraces and final farewell blessings. She had to let them go.

"I will see you again," Cassia said in defiance of the dread taking hold of her. "This isn't forever."

It couldn't be. The forever she had envisioned for herself in Orthros couldn't be gone.

Rosethorn felt so heavy at her waist as she and Lio collected their packs and gathered with Mak and Lyros around Solia. Lio's magic wrapped her close, and they stepped into the unknown.

FUGITIVES

THE COLD CALM OVER the Sea of Komne gave way to gusts of wind that still tasted of salt, and Cassia set Hesperine foot in Tenebra for the first time.

At first she didn't recognize the ragged moor and steep coastline, where waves crashed against the rocks. The moonlight was so bright, the smells so vivid. Could this really be the gray world she had lived in before?

Tenebra would never feel the same again. Her Grace's presence filled even this desolate night.

"Where are we?" Lio asked.

"Hadria," Cassia said.

Solia's cloak tangled around her in the wind. "This is the safest place I could think of to bring you. On Lord Hadrian's orders, no one will persecute Hesperines in this domain, and it's too fortified for Lord Lucis to attack…yet."

"This is a good plan," Lyros said. "Thank you. We're far from the siege, here."

"And from Rudhira's forces," Mak muttered.

Solia scowled. "Steer clear of Castra Hadria, the main fortress. There's a Charger there providing protection and communications."

Knight was suddenly alert, his nostrils flaring, but his hackles didn't rise. The aromas of blood magic and indigo warmed the night, and Karege's veils dropped to reveal him and Kella waiting with four horses. Knight wagged his tail at Tilili.

"I knew if you could escape the Maaqul, you could get out of this, too." Karege's grin turned to a frown. "But where is Tendo?"

Kella held out her hand. "You owe me twenty silver. I told you he wouldn't come."

"And I told you she would ask him," Karege returned. "Didn't you, Sunburn?"

Solia crossed her arms. "Yes, I wasted my breath asking him."

Karege crossed his arms at Kella. "You owe me snake blood. Make sure Tilili catches one alive. No Hesperine wants snake jerky."

Cassia found a smile for Standstill and Noon Watch. "The Ashes have our gratitude. Tell Hoyefe that for us when you see him."

"Don't get sentimental on us now, Shadow," Kella said. "I'm sure Lonesome and I will cross paths with you in Tenebra many times before this war is over."

"After I step Kella and Solia to Castra Patria," Karege explained, "I'm heading back to Ukocha's village with Tuura. You've been fugitives there before! Come find Peanut and me if you need to disappear."

Solia rested her hands on Cassia's arms. "I must get back to the siege now. I wish I could offer you refuge in my fortress."

Cassia grimaced. "If Rudhira catches sight of us, he'll be honor bound to arrest us and take us back to the Queens."

Solia muttered a curse. "I've half a mind to toss him and his entire Charge out on their ears."

"That's out of the question!" Cassia protested. "The Charge's support is essential to you in the war. The four of us can't give you that kind of support."

"We have to focus on what we set out to do all along," Lio said. "Find the truth about the door, wherever that may take us."

Solia embraced Cassia one more time. "I don't want to leave your side, Pup."

"I know." Cassia squeezed her eyes shut. "When I see you again, bring me a seed for the garden, just like always."

"I will. I promise I'll find something worth growing under all the flames at Castra Patria." Solia pulled back. "Remember, even if you must avoid contact with the Charge, you are not fugitives under *my* law. You are still the Queen of Tenebra's sister. I will make it clear to all my allies that whenever the Black Roses call upon them, they are to support you without question."

Cassia nodded. "Thank you."

Solia gave Knight a pat before going to stand beside Karege.

"May Ayur's blood guide your hunt," Kella said, invoking the Azarqi goddess of the moons.

Then Karege's magic flared in the darkness. Cassia, Lio, Mak, and Lyros were suddenly very alone on the windy Tenebran moors.

Mak stalked over to Bear and General, his and Lyros's matched pair of black warhorses, who were also their familiars. He loaded a saddlebag onto his mount in worrisome silence.

Lyros went to help him with their packs. "We need to determine our initial plan. The problem we must solve first is how we'll cope with daylight."

Lio fished out his astrolabe before lifting his pack onto his horse. Moonflower, white as his namesake, was not a familiar, but the gentle giant was still an Orthros Warmblood—powerful, intelligent, and all but immortal.

Cassia tallied the horses among their weapons, including her little speckled mare. Freckles might be the smallest, but she was also fast and mean. She switched her cinnamon-colored tail, looking like she wanted to bite someone, her permanent expression. Cassia found it comforting.

Lio made a couple of adjustments to the astrolabe, peering at the instrument. "With Winter Solstice almost upon us, this part of the kingdom gets only seven Tenebran hours of full daylight. Cassia will Slumber an hour or so beyond dusk and dawn, so we should have about three hours of twilight and twelve hours of night to find refuge."

Cassia fastened her satchel to Freckles' light fabric saddle, then lifted her larger pack onto her mount. Her belongings felt so easy to lift now. As a new Hesperine, she might sleep longer than the others, but she would make her new strength felt in her waking hours.

"We can't rely on Hesperine Sanctuaries," Lyros said. "No doubt Orthros will send out search parties, and those are the first places they'll look."

"I'm not so sure they will come looking. I could have sworn..." Lio hesitated. "I think Uncle Argyros knew we were there. And let us escape."

Mak went still, staring at Lio. "He what?"

As Lio described what he'd witnessed in the disenchantment chambers, images of Argyros and Lyta flashed in their Grace Union for Cassia to see. "I believe he and your mother wanted us to get away. So it's possible Rudhira will also make a point not to find us."

Mak rubbed the back of his head, his aura a tangle of emotion. "My parents…impossible."

"Not impossible." Lyros took Mak's hand. "But we cannot assume Rudhira will share their intention to let us escape."

"I'm afraid that's true," Cassia said. "What if Rudhira would rather solve this with us safely under house arrest, instead of errant in Tenebra without the Charge's support? He'll want to find us, if only because he's protective."

Lio winced. "Or because we are also breaking Charge Law by going errant without his approval."

"Marvelous," Mak said. "So all the secret Hesperine Sanctuaries the Blood Errant told us about are exactly where we shouldn't go."

"We may not need Hesperine Sanctuaries." Lio looked at Cassia. "Not when we have the Lustra."

She held up her hands, shaking her head. "My magic has caused us nothing but trouble. We shouldn't rely on it for anything."

"If we can find more Lustra passages," Lio said, "they will be the perfect solution to our dilemma."

"The Charge has access to them now," Cassia reminded him.

"To the tunnels at Castra Patria, yes," Lio replied, "but we have no evidence those connect with passages in different locations. Even if they did, the Lustra opens for whom you wish. I'm sure it would just as quickly lock someone out for you."

"And what if I spawn a forest of black roses by accident that lead the Charge and who knows who else right to us?"

Lio approached her. Closer. She had to tilt her head back to look at him. His dark blue gaze caught her like an anchor. She felt so far, far adrift. She wanted to stand in his shadow all night, soaking up the comfort of his presence. Comfort she didn't deserve.

He rested his hand on her pendant. "There's no need to conjure any roses. Simply use the pendant as you always have. It will be a small spell, unlikely to draw attention."

"We don't know what my pendant does now. You should use yours."

He hesitated, then pulled his hand back. "Very well. We'll try mine. For now."

"Where should we start looking?" Lyros pulled out his map.

Lio studied it with him. "Hadria is one of the oldest domains in Tenebra. There should be a number of structures here that date from the Mage King's time. Any suggestions, Cassia?"

Cassia pointed to a section of land that curved outward from the coastline. "We're here on the Horn of Tenebra. There's a lighthouse out on the tip of it. The legends say the Mage King lit the signal fire himself when the lords of Hadria swore fealty to him."

"Perfect," Lio said. "Let's see if the Changing Queen left her mark on it as well."

"Shall we ride instead of stepping?" Cassia asked. "I think we can reach it in a couple of hours on Orthros Warmbloods."

"Good idea," Lyros said. "You two can look for entrances to the passageways as we go. They may be spread out like the ones at Patria."

Cassia wished she could levitate onto Freckles like a proper Hesperine. Even so, mounting had never been this easy. As a mortal, it had taken so much practice to ride the Hesperine way, using her knees to guide her horse without reins. Now she felt connected to her horse through the Blood Union.

Freckles swung her head around and sniffed Cassia's dagger. She put her ears back, snorted, then proceeded to ignore Rosethorn.

"Not intimidated by liegehounds or dangerous artifacts, are you?" Cassia patted the mare's neck.

Freckles had a lively presence, but when Cassia tried to sense Knight's emotions, all she felt was solid silence. The contrast sent a pang of regret through her. Liegehounds' immunity to Hesperine magic meant she couldn't commune with her oldest friend.

As they galloped across the moors, the others let her take the lead, although she would rather have shrunk to the back of the group in silence, as Mak was doing. But given her familiarity with Hadria, she was the best guide they had.

They halted at intervals for Lio to apply blood to his medallion. No light spawned to guide them to a Lustra door. Perhaps this search would prove as disastrous as everything else Cassia had attempted.

Twilight had given way to night by the time they reached the bluff where the lighthouse stood. They approached under veils, cautious of the mortal auras within. Lord Hadrian's men might report their presence to Castra Hadria without ill intent.

The circular tower, built of heavy gray stone and Hadrian stubbornness, seemed immune to time and the waves fighting to wear down the sharp rocks below. Cassia halted Freckles at the foot of the bluff and squinted up at the firelight glaring from the top of the lighthouse. The ancient structure's presence had always given her gooseflesh, and now her arcane senses told her why.

"It's shining with magic in a literal sense," she realized.

Mak let out a low whistle. "There's something very strange about that fire spell."

Lio stared up at it with an intrigued frown. "Cassia, do fire mages come here periodically to renew the enchantment?"

She shook her head. "Lord Hadrian would never let an Aithourian war mage touch his lighthouse."

Lio's brows rose. "Are we to believe this is the Mage King's original spell? What could possibly sustain it this many centuries after his death?"

"We have a different arcane mystery to solve," Lyros said. "Did his queen leave any portals here?"

"Hmm." Lio tore his gaze from the flame and bit his hand, making another libation on his pendant.

Nothing happened.

Cassia's heart sank. Her brilliant idea had not helped them at all. "There's nothing here."

"Nothing that I can detect." Lio guided Moonflower closer to her. "Perhaps you have to let me in before the portals will accept me."

Freckles shifted testily under Cassia, and she realized she was holding the horse's mane too tight. She forced her hands to relax. "It would be unwise for me to attempt any magic."

"I can veil your casting. I'm prepared this time."

"I'm not sure I can concentrate. I'm rather thirsty."

Lio's gaze darkened. "That's easily remedied."

Her face flushed. After the ordeals of the night and the magic she had expended, she didn't dare take a bite of him here and now. Her Craving would demand more than a sip.

Lyros cleared his throat. "Perhaps after we find a Lustra portal to offer us shelter."

Sunbind the amusement in Lio's aura.

"Try a drop of your blood on your pendant," he instructed in the tone of her magic teacher.

The muscles between her shoulder blades, where she used to sweat as a mortal, now tensed painfully. There had to be a better way than her setting off her chaotic magic again.

"It was my beast magic that revealed the portals to us at Patria," she reasoned. "I can't change my eyes now. Who's to say the passages will even open for my plant magic?"

Lio's remorse saturated their Grace Union, and Cassia immediately wished she could take back her words. She should have known better than to mention her lost magic. She hadn't meant to prod his regrets about not helping her claim all her power before Gifting her.

"This is why I will never give up on your other affinities," he said too calmly. "But for now, we need you to use your plant magic to the fullest. The Lustra has shown itself willing to adapt to the changes in your power. Try."

He was right. They were out of options. It could take hours they didn't have to find a different historical location, step there, and start their search from the beginning.

Cassia's Craving would catch up to them long before dawn did. Her magic and her hunger were both burdens that only made matters worse for the four of them.

If there was a portal here, she had to find it for them, and she'd best do it before her Craving made it even more difficult to control her power.

She dismounted and planted her feet on the ground. Lifting her palm toward her fangs, she realized her hand was shaking.

Lio's aura eased up behind her, and his hands came to rest on her shoulders. "Just like we've done before."

Why did she feel as if casting spells would never be the same again?

She drew the smallest amount of blood from her hand and touched her pendant.

Magic shot up from the soil and exploded through her veins. Her senses split and spread, reaching out far. So far. As if her roots ran through all of Tenebra, and she could hold an entire kingdom in her mind's eye.

The Lustra called out to her. It knew she had returned.

Who else would know, after this arcane declaration?

We have to make it stop, she cried into their Grace Union.

I can help, but only if you're willing to let me.

Do whatever you can.

Lio swept into her mind, fast and deep, as he had when casting the mind ward. She sagged back into his arms, his body the only solid form in a world roiling with magic.

Let me help. He murmured through her every thought.

She was afraid to let go. So afraid to stop fighting the magic.

Let go.

She surrendered, her mental defenses falling for him in one gentle rush. His power encircled her, fortifying the mind ward, and the chaos went quiet.

There was nothing but the two of them, here in the Sanctuary of her thoughts.

She felt his touch on her Will, the gentlest guide. She followed where his magic led. Together, they took hold of the wild tendrils of her spell and pulled them all back to her. The magic sent a tremor through her as it shot back into the ground.

She opened her eyes. The flame at the top of the lighthouse had risen to a bonfire. She heard the shouts of men on the other side of the wards Mak and Lyros had conjured around her and Lio.

"Let's not wait for them to demand an explanation. This way." Lyros pointed.

Black roses ripped out of a crack in the bedrock under the lighthouse. The vines took hold of the stone and tore it aside to reveal a broad portal.

They all plunged inside, guiding Knight and the horses. With a rumble of stone and snapping of vines, the portal sealed behind them.

HOW NEGOTIATIONS END

MORE MAGEFIRE GLARED ON Cassia's vision. Her eyes adjusted in an instant, making the brightness bearable. In sconces all around the edges of the chamber, spell flames burned, as lively as the fire atop the tower.

The large, round room appeared hewn from the rock, with rounded arches leading off into side passages. One of the horses pawed at the ground, the soft sound echoing up to the domed ceiling overhead.

Lio crouched to examine the shapeless debris at their feet. "This looks entirely undisturbed! If we excavate, we might find artifacts from the Mage King's time."

With a snort, Freckles trotted farther inside to graze on the scrub growing through the broken stonework. Lio winced.

Lyros led the other horses to join her. "I'm afraid we'll have to treat this as our war room, not a museum."

"Our very own errant Sanctuary." Mak gave Cassia a pat on the back. "Nice find."

She only hoped no one else found it, thanks to the magical signal flare she had unintentionally sent up just outside the door. She glanced behind her. Black roses guarded the entrance, but the vine wasn't spreading, at least.

Mak had barely spoken in hours, though, so she kept her doubts to herself and smiled at him. "The Lustra will keep us safe here."

As if it sensed her words, the magic of the wilds murmured through the corridors in welcome, tinged with salt and thistle.

"It won't let anyone else in," she said with certainty.

Lio got to his feet, his aura keen with interest. "How can you tell?"

Cassia shrugged. "This will sound foolish, but…I simply know."

"It doesn't sound foolish at all," Mak said. "Intuition is powerful. Especially when it comes from the Blood Union—and whatever Union you have with the Lustra, I imagine."

Lio nodded. "Can you tell if we're in proximity to a letting site?"

"It's difficult to say." She hugged herself. "The Lustra's response was so powerful…it could be a nearby letting site. Or it could simply be that Tenebra is…glad for a Silvicultrix to return, I suppose."

Or it might be nothing more than her terrible grasp of her magic.

Lio gestured to the archways. "We should explore the corridors and see what magic we can sense."

"That's a better idea than historical research," Lyros said. "Do you think we could learn anything about the door under Solorum from these passages?"

"It's entirely possible," Lio replied. "I think we should look for magical evidence each time we encounter a Lustra portal."

Lyros nodded. "I suggest we disappear here for a few nights to search the passages and make sure no one followed us. We need to regroup and form a plan. And Goddess knows we all need a drink."

None of them argued with that.

They unsaddled their mounts, stowing their tack, packs, and weapons in the central chamber. Then Mak and Lyros took off in one direction, Lio and Cassia to search the corridors on the other side. Knight stayed within arm's reach of her at every moment. Being in Tenebra again had clearly unleashed his protective instincts, but more than that, she suspected he was still recovering from their separation.

Cassia forged ahead into a firelit passage, keenly aware of Lio behind her. She had a sudden memory of their early walks at Solorum, just the two of them with Knight for an escort, rambling in woods full of ancient sites the Mage King and Changing Queen had left behind. She had thought she was just a bastard girl who would be forgotten by history—and by this immortal. She'd had no idea her legacy had been right under her nose. Or that her Grace had already walked at her side. Following her down these dangerous paths. No going back.

"Cassia." His veil spells wrapped her close. "How much longer must you wrestle with yourself before you let me hold you?"

She halted, barely seeing the smaller stone chamber they had come to. They couldn't put off this confrontation any longer.

With a sickening weight in her belly, she turned to face him. "I don't want you to hold me. I want you to go home to Orthros as a respected diplomat and beloved son. I want you to have your life back. But that's not possible because you're yoked to me! Why wouldn't you just leave me in that cell?"

He moved toward her, his spell light casting stark shadows on his beautiful face. "You know why."

"Why wouldn't you let me protect you?" she demanded.

"That was not a sacrifice I was willing for you to make."

"It was my sacrifice to make! It was my spell that gave us away. My magic is supposed to keep you safe—but it just destroyed your life. Surrendering to the law was the only way I could shield you."

"You cannot make a choice like that on your own and expect me to go along with it. Not now that we're avowed. All your decisions affect me."

"I know that!" she cried. "That's why I was trying to repair the damage I'd done."

"By making me stand there, helpless, after I promised to always fight for you?"

"What about my vows to protect you in return? You've sacrificed for me over and over again. There are times when you have to let me shoulder that burden instead."

"Then don't demand this sacrifice of me! Don't ask me to be a respected diplomat and beloved son while our people drag you through a trial. Don't expect me to leave you in a cell, out of my reach, and try to carry on with my life without you beside me."

She retreated backward, needing more space between them. If he came any closer, she would be at his throat in a heartbeat.

His fangs grew longer with each step he took toward her. "I will not allow anyone to lock you away from me. Not kings. Not necromancers. Not Imperial fanatics. And not the firstbloods of Orthros."

Her back came up against the wall.

He was so close now that she could feel the warmth of his body. He ran a finger down her cheek. "There's no use fighting your hunger."

She fisted her hands on his chest. "It must be possible for Graces to get through an entire discussion without someone's fangs coming out."

"Perhaps in a hundred years. Not when you're my newgift. For now, this is how all negotiations must inevitably end."

"This is not the end of this negotiation. I need you to agree that you'll…" She flared her nostrils, her lips parting. His scent was dark and heavy with the musk of his own hunger.

"Is that really what you need?" he asked. "You promised to be honest with me, Cassia."

She squeezed her thighs together and realized she was already slick. How could she be this wet when everything was so wrong?

He took a deep inhale, his eyelids heavy. "I could smell how wet you were the moment we walked into this room."

She clenched her teeth, her fangs throbbing. She wanted to fight. She needed to feast.

He braced his hands on the wall on either side of her. "I'm afraid you can't go into hiding and work out your anger without me. You'll simply have to work it out on me."

She would storm out of this room right now. That would prove she had some shred of control over herself, her fangs, her magic.

But instead, her hands were on his collar. She was tearing open his robes. She opened her mouth wide, letting out her swollen fangs, and yanked him down to her. He tilted his head, giving her his throat.

His skin still tasted like the luxuries of Orthros. But when his blood burst onto her tongue, there was a new flavor that burned, thrilling, addicting. Was this what Lio's anger tasted like?

Her gentle Grace's temper, so slow to rise, now raged through him and into her. Was he angry at her? The elders? The world? She knew only that his anger was hers. Hers to feast on, like every other flavor of who he was.

She held him, moaning and fastened to his vein. He dragged her underlinens off and pushed her robes up around her waist. Yes. She wanted his fury inside her body, just like in her veins.

She let him shove her up against the wall and spread her legs. The impact didn't phase her immortal frame. He drove inside her, burying himself in her with one move.

His breath was harsh against her ear. "No one will dictate our conjugal visits, Firstgrace Komnena."

He drummed into her harder than he ever had when she'd been mortal. She clawed at his shoulders and tore at his vein. Her cries against his throat echoed back at her, a mockery of her self control. But she couldn't care, not with him working her new body over and his blood singing in her veins.

Their Grace Union fed her his emotions and imprinted them on her where his fingers dug into her thighs. She shuddered between him and the wall, reveling in the banquet of his pure, undiluted fury. He was angry that she had been taken from his sight. Angry at the door that had locked her away from him. Angry at every bit of air that came between their bodies.

His fangs broke her skin and embedded him in her fully. He growled against her throat, letting her own anger out of her. Her body laid claim to him with rough spasms, grinding closer against him. He kept pounding into her release as if he could not get close enough, deep enough.

Waves of pleasure bled her temper out of her. She sagged in his hold, still desperately suckling his vein. He caught her legs and kept up his relentless rhythm. The friction he built inside her left her whimpering, her body quivering with too much sensation, her thoughts a haze of need.

He thrust inside her one more time, pinning her against the wall. The anger in his blood heated to ecstasy. The taste of his climax drove her over the edge as he surged into her. She screamed in the back of her throat, gripping him hard inside her to feel every pulse of his release.

He held her there until she drank her fill and her fangs receded. She went limp, her belly warm and full, her core still stretched around him. She rested her face on his bloodstained shoulder.

Orthros was closed to them. And yet in this moment, she felt like she was home.

"Now do you understand?" His anger had banked, but it was still there, simmering. "It wasn't even a choice, Cassia. Of course I left everything else behind for you."

She could only pray there would not come a night when he regretted it.

FORGOTTEN RITUALS

Cassia watched Lio straighten his robes. The same festival robes they had danced in hours ago. She interrupted his precise, efficient movements to do up the fasteners over his chest for him. Or rather, she tried to. She had broken some of them.

He left his collar open in a deep vee and tied his hair back at the nape of his neck. "Now that you're well fed, do you feel ready to search the area with your magical senses?"

She shook her head. "I knew I shouldn't have tried any spells after what happened with the weapons. When I opened the portal, I may as well have raised a banner over our location."

"Not necessarily. Aunt Lyta was on watch for your roses at the border. That doesn't mean Hesperines errant will always notice you casting any spell anywhere in Tenebra."

"And what of Gift Collectors with a bounty on us?"

Lio's gaze hardened. "Whoever may be waiting for us when we leave the passages, we'll be ready. The more you practice before that confrontation, the better. This is a safe place for you to work on your spellcasting."

"If the Lustra alerts me to anything, I shall tell you."

He paused, a furrow between his brows. Not the answer he wanted, she knew.

Before her refusal could turn into another debate against the wall, the scratching of Knight's paws interrupted them. She turned to see him digging in the corner of the chamber.

Lio sighed at the hound. "Are you and Freckles both determined to turn history into chew toys?"

Knight ignored him, nose in the dirt. Then he lifted his head, his prize in his jaws, and offered it to Cassia.

"*Oedann*," she praised him. "My good sir, what have you found?"

When she took the dirt-covered object from him, she assumed it was a stick. But the instant she touched it, she knew. A shiver moved through her.

She was holding a bone. A piece of something…someone…that had once lived. She could feel the emptiness in it. The whiff of minerals and decay should not remind her of the smell of blood in the snow in Martyr's Pass, but it did.

The heart hunter she had killed would one day be bones, too.

"Cassia? What is it?" Lio drew nearer to her, then went still. "Oh. I see."

He held out his hands, but she did not surrender her burden to him. "I used things made from bone all the time as a mortal. I combed my hair with pieces of dead creatures. It feels so different now."

"Yes."

The long, yellowed bone was about the size of her own forearm. "Lio, am I imagining it, or…is this human?"

"I feel that too," he confirmed.

Who had this person been? How had this piece of their existence come to rest here for her to find all these years later? "Is this place a tomb?"

"No…" He turned the bone in her hands, gently smudging away some of the dirt. "Look at these markings."

She squinted at the carvings and gasped. "These look like the runes on my pendant."

"This appears to be a ritual object used in spellcasting."

She released it into his hands and took a step back. "Hespera's Mercy. I think you're right. Kalos mentioned that bones and such are sometimes used in Lustra rites. I didn't realize that included human bones."

"This sheds light on the purpose of these Lustra passages," Lio said. "They were some kind of ritual site for your ancestors."

That fragment of death weighed on her Hesperine senses. How could her ancestors' magic and the Blood Union run in her veins at the same time?

"What should we do for this person?" she wondered. "Should we perform the Mercy for what is left of their remains? Or would that have unintended magical consequences?"

Lio looked to her. "I think you are the best one to make that decision. What does your intuition tell you?"

She could feel the kinship between the bone and the earth under their feet, a rightness that appalled her Hesperine senses. But the Lustra's answer was clear. "I think we should return the bone to its resting place as a sign of respect."

"Then that's what we'll do."

After Cassia put the dirt back in place over the bone, she brushed her hands off on her robes, but they still felt dirty. "We should see if Knight uncovers other artifacts."

Lio did not protest, but he also said nothing in agreement. As they left the chamber, she was glad he didn't push her to cast any more spells, at least. She felt his magic stretch through the halls while they explored the honeycomb of rooms off the main chamber. He tried using his own pendant to reveal more portals, but each room appeared to be a dead end. Knight sniffed his way along, pausing to dig in nearly every alcove. He uncovered more bones—animal this time, thank the Goddess—as well as feathers, broken pottery, and wooden talismans so smoothed by time that their symbols had worn away.

In every fragment, Cassia sensed an aching weight. Could the Lustra feel sadness?

"It's all gone," she said. "No one remembers. I barely know anything."

"But you will," Lio told her. "You have the rest of eternity to rescue these mysteries from where they lay forgotten."

"Perhaps. But we don't have forever to find out how any of this relates to the door—if it does at all."

"Let's go tell Mak and Lyros what we found. Perhaps they'll have some ideas."

She nodded, and they made their way back toward the main chamber. Before they left the privacy of the hallway, Lio pulled her against him one more time. He kissed her, the deep, firm strokes of his tongue a declaration that echoed through their Union. She was in his arms again, and here she would stay.

She opened to him, letting him take the reassurance he needed and chase the taste of death from her mouth.

LIO KEPT HIS HAND on Cassia's lower back as they returned to the main chamber. He needed to be touching her, no matter the unresolved words pulling their Union taut. Those few hours with a warded door between them had been too much.

They found Mak and Lyros hanging a map on the wall, carefully avoiding the magefire sconces. Mak looked flushed and as contrite as Lio had ever seen him.

Lyros turned, looking from Cassia's face to Lio's collar. "Everyone's fangs polished? Good. In hostile territory, we need our magic at full strength, and that means no abstinence over foolish differences of opinion. Understood?"

Cassia held herself with great decorum, despite her blush. "That won't be a concern."

"No, it won't." Lio made one more attempt to straighten his collar.

"Right." Mak rubbed his jaw. "Now that we've all thoroughly crossed each other's veils, did you two find anything?"

Cassia patted her hound. "It seems Knight has a knack for unearthing Lustra artifacts. This place is riddled with them."

Lio scratched the dog's back. "My partner in historical research, after all."

"We found evidence of magic, too," Lyros confirmed.

Mak pointed toward one of the side passages. "There's some kind of casting area marked on the ground in there."

"Wait." Lio searched his packs. Bless Tuura. Of course she had packed his scroll case. "I'll record our findings."

While they told each other of their discoveries, Lio hung more scrolls on the wall beside the map, making notes and a diagram of the passages. He stared at the sketch, waiting for a pattern to emerge. But he didn't see it. Yet.

"Does any of this make sense to you, based on your lessons with Kalos?" he asked Cassia.

She shook her head. "Since we found no evidence of a letting site, I'm not sure what sort of rituals Silvicultrixes might have held here or why the Mage King would cast an everlasting flame over it."

Lyros faced the map of Tenebra on the wall and held up a stick of charcoal. "We should mark all the Lustra portals we know of."

Cassia pointed to the capital. "The first ones I discovered are inside Solorum Palace. I thought I had fully explored the passages, but there must be more I couldn't open before my magic woke. I never came across anything like the hidden door."

Lio tapped on Solia's fortress. "There are also the portals at Castra Patria, of course. We suspect they run all the way to Paradum, where the letting site is."

Lyros scrawled a few marks on the map.

Mak's serious expression didn't change. "What are those symbols supposed to represent?"

Lyros looked over his shoulder. "A door and a well. Isn't that what a letting site is? A well of magic?"

"That's accurate," Lio confirmed, biting his lip.

"But your drawing sure isn't," Mak said. "It looks like a war mage's nose after you punched him in the face."

Lyros's brows drew down. "What? How do you see a nose in that?"

Mak shrugged. "You tell me. You're the son of Orthros's greatest artists."

"I know I can't draw to save my life, but I have thoroughly studied military cartography."

"Oh, no one reads maps as well as you do." Mak snatched the charcoal from Lyros's hand. "But let me mark this one before someone bleeds to death out of their eyes."

Lyros's scowl deepened. Mak's lips twitched, his eyes glinting. Then Lyros appeared to realize Mak was on the verge of a smile and back to his usual sport of teasing his Grace. Lyros laughed, and he and Mak both relaxed a measure.

That was Mak. Quickest to anger, soonest to forgive. Except, perhaps, himself. Lio realized he and Mak might be more alike in that way than he had known.

Mak drew a door symbol over Solorum Palace, Castra Patria, and the Hadrian lighthouse. Then he added a well-shaped mark to Paradum.

"Are we certain of the locations of any other letting sites?" Lyros asked.

Cassia touched a fingertip to Corona, the Divine City, the seat of the Mage Orders' power. "We know of one in the Magelands, under the temple where my mother was a mage of Kyria."

Mak marked that with another well symbol. "Kalos said there are a few in heart hunter territory, right?"

Cassia nodded. "Jealously guarded by the warbands."

Mak added a well and a question mark in the forests and mountains near Tenebra's northern border.

After a pause, Lio said, "And one letting site in Orthros."

Mak marked Selas, his aura dimming again at the reminder of home.

They all stood back, looking at the map.

"Every location that might hold clues is heavily guarded," Lyros observed. "With Lucis still firmly in control of Solorum, going directly to the door is an unwise course of action."

"I've sneaked into Solorum Palace before," Lio said, "under a war mage's nose."

Mak snickered. "Not to research Lustra portals."

"On the contrary," Cassia said, with her most courtly expression, "he was researching a Silvicultrix's portals."

Mak laughed harder, and Lio couldn't help joining in, sliding an arm around Cassia's waist.

Lyros grinned, too. "Fair enough. But there are many more Aithourian war mages there now, and Lucis is on the alert for an invasion by Solia and her Hesperine allies."

"Cassia could sneak us in through Lustra portals," Lio proposed.

"Still too much risk," Lyros said. "The Collector is sure to have laid his own traps in the area to prevent us from beating him to his ultimate goal."

Cassia nodded. "I agree. If we approach Solorum blind, it could be a disaster. When we go in search of the door, we cannot afford to miscalculate. We must learn more about it before we attempt to reach it."

"Shouldn't we go directly there to try to stop the Collector?" Mak protested. "He could be trying to open it right now."

"This is why we require more information," Cassia replied. "We need to know how he's planning to open it now that he cannot use me. That is our only hope of outsmarting him."

"Lyros and Cassia are right," Lio admitted with reluctance. "Our lack of knowledge is our greatest weakness against the Collector."

"He always has more ancient tricks up his sleeve," Lyros agreed. "One more surprise like that might be our last. We scout first, and we don't attack until we're confident that we're ready."

Mak rubbed his brow, leaving a smudge of charcoal there. "In that case, where do you suggest we scout first, Cassia?"

All eyes turned on her, and Lio felt her tension between his own shoulder blades.

She slid her hand along Knight's ruff. "I will open Lustra portals for us everywhere we travel, to give us shelter. But roaming the countryside digging through these ruins is a shot in the dark. We don't have time to piece history together bit by bit."

"No." A grim certainty settled over Lio. "No need to hunt for lost secrets when we could ask someone who knows them already."

Mak eyes widened. "You mean Miranda."

"We need to find her." Lio searched Cassia's gaze. "Don't you think so?"

Her conflicting emotions rippled through their Union, but she nodded. "You need to finish the mind duel you started at Paradum. This time, you won't have to interrupt it to save me."

Lyros crossed his arms. "You're suggesting we go looking for a Gift Collector while the Order of Hypnos has a bounty on your heads."

Cassia arched a brow at him. "Can you deny it's the wisest strategy?"

"Wise?" Lyros returned. "Certainly not. But strategic and necessary? Yes."

"No objections," Mak said. "Let's turn the hunter into the hunted."

Their weapons, leaning against the wall nearby, were pearlescent in the magefire's light. Lyros picked up Night's Aim. "It's time for us to finish enchanting these."

Mak's face clouded. "Our fists are good enough."

"No." Lyros's tone brooked no argument. "Of all Hesperines' many enemies, Gift Collectors are the most deadly and difficult to kill. No matter our training, experience, or magic, we're walking into the greatest danger we have ever faced. We need every advantage."

"I'd be happy to leave these weapons buried down here and never look at them again," Mak bit out.

Lyros's hands tightened on the spear. "We've come this far. There's no sense in turning back now."

Mak turned away, fists clenched. Cassia stood silent, her arms crossed.

Lio fingered the moonstone in his staff. "These are intended to be Union Stones, aren't they?"

"Yes," Lyros said. "I cut them and planned to enchant them so we can use them to signal each other."

"That spell requires a mind mage, as well."

"I hoped you'd be willing."

"Of course." Lio took a step nearer his cousin. "Mak, you began this endeavor with conviction—"

"I was wrong."

"I'm not convinced you were."

Mak rounded on him. "You and Lyros still can't be charged with the same crimes as Cassia and me! I don't want either of you adding your magic to the weapons."

"That doesn't matter now," Lyros said.

Lio shook his head. "The elders can charge me with whatever they like."

Mak's jaw clenched.

Cassia touched Mak's arm and finally spoke. "I know. But after all the damage we've caused, if we don't even use the weapons to protect our people, it really was all for nothing."

That, at last, got a sigh of resignation out of Mak. He turned to them again and picked up the Star of Orthros. Cassia belted Rosethorn around her waist.

Lio took a firmer hold on Final Word and shut his eyes. He let his thelemancy rise within him to meet Lyros's casting. Four points of their power swelled within the moonstones.

He slashed his fangs across his palm and closed his hand around his staff's moonstone. The gem heated against his skin. Opening his eyes, he saw all four white stones turn red and began to pulse with a liquid glow. The crimson light reflected on an angry tear sliding down Cassia's cheek.

If this made him even more of a criminal in Orthros's eyes, so be it. He would never again find himself outmatched by an army of Gift Collectors with his Grace's life slipping away in his arms.

When the glow faded from the Union Stones, he reached out to her and ran his braid through his fingers. "There's one more spell we need to cast. We must have our Grace braids warded, like all Hesperines errant."

Her face lost some of its color. Mere nights after he had sealed his braid into her hair, he hated that she must confront this. If they died out here, their warded Grace braids would be the only thing left for the survivors to take home to their families.

"The warding of your braids is a time-honored tradition." Mak was clearly trying to soften the blow. "Everyone does it when they join the Stand or the Charge. You don't want a fire mage singing the mementos from your avowal."

"Mak and I would consider it an honor to do it for you," Lyros offered.

"We were planning to ask you," Cassia said, "when we thought we would be going errant with the Charge."

Lio and Cassia had envisioned a gallant braid-warding ceremony at Castra Justa with the Charge all around them. That was what Lio had wanted for his newgift. Not for her to stand here in this tomb, robbed of their people's protection.

But she had his protection, and they had their Trial brothers.

"The ceremony will require a blade." Lio knew the steps of the spell, having attended Mak and Lyros's braid warding with the Stand. "Shall we use Rosethorn?"

Cassia drew her dagger in grim silence, and Mak accepted it. Lio stood across from her, while their Trial brothers gathered on either side so the four of them stood in a ring.

Mak took hold of Lio's hand. "Redblood, will you sustain any wound for your Grace?"

"I Will," Lio answered.

Mak cut into Lio's hand, deeper than any common spell libation. But the pain was nothing compared to what he had endured for Cassia before. The magic of her artifact tingled in the wound as his blood spilled into Mak and Lyros's open palms.

Lyros turned to Cassia. "Whiteblood, will you sustain any wound for your Grace?"

Her face was set with grim determination. "I Will."

She didn't flinch when Lyros sliced her palm. He and Mak painted their other hands with her libation, then Lyros laid the bloodied blade in the center of their ring. Lustra magic throbbed faintly through the chamber.

Mak and Lyros each put a hand on Lio's Grace braid, anointing him with Cassia's blood. They extended their other hands to her and touched his blood to her braid. Warding magic darkened the Blood Union, binding the four of them in an unbroken circle. Their Trial brothers sealed the symbols of their love within the most powerful wards known to Hesperine kind.

Lio would keep this vow to Cassia, as surely as their avowal promises. Whether an injury to his body or his standing among their people, he would sustain any wound for his Grace.

VIGIL OF
UNION

2 Nights Until Winter Solstice

PREY

Even underground, Cassia could feel that twilight had fallen in the world outside. Restlessness in her blood made her eager to escape this place of bones and magefire. But facing the black roses that marked the portal, she felt equal apprehension.

She secured her dagger belt around the waist of her dark, sturdy travel robes. Then she turned to her longest-serving weapon and rested her hand on Knight's broad shoulders. "*Ckuundat.*"

He went into an alert stance, ready for any threat waiting for them outside. Beside him, Freckles put her ears back.

Mak led Bear to the door with a slight touch on the horse's neck. "Any ideas about where to find Miranda?"

Cassia shook her head. "She escaped the Lustra's hold under Rudhira's nose. She could be anywhere."

"We have one lead." Lio joined them, Final Word sheathed on Moonflower's saddle. "Something I heard at Mederi village. The elderly farmers there mentioned she has hiding places where she can disappear anytime her enemies get too close."

"You think they might know where some of her dens are?" Lyros asked, already waiting ahead of them by the portal.

"Or perhaps they know other people who are likely to give her refuge," Cassia added.

"We should start by asking them." Lio looked between Mak and Lyros. "Do you have any idea where the Charge took the residents of Mederi Village for safety after evacuating them from Patria?"

"Let me think," said Lyros. "Mak and I were casting wards on the walls, but I'm sure we heard where Solia planned to settle them."

Mak snapped his fingers. "Callen and Benedict had that argument about it, remember?"

Ben. Cassia had been trying not to think about him. It still hurt that the devout knight judged her for choosing Hespera's path. Their friendship had survived every ordeal but this.

Mak winced. "Callen insisted Hadria was safest because their warriors are superior, but Benedict was determined they should go to Segetia because the 'bread basket of Tenebra will keep them better fed.'"

Cassia rolled her eyes. "Typical. They can stick their swords in enemies side by side and still keep up this foolish rivalry."

"I think it's becoming their language of love," Mak quipped.

So Benedict would let go of the age-old feud and centuries of murder between Hadria and Segetia before he could accept her as a Hesperine. She should have known a holy knight would forgive warriors who had been his enemies sooner than a heretic who had been his friend.

"Who won the debate?" Lio asked.

"Segetia," said Mak. "The Charge agreed to step the evacuees past the territory Lucis controls and into the safety of Flavian's borders."

Flavian's name, on the other hand, no longer phased Cassia. Her unwanted betrothal to the future Free Lord of Segetia truly did feel like another life. But she sensed Lio bristle.

Her throat tightened. They had freed her from her mortal betrothal, only for her to ruin their Hesperine avowal.

Lyros offered the map to Mak. "Did they say where in Segetia they're taking the farmers? It's a large domain."

Mak marked a spot where two rivers merged. "Solia has placed Benedict, as a holy knight in the Order of Andragathos, in command of safety and charity toward the evacuees. I believe he and his men have gone to this area to resettle the villagers."

"Let us hope we can avoid them all," Cassia said. "I have no interest in sharing the happy news of my Gifting with Ben."

Lio scowled. "Might as well feed roses to swine."

"We shouldn't simply step to the farmers, in any case," Lyros said. "We might land in the middle of the Charge's fangs or holy knights' swords.

Cassia, do you have memories of any locations in that area that we can use as a stepping focus?"

"Yes, I can think of a place that should be sufficiently out of the way."

"To Segetia it is, then." Lyros beckoned to them. "Let's get out of here so we can step."

It was time for Cassia to open the portal. Her heart began to race. Lio rested his hand on that sensitive spot low on her back. Despite the unresolved debate between them, her treacherous body shivered pleasantly.

"A drop of your blood should work again," he suggested.

"There must be a way to get the roses to let us through without causing more magical upheavals."

He said nothing more, but she sensed that this discussion was not over, like the one her appetite had interrupted last night.

She took a cautious step toward the vine. It slithered aside, and the stone shuddered, once again opening a broad portal. She breathed a sigh of relief.

They led their horses out into the night. Dark clouds obscured the stars, but the landscape looked bright in the eerie orange glow of the lighthouse.

Fear jolted Cassia's chest, but this time it wasn't her own. She caught the scent of blood amid the rain and salt on the wind. Human fear. Human bloodshed.

They all whipped around to look up at the lighthouse. No sound came from within the monument, only suffering.

"What's happening in there?" she breathed.

"I don't know," Lio said, "but there are no other Hesperines to intervene but us."

"This could be a conflict between mortals that's outside our purview," Lyros cautioned.

"It probably is," Mak said, "but are any of us really prepared to turn our backs on these people?"

Cassia dug her hand into her breastbone, but nothing could ease the human pain pouring into her chest. "We have to help them."

"We're Hesperines errant now," said Lio. "Is there any fight in this kingdom that isn't our fight?"

Lyros, despite his cautionary words, had already drawn Night's Aim.

"We'll leave the horses here and go in under veils to assess the situation. Everyone in favor of this plan?"

They all nodded in agreement. Cassia's heart wouldn't stop pounding. In the moments they took to decide this, someone might die. But if they went in without a plan, would it cost even more lives?

Lyros pricked his thumb and smeared blood on the Union Stone below his spearhead. All four of their stones flared bright, urgent red. "If I give this signal, let's attack together. Mak and I will levitate and surprise any enemies from above. Cassia, Lio, you two take the stairs with Knight and ambush them from below. We should keep our weapons hidden until the last possible moment. No one will expect Hesperines to be armed. It's a powerful advantage of surprise."

Mak and Lyros lifted off the ground while Lio and Cassia raced up the bluff. Knight followed in three liegehound leaps up the ledges.

The door of the lighthouse hung open on broken hinges. They plunged inside and took the spiral stairs at Hesperine speed. Knight bounded ahead of her, and Lio guarded her back. Each time a doorway spun past them, she expected an enemy to spring out.

"*Hama*," Cassia murmured as they neared the open hatch at the top of the steps. Knight drew back, and she flattened herself against the wall to keep herself in shadow. The Mage King's fire cast harsh light down into the stairwell.

Good idea, Lio approved. *No telling how this specimen of our opposing element might affect our magic.*

Even if he was my ancestor, Cassia agreed.

They crept toward the opening. When she saw what awaited them above, she froze.

There was no battle. It looked like the lighthouse guards hadn't had a chance to fight. The pride of Hadria's warriors were bound and gagged on the deck surrounding the massive bronze brazier.

Four figures stood over them, armed with tools perverted into weapons. She knew those dark robes and that leather armor. For the first time, she could smell the blood that painted their breastplates with the Eye of Hypnos. Each one of those glyphs had cost a human sacrifice. She put a hand over her mouth, gagging.

Gift Collectors.

Lio put an arm out to support her. His pressed his cool hand to her forehead, his magic sinking into her thoughts. She welcomed the spell that subdued the parts of her mind sending sickening signals to her stomach. She couldn't afford to retch in battle.

They're using Lord Hadrian's men as bait! she cried. *They know we'll feel compelled to save them.*

And that's exactly what we'll do. I'll keep you veiled. Use your dagger on the guards' bonds while Mak and Lyros fight. I'll work on the Gift Collectors' dream wards.

All right.

Surprise flashed through Lio, as if he had expected her to protest. Usually, she would have. But tonight, she accepted the safest role in silence. She didn't trust her magic in this fight.

Crimson light spilled from Lio's staff and the scabbard at her belt. Their Union Stones glowed with Lyros's signal to attack.

"*Ckabaar!*" she cried to Knight.

Her hound lunged through the hatch. She pushed herself away from the wall and darted forward. Lio was already ahead of her, holding Final Word in both hands.

Knight slammed into the Gift Collector on their left. The man grunted in surprise and fell backward. He raised a woodcutter's hatchet, striking at the veiled menace he couldn't see. The swing barely skimmed Knight's fur.

Lio met the enemy on their right, this one wielding a long, sharpened stake. He aimed a flash of light magic at the Gift Collector's eyes. The man squinted, but he lunged forward with uncanny speed, his stake aimed at Lio's heart.

Thelemancy shot out of Lio. Pain flared in her head as his spell hit the first layer of dream wards that guarded the Gift Collectors' minds. Both attackers hesitated. Then the stake kept coming toward Lio's heart.

Before Cassia could scream, Lio raised his staff across his chest and drove the shaft up against the stake. Adamas met wood and snapped the stake in two. The Gift Collector took a step back, his face betraying surprise. Lio advanced on him.

Now Cassia could slip past their duel to reach the first guard. She knelt and drew her dagger. The sight of the man's bound hands made her stomach turn again. The Gift Collectors had extracted all his fingernails. They had made him suffer to draw Hesperines to his pain. And to entertain themselves while they waited for their prey.

When she touched his wrists, he jumped, then groaned.

"Don't be afraid," she whispered, slicing carefully at his bonds. "We are Queen Solia's Hesperine allies, here to fight for you."

Her words felt empty, when they were also the reason the Gift Collectors had targeted him. But the man relaxed. That simple gesture of trust made his pain in her chest hurt all the more.

A whisper cut through the air. A few paces away from her, a third Gift Collector staggered. He stared down at the spear now protruding from his chest, stained with his heart's blood.

The Star of Orthros swept out of nowhere, bright in the darkness. The man crumpled around Mak's spiked club and went flying off the side of the tower.

The first heart stopped.

Night's Aim levitated backward out of the silent organ and flew into Lyros's hand.

Cassia swallowed hard and kept sawing at the rope, cutting through the malign enchantments that strengthened it. Her spade had defeated a Gift Collector's cursed bonds before, and it would again, by the Goddess.

Lyros and Mak turned in tandem, back to back, just in time for Mak to block an attack from the fourth Gift Collector. The necromancer's pickaxe tangled with the spikes on Mak's club. Lyros, with the long reach of his spear, aimed at the Gift Collector Knight had brought down.

The hatchet wielder managed to heave off Knight's weight and rolled to one side. Night's Aim struck the stones where the man's eye had been. Rolling to his feet, the Gift Collector had to shift all his focus to Lyros to fend off his relentless spear.

"Leave this one to me," Lyros called to her. "Tell Knight to protect Lio while he casts!"

Cassia nodded and called out to her hound, *"Barda lomalii!"*

His guard bond invoked, Knight pivoted to join Lio's duel. The Gift Collector kept her hound at bay with another stake from the gruesome collection at his belt. In his other hand, he swung an iron chain that glowed with rusted light. The links caught Final Word and wound three times around the center of the staff between Lio's hands.

Lio wrenched his weapon free, and the chain snapped. But the gleaming rust clung to the staff.

What magic is that? she asked as it crept toward Lio's hands.

He hissed, but didn't lose his grip. *It's eating away my veils. He can see my weapon now.*

Cassia swore. She should be at his side, tearing through his enemy with all the power in her veins.

But would she only cause him more harm if she tried?

His voice was adamant in her mind. *Get the mortals out of here before this battle gets any uglier.*

Finally the cursed rope gave way. Cassia helped Lord Hadrian's soldier to his feet. "Can you make it out of the lighthouse?"

"Give me a sword," the warrior pleaded. "I won't run from a battle."

"Please, go. These are Orthros's enemies, not yours. Save your life and your blade for the Queen, and let your honor be satisfied."

He stood frozen for an instant, his face twisted with indecision. "You can signal for aid. There are herbs by the fire—throw them in, and help will come from Castra Hadria."

"We will," she reassured him. Even though Castra Hadria was the last place they could turn to for aid. "Tell Lord Hadrian…"

I'm sorry. I'm so sorry.

"Tell him the Hesperines known as the Black Roses did what we could for his people tonight."

"I will make sure my lord hears of your deeds." The soldier ran for the stairwell, cradling his bleeding hands against his chest.

Cassia raced toward the next warrior. His left eye socket was a bleeding mess. His right eye, rimmed in white, darted back and forth, searching the darkness.

"Don't be afraid," she said again.

She moved from one wounded man to the next, murmuring Hespera's reassurances to them, just as Hesperines had always done for her.

Lio's magic ebbed and surged around her. Knight leapt and circled, avoiding the Hesperines' most skilled enemy with the same speed and agility that made him deadly to immortals. The Gift Collector dodged each swing of Final Word, keeping his stake clear of the staff's heavy blows. The pain of their mental battle twisted his face. But the agony that echoed in Cassia's head was Lio's as he ground down the necromancer's next dream ward.

She focused on the one task she could control and forced herself to keep sawing at the ropes, keep showing the soldiers Mercy. There had been no glory or honor for them, only subjugation and humiliation at the hands of enemies far too powerful even for Tenebra's best warriors. But they were alive, and one by one, she sent them out of harm's way.

They struggled past Mak and Lyros, who were locked in a brutal dance with their two opponents, their weapons glowing with the rust-magic now. Mak grappled at close range with the pickaxe wielder. The Gift Collector with the hatchet fought on against Lyros, one arm useless at his side. She glimpsed a gash on Mak's arm that wasn't healing and a tear in Lyros's black battle robe that leaked blood onto his silver sash. She could not tell who was wearing down whom.

The last captive's leg was bent at the wrong angle. She slung his arm around her shoulders and helped him stand without putting weight on his shattered calf bone. He felt so light to her, this mortal whose life would depend on her across the last few paces to safety. She held her dagger at the ready in her other hand.

Knight's yelp tore at her heart. She looked to see him tangled in the necromancer's chain, struggling to get up. Stone clanged on metal, and the Gift Collector's weapon locked with Final Word, a hand's breadth from Lio's face. No wooden stake now. Cassia recognized the carved dagger in the necromancer's grip. A relic blade like the one Miranda had used in her twisted experiments for Kallikrates.

Lio! Cassia called helplessly in his mind.

Get the mortal to safety.

Her skull throbbed with vicarious agony. It took all the Will she possessed to keep going. At last, she and the soldier reached the stairwell, where two of his comrades who could still walk were waiting to help him.

She spun to face the battle, Rosethorn in her hand. Why had she never let Kella teach her how to throw a knife? Through the wavering flames, Mak and Lyros were cast in bronze and fighting two statues that never seemed to break. Lio was the tall, dark shadow in front of the magefire, his magic rending thoughts, his staff cracking bone. Still she wavered on the edge of the skirmish.

The Lustra reached out to her from below. At her call, it would rise up and tear this tower from its foundations. Not protection, but destruction.

A phantom pain drove into the front of Cassia's shoulder. She watched blood bloom on Lio's robe, and her entire vision seemed to fill with red. The stone dagger was buried to the hilt in his flesh.

He spun his staff and slammed it into the crook of the necromancer's arm. The man lost his grip on his dagger. But already too close under Lio's guard, he drove his stake into Lio's side.

Cassia screamed with rage, her fist tight on her dagger hilt.

A quiet magic caressed her palm. She looked down at Rosethorn. She had rubbed her fingers raw on the ropes, and her blood trickled down the blade.

She reached for that safe, familiar power. She felt all four of the weapons stir with the same energy. Just as she had in Nike's forge, she Willed her magic through her dagger and into the other three artifacts.

Black roses snaked along Lio's staff, and he let out a shout of surprise. The rabid vines tore the stake from the Gift Collector's hands and kept growing. The necromancer leapt back, but not fast enough. The roses crawled over the floor, snared his legs, and snapped him off his feet.

His head cracked back against the stone. Lio wrenched the dagger out of his shoulder, and then a bolt of thelemancy drove out of him. Through their Union, Cassia felt the last of the Gift Collector's mental defenses crumble. His poisonous thoughts flew in fragments through Lio's mind. Cassia clutched her head, nearly doubling over with the pain in her skull.

The second heart stopped.

She looked for Mak and Lyros's opponents. The hatchet wielder was impaled on Lyros's spear against one pillar, a vine of thorns tearing apart the Eye of Hypnos on his breastplate. For the third time, a mortal heart went quiet.

The Gift Collector with the pickaxe fled toward the edge of the tower, pursued by the carpet of black roses spreading out from where Cassia stood. He was ready to leap when Mak caught his throat in a powerful grip and dragged him back from the edge. He tossed the man down onto the deck and let the roses have him.

The last beat of his pulse brought silence.

Mak surveyed the carnage. "So. That's what the enchantment does."

THE BURDEN OF VIOLENCE

CASSIA STOOD THERE, SHAKING.

Lio came instantly to her side. "Are you all right?"

She tried to answer. But her grasp of words slipped. Sensations, impressions buffeted her. Anger. Humiliation. Pain. The beds of her fingernails burned. Her leg gave out from under her, and she staggered against him.

Dimly, she was aware of him catching her, of his blood soaking into her robes. Images of the battle flashed across her vision. All she could hear were those heartbeats, stopping over and over in an endless echo.

She longed to slip into oblivion, but few things could make a Hesperine faint. This torment was not one of them.

Then he was there. She saw Lio in her mind's eye, standing still in the chaos of the battle. He was a steady presence in her thoughts. Another heart, bearing the suffering with her.

The Blood Union has overwhelmed you. You're empathizing with everyone who was in the battle. Violence is always hard for Hesperines.

His calm, sympathetic voice was her lifeline. These weren't her emotions. She focused on that knowledge, fighting to break free of the ghosts of the fight.

I wish I was a mind healer, he said. *I can't make this stop. But I can make it easier.*

He waited with her, letting the horrific scenes wash over them both. His presence, a clear light in the whorl, drew her slowly back to herself.

The world came into focus again. She found herself lying across his lap with three concerned, fanged faces looking down at her and one big, furry form pressed close.

Lio stroked her cheek, his eyes dark with regret. "I'm so sorry, my rose."

Lyros grimaced. "Tenebra isn't easy on newgifts."

"How many fingers am I holding up?" Mak held up Knight's paw and pulled a face at her.

She couldn't find a laugh or a smile, but the gratitude she felt to them was an antidote to the shadows in her mind. "You shouldn't be fussing over me. I'm not the one who's wounded." She reached toward Lio's shoulder, then stopped, unsure where to touch him without hurting him. Fresh blood still oozed from the injury. "This should be healing faster."

"It will," Lio reassured her.

"These are flesh wounds." The gash on Mak's arm was still red and angry. "Sunbound nasty ones, but we'll live."

Lyros kept his hand pressed to his waist. "You rest a minute longer. We'll burn the Gift Collectors' bodies."

"Burn them?" Cassia echoed in surprise.

Mak got to his feet and helped Lyros up. "Gift Collectors can't receive the Mercy. I think the Queens would have us give it even to these carcasses, if we could. But the magic doesn't work on them."

"We can't leave them like this, though," Lyros said. "They have an unfortunate tendency to revive if not properly destroyed."

Mak shook his head. "Now that we know they're Kallikrates's Overseers, who place their loyalty to him above the Mage Orders, their uncanny abilities make more sense."

"He said that," Cassia recalled. "When someone gives him their magic willingly, as long as he holds their power, they can't truly die."

Mak shuddered. "Best leave him only ashes to work with, in that case."

As their Trial brothers returned to the corpses, Cassia reached up and touched Lio's cheek. "Are you all right? In your mind? That's the first time you've ever broken a Gift Collector's dream wards on your own."

His gaze grew remote. "When he struck his head, his control slipped. That gave me the upper hand for an instant."

That didn't answer her question. "I felt how hard it was for you. I don't mean magically difficult."

"I'm sorry, my Grace."

He was spiraling into apologies now. Never a good sign. Clearly this was not the time to press him about his own well being. "I'll help you all burn them. Then we need to signal for help—one of the men told me how. The mortals need a healer."

"I can do that." He brushed her hair back from her face. "You need to recover."

"You all spent our entire time at Patria dragging around my ailing human body. I'm a Hesperine now, and I refuse to be carried. We all promised to bear the burden of violence together, remember?"

He sighed. "I will not let my protectiveness interfere with your honor."

She made it to her feet, but she couldn't help leaning on Lio and Knight until her dizziness faded. They joined Mak and Lyros by the nearest Gift Collector's body. The roses had disappeared, leaving behind black petals scattered across the corpse. The stone dagger lay in fragments at his side. Had his death shattered it?

Cassia looked away from the thorn punctures on the Gift Collector's face. Her gaze fell on a barrel of unlit torches beside the brazier.

From her ancestors' fire, she lit four brands and placed them in Hesperine hands.

THE MAGEFIRE ATOP THE lighthouse now burned Hadrian blue. In the shadows cast by the enchanted signal fire, it was easy for Lio to make four Hesperines and a hound disappear into the shadows. But not completely. Their plan to draw the threat away from mortal bystanders would only work if the enemy could detect them.

Their Warmbloods carried them fast and far away from the sea, out onto the moors. Knight wove among them, on guard. Lio prayed any Gift Collectors lingering in the area would follow, as much as he dreaded another confrontation.

Even the Warmbloods' smooth gait prodded the dull ache in his side. With every mile, pain shot deeper into his shoulder. Then his chest. Flashes of the battle kept playing on his mind, amplified by Cassia's response to the conflict.

Eventually Cassia pulled close alongside him on Freckles, reaching out to take hold of Moonflower's mane and slow Lio down. They all drew to a halt around her. Suddenly still, he realized how much effort it was taking to stay in the saddle.

"We're stopping here," Cassia announced. "Your wounds need tending."

"I agree," Mak said. "The weapons must have been poisoned. If we leave our wounds too long, they'll fester."

"This isn't a defensible location," Lyros protested.

Lio scanned the lonely landscape. There was no shelter, only a field of grass and thistle broken by jagged boulders and cleaved by a narrow stream. Knight sniffed the wind, his body tense and ears perked.

"If Gift Collectors were following us, they would have attacked by now," Cassia reasoned.

Lyros's tan complexion looked sallow in the moonlight. "They might be waiting for our condition to worsen so they can take us by surprise closer to dawn."

"That's why we need to treat your wounds," said Cassia. "We'll find somewhere safer before daybreak."

"But if they ambush us here—" Lyros began.

Mak dismounted and reached up to his Grace. "You're overthinking everything because you're in pain. Stop being General Lysandros for a minute and let me take care of you."

Lyros pressed his lips together, but let Mak half-lift, half-levitate him out of the saddle. Mak eased him down onto the grass against one of the boulders and untied Lyros's bloodstained sash. Lyros let his forehead fall to rest on Mak's shoulder.

"I wish I could levitate you," Cassia said to Lio, along with a few of the Ashes' favorite Imperial curses.

He suppressed a laugh, knowing it would hurt. "Levitation isn't the sort of help I'd most enjoy from you at the moment."

She shook her head at him. "How are you the only person who becomes sweeter and more flirtatious when you're in terrible pain?"

"I drink the sweetest blood every night."

"You're incorrigible, Glasstongue."

She guided him to sit near the stream and set out some of Tuura's supplies from their pack. While the horses took a drink, Knight patrolled around their party incessantly. His hackles were up. With an effort, Lio focused on strengthening their veil spells.

"Stop that," Cassia scolded. "Your wound bleeds more every time you use blood magic."

"Oh." He looked down at her short, freckled fingers peeling the soaked fabric away from his shoulder. "So it does. This mess is resisting my cleaning spells, too."

She swore again. He could feel her mustering all her anger as a defense against her fear for him.

"I'm all right," he said.

"You're not all right. Lyros isn't this ill. That relic dagger must have put some kind of malign enchantment into your bloodstream, and this wound is too close to your heart. I need to cleanse it before I give you blood to speed your healing."

She tore what was left of his robe, the new strength in her hands quickly opening a gap between his shoulder and abdomen. She eased his sleeves down his arms, fast and careful. Her Hesperine hands were so agile, he barely felt the movement. She made a quick examination of the shallow cut on his side before focusing on his shoulder.

"You're good at this," he said. "I can tell you assisted in the infirmary at the Temple of Kyria."

Her frustration only intensified. "I had hoped to spend more time in Orthros's Healing Sanctuary by now."

He fell silent, unsure what words would land wrong amid her fraught emotions.

With a rag soaked in the stream, she washed the tainted gore from around his shoulder wound. Her gentle strokes on his chest mesmerized him. He should be concerned about the lethargy spreading through his limbs, but it was so pleasing to sit here and watch her hands.

His eyelids grew heavier, and the world tilted. She caught him, easing him down onto his back.

"Lio?" Her voice was sharp, echoing through their bond. "Stay with me."

"I'm here." He forced his eyes open.

"This will sting." Cassia uncapped one of Tuura's cleansing potions, then offered him her wrist. "You may want to bite down on something."

She wouldn't get a protest out of him. He opened his lips on the inside of her wrist. Her skin was so soft.

She tapped a few drops of the potion into his open wound. Fire shot deep into his shoulder. With a hiss, he sank his fangs into her flesh. The flavor of her blood soon eclipsed his pain.

She tasted of regret. The battle plagued her, endless imaginings of it that had never come to pass. Her wielding her dagger a moment earlier and preventing his wound. Using her magic a moment later and watching him die.

Her power engulfing the entire lighthouse, taking mortal and immortal lives.

He wanted to wash all those thoughts away and give her comfort from his veins. He cursed the stone dagger. It wouldn't be safe for her to drink until they were sure his blood was pure.

He wrapped his good arm around her and pulled her down against his chest. *Stop. Don't torture yourself. Your magic is what turned the tide in tonight's battle.*

No. It's what caused the battle in the first place.

We all expected our first encounter with Gift Collectors to go much worse. Thanks to Mak's weapons and your roses, we survived.

Despite his attempts at reassurance, her pain only cut deeper into their Union. *You're a fugitive. You're wounded, mind and body. Because of me. Why aren't you ever angry at me?*

I…I'm afraid if I answer that question, it will only make you hurt more. Goddess help him. For once, he didn't know what the right words were.

A silence fell between them. She turned her face away, but he kept holding her. The sting in his side disappeared, and he felt his shoulder knit back together. The silence remained, a wound on their vows.

Cassia helped him sit up and examined the new skin on his shoulder. A chill crept over him.

"You all right?" Mak was watching him.

Lio rubbed his chest. "Cassia stopped it before it reached my heart."

"He's still tired and weak," Cassia said.

"That will pass," Lio said. "How is Lyros?"

Lyros sat with Mak's arms around him. Mak wiped a stray bit of blood off the corner of Lyros's mouth.

Lyros's cheeks darkened. "I'm excellent."

Cassia pointed to the bandage on Mak's arm. "What about your gash?"

Mak flexed his arm gingerly. "Not bad. I'll let Tuura's poultices work on it a while, then have a drink at our next stop."

Cassia glanced up at the night sky. "We still have hours of darkness. After Lio and Lyros rest a bit longer, will they be in any condition for us to step onward tonight?"

"We're right here," Lio protested.

"And still denying how serious your wound was," Cassia said crisply, "which is why I'm asking Mak."

"I think they're safe to step." Mak gave Lyros a stern look. "But no unnecessary exertion."

"Belly wounds aren't as serious for us as heart wounds." Lyros lifted his hands to ward off Mak's scolding. "But I'll save my strength for our next battle."

Cassia pushed her hair out of her eyes, then appeared to notice the blood on her hands. She scrubbed them in the stream. She seemed tired. The sort of tired that could affect immortals, a weariness of spirit.

Lio didn't want that for her. "That was more than enough violence for one night. We need to find another refuge and recover until tomorrow."

Lyros nodded. "We won't survive four Gift Collectors again without time to prepare. Now that we know they're hunting us in groups, we need to rethink our tactics."

"Four!" Mak said. "One is deadly enough, but we get a party of *four*."

"I can scarcely believe it," Lyros said. "They're usually at each other's throats too much to cooperate like that. It seems the Collector isn't taking any chances against the four of us."

"But we still managed to take his Overseers by surprise," Lio said.

Cassia's hand came to rest on Rosethorn. "We won't have that advantage again. The Collector is always in the minds of his Overseers. He knows what we can do, now."

Lio was silent, unwilling to confirm her fears. But he knew she was right.

The next battle against Kallikrates would be harder.

THE MOURNING CIRCLE

A GROWL FROM KNIGHT MADE Lio fumble for his fading veil spells. The hound faced the way they had come, leaning forward, his whole body alert.

Mak and Lyros already had their wards up. Lio levitated to his feet and summoned his staff to hand, pushing through a wave of dizziness and the weakness in his limbs.

With her fangs and dagger out, Cassia moved in front of him, a small, vicious obstacle between him and unnamed danger. Goddess, she was beautiful. Every protective instinct in him demanded he pull her behind him where she would be safe.

But if he kept treating her like a mortal, that wouldn't encourage her to embrace her immortal power. He moved forward and stood at her side.

Knight let out a fretful whine, then barked.

"I think someone is following us," Cassia said.

Lio cast veiled thelemancy across the moor. "I can't get a sense of them."

Mak fingered his morning star. "Anyone who can hide from your mind magic isn't to be trifled with."

"I don't like this," Lio said. "If they're Gift Collectors, why aren't they attacking?"

"Whoever they are," Lyros said, "we've drawn them out here where they can't harm any mortals. Now we should get to Segetia and look for shelter there. Cassia, do you remember a location we can use as a stepping focus?"

She nodded and shut her eyes. Her senses opened for Lio, letting him deeper into their Union.

She envisioned a road in her mind's eye. He sensed her past emotions tied to that place. She had traveled through there with the king's entourage on the way to the Solstice Summit, where she hoped she would meet a Hesperine.

That memory of her journey to him made a powerful focus. They stepped from Hadria's harsh landscape to a road bordered by Segetia's gentle fields.

As they picked up their belongings and mounted again, Knight sniffed their surroundings, pausing over refuse left behind by whoever had ridden here during the day. But few dared travel the roads of Tenebra at night in wartime, except Hesperines.

"This is King's Road, which runs all the way from Namenti to Solorum." Cassia pointed not far into the distance, where moonlight gleamed on water. "That's where the Silvistra and Cerera Rivers meet."

"So the knights will almost certainly have to bring the evacuees along here," Mak said.

Cassia turned Freckles. "We should be able to intercept them."

"Good," Lyros said. "We'll try that tomorrow night after we've found another refuge."

Lio wrapped a hand gently around Cassia's where she still held Rosethorn. "Let's think where a Lustra site might be in Segetia."

Her grip on the dagger only tightened, and he knew he was in for another debate about the use of her magic.

He tried to keep his tone patient. "Do you know of any possibilities? This domain isn't as old as Hadria, so it didn't exist in its current form during the Mage King and Changing Queen's reign. But there could still be fortresses built by the lords of that time."

"Right." Cassia's voice was too calm. "It was settled very early because it's the most fertile land in the kingdom. Many bitter feuds were fought over it until Flavian's ancestors prevailed and consolidated power to rival Hadria's."

Mak waved at the surrounding fields. "If everything grows so well here, does that mean the Lustra is more powerful in this region?"

Lio shook his head. "I fear it may be the opposite. It's one of the least wild places in all of Tenebra."

"Men tamed it so long ago. The Lustra feels..." She seemed to search for words. "Diminished."

"It can't be *gone*, though," Mak reasoned. "The letting site under your mother's temple is still there, even though Corona is one of the most populated cities."

"True," Lio said, "but it was tended by generations of Silvicultrixes disguised as mages of Kyria. The Lustri sorceresses were surely driven out of Segetia ages ago."

"Yes." Cassia paused.

Lio leaned closer to her. "You have a theory."

She hesitated. Knight barked suddenly, then circled them. He pushed against Cassia's leg.

"He wants us to leave," she said. "It's as if someone is still on our trail. How could they follow us when we stepped?"

"We need to find shelter," Lyros said. "Quickly."

Cassia finally replied, "Segetia is dotted with circles of standing stones so old no one remembers who built them. Could they have been ritual sites for the Silvicultrixes?"

"Stone circles!" Lio exclaimed. "Certainly. I wish we had access to a library right now so I could refresh my memory on Tenebran megaliths. They're sure to date from the Hulaic Epochs, when the Silvicultrixes were at their most powerful."

Cassia frowned. "I should have thought of this before, but I've never actually been to any of them. Genie mentioned them when she was telling me about places she wanted to show me in Segetia. That was before I knew anything about my magic."

Lio could believe Lady Eugenia's imagination would be captured by some ancient site with mysterious origins. Flavian's younger sister was quite the romantic. Lio would never know what she saw in narrow-minded Sir Benedict.

Lyros levitated the map over to Cassia. "Do you know the locations?"

She furrowed her brow, studying the map. "Genie told me about a few near her family's estates, but that's too far to ride in one night and we can't step there without a clear focus."

"May I make a suggestion?" Lio asked.

She met his gaze, her chin set. It was clear she was already prepared to resist his advice.

Lio continued anyway. "If the stone circles are Lustra sites, your senses will draw you to them. You should try stretching your awareness and see if you can detect any within riding distance. This is also a good opportunity to test your range."

She let the map roll shut with a snap. "We are not performing any magical tests after a narrow escape from Gift Collectors, with more of them possibly on our heels. Do you want me to bring the next Hesperine-baiting party down on our heads?"

"If you do, we'll take care of them."

"Fight when we *must*, Lio. That's what Uncle Argyros said to us. I won't incite any more violence if I can avoid it."

Lio wanted to peel away the layers of guilt in her aura one by one until she realized just how wrong her words were. But that would take time. Right now, he had to make the argument that would change her mind. Her mind, which he knew so well.

He made a point that he knew she would not be able to refute. One that was close to her heart. "The villagers are headed here for safety. Better to draw any of Kallikrates's hunting parties to us before they have a chance to hurt the mortals."

Anger flashed in her hazel eyes, glinting half gold in the moonlight. *Sunbind you, Glasstongue*, she told him privately before saying aloud, "Very well. I will ask the Lustra to show us the way. That is all. No channeling."

She jumped off Freckles, giving him no opportunity to help her down, and strode a few paces away from them. Knight followed her, darting to and fro, clearly anxious at the delay. Mak and Lyros fanned out on their horses, and shadow wards rose to encircle their party.

Lio dismounted and followed Cassia with Final Word at the ready. He slipped up behind her and rested one hand on her shoulder. "I'll protect you while you cast. If you need help with control, I'm here."

She didn't turn to him, but he heard her little intake of breath. "I will not need help. It's not even a casting."

He resisted the ill-timed temptation to kiss the sensitive spot between her neck and shoulder. He wanted to lick her anger from her skin.

She pointed the tip of her dagger toward the ground, adjusting her grip on it. There came the barest stir in her aura, slipping down her blade.

That meek ripple of magic sent a sudden rush of anger through Lio, this time all his own. This tentative creature was not Cassia. She had left those days behind in her human life. As an immortal, she should hold her head high and unleash her power. That was what Orthros had promised her. That was what he had promised her.

She glanced over her shoulder at him, her eyes full of hurt. He pulled back. What had he said—or not said—to put that fresh wound in her aura?

Before he could respond, she gasped and swayed on her feet. He reached to catch her, but she steadied herself.

"The Lustra is still here, buried deep." She sounded a little breathless. "No one has woken it in a long time. It's tired. Desperate."

"Is it willing to guide us?" Lio asked.

"Eager." She turned slowly, holding out Rosethorn like the point on a compass. "That way. I think we can reach it before dawn."

"Then we ride northeast," said Lyros.

"Cassia—" Lio began softly, reaching to catch her hand.

"Not now. Not here." She slipped from his grasp.

THE LUSTRA'S GUIDANCE WAS a faint, keening thread pulling Cassia along the next mile. Then the next. She had to focus all her Will on it, or she would lose the trail. But that meant she had no concentration to spare for the unbearable emotions lodged in her chest.

At last they spotted gray, jagged teeth against the violet horizon. By the time they approached the standing stones, twilight muffled her thoughts and dragged at her limbs. She prayed this would prove to be a safe place. They were out of time to find another before dawn.

Mak gave the crumbling slabs a dubious look. "It's just a pile of rocks."

"This is a masterpiece of prehistoric engineering and astronomy!" Lio guided Moonflower around the perimeter of the circle at a trot. "See the arrangement of the stones? They align with the heavens somehow. Perhaps related to the equinox and harvest season? If we count the broken stones, there are nine in all—three times three. That suggests a Silvicultrix site."

"Huh." Mak tilted his head. "You *may* be onto something. That ritual circle under the lighthouse had nine nodes, too."

Lio rejoined them. "See? Your brain isn't a pile of rocks, either."

Mak gave him an affronted look. "My brain keeps your hide safe while your brain is stuck in prehistory, scrollworm."

Lyros's mouth twitched. "The question is, does this place offer any of our brains protection?"

Cassia's dulled reason somehow made her more aware of the Lustra's pull. Her voice came out hushed. "It's not just rocks. Each standing stone has a presence. Even the broken ones."

The others grew quiet. Acting on instinct, she slipped off of Freckles and put Knight in a sit stay. "I think it's best if you all wait here at first."

"I should come with you." Lio was already dismounted and at her side.

She held up a hand. "The Lustra here doesn't know you yet. It's... suffered a great deal, I think."

Lio's brows descended, and she knew there was a protest in his exquisite mouth. Two could play this game of unfair negotiations.

"If you want me to use my magic," she said, "you have to let me use it. Trust what my intuition is telling me. Let me see how the magic in this place responds to me before you try to enter the circle."

His eyes narrowed. "Well played, my Silvicultrix."

He waited with Mak and Lyros as she walked alone into the ring of megaliths. The dewy grass gave softly under her feet, and the scent of damp stone touched her senses. As the magic of the place enveloped her sleepy mind, she felt like she walked into a dream.

Power. Ancient, frightening. Familiar. Mourning soaked the earth, while the stones whispered comfort. She knew this place, and yet it reminded her of the farthest corner of the world where she had ever set foot.

Btana Ayal. The majestic megaliths of the Diviner Queen's ancient city made Tenebra's standing stones seem like small children. But with this circle's magic murmuring around her, Cassia could not help but recall how she had felt, standing on the cusp of the broken gate in Shattered Hope.

The stars glittered at her feet, and the heavens above felt rife with new seeds waiting to bloom. Her blood wheeled with the earth and sky.

"Cassia!" *Cassia!*

Lio's shout, in her ears and her mind, brought her back to reality.

Lio? she called back.

His fear sent a chill down her spine, breaking the dream. *Cassia, I can't find you. Can't step to you. Where have you gone?*

THE SORCERESS'S DUTY

Cassia turned toward the sound of his voice. But as far as her immortal eyes could see, there was nothing but empty fields and dark sky.

She clung to their Grace Union, the one law of magic that prevailed in this place. *I'm here. I'll find you, I swear.*

She ran to the edge of the circle, but careened to a halt just before she left the ring of stones. If she set foot outside now, would it only make matters worse? Gazing out at the horizon, she feared she might go spinning out into yet another world even farther from Lio.

She directed her Will at the Lustra, at the silent stones.

He is my mate. Let him in!

The strange world wrapped closer around her. Power soaked her like a sudden rain, running through the arcane paths inside her and slipping over her skin, dragging her into the rhythm of this season out of time.

She gave her head a shake, pushing back at the magic with her Will. *No! I am not yours. You are mine.*

If this place was so hungry for a sorceress, it would have to take her on her terms. She dragged her fang across her hand and flicked her blood onto the ground.

I am your Silvicultrix. He is my mate. Let him in.

Lio flickered into sight. He seemed disoriented for a moment, then snatched her into his arms. There came an echo from the stones, and the magic around them waxed.

Mate. Cassia didn't know if the word sprang from her own mind or the ground where she stood.

She pulled Lio's mouth down to hers. The world disappeared a second time. She kissed him hard. He surrendered to her in an instant, parting his lips, and their tongues clashed.

Mate. On instinct, she drew magic up from the earth and into their bodies. Yes, this was right. She marked the arcane paths inside him with her power.

He groaned and grasped her buttocks, holding her against him. He was already hard for their ritual, the ridge of his erection pressing into her belly. Hunger burned from her tongue to the core of her body.

Distantly, another shout reached her ears. Someone calling their names.

Lio pulled his mouth back with a gasp. "We can't. My blood isn't safe for you yet."

She slid down his body to stand flat footed, her canines throbbing. She couldn't make herself let him go.

He stared down at her, dazed, his fangs out and a trickle of blood trailing from his lip. "What just happened?"

"I think the circle needed me to demonstrate my claim on you."

The magic around them flared and ebbed in time to their heartbeats. Images flashed in their shared mind's eye. Naked skin, bared teeth. Her on all fours, him covering her. Them mating on this ground, here and now, forever.

Cassia pulled out of his arms and took a step back. "This part of the Lustra acknowledges you now."

He rubbed his mouth. "It seems to have a very clear idea of my role, yes."

"Lio! Cassia!" Lyros's voice drifted into their hearing.

"Just a moment," Lio called back.

"Don't you dare leave us behind!" Mak's shout sounded far away. He gave no sign he had heard Lio.

Cassia put the breadth of the circle between her and Lio to stop herself from pulling him down to the grass with her. She gulped at the cool air, trying to close her arcane senses to the Lustra.

He turned away from her and adjusted himself. "Bleeding thorns."

"Sorry."

When he faced her again, his fangs were somewhat tamed, but there was still heat in his gaze. "Don't apologize."

She tried communicating with the stones' magic again, holding Mak and Lyros's arcane signatures in her thoughts. She had taught the Lustra passages to recognize other Hesperines besides her Grace. Would these even more ancient stones understand the same?

Nothing happened. Mak and Lyros's shouts grew more urgent. Cassia was out of options. She fingered Rosethorn, her artifact that held both Mak's and Lyros's magic, as well as hers and Lio's.

She drove the dagger into the ground. *They're my pack. Let them in.*

There came a shift, not one she could see, but one that made her arcane senses spin. And there were their Trial brothers, Knight, and the horses, right where they had left them, a few paces away in another time or place.

Knight trotted to her side, wagging his tail and nudging her for attention. He did not appear troubled by the Lustra's tricks.

She rubbed his ears. "You liegehounds have something of the Lustra in you, don't you?"

He looked into her eyes with his earnest, honest ones. On impulse, she reached for that sense she'd once had as a human. As if she could speak to him without words. As if he might speak back.

But that awareness of their bond eluded her now. A sense of loss cut her deeper than she had expected. She had known she had given up her beast magic when she had accepted the Gift. She had meant it when she told Lio she was satisfied with her plant magic and the power of Hespera's blood.

But looking into Knight's opaque eyes in the dreaming circle of her ancestors, she caught a glimpse of what she had lost.

Mak and Lyros rode into the circle, leading her and Lio's horses. Mak leapt off Bear and marched up to Lio. Taking hold of Lio's shoulders, Mak gave him a shake. "Did you learn *anything* in the Maaqul? Didn't you swear to us you wouldn't charge off on your own anymore?"

"Mak, I didn't mean—"

"I can haul your ass out of a jinn prison, but not out of—whatever in the Goddess's name the Lustra just did. We don't know what we're dealing with here. You could have been dying a horrible death in front of us, where we couldn't find you."

"I'm usually safe in—"

"The Collector is trying to break down a Lustra door. Do you think anywhere is safe?"

Lio fell silent. "I'm sorry, Mak. It was blind instinct to find my Grace."

"Hespera knows we understand how that feels. But don't be an idiot about it. Do you think it helps your Grace if you run into the unknown? All of us are safer if we stay together."

Lio looked stricken. "I'm so sorry. I should have realized I wasn't only putting myself at risk."

"For a scrollworm, *your* brain is full of rocks sometimes."

"It won't happen again."

Mak collared him in a hug, then set Lio away from him.

Lyros came to check on Cassia, and she offered him her own apology. "I didn't realize coming in here would cut me off from you."

"You went in as a precaution," Lyros replied. "You negotiating with the Lustra first made more sense than Lio charging in after we realized what it would do."

"That wasn't entirely Lio's decision." Cassia avoided her Grace's gaze, trying to keep the mental images at bay. The Lustra's demands could so easily make her forget the hurt and anger in their Union. "Once the stone circle realized who he is to me, it was rather demanding about him joining me."

"I'm prepared for it now," Lio said.

She arched a brow at him. He cleared his throat into his hand, but she suspected he was surreptitiously rubbing his fangs.

Neither of them was prepared to remain in this circle for hours, fighting the insistent magic. But they didn't have a choice. "We can spend the Dawn Slumber here."

Lyros eyed the open sky. "Not under direct sunlight. It would be best if we sleep in the light-resistant Azarqi tents Kella sent with us. But underground would be better. I suppose there's no chance of finding a portal here?"

Cassia shook her head. "I don't think so. Not one of the Changing Queen's doors to her secret passages, in any case."

"This circle is something much older. More primal." Lio's voice sent a shiver over her skin.

"Yes." Cassia's mouth was dry. "It almost seems as if it is a portal in some way of its own."

"A portal to what?" Mak asked. "Where?"

"I don't know," Cassia answered. "I don't know nearly enough."

WHEN LIO OFFERED TO pitch his and Cassia's tent, he expected her to protest. But for once, she didn't insist on helping. She stayed on the opposite side of the circle from him. That made it only a little less difficult to keep his hands off of her.

Their Blood Union saturated the ring of stones, a churning mix of hurt, anger, and need. Mak and Lyros pitched their tent without commenting, but he noticed their worried glances.

Finally Cassia padded over to join Lio at the tent flap, her eyelids heavy. The magic of the stone circle hummed up through his body, demanding, right. There was still time for him to follow her into that tent and turn her over for a fast, hard feast before she fell asleep.

He shook his head, trying to clear it. He couldn't let her drink from him, not with the Gift Collector's magic still in his body. But if he drank from her first, that might finish healing him so his blood was safe for her…

No. With this magic manipulating their minds and desires, could she trust herself to wait? Could he trust himself to stop her?

She looked up into his eyes, and her throat worked as she swallowed. *If we give in, I think it could interact with the magic. Even activate it. We shouldn't do that without knowing the consequences.*

She was right to hesitate this time. He knew that. But the sight of her tongue darting out to wet her lips almost undid him.

This is one experiment I'm not in favor of, he made himself say. *Riling up prehistoric spells we don't understand could cause…trouble.*

He couldn't think clearly enough to theorize about the possible outcomes. He only knew that the moment she got her fangs into him, the remnants of their self control would break, and he would be inside her in a heartbeat.

Her cheeks flamed. *I'll go into the tent alone. Wait till I fall asleep.*

He nodded mutely. She slipped inside with only her liegehound for company.

Lio stalked to the other side of the circle and sank down onto the grass, propping his back against one of the stones. They had made the right decision. Hadn't they?

Or had she seized on the Lustra's interference as an excuse to keep her distance?

Lio looked out over the surrounding fields and tried to think who might be out there following them. More Gift Collectors. Lucis's war mage allies. Some threat from Kallikrates they hadn't imagined yet. He tried to distract himself from the fact that his Grace was falling asleep alone mere paces away, and he had hurt her.

Mak flopped down beside him, then Lyros sat on Lio's other side.

"I should have known you two would corner me," Lio said.

Mak stretched his bandaged arm. "What are Trial brothers for?"

"Don't bother avoiding our questions. You know we'll get answers out of you by any means necessary." Lyros pointed at Lio's shoulder. "First, how is your wound?"

Lio rubbed it gingerly. "Sore. But the fatigue is getting better. You?"

"Same. Another drink and I won't feel it anymore."

"Speaking of," said Mak. "Next question. Why are you moping out here instead of letting your newly avowed Grace tend your wounds some more?"

Lio grimaced. "Remember the bones we found under the lighthouse? Those rituals involved death."

"Yes," Lyros said with a puzzled frown.

"Well." Thorns, it was really unnecessary for him to blush like this. "I think the rituals here involved, ah, fertility. The magic wants Cassia and me to perform our duties to the Lustra. We're being stubborn."

Mak burst out laughing. "Well, that explains why you were in such a hurry to get in here."

"It wasn't intentional!" Lio put his head between his knees. "The Lustra has acknowledged I'm the Silvicultrix's mate, and apparently that involves certain responsibilities. Magical and physical ones. Unless this is the site of ancient Lustri orgies, and it makes everyone who sets foot here mindless with lust. Do you two feel any irrational urges to tear each other's clothes off?"

Mak laughed harder.

Lyros gave his Grace a warm look. "We don't need a stone circle for that. All we're feeling is what we feel every night."

"Wait," Mak said, "do *any* 'pleasure rituals' in the circle affect the magic? Or only the Silvicultrix's 'duties'?"

Lio sighed. "I believe it's safe to assume you may do whatever you like tonight. Have fun. Spare some sympathy in your hearts for your poor, hungry Trial brother."

Mak patted Lio's shoulder. "If we feel any magical earthquakes through your veils, we won't judge."

Lio punched Mak's uninjured arm.

He recalled the three of them sitting like this in the gymnasium the night they had extracted his confession that Cassia was his Grace. They had all been so full of themselves, the youngest to be promoted from initiates to full rank in the diplomatic service and the Stand.

They had thought their titles made it possible for them to protect their people. That their mentors trusted them to use their power wisely. What did those accolades mean now? Adamas was all that stood between them and the Gift Collectors' blades.

Lio wanted to ask his Trial brothers a few nosy questions of his own. Was Mak still blaming himself for all of this, or was he listening to Lyros's reassurances? But hearing his cousin rib him, Lio couldn't bring himself to banish Mak's humor. He might only make Mak feel worse. Just like Cassia.

Lio waited until her breathing went silent in Slumber and her hurting aura gave way to fretful dreams. He got to his feet. "She's asleep."

"Can we trust you to behave yourself in there?" Lyros teased.

Lio made a face. "With a liegehound sleeping between us, yes."

"Good old Knight," Mak said, "an unfailing deterrent against enemy mages and thorny young Hesperines."

Lio laughed with them and slipped away without them realizing Glasstongue had won this negotiation. They hadn't questioned him about the real reason for this new rift between him and Cassia.

If they had, he wouldn't have known the answer.

VIGIL OF THE GIFT

1 Night Until Winter Solstice

NO ESCAPE

Cassia woke to a parched tongue and a cold bedroll. Her body worked itself out of the Dawn Slumber without Lio there to hold her. He was everpresent at the boundaries of their Union, fretful, distant, his self-control a seething thread ready to snap.

When she could move her arms, she wrapped them around Knight and buried her face in his fur. The scent of the herbal rose bath she had given him before the avowal ceremony was finally fading from his coat. He rolled onto his side, sprawling across Lio's place.

She rubbed Knight's belly. "Still occasionally jealous, darling? Happy to have me all to yourself now and then, like old times?"

Her hound let out a sigh, his tongue flopping out in a dreamy expression.

"What would I have done if you'd been wounded in that battle, hm? This kingdom is harsh, even on liegehounds. I wish I could do more to protect you."

He licked his nose and settled more comfortably against her.

"Are you tired? This is a lot to ask of you. I wish I could make you immortal."

The thought squeezed her heart. She would have him with her for another decade at least, given how much longer a liegehound's lifespan was than a mundane dog's. But that didn't sound like very much time now that she would live forever.

She stroked his side. "Do you suppose you could reconcile yourself to becoming a Hesperine's familiar? Would that magic even work on you?"

The awakening potential of her beast magic, not even her full power, had been enough to convince Knight to protect Hesperines instead of hunting them. But she did not have that power now.

"Muster out, Shadow!" came Mak's very cheerful, very loud voice from outside the tent. Karege would have been proud.

Knight chuffed with displeasure. Cassia rubbed her sensitive ears. "Are you trying to wake the dead, Wisdom?"

At the mention of his honorary fortune name bestowed by the Ashes, he only sounded more cheerful. "Lazy newgifts are harder to wake than the dead! Up and at it!"

She did her best to smooth her rumpled travel robes before leaving the tent. Would she ever learn Hesperine cleaning spells? At least she wasn't a mortal in need of a privy first thing in the morning. Or rather, at twilight.

In the deepening dusk, her eyes instantly locked on Lio's. He looked back at her across the stone circle, searching her gaze. His confusion and pain throbbed in their Union, and she knew she was the cause.

The site's ancient power uncoiled inside her. Heat throbbed deep in her body, in her magic. Before she thought, she took a step toward him.

Winter rain spattered down between the stones, and the cold drops on her cheeks brought her to her senses. They had to leave this place.

Mak eyed her fangs. "Do I need to give you a bottle of thirst suppressant?"

She slapped her hands over her mouth and mumbled a curse.

Lyros slung one more pack onto General. "Get a veil at our next stop. We're nearly ready to go."

Lio, his high, pale cheekbones painted with a handsome flush, focused his attention on dismantling their tent.

They led their horses out of the circle and back into the world as they knew it. The Lustra's compulsion faded but left Cassia with her Craving.

Lio drew near. She wished he wouldn't. He didn't touch her, but she felt his mind voice all over her body. *Can you make it until we find a safer place to camp?*

Her gaze fixed on his throat. *I drank from you last night, just before we left the lighthouse. And we'll find somewhere I can drink later tonight. Hesperines are fine with one dose of blood each night.*

Not newgifts, and not after a battle.

The look he gave her made her wonder if he was considering carrying her off right this moment, covering them in veil spells, and feasting with her on the nearest patch of grass. Her face flamed.

We'll wait a few more hours to make sure my blood is safe, he said. *But I will not leave you in withdrawal longer than that.*

When Lyros pulled them over for a quick strategy session, Cassia was grateful for the interruption.

"You two didn't have much time to sharpen your combat skills before we left. Mak and I will continue your training when we find a safe enough place. Until then, trust your experience from past battles, but follow our instructions, understood?"

Cassia and Lio both nodded in agreement. Despite all the dangers they had survived until now, she didn't feel prepared.

Now that they had left the circle, they were able to step back to the road. Knight was the first to notice the tracks leading southwest. He nosed around the imprints left by horses, carts, and shoes.

"A large group passed this way while we slept," Lyros observed.

"Looks like it could have been a group of knights and villagers," Mak said.

Cassia frowned. "It does, but I expected to find them farther northeast of here. Flavian has holdings there where Ben would be likely to settle them. Why would they travel this far southwest? There's nothing in that direction but the rivers."

"Let's find out," said Lio. "I'll try to sense any minds as we ride. Hopefully we can pinpoint the auras of the couple we're looking for."

"Warn us if you feel the person following us," Lyros said.

"Or any Chargers," Mak added. "I hope we're not serving ourselves up on a platter by seeking out the evacuees."

"I doubt the knights will still have Hesperines with them," Lyros replied. "The Chargers probably returned to the front lines once they were able to leave the villagers in safe territory."

They followed the tracks the large group of mortals had left. As they rode, Lyros and Mak drilled Cassia and Lio on combat tactics. The warriors described scenarios, then asked how their party should respond in that situation. When Lio and Cassia made the wrong call, their Trial brothers patiently explained alternatives. Cassia's head was soon swimming with creative ways to use the few, basic fighting moves she had mastered.

Some time after twilight gave way to night, Lio's thelemancy swept out around them again, a shadow stretching far across the countryside. He sucked in a breath.

"What is it?" Cassia asked.

"I can sense them ahead of us," he answered. "They're moving faster than I expected."

Cassia pulled Freckles alongside him. "If they go much farther, they'll be at the ferry. Surely they wouldn't try to cross the river with exhausted villagers in the middle of winter."

"They would if they're running from something," Lio said.

What danger could have found Solia's forces here in the heart of a powerful ally's domain? Without further debate, they rode toward the disturbance. Their veil spells swallowed the pounding of the Warmbloods' hooves.

As they neared the vee of the rivers, a bright flash lit the night. Suddenly the air smelled like a storm. But it felt like magic.

Duck, Lio shouted in her mind.

Cassia flattened herself against Freckles' outstretched neck. The revelatory spell struck her like a hot breath, and she shuddered. The next instant, a jagged streak of lightning followed it. A crash tortured her ears, and the hairs on her arms stood on end.

The spell shot over her head. The enemy had expected a taller rider.

The next fork of lightning broke against a shadow ward in front of Lyros. "Weapons out!"

Another ward swept up from Mak. "Focus on keeping the enemy away from you, and let the Warmbloods help."

Cassia drew Rosethorn and tried to spot the mage in the chaos of men and horses ahead. Knights in the white surcoats of the Order of Andragathos clashed with soldiers in Lucis's sky blue. Behind the knights' line of defense, the population of an entire village cowered on the riverbank.

Scorched planks spun away on white-capped water. What was left of the ferry. The coward of a weather mage who was throwing lightning bolts lurked at the back of Lucis's warriors.

"Leave the robe to Mak and me," Lyros called out. "Help the knights."

Lio's magic washed over their enemies, and a shudder seemed to move through Lucis's forces. But they kept fighting.

Kallikrates is here, Cassia guessed. *In whom? All of them?*

He's toying with us, Lio answered. *Darting in and out of their minds. Stay close to me.*

Freckles slipped past the larger mounts and pranced into the fray. Lio cried out a protest in Cassia's mind. She grabbed for Freckles' mane, squeezing with her knees. But the mare merely smacked Cassia's leg with her tail and plunged onward.

Lio charged after them. Over her shoulder, Cassia saw one soldier turn his horse to face the oncoming mass of white that was Moonflower. The mortal lifted his longsword and aimed at Lio's heart.

Lowering his staff like a lance, Lio drove the end at the man and flung him out the saddle before he ever saw the veiled weapon.

Instead of a scream of pain, the soldier let out a smooth, deep laugh that Cassia recognized. Through her Union with Lio, she felt the presence his thelemancy revealed.

Concentrate on the Collector, she urged him.

Stay. Close. To. Me.

But her mount danced deeper into the battle with confidence twice her size. She was the descendant of Celeris, the steed who had carried the Guardian of Orthros through the Last War. Lyta had trained Freckles herself. This horse was better prepared for battle than Cassia.

She relaxed her knees and eased her grip. *Trust Freckles to protect me.*

The little mare dodged blades and, with a vicious kick, left one macer clutching his head in the dirt. Cassia called out commands to Knight in tandem, and his lunges and bites widened the swath her horse carved through the skirmish.

Another bolt of lightning reached for them. Cassia pressed herself against her horse until they felt like one creature. By the time the spell blasted a small crater in the riverbank, Freckles had already leapt a pace away.

Another horse screamed. One of the knights went down, trapped under his bleeding mount. Pure suffering crushed Cassia for an instant. The battle wavered before her eyes, her vision going dark.

She couldn't see the knight's face. Could he be…

A sharp pain in her leg brought her back to herself. Freckles bared her teeth at Cassia.

"Thank you," she whispered.

As if understanding her pure Will, Freckles raced toward the fallen horseman. A soldier in sky blue yanked his sword out of the knight's body, then turned to swing at Cassia.

Panic seized her mind, even as her arm came up on instinct. She made a mad flail with her dagger and dodged. Pain sliced along her hip.

Only Hesperine agility had saved her from a sword in her gut. The slash of pain faded by the time she straightened on Freckles' back.

Her horse surged under her, lashing out with her front legs. The hoofprints of an Orthros Warmblood marred the king's emblem on the man's surcoat. Ribs cracked. The warrior staggered back into Knight's range, and his sword arm was the next to break in the grip of the hound's jaws.

Cassia's Blood Union with the knight faded as his blood slowed. Helpless empathy drove her out of the saddle and down on her knees beside his body.

She had to know. She touched his mud-spattered helmet and turned his face toward her.

Not Ben. Someone else's friend or sweetheart or brother. But not Ben.

Cassia, get back on your horse!

At Lio's warning, she realized three of Lucis's soldiers were closing in on her. She sat alone in the gap the knight's death had left in the defenses. Behind her, a villager's infant wailed.

Enraged for people whose names she didn't even know, she surged to her feet with a cry of anguish. She pushed power into her dagger.

Three vines broke out of the soil of the riverbank. Black roses ensnared the trio of warriors and dragged them to the ground. Their screams joined the battle's cacophony.

The man right at her feet choked, yanking at the rose vine around his throat until the thorns shredded his hands. Cassia's stomach heaved. She swayed where she stood, looking down at him.

He was younger than her. Was he like Lucis's personal guards, known for their cruelty? Or had he been a frightened subject impressed into the king's service?

She tore her gaze away from him and found herself face to face with Benedict.

A SPREADING FIRE

BEN STOOD FROZEN, HIS sword upraised. Her roses had made his kill for him. He stared at her with wide eyes. She could guess how she looked to him, spattered with blood. Dagger in hand. Fangs bared. The antithesis of the devout maiden of Kyria he had once believed her to be.

"Cassia?" There was a note of plea in his voice.

His emotions pummeled her. Shock. Horror. Grief.

She didn't want to feel his censure. She didn't want to feel how much he cared.

In his moment of distraction, another soldier in blue attacked from his blind side. Cassia raised Rosethorn, summoning another twirl of vines around the swordsman. She tossed him at Benedict's feet and turned away.

Mak and Lyros sat on their horses over the body of the mage. A swath of fallen soldiers surrounded Lio and Moonflower. The battle was over, the surviving knights trying to gather and calm the villagers.

Cassia went to Lio's side. Knight shadowed her, murmuring a final growl.

Lio slid down next to her and examined the slice in her robes. *Are you all right?*

It was a mundane sword. I've already healed.

He wrapped his arms around her. *Two battles in two nights. This is too much.*

She couldn't fall to pieces. Not yet. She had to focus. *Kallikrates—?*

Gone. Curse him and his games. He kept me distracted so I wouldn't end the battle with thelemancy.

He could have done far more damage than this. Why is he toying with us? I wish I knew.

"What happened here?" Lyros asked Benedict.

The knight ignored him. He stalked toward Lio and Cassia. He hadn't sheathed his sword. Lio tucked Cassia closer against him, gripping Final Word in his other hand.

Tension moved through every human and immortal around them. Mak and Lyros's latent warding magic hummed in the air.

"I heard the rumors," Ben said, "but I didn't expect…"

Cassia's icy court manners came back to her. "How glad I am to see you alive, as well."

He didn't have the grace to look abashed. He appeared to still be in shock at her transformation.

"I trust Solia told you that Lio saved me with the Gift?" Cassia said.

"Is that what you call this?" Ben's voice cracked.

"I call it respecting her choice," Lio cut in.

"You," Ben spat. "You've taken her humanity. She deserved so much better than you."

Lio didn't answer. He just looked at Ben. Cassia realized in that moment that Glasstongue had a stare worthy of his mentor that could make a man quail in his boots.

Ben took a step back.

"Sir Benedict," Lyros said sharply, "are you in command here or not? Your fellow knights and your queen's subjects need leadership, and your Hesperine allies need an explanation. Remember yourself."

Ben drew himself up, although he emanated resentment. Of course it didn't go down well that a heretic had reminded him of his honor. "I won't thank you for what you've done to Cassia. But out of fealty to my queen, I will continue to treat you as allies."

"What are a war mage and Lord Lucis's soldiers doing here?" Mak asked.

Ben pointed to the river with his sword. "The weather mage sailed them in against the currents. I expect more will slip in to turn our villagers into Hesperine bait."

"How did they get past Segetia's defenses?" Mak demanded.

"Our defenses are doing the best they can," Ben shot back. "At dawn, Lord Lucis and the Mage Orders launched an invasion of Segetia. Their forces are coming down on us from Solorum like a hammer."

The air rushed out of Cassia's lungs. The war had finally spread. Who knew what part of the kingdom the fire would engulf next?

"I'm sorry," she said.

Ben didn't look at her. "We're trying to get the evacuees to a safer area south of the river, where Lord Flavian's allies and my knightly order are preparing their fortresses to receive refugees. If we can get this group to Castra Augusta, we can protect them."

Cassia gazed back at him in silence. Lio and their Trial brothers seemed to have the same idea as well. If Ben wanted their help, let him ask for it.

"The ferry is gone," Ben bit out. "Will you step them across?"

"We will always protect Solia's people," Cassia said, her chin high.

She and Lio went to help the other knights organize the villagers, keeping their distance from Ben. Mak and Lyros, on the other hand, seemed inclined to breathe down his neck while the three of them escorted groups of evacuees across the river.

"I sense the couple from Mederi somewhere here." Lio's words pulled her thoughts back where they belonged.

Cassia helped him search the passing crowd as the night wore on. It was no swift task to move that many mortals, including elders and children, especially when they were unaccustomed to stepping. About half of the villagers were safely across when they encountered the elderly farmers and pulled them aside.

"I'm so glad we found you," Cassia said. "We're searching for Lady Miranda and hope you can help us."

The farmwife pressed her hands to her chest. "Oh, that sets my heart at ease. We've been so worried for her since she disappeared. But you can make sure she's safe."

Regret bit at Cassia. She hated to use these people's trust to hunt Miranda down.

But Miranda was part of the conspiracy tearing everyone's lives apart. These people would also be safer when she was brought to justice.

Lio said, "You mentioned she has safe places where she can go into hiding. Could you tell us where any of those might be?"

The husband scratched his chin. "She never plainly said where they were, but her hints might mean something to you."

Lio gave an encouraging nod. "Any detail could be valuable."

"Somewhere abandoned," the man said. "Forsaken, she called it. As if it were a place others feared to tread."

Can you think of a place with such a reputation? Lio asked silently.

Tenebra is such a superstitious kingdom, she replied. *That could refer to any marsh, graveyard, or field with a cross-eyed goat.*

"Did she say anything else about this place?" Lio's tone was patient, despite the frustration in their Union.

The woman rubbed her back as if it ached. "I got the idea it was quite a ways from Patria. It would take her weeks to come back. We worried about her, asked her if she had anyone like us there to look after her."

Her husband put a supportive arm around her. "She told us no. 'Nothing there but salt and bones,' she said. No place for our lady, if you ask me."

"I wish we could tell you more," the woman fretted. "But she does keep her secrets. To protect us, you know."

"It's all right," Lio reassured them. "You've been a great help, and you have our gratitude."

"Please find her," the man implored them before the couple joined the next group Mak and Lyros were stepping across.

"Salt and bones…" Cassia murmured.

Lio's gaze sharpened. "Does that mean something to you?"

She glanced at Ben. "Later."

By the time the last family made it over the river, night had turned into twilight again. Mak and Lyros pulled Cassia and Lio aside for a veiled consultation. Lio cast an uneasy glance at the knights who lingered nearby to see to their fallen comrades.

"We need to discuss our options," Lyros said. "Do we want to risk staying with the knights and villagers during the day?"

Lio's nostrils flared. "I would sooner spend the Dawn Slumber in Cordium. I don't want Cassia anywhere near Benedict, especially while we're all asleep and vulnerable."

Mak shook his head. "Slumbering surrounded by Knights of Andragathos sounds like a good way to wake up with holy daggers in our hearts."

"These knights have sworn fealty to Solia," Lyros said. "They've fought with the Charge. I doubt they would try to punish us for heresy. I'm more worried about who else might find us if we sleep outside a Lustra site."

"I agree," Cassia said. "I can deal with Ben, but there's no telling what enemies might ambush them if we linger. These mortals are already pawns in Kallikrates's game with us. The sooner we leave, the safer they'll be."

Lyros nodded. "Unfortunately, we don't have time to find another refuge before dawn. I'm afraid our only option is to return to the stone circle."

Lio and Cassia looked at each other.

I'll suffer it to keep you safe, he said, *but I don't want to put you through another night of Craving with the circle's magic making it more difficult for you.*

What a moment for a laugh to bubble out of her, if a slightly hysterical one. *I would rather return to the stones of unholy lust than stay here and suffer through more judgmental, holy stares.*

She sensed Lio groan inwardly. *We'll manage. I'll wait outside the stones until you fall asleep and leave before you wake.*

Will you be safe?

Yes. I'll come inside the circle before the Slumber hits me.

She sighed. *It's the best we can do.*

"We'll go back to the standing stones," Cassia agreed, "but there's one more thing I need to do here first. This might be our only chance to send word to Solia for quite some time. We should ask Ben to reassure her we're all right."

"Do you even trust him with that?" Lio asked.

Cassia shrugged. "We can rely on him to take a message to her, at least. Whatever Ben thinks of us, he will never break his oaths to my sister. His quest not to become his traitorous father is what defines him."

Anger still darkened Lio's expression. "Even if that's true, I can't forgive him for being disloyal to you."

She squeezed his hands. "Just give me a moment. Then we'll leave him in our dust where he belongs."

"I'll ask him for you," Lyros offered.

"That's all right," said Cassia. "I'll take care of it."

She approached Ben. The stench of the dead threatened to make her retreat to the river and retch. But she would not let these battle-hardened mortals mistake her newfound Hesperine empathy for female weakness.

She halted in front of Ben. His lips parted, then he hesitated, his aura fraught.

"Sir Benedict, I would ask a favor of you, for my sister's sake, if not mine. None of us need enjoy the situation."

"What do you need?" His voice was quiet, as if his anger had gone and left him drained.

Cassia considered her words carefully. She didn't want to tell him anything their enemies or the Charge could use to find them if her message reached the wrong ears. "Will you send word to Solia that the Black Roses are making progress?"

He swallowed. "Now I understand why you call yourselves that."

She felt the urge to shake him. He had no right to look so uncomfortable after she had saved his life. Would he rather die than be rescued by the unholy flowers his order referred to as harlot's kiss? "Can you get our message to her or not?"

"I told you, there's an invasion force between us and her fortress right now. I don't know when or if my couriers will get through to her."

"This is the first contact I've had with my sister's forces in nights, and might be the last for weeks. You'll have the chance to communicate with her long before I do. Will you at least tell her I'm still alive? Will you give your queen that much kindness, even if you have none left for me?"

His gaze dropped. "Cassia, I... Of course. I'll reassure her."

His anger had been easier to bear than the familiar way he said her name.

She turned away from Ben and marched back to her fellow Hesperines.

LIO PULLED CASSIA INTO his arms. She wasn't shaking this time. She seemed frozen, her spine rigid. That worried him more.

Lio second-guessed his decision not to put a fist in Benedict's face.

After holding onto him for a long moment, Cassia made to pull away. He didn't let her go. Brushing her hair back from her forehead, he felt how warm her skin was. For the first time in her Hesperine life, she had a Craving fever, and Lio hated it with every fiber of his being.

"Ride with me," he said.

She glanced at Freckles. "I can make it back to the stone circle on my own."

"I know you can. I need you in my arms for a while before we have to sleep apart again."

She softened against him and nodded. He had known if he made arguments about her own needs, she would only get more stubborn to prove she could hold up. But she had been willing to give in for his sake.

He scooped her up in his arms, then levitated into the saddle and settled her across his lap.

She arched a brow at him. *You're showing off.*

Surely you're getting equal satisfaction from putting Ben's underlinens in a few more twists?

She gave Lio her secret smile and settled against him. *Yes. I refuse to be less Hesperine to appease him.*

As Lio urged Moonflower forward, Freckles and Knight fell in behind him without a command. Mak and Lyros flanked them, and the mortals parted to let them through. They rode shoulder-to-shoulder past the staring knights. Ben's gaze tracked them, fixed on Cassia in Lio's arms.

They galloped until they couldn't smell death any longer. Then Lio slowed Moonflower to a walk. Mak and Lyros exchanged concerned glances with him, and he nodded. His Trial brothers fell back a little, and he layered more veils with their wards.

Cassia's gaze flicked from the open fields to Lio's face. "Why are we slowing down here?"

"For the same reason you stopped us on the moors last night to tend my wound." He offered her his wrist.

As he had expected, she protested immediately. "We're not safe here. There could be more mages in the area."

"The safest place for you to have a drink between the battlefield and the stone circle is right here in the saddle with me."

"We need to step back to the Lustra refuge."

"You will not go a single night without my blood. Not when we're safe at home. Not when we're in enemy territory. I will not allow our quest to deprive you of what you need, my newgift. If a war mage tries to come between me and your Craving in the next five minutes, I will kill him and keep feeding you."

A shiver went through her whole body. She looked up at him, her lips softly parted. He watched her fangs unsheathe at his words.

This time, when he held up his wrist, she seized him in shaking hands and sank her fangs in. She made a stifled sound of relief in her throat and drank him down. He wrapped his other arm closer around her and kissed her hair.

He watched his powerful Grace drink long and hard. Her aura swelled with renewed magic. He'd been right. She never could have borne another day in the stone circle without this drink, especially after how much she had channeled in their two battles.

When she finally had her fill, she sealed her bite and rested her face against his chest. He offered her his handkerchief.

Her cheeks flushed, she wiped her mouth, staining the white silk red. "Trust my champion to never be without a clean handkerchief, even under these circumstances."

"All those times when I handed you one as a human, did you ever imagine you might need it to wipe my blood off your lips?"

"Often."

He smiled.

She folded the handkerchief, not looking at him. "Thank you."

"Of course. You have nothing to prove, my rose. Trying to outlast the Craving longer only makes you miserable and more vulnerable to our enemies."

"I know. I just...need to feel in control of something right now, if only my own body."

He grimaced. "I understand."

He thought of all the nights he had hesitated to tell her she was his Grace for this very reason, among other fears. Neither of them would ever be fully in control of their Craving. Now that he had Gifted her, she was living with the full effects of that curse, the price of their bond.

Everything was out of control now—their futures, the war, the Collector's conspiracy. Except for one thing.

"I can help you control your magic," he said.

She tensed in his arms. "We can't afford magical experiments right now."

"You saved Benedict's life with your spells tonight, not that he showed you any gratitude. You used your magic as effectively in this battle as you did at the lighthouse."

"That wasn't control. It was instinct. Last night, when I saw you wounded with that dagger like the time Miranda captured us…I was enraged. And tonight, the mortals' suffering tore those roses out of me."

"Your magic answered to your protective instincts again."

"I can't let my instincts take control of me in every battle. It worked in our favor—this time. What about the next time my magic betrays us?"

Their own people had betrayed her, and now she felt like her power was a traitor, too. Goddess help him, this anger in him was enough to fill centuries.

She turned her face away. "It's not fair of you to debate this with me right now. Dawn is so near, I can hardly put two words together."

Lio wanted to break something. But he couldn't break down the wall she had built inside her. He would have to coax her to let it down for him.

"No more negotiations tonight," he agreed.

She was a knot of tension against him until she slipped into the Dawn Slumber in his arms.

WINTER SOLSTICE

SALT AND BONES

CASSIA BEGAN HER FIRST Winter Solstice as a Hesperine by saddling her warhorse. She should have been home, celebrating Lio's Gift Night and going to House Annassa for Ritual with the Queens. She had only herself to blame for the Black Roses being on the run in wartorn Tenebra instead.

She and Mak rode out of the circle to meet Lio and Lyros where they waited. She couldn't bring herself to wish her Grace a happy Gift Night when there was nothing happy about it, and all thanks to her magic.

Lio sat astride Moonflower in his midnight-blue battle robe and Imperial trousers, his hair windblown. He looked unfairly handsome and infuriatingly unrepentant about having his way the night before. But she was more grateful than she would ever admit for that drink from him. She didn't know how she would have made it through the day otherwise. The circle's magic had plagued her Slumber with dreams of dragging Lio into the ring of stones for a more intimate sort of ride.

The smile he gave her suggested that if she never confessed any of this in a hundred years, he still knew.

Mak cleared his throat. "So, where's our next stop? Anyone know what Miranda could have meant by 'salt and bones?'"

"I might," Cassia said. She'd had a lonely time in the tent to mull it over. "I think I know where to find Miranda and probably another Lustra portal. There is a forsaken place where the fields are sown with salt and the bones of the defeated were left where they fell."

Lio's eyes widened. "You mean…"

"Traitors' Grave," she told them. "That's what they call it sometimes.

The site where Castra Roborra once stood."

She hadn't wanted to discuss her theory last night with Ben nearby. His father had died there. Bellator's remains still lay among the rubble with those of the other lords who had kidnapped Solia and revolted against Lucis.

"Thorns," Mak said, "I wouldn't have expected that. But it makes a twisted kind of sense."

Cassia nodded. "Given Miranda's personal vendetta against me, she might be drawn to such an important place from my past. She knows it's where Hesperines saved my life—the reason I refused to join her in service to Kallikrates."

"She's devious," Lyros said. "That would make a good hiding place for any renegade. I doubt anyone goes there, not after the king leveled it and left it as a warning to would-be rebels."

"It's still under royal control, though, isn't it?" Lio asked.

Cassia nodded. "All of Roborra, Lord Bellator's domain, reverted to the crown upon his defeat. We'll need to watch out for royal forces and Gift Collectors."

"So we might be stepping into another battle," Lio said.

"I hope to avoid that. Lyros, let me check something on the map."

He handed it to her. "Is there somewhere you've been in that region that would be a safer arrival point?"

She ran her finger along the eastern edge of the kingdom, where the settled areas gave way to the wilds of the eastern Tenebrae. "Stepping blindly to Castra Roborra and possibly into Miranda's traps would be the most dangerous thing we could do, yes?"

"Like Paradum all over again, I fear," Lio said.

She tapped a point northeast of Castra Roborra. "The lesser evil would be to step to a small keep guarded by a few of Lucis's soldiers."

Mak nodded. "Good idea. Only thick mortal heads to knock together."

"How many soldiers?" Lyros asked. "Are they likely to have mages with them?"

Cassia considered this. "It's a remote fort for guarding against wild animals and brigands coming out of the east. It was one of Lucis's favorite places to stash me when he wanted me out of the way. I doubt he'll bother with it at a time like this. He may even have recalled the garrison to the warfront."

Lio drew Moonflower closer, looking at the map. "Stepping there could give us a real advantage."

"Yes, the Lustra will be stronger in the eastern wilds, won't it?" she speculated. "We'll have a higher chance of finding a Lustra portal there."

"Only one way to find out." Lio held out his hand to her.

He could step her without touching her. But she gave into his game, letting them both have this excuse to touch each other. She allowed herself the brush of his palm against hers, the grip of his fingers.

"Focus on another memory for me," he invited.

Cassia reached into her mind for a clear image of their destination. Her memories from before her Gifting were amorphous things, she'd found. Some were crystal clear treasures she had brought with her into eternity. Others were phantom pains, left behind on the other side of a veil of stars.

This one felt distant, but she dug deep and brought the bare tower to her mind's eye. The emptiness. The feeling of being forgotten on the edge of the world. Lio's magic pulled at her, and they stepped into her past.

LIO DIDN'T LET GO of Cassia's hand, even after they arrived outside the keep. Snow topped the walls, bright in the moons' light. The four of them held their horses back in the darkness under the dense trees that surrounded the outpost.

Do you sense anything? Lio asked her.

I'm not sure yet.

Of course she was unsure. She wasn't even stretching her senses, he could tell. He tried to keep his frustration in check.

"A dozen auras," Mak commented. "No mages."

"Can you sense any hidden minds?" Lyros asked Lio.

He kept his veils about them and let his thelemancy slip uninvited through the gates. The fort consisted of a small bailey and keep built around a derelict tower that appeared much older. The twelve mortal minds in the garrison were preoccupied with their dice game and how long it had been since they'd touched any women. At his glimpses of their fantasies, Lio hoped they got frostbite on the relevant appendages.

His lip curled. "No one but Tenebran boors who deserve to be banished out here for the winter. These soldiers won't pose much of a threat. They don't even have liegehounds."

They all paused. Mak was the first to ask, "Is anyone else having a moral dilemma?"

"Yes." Lio hesitated. But someone had to say it. "It would be very easy for us to make sure these soldiers never fight against Solia's forces."

Mak's breath clouded in the cold. "If we leave them be, who's to say they won't drive a sword through one of our friends?"

The snow crunched softly as Freckles pawed the ground. Cassia stroked her neck. "What if they don't want to serve Lucis? What if they come from a village that welcomed Hesperines and killing them will only hurt people who were kind to us?"

"Spoken like a true Hesperine," Lio said.

Her aura softened a little at those words.

"Twelve mortal warriors are no match for us," Lyros said. "There's little risk in confronting them and giving them the opportunity to choose their side."

Mak cocked his head. "Is it really a choice, when confronted by fanged heretics likely to make them piss themselves in terror?"

Cassia smiled, her fangs pale in the darkness. "I have no objection to encouraging them to make only good choices."

"They need some encouragement in that area," Lio said darkly. "I'd like to scrub out their brains. But I'll settle for humbling them."

Leaving the horses in the woods, they stepped through the closed gate of the fort and trod lightly across the bailey under veils. Entering the garrison, they found the men gathered around a trestle table. A roaring fire drove back the winter cold and cast their unshaven faces in brash light. The place stank of stale beer and staler sweat.

Lio, Cassia, and their Trial brothers fanned out to surround the mortals, careful to keep their distance from the fire pit. Knight stalked at Cassia's side.

One soldier rolled a high score to the guffaws and curses of his comrades. Lio bared his fangs and dropped his veils in unison with Mak and Lyros. The men's outbursts turned to shouts of terror.

The scent of sweat intensified. True to Mak's prediction, one of the mortals would need a clean pair of breeches. The men put their backs to the table, swords out in every direction.

Cassia gave them a fanged smile. At her side, Knight snarled, a fearsome sight with his hackles up and spittle dripping from his jaws. The slurs the men spat at her made Lio discard the idea of scrubbing their brains. He would rather twist their minds into painful shapes. But at their insults, Cassia's smile only widened.

You're enjoying this, Lio said.

These are the very men who used to leer at my handmaiden and me whenever I had to stay here. It is a delight to watch them cower.

"Hello, Commander," Cassia said to the drunkest of the men. "Do you remember me?"

He signed a glyph of Anthros over his heart. "You're the king's bitch. No lady now."

"I am no one's bitch, and he is not the king any longer. You will address me as Ambassador."

A smile spread across Lio's face as he watched her. This was his blood sorceress, his witch of the wilds.

She took a step closer to the man, fluttering her fingers in a spellcasting gesture.

He cowered back against the table. "As you s-say, Amba-bassador."

"Her Majesty Queen Solia the First is now the rightful monarch of Tenebra, and you are aiming that sword at the wrong side of the war. But we, her Hesperine allies, are prepared to grant you clemency."

One of the other men laughed. "Dead princess Solia back from the grave? Hesperines fighting a war in Tenebra? She's a heretic and a seductress, playing with our heads, men. Don't listen to her."

Mak rolled his eyes. "So that's what you meant by a remote garrison."

"Unfortunate," Lyros said. "It seems word hasn't traveled out here yet."

"It falls to us to bring tidings from Patria, then." Lio joined Cassia in a bit of theatrics. With a pull of his light magic, he cast the entire room in dramatic shadows, obscuring even the firelight. At the soldiers' fearful gasps, amusement danced in Cassia's aura.

Lio painted Solia's coat of arm above their heads in blue and gold light. "What we say is true. Solia's tomb has been empty for fifteen years. She has returned to her people, and the Full Council of Free Lords has given her their mandate. Hadria and Segetia fight side by side under her banner."

"Lucis will fall." Cassia's voice filled the room with quiet menace. "When he does, where will your fealty lie?"

One of the men tried to bolt for the door. Lio didn't see Mak move. The man ran headlong into Mak's grasp, and he tossed the mortal back at his comrades like a sack of potatoes. They dodged aside, managing not to impale any of their own men on their tangled blades.

"No one leaves until you choose your side." Lyros had shifted to block the doorway.

"We will show you Mercy if you do exactly as we say," Cassia declared. "Leave this place and ride for Patria, stopping only to rest when you must. Find Queen Solia at the fortress there and pledge your loyalty to her."

Lio levitated toward the warriors, letting the shadows gather around him to make him seem even taller. They craned their necks to look up a him.

"Do no harm to Solia's subjects on your way." He strengthened his voice with mind magic, and his words echoed deeply through the room. "If you steal from a family, we will know. If you lay a hand on a woman, we will know. And we will find you."

"What's our other choice?" demanded the bold one who had called Cassia a seductress.

"Choose Lucis's side," she said, "and fight us here and now."

The commander's eyes were rimmed in white. "If we do as you say, you'll let us leave? With our throats in one piece?"

"I have no desire whatsoever to taste your fetid blood," she informed him.

"We guarantee you safe passage," Lio promised, "if you adhere to our terms."

"We have conditions." The commander drew himself up, wiping sweat from his brow. "We'll go to Patria to see if what you say is true. That much we'll do. And we won't trouble anyone on the way. As long as you leave us be."

Lio and Cassia exchanged glances with their Trial brothers.

"Good enough for me." Mak cracked his knuckles, and the men startled. "Once they get to Patria, the Charge can encourage them to make good choices."

"I agree." Lyros crossed his arms. "We can rely on Solia's forces to give them a warm welcome."

"We'll be watching," Lio warned.

Cassia gave the mortals a dignified nod. "As the queen's sister, I give you my permission to leave our presence. Do not make me regret my kindness."

They bolted for the exit. Knight snapped at their heels, chasing them. Mak and Lyros flanked the door, making the terrified mortals scramble between them to escape.

Lio made sure they passed through a wave of his mind magic on their way out. They didn't feel a thing as he worked through their thoughts. He was careful, precise. With so much at stake, there was no room for error.

When he released their minds from his spell, he paused to consider the magnitude of the small act had just committed. He had rewritten a little piece of their lives. He acknowledged the gravity of it. But he did not regret it.

The four Hesperines waited, listening to the commotion down in the stables, then the pounding of hooves. At last the gatehouse shut with a final thud.

Cassia, Mak, and Lyros all burst out laughing.

"The looks on their faces!" Mak's shoulders shook.

"Nice aim," Lyros told him, grinning. "You tossed him between those swords like you were playing discus throw in the gymnasium."

Mak drew nearer to Lyros. "Do I get extra points for human throwing?"

"You won that match, to be sure." Lyros gave him a flirtatious salute to the victor. "And winner picks the prize, even when we're Abroad."

Cassia was smiling like a cat who had caught her mouse. She scratched Knight's chin, praising him for his performance.

Lio smiled back at her. *Have I mentioned that you're beautiful when you threaten people?*

A few times.

Allow me to mention it again, my fearsome Grace. I wonder how they would have reacted if you'd had your roses chase them out of the room?

Her momentary joy flickered out. He cursed inwardly. But no, he decided. He wouldn't apologize for reminding her of her power.

"The keep is ours," he said. "There are no mortals at risk anywhere near. We can disappear here without putting anyone at risk."

Lyros righted one of the spilled mugs. "This will make an excellent base of operations while we continue searching for Miranda."

"Yes." Mak examined a bow the mortals had left behind. "We should cast thelemantic wards around the fort before we do anything else."

Lyros nodded. "If the mortals carry tales and Gift Collectors come looking for us here, we need to be prepared."

"They won't carry any tales," Lio said.

Cassia gave him a questioning look, her brow furrowed.

"I was gentle," he assured her. "I simply made sure they are confused about a few key details. If anyone asks, they'll recall us ambushing them not far southeast of Patria. If they mention that to any Hesperines, the Charge will look for us in within their own perimeter. And if Kallikrates raids any minds to find us, a false location is all he will see."

Cassia looked stricken. "Lio. I'm sorry you had to do that."

"I am not. If I must cost them a few thoughts so we can spare their lives, I will."

"That was…" Lyros hesitated. "Necessary, I think. We can rely on their superstitions to make them obey our commands. But we can't trust the Collector not to exploit them."

Mak nodded. "The less they remember about us, the safer they are."

But everyone's amusement had died.

Lio looked at Cassia. "After we've veiled and warded the place, we can start looking for Lustra portals."

She made no promises about using her magic. Avoiding his eyes, she looked down at Knight again. A useless evasion, when their Grace Union was his window on her soul—and her regrets.

THE MOST IMPORTANT LESSON

Once their spell was finished, Lio found Cassia in the stables. Knight drowsed on a pile of hay while the Warmbloods munched grain in their stalls. Cassia had found a brush somewhere and was running it over Freckles' side with steady strokes. The little mare preened under the attention.

All Lio could see in Cassia's thoughts was the smooth rhythm of those brush strokes. Her utter concentration on the repetitive task was as effective as greenhouse diagrams at deflecting his mind. Almost.

He stroked Moonflower's nose. "Thank you for seeing to the horses while we were casting."

"This place is hardly up to Warmblood standards, but I did my best. The provisions the men left behind will keep our horses and Knight fed. Where are Mak and Lyros?"

"They want to keep watch until they're confident no one is probing our defenses."

Before he could say more, she pressed on. "Are you ready to look for Lustra portals?"

So she was determined not to talk yet, was she? Using arguments about her magic to get him to do what she wished would not work a second time. Especially when he knew she didn't actually want to use her power. By the time they finished their search, he would coax her to open up to him.

"The tower looks quite ancient," he said. "Let's start there."

She put the brush away and turned toward the door, giving him a glimpse of her neck before her long hair swung to hide it again. He followed her and Knight out of the stables, ducking to avoid hitting his head on the door frame. Her hound's paws left broad tracks in the dirty snow as they crossed the bailey, while Cassia's light steps left hardly any imprint at all.

She paused, looking to the sky. He followed her gaze to see a large hawk circling above. That was the animal form which had earned her ancestor the title "Changing Queen." Cassia herself had transformed into a hawk when Ebah's spirit had briefly granted her shape-changing abilities. He wondered if it was a sign.

As they watched, the hawk took a dive into the trees, oddly silent. It emerged a moment later with a small, broken shape clutched in its talons. Cassia shuddered and headed up the front steps of the keep.

"When did you last stay here?" Lio asked.

Her aura stirred with memories. "Three years ago."

"How many times?" He opened the weathered door for her and propped himself against it, half filling the doorway.

She slipped through, so close to him that their bodies almost brushed. "Twice. The winter of the Equinox Summit would have been my third, if I hadn't made it to court instead."

Before she was out of reach, he caught her cheek in his hand and turned her face toward him. "You almost spent that winter here instead of with me."

"But I didn't."

"Thank you for the risks you took to make that happen."

She clutched his hand briefly, then turned and went further into the keep.

"Will you show me the room where you stayed?" he asked.

"If you think it's useful." She led him past a broad, empty chamber on the ground floor and up a curving staircase, higher into the tower. Knight leapt upward ahead of her. Lio walked close behind her, and her aura tingled with awareness of him.

They entered a shadowy room, and he pricked his thumb on his fang to conjure a spell light from his blood. The warm glow illuminated a round room with one bed, one trunk, and a washstand. It was even worse than her rooms at Solorum. Old anger simmered in him at the neglect she had suffered in her mortal life.

There was something about this claustrophobic room that bothered him. Something wrong about it. But he couldn't put his finger on precisely what that wrongness was.

He only knew he ought to pull Cassia down onto that bed and replace her memories of lonely nights here.

Knight embarked on a thorough sniff of the place and sneezed. Cassia patted him as he passed her to investigate another corner. "Yes, you remember this place, don't you, love? Not fit for dogs or ladies."

"But perhaps it once was." Lio cast a cleaning spell over the room to peel away the layers of dust and old torch grime. Flakes of plaster crumbled to the floor, revealing the ancient stones beneath. The leather flaps over the windows blew back, letting moonlight in through their rounded arches. "There is neglected beauty here."

"And magic too, we can hope." Cassia set her gardening satchel down on the table by the bed. "Strange to think I might have walked past portals here without ever knowing it. I'll see if the Lustra is telling my intuition anything."

He rested his hands on her tense shoulders. "No, Cassia. I want you to cast."

She whirled to face him. "We just found what might be a safe place for us, and you want me to draw attention with a spell?"

"We've covered this place in thelemantic wards. No one will detect your casting."

"The spells at Nike's forge did nothing to cover my magic!"

"Those were not my spells."

As they stood there facing each other, the air grew full of their latent magics. Knight put his ears back and trotted off to keep watch outside the door.

Lio leaned closer to Cassia, shrinking the small, taut distance between them. "I am your Grace. Your blood is in my blood, your magic in my magic. We know the Lustra has marked me. If any spells can conceal your magic, mine can."

Her canines were so far extended, they must be aching for him. "Now is hardly the time for testing theories! I have no wish to repeat what happened at the lighthouse. We cannot afford to take that risk."

"Why, Cassia?" he demanded.

Her hands closed into fists, and her voice rose. "Because every time I let go of my power, I hurt someone. I hurt *you*."

He gritted his teeth, on the verge of releasing the magic in his own veins. The trunk lid rattled.

Cassia retreated to the window, flattening her hands on the sill. Her voice fell. "I don't blame you for being angry."

He stayed where he was for the moment, giving her more space. "You know I'm not angry with *you*, don't you?"

"Yes," she said, her voice small. "After the way my father treated me, I know I have a tendency to assume that when someone is angry, they must be angry at me. But the mind healers have reminded me again and again to stop doing that to myself."

"I never want you to think my anger is directed at you."

"I know you better than that. You always give me the benefit of the doubt. You are never disappointed in me. It would be easier if you were."

"What do you mean by that?"

"I can feel how angry you are over everything we've lost, over how my magic is nothing like what we hoped for. Yet you are so unfailingly gentle with me. It makes my heart break even more at what I've done to you."

"Oh, Cassia." He dragged his hands through his hair. "My newgift. This is something you need to understand about the Blood Union. It only tells us what someone is feeling, not why they are feeling it."

"Grace Union is different."

"Not when we're hiding from each other. Just as you said when you proposed to me, our words are so important, even now that our souls are bound together."

She half turned to him, wrapping her arms around herself. "Then tell me. Why are you angry, if not because my magic cost you everything?"

He strode to her side and turned her to face him, pulling her against him. Their gazes locked. Her eyes were dilated.

"You have that backward," he said. "You did not cost me everything. Everything has always tried to cost me you."

"Lio." She sounded breathless. "I will not allow this negotiation to end against the wall."

"I agree. The bed would be better. Those visions we saw in the stone circle will give us no mercy until we act them out."

"No," she gasped. "I won't take from your vein again. Not until we talk."

At last, he had persuaded her to talk. He had hoped her sheer stubbornness to resist her Craving would prove a powerful motivation.

"Tell me why you're angry, then," she demanded.

"Orthros promised that you could embrace your magic without fear. That it would be safe for you to be powerful. Then the moment you spread your wings, they punished you for it. I am so angry at how our own people have treated you."

"Oh." Her surprise was a flicker of light in their Union, but her gaze fell. "It's not their fault. I knowingly broke the Queens' laws."

"Our laws are supposed to be just. Where is the justice in punishing you for your own nature? Our elders taught us that all are welcome under Hespera's Eyes. When did they decide our profane goddess would not accept your thorns?"

"They accepted my roses. Just not our weapons."

"They, who have killed war mages with their bare hands and even now have voted that Hesperines should march to war."

She pressed her hand to his medallion. "We were always supposed to be diplomats. You worked your whole life for the title of Ambassador. You were born into Blood Komnena, the long-awaited hope of our elder house. Don't tell me you do not feel the loss."

"I do. I feel it so bitterly. I gave all of myself to the diplomatic service, and I earned my seat in the Firstblood Circle as Firstgift Komnenos. I proved to our people over and over that they can trust my judgment. And this is how they repay me. By casting out my Grace."

She drew a sharp breath, and he felt the stab of pain in her aura. "Oh, Lio. This is so much worse than if you were angry at me."

"What? Why?"

"You're not angry at me. You're angry at our people." Tears welled in her eyes, wavering gold. "I haven't merely cost you Orthros. I've cost you your love for it."

"You know that when faced with unbearable choices, I will always choose your love. My first loyalty is to our Oath, my Grace."

She hid her face against his chest, her sobs quiet against his heart. He held her while her weeping wracked her and waves of grief tore out of her. They'd had everything they ever wanted for a night, only for it all to disappear.

Lio bared his fangs, his blood pounding with the injustice of it. "I will not let anyone punish you for who you are. Remember what I said, Cassia. I want you to break everything in your path."

"I can't bear to hurt anyone again."

"Look at me, my rose."

At last, she lifted her tear-stained face.

"You taught me something, one of the most important magic lessons of my life. And now it's my turn to teach you."

She scrubbed her hand over her eyes. "What could I have taught you about magic?"

"Think of that night after Martyr's Pass, when I believed I had slaughtered hundreds of mortals with my magic. What did you tell me?"

"That you could never hurt anyone like that. It's not in you."

"You were right. It turned out I was not to blame for their deaths. You taught me not to fear my own power. And I will not ever allow you to fear yours."

"You understand." The words rushed out of her. "I do fear it."

"I know. The first time you touched your roses, their thorns cut. Now you're afraid to repeat that pain. But that is the nature of your magic. It is not easy. It is not tame. Do not expect it to be. Let it be what it is."

"What if it is not Hesperine?"

"That doesn't matter. *You* are Hesperine. Trust yourself, as you told me to do in Martyr's Pass. If you unleash your power, your Hesperine heart will set its limits, just as mine did."

She swayed against him, as if standing on a precipice. "That is such a terrifying risk to take."

"I will take that risk with you. But in return, I need all your courage. I need you to *try*. You will never learn if you do not cast. Will you do that for me?"

"For you, Lio, I will do anything."

"Then let go," he said against her lips.

She raked her mouth over his, his starving queen, finally allowing herself to her own banquet table. He served up his tongue to her, and she lit into his mouth. Her kiss made his fangs unsheathe. She sucked them, turning his canines into her next course.

She pushed him, putting him where she wanted him with all her strength. His back hit stone, and he smiled into her wicked kiss. All her resolutions about not ending up against the wall had been in vain. And he intended to make the most of it.

ON WING

*L*ET GO. LIO ECHOED his demand with a flash of power in her mind.

Cassia's magic flared back at him, and she let out a sharp groan.

Yes. He caressed her with his thelemancy again. *Your magic feels so good.*

Another measure of her power unfurled. She slid her knee up his body, the inside of her thigh rubbing his leg through their robes. He found her bare knee with his hand and pushed the fabric out of their way.

He let waves of his magic roll into her, coaxing out hers. *Is this what you need?*

Pleasure eddied through her aura, and her magic waxed. *Oh, Goddess, yes.*

You know it's safe to lose control with me. Let's remind your magic of that. He kissed his way down her neck.

He bit her throat slowly, not breaking her skin, and listened to the guttural sound she made. Slipping his palm up and down the soft skin of her inner thigh, he matched the intimate touches with strokes of magic in their Union. Ephemeral tendrils of power pressed up under the surface of her aura. He could almost taste it, and his mouth watered.

He cupped the tender curve of her breast through her clothes. Massaging her, he bit harder.

You're torturing me, she accused.

He trailed his other hand all the way up her thigh and slipped his fingers into her curls. He found her warm but tight.

I want you, she protested. *I want you* now.

Your fear of your power is making it hard for you to relax tonight.

That's not fair.

Our magic and our bodies are one. You have to release one for the other to follow. He smiled down at her. *Fortunately, I can help with both.*

He tugged her collar down and pressed her breast up out of her robes. Holding the small handful taut, he rolled her bare nipple between his fingers. The heady sensations flowed into their Union. Between her legs, he stroked into her slight dampness over and over until she was wet enough to slick his entire hand.

His body was torturing him now, ready to feel that wet heat wrapped around him. She squirmed on his fingers, and he groaned at the wanton invitation.

Unreleased magic shuddered through her, and her fear broke through the haze of their pleasure.

That made him even angrier. She should *never* feel fear in his arms.

Do you want me to stop? he asked.

She threaded her fingers through his hair. *No. I refuse to stop.*

Your determination is one of the most beautiful things about you.

He feathered reassuring kisses over her neck. Keeping up a slow, teasing rhythm at her breast, he began to swirl his fingers around her most sensitive bud.

She brought her knees up on either side of him and pushed him more firmly against the wall. Her breath warmed his throat.

He lifted his head, his eyes widening. Her feet weren't touching the floor. An elated laugh came out of him. "Look! You're levitating."

She looked down at herself. Then she wobbled against him, grabbing at the front of his robes.

He caught her with a touch of his magic. "Look at me."

She met his gaze, and he saw hope in her eyes at last.

"Forget about everything but how much you want this." He drove two fingers inside her, stroking her kalux with his thumb. "Trust your instincts."

She canted her hips into his touch, her knees clamping around him. Supporting her back with one arm, he lowered his mouth to her breast to suck her nipple, letting his fangs tease against her soft flesh.

The barriers in her mind fell, and all her fearsome Will honed in on them, on *him*. He had captured all her attention. This feeing was worth tearing apart kingdoms for again and again.

She became buoyant in his arms. He eased off his levitation spell, and she hovered on his hand, at his mouth, arching into his licks and touches with leverage from her newfound power.

He laughed again and wrapped his arm more securely around her. When he swept them up toward the ceiling, she let out a cry of delight. They spun together, floating on her power and his.

"Eyes on me," he said.

She didn't look away, but when he turned her onto her back, she wrapped her arms and legs around him.

"Trust yourself," he reminded her.

They held their breaths as slowly, surely, they let each other go.

She hovered beneath him, her fangs untamed and lips rosy from their kisses. Her hair floated around her, his braid wavering on the unseen current of her blood magic. She reached out slowly, touching his chest.

"I'm not going to fall," she said, her aura shining with wonder.

"You've found your wings."

"For you," she said.

"Will you tell me…" He hesitated, afraid of the answer. But selfishly, he wanted to know. "Does this feel as good as changing into a hawk and flying on real wings?"

She spread her arms wide, as if testing the air, her gaze never leaving his. "This, my Grace, is better."

"Take me like this." His voice came out low and rough.

With fearless touches and hungry tugs, they stripped each other in midair, letting their robes flutter down to the floor below. When they were bare, she pressed herself against him, skin to skin. With a tentative push, she rolled them over, and again. A fanged smile spread across her face, and with a confident shove, she levitated them upward until she had him pinned against the ceiling.

"I hope you know this is the most erotic moment of my eternal life," he said.

"No." The green-gold rings of her irises shrank even further. "This next moment will be."

She floated down his body until she was on eye level with his erection. Like a sorceress summoning him to her, she gave the underside of his shaft a luxurious stroke with her hand. He bit back an oath.

Holding his shaft, she bared her fangs at his head. Her tongue darted out from between her sharp canines to lick the damp tip.

"Your prediction"—he managed—"was correct."

Her power enveloped him, and he floated entirely on her magic. She brought her free hand down to cup his moskos, caressing him with her dexterous immortal fingers. He was entirely in her hands.

She swirled her tongue in slow circles around his head. He didn't breathe, didn't move, as if caught in an enchantment. Her every careful stroke sent him spinning deeper into her spell.

Her eyes glowed up at him from beneath her lashes. *Oh, Lio. This flavor of you...I've been deprived.*

This was...worth the wait.

She hummed her agreement, then dipped lower along the underside of his shaft. She ran lascivious licks along the full length of his vein, ending with little flicks of her tongue just under the tip. He forgot what words were, riveted to the vision of his fanged Grace dining on his erection.

She adjusted her grip on his shaft, then boldly took his head in her mouth. He felt the soft brush of her puckered lips and the damp glide of her tongue, shielding him from her fangs. With exquisite control, she withdrew, then skimmed him into her mouth again.

His nails dug into the stone as he held himself still. His eyes were about to roll back in his head, but he focused on her, unwilling to miss the sight of her sliding him between her lips. A shudder went through him, and he arched into her grip. She guided him with her hands and tongue, floating back to adjust how deep she took him.

She was in perfect command of the intimate magic she was performing on him. Her every little motion seemed to anticipate his fantasies as the thoughts formed in the primal parts of his mind. Every time he thought he would explode and this would be over, she gave him a reprieve to prolong his pleasure. Then she took him again, working him nearly to his limit. Their Union grew richer still, and he tossed his head back, surrendering another, deeper part of himself to her.

Just when he thought she would withdraw again, she didn't. She gazed up at his face and worked him with her relentless tongue until he broke. He poured into her mouth, her name pounding through his mind. *Cassia.* She held him through the spasms of his release, swallowing hard.

At last she pulled back, licking her lips with a moan of delight. *Now I know what all of you tastes like to my immortal tongue.*

He tried to remember how to speak. To think, she had been worried about trying this with her new fangs. *Cassia, that was…*

Amusement danced in her eyes. *Orthros's canon of erotic texts is full of excellent advice on how to manage one's fangs in these situations. Did my studies pay off, Sir Scholar?*

He pulled her up his body and gave her his answer with a heated kiss on her throat.

"Did I make you hungry?" she breathed.

When he bit her, she gave a little cry, and her levitation lifted her higher against him. He drank the afterglow of her feast on him, slipping a hand between her legs to feel how wet his pleasure had made her. The confidence she'd found in this moment was a warm, heady flavor in her blood. And beneath it, the promise of her magic, ready to be set free. His body woke to the taste of her power, ready to make her lose control in return.

He flipped her around. Her gaze fell to the room below. He felt her weight again as her levitation slipped.

"Don't look down," he said. "Eyes on me."

That drew her gaze to his again. Now he watched her eyes glaze as he thrust up into her. They rode their combined levitation spells, grinding together against the ceiling. He gritted his teeth against the ache in his fangs, watching her face to see her expose her canines in a grimace of pleasure. Her hunger and magic swelled in their Union, her control slipping away.

Stop resisting, he said. *Give in to your hunger. It's all right.*

She brought her fangs down and opened his vein. As his blood spilled into her mouth, her magic broke through her fear. Her power exploded into their Union, into the stone above them and the earth below. Into him, the most exultant rush in his every vein, muscle, and bone. A growl tore out of him against her throat.

That's my queen.

Suddenly they were no longer weightless. The Lustra pulled them back down toward the ground. They gasped together, losing their hold on each other's throats.

He landed on top of her on the bed, catching himself on his arms. She threw her head back and arched under him on the waves of power crashing out of her. Every dark, lush crest of her magic slammed into him.

He watched her, wild beneath him, and drove deep into every undulation of her body. *That's right,* he urged in her mind. *No fear. Just power. Let it all out for me.*

Her moans of relief seemed to well up from her very soul. He covered her mouth with his to swallow her cries and the magic. She clamped her legs around him as she climaxed, her hips bucking with one final rush of magic. The grip and release inside her pulled him out of control with her, capturing him in the current of her power. He sank his fangs into her throat again, needing to bite through the pleasure tearing him apart.

Aftershocks moved through them both as her channeling faded. They lay tangled on the creaking bed, and she framed his face her hands. "Lio."

She flexed her power in their Union again, a bold, exploratory touch. Sensation rippled along his body, a tease where they were joined.

"I'm not out of magic," she whispered. "Does it ever end?"

"Let's find out," he dared her.

A look of determination came over her flushed face. The next infusion of magic she gave him left him gasping.

They made love again, this time on gentler currents of her power, with heated sighs and soft, intense touches. They left bites on each other and blood on the blankets. At last their Craving and their magics were satisfied, and they lay still.

He rolled them onto their sides. "What you just gave me is all I need this Winter Solstice."

She touched her brow to his. "Happy Gift Night, my Grace."

When she didn't follow those words with any apologies, he felt he had won a victory against her guilt.

She pushed up on her elbow, coming out of her daze to take in the room around them. "No roses have gone wild in here."

"I told you I'm a safe container for your magic."

She rubbed at a smear of blood on his bicep. "I suppose I should stop fearing the consequences of this particular magical experiment."

"Try," he encouraged her softly. "Goddess, please stop worrying about it. You know how much I want it."

"Then I won't deny you." A small smile came to her face. Then her gaze fixed on something behind him. "Oh. I think the tower absorbed some of my magic, too."

He rolled over to look. Where the new plaster was crumbling off the ancient stone, a few tendrils of ivy had sprouted out of the wall. Spreading along the cracks in the mortar, the fresh green leaves promised that the magic they had come looking for was waiting to be found.

THE IVY REAWAKENED SOMETHING in Cassia that her fear and horror had beaten out of her in recent nights. A yearning for her power.

Lio smiled at her. "I think this is a clear sign we'll find portals here."

She smoothed her hair. "I wonder if it's common to mate the portals out of hiding or if that's our special talent."

His smile turned to a sly grin. "I believe more testing will be required."

She laughed. "Alas, further experimenting will have to wait. Mak and Lyros will be back anytime now, and they'll be ready to see what's through the portal."

They collected their clothes, and Lio cast more cleaning spells. Just in case, they buckled on their weapons again as well. Knight padded back into the room at last.

"Ohh," Cassia cooed, rubbing Knight's ears. "That was rather too much magic for your keen liegehound senses, wasn't it?"

Knight gave Lio a decidedly reproving look.

Cassia stifled a laugh. "It wasn't entirely his fault, you know. We were mutually responsible."

Lio crossed his arms and gazed back at her dog. "You'd best get accustomed to it, Sir Knight. I won't have your lady holding back her power to soothe anyone's feelings."

Knight huffed at him, but looked away first.

Cassia covered her smile with a hand. "You just won a staring contest with a liegehound."

"That might be my greatest accomplishment yet, after persuading him to make room on the bed for me."

Cassia gave Knight an abundance of consolation pats. But his anxious need for her attention prodded her worries again. He had seemed to accept her after her return from seclusion. But tonight, unleashing her magic had sent him retreating.

"His kind are sensitive to magic, that's all," Lio reassured her.

He was right. But liegehounds were more sensitive to their opposing magic than anything else—the blood magic that now fueled her every heartbeat.

It had taken Knight time to adjust to being around other Hesperines' magic. Would he ever be fully comfortable with that magic being a part of her?

Lio put a soothing hand on Cassia's back. "Come, let's see about the portals."

Cassia turned her attention to the ivy growing out of the stones. Her magic now saturated the walls, and another's power had come to life in response. She could feel someone else's spells spidering through the tower as if the ivy's roots grew all through the stone, guiding her along currents of magic.

"Hawks hunt these woods," she said, "and ivy thrives in the walls. Those are Ebah's symbols."

"I think this tower belonged to the Changing Queen, as surely as the Mage King lit the fire at the lighthouse."

"This isn't the portal, but it is a…" She searched for words from their magic lessons. "It's a manifestation of the tower's magic."

"Astonishing."

She put her hand over his and rested his palm amid the ivy leaves. "Can you sense that, too?"

His power flared in their Union, seeking. "I'm aware of the sheer amount of Lustra magic here, but the details aren't clear to my senses."

She thought back on what he had taught her about the paradigms of magic: mageia like Solia's affinity for fire, manteia like his thelemancy, and hulaia—her Lustra magic. "This ivy is an arcane link to the various spells here. They aren't anchored like mageic or manteic enchantments are. I would describe them as rooted, with hulaic magic running through them."

He let out a soft breath behind her. "What an incredible discovery. These spells have endured for untold centuries without a living mage to replenish them. This tells us that Silvicultrixes have the power to create enchantments that are sustained by the Lustra itself."

"The strongest concentration of magic is somewhere above us."

His aura was bright with excitement. "Let's follow it."

Cassia took the lead up the spiral stair. When they entered the chamber at the top of the tower, Lio had to duck under the sharp slope of the roof. Knight, rather than sniffing their new surroundings, froze on the threshold, ears perked and tail out.

Dust tickled Cassia's nose, and she wrinkled it at the piles of mundane barrels and crates. "Really? The men of this epoch turned the most magical chamber in the Changing Queen's tower into a storage room?"

"Foolish mortals." Lio knelt between a moldering rug and a rusted trunk and ran his fingers over the planks of the floor. "Can you feel this?"

She crouched beside him. No spell marks were visible on the grimy wooden floor, but she could sense them. "Oh, yes. There was a ritual symbol here."

"How many nodes?" he asked.

"Three times three," she answered.

"Another nonagram like the one Mak and Lyros found at the lighthouse."

"Like the nine standing stones, too."

Lio got to his feet, bracing one hand on the ceiling. "Our Trial brothers will have our fangs if we experiment on this without them."

Cassia nodded. "Let's wait for them."

They had moved a few of the crates and barrels out of the way when they heard Mak and Lyros calling them from below. They headed for the stairs.

Cassia paused at the top. "I wonder if I can levitate down, on purpose this time."

Lio gave her a kiss that left her blood pounding and her magic singing. "There. That should give your new instinct for levitation some encouragement."

She realized she was nose to nose with him and glanced down to find her feet hovering off the floor. Blushing, she didn't try to concentrate on the spell, but let her intuition take over. She didn't sink.

Knight circled her fretfully, nosing the bottom of her shoes. Lio shook his head and put a reassuring arm around Knight's neck.

Cassia managed to float down a few steps without falling and breaking an ankle. Holding her arms out slightly, she tried a pirouette. Lio caught her before she knocked one of the torches off the wall.

"Perhaps try floating in a single direction for now," he suggested with an affectionate smile.

"Good idea." She focused her Will on *down.*

She swept along the curve of the stairwell while Lio walked down with a very puzzled Knight.

They found Mak and Lyros waiting on the first floor. When Cassia floated in, Mak beamed at her. "Well, look who learned to levitate!"

She gave them a bow midair, and they all clapped for her. Looking down, she tried to lower herself to the floor again. She floated a bit higher. "Oh dear."

Lio pulled her down and held her until she was sure she wasn't going to float off again.

"Good timing," Lyros said. "That will certainly be an asset out here. How did you manage it?"

"It turns out I simply needed motivation," she replied.

Lyros looked at Lio. "Did you toss her off the top of the tower?"

Mak shook his head. "We would have heard screaming."

"Not under my veils," Lio said innocently.

"He did no such thing." Thorns, Cassia really needed to learn veils next so she could conceal it whenever she blushed like this.

"Ahh." Lyros gave a knowing nod. "That kind of motivation. Clever, Lio."

Mak snickered. "That was certainly a more pleasant way to learn than jumping off Wisdom's Precipice."

"We also looked for portals," Cassia interjected.

Lio held up his hands. "And we waited for you before experimenting with anything."

"Diligently searching for portals this entire time, were you?" Mak inquired. "Mmm hmm."

"Say you two," Lio replied, "returning from a one-hour watch that lasted much longer than an hour."

"My Grace is very diligent in his duties," Lyros said with an amused tilt to his brows.

They climbed the stairs, finding nothing but more abandoned rooms on their way up. At the top of the tower, they gathered in the center of the chamber where everyone could stand up straight.

"It's definitely like the nonagram we saw at the lighthouse," Lyros agreed after Lio had explained their findings.

"Any ideas what to do with it?" Mak asked Cassia.

She opened her senses to the faded ritual pattern still perceptible to her mind's eye. Nothing happened.

Lio took up his position behind her and rested his hands on her shoulders. "Ready to try an active casting?"

Her fears stirred again, but she drew a steadying breath and leaned into his hands. She sank into herself, and her connection to the Lustra felt like a steady stream, not a river raging out of its banks during flood season.

Lio squeezed her shoulders. *See how much better you feel when your power isn't bottled up inside you?*

I suppose we'll simply have to wear it out in bed prior to any spell I cast.

Your magic tutor approves this plan. I would also like to point out that channeling into me when we feast does more than take the edge off your power. That helps you build your intuitive ability to manipulate the magic, the same way rigorous training exercises teach a warrior's muscles what to do in battle.

In that case, you're welcome to train my magical muscles anytime.

You know I always make our magic lessons as pleasurable as possible.

The Lustra's power seeped up into her. Beneath that gentle trickle, she sensed a deep, vast reservoir.

"The tower is built on a letting site," she realized.

She was unprepared for Lio's reaction. His determination hit their Union with a force she felt to her toes.

"We found one." His voice was tight with emotion. "Is it damaged like the one at Paradum?"

"No."

"Kallikrates never got to this one. Can you sense the beast magic and soothsaying in it?"

She hesitated, also unprepared for her own deep sense of frustration. "I don't know. It all feels like power to me. It's not like my letting site, where I can feel my blood magic and plant magic. My real affinity."

"The completed triune affinity is your real magic. One of the Silvicultrixes' original, intact letting sites could hold the key to awakening the rest of your power."

"Right now, the key to that door is what we need to focus on."

"We'll talk about this more later."

Cassia bit her lip and opened herself cautiously to the new and unknown letting site. The power she left untapped loomed below, tempting, terrifying. She let a mere rivulet of Lustra magic flow through her and Rosethorn into the nonagram.

The fabric of the world shifted. The stones beneath their feet turned to rich soil. Vines snapped around them, and the walls were gone, replaced by walls and arches of ivy, so tangled she could see only glimpses of a strange sky above them.

Lio, their Trial brothers, and Knight were still beside her, trapped with her in a labyrinth of her ancestor's making.

TRIAL BY LEAF

"Right," Mak said, "I'd say that's a sign the Changing Queen wanted this secret to stay secret."

Knight didn't move to investigate their surroundings. Calm but alert, he stood close to Cassia. She put a hand on him. "Is this like the other Lustra passages? None of you can step right now?"

The other three shook their heads.

"This is astonishing." Lio reached out toward one of the ivy walls.

Cassia tried to catch his hand and stop him, but her new immortal reflexes weren't quite as fast as his yet.

He rubbed a leaf between his thumb and forefinger. "It's solid. Not an illusion, then. I can also tell it's not some kind of waking dream created by mind magic to trick our brains into thinking all of this is real. It *is* real."

Lyros shook his head. "No elemental magic or other mageia can manipulate reality like this."

"This isn't mageia or manteia," Lio said. "It's hulaia. The raw power of creation. We're walking through the lost paradigm of magic right now, as it hasn't been seen since the Silvicultrixes were at the peak of their power."

Cassia drew Rosethorn. "I'll have more appreciation for the magical significance after we find our way out of this. All of you stay close to me."

Lyros nodded. "If we search each turn and mark the ways we've already tried, we should be able to find the correct path."

"I'll draw a map as we go." Lio pulled a scroll out of his case.

"How shall we mark our way?" Cassia asked.

"Not with anything magical," Lio suggested, "including blood. We don't know how other powers interact with this spell."

Mak pulled a small pouch out of his pocket and gave it a forlorn look. "All I brought with me are Tuura's candied almonds."

Lyros patted his arm. "A necessary sacrifice."

Mak sighed and dropped one of the treats on the ground.

"All right. Might as well try forward first." Cassia led the way along the twisting path ahead of them.

Their steps sounded muffled in the maze. The only other sound was a whisper of leaves against leaves. They'd walked several paces when Lyros, bringing up the rear, cursed.

She looked back. Their starting point and the almond they'd left there were nowhere to be seen. A completely different intersection of three paths lay behind them now. Cassia whirled to look ahead, only to find the single trail had changed into a fork in the path.

"So much for marking our way," Lyros said grimly. "We can't map a labyrinth that grows into a different shape with every step we take."

Mak popped one of the candied almonds in his mouth, then slipped another one to Knight. "Tuura's provisions are saved."

Lyros's expression betrayed a hint of frustration as he glanced at Mak.

Mak shrugged too casually. "Maybe thinking isn't the right tactic in here. Cassia, what feels like the right way to go? Your intuition seems to be working just fine, at least."

Cassia knew when someone was having two conversations at once, the one you could hear and understand and the hidden one beneath. She aways knew what to do with a secret layer of meaning that held political significance.

But hearing the layers of hurt in Mak and Lyros's conversation, she felt out of her depth. Love was always harder than politics. She had to figure out how to help.

They're veiling their emotions, she lamented to Lio silently.

I don't understand. They seemed all right when they got back from their patrol.

Have they said anything to you about how things are between them since… we left Orthros?

I wish. Perhaps if we each try talking to one of them when the other isn't listening, we can get them to confide in us.

All the more reason we need to get out of this maze.

Cassia gave them both a reassuring smile. "That was a clever plan, Lyros. I'm sorry my ancestors' magic is so tricky. Let's try Mak's excellent suggestion next."

Very diplomatic, Lio said in her mind, putting his scroll away.

Lyros rubbed his neck and nodded. Mak sighed.

Cassia consulted her intuition again, as she had when they'd searched for the stone circle. She felt a tug and started walking. Several paces brought them to an open circle in the ivy maze.

"This looks promising," Lio said.

A soft rushing sound chased his words. The rustle became the groan of vines.

The circle of ivy started to grow, shrinking the space around them.

"No. Hurry, back this way!" Cassia dashed for the archway they had just come through.

The ivy grew together faster than immortals could run, sealing the only way out.

They retreated to the center of the circle and put their backs to each other to face the advancing ivy.

"Our wards aren't working!" Mak cried. "We can't cast anything in here."

Chain belts rattled as the other three drew their weapons. The ring of vine walls coiled tighter. stealing their time to strategize as Cassia wracked her mind for a plan.

Yet Lio's voice was calm. "Pretend the ivy vines are those roses you retrained in the Ritual hall. Use your magic to make it grow where you Will."

It had taken her many nights of effort to achieve that. Now she had mere moments.

But she didn't confess her self-doubt aloud in front of their Trial brothers, who had so bravely defended her before. She wouldn't let everyone down this time. She couldn't.

There was only one person here who could save them from rabid Lustra magic, and it was her.

This time her emotions didn't hold her power back. They drove her magic deep down into the letting site. The instant she tapped it, the full force of its power shot up through her, rooting her to the spot where she stood.

Not her letting site, with its gentle, ravenous blood magic. Not the wounded beast at Paradum. A living letting site, ancient and lush, pouring forth the power of the Lustra through the stems and branches of her body. She held out her hands, her breath coming hard. She felt so alive.

"Cassia, it's only growing faster!" Mak's warning reached her from a distance.

A coil of ivy slid around her throat, caressing. Then began to tighten.

She gasped and clutched the tendril, but it was too strong even for her immortal hand to break. She sliced at her ivy noose with her dagger. Where she cut off a branch, two more grew in its place.

She looked frantically around her. Lio held off a branch with Final Word. Knight snapped, growling, but every time his jaws tore through a vine, there was always another.

She bared her fangs at the vicious plants. She had not reclaimed her magic only for her own legacy to defeat her now. She would not let the Changing Queen's power treat her like a foolish apprentice, not when she was the last and only Silvicultrix it had.

And yet, she was an apprentice. None of the skills she'd learned so far were of any use. Not intuition. Not a battle of Will with the raw power of a letting site. Least of all her dagger, the most basic of her artifacts, which she had clumsily wielded when she had no knowledge of magic at all.

She needed advanced magic. Kalos's lesson came back to her. *...you need a triune focus...the most powerful Lustra artifacts...*

She closed her hand over her pendant so tightly that the ivy carvings dug into her skin. Its magic, familiar and yet unknown, whispered to her. She tried to feed her power into it.

It didn't respond except with those whispers, almost but not quite understandable, mocking her.

She let out a cry of disbelief. What good was the Changing Queen's focus if it did nothing against her traps?

Lio and Lyros stood on opposite sides of the group, their staff and spear braced against the oncoming wall of ivy, their arms straining. Mak swung the Star of Orthros at the green mass, leaving a swath of damage that closed in an instant. A vine snaked up his leg, tracing the laces of his sandal.

She tightened her hand on Rosethorn's hilt, remembering his kind words.

I couldn't bear for you to lose it. You can't replace an artifact like that, not when your battles have created it for you.

What had Kalos said? *A focus has to be made. You give it life by using it during rituals.*

Perhaps the pendant wasn't the only focus she had. Perhaps it wasn't the right one for this ritual.

Perhaps Rosethorn was not a beginner's artifact at all.

She let her eyes slide shut and placed her trust in the constant power of her spade.

The letting site honed in on the blade. Its staggering power concentrated into a focused current. She Willed it out at the vines.

As if time had stopped, they froze. The air seemed ready to explode with a single held breath of magic.

She pushed harder with her magic through the dagger. The vines whipped backward, retreating. They reformed themselves into still, tame walls.

Lio faced her and took hold of her arms. Only he could be smiling at a time like this. "Well done, Silvicultrix."

She wrapped her arms around him. "That was too close."

"It was brilliant casting." Lyros leaned on Night's Aim. "Not everyone can learn and adapt under duress like that."

Mak ran his hands through his hair. "I'm sorry my suggestion got us deeper into trouble."

Lyros put an arm around him. "Mine wasn't any better."

Cassia held out her dagger. "Mak, you're the one who got us out of trouble. I don't know what I would have done if you hadn't saved my spade and reforged it for me."

He frowned in confusion. "But cutting the vines with the weapon didn't work."

"Casting through it did. It's not just a weapon, Mak. It's one of my three foci."

The regret on his expressive face cleared, giving way to a hint of a smile. "Really? Those artifacts Kalos told you about?"

She nodded. "I need three to form a complete triune focus. They're incredibly hard to make, especially since so much knowledge is lost. This one was forged through all my experiences. It's irreplaceable. And it just saved our lives."

Mak put one arm around her and hugged her. "I'm glad."

Lyros pointed at Rosethorn. "Can it lead us out of here?"

"Perhaps something better." Cassia closed both hands around the hilt and directed the letting site's magic through the blade again. She let the power permeate the veins of the ivy. The vines shrank in on themselves, turned back into fresh green seedlings, then ducked into the soil and wrapped themselves tight in their seeds.

The labyrinth was gone. What remained was a wild marsh wreathed in fog. The cool damp crept around their ankles, and night insects hummed. A semicircle of standing stones blocked the path behind them, and a single trail led ahead of them into the mists.

"This can't be inside the tower," Mak muttered.

"It's not anywhere in the surrounding woods, either," said Lyros. "We would have smelled the water."

"It's a world of the Changing Queen's making." Lio started forward, holding his staff like a walking stick, his robes swirling behind him. "Let's go further in and see what mystery she has in store for us next."

Cassia held on to his fearless curiosity, so strong in their Union. Together, they all forged deeper into her ancestor's strange testing ground.

TRIAL BY CLAW

Lio conjured a spell light to illuminate the narrow path through the marsh. The glowing orb dissolved into the pale mist as if the Lustra had consumed it. He sighed. His magic was as useless in here as Mak and Lyros's wards.

Knight splashed through a stand of reeds ahead of them, sending mud flying. Mak paused at the edge of the soggy ground. "Thorns. We can't levitate, either?"

"Seems not." Lyros waded through the puddle.

"I'm sorry," Cassia said.

Lio laughed softly. "You needn't apologize for your ancestors, my rose."

She scowled. "I'd like to have words with Ebah right now. When she appeared to me in Btana Ayal, all she gave me were cryptic commands. Nothing so useful as, 'By the way, if you ever need to get into that long-lost tower of mine in the eastern Tenebrae, just pull out a focus imbued with plant magic and that bloodthirsty ivy will be docile as a lamb.'"

Mak huffed. "And while she was at it, she could have told us what all of this is actually guarding."

"It will be worth it," Lio said. "She wouldn't have gone to this much effort to hide it unless it was very important to her."

"Any theories?" asked Lyros.

"Another ritual site, perhaps." Lio held the drooping branches of a marsh tree out of Cassia's way and let her go ahead of him. "One even more important than the last two."

"We didn't learn much from those," Cassia grumbled.

"Didn't we?" Lio asked her.

Mak rolled his eyes at Lio. "Anytime you get tired of his magic teacher tone, Cassia, let us know. We'll knock it out of him for you."

She gave Lio her secret smile over her shoulder. "That won't be necessary."

Lio smiled back. *I do believe you like my magic teacher tone.*

I can't decide which part I enjoy most, you glass-tongued scrollworm. When you instruct me like a student, or praise me like a queen.

I will do either one you like if you can answer my next question.

Their faces must have betrayed their private conversation, for Mak whistled. "Why weren't our magic lessons this interesting, Lyros?"

"Not fair at all," Lyros said. "We might have become scholars if we'd gotten to polish our fangs instead of having to read boring scrolls."

Lio cleared his throat, pulling his thoughts away from that bed in the tower room. "Can you name at least one thing we learned from each of the ritual sites we've visited?"

Cassia's aura grew thoughtful. "Fighting for survival is what brings on a Silvicultrix's beast magic. The ritual site under the lighthouse where we found the bones could be aligned with that affinity. Fertility and the stone circle might be connected to plant magic. Would that make sense?"

"Certainly," Lio agreed.

She looked at him askance. "That's not the answer you're looking for."

"All of that is important, but I think we learned something even more interesting from each site. Trust your intuition like Mak suggested. What did you feel?"

She paused to think again. "What didn't belong was more interesting that what did."

Lio nodded in encouragement.

"The Mage King's fire was so strange to find in a Lustri ritual site. That tells us he wasn't just a guest in Ebah's passageways. He was a participant. They blended their magic somehow. As for the stone circle...no, this sounds ridiculous."

"Try us," Lio said.

"The standing stones reminded me of Btana Ayal."

Lio was about to reply when Lyros broke in softly. "Do you hear that?"

They stopped speaking, and Lio listened.

Mak said, "There's only one four-legger with us, but I can hear nine more."

Such heavy footfalls could only belong to large creatures. The beasts were closing in from all different directions. Their party was already surrounded.

"I can't feel their auras," Lio said. "They aren't normal animals."

Lyros lifted his spear. "If they're as friendly as the ivy, get ready to fight."

Cassia's horror crept over Lio. She said nothing, but he could feel her terrible realization. If the Changing Queen's traps required all three of her affinities to escape, then this test of her beast magic was one they wouldn't pass.

"We'll find a way," she said with bravery he knew she didn't feel. "That's what Hesperines do, isn't it? Ebah may have designed one solution to this puzzle, but we heretics will invent our own."

"That's right!" Mak called into the night. "Come and get us, you doddering spell-beasts. I bet you've never met a Hesperine before, have you?"

They fell into their fighting formation, back-to-back in a circle again. Knight let out a howl unlike any sound Lio had heard him make before.

Unearthly howls answered him. Wolves.

The pack emerged from the fog, nine beasts as large as Knight. Their eyes, orange as magefire, held uncanny intelligence.

"What are they?" Lyros whispered.

"Not illusions," Lio murmured back, "nor similacra. Not mundane wolves, either."

"Creations," Cassia breathed.

Knight howled again, and the pack took up his song. Dare they hope the wolves were their allies?

A single wolf turned away from them and trotted a few steps along the path. As one, the others surrounding them faced forward.

"This feels more like an escort than an attack," Cassia said with relief. "I think they're offering to lead us out of the marsh."

The wolf in the lead, surely the alpha of the pack, looked over his shoulder at her expectantly. When she hesitated, he spun to face her. His teeth peeled back, and his warning growl sent a chill down Lio's spine. They all stood very still.

Cassia took a slow breath. "I think he wants me to communicate with him using my beast magic but I...I can't."

Lio put a reassuring hand on her back, trying to think of a plan. "You communicate with Knight intuitively even without your beast magic. Perhaps the wolves will respond as he does?"

Her misery intensified. "It's not there anymore."

"What's not there?" he asked, trying to understand.

"The connection I felt with Knight."

"No! That was your latent power—your innate capacity for your future beast magic. That should still be there."

She shook her head.

He couldn't bear her looming sense of failure, her fear that she couldn't protect them. He was the one who had Gifted her before she had claimed all her power, without knowing what the consequences might be. He cursed everything they still didn't understand.

The promise he'd made to her the night of her transformation burned through his veins. He would not rest until she claimed all her power.

The wolf took a step forward. This time, his howl sounded like a war cry. The pack turned on them and attacked.

Lio swept his staff out at the three wolves lunging toward him and Cassia. There came no impact of adamas on muscle and bone. The staff passed right through their bodies.

He dropped his weapon and threw himself in front of her, his arms up to shield his heart and throat. The fangs that closed around his forearm were no spectral touch. Pain tore through his flesh. A sickening crack rang in his ears, punctuated by Mak and Lyros's shouts.

Lio swung his other hand, aiming a fist at the wolf's jaw. His knuckles passed right through its head.

Then there was a heavy thud, and something jostled the wolf off Lio's arm. Fresh agony burned through his wound, but he was free.

Knight wrestled the wolf to the ground, aiming his bite at its jugular. The other two wolves had already retreated a pace with scrapes marring their fur.

"*Oedann*," Lio barked out, then whirled to check on Cassia.

She had her eyes closed, one fist around her pendant and the other around Rosethorn's hilt. Two points of Lustra magic grew in her foci.

The magic flew outward from her all at once. Black roses tore out of the marshy ground, forming a barricade between them and the wolves. Knight's opponents leapt over the rising thicket just before the roses grew too high for any wolf to jump. The beasts harrying Mak and Lyros retreated, yelping at the sting of the thorns.

"They can feel that," Mak snarled.

But Cassia's face crumpled. "I can't make the roses attack the wolves. The Lustra vines won't turn on their own. I'm sorry. All I can do is buy us time."

Another howl sounded from outside her barricade. Bloodied jaws tore through. The roses grew closed again, shutting out the beasts. But on every side, Lio could hear their teeth and claws working at the vines.

"Now would be a good time for obtuse arcane theories, scrollworm," Mak called over the growls.

Lio had walked into this trap with nearly a century of knowledge from the greatest libraries in the world stored in his head. All of that meant nothing in the face of ancient power from a lost epoch. He didn't know enough. He didn't understand *anything*.

He dragged a hand over his face. "What's happening here defies every known law of magic! If they obey any law at all, it's some primal code we don't understand."

"Primal laws..." Mak echoed. "What's the oldest law there is?"

Something passed between him and his Grace, and Lyros answered, "Trial by combat."

"What?" Cassia protested. "No, I won't let you—"

"Let us try," Mak said firmly.

She shook her head, her magic growing stronger in the ground under their feet. Her rose barrier grew higher.

Mak eyed the vines. Then he slashed his finger on one of the thorns. "We, Telemakhos and Lysandros, warriors of Hespera, challenge your wolves to trial by combat, Silvicultrix Ebah of the Lustra."

The rose vines parted and sank into the ground. The wolves stood in a ring around them. Torches that hadn't been there before now encircled the area. They burned not with mundane flame but with magefire that felt akin to the lighthouse.

His heart was in his throat. All he wanted to do was reach out to hold his Trial brothers back from this battle. But he was beginning to understand the laws at work here.

I think Mak just found the alternate solution to the puzzle, he told Cassia.

If the wolves hurt them—

Time to trust our warriors.

The alpha wolf and a fearsome female who must be his mate stepped out of the formation to face Mak and Lyros.

Mak squeezed Cassia's shoulder, and his reassurance flowed through the Blood Union. "They've accepted our challenge and chosen Lyros and me as their opponents. It would be dishonorable for you and Lio to intervene."

Her jaw tightened, but she nodded.

Mak approached the alpha as Lyros faced off with the vicious mate. Even Knight stayed back as if he had understood this law all along.

Lio could do nothing but stand helpless and watch. Cassia took his hand, and they held on tightly. His vow pounded with his pulse, a wordless determination now. He would learn. He would know. When they finally faced that door, his ignorance would not be the death of his Grace and Trial brothers.

The two wolves moved as one, launching themselves at Mak and Lyros. Lio's muscles braced for the pain his Trial brothers were about to meet.

Mak turned his powerful frame with graceful precision. He moved into the wolf's attack, merged with it as if he too was a force of nature. The beast's pounce carried them both to the ground.

His hands closed around the wolf's two front legs. Solid. The beasts truly had accepted the challenge. His biceps strained as he forced apart the claws trying to pin him down.

The alpha's mate had landed behind Lyros to nip at his heels. He danced out of the reach of her jaws. With his own predatory gaze, he watched her every move. They circled each other, her eyes calculating.

Mak emerged on his feet. His face was utterly calm despite the fresh claw marks on his barely-healed arm. This time, it was he who pounced.

He wrestled the alpha back to the ground, and they rolled in a whirl of black fur and blacker cloth.

At last, Lyros struck, a blur of immortal speed. His fist connected, a rapid strike at the wolf's muzzle. It must have been a vulnerable spot, for she let out a yelp that promised revenge.

A glint of firelight on water revealed the wolf's strategy to Lio too late for him to call out a warning. Lyros's sandal slipped on a patch of muddy ground hidden in the reeds. He lost his grip on her muzzle. Lio was sure the wolf had lured him into that position on purpose.

She forced Lyros to the ground with her front paws on his chest. His leg, trapped in the mud, twisted at an unnatural angle. Lio shuddered at the pain that contorted Lyros's face. He took a step forward.

Cassia grabbed his arm. *They're right. If we intervene, we'll all fail this test.*

The clever wolf bared her teeth and aimed for Lyros's throat. Lio didn't know what oath he shouted as the beast's teeth connected with Lyros's jugular.

But it was she who leapt back, whining and pawing at her muzzle. With a savage smile, Lyros made it out of the mud, favoring his broken leg. The torn collar of his battle robe revealed what he'd hidden there: a vine of black rose thorns, the Lustra's own armor.

Mak's pain raked across the Blood Union, yanking Lio's attention back to his battle. His blood flew, a spray of bright red in the firelight. He broke free of the alpha's grasp, rolling away from the wolf, only to fall still on the ground.

His hand moved. He pressed it to his chest in a vain effort to staunch the blood streaming from his heart wound.

IN HESPERA'S HONOR

Lio's thoughts hung suspended, trying to make sense of the blood on Mak's chest, the pain in their Union. Cassia stood frozen at his side, both hands clapped over her mouth.

How deep was the wound? Had the wolf hit Mak's heart?

Lyros's gaze never left his opponent. His face was cold, his knuckles white on the branch he had snatched up to use as a crutch. The female wolf snapped at his bad leg, but he swung the branch with perfect aim, and her bite sank into wood instead.

With a battle cry, Mak barreled to his feet an instant before the alpha wolf crushed him under its weight. He threw himself on the alpha's back, his arms locking around the beast's neck. The name of that fighting move flitted through Lio's mind, a memory foreign to this brutal contest. Mortal Vice, the headlock that could choke a mortal or decapitate a Hesperine.

Mak held the wolf, the heartbeats ticking by. The alpha's mate howled with fury. Lyros gripped her ears with both hands, exploiting another sensitive point. With a frenzy of paws, she flicked blood and mud into his eyes.

No use against his immortal senses. He didn't release her. She retreated, but he held on, letting her drag him along with her.

They inched closer to the nearest magefire torch. This time Lio tried to yell a warning.

No sound came out of his mouth. The Lustra had truly disqualified him and Cassia from this duel.

The wolf crouched, then with a heave of her shoulders, made to hurl Lyros at the fire. He let go just in time to spare his face from the flames. His back hit the shaft of the torch. Wood splintered.

The top half of the torch landed in the reeds. Magefire began to lick at the wet plants.

Lyros fumbled for his crutch, which had fallen to the side of the path, but not into the water. While the wolf gave her tortured ears a shake, Lyros scrambled to his feet, leaning heavily on his crutch, and limped away.

Her eyes filled with triumph. Her pack howled with hunger. And she pounced to down the weakest prey in the herd.

Lyros dropped to the ground. An ember of light flashed in the night. The wolf's leap took her too high, while Lyros rolled onto his back under her and brought up his crutch to strike her belly.

The end of the branch was alight with magefire. The flames ate through the wood in a breath, and Lyros dropped the crumbling branch just before the deadly element reached his hand. But not before the wolf's fur caught fire.

The king's flames scoured his queen's wolf. She landed on all fours and lifted her face to the sky of this otherworld like some burning specter. She and her pack sang in one voice that sounded of ancient fire and older hunts. An ember flew from her fur to land on Lyros's brow, and he hissed in pain, flicking the spark away with one hand.

Her mate slumped in Mak's hold at last. He released the alpha wolf's body and fell back, bracing a hand on his chest wound again.

The burning queen wolf streaked past Lio and Cassia to the side of her fallen mate. She licked the alpha's throat, and the magefire danced across his fur.

His chest lifted. Breath filled his lifeless body. He got to his feet and rested his open jaws lightly on her jugular. Flames spilled into his mouth. As he drank the fire from her fur, the burning glow faded and went out.

Each wolf turned, facing Mak and Lyros, and went down on their bellies in an unmistakable gesture of submission to the victors.

The pack surged around their leaders, and the nine wolves raced away, disappearing back into the fog. Their howls sounded through the marsh, and Knight called after them, his voice blending with theirs as if they were one pack. The mist followed the wolves, peeling back to reveal nine standing stones in a ring around them.

Lyros's calm broke, and he made the first sound he'd uttered the entire battle. He let out his own howl of rage and staggered toward Mak.

Cassia fell to her knees beside Mak and helped him apply pressure to his wound. Pushing through his own pain, Lio slung Lyros's arm over his shoulders. He helped Lyros hobble over to their Graces and eased him down at Mak's side.

"Let me," Lyros ground out.

Cassia nodded and took Lyros's hand, pressing it over Mak's in her place. Then she scrambled away to give them more room.

She shook her head. *No natural wolf can do that—I've never seen a wound like this—*

Lio sank down beside her and pulled her close with his good arm.

Mak was trembling. The sight of his powerful cousin shaking frightened Lio in a way he had never felt before.

Lyros took one look at the blood spilling from between his fingers, then put his other hand behind Mak's head to support him. Lyros held Mak's lips to his throat. But Mak's eyelids drooped, the color draining from his face.

"Don't you dare!" Lyros massaged his Grace's jaw with desperate motions.

Finally, Mak's fangs locked onto his offered vein. Lyros released a sharp sigh.

Lio let his face fall to rest on Cassia hair. *Mak is conscious enough to bite. That's what matters.*

I can't bear this.

Lyros will heal him, Lio said, as much to reassure himself as her.

After a moment that seemed to last forever, Mak dug his fingers into Lyros's hair, holding on. With a soft groan, he pressed his face closer against Lyros's neck, his throat working.

Where their joined hands rested on Mak's chest, the flow of blood slowed, then ceased. But how deep did the damage go?

At last, Lyros eased Mak's jaw open and rested his Grace's head on his lap. Mak caressed his face, then let his hand drop and felt his chest.

"Are you all right?" Lio asked.

"That beast tried to rip out my heart," Mak answered hoarsely, "but trying isn't enough to best a Hesperine warrior."

Lyros gripped Mak's hand. "I would take you to a healer if I could."

"Your blood and my Gift are all I need. Who knows if a healer's affinity even works on doddering wolf wounds? Help me sit up."

"You should lie still," Lyros insisted.

"I can rest when we're out of here."

Lyros narrowed his eyes, but he helped Mak into a sitting position. Gently, Lyros parted the torn front of Mak's robe. A scar was all that remained of what might have been his death wound. Four neat slashes crossed Mak's heart, the unmistakable marks of a beast's claws.

"How can this be?" Cassia shook her head. "I thought nothing could scar a Hesperine."

"Only anti-haimatic magic can," said Lio. "Magefire. Lustra magic."

With a bemused look, Mak pushed the hair back from Lyros's forehead. "You've got a handsome new scar, too. Does that burn mark hurt still?"

"No," Lyros said tightly.

Mak looked from Lyros's brow to his own chest. "Well, it seems the Lustra gave us tokens of approval, too. I like these better than fancy necklaces."

Lyros didn't laugh. Saying nothing, he pulled Mak's face against his neck and held him for a moment longer.

When they were sure Mak was hale enough to stand, Lio and Cassia helped him and Lyros up. Lio supported Mak while Cassia handed Lyros his fallen spear to use as a crutch. The four of them made their weary way over to a pair of standing stones with a broad gap between them. Knight already sat there waiting for them. Beyond the gate, more magefire torches lined the path.

"This looks like the way forward," said Lio.

"I expect the next trap to require soothsaying," Cassia warned.

"You two are the diplomats," Mak said. "I dare say you can talk our way out of it, with or without an affinity for soothsaying."

Cassia glanced back the way they had come, but Lyros shook his head. "The only way out is forward."

Lio took Cassia's hand. *We'll find a way.*

They walked between the stones to face the next challenge.

Cassia took one step forward, and the marsh was gone as if they had left it behind inside the standing stones. But those had disappeared, too.

They were back in the top chamber of the tower. Only it wasn't a dismal storage room any longer.

The room was empty and dark save for the nonagram, which now glowed with verdant green light. The symbol was drawn on the floor in a luminescent powder that smelled of ash trees and bone. The complex, interlocking pattern formed a sort of nine-pointed star, and at its center rose a small standing stone.

"Why does that look more dangerous than Hesperine-eating ivy and unkillable wolves?" Mak asked.

"Because we understand it even less," Lio answered.

Lyros eyed Knight, who was keeping his distance from the glowing lines. "No one set foot inside it."

Lio nodded in agreement. "Not until Cassia has a chance to examine it with her power."

She circled the symbol, studying the standing stone from every angle, and consulted the letting site again. As if the Lustra's power amplified her hearing, she was able to make out a sound in the quiet room. A murmur that seemed to echo along the twists and points of the nonagram.

"Do you all hear that?" she asked.

Lio frowned, shaking his head. "What?"

"The tower has a voice," she said.

The murmur grew more urgent, and she drifted closer to the outer edge of the symbol.

Lio caught her hand, holding her back. "What is the voice saying?"

"I don't know." The fleeting words seemed to hold a revelation just beyond her understanding.

She couldn't help remembering the whispers that had permeated Btana Ayal, the voices of all the ancestors who had walked in that once-great city. She hadn't been able to understand them until one of her own ancestors had manifested and briefly gifted her the power of soothsaying.

She would never have that ability again.

"This is definitely a soothsaying test," she said.

"May I listen with you?" Lio asked.

"Please." She opened her senses to him.

He drew nearer through their bond, and their Grace Union heightened. She felt him behind her eyes, under her skin. His voice echoed silently in her ears. *Is this what it sounds like to go through a spirit gate when you're human?*

Yes. And what I heard at the shattered gate. But that's impossible. The ancestors can't speak in Tenebra.

He leaned nearer with a puzzled frown. *It must be some manifestation of soothsaying magic we've never seen before.*

If I make the wrong move, the consequences could be far worse than the other traps. The ivy and the wolves threatened us physically, but soothsaying could affect our minds.

"All we can do is face this challenge as we did the others." Lio moved behind her and wrapped one hand around hers over her pendant, holding her dagger with her in the other. The motion had to cause him pain in his healing arm, but he didn't hesitate.

"Wait." Lyros held up a hand. "Our wards are working."

Mak nodded, his face still pale.

"Let me manage the spell alone," Lyros told him.

"Not a chance, my Grace." Mak's magic rose to join Lyros's, and the dark steadiness of their wards wrapped around everyone.

"Does this mean we're really back in the tower?" Cassia wondered.

Lio's thelemancy touched her mind, adding new dimension to their Union. "I believe so. My magic is working, too. We must have left the Lustra's creation and re-entered the world."

"How is that possible? The tower looks completely different."

"We still can't step, so this place is clearly under the influence of Lustra magic, as well."

"Yes. Yes, I can feel it. I could be wrong…" She gave a humorless laugh. "I could always be wrong about any of this. But I don't think this is the final trap guarding the tower's secrets. I think this might be the secret itself."

Lio's power filled her mind ward. "If this soothsaying enchantment affects our Wills, I'll try to protect us."

"Our wards are ready," said Lyros.

Cassia channeled magic up from the letting site, directing it into her incomplete foci. Her dagger and pendant stemmed the measureless flow. The whispers grew louder.

They called her forward. She stepped into the symbol, and Lio moved with her so they both stood inside one point of the star.

"The spell feels off-balance," she said. "Mak…Lyros…would you be willing to join us inside the symbol?"

"Anything you need," Mak replied.

"Where shall we stand?" asked Lyros.

"Each of you take one point of the star to form a triangle with us."

Mak stepped into one section of the nonagram, and Lyros limped into the other, his staff tapping on the floor. She could feel their auras pass over the border of the symbol. The magic grew stronger, but it felt like an erratic heartbeat to her.

Cassia drew her brows together. The uneven magic was forming a headache behind her eyes. "No, this isn't right either. Why doesn't it feel right?"

Lio's magic reached through her senses again. "I'm not sure. I've never encountered anything like this nonagram. No other magical paradigm has spell patterns based on threes."

The enchantment demanded she use three affinities. Was there any hope of answering the voices with only one?

No, Cassia had more than a single Lustra affinity. She had blood magic, too.

"Hesperine spell patterns are based on unions," she murmured. "Unions so powerful, they can even bind together opposing forces…"

"Flesh and spirit," Lio said. "Thorns and roses. Hulaia and haima."

Haima, the paradigm of blood magic. Cassia's fangs slid down. "We shall do this the Hesperine way, and if the Changing Queen doesn't like it, she can keep her secrets."

She felt Lio's fierce smile in their Union. "If you think committing heresy in the symbol of your ancestors is the answer, then that's what we'll do."

"With you all the way," said Mak, although he was barely on his feet.

Lyros was a ball of worry for his Grace, but he didn't hesitate either. "Let's give the Lustra a taste of Hespera's thorns."

Cassia motioned for her Trial brothers to move closer together. "You two stand inside the same point across from Lio and me."

They did ask she asked, sliding a supportive arm around each other.

Cassia lifted Rosethorn and made a slash on both her hands. Droplets of her blood flew from the cuts and hung suspended in the air, caught between the pull of the enchantment and the push of her Will.

Her new ability for levitation won the contest. Her blood obeyed her, sweeping through the air and down to the floor. She traced over the glowing green lines of her choosing, forming her own symbol out of the nonagram. Five petals and five thorns, Hespera's Rose imprinted in crimson over her ancestor's tracings. She looped one petal around Mak and Lyros, pointed a thorn at her and Lio, and drew the center of the rose around the standing stone.

"Yes," Lio said, "this could work!"

She pressed one bleeding hand to her pendant, the other dripping blood down Rosethorn. The letting site's power split and funneled into her foci. A wild, chaotic third current of power sought for her missing focus.

"I have a unified duality and two foci," she told the Lustra through gitted teeth. "Take them or leave them."

She braced herself and drew on the blood magic flowing in her veins.

Her Hesperine power flowed into the lines of the rose, and the rightness of it, the relief made tears prick her eyes. The current of her blood magic pulled her plant magic along with it. The letting site's power shuddered and built, a raging river trying to crash through the narrowest ravine. Lio folded himself around her, holding her against the onslaught.

She felt small. The vast Lustra threatened to roll over her and return her to dust.

No. She was immortal. Recreated by Hespera, she had nothing to fear from the power of creation.

The unanchored third current snapped into place, melding with the two channels pouring through her artifacts. The force of nature pouring from the letting site followed her blood magic into the thorns and petals of Hespera's rose.

Lio gasped. "Goddess bless. It's working. You can do this, Cassia."

Flecks of blood floated around her. She caught their scent and realized they were Lio's blood. Every stain their battle had left on him rose from his skin and hair and robes to fall, wet and bright, into the center of the rose. Mak made a surprised noise, watching the gore on his chest lift away and stream into the center, mingling with the blood the spell pulled from Lyros.

The green lines of the nonagram faded to darkness. The spell wrenched itself out of Ebah's ancient pattern and reformed along every petal and thorn of Hespera's Rose. It sang, with two nodes keeping the whole chaos in balance—one concentration of power swirling around her and Lio, the other encircling Mak and Lyros.

She heard her pendant and the stone speaking to each other in that language she couldn't understand. This enchantment was created by soothsaying, the wisdom of people. The magic of words. She grasped at the few words of the old tongue she knew.

"Ebah," she said, the name of ivy, of the sorceress who had crafted this spell. An invocation of her matriarch. Then she said in Divine, the mother tongue of Hesperines, "I am your daughter in this epoch. Your past is mine by right."

The pendant was warm, almost too hot against her hand. Lio ran his thumb over hers and didn't let go.

"Ebah," Cassia demanded a second time. "I am your immortal daughter. Trust me with your secrets, and they shall live forever with me."

The whispers grew to a cacophony. They spilled forth from the stone and rushed toward Cassia. The channeling hit her pendant and sent her staggering back against Lio. He held her tightly as magic poured into her chest.

Light raced along the patterns of the nonagram, erasing the symbol line by line. The standing stone crumbled to dust before their eyes.

"No, no—" she began.

But the whispers interrupted her. Now they were coming from her pendant.

The current of magic faded and left her feeling light and unsteady. The whispers quieted, as if going to sleep. But the feel of the magic inside her pendant had changed. Grown.

Slowly, Mak and Lyros lowered their wards. Lyros was the first to speak. "What just happened?"

"Incredible." Lio, immortal as he was, sounded breathless. "The enchantment in the stone was designed to be transferred to another artifact. It merged with the spells inside Cassia's pendant."

She flicked her hand and left one more emphatic splash of blood where the stone had stood. "And we did it on Hespera's terms."

The floorboards creaked, then the wood under the fresh bloodstain cracked, and a vine of black roses blossomed in the center of their defiant Ritual circle. Magic echoed in the vines, in the bloodied lines of their spell, and in the Union between the four of them, which battle had only strengthened.

"I know this isn't how any of us expected to spend Winter Solstice," Cassia said, "but let this be our Ritual in Hespera's honor."

THE REAL TOWER

Cassia traced the intricate carvings on the pendant. Power. Answers. Right under her fingertips yet out of reach.

"There's only one problem," she said. "I have no idea what this enchantment is for. It's still useless to us."

Lio's smile faded, giving way to the harsh determination she had come to recognize. His impossible vow to restore her lost magics. As if he would shake the world with his bare hands until it yielded up her power.

"So much has been preserved here," Cassia said. "Perhaps we can learn more than we did at the other Lustra sites."

"Yes," he replied. "Let's search the rest of the tower. There could be clues that will help us understand the enchantment."

Knight was waiting for them outside the Ritual circle. She stroked the soft fur of his ears to reassure him, then reached for the door to the stairwell. It opened before she touched it. "I take it the entire tower has recognized me as Ebah's descendant. It's about time."

Cassia finally sheathed Rosethorn. Mak surrendered his heavy weapon belt to Lyros and let him carry it.

Her heart ached at the sight of them leaning on each other for support. "This tower is our errant Sanctuary now. Let's find you a place to rest."

They made their way downward through other rooms just as impossibly transformed from their abandoned state. In the bedchamber, a bronze chandelier cupped spell flames that cast a warm glow over the ancient tower's glory. Luxurious furs covered a large bed carved from thick beams. Ivy flourished on the walls, and the cold floor was now warmed by rugs woven in designs like the triquetra on Cassia's pendant.

"What in the name of all the stars of old…" Lio went to the window and looked out.

There was a look of uneasy wonder on Lyros's face. "It feels like we stepped into another time. But that's not possible, is it?"

"No." Lio pointed out the window. "We're in our own epoch, in the same tower."

Cassia joined him there, looking down to see the snow-dusted forest, the dreary bailey, and the thatched roof of the stables.

"All of this should have disintegrated," Lyros protested. "Without Hesperine tending, cloth and wood and such don't last sixteen hundred years."

"Cassia's pendant lasted," Lio pointed out. "The magefires are still burning. The Lustra sustains all of this somehow."

Cassia turned in a circle, taking it in. "So, this…version…of the tower was here all along?"

"The real tower," Lio said, "protected by the crumbling facade that men can see. Just like the passages at Solorum and Patria, only concealed in a much more complex way."

"None of that makes any sense." Mak yawned.

"No, it doesn't." The grimness in Lio's aura hadn't lifted. "But it will by the time we're done, mark my words."

Cassia's mind whirled, thinking of all the nights she had slept within the Changing Queen's secrets without knowing it. She ran a hand over one of the woven blankets on the bed. Had Ebah made it with her own hands? "This place is different from the other sites. More personal, somehow. As if she only just stepped out the door and will return at any moment."

They found another spacious room across from Ebah's bedchamber. This one had a decidedly masculine touch, from the empty weapon rack to the tidy bed that did not appear much used.

Lio raised a brow at Cassia. "Seems like Lucian visited his queen in her room most of the time."

Lyros, although still limping, guided Mak to the bed and sat him down on the edge of it. "You need to get off your feet now."

"We should finish searching the tower," Mak protested.

"Cassia and I will do that," Lio said.

"We're safe here now." She headed to the door with him by unspoken agreement.

"The horses," Mak called after them. "We should bring them inside the keep so they're protected by the Lustra's spells too."

"We'll make them a place on the ground floor," said Lyros. "Later."

Mak started to grumble again.

"You need more blood," Lyros interrupted in his most commanding tone. "Now."

A grin tugged at Mak's lips. "In that case, I might be persuaded to put up my feet in an ancient warrior's bedchamber, as long as I won't be resting alone. Not everyone can say they got their fangs polished where the famous Mage King slept."

Smiling, Cassia closed the door behind her and Lio.

They drifted through the lower levels of the tower. In one room, the vacant armor stand spoke of a king gone to war. A collection of Lucian's shields and banners still adorned the walls, perhaps trophies of victories that gave him particular satisfaction.

But it was clear this tower was the domain of a sorceress. There was a weaving room with a half-finished tapestry still on the loom. One chamber appeared entirely dedicated to her alchemy, with still-fragrant herbs hanging from the rafters.

Lio paused to examine the mortars, pestles, and jars. "This is definitely Lustri pottery dating from the end of the Great Temple Era! I've only seen broken fragments in Prince Iulios's museum!"

Cassia tried to close her jaw, but she was too much in awe of everything they found.

When they reached a dining hall on the first floor, Lio sighed. "No library. I suppose it was too much to hope for, considering that the Lustri had a primarily oral culture."

"So much died with them," Cassia murmured.

Two high-backed wooden chairs stood in front of the hearth. Knight lay down on the fur rug in the glow of the flames. For the eternal magefire of a dead king, it was remarkably cozy, although her Hesperine senses warned her away. Like all the magic here, the flames both called to her and repelled her.

Her arm throbbed with the pain Lio had been ignoring. She patted one of the chairs. "Come here. Let me see to your injury."

He sank onto his seat. Even weary from battle, he looked noble and powerful sitting there. No fire mage for her. This Silvicultrix now ruled the tower with an immortal sorcerer king at her side.

She sat on his lap and examined the break. "It doesn't need to be set. A good long drink should set you to rights."

He traced the vein on the inside of her wrist. "And you, my rose? Are you all right?"

She knew he wouldn't accept her blood until she set his mind at ease. But she struggled to find any reassuring words. "I'm not sure I can forgive my ancestor for what her magic did to Mak."

"It's not your fault."

"You are not allowed to tell me to stop blaming myself when you are so occupied with your own self-blame."

He sighed and looked away, the fire casting his elegant profile in gold.

She turned his face back to her. "We learned this already, my Grace. Hespera taught it to us at the End, when my Gifting might have destroyed me. We have to forgive ourselves. Can you help me remember that?"

"You're right. That lesson is a gift we must carry with us always." He gave her a sad smile. "Let us remind each other of it, every time we have a new regret, until our stubborn minds finally learn."

She ran her hand down his chest. It was not their minds that were the trouble, but their broken hearts.

"I know," he whispered.

"Since we had to leave home, we've done nothing but get ambushed. We cannot afford to go into our next battle so blind."

"No," he agreed. "But we don't have much time."

"No," she replied tightly.

Peace and war. Preparation and time. So many imperatives pulling them in opposing directions. So many conflicts that seemed to have no solution.

"I don't think we have a choice," Lio said. "We have to stop here until we're ready to face Miranda. When we go to meet her at Castra Roborra, we need to be prepared for anything."

Cassia traced the furrow on his brow, and he closed his eyes. "How close do you honestly think Kallikrates is to the door?"

"Closer than us," Lio confessed.

"Yes."

The magic inside her felt so heavy suddenly, too much even for her immortal frame to carry.

She saw the heart hunter's lifeless body in the snow. The broken bodies of innocent mortals at the lighthouse.

The blood pouring from Mak's heart. Her own bleeding hand, reaching toward the door.

"I'll keep trying," she promised Lio and herself and everyone Kallikrates would destroy if she laid down to rest.

"And I will keep trying with you," her Grace swore.

10
nights after
WINTER SOLSTICE

WEAPON MASTER

CASSIA WONDERED IF THE Mage King had ever imagined an errant circle of Hesperines would turn his armory into their practice room. She doubted anything about this epoch resembled what he and the Changing Queen had envisioned.

Especially their descendant standing there with her fangs out, her hand stinging from impact with her Grace-cousin's immortal jaw.

"How can your face be that hard?" She watched her split knuckles heal. A new spatter of bloodstains now decorated the red-brown fabric of her battle robe.

Mak was unfazed by the one punch she had managed to land. "You're getting better."

"I think you let me hit you."

"If I ever did such a thing," he said innocently, "it would be for teaching purposes. You still have the muscle memory of a human. You need to learn to move like a Hesperine and do it intentionally, not only when your immortal reflexes come to your rescue."

"Thank you for the lesson. Maybe I'll make it through our next battle without a sword slicing my hip open."

He gave her an affectionate push toward the bench where Lio and Lyros were watching. "All right, Lio, your turn. Get out here, you overtall, undermuscled scrollworm."

Lio paused to kiss Cassia's bloodied knuckles. She watched him tread barefoot onto the leather mats wearing nothing but his Imperial trousers.

He faced Mak, looking down his nose from his bloodborn height. "I gained at least a few new muscles when I broke Flavian's face this past autumn."

"You need more muscles than you can get turning that limp rag into your punching bag. Prove you learned something from the times Tendo smashed your face in the dirt." Mak crossed his arms over his bare chest. He too was sparring in trousers tonight, with everyone's robes the worse for wear after their battles.

Cassia flopped down onto the bench next to Lyros and picked up Lio's folded battle robe, examining the damage. She resisted the urge to bury her nose in the fabric and sniff her Grace's scent like a thorny youngblood. "We really need to see to the mending."

Lyros's gaze drifted over Mak. "I'm not in a hurry. Are you?"

Cassia watched Lio's back as he warmed up with a couple of stretches. He had just the right amount of muscles. "On second thought, sewing doesn't seem very important in our dangerous circumstances. Clearly, bare-chested training sessions take priority."

Lyros half grinned, and she was glad. He hadn't smiled much since Mak had been wounded.

Mak raised his fists, but Lio shook his head. He extended his hand toward their pale adamas weapons, which now hung among the Mage King's armaments of bronze and iron. Lio's staff levitated into his grasp. "What I need is a lesson from our weapon master."

Mak's teasing humor faded.

"When you set your mind to something," Lio said, "you don't do it by halves. You wouldn't forge weapons without developing a Hesperine combat style to make use of them."

Mak shifted on his feet.

"He has," Lyros spoke up. "How do you think I knew how to throw a spear at those Gift Collectors?"

"It's a work in progress," Mak said. "It's not as if I could show the Blood Errant what I was working on and ask for their advice."

Lio lifted Final Word in both hands. "You can show the Black Roses."

Mak's veils slipped, and Cassia felt his grim acceptance. She understood. Just as she must embrace her power, it was time for him to teach them to use their weapons to the fullest, for better or worse.

A look of decision came over his face, and he nodded. "One thing I was able to learn from the Blood Errant is how Gift Collectors use their makeshift weapons. I'm designing our combat style as a defense against the necromancers' tactics, built on the Hesperine battle arts, with a few tricks from the Ashes thrown in."

"That sounds brilliant," Lio said.

Mak gestured to Lio's staff. "I chose a staff for you because its long reach will help you keep opponents off you while you cast. When wielded well, a quarterstaff like this will let you dominate the space around you. Never underestimate how dangerous a human with a wooden stick can be…"

Lio laughed. "And a Hesperine with an adamas stick…?"

"You have the potential to be a terrifying enemy. But one disadvantage is that it leaves your hands vulnerable, so let's start with how to hold it properly." Mak began a patient demonstration, adjusting Lio's grip.

"He's a good teacher," Cassia commented to Lyros.

A fond smile came to his face. "He's the best trainer the Stand has had since Lyta herself, and he doesn't even realize it."

Mak was such a good mentor for Bosko. When would they see him and Zoe again? Cassia longed to wrap her arms around her little Grace-sister right now.

Lyros must have been thinking of the sucklings, too, for he said, "Mak began his Stand training when he was younger than Zoe, you know."

"Didn't you?"

Lyros made a face. "No. I was still struggling through my art studies. Or rather, ditching them as often as I could to follow Mak to the gymnasium. Goddess, I was such a little idiot, sweet on him and clueless about why I wanted to punch him so much."

Cassia laughed, envisioning them as two innocent sucklings full of feelings that were too big for them. "Is that why you started training? Because you didn't know how to tell your childhood sweetheart you liked him?"

"More or less. But you know, it wasn't Lyta who taught me how to throw a punch. It was Mak who gave me my first lesson in the battle arts."

Cassia leaned closer. "I didn't know that."

Lyros nodded. "I had failed another attempt at clay modeling. I was so angry. Mak, being Mak, wanted to cheer me up. So he showed me what he had been learning that day. I understood it, and I *enjoyed* it."

"And not only because you were sweet on Mak."

"Yes, I enjoyed the actual training, too. So he kept giving me lessons after his practice sessions. When Lyta noticed how I took to the battle arts, she spoke to my parents about formally training me."

Mak had now taken Lio's staff to show him a series of guards, high and low, left and right. His demonstrations made the defensive postures easy for even Cassia to grasp.

"How did Timarete and Astrapas react?" she asked.

"They deemed it a good outlet that would help me concentrate on my studies." Lyros snorted. "Then they thought my obsession with the battle arts was a youthful phase. I think they were in denial until I told them Mak is my Grace. They finally had to accept I had no aptitude for art whatsoever and that they had no hope of prying me away from my future in the Stand with him."

Cassia leaned her shoulder against his, shaking her head. "How did you end up in Orthros's most artistic bloodline?"

"Because of these." Lyros held out his hands and wiggled his fingers. "You know that when I was an urchin in Namenti, I pickpocketed Basir, and that's how he and Kumeta found me."

"And of course, being Hesperines, they repaid your attempt at theft by taking you to safety in Orthros."

"My parents thought any hands deft enough to pickpocket a Hesperine would be better suited to crafting great works of art."

"Hmm. But they turned out more suited to breaking noses."

"As Mak taught me that day." Lyros gave a huff. "He still keeps that hideous lump of clay in our residence. I can't convince him to throw it out."

Mak tossed Lio's staff back to him so he could practice the guards. As Lio went through them in turn, Mak watched, pausing to correct Lio's posture here and there.

Cassia wrapped her arms around her knees. "We've scarcely had a chance to talk like this since we had to leave Orthros."

"Not much time for that while trying to stay alive," Lyros agreed.

Cassia considered her words. The Blood Union was helping her get better at understanding and supporting others. But her new empathic abilities weren't much help when Lyros was keeping his feelings so close to his chest.

So she tried simply asking. "How are you holding up?"

Lyros put an arm around her shoulders and gave her a brief hug. "As well as any of us, I suppose."

"I owe you an apology. I can imagine how you feel watching your careful plan about the weapons fall apart like this. You and Mak had everything under control until my spell gave us away. I know we all share responsibility for what happened, but I want you to know how sorry I am for my part in it."

"I should have my head examined for agreeing that weapons were a good avowal gift for you and Lio. I'm so deeply sorry for what this has cost you, too."

"Well, now that we've both dissolved into a puddle of apologies, how about a promise? We'll work together on strategic preparations to keep our Graces out of further trouble."

There was something hopeless in Lyros's smile. "A whole lot of good my strategies have done so far."

Cassia turned her attention away from Lio's lesson and studied Lyros instead. She saw his devotion in the way he watched Mak. His heartache in the strain at the corners of his mouth and eyes. The tension in his posture. "You're so in love with everything about him. Even the weapons."

"It's hard to protect our Graces when we're such fools over them."

"I understand why you supported Mak when he started forging weapons. I've thrown all my better judgment to the winds for Lio on plenty of occasions."

"But that's not the promise I made when I joined the Stand and when I avowed into his family. Not the vows I made to my Grace. I swore to protect him."

"You do that every night, Lyros."

"Not this time. I'm the one who's supposed to be a good influence when he gets impulsive. But I failed to protect him from himself."

Cassia frowned, considering. She knew what it was like to pull Lio back from the brink of his power. But together, they were also learning the importance of not fearing everything they were capable of.

"Don't you think that's a great deal to take on yourself?" she asked Lyros. "And don't you think Mak is capable of making his own decisions?"

Lyros's expression shuttered, his veils tightening. "If you'd seen how things were when we were younger, you would understand. Mak's relationship with his family, especially his father, has gotten better only recently. There have been so many times when his hot-headedness caused…friction…among Blood Argyros. And now all that progress he made is gone."

Nothing about Lyros's tone was unkind, but his words still stung. Perhaps because he wasn't wrong. She was the newcomer in their Trial circle. And family was one area of diplomacy she was still learning to navigate. Her attempt at encouraging him to confide in her had only resulted in him closing himself off even more.

Mak took up his morning star. Now he went on the attack so Lio could put the defensive staff moves to use. Adamas rang against adamas as they began to practice in earnest.

The tower suddenly felt less like a refuge.

A ball of solid adamas covered in deadly spikes swung toward Lio's heart.

He brought his staff up as Mak had shown him. The shafts of their weapons collided. The spikes stopped a hand's breadth from his chest.

"Good block," Mak said, "but why was it the wrong one to use?"

Lio poured all his strength into holding off his cousin, realizing his mistake with chagrin. "I've already let you in too close."

Mak looked like he could hold this position all day. "Right. This is why a Gift Collector was able to reach you with a dagger. You aren't making proper use of your staff's greatest advantage: range."

The Star of Orthros inched closer. Lio gritted his teeth, the muscles in his arms burning. The spikes brushed the hair on his chest.

Mak snatched his weapon away. The force holding Lio back was suddenly gone. He tipped forward into the path of Mak's next swing.

The Star of Orthros swept past his kneecaps. Mak could have broken his legs if he'd been aiming to. Too late, Lio recovered his footing and dodged backward.

"That was close, but good backup plan." Mak pressed his advantage, advancing on him.

Lio adjusted his grip closer to his body and swung the end of his staff out. Just as Mak had explained, the small movement of Lio's hands on one end of his staff rewarded him with a wide motion at the other. The far end of Final Word knocked the Star of Orthros away before Mak could reach Lio.

"Much better," Mak approved. "Fight like a Hesperine. You're trying to keep violence at bay, not welcome it into your heart."

"Yes," Lio said, his voice far more strained than his cousin's. "That's the spirit of your proposal, isn't it?"

Mak didn't miss a beat in their fight, attacking Lio from the right this time. But his veils wavered again. "You read it?"

Lio blocked Mak with a right guard. "I told you I would."

"Even after…everything that's happened?"

"Especially after that."

Lio focused on defending himself from Mak's next several attacks, waiting for his cousin to speak.

"Well," Mak finally burst out. "What did you think, then?"

"It's brilliant. The Blood Errant should have brought this before the firstbloods eight hundred years ago. But they didn't. You're the first Hesperine who has ever dared."

"I doubt that makes me braver than them. Just more impulsive, and that's saying something."

"If Hespera worshipers had taken the safe path and respected authority, we would have been crushed under the Orders' heels long ago."

"You sound like Kia."

"She's not wrong, Mak. Orthros has forgotten that heresy is our greatest strength." Lio saw Mak's morning star sliding low again and braced himself for the impact.

Mak trapped the end of Lio's staff between the spikes on his club. "Maybe her mother is right. If we don't follow some rules, we're no better than the Orders, throwing our might around for our beliefs."

Their weapons locked, and they stood in another stalemate. "I'm a diplomat with a weapon in my hands. I'm in no position to philosophize about whether we're hypocrites or not. But I'm certain of one thing. I trust the warrior who made this weapon."

Mak closed both hands around the grip of his club and heaved Lio's staff away.

Lio danced backward under the momentum and just managed to keep the staff balanced in both his hands.

Mak didn't push forward this time. "Why?"

"You made this weapon for only one reason."

Mak snorted. "To get us all exiled, apparently."

"No, you lunkhead. You crafted them out of love."

"I thought you said you weren't going to philosophize."

"I'm not. That's simply a fact. Your love for all of us is evident in every line of that proposal."

"I want to know what the proposal says," Cassia spoke up from the sidelines.

Mak let his club dangle from his hand, looking from Lio to their watching Graces.

"So would I," Lyros said.

"What?" Lio turned to him. "You mean you haven't read it?"

Lyros shook his head. "I picked up some of it from our Union while Mak was writing it. But he won't show it to me."

"Love." Lio gave Mak a look. "You were trying to protect your Grace."

Mak sighed. "Fine. I'll summarize for everyone because if I let Lio explain it, we'll be here all night. My proposal requests approval from the firstbloods and the Queens for the Stewards to carry weapons. Only the Stewards, mind. I'll turn in my speires before I let just anyone stroll through Orthros with blades. That would only make our Sanctuary less safe."

"That's a good policy," Cassia said. "The Stewards are rigorously trained and already understand what it means to bear the burden of violence for our people. You have learned to fight with Mercy and proved you will wield weapons with compassion."

"My proposal also requires the Stewards to be of age, with full rank in the Stand. Trainees shouldn't have weapons."

Lio chuckled. "You wrote that line for Bosko, clearly."

Mak's gaze fell. "I want him to have the same experience we did, learning how to use his fists for the Goddess, before he ever touches adamas."

"Tell them about your plan for crafting more weapons," Lio encouraged.

"They're to be forged and stored within the Queens' Ward," Mak explained, "but on the other side of the Sea of Komne, where Nike's forge and Waystar already are. In southern Orthros, we can build a forge on one of the islands, like the Armory of Akofo. Stewards can take their arms with them on patrol, but leave them in the armory when off duty."

"This sounds like a sensible extension of current policy," Cassia said.

Mak pushed his hair back from his face. "The Stand could also supply Hesperines errant with arms under the First Prince's supervision. I thought Rudhira might even want a forge at Castra Justa."

"He's being modest," Lio put in. "He outlined suggested changes to Charge Law to make this reform with the lowest risk."

"The Prince would have to approve them," Mak replied.

"No doubt he would find it a plan after his own heart," Lio said.

Cassia nodded. "Rudhira chooses his forces carefully and can judge who should be trusted with armaments."

Lio took a step closer to Mak, planting his staff on the floor. "Hesperines can be trusted with armaments. For the same reason we can be trusted with immortality. Hespera blessed us—or cursed us—with the ultimate limitation on our power. The Blood Union."

"Empathy," Cassia said.

It felt more like a curse in a room full of people Lio loved who were hurting. All their emotions were running high, throbbing out of the raw edges of their flagging veil spells. In the center of it all, Cassia's unconcealed heart beat. Once the most closed of them all, but now the most open.

When Mak didn't reply, Lyros broke the silence. "It's a good proposal." He paused. "I wish you'd told me."

"It doesn't matter now," Mak replied lightly. "Fugitives can't march into the Firstblood Circle for a cordial policy debate."

But Lio knew that whether or not the firstbloods ever saw that proposal, it would never cease to matter that Mak had not made Lyros a part of it.

21

nights after

WINTER SOLSTICE

CALL OF GLASS

"No," Cassia pleaded.

She couldn't see the Collector. But she knew he was here with her before the door.

"No, please," she begged him. "Anything but this."

She couldn't hear his laughter. But she felt it. He savored her desperation like a fine wine.

Pain erupted out of her heart, and she clutched her chest. His icy, unseen hand reached for the spark of power and promise inside her. His nails dug into her magic.

"No, please," she sobbed, grasping at her magic, at herself.

It slipped through her fingers. So beautiful. He was taking it from her, the only treasure she'd ever had, and she would be empty forever.

The door shuddered. Her hoarse screams and the rumble of stone echoed through the halls. She went down on her knees as her power bled out of her throat and the door cracked open.

Through the blur of her tears, she saw what lay beyond the portal.

A second door, sealed tighter than the last.

"Cassia!"

Another presence filled the halls. So much power. His resonant voice could bend the world to the shape of his words.

Glasstongue.

"Cassia!" he called her again.

She tried to answer, but she couldn't get air into her chest. Couldn't push words through the agony in her throat.

His Will cut through the stones and the pain. The Collector's hold on her shattered. She felt Lio's arms around her as the vision of the breached door—and the next portal behind it—shredded into nothing.

Cassia came out of the Slumber all at once, heaving at the air. Lio held her shuddering body tightly against him.

"It's not real." His voice, potent with thelemancy, oriented her. "It was a day terror. I pulled you out of it as soon as I could."

Not real. She dug inside herself, scrambling to feel her magic.

Her power welled up from within her, lush and verdant. Dark and eternal. Her plant magic, but more than that. She felt her mouth, and when she cut her finger on one of her fangs, she sobbed with relief.

"You are whole." Lio rocked her in his arms. "You are powerful, my immortal. He can never do that to you again."

Her Grace's presence flowed through their Union, immersing her in his closeness. Together, they traced the arcane paths in her veins, reassuring her that her magic thrived. He held her until her weeping calmed, and she could breathe again.

She sat up in the luxurious bed of the Changing Queen, which they had claimed as their own. The fading glow of twilight came in through the window. "You pulled me out of the Dawn Slumber early?"

Lio sat up beside her. "That's the first time I've ever cast a Night Call. I'm thankful it worked."

"So am I." She wrapped her arms around herself.

He stroked her bare back. "I tried to be gentle, but I'm afraid having another Hesperine use magic to yank you out of your sleep is never pleasant."

"I've heard the stories of an elder jolting a youngblood awake with a shout that feels like a blizzard in your veins."

"That's how my uncle does it."

She caressed Lio's face. "Your Night Call was nothing like that. You sounded like…rescue. Thank you."

That power echoed in Lio's aura still. "I will make him pay for that dream."

Cassia swallowed. "I'm not sure it was a dream."

He pulled her close again. "Talk to me about it."

She described what she had seen, their hearts racing faster together as the realization sank in.

"Was it a premonition?" Lio asked tightly. "A warning from the Lustra about what he has yet to do? Or…"

"Or a vision of what he's already done." Cassia spoke their greatest fear aloud. "I don't know. I only know he has the power to open the first door. Because he took it from me."

"We have to stop him before the next door falls."

"We're not ready." Lyros leaned both hands on the table in the dining hall.

"I know." Cassia glanced over their scrolls and maps in the wavering light of the hearth. She saw only their questions, not any of the answers they were searching for. "You know I would rather train more before we go to Castra Roborra. But I can't tell from the dream how much time we have left."

"We can't afford to wait any longer," Lio said. "We must face Miranda and do the best we can."

Mak put his hand over Lyros's. "We still have one advantage. Surprise. As long as the Collector believes we were last seen in Patria, he'll think we're focusing on the war. The longer we wait, the more time he has to realize we're not there—and that we're racing him to the doors."

Lyros bowed his head, his brow furrowed in thought. Then he straightened. "Right. We don't have a choice. We'll make the best of it. Let's adhere to the strategy we agreed on, even though we didn't have time to finish practicing. We'll work together to wear Miranda down enough to capture her, then bring her back here for questioning. Are all of you clear on your roles?"

Mak nodded. "While you focus on defensive wards, I'll cast Blood Shackles on her to prevent her from traversing away."

"I have something that might help." Lio set down a pair of heavy iron cuffs linked with a chain. "Mak, can you tell us if these are still in working condition?"

"Traversal cuffs!" Mak examined them. "Yes, the metal and enchantments are sound."

"How did you get your hands on a pair?" Lyros asked. "These look ancient."

Cassia gestured downward. "We found them in the cellar. We're not sure if they were Ebah's or Lucian's, but it's no surprise they'd have such things to use against their enemies."

"Excellent find," Lyros replied. "Snapping these on Miranda may be easier than casting Blood Shackles, depending on how the battle plays out. Lio, Cassia, any questions about your part of the battle?"

Lio shook his head. "I'll focus my thelemancy on helping Mak disable her. Fishing for secrets can wait until we secure her in the tower."

Cassia shifted on her feet. "I'll watch for your signal of when to activate my enchantment on our weapons."

Lyros put a hand on Cassia's shoulder. "We'll need your roses."

"You can trust me not to hesitate," she promised.

"Good." Lyros gave her shoulder a squeeze.

"You two will still need to be careful," Mak told Lio and Cassia. "A few weeks of intense training can't catch you up to the lifetime of professional skill Lyros and I have." He lifted a hand to ward off Lio's protests. "That's not a criticism, just common sense."

Cassia put a hand on Knight, but she knew that even with a liegehound at her side in battle, Mak was right.

"Let Lyros and me take the hardest hits," Mak said. "This isn't the time for noble self-sacrifice, understand? Let the warriors do what we do best. You two focus on using your magic and fall back on your combat skills when you're in a tight spot."

Lio nodded in acquiescence.

"All right." Lyros stepped back from the table. "Let's saddle up. We'll step there, a safe distance from the ruins, then approach on horseback. We'll need to scout our path carefully to make sure we don't spring any traps."

Cassia shuddered, recalling the necromantic traps that had been waiting for her and Lio at Paradum when Miranda had tricked them into stepping there with her. Lio's memories of it also flashed across their shared mind's eye. Excruciating pain, followed by blackness. Then they had woken with Lio chained to a wall and her strapped to the Gift Collector's work table.

Here they were, following Miranda into another ruin from Cassia's past. The Gift had helped Cassia forgive Miranda and herself for the betrayals that had brought them to this point. But she knew Miranda's pain and rage would only burn hotter after their last encounter.

"We held our own against four Gift Collectors," Lio reminded them, "and Cassia and I have defeated Miranda before. Victory isn't impossible."

"It's never impossible," Lyros replied, "but it's always a question of what it will cost."

"As long as we capture her alive," said Lio, "it will be worth it."

The different outcomes they had prepared for ran through Cassia's mind like another terrible dream. She didn't like any of her and Miranda's possible futures.

Cassia's throat tightened. "Do you think there is any hope of freeing her from him?"

Mak and Lyros exchanged glances.

Lyros spoke gently. "There has never been a Gift Collector whose loyalties changed. Not one, in sixteen hundred years."

She gave a numb nod. "Thank you for being honest with me."

"We know you prefer the truth," Lyros said. "In our opinion, once Lio gets the information we need from her mind, the best possible outcome is to defeat her to the point that her master must revive her. Perhaps then you'll have a reprieve from her quest for revenge, for a time."

Was this to be their fate? Both immortal and doomed to an eternal duel through each round of the Old Masters' game?

Lio's touch on her cheek fetched her gaze to him. *I freed Eudias. If my thelemancy can break the Collector's hold on Miranda, I'll try.*

Cassia clutched his hand. She knew why he was whispering this intention into her mind. Lyros and Mak would never agree to it. She wasn't sure she should, either.

This is different, she protested silently. *Miranda isn't an innocent victim* like Eudias. She gave her magic to Kallikrates and asked him to possess her. She won't fight him with you as Eudias did.

I know. But imagine if I could discover a way to sever an Overseer's bond with Kallikrates. We could rob him of his most powerful playing pieces and make the Gift Collectors mortal again... and perhaps give Miranda some hope of a different future.

I want to believe that's possible, but I don't think it ever will be unless she makes a choice. Don't fight him for her freedom if it puts you in greater danger. He's waiting for his chance to take revenge on you for freeing me.

I'll be careful, her Grace promised.

So why did she feel he had left his caution behind in Orthros? If her words of compassion toward Miranda came back on Lio, she would never forgive herself for that.

TRAITORS' GRAVE

Sometimes Lio wished mind magic lent itself to elaborate rituals or complex spell ingredients. There was a certain comfort in making physical preparations for a casting. Those gestures made a mage feel in control. Of magic. Of outcomes.

But all Lio could use to control his affinity was pure Will. The only way to ready himself for his rematch with Miranda was to sit quietly in his saddle and prepare his mind. Moonflower and Freckles followed Mak and Lyros's horses, leaving Lio plenty of time, or perhaps too much, with his own thoughts.

He kept thinking of that moment when he'd held Miranda's mind under his power. She was different from a nameless war mage throwing fireballs at him. Perhaps she shouldn't be—every life he had the power to destroy was still a human life.

But Miranda was someone Cassia used to love. She could have turned out like Cassia, if Hesperines had found her before Kallikrates did.

She had also taken Cassia's magic, subjecting his Grace to the torture she had relived in her day terror. It had been Kallikrates's doing, but he had used Miranda's hands to perform the spell. She had offered those hands to him willingly and painted an Eye of Hypnos on her breastplate in Cassia's blood.

Lio remembered how Miranda's head had felt between his palms and the pleading look she had given him. The pitiful way she had begged him not to bring her Master's wrath down upon her for her failure… Until Kallikrates himself had spoken through her.

You will have to duel me.

He had been ready to fight Lio, not for Miranda's sake but to keep Lio from discovering the secrets in her mind.

Could Lio have won? Perhaps. He'd had the power of a rabid letting site flowing through him, a boon from the Lustra to Cassia's mate in her hour of need. Tonight, he must rely only on his own power.

Cassia's touch in their Union pulled him out of his thoughts. *You've stopped meditating and started overthinking. Try not to make this harder for yourself, my love.*

He gave in to her invitation to focus on her instead. Amid the dread of what they were about to face, the reality of it struck him anew. They had Grace Union now. She was immortal with him.

Immortality didn't feel as certain on a night like this. But Grace Union did.

She reached over and took his hand.

Ahead of them, Mak murmured something to Lyros, then dropped back to ride on Lio's other side.

"Did Lyros send you to make sure I'm not planning anything rash?" Lio asked.

"Yes." Mak made a face at him. "Somehow it's become *my* duty to tell *you* not to be impulsive. The world has gone mad."

"That's precisely why he'll listen to you," Cassia said. "Lyros and I can't reason with him any longer. You can speak to him as one hothead to another."

"I haven't become a hothead," Lio protested.

She eyed his staff. "Whatever you say."

"There's something you should know." Mak's smile was humorless. "Nike would have my fangs for breathing a word of it, but no telling how long it will be before we see her and she has an opportunity to make me regret it."

"A secret of your sister's?" Lio asked. "Something that could help us in the battle tonight?"

Cassia leaned forward in her saddle to look around Lio at Mak. "Does this have to do with her quest to find out if Methu is alive?"

Mak hesitated. "Yes and no."

Lio raised his brows. "We always suspected she confided more in you than you were letting on."

Mak gnawed on his lip. "I do try not to cross the veil. But I'm not even sure where the veil is these nights."

"If it could keep us safe," Cassia pointed out, "I don't think she'd begrudge you telling us."

"Right." Mak sighed. "Lyros is correct that a Gift Collector has never changed sides. And no necromancer in history has every become a Hesperine."

Lio felt Cassia's heart twinge, and he frowned at Mak. "This is not reassuring us about the battle."

Mak held up a finger. "But there is a necromancer who has allied with a Hesperine."

Lio had to shut his jaw before speaking. "Nike has a necromancer ally? Your sister, who has sent so many of them back to Hypnos that he probably has a dedicated portal to the realm of the dead just for her victims?"

Mak gave a sad laugh. "Wish you'd had time to tell her that. It would have made her laugh."

Mak's homesickness washed over Lio. He tried not to wonder what his own sister was doing at this moment. It was hard not to imagine Zoe crying and frightened and confused about why he and Cassia would put her through this separation.

"What else did Nike tell you about her ally?" Cassia asked.

"Oh, she didn't tell me. I found out in time-honored younger brother fashion—by snooping. You remember all those scrolls she filled after she came home?"

Cassia nodded. "It seemed she might be writing down her findings from her travels."

"They're letters," Mak told them. "She's been writing to the necromancer. And he writes back."

Lio stared at his cousin. "Nike is pen friends with a mage of Hypnos?"

"How does she even get her messages to him?" Cassia asked in disbelief. "One does not simply send a courier into a necromancer's lair."

Mak shook his head. "The fellow uses his familiar like a carrier pigeon. It's a vulture. An undead vulture."

"A literal bloodless vulture," Lio said flatly.

"That was my first reaction, too." Mak shuddered. "Uncanny thing."

"And where *is* this apostate's lair?" Cassia wondered.

"He's not an apostate," said Mak. "He's a mage in the Order of Hypnos. In Corona."

"What in all the Divine Domains?" Lio uttered. "That's…unbelievable."

"And brilliant." Cassia's admiration and regrets tangled in her aura. "Nike has a source among the enemy."

"How does this help us tonight?" Lio asked. "We can't march into Cordium and ask him for information. And we can't ask Nike to politely write to him and request he send us Kallikrates's secrets by carrier vulture."

"That's not the point." Mak looked at Lio as if his head was full of rocks this time.

"Ah," Lio said after a moment. "Your point is that there is one necromancer who's had a change of heart. And if there's one, who says there can't be two?"

Cassia's gratitude throbbed in the Blood Union. "Thank you, Mak. That gives me hope."

Mak bowed from the saddle. "Think about that before you do anything hot-headed, will you, Lio?"

The forest outside Castra Roborra looked smaller to Cassia now than to her seven-year-old self. And yet it was richer with scents and sounds. The year's fallen leaves, ripe with decay, now trapped beneath fresh frost. The lone lament of a bird. The clack of bare branches against each other in the wind.

"The woods feel deserted to me." Her own voice sounded hushed to her in the winter night.

"I don't sense any minds so far," Lio confirmed.

She clucked her tongue softly and murmured a command to Knight to seek for enemies. Nose to the ground, he disappeared into a nearby cluster of evergreens.

Warding magic waned in the air, a spell returning to Mak and Lyros's hands. Mak shook his head. "The wards we sent out didn't activate any death magic. Yet."

"There may still be traps nearer the fortress," Lyros cautioned.

Cassia halted Freckles beneath a tree that seemed familiar, although she couldn't place it in her memories. Then she realized it was not from her own recollections of that night, but the final moments of Solia's handmaiden, which Nike's mind magic had allowed Cassia to witness.

"Iris was captured right here," Cassia said.

The other three paused around her, and they all shared a moment of silence for the brave woman who had sacrificed her life for her future queen.

"We're getting close." Cassia urged Freckles onward.

They rode between stunted saplings and once-proud oaks with scars burned into their bark. Not from the fires of battle. Cassia recognized the signs of salt damage. More than that, she felt the sickness in the soil. And yet that proved to her the Lustra was still alive here, somewhere deep, giving her a sense of the poisoned land.

Knight returned to them, falling into step beside Freckles. Cassia reached down to pat his shoulder. He hadn't bayed a warning, so he must not have found anything. But he remained alert, which also put Cassia on guard.

The forest ended abruptly at a line of dead pines. She looked across the field of snow before them to the place where fortress walls had once towered over her. She didn't need to say a word for Lio to pull Moonflower closer to her.

He reached over and clasped her hand. *I almost lost you here before I ever knew you.*

She squeezed his hand. *You gained me here.*

"This is where I first met a Hesperine," Cassia said.

Mak let out a breath. "Nike saved your life right here?"

"The arrow hit the ground in this area." Cassia gestured to the snow at Freckles' hooves, then at the trees behind them. "She carried me into the shadows, where Alkaios and Nephalea were waiting."

Lyros pointed across the field. "And that's where the fortress stood?"

"Yes."

Cassia remembered looking out across that seemingly impassable distance to the bodies Lord Bellator had catapulted over the walls. She had believed Iris's broken form was Solia.

That horrific moment had defined her human life. Now, turning over that shard of her past in her mind, she discovered it was one her Gifting had smoothed so it was no longer too sharp to touch.

She breathed, her chest free of the crushing weight of that grief and bitterness and despair. She had survived this place. She had even healed from it.

Whatever danger lay in the ruins, her past was no threat to her. She bared her fangs at the snow-covered rubble ahead. *Let Miranda do her worst.*

We'll face this place together, this time, Lio answered.

They drew their weapons and fell into the formation Lyros had taught them, with him at their back and Mak ahead, Knight and Cassia on either side of Lio.

I still protest this arrangement with every fiber of my being, Lio informed her. *You should be in the center where you're safest.*

You know the rest of us overruled you about this several training sessions ago. Let my roses throttle your enemies so you can concentrate on breaking the dream wards protecting Miranda's mind.

I will, but not happily.

I know, my champion.

His thelemantic veils descended over them while Mak and Lyros's wards swept out ahead. Cassia adjusted her grip on her dagger as they rode forward across the field.

It was too quiet. Her heart seemed lodged in her throat. Despite all their spells, she felt exposed.

They reached the snow-capped, crumbling stones that marked where the outer wall had been. Not a living creature disturbed Traitors' Grave. No magic raised the hairs on her arms. And yet there was a thick presence here, a stirring of some other power.

An instant before it overwhelmed her, Lio's magic shot through the mind ward and bled into their Grace Union. The onslaught of impressions broke against his magic, and they tugged on her heart as if from a distance.

The certainty that all was lost. The anger that this was the end. Grief, blow after blow, until the loss and the blood wore her down like visions of her own impending end repeating before her eyes.

Even held at bay by Lio's magic, the flood of emotion made her stomach sour. She swallowed hard. "Do all battlefields feel like this to Hesperines?"

He nodded. "Where blood soaks the soil, so do emotions. The residual energy of so many lives ending can be overwhelming to our senses, even years after the fact."

"I wasn't prepared for that." She took another deep breath. "I should have been."

"You'll get stronger," Mak reassured her. "I won't say it ever gets easier, but you develop the ability to cope with it."

She shook her head. "What if we'd been ambushed while I was losing my grip?"

"We weren't," said Lio, "and I'm better able to shield you from remnants of the past than from your own living experiences in battle."

"Thank you," she told him.

Lyros's aura hummed with tension that brought to mind his spear when he was just about to strike. "I'm not sure the ambush we expected is going to happen. We may be able to ambush her. Let's stay veiled and search the ruins."

They picked their way through the maze of rubble. There wasn't a wall or roof still standing, but the way the chunks of the fortress had landed, they had created plenty of hiding places where Miranda might lurk. Watching every twitch of Knight's tail for signs of danger, Cassia began to jump at shadows.

Piles of stone, shattered by the mages' enchanted siege weapons, now formed cairns for those who had died trapped under them. From between two stones, a hollow-eyed skull met Cassia's gaze, and she recoiled. Lio reached over to touch Freckles' neck, guiding them away from the sight.

These soldiers had betrayed Solia, murdered the few men loyal to her, and mutilated Iris. In Cassia's human life, she would have spat on that skull. She didn't want to feel compassion now. But she did, and she clung to that feeling nonetheless. Her path to Hespera had begun in this place, and she had not turned from the Goddess yet.

The bones of dogs, horses, and page boys left icy tears on her cheeks. She pushed herself onward with Lio and their Trial brothers until they reached the center of the ruins, where the keep had stood.

Lucis had not left this grave to chance. The body he'd put on display here had long since wasted away, but the skeleton remained impaled on a banner pole. The wind tugged at the moldering flag bearing King Lucis's emblem. The broken shield strapped to the dead man's chest left no doubt as to who he had been. That black horn on a field of gold was the emblem of the former Free Lord Bellator.

Cassia sucked a breath into her lungs. "Perhaps I was wrong about salt and bones. There's no sign of Miranda here. I'm sorry if I've brought us through this for nothing."

"There's one thing we haven't checked for," Lio said. "Do you feel able to search for Lustra portals?"

She nodded, rubbing her eyes. "Yes. We've made it this far."

"Are you sure?" Mak asked.

"We can step away to the trees if you need a moment," Lyros offered.

"No, I can cast," Cassia said. "We should be certain we didn't overlook anything. Then we can leave this place behind with no unanswered questions."

Lio dismounted swiftly and helped her down from her horse. This time, she didn't protest. All the death had left her weak in the knees. He turned them away from Bellator and kept a steadying arm around her as she raised her dagger to her hand.

Her blood slid along the blade. She let one drop stain the snow at their feet.

Her first warning was the sickening sound of bones shattering. Then Mak and Lyros's shouts. She and Lio spun to face Bellator's corpse.

It wasn't there. The skeleton had exploded, leaving a fissure in the snow and the air, a maw opening in the world. Wind blew from inside it and tore at their clothes, bathing them in the scent of belladonna.

She had seen such a thing only once before: in Orthros, when the Collector and his Overseer had opened a displacement gate.

She had an instant for the moves to make sense in her mind. A spell hidden in the bones. A trap waiting to be awakened with the one thing Hesperines would surely shed—blood.

Then a figure stepped through the portal, his spurred boots clanking in the snow. A blond man, tall and muscular, without a scar on his handsome face. She had never seen him before. But there was something familiar about his cruel smile.

When he spoke, there was no mistaking his voice. He sounded like he had spent centuries breathing down magic until it left him raw.

"I told you I wouldn't let you escape," Skleros said.

THE BARGAIN

Lio had last seen that smile on Skleros's severed head. How had Kallikrates shoved the Gift Collector's detached spirit into this new body?

"Were you expecting Miranda?" Skleros rasped. "She's out of favor after her last failure. That little bitch should have known she'll never take my place as the Master's champion."

Facing the wrong Overseer was not a possibility they had practiced for. The Union Stones in their weapons flashed with quick pulses of light. Lyros's signal to retreat.

No. A veteran Gift Collector would know even more secrets. They could take him with the same strategies they had planned to use against Miranda. Lio shot magic into his Union Stone, flashing back the sign to capture.

In that instant of indecision, more skeletons shattered all around them.

Bear's screams tore the air as he went down. Mak landed on his back, arms and legs flat against a dark hexagram that burned through the snow. A jagged bone pierced Lyros's chest and propelled him off his mount. He struck one of the stone cairns, and the shard pinned him there.

Lio's heart jolted, as if trying to beat for Lyros's. How close was the bone to his heart?

With a powerful, two-handed swing, Skleros aimed a headsman's axe at Lio's neck, and there was no ward to stop it.

Lio swept his staff out. The blade of the axe struck Final Word with a clang that made his teeth ache. Behind Skleros, something dark glinted in the snow. The traversal cuffs. The trap must have blown them from Mak's grasp.

Skleros's smile widened. "Remember what I said at Rose House. Your head is next."

"Your heart is next," Lio snarled.

They had no plan for this, but Cassia's thoughts met his in the flow of power and anger between them. Their strategy was clear in both their minds. They moved as one.

Lio retreated under Skleros's vicious swings. Cassia stood clear of the skirmish and gripped her dagger, wearing a grimace of frustration. Knight backed away, staying close to her.

Skleros's hoarse laughter taunted them. "Haven't learned much since our last round, have you? You're still too soft to survive the Master's game. And she's still a clueless chit trying to use an artifact she doesn't understand, destined to be no more than a tool in his hands."

It was working. The fool underestimated them, cocky in his new form.

In the noise of battle, Lio strained to catch his Trial brothers' faint pulses. His only reassurance that they lived was that their bodies were not returning to the Goddess in a flash of light before his eyes. Their pain fractured the Blood Union.

Pain Lio and Cassia would deal Skleros. They would show him he was not as indestructible as he thought.

Blow by blow, Lio let Skleros drive him back. The long axe had a greater range than any weapon Lio had faced before. He kept the Gift Collector at staff's length as Mak had taught him.

The man drove at him with inhuman strength and speed. But not Hesperine strength. Lio held his physical power in check even as he pushed his training to the limit to avoid losing his head. He fell into the flow of battle, as if his staff were a part of him. He watched every twitch of muscle in Skleros, trying to anticipate each swing of that deadly blade.

Just as the axe moved right, Lio shifted into a high right guard. But Skleros pivoted his weapon. Too fast. The axe swung low and sliced open the side of Lio's robes.

He spun his staff and knocked the axe back just before it broke his skin. The necromancer's breath clouded in the air with exertion, but still he smiled.

Cassia's power built under Lio's feet. Through her, he was aware of the

Lustra magic that eluded other mages' senses. Even Skleros's. The tainted ground roiled with vengeance.

Knight never wavered from his defensive stance in front of Cassia, protecting her as she cast. His barks boomed at the Gift Collector.

"Do you think a dog can protect you long enough to get off a spell?" Skleros spat. "He didn't hold up very well against me in Orthros, did he?"

An explosion rippled beneath the ground at Cassia's feet. A burst of necromancy smothered by the Lustra. Now it was her turn to give Skleros a savage smile. "I didn't have my magic in Orthros!"

"Go ahead," Skleros said. "Try your power against the Master. He's looking forward to putting you in your place."

Their ruse was wearing thin, but Skleros was far enough from the portal now. He could never outrun a Hesperine to reach his escape route.

Now, Lio said in Cassia's mind.

Ready, she replied.

The salted soil broke, and the grieving land reclaimed the ruins.

Her roses tore across the rubble, covering the snow in black. A dozen more traps set off, leaving holes in the vines, only for more roses to pour out and cover them.

Thorns ate the ground around Mak and Lyros, crumbling the death magic that trapped them. The vines rose to form protective walls around them. Another barrier grew up around the portal, cutting off Skleros's retreat.

Before he could escape with magic, Lio made the attack he'd been holding back. He went low, dodging under the path of Skleros's axe, and swept his staff behind the man's ankles. Living bone cracked this time. Skleros went down.

Cassia's roses snaked around Skleros like chains, tearing the axe from his hand. Lio summoned the traversal cuffs into his hand and snapped them around the necromancer's broken ankles.

She came to stand over Skleros, her dagger dripping blood to feed the roses that held him captive.

Lio leaned down, pressing his staff across Skleros's throat. "You're lucky there's something in your brain that's of use to me. I'll wait till I'm done with your mind before I drive adamas through your heart."

Skleros only laughed again. "You're learning. But not fast enough. I've survived every round of the game since the first. Do you think I'm afraid of an infant like you?"

"You should be," Lio said. "That many millennia of secrets will take time to extract. I won't be done with you for a long while."

"No," Skleros replied, "you won't be rid of me until the Master wins the final round."

"Don't listen to him," Cassia said. "You have to help Lyros and Mak."

Lio nodded and pulled his staff back. Knight pinned Skleros under his weight and growled in his face.

Lio levitated to Lyros first. The thorns parted to let him through.

Just in time for Lyros to stagger against him. One jagged bone dangled from Lyros's hand. Lio caught his Trial brother and pressed a desperate hand over the bleeding hole in his chest.

CASSIA DUG HER HANDS into Skleros's new blond hair and wrenched his head back. Her blood pounded with years of muddled pain. The Lustra's at the king's rape of the land. Her own at the destruction Skleros had once brought into Hespera's Sanctuary. And now the suffering he had inflicted upon her Trial brothers.

"Here's a souvenir from this round of the game," she hissed.

She traced her dagger across his unblemished face, making an ugly slice from above his left eye to his right jawline. Lustra magic welled in his blood, and more tiny cuts feathered out from the wound, like thorns.

"My first scar in this form," Skleros mused. "Do you think such a trophy an insult to me? You should know my pain only gives the Master pleasure, Cassia."

His ruined voice grew smooth and deep. His rough tone was gone, and the syllables of her name seemed almost intimate on his tongue.

Her stomach turned over. She moved her dagger to Skleros's throat, holding her magic at her fingertips.

One wrong move, and he could unleash untold magics on all of them.

"Hello, Kallikrates," she said.

The Collector studied her face through Skleros's eyes, his gaze a caress that made her want to claw at her skin. "Your Gifting has dulled your pain, but it could be sharpened again with the right touch."

She wanted to spit in his face, but an idea took hold in her mind. More dangerous than anything she had ever attempted. Perhaps the only thing that could save them now.

She *was* an infant compared to this ancient, twisted mind. He had taken them by surprise at every turn. This might also be a trap in the form of words, not spells. But even so, it was an opportunity to attempt what she had never dared before.

A negotiation with the Collector.

Lio's alarm rang in their Union. *Cassia, what are you thinking?*

She was thinking of that bone spearing Lyros. Of a wolf's claws raking Mak's chest. Of a Gift Collector's poison creeping slowly toward her Grace's heart. Would they live through the next close call?

This is my chance to spare us from a battle that might be our last, she told Lio.

Cassia, no—!

Out of the corner of her eye, she saw him levitating with Lyros across the battlefield. She had to buy them time. If the Collector grew tired of toying with them, it would take all four of them to survive whatever spell he unleashed.

"I still understand you, Kallikrates," she said. "You know I've always been a schemer after your own heart."

His rich laughter washed over her, and she felt filthy. "You are. I see that you're attempting to talk your way out of this round. Ambitious, little Silvicultrix, especially without your soothsaying power."

She leaned closer and smiled with all her fangs. "How do you know plant magic is the only affinity I have?"

His gaze sharpened on her face. She had his attention now.

She pressed the knife a little closer against his throat, just enough to draw blood. "I opened a letting site in Orthros."

He sucked in a breath, and she knew she had accomplished a great feat, even if this negotiation ended in disaster.

"I'm one of the only people in thousands of years who has surprised you, aren't I?" She traced her dagger under his chin.

"You and Lio are threatening the game's existence. You learned of our grand design and betrayed that secret to others. That knowledge is only for my Overseers—or those doomed to die. The rules demand that I destroy you."

"And yet you hate the thought of sacrificing me. It goes against your grain to waste such a valuable playing piece."

"You would have been one of my most beautiful weapons. But you've fallen into the wrong hands, and I cannot allow that. You know that."

"Perhaps there's another way." She gave him her coldest court smile. "For the right price. Tell me what's behind the doors, and I might be willing to help you open them."

She had looked into the eyes of her possessive sire, lustful suitors, and predatory enemies. But none compared to the covetous gleam that lit the Collector's gaze.

"My dear, after all these years. Could you finally be having a change of heart?"

What in the Goddess's name are you doing? Lio demanded.

Trust me.

Their Union vibrated with his protest, but he was too busy staunching the blood Lyros was losing to do anything about her wild plan.

"I'll never lick your boots like Miranda," Cassia said. "If you're counting on my devotion, you can go to Hypnos. You know what I want, Kallikrates."

He smiled. On Skleros's new face, it was a beautiful smile warped by the fresh scar she had given him. "You want your power."

"That's all I'm interested in, do you understand? The magic that's rightfully mine. All of it."

"Even immortality is not enough for you, is it? Unlimited time is not the greatest mystery or the greatest prize. I'm sure you found it a small ambition, just as I did. You know that the real goal is unlimited magic. The power to peel back every mystery of the arcane and break it in your hands until it no longer shapes you. You shape creation."

Were these words merely more poison, or could they be a valuable glimpse into what really motivated him? Either way, she had to keep him talking.

"Whatever lies behind those doors is mine," she said, "and you still need my magic to open it. I'll consider helping you on two conditions. You tell me what it is, and you spare my errant circle. If you harm any of the Black Roses, the deal is off."

"I heard that's what you're calling yourselves now. I can appreciate a flare for the dramatic."

"If a single one of us dies, you don't get anything from me."

"Bold, to make such demands of your creator."

"You didn't create me, despite your arrogance about your little plot to breed a Silvicultrix. My mother made me, and Hespera remade me. Don't forget it again, or I will remind you just whose weapon I am now."

"You've always been your own weapon, Cassia. That's why you and I are so alike. You are never without an agenda of your own, and you're willing to do whatever it takes to achieve it."

She kept her court mask in place to hide how much his words affected her. Her ends were just, now. To protect those she loved, she reminded herself. She hadn't strayed too far from Hespera's means, either. Had she?

She spared a glance toward Lio and Lyros. The thorns around Mak parted for them. Black burn marks criss-crossed Mak's arms and legs, but he was sitting up. He took his Grace in his arms, pressing Lyros's mouth to his throat. Almost safe. Just a moment longer...

"What do you think of my proposal?" Cassia prompted.

The Collector paused, as if actually considering the deal she had offered. That should have made her feel victorious. But it frightened her most of all because he seemed pleased.

Finally, he replied, "I shall consider your offer in exchange for a token of good faith."

She adjusted her grip on her dagger. "What do you want?"

"The token isn't open to negotiation. I'll name my price and take it, whether or not you are willing to pay. You've come to my negotiation table now, and that means following my rules."

A crackle prickled at her sensitive ears. Light flashed on her vision, and she screamed. It took all her Will to keep hold of her dagger and not cover her eyes.

Then pure energy blazed up the blade into her hand. A massive force threw her backward. She landed in the rose vines. But they were fizzing with the same energy, too. She heard Lio shouting in her mind, but didn't know how to answer. Her thoughts seemed to fork and shoot out of her grasp.

Through the spots on her vision, she saw tongues of lightning travel along the vines, burning them to nothing. She was helpless in the war magic's grip as another wave jolted up her arm and into her heart.

Kallikrates caressed her face, sparks dancing from his fingertips to her skin. "Your heart is the most vulnerable of all."

He seized her pendant. Her ambassador cords snapped as he tore her talisman from around her neck.

No, she tried to say.

He rose to his feet, running her cords through his fingers, and fondled the pendant with a triumphant gleam in his eyes. "Thank you for unlocking the Changing Queen's tower and retrieving this for me. Quite the token of good faith, don't you agree?"

HEART WOUNDS

Lio couldn't see Cassia through the glare of lightning magic. He only felt her pain. He clutched his chest, his senses blinded.

Mak's magic slammed between them and the onslaught. On his knees in the snow, he had one arm around Lyros, his other hand outstretched and covered in his Grace's blood. He gritted his teeth, shaking as he held his defenses against the war magic. "Go."

Lio levitated and forged through the lightning spell, wrapped in shadow wards. He poured the full force of his thelemancy at Kallikrates.

Lio's power met dream wards that felt like razors ready to shred his every thought. He flooded the maze of spells with his magic and felt the first edges of the Collector's defenses wear away.

He was halfway to Cassia when he cleaved through another dream ward. Pain frayed his veins. He drew more power from inside himself.

Skleros stood over Cassia's body and said in the Collector's voice, "Save some for the next round."

With a flick of his fingers, he tossed lightning at the roses blocking the portal. The vines fell to embers. Leaning on his axe, he strolled through the displacement gate.

Lio's magic battered uselessly against the portal, chasing the mind that was now beyond his reach. His power rebounded back on him, and he staggered. The portal collapsed before his eyes, and the lightning sizzled out.

The air was suddenly silent and cold. Mak's ward lifted, and Lio stepped to Cassia. He went down on his knees and gathered her onto his lap.

His heart beat erratically in his chest, telling him the state of hers. He felt her mind reaching for words and not finding them. Her movements were stiff and uncoordinated.

He cradled her closer, supporting her head, and pushed her fangs into his throat. Her jaw did lock, but there was a tremble in the joint. His blood escaped down his neck, but he massaged her throat until she swallowed. Not much. But enough.

Enough that she would live.

All of them would live. This time.

When Lio was certain Cassia was stable, he stood with her in his arms. Knight had joined them, miraculously unharmed by the lightning. Lio didn't understand how, but he was too grateful to wonder about it.

Mak drew near, leading General with Lyros on his back. Lyros was upright, but his face was ashen, his fangs distended. Bear limped along after Mak, with Moonflower and Freckles trailing him.

"We need to get out of here," Mak said.

Lio didn't argue this time. He and Mak joined their magic to step their Graces as gently as they could. They arrived on the front steps of the derelict tower and hurried through the front door.

They left the horses on the ground floor and headed up the stairs. Now it was Mak's turn to help Lyros into the Mage King's room. Lio carried Cassia onward to their chamber, casting a cleaning spell on the way to their bed. He rested her in the warm blankets and parted the charred front of her robes.

Her pendant was gone. In its place, there was a whorl of burns over her heart. Lio wanted to rip the portal open and hound Skleros until he fulfilled all his promises of revenge. He wanted to tear open the gates of Orthros until they gave his Grace Sanctuary again instead of judgment.

Cassia and Lyros needed healers. But there were no Hesperines he and Mak could take them to without all of them getting arrested. And an army of Chargers stood between them and Solia's aid.

All the Black Roses had now was each other.

Lio joined Cassia on the bed and fed her from his throat again. Then she fell into a kind of dazed rest against him. Knight stayed near, his ears and tail drooping, occasionally giving Cassia's hands fretful licks. Lio thought of how many times he had seen Knight sink into this despair while Cassia lay on the brink of death.

"I'm sorry," Lio said again. "I promised you I'd keep her safe."

The night wore on, and Lio roused her every couple of hours for more blood. He held her distant, muddled thoughts with care. His own hunger became a sharp, hot ache, but he pushed it to the back of his mind, giving her Gift and his blood time to heal her. All that mattered was getting more blood into her and listening to her heartbeat strengthen by a tiny measure each time.

She came to in the twilight hours before daybreak. When her gaze focused on him, he breathed a sigh of relief, blinking hard.

She squeezed his hand, her grip weak. *I'm so sorry I let him take the pendant.*

You're safe. That's what matters.

She gave her head a shake. *After my ancestors kept it secret for centuries… after my Gifting changed it…and everything we went through to retrieve the enchantment here… Now I'm down to one focus, and—*

Shh. He stroked her hair. *Don't worry about that now. Look. Knight is safe too.*

She ran a weary hand over his head. He wallowed closer to her in the bed and propped his head on her belly.

She cleared her throat. "Kallikrates spared him on purpose. He knew our bargain would be off if he hurt anyone I love."

Silence fell between them. Lio harnessed the raging magic inside him and used it to veil his anger from his Grace. Or at least dull the effect of it in their Union.

When he spoke, he managed to keep his voice gentle. "Did you mean what you said to him? About wanting all your power?"

"No."

"Cassia, you know I wouldn't blame you if you did. I want you to have all your magic."

"I don't want it. But it's a motivation he understands, so I let him believe it. You know I didn't mean anything I said to him, don't you?"

"Of course I know that."

"Then why are you so angry?" she asked.

He swore under his breath, his veils shredding at her words. There was no point in hiding. They had promised each other they wouldn't, even when it caused them pain.

"You opened a negotiation with Kallikrates," Lio said.

"Negotiating is what we do. Even now. Or has that staff made you forget it?"

"That staff is for keeping you safe!" Lio's voice rose. "You made a bargain with Hypnos himself! He will make you pay for it, Cassia, and I cannot bear to imagine what the price will be."

"I gave him a reason to spare us." She hugged herself, hiding the fading mark on her chest. "Would you rather he have taken the pendant and left us all dead? At least he let us keep our lives."

"Better to fight our way out than you make this kind of pact with him."

"Do you honestly think there was another way out of that battle?"

"Yes! The moment the Collector manifested through Skleros, you should have let me fight him with thelemancy instead of listening to a single word he said."

"You were too busy holding Lyros's heart inside his chest!" Cassia covered her face with her hands but not before Lio saw her tears.

He bit his tongue. Goddess, this was not what she needed right now.

"I'm sorry," Lio murmured.

He reached out to touch her shoulder. When she didn't flinch away, he pulled her close again.

The minutes slipped away, and the sky lightened. He thought of all the things he might say but spoke none of them, unsure of whether his words would only wound her more. He watched helplessly as she slipped into Slumber.

Before sleep claimed him too, he needed to ask Mak how Lyros was. Lio dragged himself out of bed and went to their door, where he waited for them to sense his aura.

When Lyros opened the door, Lio breathed a sigh of relief. Until the cold anger in Lyros's aura swept over him.

"How are you feeling?" Lio tried.

Lyros leaned one hand heavily on the door frame. "It grazed my heart, but didn't go through it. Hard to aim a corpse. Is Cassia all right?"

"She'll mend. Slowly. Lightning magic isn't fire magic, but it's bad enough."

Lyros looked at him for a long moment, his jaw clenched.

"Think about when Solia ignored you in battle," he said at last. "What happened?"

Solia hadn't heeded Lio's pleas to be patient and strategic. An innocent healer mage had paid the price when the Collector had ripped out her magic. Pakhne continued to exist, hollow and suffering, without hope of a cure or even comfort.

Heat flushed under Lio's collar. "That would have been Cassia's fate if I hadn't Gifted her. Don't compare that to tonight."

"People get hurt if we fight before we think."

Lio thumped his hand against the door frame. "Cassia did get hurt. Over and over again by Kallikrates and his Overseers. Don't tell me not to fight them."

"Throwing yourself at Skleros won't get Cassia's magic back. Do not ever ignore my retreat signal again. Do you understand?"

"Kallikrates knows more about the Lustra than we do. If there's any chance his secrets could help me restore Cassia's power, I will tear apart every Overseer's mind, and I will not retreat until I'm done."

Lio turned on his heel and walked away. Behind him, the door slammed.

Lio fell back into bed beside Cassia, gazing at the burn on her chest. Would it be there, if he had heeded Lyros? Would they have captured Skleros, if Cassia had heeded Lio?

He thought through everything they could have done differently until day closed his eyes for him and banished him into uselessness.

22
nights after
WINTER SOLSTICE

HER ONLY PROTECTOR

Lio tasted sparks on his tongue and jolted toward consciousness. Snow. Bones. Cassia. He felt like he was running through lightning and feared he would reach her too late.

He got a breath in him and scented her lifeblood. She was alive. Her heart beat against his at the slow pace of immortal rest. Fumbling for her, he found her lying beside him and wrapped his sluggish arms around her. Safe.

He opened his eyes and saw her face. Her chin was set at a stubborn angle, as if she remembered why she was angry at him, even in Slumber.

Lio brushed his fingertips over her heart. The dark scar had turned to angry, red new skin.

As he stirred, so did Knight, lifting his head from his paws. He drowsed on the floor in the pile of furs Lio and Cassia had cast off the bed. He certainly didn't share their Hesperine aversion for the pelts.

"She'll be back with us in a little while," Lio said. "You'll have to make do with my company for now, I'm afraid."

Knight laid his head back down with a grumpy chuff.

"I know," Lio said. "The Dawn Slumber makes us all miserable."

After everything she had suffered yesterday, at least he could make her awakening easier. Would her mind wake caged in the stasis of her body tonight? Or would the Slumber continue to inebriate her while her physical instincts awakened first? Either way, he knew how she hated those moments of pure vulnerability.

"Wake under my protection," he murmured to her.

He felt her mind first, a flutter of thoughts cupped in his power. Seeking escape from the grasp of sleep. Seeking him. He nudged her mind with his magic, and her thoughts sharpened.

Lio. There was her mind voice, edged with hunger and panic.

You're safe. He covered her in a heavier blanket of thelemancy until her racing heart calmed.

I hurt, she said. *Why...?*

He squeezed his eyes shut. *Your body is still healing. But you're safe.*

Battle—!

It's over. Let me give you more blood to ease your pain.

Hungry, she groaned. *Can't move.*

He framed her cold cheeks in his hands to give her warmth. *I know, my rose. But I'll take good care of you.*

He guided her mouth to his vein, but her lips rested cool and still on his throat. To help her become more alert, he nudged her thoughts with gentle, rousing waves of magic.

When she finally moved, she shifted her hips, rubbing her lower belly against him with the rhythm of his magic. Well, it seemed the rest of her body was waking before her fangs tonight. At her soft invitations against his rhabdos, he hummed in the back of his throat. He wanted to accept far too much. But he had to stop her.

"You need to drink first." He slid away from her in the bed.

She hooked her leg around him and dragged herself on top of him.

He groaned. "We shouldn't do this right now. You're half asleep and entirely angry with me."

I need you.

He didn't have it in him to deny her anything, not when she made such a demand in his mind.

He wrapped his hands around her buttocks, then slid his palms up over her hips and let his fingers play along her back. Inch by inch, he stroked her immortal body awake, his own hardening to an ache. Goddess, she was so beautiful. When he reached her breasts, sliding his hand between their chests to tease her nipple, she drew her first breath.

She splayed her legs and shifted on him again, searching. He fondled her other breast, kissing her neck, and flared his nostrils. Bleeding thorns, she was so ready.

Fill me, she pleaded.

He took her hips in his hands and lifted her onto his erection. Pulling her down onto him, he thrust up into her slick, pliant heat. Her voice woke with wanton little moans, and his fangs shot farther down.

I'm so addicted to everything about you, he confessed in her mind, driving deep until he was completely buried in her.

Her hands came to life. She pushed herself up, digging her nails into his chest, and stretched her back with a sigh of pleasure. Her eyelids still heavy, her gaze hazed with sleep, she began to move. He lay back and watched her pleasure herself on him.

I'll never get enough of this, he told her. *You, without inhibitions.*

She tightened her inner muscles around him and shifted her angle. Chasing her release, she sent cascades of pleasure through his body. The death of the night before faded, and he felt alive.

When the Slumber fully cleared from her mind, her gaze focused on his face. A flush swept from her cheeks to her nipples. Her mouth rounded in sensual O that made him want to bite her.

"Good Moon, my Grace," he said.

His name was the first word she spoke. Her jaw dropped, and she rode him harder. He showed her his fangs.

She pulled her little feet higher along his sides, her toes curling. As she bowed her head, her hair and his braid fell around her face. Then she shuddered hard, and the pulses of her release traveled along his shaft.

As she climaxed, her canines shot down at last.

"There are those beautiful fangs," he said, breathless.

He listened to her rough groans of gratification. He was addicted to this most of all—knowing he was her addiction.

"I'll take care of you," he promised.

She panted on him, going still, and a furrow appeared between her brows. Her arms were trembling. He felt a ghost of pain in her joints.

"I've got you." Rolling them over, he eased her onto her back. He adjusted their position until the flares of her pain in their Union faded.

When he bared his throat for her, she sank her fangs into him desperately. Goddess, he would give up everything again for this. Under the pads of his fingers, the delicate muscles in her jaw tightened as she locked onto him.

The more blood she downed, the more her body relaxed under him. He couldn't hold back his need to thrust into her, hard and deep with every rush of his blood into her mouth. He let her suck his control away until all the built-up pleasure surged out of him.

He sank his fangs into her throat as he came apart. Tremors moved through the depths of her body again, an echo of ecstasy that only amplified his. Through the waves of his release pounding through him, he heard the lascivious sounds she made against his neck.

Oh, Goddess, she purred in his mind. *Your climax...*

When they collapsed together, well fed on pleasure, he kept drinking hard. He needed to cycle more of his fresh blood into her healing body. He needed more of her. As long as the taste of her was running through him, he could ignore everything else. She whimpered her agreement, licking her way to the other side of his neck to bite him again.

Some time later, he lifted his head to gaze down at her. There was no sign of her wound on her chest. He kissed her there, leaving the bloody mark of his lips over her heart.

She traced her fingers through his hair. "Are you still angry with me?"

"I will always be angry at things that endanger you. Even things you do. Are you still angry with me?"

She paused, then, "Your anger at yourself is enough for you to bear."

25

nights after

WINTER SOLSTICE

PEACE OFFERING

AFTER CASSIA AND LYROS had a few nights to heal, Lio took it upon himself to make a peace offering. He silently thanked Tuura for packing coffee as he set out a travel pot, geomagical warmer, and sack of beans on a table in the dining hall.

He ground the beans with a mortar and pestle borrowed from the Changing Queen. This would either be the most delicious coffee in sixteen hundred years, or drinking it would inflict anomalous arcane effects on them all.

Once the coffee was steeping, he waited. As he had hoped, the scent of Imperial Roast had the effect of a magical summons.

He sensed Cassia's aura drifting out of their bedchamber. She padded into the hall in her veil hours robe with Knight at her side. "Is that coffee?"

Lio poured her a cup and gestured in invitation toward one of the chairs in front of the fire.

Knight stretched out on the warm hearth stones. Cassia took a chair and accepted the coffee from Lio, wrapping both her hands around the cup. For a moment, she just breathed the scent. Then she took a long sip. "Mmmm."

"How are you feeling?" he asked.

"Revived."

Lio sat down at her feet. He checked to make sure she had put on stockings, then leaned back against her legs.

She looked down at him over the rim of her cup. "I'm a Hesperine. I will not catch a chill if my feet get cold."

"You're healing, and you deserve comfort."

Her eyes crinkled with affection, and she ran her fingers through the hair at the nape of his neck. He closed his eyes, enjoying her touch.

A moment later, Mak and Lyros's voices drifted down the stairs.

"No," said Lyros, "I really don't need you to carry me."

"Don't go all hardened warrior on me yet."

"I am a warrior, not a human bride, and I can go down on my own two feet."

"Won't you let me enjoy carrying you?"

Their conversation halted abruptly, and it seemed Lyros had offered Mak a kiss as a consolation.

"No," said Lyros.

A moment later, they entered the dining hall hand in hand. Despite Lyros's assertions that he was in a hardened warrior frame of mind, they weren't dressed for battle. They'd come down in their veil hours robes as well, the attire Hesperines only wore at times of relaxation among their confidantes. That gave Lio hope they hadn't come for a fight. Then again, maybe those were the only clothes they had left that hadn't been torn to shreds in a skirmish by now.

They poured themselves some coffee, and Mak took the other chair by the fire. Lyros sighed as if he'd lost the argument this time. He slid onto his Grace's lap, and a grinning Mak gave him a kiss.

For a moment, it felt like they were all at ease in one of their coffee rooms back home.

But Lio knew that illusion wasn't enough. "I owe you all an apology. I will not make the same mistake again."

"We all owe each other enough apologies to go around," Mak said. "Call it even?"

Lyros said nothing, but he nodded.

Cassia's face was impassive, the expression she got when she was trying not to show weakness. "I owe you all an explanation before you hand out forgiveness."

She didn't look at any of them as she related her conversation with Kallikrates.

Lyros got up and began to pace. There was still so much anger in the way he moved, although his aura was veiled. Lio couldn't blame him.

At last, Lyros faced Lio and Cassia. "Mak and I are trying to keep us all alive."

Her hand went to her chest, where her pendant no longer hung. "Whatever the consequences of my negotiation with him, it will only come back on me."

Lio's own anger flared again. "That is not how this works."

"It is," she insisted. "He knows if he harms any of you, our deal is off. I bargained with him for your protection."

Lyros's gaze flashed. "Do you think 'keeping us all alive' excludes you? We're trying to ensure your safety, too. Will you two stop making that so sunbound difficult?"

"Thank you." Cassia's voice was small. "Yes, we'll try."

Lyros stalked back to Mak's lap.

Their quest was in shambles. Roborra had reminded all of them what their enemy was capable of. They were woefully unprepared and outmatched. They had lost Miranda's trail, and their most precious resource—each other—was under strain. Over the past few nights, Lio had taken plenty of time to think about how he could fix this.

"We need a new plan. The least I can do is suggest a way forward." He held up a hand before Lyros could protest. "You can reject the idea if you think I'm being a hothead again."

Lyros crossed his arms. "We'll consider it. That's all I'm promising."

"Thank you. I think we all agree we should avoid Skleros."

"Yes, but Miranda is a Gift Collector, too. Kallikrates could just as easily manifest through her and fry us all."

"We'll plan wards for that," Lyros interjected.

"Of course," Lio agreed, "but think about what Skleros said. She was their master's favorite, but now he's displeased with her. Perhaps Skleros is more dangerous than she is right now because he has Kallikrates's favor."

Mak looked dubious. "That could simply be his pride talking. Can we believe what he says about his rival, knowing he sees her as a threat to his status?"

"I think Lio's right." Cassia weighed in finally. "Miranda made a catastrophic mistake—she failed to take the rest of my magic, lost a mind-duel with Lio, and let us escape. Kallikrates is sure to punish her, and that puts her at a disadvantage. But however she's planning to earn his forgiveness, it's sure to be painful for us."

Lyros frowned. "And here we are, planning to chase her right into the trap she's set for us."

"Is she hunting us, though?" Mak wondered. "Or running? We've seen little sign of her."

"Oh, Mercy," Cassia said suddenly. "I am such a fool."

Lio looked up at her. "What is it?"

Cassia put her face in her hand. "She has been hunting us all along. The arrow that shot Kalos was made of apple wood."

Lio swore. "I should have realized. She's left us an apple as a taunts before. No surprise, given the importance of Paradum's apple orchard in your shared past."

Cassia bit her lip. "Let us assume that either Skleros or Miranda had a hand in each of our encounters with the Collector's forces."

Lio nodded. "Miranda must have been hidden among the archers who attacked the Patrian villages. She shot Kalos, but perhaps also tried to mitigate the harm upon Mederi."

Cassia set aside her coffee cup as if she felt ill. "Skleros must have been responsible for the heart hunters in Martyr's Pass. That's the same tactic he used when he came to Orthros with the embassy."

"What about the Gift Collectors at the lighthouse?" Mak asked. "It's so rare for them to work together. Could Skleros and Miranda have made sure those four discovered our location? They might have set them on us to eliminate some of their lesser competition for the bounty."

"That makes sense," Lyros said. "Then Miranda's villagers led us to Roborra."

Cassia shook her head. "She wouldn't exploit them to get at us."

"But Skleros would," said Lio. "He'd take particular satisfaction in using her own people against her. With Kallikrates's help, he could easily have planted that clue about her supposed location in the villagers' minds to lure us to him."

"Kallikrates knew I would understand the clue about salt and bones. He wanted to confront us in the place where I met the Hesperines who turned me against him." Cassia's gaze fell. "He also lured us to this tower. He and Lucis must have known it was a Lustra site. I think that's why the king was so determined to send me here during the Equinox Summit."

"That was around the time he was watching for your magic to manifest," Lio said.

She nodded. "I overheard them discussing it in Lucis's solar while Kallikrates was possessing Dalos. I thought they were talking about executing me, but in hindsight, I realize they meant the Collector's plan to take the rest of my magic."

Lyros's eyes narrowed. "That's why the tower was so poorly guarded. He and Lucis wanted you to retrieve the enchantment."

"How could they be sure we would think to come here?" Mak asked.

The ease with which their enemy predicted their thoughts sent a chill down Lio's spine. The Black Roses had retrieved the soothsaying enchantment and then escorted Cassia right into Skleros's ambush so he could take it from her. "They must have known this would be our most likely place to find shelter before approaching Roborra."

Mak blew out a breath. "So Miranda was never at Castra Roborra at all. That leaves us with no leads about her real whereabouts and two Gift Collectors with personal grudges on our tails."

"They also know we're here at the tower," Lyros added. "We need to fortify our thelematic wards around the keep. But no matter how strong we make them, Kallikrates has enough power to break through them if he decides to. We're only safe inside the Changing Queen's spell."

The fire glinted in Cassia's troubled eyes. She was drawing a Hesperine Ritual circle in her mind's eye, five petals and five thorns over and over. Under the distracting thoughts, Lio caught her worries. Her bargain with Kallikrates had spared their lives, but there were still many ways he could twist her words and make them suffer without killing them.

Lio said it aloud. "Their goal has probably changed. They were bent on destroying us before, but after Cassia's conversation with him, we should consider the possibility that he wants to capture us all instead."

Despair weighed deep in her aura, but she gathered the armor of her pride around her thoughts. *I know you don't agree with what I did. You needn't remind me.*

I'm not trying to torture you for your choice. I just don't want you to carry it inside you in silence. You don't have to bear it alone.

Her gaze flashed. *Just like when you wouldn't let me get myself arrested alone.*

Yes, exactly like that.

Lyros lifted his hand, as if to rub his chest, but then let it drop. "The heart wounds they keep dealing us in every battle aren't a coincidence. They're a terror tactic. Kallikrates is trying to make us feel vulnerable."

Cassia finally looked away from Lio, and her gaze went to Mak. "One of us got a heart wound from the Lustra instead. Does that mean my ancestors are trying to scare us, too?"

"I don't pretend to understand the Lustra's strategy," said Lyros.

Mak raised a brow at Lio. "Maybe our philosopher has an opinion."

Lio nodded. "I think the Lustra's heart wound was a mark of honor."

Mak thumped his chest. "I'll take it."

Lio pointed at Lyros's forehead. "That's a sign of respect, too. The Lustra acknowledged your insight. The rest of us should take a lesson from it."

Lyros narrowed his eyes. "You're trying to flatter your way back into my good graces, Glasstongue."

"You know I mean it, too," Lio replied.

Lyros sighed again. "So what's your new plan?"

"We focus on our original goal," Lio said. "Finding Miranda. Without the Collector's favor, she's vulnerable."

Lyros opened his mouth, then threw up a hand. "There are so many ways this could go wrong, I don't even know where to begin."

"If you have a better plan, I will listen," Lio promised.

Lyros had no reply.

"All right," said Mak, "looks like we're going after Miranda again. Any ideas on how to find out where she really is?"

"We have an ally who can help with that." Lio pointed at Knight.

Cassia raised her brows. "Tracking her the old-fashioned way is simple, but brilliant. However…"

"Yes," Lio said. "It will require starting somewhere we know Knight can pick up her trail."

"Patria," Cassia concluded.

"That's madness," Lyros protested. "We'll have to dodge Rudhira, the king's forces, and Gift Collectors. Not to mention the Lustra passages there are full of people who want to arrest us."

Cassia's chin was set. "It's also the location of a rabid letting site. The Lustra will get us in. I will see to that."

Lio should have been filled with triumph that she was finally ready to use her magic. But thinking of her words to Kallikrates, he could not deny he was afraid for her. If she took matters into her own hands again, what might she do next?

26
nights after
WINTER SOLSTICE

CHASING GHOSTS

As Cassia saddled her horse, she felt like their history at the lighthouse was repeating itself. The Black Roses were once again about to leave a Lustra refuge and face a possible ambush. She felt trapped in the moves playing out on the game board. Were they doomed to dance to the patterns Kallikrates dictated until the doors came crashing down?

"Here." Mak handed her a morsel of dried apple. "You and Freckles both need to sweeten your moods."

With a rueful smile, she gave the fruit to the mare. Freckles looked no less grumpy afterward, but Cassia found comfort in watching her horse enjoy the treat. "How is Bear after his fall at Roborra?"

Mak examined his horse's leg. "The sprain has healed, but I'll give him one more dose of my blood before we ride out, as a precaution."

He pricked his hand with one fang, then put a slice of the dried apple on his palm and held it out to Bear. The horse ate up the treat, swallowing Mak's blood along with it.

Cassia watched with interest. "So that's how you care for him as your familiar?"

Mak nodded. "You know that animals can't receive the Gift? When they drink our blood, they don't transform like humans do."

"Yes, Lio explained that to me. He mentioned that our blood gives them healing and longevity."

"Right. It maintains them in the peak of health and prevents aging. Helps them recover faster from injuries, too, although there are still times when they need a healer."

"So Bear really is immortal."

Mak stroked the stallion's head. "He's stuck with me forever, as long as I keep giving him my blood every now and then."

"If you stopped…"

"He'd start aging again and have the normal lifespan of an Orthros Warmblood, which is still quite long."

Cassia fed Freckles another piece of apple. "Can a Hesperine have more than one familiar?"

"Certainly. Uncle Apollon gives his blood to his horse, Patriarch, although the familiar he relies on most during spellcasting is his lion."

The mention of her Grace-father made Cassia's heart ache.

Mak winced. "Thorns, I'm sorry. I didn't mean to remind either of us of home."

"It's all right. If I ever stopped remembering, I'd be far more worried about myself. Tell me about casting spells with familiars."

Lio groaned. "Don't ask him that. We'll be here for hours while he talks about how the Stand uses horses in warding drills."

Mak put on an expression of affront. "You talk my ear off about your research treatises. The least you can do is not fall into Slumber when I'm talking about horse wards."

"That's fair," Cassia said.

Lio put his hand to his heart. "My Grace, the betrayal! Are you taking his side?"

She levitated to place a quick kiss on Lio's mouth. "I'm saying I find both your research treatises and his horse wards very interesting."

His mouth curved in a smile. "Clever words, Ambassador."

Mak laughed, and home felt a little less far away. They might be riding into more death traps, but by Hespera's Cup, at least they could still find ways to laugh with each other.

Lyros, however, seemed in no mood to join in. He came around to each of them, checking to make sure they had packed everything, then grilled them on the tactics they had practiced for the past few nights. She thought he might keep them there a week longer, but at last he seemed satisfied enough with their preparations.

He drew his spear. "Wards and veils up."

"Here we go again," said Mak.

Lio lowered his staff, once more holding it like a knight's lance. "Ready."

"Ckundaat," Cassia said to Knight.

The door of the keep forced them to ride single file. Cassia held her breath as Lyros went first out of Ebah's spell. The rest of them charged after him and leapt down the steps.

They landed in the muddy snow. There was no sound except the call of the hawk hunting in the twilight.

"The thelemantic wards haven't been disturbed," Lyros said.

Mak turned Bear in a circle. "They know we're here. Why haven't they made their move?"

Lio's gaze, sharp with magic, scanned the walls. "Perhaps they are here, but we haven't detected each other yet."

Knight made a quick patrol around the courtyard, but he sounded no alarms.

"They might be choosing a different battleground," Cassia guessed.

"We can hope," Lyros said. "Let's step."

She saw their destination in Lio's mind, a remote area in the domain of Patria where they had searched for a letting site that summer. They stepped and left their errant Sanctuary behind.

Clouds obscured the stars, but Cassia's eyes adjusted quickly. She saw no one and heard no heartbeats in the rolling fields. Lio's magic swept the area, a veiled probe she could only sense in their Grace Union.

"There's a patrol headed this way, about half an hour to the north," Lio said. "No one else."

"Whose patrol?" Lyros asked.

"Rudhira and Solia's. One Hesperine and six mortals. We're clear to ride south and search for the tunnel entrance where Kalos was shot."

Lyros turned General southward, and they all set off with him. As they rode, Cassia opened her senses to the Lustra. She sucked in a breath.

"What is it?" Lio asked.

"Now I can feel how powerful the magic is here. The letting site feels like…a nearby storm. And its rain is running all through the ground."

"The passages," Lio said.

She nodded. "It won't be difficult for me to sense the entrances, but you'll have to open them with your medallion."

He reached out and touched her hand. "I'm certain you could open them without your pendant. But you're wise not to cast any spells this close to the Charge."

She kept her magic in check and let the Lustra guide them. The Warmbloods, already familiar with this territory, required little direction. But Knight kept stopping, his nose to the wind. She could only imagine how confusing it was for him now that their allies were the threat they must avoid. She called for him to come, and he stayed by her side this time.

After half an hour, Cassia spotted Castra Patria in the distance. "With Rudhira and Solia's patrols so near, that must mean they still hold the fortress."

"No fire coming from the walls tonight," Mak observed. "Hopefully that means a lull in the siege and a respite for your sister's forces."

Lyros said darkly, "That also means the Charge is not distracted by the enemy, so they're more likely to detect us."

It hurt to be this close to Solia with no hope of seeing her. They would be lucky if they managed to ride past without getting arrested. Trying to infiltrate the castle would be madness.

Lio sent her comfort through their bond. He had always been her greatest solace when missing her sister. She could bear anything as long as she was with her Grace.

Lyros cast another wary glance at the fortress. "How much farther?"

"I sense another portal up ahead. I think it's the one we're looking for." She showed Lio the passage's route in her mind's eye.

He nodded. "That should be the one where I found Rudhira healing Kalos."

Lyros looked from him to Cassia. "Can you tell if there's anyone inside?"

They both shook their heads.

Lyros's aura was grim. "We'll have to keep our veils up and hope no surprises come out of the portal."

The glowing symbol in the hillside came into view, and they guided their horses cautiously toward it.

Mak frowned. "I can't sense whether there are auras inside either. The magic running through those passages confuses the senses."

"How much time do we have before that patrol behind us catches up?" Lyros asked.

"A quarter of an hour," Lio answered.

"We'd better find Miranda's trail fast, then," Lyros said.

Cassia scanned the surrounding hills. "Any ideas where she was standing when she shot Kalos? We need to get Knight as close as possible to her scent."

"We can easily narrow it down," Mak replied. "An apple wood arrow shot from one of the standard issue bows Lucis's soldiers use, possibly enhanced with malign enchantments…"

"You've been researching archery, too." Lio sounded impressed. "Did you have in mind to craft bows next?"

Mak shrugged. "Not at the forge. The archery research was in case Rudhira or other woodworkers wanted to try crafting bows for the Charge."

"We'll follow you." Lyros gave Mak a look like he was holding back more he wanted to say.

Mak turned Bear and set off across the dry winter grass, guiding them to a slope some distance from the portal. They had just reached the crest of the hill when an impression came to Cassia through the Lustra. The hint of a Hesperine aura.

She drew Freckles to an abrupt halt and looked back the way they had come.

"What is it?" Lio pulled Moonflower near to her.

"The Lustra is warning me," she replied quietly. "I think there's a veiled Hesperine near the portal where we were standing a moment ago."

"How did the patrol get here so fast?" Lyros demanded.

Lio shook his head. "I can still sense the patrol a quarter of an hour away. This is someone else."

"Can you tell who it is?" she asked.

"I can't feel their mind at all. Without your magic, we would never have known they're here."

"Whose veils can hold against your thelemancy?" she asked desperately, knowing it was a short list.

"The Queens' most powerful scion," was Lio's first guess.

"You have to step us away, now!"

Lio set his jaw. "No. See if Knight can catch Miranda's scent."

"If that's really Rudhira, will your veils hold?" Lyros pressed.

"Nike taught me her experimental veils, remember? She evaded him for nearly a hundred years with those spells, and so will we, if that's what it takes."

Cassia wasted no time leaping down from Freckles. She called Knight to attention. *"Ckuundat!"*

For once, it was an advantage that Miranda had painted her breastplate with Cassia's blood. They could only hope the difference between the human blood on the armor and her Hesperine blood didn't confuse Knight.

Cassia bit her hand and held it out to her hound, ready to snatch it back if he tried to do more than smell it. She longed to know what would happen if he licked it, and yet she was afraid to find out. She couldn't risk harming him.

He breathed sharply and took a step back.

Her heart sank. Clearly, she needn't have worried about him being too eager to taste it.

The Lustra hummed another warning. Cassia's pulse pounded. "He's coming closer."

Lyros vibrated with frustration while Mak cursed vocally.

Lio's eyes fell shut, and shadows gathered around him and his mount. "Keep trying."

"*Soor*," Cassia soothed her hound. "It's all right, darling. I know it seems like I'm hurt and my blood smells different now. But I'm safe, and I'm still your *kaetlii*."

Knight moved closer, stretching out his neck and flaring his nostrils.

The Lustra tracked the veiled Hesperine's passage. Their pursuer was crossing the distance with alarming speed. The shadows spilled out from Lio to encircle them all.

Cassia stood still in front of Knight, her blood drying on her hand, her heart in her throat.

"*Seckkaa!*" she tried at last.

He put his nose to the ground. The veiled Hesperine started up the hill.

"My spells will hold." Lio's voice echoed with thelemancy. He was so wrapped in darkness, he looked liked a specter riding a wraith.

Knight sniffed in circles. Cassia's nerves frayed with each moment they stood in the open with a thin veil of darkness between them and the powerful immortal closing in on them.

As her Grace sat locked in a covert duel with a fellow Hesperine, the air became so saturated with magic that Cassia thought she would drown.

"*Seckkaa,* Knight!" she commanded again, uselessly.

Her hound returned to her feet, his tail drooping.

"There's no trail here," Cassia ground out.

Just as their pursuer crested the hill, a Hesperine step swept her away, and their surroundings disappeared.

She and Knight and Freckles landed back where they had begun the search, with Lio, Mak, and Lyros still surrounding them on horseback.

She reached up and took Lio's hand. "How much longer can you keep this up?"

His blue eyes glowed down at her from within the darkness of his power. "Long enough to make sure we aren't followed."

Lyros gazed at Mak. "How sure are you that was the hill she shot from?"

Mak hesitated.

"I need you to be honest," Lyros said.

Mak replied at last. "She shot from that hill."

General danced uneasily under Lyros. "You didn't learn this much about archery from books."

Mak sighed. "I've been picking up some things here and there. From the Ashes and the Tenebrans."

Lyros dragged a hand through his hair. "Bleeding thorns, Mak."

Mak's brows drew together in his most stubborn expression. "I know I should have told you sooner. But I'm telling you now."

"We'll have time for confessions later," Cassia cut in. "We need to keep searching for Miranda."

"Two more attempts," Lyros declared. "If we can't find her trail after that, we go back to the tower. We can't risk more than that if Rudhira is looking for us. Agreed?"

"Agreed," Lio said.

"We only need one more attempt." Cassia levitated into her saddle again. "There's one place in Patria where we know without a doubt that we can find evidence of Miranda."

"No," Lio replied immediately.

"Yes." Cassia turned her horse toward the northeast. "The place we last saw her—Paradum."

"It's too dangerous," Lio protested. "Rudhira surely has it under guard. For all we know, our side of the war has turned it into a garrison for troops, and it's overflowing with Chargers or holy knights or—"

Cassia drew her dagger. "Then they're squatting in my keep. The letting site is mine. I will get us in and out."

Lio closed his mouth. A slow smile spread across his face. "Well, I cannot argue with that. Lead on, Silvicultrix."

CASSIA HALF EXPECTED TO find Paradum in ruins. During her Gifting visions, she and Lio had watched her inner conflicts tear the place stone from stone. But outside that dream world, the small castle still stood, locked tight and eerily quiet. As the Black Roses approached on their horses, not even a night insect chirped.

All that had been destroyed was the letting site. The Lustra magic leeching from its wounds reached out, trying to catch Cassia. She held herself back, her grip firm on her dagger to aid her self-control.

When they halted their mounts a safe distance from the castle, Freckles put her ears back. Switching her tail, she picked up her feet as if the ground were covered in nettles. The other Warmbloods were equally restless.

"It's empty," Lio said in surprise.

"Are you sure?" asked Lyros.

"Yes," Cassia confirmed.

Knight let out a growl, pacing round and round the four riders.

Mak frowned. "If there's no one here, what is he trying to warn us about?"

"*Dockk*," Cassia called.

Knight backed away from the castle to stand close to her. She reached down to stroke him. The fur along his back stood on end.

A frisson of alarm went down Cassia's own back. "This isn't how he behaves when warning us of an enemy. It's almost as if he's…frightened."

She nudged her horse to continue forward. Abruptly, Freckles shied. Struggling to keep her seat, Cassia patted the mare's neck, murmuring reassurances.

Moonflower let out a whinny and began to buck. Lio levitated out of the saddle, landing a bit hard on his feet, and watched his horse bolt in the other direction.

Bear and General galloped after him with Mak and Lyros still on their backs. They were nearly over the next hill before the two warriors gave up trying to control their mounts and rolled out of their saddles.

Lio beat dirt off his robes. "Moonflower has never done that, not once."

Mak popped back into sight next to them with Lyros at his side. "I can't believe this."

Lyros shook his head. "Nothing spooks Warmbloods!"

Only Cassia was still in the saddle. Perhaps it was the strength of Celeris in Freckles' veins or her connection with Cassia. The little mare stood her ground, although she wouldn't go a step nearer the castle. Through the Blood Union, Cassia could feel just how afraid Freckles was and how much determination it took her not to flee.

Cassia leaned down and pressed her cheek to Freckles' neck. "You've proved your bravery today. I know you don't want to be here. It's all right if you go wait with the other horses."

Freckles waited for her to dismount, then shot away and disappeared over the hill.

"What in the Goddess's name is in that castle?" Lyros asked.

Cassia hugged Knight to her. "It's the letting site. Animals can feel that there's something wrong with it."

Mak raised his eyebrows. "No wonder they aren't using this place as a garrison."

Lio rubbed the back of his neck. "I can feel the wrongness too."

"You can?" Cassia asked.

He shivered. "Our bond makes me aware of it now."

The four of them continued on foot, Knight growling at every shadow. Lio led them to a discreet entrance in the back wall. The door lay in pieces, the postern blasted apart and marred by scorch marks.

"Solia did that?" Cassia guessed.

"Yes. This is where we carried you out during the battle." Lio took her hand. "Are you sure you can bear to enter this place again?"

She wasn't afraid, she realized. Far from it. She had to go through that door. She wanted to stand victorious in this place where Kallikrates had once violated her magic.

"I need to do this." She levitated over the debris and set foot in Castra Paradum again.

Knight whined, but followed her, the others close behind. Before she walked further inside, Mak put a hand on her arm. "Let me check for traps."

She glanced at the bow he held. "Where did that come from?"

"The Mage King's armory." He nocked three bloodied arrows and shot the volley into the ground ahead of them. "All clear."

They levitated over the bare ground, Mak checking for traps along the way. Cassia kept Knight heeled, fearing he would go ahead of her and into danger, but her poor hound showed no sign of wanting to leave her side.

She led them through the inner walls overgrown with thorn vines. Her thorns. Those were alive, sprouted from her need the night she and Lio had fought Miranda here.

They passed through the dead apple orchard, through Cassia's youthful memories of Miranda when they had been friends, past the ghosts of her Gifting visions. At the edge of the garden, she paused, looking across to the doorway of Agata's empty kitchen. The cook had looked after her and Miranda like a mother.

Cassia believed Miranda regretted causing Agata's death. It was sickening that she had reanimated their friend as a bloodless, but perhaps preserving her in undeath had been Miranda's twisted way of trying to atone.

Lio put his arm around her. "I'm so sorry about Agata."

Cassia leaned into him. A gentle, aching magic emanated from the kitchen like a lament. She recognized royal Hesperine magic, the cool and powerful traces of Rudhira's power. She knew he was always compassionate when sending the undead to their final rest.

"He freed her here," Cassia murmured.

"Yes," Lio said.

Cassia drew a shaky breath. "I hope she is happy in Mother Kyria's embrace."

"Which way should we go next?" Lyros asked gently.

Cassia pointed to the other side of the garden. What had once been the window of her sickroom was now a gaping hole where vines had destroyed the wall to free her and Lio. "That's where we last saw Miranda."

She set out across the garden. When she reached the patch where her pea plants had once grown, the feathery touch of the letting site became a tangled grip.

She gasped, going down on her knees. She heard Mak and Lyros's voices, felt Lio's alarm in her heart. Knight was baying like a wild thing. But all her senses roared with the power pouring up out of the ground, here where she had channeled Lustra magic for the first time.

The letting site was crying for her. It was a force of nature, without morals or emotion. But she had a heart, and the letting site's pull dragged a chaos of emotions out of her. Grief and anger and joy and recognition.

All of that flowed down her arm, and she plunged her dagger into the ground, returning her first focus to the soil that had forged it.

It didn't tap the letting site. It tapped her. The channel that always ran through her from the Lustra now reversed, the world spinning the other way on its axis. Magic poured out of her and back into the letting site.

She knelt there, caught in the force of it, as if her heart had burst open to feed the land. She saw blood running down the inside of her arms, watering the soil. She wept, not with pain. She had never felt more powerful.

She was healing the letting site.

Cassia. We have to go!

At Lio's warning in her mind, she looked up from the ground. And met a familiar gray gaze.

Rudhira's mouth moved, but she couldn't hear him over the howl of her own magic. He held out his hands, as if trying to approach a wild creature.

The Blood-Red Prince had found them.

RITUAL GROUND

Lio's protective instincts roared, and he stepped in front of Cassia. For once, he didn't understand what she was doing with her magic. He only knew he would defend his Grace until her casting was complete. Even against someone they loved.

Mak and Lyros spread out to Lio's left and right. Knight had Cassia's back, whining in confusion but standing firm by his lady.

Cassia's power rushed through Lio's senses. He wished it would drown out the disappointment in Rudhira's words.

"Let me take you home," their Ritual father said.

"Home?" Lio didn't think before he spoke. His anger pushed the words out of him. "What home do we have anymore?"

"We want you safe. That's what matters now." There was so much grief in Rudhira's voice.

Lio didn't want that grief. That love. Anger would have been easier to fight.

"My Grace isn't safe in a prison cell!" he shouted.

"Think of Zoe and your parents. I don't need to tell you how afraid they are for you."

How could Rudhira twist the knife like this? Of course Lio knew what this was doing to their family. "What do you expect Zoe to do if we return? Come to play with Cassia—where? Under house arrest? In exile?"

"Is abandoning her to go errant any better? If you come back with me, at least she'll get to see you again."

"We didn't abandon her!"

The Lustra magic pounded in Lio's ears, and Rudhira's condemnation hammered on. "Running is always easier. Do the brave thing and face the consequences of your actions."

"None of us are cowards!" Mak shot back. "I don't see anyone else facing off with the Collector to save us all from whatever is behind the doors. Don't you understand that's more important right now?"

"More important than the law you swore to uphold?" Rudhira asked. "More important than your mother's honor? It was so hard for her to explain your actions to the Queens. And think of the example you're setting for Bosko. Is this the kind of warrior you want him to grow up to be?"

Mak faltered.

"I spoke to your father," Rudhira went on.

"I'm not interested in his opinion right now," Mak snarled.

"Argyros misses you. He just got Nike back. He can't bear to lose you."

"I said I don't want to hear it!"

"He believed in the person you could become. Don't prove him wrong."

"That's enough," Lyros cut in.

Rudhira turned to him. "You should know that your parents have intervened on your behalf. They understand you were drawn into this out of love for Mak. It would mean a dishonorable discharge from the Stand, but you could avoid arrest. They'll help you move forward in a different service."

Mak looked at his Grace. "There's still a way out for you. You know all that matters to me is what's best for you."

Lyros let out a bitter laugh. "Lose my speires and spend eternity accepting pity commissions from my firstblood parents' patrons? Not on your life or mine."

Lio took a step forward, Final Word in his hands, an ocean of magic at his fingertips.

There was so much pain in Rudhira's eyes. "Lio, please don't make this harder for me."

"I won't let you arrest a single one of us," Lio said.

Cassia's magic had betrayed them again. But she would not let anyone, Hesperine, mortal, or undead stop her from healing the wound Kallikrates had dealt her and the Lustra here.

She reached deeper into the letting site. And found herself. Her dual power was filling the emptiness the Collector had left behind. The Lustra was drinking down her plant magic as her blood magic washed over its wounds.

With a thought, she raised a barrier of black roses between her and Rudhira, closing Mak and Lyros, Lio and Knight in her protection. Magic coursed from her immortal veins down into the land where her power had been born.

The letting site filled, and at last it overflowed back into her. The Lustra's power, natural and whole, slammed through her heart. With a cry of victory, she pulled her dagger out of the ground and got to her feet.

On the other side of her roses, there was a nova of Hesperine power. Her prince.

"We have to go before he finds a way in," Lyros called out.

A powerful instinct held Cassia where she stood. This place was her ritual ground now.

"We're not leaving empty-handed." She closed her eyes.

She focused on what Miranda's aura felt like and conveyed that impression to the Lustra. It stirred, snapping. It knew Miranda, the predator who had hurt them. Smells, sounds, and finally images stirred within Cassia.

Miranda sat helpless, bound to the wall of the sickroom by thorns. Her undead crow familiar ran its beak through her hair, its hollow, silent chest somehow filled with concern for her.

The door opened. In walked the farmer Miranda had healed, his wife at his side. The two villagers stood over their beloved lady. The crow fled, cowering in the farthest corner of the room.

"You failed me," the farmer said in the voice of Kallikrates.

Miranda's fear told the Lustra she was prey now. But she looked the Collector in the eye. "Yes, Master. I failed you."

"You know I will not tolerate excuses. You should have been prepared for any unexpected resistance from Cassia and Deukalion."

"I've always known I am imperfect. That's why I gave myself to you, Master. I am yours to shape into your perfect playing piece."

The farmer took Miranda's face in a bruising grip. "I will only tolerate so many mistakes before I deem a piece unviable and destroy it."

She didn't flinch. "No matter how many times you destroy me, Master, I will survive for you."

The farmer released her. His wife ran her hand over Miranda's head with the tenderness of a mother. Kallikrates's voice came from her mouth, too. "Miranda. My vicious girl. You understand the rules of the game so well."

"You need the survivors, Master. Nothing else matters. I accept your punishment, in the name of the game."

The farmwife kept stroking Miranda's hair. "You know what this means for your people. Mederi will be without my protection until your punishment is complete."

The slightest tremble went through Miranda. "Yes, Master. I know I must earn back your favor for them."

"And for yourself." The farmer took a step closer, looming over Miranda. "I will not come to you until you correct your mistake."

Her wild panic stoked the Lustra's hunger. The vines tightened on her arms.

The farmwife stepped back, her expression sad, and stood behind her husband. His face was stern. Kallikrates spoke through both the villagers in unison.

"This is your punishment. You must defeat Cassia and Deukalion on your own. Collect the bounty for them before my other Overseers, and you will receive my forgiveness."

"I will not disappoint you this time, Master," Miranda promised him.

Fire danced along the thorn vines, turning them to ash. Miranda fell to the floor in a heap, hissing, her arms riddled with burns.

The farmers were gone. The room seemed like a tomb.

Miranda's hands went to her chest, clutching at her bloodstained breastplate. She began to pant. Then she grasped her head in both hands and let out a pitiful wail.

"Master. I can't hear you. Master!"

She cried out for him until she was hoarse, but no voice filled the room but her own. Her crow returned to her side, hopping fretfully to and fro by her crumpled form.

Finally the sound of blades clashing made her look through the broken wall. Out in the garden, Hesperines errant and Gift Collectors were locked in battle.

"Survive," she whispered.

Miranda dragged herself to her feet, and her crow took flight in her wake. Leaving her fellow Overseers to die on the Hesperine prince's sword, she fled through the door that led deeper into the castle.

Magic from the letting site nipped at her heels with every pounding step she took through Castra Paradum. But the thorn vines, weakened by the Lustra's wounds, could not catch her. Miranda slipped through servants' corridors and down narrow stairways, then crawled through a drainage ditch to a grate that was already loosened. The Lustra's deep roots marked her passage, even as she made it beyond the walls.

The Lustra was everywhere, and she was prey now.

The images faded from Cassia's mind's eye. She saw her roses in front of her and heard Thorn's blade hacking at vines.

Lio held her shoulders, searching her gaze. "Is your spell complete?"

She cast her power back into the ground. "Let's go."

The rose vines fell an instant before they stepped. The last thing she saw was Rudhira's face, haggard with regret.

Lio's boots sank into the mud in the bailey. Once again, no ambush was waiting for them outside the tower, but they hurried up the steps nonetheless.

The door banged shut behind them, closing them back in the safety of Ebah's spell. But he could still hear Rudhira's words echoing in his head.

Lyros kicked a pile of hay. "We can't risk going back for the horses."

Mak looked at his usually-composed Grace with furrowed brows.

"My gardening satchel was still on my saddle," Cassia murmured.

Somehow, that small loss made Lio angrier than anything else. He know how vulnerable she felt without her satchel, for it had been her survival kit during many ordeals. Now it held her few mementos from Orthros. She had lost what was let of home.

"Are all of you in one piece?" She was still shaking, her aura popping with little flares of residual magic. Fresh blood slipped down her arms.

Lio wanted to pick her up and hold her, but felt that was somehow inappropriate when he had just watched her make a stand so powerfully. He settled for gathering her close to him. "Let me see to your arms."

"You didn't answer my question," she said.

"I'm fine, my Grace." Physically, in any case. Lio didn't know how long it would take his mind and heart to recover from that encounter with their Ritual father.

"Not a scratch on us, either." Mak waved them away. "Go get patched up, all right?"

Cassia hesitated, then nodded. She let Lio lead her toward the stairs. Mak pulled out the flask of ora that Tendo had sent with them, offering it to Lyros.

"Still not strong enough for Hesperines," Lyros muttered, but he downed a swig in any case.

Lio took Cassia up to the dining hall and sat her in a chair at the hearth. Knight sank down by the fire's warmth as if he were a tired, relieved old dog. Lio gave him a comforting pat before kneeling on the floor in front of Cassia.

He turned her hands over, palms up. The veins on the inside of her arms were split open and healing sluggishly. How had her magic done this to her?

There would be time to ask for an explanation later. Right now, she needed his care. He lowered his mouth to her skin and gently laved at her left wrist, where the bleeding was heaviest.

He wasn't prepared for the kick of Lustra magic in her blood. Her power thrummed through him. The sensation drove all thoughts of Paradum out of his mind for a blessed moment.

Lio raised his head, licking his lips, to look at his Grace in wonder. Her hair was tousled, and there was a streak of dirt across her face. She looked back at him, not with her kingdom-destroying look, but a kingdom-claiming one.

"Your power intoxicates me," he whispered, then glided his tongue up the inside of her arm.

She stroked his head. "I felt so much power tonight."

Did you like it? he asked in her mind, unwilling to take his mouth away from the delicate trail of magic bleeding from her right wrist.

Yes.

Your confidence tastes so good, Cassia. He returned to her left wrist, sucking a little at the gradually healing wound.

You can still taste my spell? she asked.

Yes. Goddess, he had to focus. He was supposed to be healing her, not indulging himself.

But she held him to her vein. Under his tongue, the muscles in her wrist tightened. She was still holding her dagger in that hand, he realized.

Magic traveled down her arm, and the flavor of her power bloomed stronger in her blood. He groaned, opening his mouth wider on her wrist.

"Go ahead." Her voice was husky. "Enjoy it."

He couldn't resist. He reopened the Lustra's wound with his fangs and sucked.

Controlled waves of her magic surged through her blood. Her control tasted as good as her power. His head spun in the arcane currents, and pleasure tingled over his skin.

He wrenched his mouth back before he lost all vestige of his own self-control. Another sip, and he would be too tempted to feast on her in this chair. She gazed down at him with dilated eyes, her fangs out.

He smiled at her. "Does using so much power make you hungry, My Queen?"

Her chest rose and fell with a rapid breath. "It also makes you hungry for me, doesn't it?"

"You know it does." He rose up to nuzzle her neck, taking in her scent. "The fact that you're so powerful arouses me."

Her awareness of her power over him was a heady musk in her aura. "Take me upstairs."

When he stepped them, her eyes widened, and she clutched the arm of the chair he had brought up to the room with them.

"Feast on me from your throne," he said.

She slid both her hands into his hair and tilted his head back. Her lips met his throat, soft and rough at the same time. She bit him once, and the pleasure of it was still stinging when she withdrew and slid up his vein to bite him again.

He reached down and yanked his trousers open for her. "Let me feed you on my knees."

She moaned and scooted closer to him. Her gripped her knees and spread her legs. They came together hard and fast, her core already slippery with need. She locked her legs around him, canting her hips with a hungry growl.

He clamped his hands on the arms of the chair. Flexing his back and hips, he gave himself up to her. She held his head where she wanted him while she ravaged his throat, gripping his body deep inside hers.

She wrapped her other arm around him, and he felt her dagger hilt press into his lower back. Another wave of her magic crested up from the letting site beneath the tower, then rolled through his body with exquisite intention.

Do you like that, my Grace? she asked.

His jaw dropped, and he arched into her harder. Her satisfaction hummed through their Union.

She dragged another wave through him, turning her growing mastery of her power into a new method for pleasuring him. If she kept this up, he would spend himself like a newblood.

It's only fair, she murmured in his thoughts. *You can make me climax with one touch of your thelemancy.*

The third stroke of her power undid him. He shouted a curse at the ceiling before words deserted him, and his magic and body spilled for her. He was free again, suspended on the currents of her power without need for control.

When he was spent, his head fell to rest on her shoulder. He rested there for a blissful moment, numb to anything beyond her embrace. She licked her marks on his throat tenderly, her magic lapping at the edges of their bond. He didn't move, allowing himself his Grace's care.

She pressed her face against his healed neck. *Thank you for loving my power.*

Your magic is one of the most beautiful things about you. Will you explain the spell you cast tonight?

Yes. I need your opinion.

He eased back, disentangling himself from her. But when she paused to lick his blood off her fingers, his body warmed for another round. With her robes still rucked up around her waist and her knees splayed, he thought about having the next course of their meal with his mouth between her legs.

He gave his head a shake and tried to gather his thoughts. They were out of time to drown their sorrows.

"More later." Her voice was a sultry promise.

He cast a cleaning spell over them both, and they resettled in the chair with her on his lap. "There was a massive power exchange between you and the letting site. It was one of the most amazing arcane phenomena I've ever witnessed."

She kissed his lips. "I needed to hear that, my beloved scrollworm."

"I will never stop reminding you how wonderful your magic is."

Her gaze fell. "Rudhira looked at me like I was a threat."

Lio searched for words of comfort where there were few. "I think that look was directed at all of us."

"But it was my roses that he attacked. I did something good tonight. Why couldn't he see that?"

"I can see it, Cassia. Tell me everything you did."

She turned her dagger over in her hands. "Lio, I...healed the letting site."

"You what?" he breathed. "You restored it to what it was before Kallikrates harmed you both?"

She shook her head, her eyes lighting up. "Something better. Now it's like our letting site in Orthros. It has my blood magic in it, too. Do you realize what this means?"

"Goddess bless." The implications whirled through his mind, the beginnings of countless theories.

"I can do more than channel magic from the Lustra," she said. "I can channel my power into it. I don't know if all Silvicultrixes could do that... or if it might be some unique effect of my dual magic...but don't you think the possibilities are astonishing?"

"Yes. You're incredible."

A ghost of a smile touched her face. "If my Gift can somehow share Hesperine restoration with the Lustra itself, imagine what I could achieve."

He held her gaze. "If you can heal yourself and a letting site, then I have no doubt you can heal your missing affinities, too. You can reclaim your other magics."

The spark of joy behind her eyes faded. "I don't need those for what I want to do. I could undo so much of Kallikrates's harm with only my dual magic. Perhaps I could repair the fallen door and close it again so he'll never get to what the portals are guarding."

Lio bit his tongue about her lost magic. He didn't have the heart to debate that with her right now, although that negotiation was still far from over.

"You're right," he said for now. "We left Paradum with a greater discovery, even if we lost Miranda's trail."

"We didn't lose it. The Lustra showed me how to find her."

DANGEROUS EXPERIMENTS

WHEN THEY FOUND MAK and Lyros in the practice room, Cassia cast a questioning glance at Lio. He gave his head a slight shake. She agreed with him. The warriors didn't seem in the mood for interruptions.

Mak and Lyros danced around each other in complete silence, their feet barely making a sound on the mats. Then every muscle in Lyros's body seemed to engage. He rolled forward and sprang to his feet to launch a close attack on Mak, so fast that Cassia's eyes could barely track him.

Lyros froze with his heart a hair's breadth from Mak's outstretched palms.

"Again," Lyros said.

"Lyros—" Mak began.

"Again," he insisted.

They returned to their positions and repeated the drill. Cassia didn't understand the advanced move they were practicing, only that it took astonishing strength and skill to be so precise at such speed. She and Lio watched Lyros repeat the attack over and over, each time ending up with Mak's hands nearly striking his heart.

Lyros rolled and lunged again. At the last instant, Mak opened his arms and caught Lyros against his chest. "That's enough."

Lyros's hands curled into fists against Mak's back. "Martyr's Heart is the only way to confront a mage head-on when we're out of options. We'll need it."

"No one has ever mastered it before the age of one hundred and sixty. You aren't going to learn it tonight."

Lyros pulled away. "You can stop me from training tonight. But I will never give up the battle arts. Don't you dare suggest it again."

Lyros stepped out of sight.

Cassia looked at Mak in confusion and tried to keep her tone tactful. "You've never told him to give up being a warrior. Have you?"

Mak slumped onto a bench. "That's not what I meant."

Lio sat down beside his cousin. "I think that's how Lyros interpreted what Mak said in front of Rudhira tonight."

She supposed she couldn't avoid that topic any longer. "What did Rudhira say?"

"You didn't hear him?"

She shook her head. "I was too absorbed in my spell."

"Good." Lio's gaze fell. "None of it bears repeating."

She had a flash of understanding, finally. How right he had been to caution her that their Grace Union didn't always reveal the reason behind his emotions.

So she spoke through their bond. *That's why you were so affected by what happened tonight. I thought you were angry and hurt because of how he reacted to my spell.*

I was, he insisted. *I still am.*

But Rudhira said something that hurt you, too.

"Don't be close-lipped about it, Lio," Mak said. "You can see how much trouble secrets have gotten me into lately."

Cassia crossed her arms. "Did you two learn nothing from Lio waiting too long to tell me I'm his Grace?"

"The things I've been keeping from Lyros aren't as important as Grace," Mak said defensively.

"And I had good reasons for waiting to tell you about our bond," Lio protested.

She gave them both a pointed look. "'For their own good' is never a good reason."

Mak groaned. "You're right."

Lio sighed and gave in. "It's just as we feared. Rudhira wants us to turn ourselves in so he can to take us back to Orthros to face trial."

She wrapped her arms around herself. "He really tried to arrest us, then."

Lio and Mak relayed the rest of their standoff with Rudhira. By the time they finished, Cassia was fighting tears.

"I'm sorry," she said.

"So am I." Lio sounded tired.

She sent him her warmth through their bond. "I never imagined Rudhira would be so hard on us. He's the one who heals wounds, not someone who rubs salt in them."

"We made this hard on him," Mak said.

"I'm still surprised he wasn't gentler with us," Cassia replied.

Mak snorted. "The Blood-Red prince doesn't have a reputation for being gentle."

"Not with his enemies. But with the people he loves…" She thought of how, without judgment, he had helped her tame her spell at her first Ritual. Then of how he had fought against her magic tonight. It seemed all wrong. "That was so unlike him."

Lio nodded. "I expected him to have more sympathy for our choice to carry weapons, even if it does put him in a difficult position."

"We didn't exactly handle it as well as the Blood Errant did," Mak said, his gaze downcast.

"I truly thought he would understand." Cassia swiped at her eyes, wondering where the armor over her heart was now.

I cannot bear this, Lio told her privately. *A Hesperine has made you cry. Our Ritual father, no less!*

The Gift makes us good, but not perfect. I can point fingers least of all.

"I didn't mean Lyros should give up the battle arts," Mak said. "I just want to protect him from what I've done."

Cassia rested a hand on his shoulder. "I know."

She had lost her own battle to make her Grace put himself first the night they had gotten arrested. Looking at Lio, knowing she would do anything to protect him, she thought she finally knew what to say to Lyros.

"I'll try to talk to him, if that's all right with you," Cassia said.

"Thank you," Mak replied. "Goddess knows I can't say the right thing to him tonight."

I'll talk to Mak, Lio promised.

Knight is still napping by the fire. I'll let him sleep. Would you veil me?

Yes, I agree an ambush may be necessary.

Concealed by Lio's spells, Cassia headed out of the practice room. She levitated up through the tower and found Lyros out on a parapet. He had his fists propped on the stone as he stared out over the bailey and front gates of the fort.

This tower was too small for three brooding immortal males. Cassia smiled with affection for all of them.

I'm not brooding, Lio protested.

She couldn't keep her amusement from filling their Union. *You are the most brooding of all, my mind mage. You can drop the veils now.*

Done, he grumbled.

Lyros actually started, and Cassia bit her lip to keep from laughing.

"Hespera's Mercy," Lyros said. "You were a sneaky mortal. I should have known no one would stand a chance against you as a Hesperine."

"I was afraid you'd storm off again before I had a chance to tell you that I know where to find Miranda."

Lyros stood up straighter. "How?"

"The Lustra showed me her trail." Cassia waved a hand. "It has decided she's its prey, and it is all too happy to help us hunt her down."

Lyros leaned against the parapet and crossed his arms. "Is this like Kalos's tracking methods?"

"No. This is a Silvicultrix's method."

Lyros gave her a nod, respect in his gaze. That look meant more to her than she could say. Despite all her mistakes, he trusted her to make this right. No matter what the elders thought, her Trial brothers and her Grace had faith in her.

She drifted forward, looking out over the fort with Lyros. "Being fugitives like this…it's different for you and me than it is for Mak and Lio. You and I remember when we were human."

Lyros shook his head. "I was Gifted as a child."

She touched his arm. Seeing her olive skin against his, she was struck again by how much they had in common, two bastards of Tenebra and Cordium's conflicted couplings over the centuries. "You were old enough to have some memories of your human life in Namenti. Those early years leave powerful marks on us. Surviving as an abandoned child on the streets of a border city must have hurt you as much as losing my mother and Solia hurt me."

Lyros crossed his arms. "I've had decades of growing up as a Hesperine to leave all that behind."

"There is no shame in remembering that pain, Lyros. It makes us fight harder."

His green eyes slid toward her again. He gave a short sigh. "You're right."

"Both of us remember when we were truly alone, treated like castoffs by someone who should have nurtured us."

"All my human parents did was birth me onto the streets and walk away. I've always thought I was better off never knowing them. You went through much worse with your sire."

"Would you stop trying to be a stoic warrior for a moment? I know we can both recall the first time Hesperines made us feel like we mattered. I dare say you could tell me the exact night you stopped fighting for your own survival and started fighting out of love for them instead."

He didn't tell her, but she could feel it in his aura. A powerful memory of when he, young and vulnerable, had discovered his cause for the rest of eternity.

Cassia poked him in the arm. "I bet it was when Mak made those matching heart pendants when you two were sucklings."

"It was not," Lyros protested with indignation, dodging her next poke. But now he was laughing more and brooding less.

He caught her around her shoulders and gave her a squeeze. "You don't have to play mind healer for me, Cassia. The theramancers already went through all of this with me when I was a suspicious little brat, unwilling to trust my Hesperine parents."

"And prone to thieving their valuables to hide in a treasure stash in your room."

Lyros flushed. "Lio told you that story?"

Cassia tried not to chuckle. "I'm impressed. You managed to snatch a small fortune before Timarete and Astrapas found out. You could have run away and become a very wealthy child-king of your own ring of thieves. But you didn't. Because you loved your new parents already."

"Of course I did. And like all angry sucklings, I eventually realized they love me, even if they don't love all the worry I've caused them over the years."

"That's the only reason your parents offered you a way out of the battle arts," Cassia said. "And the only reason Mak suggested you take it. They love you."

"I know that."

She nodded. "Of course you do. But it still hurt."

"I'm not hurt. I'm offended."

"It wasn't an insult to your skills as a warrior."

"It was an insult to my honor. I may be a failed artist and a derelict Steward, but I will not desert my Grace."

"Lyros, it wasn't failure that turned you into a Steward. The battle arts are your calling. We all know you belong in speires. Mak wasn't questioning that."

"I know that," Lyros insisted.

She suspected he knew it but didn't feel it. When Timarete and Astrapas had chosen him as their son, he had gained a family at last, only for his talents to be incompatible with their hopes for him. She knew from spending time around Lyros and his family that he still didn't feel like he belonged in his own bloodline.

He hadn't found his place as a Hesperine until he'd taken up the battle arts and become one of the few in Orthros's history to join the Stand from outside Hippolyta's family.

And now he felt as if the people he loved the most were telling him he didn't belong there, either.

He was right—she was no mind healer who could talk him out of years of lies he told himself. Not when she was still so prone to lying to herself. But she was family, and she could listen and give him the gift of her new empathy.

He turned away, bracing his fists on the parapet again, hanging his head. "How could Mak imagine I would abandon him?"

His hurt filled the Blood Union, squeezing Cassia's heart. "All I can tell you is what went through my mind when I told Lio to let me get arrested without him. Nothing. I wasn't thinking at all, Lyros. With my whole heart, I was feeling the need to protect him at any cost."

He narrowed his eyes at her. "And here I thought you were being strategic."

"Well, ensuring you and Lio went free did prove to be a good plan, but my point still stands. I'll be the first to admit it's difficult to be rational when the protective Grace instincts come over you. Mak wasn't thinking either, I suspect. Only feeling. Even though he should have thought before he spoke."

"Yes. He should have." Lyros grimaced. "But I…could have taken it as he intended it."

"It's difficult to do that, too, when his words hit a sore point. Lio frustrates me so much when it seems he won't let me protect him the way he protects me. He was born to protect our people. But I chose to, and that is no less powerful."

If Lyros realized she was talking about him and Mak, too, he gave no sign. She hoped her words had gotten through to his analytical mind, even if they hadn't yet reached his heart.

Lyros drew himself up. "I'm sorry I let my temper get the best of me when we have work to do. Get some rest. We'll start tracking Miranda tomorrow night."

She arched a brow at him. "No more brutal training sessions before our next excursion, General Lyros?"

"You and Lio are dismissed," he said. "Mak and I need the practice room until dawn."

The glint in his eye reassured her that sparring was not what he intended to do with Mak for the rest of the night.

AT THE TOP OF the tower, Cassia stood in the center of the ritual markings. The Rose of Hespera she had created from her ancestors' nonagram glowed red in the dark room. She let her dual magic flow along the lines of the rose and down through the spell patterns of the tower to touch the letting site.

"I know I should look for Miranda first," she said, "but there's something else I want to try. *Need* to try."

Lio spoke from just outside the ritual circle. "You want to infuse this letting site with your blood magic, too."

"How did you know?"

Her senses were so alive with power that his voice seemed to fill the shadows. "I can feel your thirst to know what's possible. I understand it, Cassia."

"Experimenting with a letting site is like baiting a wild animal."

His fanged smile flashed at her. "Then show it you bite back."

That made her smile. His excitement for their magical experiment was infectious. "Thank you for being willing to try my dangerous idea."

"You know I will take any risk in this world to help you become more powerful."

She didn't miss the implication in his words. He was thinking of her other affinities, as well. She let that debate lie and hoped it would not wake anytime soon.

She probed the letting site, and the Lustra rose, ready to come to her. "It feels like plant roots, made for pulling nourishment out of the soil. The channeling only goes in one direction."

"But you know it can be reversed. Your experience at Paradum proved that."

This time, she reached deep within herself. Her Gift was everpresent, permeating her bones and veins and skin, sustaining the plant magic within her. She pushed her dual magic down toward the letting site with all her might. Her feet left the ground, and she hovered on the outpouring of power.

She felt as if she dissolved into the wave of her magic and crashed down into the letting site. When she struck the Lustra, the impact slammed through her. Her blood magic rebounded, chased by a massive wave of Lustra magic.

Her back and head struck something solid, bringing her back to her body. Stars exploded on her vision, and her dagger flew from her hand. Then she was in free fall.

She landed in Lio's arms, numb all over. As feeling returned, she felt pain. Everywhere. Where he cradled her head, her skin and hair were wet with blood.

His calm was like a sure grip on their Union, holding fear at bay. "Cassia, can you hear me? Try to answer aloud."

She wasn't human anymore. A blow to the head couldn't kill a Hesperine. "I can hear you."

He lifted her eyelids. "Can you see me?"

"Yes, you handsome creature."

He grinned. "You're going to be all right, I can tell. Have a drink so that nasty bump heals faster."

She reached for his wrist, then hissed in pain. "I think my dagger hand is as broken as my head."

He caressed her cheek, putting his wrist to her mouth. "Hesperine magical experiments can be rather damaging, but fortunately, we are very hard-headed."

As his blood flowed into her, she let out a sigh. She could do much worse than lay broken in his arms with him gently feeding her till she healed.

His blood drove away every trace of pain and left her body feeling warm. She wondered what the magical results would be of pushing him onto his back and mating him right here on the ritual markings.

Thorns, she was definitely an immortal if she could go from concussed to lustful within minutes.

He arched a brow at her. "I do think that might confuse the results of our current test. But we can certainly make that a future experiment."

She licked the last drops from his wrist and her lips, gazing up at him. She could see the little betrayals of tension around his eyes and mouth, although they were hidden deep in their Union.

"I know it's hard for you to see me get hurt," she said, "even when you know I'll be all right."

He helped her sit up and ran a cleaning spell over the matted blood in her hair. "Nothing is harder for me. But there is always pain on the path to power. Accepting your pain is part of my promise to help you become as powerful as you can."

"Thank you for never treating me like I'm fragile."

"How could I, when you are so unbreakable?"

She kissed him, and she tasted his anger at the Lustra on his tongue. But also his admiration for her.

"I want to try again," she said.

"Then we will."

She retrieved her fallen dagger. Lio joined her in the center of the rose this time and put his arms around her.

"I won't let the sunbound Lustra toss you against the ceiling a second time," he grumbled.

She poured her power into the Ritual rose again, joining with the tower and the letting site once more. She fingered the myriad arcane paths of the tower's enchantments. They came easily to her hand now, willing to do as their Silvicultrix bade.

They all drew from the letting site as well, but…

"What if I can transform the tower enchantments?" she said. "I was able to redraw the nonagram into Hespera's Rose. Could I subvert the spells on the tower to work with my magic, too, and use them to siphon my power back into the letting site?"

"That's brilliant. I don't know if it will work, but we have evidence that it *could*. So we should test it."

She thought aloud with Lio. "Last time, casting with two avowed pairs of Hesperines in Union, using blood from all four of us, made the hulaia here conform to the paradigm of haima."

"Yes, exactly."

"But what we're trying to do now is more like when you Gifted me and we opened a letting site fed by our combined power. So I think only you and I should be necessary for this casting. What do you think?"

"I agree we should try it that way first." He gave her waist a squeeze. "Let's shed our blood, and if that doesn't produce results, I'm happy to try mating rituals."

"I like this plan."

She slashed her hand with her dagger, then made the same cut on his hand. They twined their fingers together, squeezing their mingled blood onto the rose. The current of her Gift, flowing through the markings, strengthened and spread through the tower's enchantments.

She grasped the whole tangle of spells and Willed her magic into them.

Her power set the tower alight. The enchantments glowed in her mind's eye, a delicate but powerful web strung between her and the letting site.

She pushed until the strands of the web vibrated with her power. The letting site pushed back, and the spells shook. Her dagger grew hot in her hands. She had that feeling again that the spell was unstable, unbalanced. Something was missing. Two somethings.

She released her hold on the casting before the straining tower broke. The Lustra's natural patterns took over again, channeling magic into her. With it came an awareness of Miranda and a sense of direction.

She released the channeling and opened her eyes, swearing.

"What happened?" Lio asked.

"I can't manipulate the connection between the tower spells and the letting site. Not yet." She gritted her teeth.

He brushed her lips with a finger. "What's wrong?"

She looked away. "I need all three of my foci. But I was a fool and lost one. And I don't even know how to make the third."

"You'll learn."

She lifted her gaze to his again. "But can I learn in time?"

"I have faith in you."

She wouldn't fail him. She couldn't. Not after everything he had sacrificed to stand here with her, pushing the limits of forces they didn't understand.

"Hopefully Miranda's secrets will yield some answers," she said.

"Did the Lustra show you which way to go?"

"Yes. But none of us will like the answer. We need to travel west. To the warfront."

nights after
WINTER SOLSTICE

FOLLOWING SMOKE

Lio smelled soil and *decay. Was he in a tomb?*

He opened his eyes. Magefire glared on his vision. He took a wary step back from the brazier that revealed where he was.

The flames shone on the stone door. The runes carved into the portal seemed like bottomless shadows.

He was somewhere worse than a tomb. He must be in Miranda's mind.

A soft, familiar hand took his. "No, my Grace. Your first duel with her is over, and your next is yet to come. This is my mind."

His breath of relief disturbed the dead air. He turned to Cassia. She stood beside him holding her dagger, her tattered ambassador cords at her neck where her pendant should have hung.

"This is a shared dream," *he realized.* "Our Grace Union has blended our day terrors."

"I'm so glad we're together here."

"So am I."

She squeezed his hand. "Does this vision feel different to you? It's as if we're more in control of our thoughts and actions."

Lio nodded. "A lucid dream."

Cassia turned to look behind them, and he saw her shiver. The first door lay in ruins. Blood had dried on the floor at its threshold. He could smell that it was her blood. He put an arm around her and pulled her closer.

A cracking sound made them spin to face the second door again.

"No!" *Cassia cried.*

Fractures appeared in the surface of the stone. The thin cracks spread before their eyes.

Lio felt no hint of the Collector's presence here. "How is he breaking it?" She moved in front of him. "We have to stop it."

"How?" he asked.

"Help me cast," she said.

He wrapped one arm around her and held his wrist to her mouth. She sank her fangs into him, and as she swallowed his blood, her magic rose to life. She sliced open both her hands and squeezed her blood onto the ground. Her power swept out of her, through his veins and the soles of his feet into the ground below. Her essence seemed to soak the walls and the stone overhead.

Blood ran through the cracks in the door, gleaming red in the firelight. Their blood. It traced each rune and filled every fissure until it dripped down the surface of the door. But no matter how much blood they shed, more cracks split open.

"No!" she shouted again.

The embers in the braziers collapsed into ashes, and the fire went out. All that remained was the scent of death.

CASSIA WASN'T SURE HOW much longer she and Lio could withstand their recurring day terrors. The deeper they traveled into wartorn territory, the worse their shared dreams became. A fortnight of troubling visions had worn her down and sent Lio spiraling into dark thoughts.

Their hunt for Miranda had proved fruitless so far, fraying everyone's morale even further. Her trail was vivid to Cassia, a whiff of violence on an arcane wind, a vengeful footstep imprinted on the land. It always felt as if she was just ahead, and yet the Black Roses had seen neither hide nor hair of her.

Tonight they tracked her through an orchard in Segetia. The four of them levitated between the trees with rain slicing at their cloaks while Knight splashed along the rutted trail below. They had met no one so far except raiding parties of Lucis's soldiers, each with a war mage and many with liegehounds, bent on flushing out Hesperines.

Cassia started to shove her tousled hair back under her hood, then realized there was still blood on her hand from the last skirmish. She shuddered.

"I'm sorry I missed that." Lio hovered nearer, and his cleaning spell banished the mortal's blood from her hand. "How is your arm?"

"It was only a small singe. The soreness has faded."

Despite her reassurances, Lio's aura was still full of anger. "I would give anything to step to Miranda right now. Thorns, I'd settle for Tendo flying us to her like baggage if it meant I didn't have to watch another war mage hurl a fireball at my Grace."

Mak laughed. "I doubt our favorite vulture would agree to that."

"I do not need help flying now." Cassia spun in the air and gave Lio a smile she hoped he would find comforting.

Knight bounded through a patch of mud, and Lyros floated aside to avoid the spray. "I know this is frustrating, but we must keep to our search strategy. Being methodical is our best chance of finding Miranda."

"It's begun to feel useless," Cassia confessed.

Lyros shook his head. "We'll do the same thing tonight that we've done every night. Follow Miranda's trail as far as we can until dawn, then return to the tower to Slumber. And tomorrow, we'll step back to where we left off tracking her and pick up her trail again."

If Lyros drilled them on their strategies one more time, Cassia thought her mind would melt. If Mak and Lio were equally weary of it, though, no one protested. They knew Lyros was being protective and that he drove no one madder than himself. The farther they went into danger, the more he seemed to need to control every little decision they made.

"Our strategy is good," Mak said. "If we could step to her, we wouldn't have been here to take care those raiding parties. There aren't any other Hesperines this far out to stop them from pillaging everything in their path. We all know what they do to any people who can't defend themselves. Especially women."

Lio grimaced. "You're right. At least we can do a little for the war effort on our way and keep a few innocent people safe."

They emerged from the trees to find a small cluster of homes, which must belong to those who tended the orchards. The settlement appeared undamaged, but deserted.

Lio's power flashed among the cottages. "No one here. These families must have evacuated already."

Cassia stroked Knight's back as he sniffed heavy tracks left behind by horses and boots. It looked like the Knights of Andragathos had been through here, gathering up the villagers. "Let us pray they made it to safety with one of Flavian's lords. I fear not everyone will reach a fortress before Lucis's forces find them."

Mak shook his head. "These raiders are like strikes of lightning. No rhyme or reason to their ambushes. It must be hard for Benedict to organize the evacuations."

Cassia tried to shut out the fear and sadness that still drifted out of the abandoned homes. "It's as if the whole domain is under siege. An entire population can't survive locked inside Segetia's castles all winter…or longer."

"I know." Lio touched her back. "I wish we had news from the front lines, too."

She nodded. As usual, he knew what she was thinking. "I wonder how Solia and the Charge are faring. It's hard to tell from here."

So far, Miranda's trail had gone around the main warfront, avoiding the territory where the bulk of Lucis's army was clashing with Solia's forces.

"We can't draw any conclusions," Lyros agreed, "but I don't like what we've seen."

"Neither do I," Cassia said. "Too many raiding parties have already infiltrated Segetia's defenses."

Lyros picked up a doll lying on the path. The door to the nearest home hung open. He set the toy inside the house and shut the door. "There is no honor or courage in this war. Instead of facing his equals in battle, Lucis is bent on slaughtering those powerless to fight back. The world has never seen a war quite like this."

"Or perhaps we have," Lio said quietly, "but all memory of it was buried with the last civilization the Old Masters' game destroyed."

Cassia shivered, thinking of the last raiding party they had killed. Lucis's soldiers and the Order of Anthros's mages had died as pawns. The gauntlet of violence and death was taking its toll on her, night by night.

She knew this was part of her calling as an immortal. It was one of the oldest promises the Hesperines had made to Tenebra in the Equinox Oath. Criminals who hurt honest people were fair game for Hesperines errant. When Tenebran law failed, immortals enacted Orthros's justice.

She did not know how that promise coexisted with the guarantees of peace she cherished from the treaty. Every time another mortal fell before her power, she tried to understand. But she found no answers in the hollow eyes of the men who had no more future, no more hope that they might one day transform into their better selves.

Lyros unrolled their map, pulling her out of her thoughts. "We're nearing the area where the knights were headed with the refugees we helped across the river."

Cassia ran her finger south of the River Silvistra. "The defenses here will be better. Segetia's strength lies in their alliances and trade agreements. All across this region, there's a swath of fortresses that belong to Flavian's most loyal lords."

"I remember reading about those," Lio said. "For centuries, they've been the main line of defense against invasions from the south. They've held out through countless wars."

"Here's Castra Augusta." Cassia pointed to the fortress. "That's the stronghold of a Knight Commander in Ben's order, where he said they were taking the Mederi villagers."

"Good," said Lyros. "We can hope that raiding party from earlier tonight will be the last one we meet for awhile."

"But that also means there might be Chargers near," Mak reminded them. "If Rudhira has been able to spare any Hesperines errant to fight in Segetia, they're sure to be protecting the fortresses where the refugees are."

Lyros nodded. "Let's be on our guard."

Lio looked to Cassia. "Where to next?"

The Lustra was pulling her toward the fields past the village. The farmland felt too open and exposed. But she squared her shoulders. "This way."

They swept over the fallow fields of Tenebra's bread basket. It seemed dead now, with animals in their burrows for the winter and the humans gone. Would any of the farmers make it back in time to sow their fields in spring? Would Lucis's armies leave them any fields to return to, or would they come home to find their livelihood trampled by armies? Cassia feared there was famine in the future for Solia's kingdom.

It was midnight when they scented fire. There was no cover to be had, so they gathered close under veil spells. Knight paced restlessly, and Cassia could hear his heart beating faster.

Mak scanned the horizon, where a column of smoke rose. "That seems like something worse than another skirmish between the knights and a raiding party."

"Miranda's trail leads right toward the fire," Cassia said.

Lio's magic stretched out from him. His dread crept over their Grace Union before he spoke. "I don't sense any minds. Whatever happened out there…I don't know if anyone survived."

A weight settled in Cassia's belly. "We have to find out."

Mak nodded, his aura grim.

"No one drop any veils until we're sure what we're dealing with," Lyros said.

They drew their weapons and moved into their defensive formation. This time, the smoke was the guidance they followed across the fields.

When Cassia smelled the bodies, she nearly gagged. She put a hand to her mouth, swallowing hard. This was different from any of their battles so far. There was more death here. So much more.

The source of the smoke came into sight ahead. They all came to a halt as shock reverberated through their Blood Union.

A castle stood battered and scorched before them. Fire magic had made short work of the outer palisade and left its fresh timbers snapping with hot sap. The old stones of the inner wall had succumbed, and the Charge's wards were long gone, too. Smoke swirled up from the keep.

Through the odor of burnt flesh, Cassia comprehended what she was seeing. Bodies lay amid the broken remnants of tents. She glimpsed dark hair and white hair, rough homespuns and fine surcoats.

This was Castra Augusta, the fortress where Ben and his knights had brought the villagers for safety.

LIO HELD HIS MAGIC taut, striving to catch any hint of a living mind. He could feel nothing but the memories of suffering that flooded the Blood Union.

He withdrew into his bond with Cassia and focused on shielding her. That was one thing he could do, besides stand here helpless in the face of destruction they were too late to prevent.

"An army did this." Mak sounded numb.

Lyros dragged a hand over his face. "Let's spread out and listen for heartbeats. We may be able to detect survivors the enemy missed."

Cassia didn't open her mouth, but she nodded.

You can come with me. Lio made the offer privately so as not to wound her pride in front of the warriors.

Her throat worked as she swallowed again. *No. If there's anyone left to save, every moment counts. I'll search on my own so we can cover more ground.*

None of them were safe fighting alone, but Lio knew she was right. At least she had Knight with her. Fighting his Grace instincts, he let her out of arm's reach and forced himself in a different direction.

He levitated over the mortals' remains. His magic seemed blind in the face of their terror and despair. He stopped breathing and listened. But the bodies were lifeless.

They had come from all over Patria and Segetia to find safety here, only for their last Sanctuary to fall.

Lio felt as if he were seeing into the forgotten past and the inevitable future. Was this what the beginning of the end looked like each time the Old Masters prepared to destroy the world again?

All these lives, wasted for the game. Their loved ones would grieve out their mortal years, while the necromancers continued their schemes, untouched.

Lio didn't know the names of the fallen. He didn't have room in his chest for all their pain. But he tried to memorize their faces as he searched. He had to do something for them, if only remember them for as much of eternity as he and Cassia survived.

Have you found anyone? she asked.

No. Have you?

Only more fallen knights.

Is Ben...?

I don't know. I haven't found him yet. That means there's hope.

When Lio checked the next body, recognition jolted him. He would never forget how this young woman had smiled at him after he had soothed her fears with his thelemancy. Rudhira had helped her grandmother up from a fall.

Now the girl's expression was blank of either joy or fear. She lay across the elder woman's body, the young trying to shield the old, love trying to defy fate.

Lio searched through familiar faces now. He reached into every person with his magic, sending his own mind into their emptiness again and again.

Goddess, let even one be alive.

When he found two gray heads bent together, he sank to his knees on the ground. The elderly couple who had loved Miranda lay in each other's arms with matching wounds. The same sword had run them both through.

Cassia wrapped him in their Union. *Who is it?*

I found the villagers from Mederi.

Oh, Lio. I'm so sorry.

We tried so hard to save them.

She had no answer for that. Neither did he. But they had each other. Grace Union was the cord of life that pulled him to his feet and gave him the strength to forge ahead.

When he found the little girl's goat with its throat cut, he dug the heels of his hands into his eyes. *I can't find the children. I don't see them anywhere.*

We'll keep looking, Cassia promised.

He took the goat in his arms and laid it next to the girl's parents. Then he got up again and kept putting one foot in front of the other.

S<small>PLINTERS DUG INTO</small> C<small>ASSIA</small>'s hands, but she pressed on into the ruins of the keep. With her Hesperine strength, she shoved more scorched beams out of her way.

"Baat!" she commanded Knight again.

He whined and scratched at the rubble in the demolished doorway.

"No, darling. You may not come in here with me. This mess is no place for a big dog."

She feared he would hurt himself or get trapped. But her Hesperine agility let her shimmy safely under fallen pillars and levitate over broken stones.

The residue of war magic was everywhere, acrid to her arcane senses. This was the work of an enchanted siege engine. She knew what the chances were of finding anyone alive. Not a soul had lived through the siege of Castra Roborra.

But they'd had no Hesperines to protect them. There had been Chargers here at the refugee camp, just like at Patria, which had held out for months against the Order of Anthros's trebuchets. Surely the Hesperines had managed to survive, to save someone.

An arcane glimmer caught her attention. She pushed her awareness deeper into the ruins.

Did you find something? Lio asked.

I don't know...

She navigated around a pile of fallen stones and nearly tripped over another body trapped in the collapse. A Knight of Andragathos she didn't know. She turned away from the sight and tried to focus on the gleam of magic she'd felt.

There. Yes, thank the Goddess. That was a trace of Hesperine magic.

She crept further into the keep, coughing in the ash she stirred. At last the rubble opened up to a clear space, a cocoon of safety inside the devastation. Stones had piled up around it in a perfect sphere.

She could still feel the imprint of the shadow wards that had held the collapse at bay. But there was no Hesperine to be seen.

She drew a shallow breath and tasted light. That radiance filled her lungs and veins, a shout of triumph and a final cry of despair. She put a hand to her chest, her fingers twisting in the front of her robe over her heart.

Cassia, what is it?

She let her tears fall. *One of our people died here.*

Complete silence fell over the Blood Union between her and Lio, Mak and Lyros. They stopped together, holding a moment of eternity for this Hesperine who should have had forever.

Who? Lio pleaded.

She knelt and dug her fingers into the soil, reaching for the weary Lustra. Could it give her a sign of what had happened here?

A vision ghosted through her mind. A Hesperine with a lean warrior's build and shoulder-length black hair. She knew him.

She held his image in her thoughts. *It was Azad.*

No! Lio's sorrow overflowed their Union.

They shared a memory of the last time they had seen Azad. He had danced the night away at their avowal celebration with Neana, his Grace.

One of their own had been martyred here. Azad had been a Ritual tributary of Blood Komnena. Apollon's Gift had flowed in his and Neana's veins, as surely as in Lio and Cassia's.

Through the Lustra, she saw Azad standing alone at the heart of the keep. Fire and stone rained down while his wards held back the destruction. But every ball of magefire the trebuchets hurled at him brought new lines of strain to his face and wore at his protective spells.

Another flaming stone shattered against his magic, and burning fragments sprayed his ward. One ember made the smallest breach in his spell.

The next gout of flame washed over his defenses. The fire found that vulnerable point and ate at it.

No, no, no, Cassia chanted in her mind as the fate already written played out in her mind's eye. Lio watched with her, sharing the horror in her every thought.

Fire spilled through the breach in the ward, and Anthros's element engulfed Azad. His once-immortal body returned to the Goddess in a blinding flare of white.

Cassia blinked hard, as if she could clear that flash of light from her sight and her soul. On her hands and knees, she began to search the ground around her.

A few pebbles broke free and skittered down over her head.

She slowed down and searched more carefully, relying on all her Hesperine ability to move lightly through the space.

Finally, she found what she was looking for. She lifted her precious find with reverent hands.

She shook with the effort to hold in her angry sobs. She tried to brush the dirt off the thin golden braid she held. All that remained of the fallen Hesperine errant was his beloved's hair.

THE LAW OF LOYALTY

Loss saturated Lio's blood and paralyzed his limbs. He stood there grasping his Grace braid, holding on to Cassia in their Union.

He looked around at the bodies of everyone Azad had tried to save. He had to find survivors. Even one person who was still alive. Azad and Neana's sacrifice could not be in vain.

Lio stumbled forward. More timbers crashed into embers around him. A murder of crows flapped overhead, cawing. In the hush between every sound, he heard the silence in the minds and bodies that surrounded him.

Until a vibration broke the quiet, the faintest touch on his hearing.

One heartbeat.

He held his breath, straining toward the sound. Slow and faint. But still beating.

He lifted off the ground again and levitated toward that hint of life. Even the air soughing against his ears made him curse.

"Lio!" Mak called. "You need to see this."

Lio gritted his teeth. "I can't. I think I hear a heartbeat."

"They're here," Mak said.

Lio held on to that flicker of hope and stepped to his Trial brothers.

When he saw whom they'd found, his prayer of gratitude died on his lips and turned into a snarl of fury. There were five survivors, all wearing the flame-red robes of the Aithourian Circle.

Lio whipped Final Word into his hand before he realized their was no need. The mages were on their knees, bound to a ring of stakes. Mak and Lyros stood on opposite sides of them, maintaining a ward around the war mages.

Lio's magic boiled. All the suffering that had bled into this ground gathered inside him. With a thought, he could flood the war mages' minds with the pain they had caused. He could make these men live out the deaths of their victims until they wished they had never survived.

Are you all right? Cassia voice slipped into his heart. So close. Too close to all the ugly things there.

He veiled his thoughts. *No. Are any of us?*

No, she agreed.

Lio felt a hand on his shoulder, then. Mak's voice pulled him back from the brink. "We need your opinion. We found them like this, as if someone staked them out to make an example of them. Their auras feel wrong. Can you tell if the Collector stole their magic?"

It took a moment for Mak's words to reach Lio's rational mind. "You think someone performed essential displacement on them?"

Mak nodded. "They remind us of Pakhne after Kallikrates displaced her healing magic."

Lio took a step toward the nearest mage. The Aithourian whimpered. Tears streaked through the blood and ash on his contorted face. He lifted his haunted gaze to Lio in a wordless plea. The mortal's aura was hollow.

"I think you're right," Lio said.

"Can you confirm it with your thelemancy?" Lyros asked.

With a grimace of distaste, Lio dug into the five mages's minds. Pity he didn't want to feel tempered his power. The arcane pathways inside the men were scarred in a way he recognized. "One of Kallikrates's Overseers definitely did this."

Lyros shook his head. "This doesn't make sense. Why would the Collector do this to his and Lucis's mage allies?"

Mak gestured at the war mage in front of him. "I recognize this one. We faced him at Patria."

Recognition came over Lyros's face. "You're right. This is the war circle from the siege, or what's left of them, in any case. The other two of their brethren died the night they attacked Mederi—one to Rudhira's blade, the other to Lio's magic."

Lio tried to think through the roar in his ears. The war mages were surrounded by parts of bodies. It was difficult to make sense of the dismembered remains. But he made himself study their clothes and wounds. All of them were Lucis's soldiers, and it looked like they'd been butchered not with the professional instruments of war but by a Gift Collector's brutal tools.

"Miranda did this," Lio said. "She took revenge for her people."

Mak blew out a breath. "What are we going to do with them? I want to make them pay as much as you do, but it doesn't seem like justice to kill them when they're no longer a danger to anyone."

Mak was right. Miranda had already subjected the mages to the worst punishment any of them could imagine.

So why did Lio still want to punish someone, anyone, for all the nameless pain he had swallowed?

The war mage nearest him strained against the ropes that bound him to the stake. His lips moved. At last, words emerged from his mouth in a haunted echo of a human voice.

"Please," he begged, "kill me."

Lio's hand curled tighter around his staff.

Lyros eyed Lio. "We'd best leave our wards up. Just in case."

A veil spell settled over the men, then. Mak's power cut off their pleas for death from Lio's hearing. The silence of the grave fell over the battlefield once more.

All these lost lives. And five of their murderers were the only survivors.

The distant heartbeat fluttered in Lio's ears again.

"The pulse I'm hearing isn't one of theirs! There must be another survivor."

Lyros clapped him on the shoulder. "We'll keep looking."

The three of them headed across the outer bailey. Mak paused by soldiers in unfamiliar colors and knelt to check for pulses. He shook his head, then swore softly. "Their swords aren't of Tenebran make. These are Cordian soldiers."

Dread settled in Lio's stomach. "The princes of Cordium have sent soldiers to fight with Lucis?"

A few paces away, Lyros stood over the bodies of men in flamboyant, colorful clothes. "And some of Cordium's infamous mercenaries, it looks like."

The people here had never stood a chance. But one slow heart still defied the odds.

"The heartbeat is fading," Lio said. "We should split up again to search faster."

Mak and Lyros exchanged a look.

"What is it?" Lio asked.

"We can't hear it," Mak answered ruefully.

"I'm not imagining it," Lio insisted.

Mak held up his hands. "We're not saying you are. We'll go this way."

They circled the outer bailey, while Lio forged into the area within the remains of the stone wall. He levitated again and swept left. No, the sound got fainter that way. Right? Ahead and to the right.

The sound grew less faint as he approached a pile of bodies by a blasted-out portion of the wall. Knights and village men had died together in the defense. Their enemies had paid dearly to gain this ground. Dozens of Cordian soldiers lay dead on the threshold of the breach.

The princes' forces had come prepared for Hesperines. Their liegehounds rested at their sides, bloodied and still. Poor, noble dogs. They had lived by the law of loyalty and died out of love for their masters, no matter whose side they fought on.

Lio quickly strengthened the veil over his thoughts and emotions. Not fast enough to escape Cassia's notice.

What did you find? she asked.

There is no reason for you to see this.

The sight of the dogs was not something she needed in her memories forever, nor haunting her when she worried about Knight.

She hesitated, a protest brewing in her mind.

Please, Lio said. *Let me spare you this one thing.*

Her aura gentled. *All right, my Grace. Thank you.*

Lio wiped his eyes and sank back to the ground. Listening closely, he picked his way closer to the breach.

A growl halted him in his tracks.

He went still. Then slowly, he turned his head, careful not to meet her hostile eyes.

Red stained her fur. Lio hadn't noticed her lying in despair by her master as if she too were dead. Now she crouched over the soldier's body, her lips peeled back.

Lio and the liegehound eyed each other.

She didn't lunge. He realized her back legs were barely holding her weight. She was panting too hard for such a cold night. Even as he stood there, her heartbeat grew weaker.

No. By the Goddess, he would not let one more innocent life end tonight. He would save one creature, if it was the last thing he did.

He thought of Martyr's Pass, when he had crossed his first battlefield to rescue Knight from a heart hunter's trap. He had managed to secure the dog's trust and bring him safely to Cassia.

But this liegehound was not Knight, who was bonded to a Hesperine's Grace and persuaded by her Lustra magic to love their kind.

There was nothing Cassia could do for this dog now. If Lio asked, it would only give her further cause to mourn the loss of her beast magic. He didn't want Mak and Lyros to cast wards over the hound, either. That much blood magic would only make her more frightened and aggressive.

There had to be something Lio could try. He knelt down to make himself smaller and less threatening. "Good dog."

She snarled at him.

"*Oedann*," he murmured softly. "*Oedann*. You fought bravely by your *kaetlii*."

She let out a whine that tore at his heart.

Lio kept his voice low and soothing. "I know you loved him. But this needn't be the end for you, Lady Hound. There are other safe places. You can find another *loma*."

The dog crouched lower over her master's body. To protect him? Or in surrender to her pain and weakness?

"*Loma*," Lio repeated, thinking of every calming word he had ever heard Cassia say to Knight. "*Het. Soor het.* Down, girl. There's no threat here. I'm a friend, I swear, although nothing has ever taught you to believe so."

She whined again, as if terribly confused to hear familiar words coming from a Hesperine's mouth. He wasn't sure if he was calming her or agitating her.

"*Toaa*," he soothed. "*Toaa*."

Lio inched closer to her, keeping to one side instead of approaching directly. Her gaze tracked him.

"Your master is with his gods. You can let him go. *Obett*." Lio was within arm's reach now.

She snapped her jaws at him in warning.

Thorns. He could stand to lose an appendage if she got rough with him, but he couldn't afford for her to rip out his throat. Clearly her wounds were the only reason she hadn't tried. It would take more than a calm voice and liegehound commands to prove to her he wasn't the enemy.

All her breeding and training hinged on magic, didn't it? The arts of hedge warlocks, the crueler descendants of Lustra mages.

Lio braced himself and opened his arcane senses to the hound. The battlefield's tragic emotions shuddered through him. He pushed through them to focus on the grieving creature in front of him.

She was opaque to him, as he had expected. Liegehounds had as much resistance to mind magic as they did to poisons and frost. But had one of the three most powerful mind mages in Hesperine history ever tested their full power against that of the ancient liegehound breeders?

Lio's stomach turned at the prospect of what he was about to do. It went against everything in him to subject the innocent animal to any more fear and suffering.

But the alternative was to leave her here to die in pain. It was clear to him which was the cruel choice and which the kindness.

"You will be all right," he promised her. As gently as he could, he let his full power wash over her mind.

He was prepared for her to snap at his neck or torture him with yelps of pain. But all he heard was her sigh. As her exhausted mind opened to him, he felt an answering sigh from deep in the ground. Was the Lustra helping him?

The hound eased to sleep under his spell. Lio, too, let out a breath of relief, knowing he had given her an escape from her pain.

He knelt beside her and carefully examined her wounds. Curse the mortals who had brought her into this fight to get battered by blades.

Working as quickly as he could, he scavenged among the bodies to make bandages. Once he had bound the dog's bleeding back, he kept applying pressure to her wound while he studied the magic inside her. There was a distinct cord twining from within her chest toward her master. It reminded Lio of the patterns of Lustra magic he and Cassia had encountered on their quest.

The end of the spell-cord was frayed, broken. And yet it still bound the dog to the dead man. What an injustice that her life was fated to end with his. As long as she was tied like this, there was no hope for her.

Lio took hold of the magical bond with all his Will. *Goddess, please, let this free her and not doom her to die even faster.*

With the gentlest thelemancy, he unraveled the cord bit by bit. Fast asleep, she knew no discomfort while he worked. But with each filament of the bond that he snapped, a lifetime of pain wore at Lio.

He bore it. Welcomed it. *Goddess, let me take someone's pain tonight.*

He unwove every harsh word and brutal training exercise that had defined the dog's existence. As her cage of discipline crumbled, the fog over her mind began to clear. He caught sensory impressions, familiar and foreign. Warm fire. Satisfying bone. Open grass, running, joy.

He stroked her head as he worked. Her ears were so soft. "You'll be all right," he said again, praying it was the truth.

At last the bond that had defined her life and death frayed to nothing under his power. She drew a deep breath in her sleep.

"I think it worked," he said to her.

But her blood had already soaked the bandage and pooled between his fingers. Goddess, if only they had a healer with them. After giving her hope to outlive her master, he couldn't let her die of her wounds.

In that moment, he came to a decision. He would fight for her life with everything he could offer her.

He ran his hand along her cheek. "I don't know if this will help you, but it's our only chance. And if it does work...I promise being bound to me will be a much kinder fate."

Lio bit his hand and lowered it to her muzzle. He opened her dangerous jaws and pressed his bleeding cut to her tongue. With his thelemancy, he touched the part of her mind that controlled her swallow reflex.

The Lustra had helped him into her mind, and he had given her the healing power of Hespera in his blood. Now all he could do was wait.

He didn't move until he realized the blood under his hand was drying. Her wound had stopped bleeding.

He sat there and listened to his familiar's heart beat stronger.

CASSIA TUCKED AZAD'S GRACE braid close to her heart. She wondered where Neana was and shuddered. If she survived, she had no future now, only the Craving that would slowly end her life.

It wasn't right. Azad had died here in this dirty hole without his Grace at his side. The knights hadn't even fought with him as he had tried to save Castra Augusta.

None of this made sense. What had Azad been doing in here while the slaughter went on outside? Why had he made his last stand alone?

Cassia could think of only one explanation. While the knights had tried to hold off the attackers, Azad must have been protecting someone inside the keep.

Cassia listened, straining her Hesperine senses. She couldn't catch a hint of hearts or auras.

But of course she wouldn't, if a Hesperine had veiled someone to hide them from the enemy.

Cassia drove her dagger into the soil. *Does any creature survive here?*

Proof of life welled up through the veins of the earth.

There are survivors, she called silently to Lio, afraid her voice would disturb the delicate balance of the stones.

His heart leapt in her chest. *We'll come help you.*

There's not enough room, and we don't want to risk a cave in with too much movement rattling the debris.

His aura rang with alarm. *Cave in? I'm coming to step you out of there.*

There's no danger to me, my Grace.

She brought her roses gently out of the soil. Vines spread across the sphere of stones. Thorns fortified the bubble of safety Azad had left behind, and black roses bloomed where he had died.

Cassia kept pulling. She parted the ground with her roses and guided their strong vines to hold back the layers of dirt and rock. By the light of Rosethorn's Union Stone, she could see a stairway leading down into darkness.

The cellar. Cave-ins from the siege must have sealed it off. How long would the roof hold?

"Hello?" she called as softly as she could. "Is anyone there?"

"Cassia?" came an astonished murmur. A figure crept up the stairs. Red light fell across her disheveled chestnut curls.

"Genie!" Cassia whispered.

Flavian's seventeen-year-old sister crawled out of the hole, breathing hard, and threw her arms around Cassia.

Cassia held her tightly. The last time she had seen Genie, the vibrant young woman had been in Solia's retinue of ladies. How had she come to be on a battleground?

"We have to get you out of here, quickly and quietly," Cassia said. "The rubble isn't stable."

"Thank all our gods you found us. We had no water—we were running out of air..."

"We?"

"The children. The children are the only ones we got into the cellar before...before..."

"Lady Genie?" called a small voice from below. "Is it safe to come out now?"

The glow from Cassia's dagger illumined the faces of Patria and Segetia's children. Tenebra's newest orphans.

Cassia held the image for Lio to see. *The children are alive.*

His relief and gratitude filled her, powerful and pure. *What can we do?*

Is there any way you could clear a path outside the keep? I don't want the first thing they see to be...

Of course.

"We must all be as still and quiet as we can," Cassia explained to Genie and the children. "I shall work some magic now. Don't be afraid—my spell will keep us all safe."

The children huddled closer together, but nodded. Avoiding Genie's gaze, Cassia kept her lips tightly closed over her unsheathed fangs. The last thing she wanted was for her canines to frighten them. Her magic was terrifying enough.

She eased her roses down through the crumbling cellar entrance and let them climb the walls and ceiling, fortifying the structure around the little ones. Once she was sure they were safe, she expanded the vines inside the sphere of stones around her and Genie. They grew through the space where she had crawled in, and the breach in Azad's defenses filled with thorns.

At last she let her roses tear through the keep, shoving aside every rock and timber in their path. When her spell was complete, she looked down the tunnel she had made. Moonlight shone at the end of it, and Knight stood silhouetted there, guarding their escape.

She motioned to Genie. "It's safe for us to lead the children out now."

When Genie didn't reply, Cassia braced herself and finally risked a glance at the young woman.

Genies was staring. Cassia had been so prepared for a horrified stare like Ben's that it took her a moment to realize Genie was wearing a different expression.

She looked…awed. She opened her mouth, as if at a loss for words.

Cassia smiled. "Ready to go?"

Genie gave her head a shake, her dirty curls bouncing. "Right. We need to get out of here."

Genie stationed herself at the cellar entrance and guided the children out, organizing them in a line as they went. "Everyone take the hand of the person in front and behind you. Just like that. Now, would you like to be the leader and take Cassia's hand? Very good. Your mama and papa will be proud."

Cassia's throat tightened. She took the hand of the little girl in the lead. She had seen this child in Lio's thoughts the night he had helped evacuate Mederi.

Now the girls' round face turned up toward Cassia, pinched with exhaustion and anxiety. "Have you seen my goat?"

Cassia willed her tears not to fall and stroked the child's hair. "We'll have time to look for everyone else later. Right now we need to get you and the other children to safety. Thank you for being the leader. You're very brave."

Cassia led her through the tunnel, moving patiently so the whole line of children could follow. When she and the goat girl made it out of the keep, Lyros was waiting. Cassia gave his arm a squeeze.

There was no sign of the bodies. He and Mak guarded a wide, clear space around the half-demolished castle well. Her Trial brothers' wards held back tall piles of debris, and Lio's veils lay heavy over the devastation beyond.

But where was her Grace?

Coming, he said without further explanation.

Lyros knelt in front of the little girl and smiled. He had veiled his fangs to look like a human's canines. "Hello there. I'm Lyros, and this is Mak."

The child clenched her fist, holding something tightly in her hand. "I need to find my family."

"We're taking care of you for them tonight," Lyros said. "If you come over here, we can give you some water and make sure you aren't hurt."

Mak, clearing stones from around the well, waved at her.

She nodded mutely, but before she went with Lyros, she turned to Cassia again. The child opened her hand and offered up what she held.

The sight of the black feather on the girl's palm sent a chill down Cassia's spine. "Where did you get this?"

"Lady Miranda gave it to me. She said to keep it safe, and if we need her, we can use it to find her. But I don't understand how, and I don't know where my parents are. Please, will you tell her to come help?"

Cassia took the feather and kissed the child's brow. "I will find her."

She and Lyros shared a look of regret over the girl's head. He held out his hand, and the child let him lead her to the well.

Cassia hugged Knight to her. "*Barda. Ckada.*"

His protective instincts awoken, Knight wove among the children emerging from the keep and herded strays back toward the group. But he also let the frightened little ones pet his fur for comfort. That was something he had learned not from liegehound training but from Zoe and the sucklings. Cassia wanted nothing more than to cuddle her Grace-sister on her lap right now to reassure Zoe and herself that everything would be all right.

Lio stepped into sight by her side and wrapped his arms around her.

She hid her face against his chest and held him tightly. Oh, Goddess, how she needed to hold her Grace. *Where were you?*

I'll show you as soon as we see to the children. For a long moment, he didn't let go of her.

Then they sprang into action again and guided the rest of the children out of the tunnel. When all of them were finally out in the open, the area was packed with scraped, thirsty little humans. Cassia lost track of how many villages they represented.

Lio touched her back. *Mak and Lyros and I can take care of them. Could you find out what happened from Genie?*

Yes. Will you veil our conversation? None of us are ready to tell the children what happened.

Lio nodded, and his magic enfolded her.

Cassia drew Genie aside and convinced her to sit down and accept a waterskin. She let the young woman drink and catch her breath before broaching the difficult questions.

"Did anyone hurt you?" Cassia asked gently.

Genie shook her head. "Thanks to you. How did you do that? With your magic?"

Cassia tensed before she could help it.

But there was no condemnation in Genie's aura. "Did becoming a Hesperine give you that power?"

Cassia relaxed a little. "Plant magic was my affinity as a human, but the Gift made it much more powerful and gave it unique Hesperine effects."

"I've been hearing all sorts of marvelous tales of the Black Roses' deeds. Now I see why. When I saw your fangs tonight, I knew rescue had come."

Cassia had thought she didn't possess enough tears for what had happened here, but Genie's words put a lump in her throat.

"Where is everyone else?" Genie's tone was so grim, she seemed to already suspect the answer.

Cassia knew this would be the first of many times during this war when she delivered the news that the worst had happened. She was far more accustomed to facing the worst herself, rather than trying to help others face it. Would every time be this hard?

She sat down and put an arm around Genie. "I am so sorry. You and the children are the only survivors we've been able to find."

Genie pressed a hand to her mouth. Denial filled her aura.

"Forgive us," Cassia said. "We were too late."

"No." Genie took a deep, shaky breath. "You were just in time. If you hadn't saved us with your spell…"

She was shaking. She bowed her head over her knees. Cassia gathered Genie's hair back from her face and gave her sips of water, stroking her back.

"How did you get here?" Cassia asked.

"I came to run the refugee camp with your sister's permission. She knows I need to be here for my people and the families need"—Genie's face crumpled—"needed a lady to make sure the conditions were fit for women and children. The queen is the only one who understands."

"Your family wanted you somewhere safe," Cassia guessed.

"Of course." Genie swiped at her eyes, and silent fury cried out from inside her. "When the enemy came, the knights put me down there as if I'm one of the children, not a woman responsible for these people's lives."

"It was wrong of them to treat you like a child. But at least the little ones had you with them."

Genie's gaze swept over her young charges. "We have to get them somewhere safe, but I don't even know where that is now."

"What happened here?" Cassia finally asked.

Genie looked at her. "Cordium."

A hand closed around Cassia's heart. "Reinforcements from the Magelands?"

"No. Seven full war circles of mages with siege engines, soldiers in the colors of at least three princes, and an army of Cordium's infamous mercenaries. Not reinforcements. An invasion."

Cassia's pulse pounded. It couldn't be.

After centuries of political and religious factors had stayed Cordium's hand, after generations of Tenebrans had held their ground against the Magelands' attempts to subjugate them, the time had finally come. Cordium had no more caution or mercy. They were here to win the Last War.

"All our goddesses preserve us," Cassia breathed.

"We'll need all of them." Genie's voice wavered. "They moved through here like a wildfire. Nothing could have stopped them."

"Did anyone make it out before the attack to get word to the queen?"

Genie pressed her trembling lips together and shook her head.

Until now, Cassia had held on to a little hope. She finally asked the question she had been avoiding. "Was Ben here?"

Genie gripped her hand. "No. He leads the knights who escort the evacuees to safety. They left with a Hesperine days ago to bring in another village. They should have returned by now."

So they were out there, somewhere in the path of the army bent on crushing Solia's kingdom.

"We have to warn my sister," Cassia said.

ATONEMENT

Kneeling amid the orphans, Cassia sliced up another tunic, turning a lost parent's shroud into bandages and diapers. "We only have one option. We have to find Ben."

"No," Lio said.

"We need him to take responsibility for the children and warn my sister."

Lio handed a toddler to her older brother. "I will sneak into Castra Patria and warn Solia myself before I trust him."

Cassia tried to keep her voice calm. "We don't even know if the fortress has fallen. And wherever Solia is, you'd have to sneak past Rudhira."

Lio's expression hardened. "Then I will."

"Cassia is right." Lyros refilled a waterskin from the well for the next child. "Dawn is coming. We need to entrust the children to the knights and go back to the tower."

Mak glanced at Genie, who was gathering the children to sit in circles by village, appointing the eldest in each group as the leader. "Ben is an idiot, but they need him."

Lio's jaw was set. Her gentle Grace could be more stubborn than any of them when pushed past his limit.

Cassia reached for him in their Union. *Lio, we can't leave him out there to die.*

Lio's anger softened. *Of course not.*

She rose to her feet. "Lio and I will find him. With his veils and my roses, we should be able to bring Ben and his knights back safely."

"What's your plan to deal with the Hesperine who's with them?" Lyros asked.

"This is why we diplomats should go," she said. "It will take some negotiation. My hope is that the Charger will realize it's more important to get the children to safety than to arrest us, and there's only time to do one of those things before dawn."

Lio dusted off his hands and drew his staff. "And if negotiation fails, we are a match for them."

Cassia looked at Genie again. She knew the young woman harbored as much unrequited love for Ben as he did for her. "Don't tell Genie where we're going. I don't want to get her hopes up."

Mak and Lyros nodded in understanding.

Cassia drew her dagger and called Knight to her. She focused on Ben, recalling her soulful friend, not the judgmental man they had last met. Lio's magic picked them up and carried them away from the scene of slaughter, toward the knight's aura.

She breathed, but the air was still heavy with fear and death. The fallow field under their feet smelled of bloodshed. Amid the bodies of warriors and mages, five knights and one Hesperine still stood. A contingent of the invasion force had found Ben's party.

The nearest knight pulled his sword out of a Cordian mercenary and rounded on Lio and Cassia.

Cassia raised a low barrier of roses. Lio held out his staff in one hand, lifting the other in a placating gesture.

"Peace!" Lio shouted.

The Charger stepped in front of the knight, warding magic emanating from her hands. "You dare speak of peace with weapons in your hands? You know nothing of peace or war. Of sacrifice."

Blood and ash streaked the Charger's golden hair, but finally Cassia recognized her and the black braid she wore. This gaunt being bore no resemblance to the bold, happy woman who had danced all night with Azad in the gardens of House Komnena. Her heart labored on, but she had already died in Union with her Grace.

"Neana." Cassia met her fellow immortal's hollow eyes as if looking into a mirror. This would be her own future, if she ever lost Lio.

Neana slashed her hand with her fangs and took a step toward Cassia and Lio, her magic rising.

Cassia dropped her dagger. Lio's protest flashed in their Union, but she held out her empty hands. "I found your braid."

Neana went still. If Cassia lived forever, she would never be able to describe the anguish that flowed out of Neana, a flood devastating the Blood Union.

Cassia managed to speak. "It is my sacred duty and my privilege to return your Grace braid to you, in honor of Azad's sacrifice."

Neana drew a rattling breath. "Did anyone survive?"

Cassia took a step forward. "His death was not in vain. Lady Eugenia and the children are alive because of him."

The knight pulled his helmet off. Ben looked at Cassia with a pleading gaze. "Genie is safe?"

"Mak and Lyros are with her," Cassia replied. "We came to find you and take you back to her."

He sagged where he stood. "Everyone else at Castra Augusta?"

"I'm afraid there were no other survivors."

Ben's mouth moved, although he made no sound. Cassia read the words of an ancient prayer on his lips.

Lio's gaze swept the defeated mercenaries. "These men were only a scouting party. The rest of the army could find us at any moment. We need to get back to Castra Augusta."

"Where are the villagers you were taking to the camp?" Cassia asked.

"The army found them first." Neana sounded so angry.

"We tried—" Ben began. "When Azad warned Neana of what was happening at Castra Augusta—we tried to get back—but the mages ambushed us mid-step."

Cassia reached out and put a hand on Ben's arm. "You did the best you could. Come back and reassure Genie you're alive."

Neana closed her fists, red dripping between her fingers. She took another step toward Lio and Cassia. "Back to Castra Augusta is not where our prince ordered me to take you."

Lio faced her, his staff ready. But all he said was, "Your grief runs in my veins."

She lowered her hands. The blood she shared with Azad, with Lio and Cassia, began to dry on her skin. "So it does, son of Apollon."

Slowly, Cassia reached into the collar of her robes. Neana made no move to stop her. She retrieved Azad's braid and offered it to Neana.

She gathered her promise to Azad in her hands. "You have my gratitude."

Cassia closed Neana's fingers around the braid. "If there is anything we can do for you, ask. Anything."

"I am beyond help. Now there is nothing our prince can do to reprimand me if I don't arrest you. I would rather see you out here, bringing Othros's justice upon those who took my Grace from me."

Cassia squeezed her hands. "Thank you."

"All that matters to me is finishing what Azad and I started."

"If you're willing to warn my sister about the invasion, you will save countless lives."

Neana nodded once. "I will go to her."

"You have our gratitude as well," Lio said.

Neana put one hand to his cheek, the other to Cassia's. Azad's braid touched her skin. "Farewell. Survive to dance the night away, for all of us. May we never meet in Sanctuary."

She disappeared with a whisper of a step.

We'll never see her again, Cassia said.

Lio put his arm around her and held her against him. *Not in this life.*

One of the other four knights looked to Ben for guidance. "What will we do with the bodies, Sir?"

"Leave them," Ben answered, "and let us remember them in our prayers. We have to go."

The air swelled with Lio's power as he stepped them all back to Castra Augusta. When they arrived beside the well, Mak and Lyros's sighs of relief were audible.

Genie's eyes filled with tears. Ben dropped his helmet and his sword. As if no one else in the world existed, he ran to her and pulled her into his arms.

LIO LISTENED FOR THE hound's heartbeat through the children's weeping and the adults' worried voices. She still slept where he had settled her, away from the chaos around the well. She still lived.

Cassia kept her arm around him. *Where do your thoughts keep drifting? I'll explain as soon as I have a chance.*

"We only have an hour till dawn," Lyros was saying to Benedict. "Is there somewhere we can step you?"

The knight rubbed his face. He now stood at a distance from Genie that mortals would consider appropriate. Barely. "What do you think? Could we try Lord Avar's keep?"

Genie blinked, as if realizing his question was directed at her. Well, it was about time the man started showing some respect for her judgment.

"No," she said. "His loyalty is wavering because of his trade with Cordium."

Ben scowled. "When did this start?"

"Since his ancestors swore fealty to mine. They've always been a money-minded lot. We should go to Lord Septimus. He will stay loyal to my family and the queen because his temples have chosen Solia's side, and the mages know all his sins."

Lio suppressed a smile. Someone had been paying attention, and she was well on her way to becoming a cunning politician like the rest of her family.

"Then we go to Lord Septimus." Ben gave his knights a look. "Is that understood?"

No one protested his decision to follow the advice of a seventeen-year-old girl.

Mak glanced at the twilight sky. "It will take time to move this many children. We need to hurry."

Before Lio could reply, pressure built on his arcane senses.

"Mages!" He shouted the warning at the same time as Mak and Lyros.

Five knights and four Hesperines had their weapons out before the traversal spell popped Lio's ears. He tasted a storm on the air.

A mage in red-gold robes manifested with lightning crackling around him. The forks of magic darted across his tan skin and black hair, then shot back inside him. Through the abating heat, Lio recognized the mage's aura.

"Eudias! Thank the Goddess it's you." Lio sheathed his staff and reached out to steady the young man.

Eudias grasped Lio's arm for support in the wake of the exhausting spell, but he kept his balance. "I'm glad to see you too, my friend."

Now that the glare of the lightning had faded, Lio realized who had been standing behind Eudias. The young mage of Kyria in blue robes was Ariadne, his respected colleague and secret sweetheart. Her eyes, visible above her veil, gleamed with tears.

Ben gripped Eudias's shoulder. "What are you doing here?"

"Neana brought word of what happened," Eudias said. "Queen Solia agreed to spare us so you'll have a healer to help with the children and a lightning mage to protect you while we get them to safety."

"How is my sister?" Cassia's heart made Lio's race with fear of the answer.

Ariadne clasped her and Genie's hands. "Our queen prevails."

Cassia let out a breath. "Does she still hold Castra Patria?"

They couldn't take any more bad news tonight, and yet Eudias shook his head. Such a small sign, but a great blow.

"What happened?" Mak sounded as devastated as they all felt.

"Our forces are divided between the queen's position and Segetia," Eudias explained, "and Lucis's army stands between us. Even with Hesperine aid, fighting a war on two fronts is wearing us to the bone. We can't hold Patria. The queen has ordered us to abandon the domain and retreat to Hadria."

Lyros's shoulders slumped. "What else can she do?"

"Hadria will never fall," Cassia said fervently. But Lio knew she was trying to convince herself as much as the rest of them.

"Where are we taking the children?" Ariadne asked.

"We're trying to get to Lord Septimus's estate," Genie answered, "but you two will exhaust yourselves traversing this many, and our Hesperine friends must leave before dawn."

"I can traverse to the Kyrian mages there," Ariadne said. "The leader of their temple is a staunch ally of my own Prisma. Let me gather more of my sisters to help traverse the children."

"Are you sure you all can manage?" Cassia asked.

Ariadne's eyes flashed. "We will do better than manage. This is our goddess's fight now. Did you not hear of Cordium's ultimatum?"

Everyone shook their heads, although Lio had a guess as to what machinations the Magelands would try next.

Ariadne continued, "The Mage Orders issued a unanimous decree from the Divine City of Corona. Cordium demanded that the temples of Tenebra repudiate Queen Solia and her Hesperine allies and reaffirm our obedience to the Orders. All who refuse will be branded apostates. But their threats of arrest and persecution won't sway us from our cause."

"It's as I feared," Lio said. "If Solia was not associated with Hesperines, the religious authorities would have no grounds to intervene in a Tenebran political conflict. I'm sorry."

"Don't be," Eudias replied. "They would find any excuse to prey on Tenebra. They've already trampled on the law with their enchanted war machines and magefire arrows. And if no Hesperines had been here to defend us from them, we would have lost already."

Ariadne nodded. "They may try to place Hesperine heresy at the center of this conflict, but they know it's about so much more. The Mage Orders have been trying to subdue Tenebra for centuries, just as they brought Cordium under their thumb."

"How did the temples respond?" Lio asked.

The proud gleam in Ariadne's gaze told them the answer. "At the Temple of Kyria at Solorum, we shut their gates to Lucis and declared our walls a sanctuary for Solia's supporters."

Eudias crossed his arms. "Then the mages of Anthros at Lucis's capital abandoned the Sun Temple in protest and came to our Kyrian sisters' defense. Most other temples in the kingdom have followed their example."

"We will defend our right to worship free of the Mage Orders' dictates," Ariadne swore, "even though we know the cost. There's no doubt Cordium will cite our temples' rebellion as a justification for the invasion they have longed to launch for centuries."

"We know the price you pay," Lio said. "The only comfort I can offer is this. Hesperines dared to resist, and we are still standing."

"And we stand with you," said Cassia.

Ariadne squeezed her hand again. "We know."

Lio could feel history shifting around them. The temples that had abandoned Hespera worshipers during the Ordering now fought at their sides. Could this be the sixteen-hundred-year conclusion of the Last War? Or was it only the beginning of the next one?

Mak glanced at the sky. "I'm afraid it's time for us to go."

"Wait." Ariadne handed Cassia a small fabric pouch. "The queen told me to give you this."

Cassia peered inside, then pressed a hand to her mouth. "Seeds."

Ariadne nodded. "Her Majesty plucked every winter weed that prevails in the scorched earth of Patria. She said you would find hidden power in the plants that others cast aside."

Cassia held the pouch close. "I will. Give her my love."

Eudias smiled. "She speaks of you all the time. She can't stop boasting of your fangs and had lovely tales to tell of your avowal celebration. I wish I could say this under better circumstances, but congratulations to you both."

The words reached Lio through the horror around them and proved there was still gratitude in him. "Thank you."

"We've heard wondrous rumors of your spells, Cassia," Eudias added. "I hope for better days when you two can tell Ariadne and me all about your magic studies."

"I'll hold that hope with you," Cassia said.

As they prepared to go, Benedict approached her. He had the look of a supplicant, but Lio still moved closer to her and glared at the knight.

Benedict avoided his gaze and addressed Cassia in a surprisingly humble tone. "Genie told me what you did with your magic."

Cassia said nothing. The silence became uncomfortable.

Benedict looked away, at Genie. Then back at Cassia. "When I knew Castra Augusta was under attack, and I couldn't get to her... I would have done anything to save her. I would have broken my vows as a holy knight and used any magic, no matter how forbidden."

Cassia's aura softened. "You should tell her that."

His gaze fell. "I have work to do to be worthy of her. But after looking into my own heart tonight, I cannot fault any of the choices you have made for love."

"I hope you will not fault your own choices either, Ben. Love is nothing to be ashamed of."

"I am sorry I shamed yours. I beg your pardon and your patience as I continue trying to understand your true beliefs. Can you forgive me?"

She held out a hand to him. He took it, and instead of kissing it as if she were a lady, he held her hand in both of his like a friend.

"Yes," she said warmly.

"You have always been too generous to me," he replied.

"Someone ought to be, when you are so hard on yourself. I'm sorry I lied to you."

"I cannot fault you for that, either, when I gave you no reason to trust me with the truth."

"Can we trust each other again?" she asked. "Can I still call you friend?"

"If you will have my friendship, Cassia Komnena."

At his use of her true name, she smiled at him.

Lio would have liked to see Benedict grovel longer to earn back Cassia's goodwill, but if she was satisfied, he would call a truce. He extended his hand to the knight. Benedict clasped his wrist the Hesperine way.

When they had all said their farewells, Mak put an arm around Lyros's shoulders. "Ready to return to our tower, Black Roses?"

Cassia clicked her tongue at Knight, and he somewhat reluctantly left the children. "Ready."

"Almost," Lio said. "There's someone I'm bringing with us."

Lyros frowned at him. "What?"

"Who?" Mak demanded.

"The survivor I found," Lio replied.

Cassia's brow furrowed, her mind probing his veils. He hadn't wanted her to know about the hound until he was sure she would survive the night. But he couldn't keep his new familiar from his Grace any longer.

Lio rubbed the back of his neck. "I'm not sure how Knight will take to her."

"I'll make sure he behaves. *Hama.*" Cassia heeled Knight and followed Lio.

He led her and their Trial brothers away from the mortals, to a quiet place around the corner of the ruined keep. He had laid the hound there in the lee of some fallen stones and covered her in veils. Now he pulled back his spells.

"Oh, Lio." Cassia put a hand to her chest, tenderness welling out of her aura. Just as he'd expected, one look at the hound was all it took. She was already in love.

Barks erupted from Knight. She moved in front of him, holding his gaze.

"*Het!*" she barked back. "*Soor het!*"

He bared his teeth, and his haunches bunched. Lio tensed, prepared to shield his familiar if Knight tried to lunge past Cassia.

"*Barda acklii,*" she commanded.

At those words, Knight fell silent. His posture was still tense, and he kept his eyes on Lio's hound. But he made no more aggressive moves.

"What does that mean?" Lio needed to pay more attention to the training tongue from now on.

"I told him to guard her as an ally." Cassia crouched and put her arms around Knight's neck. "Shh, darling. She suffered a great deal. Be kind to her."

Reassured, Lio knelt to check his dog's bandages. No blood has soaked through.

"Where did you find her?" Cassia asked.

He sighed. "Next to her fallen master—a Cordian."

Mak gave Lio and his new familiar an apprehensive look. "She's one of the enemy's war dogs?"

"Lio." Lyros's tone was gentle. "There's only one kind thing we can do for her."

"That's out of the question. I won't let her die."

Lyros turned to Cassia with a plea in his voice. "You know how a liegehound suffers when it loses its master."

Cassia looked at Lio, and he could feel her looking into his soul. His Grace saw all the things inside him that were too raw for words, and he knew she understood why he had to save this animal.

"Lio is keeping her," she informed Lyros and Mak.

"She's a danger to us," Lyros protested, "and always will be."

"Not anymore." Lio got to his feet, lifting the massive dog in his arms as gently as he could. Laying limp across his chest and shoulders, the dangerous beast, now defenseless in her sleep, was less a burden than he had expected. "Now she's my familiar."

"What?" Cassia breathed. "You gave her your blood?"

"Did it work?" Mak asked.

"I don't know. I only know I was able to break her bond to her master with my thelemancy and that her wounds are better since I gave her my blood."

Lyros frowned at him in consternation. "Is that even possible?"

"For a Silvicultrix's Grace in favor with the Lustra, apparently so."

Cassia reached out a hand and stroked the dog's face. "We're keeping her. Forever."

If Lyros and Mak still had their doubts, they made no further protests as they stepped back to the tower together. Lio carried the hound up to the dining hall and laid her on one of the furs in the warmth of the fire.

His hands came away from her stained with blood again. Moving her had reopened the wound. "What can I do for her?"

Cassia hovered just beyond the fire's reach with a staying hand on Knight. His hackles were still up. "I'll get us some supplies."

She left, taking Knight with her. Lio sat on the floor with his back against the hearth stones and the dog's head on his lap. Her heartbeat filled the emptiness in his mind.

"I won't let anyone hurt you again," he whispered, wondering if his promise was empty, too.

He gave her more of his blood while he waited for Cassia. When she returned, she set clean rags, water, and a pestle full of herbs within his reach, then retreated to sit with Knight several paces away.

"I prepared some healing plants in the Changing Queen's alchemy room. This mixture always helps Knight when he's injured. You can put it under her bandages."

Working the soaked bandage carefully off the dog's side, Lio paused and looked at her. "Thank you, Cassia."

"I've known her for minutes, and I already adore her. Knight will, too, once he grows accustomed to the idea that there's one more member of our pack."

Lio let himself believe her reassurances that his familiar would live long enough for Knight's reaction to matter.

Once he finished changing the bandage on the dog's back, he gave her yet another dose of his blood. He saw no sign it was hurting her, at least. He could only hope it would stop the bleeding again.

"Try to get some water into her," Cassia said. "Even little sips will help. If she tolerates that, we can try some morsels of meat next."

Twilight brightened beyond the clerestory windows while Lio worked tiny swallows of water into the dog's mouth. Cassia's presence abided with him. His eyelids grew heavier as the last hour of the night slipped away. He forced his eyes open with a sudden burst of anger.

"Lio."

At Cassia's quite voice, he looked up from the hound. His Grace was within arm's reach now. She must have been working her way gradually nearer for the last hour. Knight lay on a fur on the other side of the pool of firelight. But closer than before. Lio lifted his arm.

Cassia slid under it and leaned against his side. "We can give her some meat tomorrow."

"What if she dies in our Slumber?" he whispered.

Cassia ran her hand down his chest. "Hespera's healing will fight for her while we can't."

He found no comfort in those words. He felt so helpless. Where had Hespera's healing been tonight?

She stroked his hair back from his face, her fingers gentle on his brow. "I know, my mind mage."

His throat closed. A sob wanted out of him, but couldn't escape. Weeping was useless. His power was useless.

"It's not," Cassia said fiercely. "You saved them at Mederi. You gave them more time. That time means so much to mortals."

She stroked his face until they fell into Slumber in each other's arms.

41

nights after

WINTER SOLSTICE

DAME

THE DOG'S HEART WAS still beating when Lio woke from his day terrors. She stirred a little on his lap and let out a faint whine. Mustering his thoughts and magic, he slid her into painless sleep once again.

When Cassia woke, her embrace told him she had seen his dreams. She kissed him gently, as if he might break.

"I'll feed Knight and bring back some meat for her, too."

He gave his familiar more blood. More water. He tried to keep track of time. Time was important. But he wasn't sure how much went by before Cassia returned.

She handed him a small plate of shredded venison softened in warm water. "Try this now."

The night passed in a blur of changing bloody bandages and soiling his fingers with dead flesh. He knew Miranda was out there, their true goal. But nothing felt as important as keeping this one creature alive.

At some point, Cassia went to the door to speak with Lyros in low tones. Lio couldn't catch their words through Lyros's veils, only their worry.

Lio felt a heavy, soft weight press against his leg. He looked to see Knight laying at his side. Cassia's hound leaned his head across Lio's lap to sniff his sleeping familiar.

Lio stroked Knight's head, and a different fear replaced his worry that Knight wouldn't accept the new hound. What if Knight grew too attached, only to lose his new companion?

Cassia sat down with him in the pile of dogs. "What will you call her?"

He doubted anyone but his Grace would have urged him to name a dying thing.

"You should name her," Cassia said firmly.

"Every champion needs a lady," he said. "What do you think, Knight? Shall we dub her your Dame?"

Knight licked the other dog's muzzle.

"That's perfect," Cassia said.

"Dame, then." Lio stroked her soft ears again. "How much longer will Lyros tolerate my madness, do you think?"

"He didn't come to argue. He came to ask me how you are."

"Are he and Mak all right?"

"None of us are. But they have the training for coping with death."

"So should I, after so much of it."

"Mak and Lyros and I aren't mind mages."

She reached for him in their Union, the touch of her thoughts and emotions the gentlest offering. He sucked in a deep breath and let his Grace's presence fill the void inside him.

nights after
WINTER SOLSTICE

THE REAL GOAL

LIO STUMBLED THROUGH THE bodies. *The battlefield stretched as far as his eyes could see. The silence reigned as far as his ears could hear.*

His magic swept out of him like a wind, beyond his control. It carried him through the vacant husks that had been people.

His only hope lay on the horizon. The stone circle where he would find his Grace. He had to get to her before it was too late.

He waded ahead on foot. The blood of the fallen stained his avowal robes.

At last he staggered into the circle. The stones lay in broken pieces around him. At their center was Cassia in her ceremonial white robes. His beautiful Whiteblood was now on her knees and bound to a stake.

"No." He let his power flow into her, Craving her life force.

But her vibrant magic didn't fill their Union. She, too, was hollow.

"No!" His shout echoed across the devastation Kallikrates had left in his wake. "I will wrest her magics from you and leave you empty."

WHEN CASSIA EMERGED FROM the Slumber this time, she was no longer on the floor with Lio and the dogs. It seemed he had carried her to a chair and covered her with one of the Changing Queen's woven blankets. He still sat by the hearth with Dame and Knight.

"Her bandage is off!" Cassia exclaimed.

The despair in Lio's eyes quelled her hopes. "Her wound is gone, and I lifted my sleeping spell. But I can't wake her."

Knight licked his fellow liegehound's face and looked up at Lio with soulful eyes.

Cassia knew what it would do to Lio if Dame didn't survive. Swallowing back tears, she joined him by the hearth and rested her hand on Dame's side. Before she could stop the thought, she found herself wishing she could help with her magic.

"I know." Lio wrapped his arm around her, his hold fierce. "I'll make it right, Cassia, just as I swore."

"Stop." She stroked his face, where a hint of stubble had begun to appear. He looked exhausted sitting here with tousled hair and bloodstains on his robes. "That was just a day terror. You mustn't torture yourself every time I have a thought about my other affinities. I was sincere when I told you my plant magic and the Gift are enough for me."

"I know you were. But you won't always be content with only part of your power."

She released him. "Yes, I will."

"I know you, my rose. The night will come when you hunger for more. And when it does, I will move the sun and moons to make sure you have everything your heart desires."

She rose to her feet. "I don't want more power. Ever. I'm better than that."

Surprise flashed in his gaze. "It's nothing to be ashamed of. You know there's nothing wrong with wanting to be powerful."

"It's right for me to want you and the Gift and the magic Hespera blessed in me. But I must stop there, Lio. Don't you see?"

"No, I don't see at all."

"I don't want to channel two more powerful affinities. What will that make me?"

He stood and took her hands. "We can work through those feelings together, just as we did with your plant magic. Since the first night we met, I've always helped you overcome your fear of wanting more."

She pulled out of his hold. She couldn't bear his sweet words, tempting her with the purest intent. She had refused the Collector's poison again and again, but she could not resist her Grace.

Lio's confusion filled their Union. She was hurting him, and he didn't understand. "I swore to give you everything. Unlimited time. Unlimited power."

Cassia recoiled. "Don't say that!"

He shook his head. "What did I say?"

The Collector's words whispered in her mind, and she felt sick. *Unlimited time is not the greatest prize... You know that the real goal is unlimited magic.*

"If I keep wanting and wanting, where will I stop?" she cried.

"Talk to me about these fears," Lio pleaded. "You just saved a castle full of children with your magic. Even your friends from your human life have acknowledged the good your power can do. Why this sudden aversion for more magic?"

"We just beheld the casualties of the game. The consequences to humanity and Hesperines when a few mages have too much power."

Shock flashed across his face. "You cannot be comparing yourself to the Old Masters."

"What is to prevent me from reaching for more and more magic until it turns me into a heartless being like them?"

"You are *nothing* like them," Lio said fiercely. He took a step toward her. "After what you came through during your Gifting, you can't really believe that you would ever become like Kallikrates. You have fought him more bravely than anyone."

"The Gifting purifies us, but it does not perfect us. Isn't that why we have so many rules about how to use our power?"

"Of course we aren't perfect. But we've tried to follow Hespera's tenets for sixteen hundred years. Hesperines have possessed immortality and incredible power all this time, and we have never become a force of evil in the world. We are still striving to be our better selves."

"Are we, Lio? As fugitives who have broken those sacred laws?"

Anger flared in his aura. "The Goddess's laws and how imperfect Hesperines apply them are two different things. I no longer have qualms about breaking laws that make you ashamed of who you are."

She felt as if she were teetering on the edge of a dangerous slope, and there was nothing to keep her from plummeting. Except her own Will. "No Hesperine has ever had power like mine. How do we know one of our own kind will not become a New Master in the next round of the game?"

He caressed her cheek, and she needed him too much to pull away. "Not you, Cassia. No matter how many times he has tried to corrupt you, you never break."

She forced herself to step back. "Nothing in this world is unbreakable. Standing on the ashes of past epochs, we know that."

"My faith in you in unbreakable."

Tears burned her eyes. "You have always trusted me too much. No one should have that much magic, not even me. Especially not me."

"You will. I made a promise."

He looked down at her with a dark fire in his aura, his eyes hard with conviction. The two of them might break, but not before his love for her broke the world.

She knew her magic might be her downfall. But that was a small fear compared to the sense of foreboding that came over her. Her power would destroy her Grace, too.

A FOOTSTEP IN THE shadows was all that kept Lio from fighting her—fighting for her—all night. Before he could say more, their Trial brothers approached.

He and Cassia stood there, gazes locked, anger and hurt and Craving throbbing between them. He fought his instinct as her Grace to say whatever he could to soothe this conflict in their bond. He would not give in. He would debate this with her for as many battles or as many centuries as it took for her to seek her magics, the missing parts of herself.

Mak stepped between the two of them. His quiet presence banked the tensions in the Blood Union, but nothing could calm the turmoil in Lio and Cassia's Grace bond.

"How's your familiar?" Mak asked.

"I've done all I can do for her," Lio replied. "Either she'll wake, or…"

Mak gave him a sympathetic look. "She'll be safe here if you're willing to leave her for a few hours."

Lio rubbed his face. "How long has it been since the attack on Castra Augusta?"

"Three nights," Lyros answered. "When you're ready, it would be wise to pick up Miranda's trail again before it goes cold."

"Yes," Lio agreed. "We should go."

Cassia gave a nod. "I shall find her tonight. It's time to finish this."

A hint of necromancy brushed Lio's senses. It came from Cassia's fingers. She held up a crow's feather.

Lio caught her hand. "What is this?"

"I think it's from Miranda's familiar."

"Where did you get it?"

"From the children. Miranda gave it to them and promised it would help them find her in a time of need. I don't know if that's true or if she left it to lure us into a trap." Cassia looked at each of them. "Are we willing to spring it?"

"If we're all willing to follow a plan and not take any foolish risks." Lyros's gaze was on Lio.

Lio's jaw tightened. "We've drilled for every possibility and plenty of impossibilities. No one is more prepared than we are, General Lyros."

"You'll thank me if we survive this."

Mak hugged Lyros's shoulders and shot Lio a look. "We're all grateful we have each other's backs. Go ahead, Cassia."

Cassia drew her dagger.

Let me help you, Lio said.

She shook her head, squeezing her eyes shut. *I can't afford to lose control right now.*

I won't let that happen.

That is exactly what will happen if you keep pushing me.

Cassia, there could be dangerous curses on that feather. Please let me keep you safe from it.

The Lustra is greater than Miranda's curses.

Her magic built around the feather in her hand, eclipsing the faint aura of Miranda's power. Knight backed away, his ears flat against his head.

She slashed her hand with her dagger and wrapped her bleeding fist around the feather. Blood magic unfurled from her and twined through the tower, clashing with the Lustra magic that welled up from the letting site.

The swell of her power made Lio's pulse pound. Standing on the outside of her spell, he hated the distance between them.

Her cry of fury released the pain inside of him. Why couldn't she see that her ferocity was not wrong? Hespera had always had fangs.

She hurled the feather into the Mage King's fire, her blood sizzling in the hearth. The fire rose in a white-hot surge. Lio thought he glimpsed images in the flames. But they were gone before he knew what they were. The fire collapsed on itself and fell to its quiet orange glow.

Had her spell worked?

Cassia spoke in the stillness. "There you are, Miranda."

Lio took a step closer to his Grace. "Where is she?"

"Hierax Temple," Cassia replied. "Right now."

A frisson skipped over Lio's skin. "That's the site of the decisive battle where the Mage King stopped Cordium's invasion during the Last War. He built a temple there to thank Anthros for his victory, but historical sources suggest it was a site of worship long before his reign. There's no record of which cult held it sacred before he claimed it."

Cassia turned to them, silhouetted against the fire. "What if he never claimed it? What if the earlier worshipers wanted him to build his temple there?"

"Yes. That would make so much sense. It could have been a Lustra site. Then he and the Changing Queen could have built another structure there that blends their magics, like the lighthouse and the tower."

"It has to be. Doesn't 'hierax' mean 'hawk' in the Divine Tongue?"

"Cup and thorns. The evidence has been right there in the name all these centuries."

Mak grimaced. "Lustra site or not, it's too close to Cordium's border for comfort."

"The invasion force may have already been through there," Lyros said. "We'll need to be more careful than ever."

Mak gave his Grace a squeeze. "We will be."

"We need to scout the place under veils before we attack," Lyros insisted.

Lio held up his hands. "I agree. I don't want us to scare Miranda off with any hasty moves."

Lyros didn't reply, but Lio didn't miss the warning in his Trial brother's eyes.

"I have a focus on her through the Lustra," Cassia said. "Lio, can you use that to step us before she's on the move again?"

"I'll go," Lyros broke in.

Lio frowned. "I'm the only one who can use Cassia's thoughts as a stepping focus."

"He's been there," Mak told them.

Lyros shrugged. "That's the part of Tenebra where I spent my mortal childhood, remember?"

Cassia moved away from the fire. "I hadn't realized you ventured that far out of Namenti."

"I tried to get out of the city once. I stowed away on a wagon headed for greener pastures, or so I thought. The caravan made it all the way to Hierax Temple before the traders found me and put me out on my ear. I decided I'd rather try my luck on the streets than in the wilderness, so I hopped into another wagon heading back to the city."

"With the traders' coin purses," Mak finished.

Lyros rubbed the back of his neck. "I'll get my spear and scout the temple. Wait here."

Mak didn't protest, so he and Lyros must have agreed on this privately. Lio started to say something, but Cassia caught his hand and held him back while Lyros headed for the armory.

Did they think Lio such a fool that he couldn't be trusted with a simple scouting mission?

Save your thelemancy for Miranda, Cassia said in his mind.

When Lyros returned with Night's Aim, Mak held him close for a moment. Lyros gave Mak a tender kiss, then stepped away.

The minutes slipped by. Mak sat down and failed at pretending he wasn't worried for his Grace. Cassia paced. Lio nursed his pride and his fear for their Trial brother.

At last, Lyros appeared by the fireside again. Lio sent up a silent prayer of thanks.

Mak jumped to his feet and pulled Lyros into his arms. "What did you find?"

"Nothing good," Lyros reported. "It appears the invasion force vanquished the temple on their way up from Cordium. The Aithourians have made themselves at home. Their leader is playing a game of kings and mages with Skleros over a bottle of wine."

Cassia curled her hands into fists. "Skleros is there? Could you tell if he has my pendant with him?"

Lyros nodded. "He was boasting to the war mage about taking a witch's artifact."

"This witch will send his pretty new body back to Kallikrates in pieces. What about Miranda?"

"No sign of her."

"She's there somewhere. I can tell."

"Marvelous," Mak said. "A temple full of Aithourians and two Gift Collectors. Our odds just keep getting better and better."

Lio resented every war mage between them and their goal. But he was not a reckless idiot, contrary to others' belief. "What do you recommend we do, Lyros?"

Lyros narrowed his eyes. "I would prefer to continue avoiding Skleros since our last battle with him was such a disaster. We can't afford to lose another of Cassia's foci to him. But it seems we have no choice. We'll have to face him tonight."

Cassia's temper flared. Lio knew the flavor of her anger when she was using it as armor. He alone could sense the regrets she was trying to hide.

He glared at Lyros. "Now is not the time to berate ourselves or each other for past decisions."

"I'm simply stating facts. Skleros is the greatest threat in the temple tonight, especially since we don't know how he might use Cassia's pendant against us. We should concentrate our power on him."

Cassia crossed her arms. "This might be our only chance to get my focus back. Could we steal it from him and then pursue Miranda?"

"No," Lyros replied, "there's no hope of using stealth. The temple is a maze of fire traps and revelatory spells. We'll have to fight our way to Skleros and take the pendant by force."

Cassia fumed, "I hate the thought of Miranda slipping our grasp while we're fighting him."

"I wouldn't count on it," Mak said. "When we confront him, I doubt she'll let him steal her prey."

Lyros nodded. "She's sure to make her move. With her in the wind, following a plan is vital."

"We're listening," Lio said.

Lyros explained the temple's defenses in detail and gave each of them instructions. The look in his eye said that if any of them put a toe out of line, he'd put them in their places with the sharp end of his spear. But he wouldn't hear any complaints about this plan from Lio. He was spoiling for a rematch with Skleros.

Finally, Lyros's voice lost its commanding edge. "Cassia, you'd best leave Knight here. Levitation is key to our survival. He won't fare well on the ground against fire mages. I wish Mak and I could ward him, but it will take all our power to protect the four of us from a full war circle of Aithourians."

She crouched and hugged her dog. "You're right. He'll be much safer here, and Dame won't be alone."

She murmured commands and pleas to Knight, and at last he stretched out beside Dame. Lio drew a bit of comfort from the sight the two hounds together.

While Cassia and Mak retrieved their weapons, Lio set out food and water for the dogs. He gave Dame another dose of his blood, but true to his fears, that did nothing to wake her.

"Keep an eye on her for me, will you, boy?" he asked, rubbing Knight's ears one more time in farewell.

Lio joined the others outside the tower, where Mak and Lyros stood holding hands with their weapons at the ready.

Cassia offered Lio his staff. "I'll show you the temple."

Images, smells, and magical imprints took shape in her mind. A stone face. Magefire. Miranda's arcane scent as the Lustra understood it.

Lio took the invitation, drawing so near in their Grace Union that she flushed. Her emotions slipped through to him, interlaced with her thoughts. More than the hurt and anger he had expected. Fear. For him.

Wrapping his arm around her waist, he pulled her back against his chest. He ran his hand down his braid in her hair. Her face was turned away from him, but she leaned into his touch as if it were pure reflex.

The four of them stepped, arriving in a copse of cypresses that provided good cover. Between the tall trees, Lio glimpsed a structure built in a style of the Great Temple Era, with fluted columns and a peaked roof.

Cassia knelt and ran her fingers over the trees' fallen needles. Lio couldn't see or sense anything, but she said with certainty, "Miranda hid here on her approach."

"Can you tell where she is now?" Lio asked.

Cassia shook her head. "I know she's here, but not precisely where. If I sense her close, I'll warn you all."

"That's the best we can do," Lyros said.

"Stay as safe as you can, everyone," Mak bade them. "May the Goddess shield us."

Lio spun thelemantic veils around them, the last advantage of surprise he could give them. It wouldn't last long.

They shot into the air on a burst of levitation. As they rose past the tops of the cypresses, the temple's many flames shone in Lio's eyes. Braziers of magefire lit the spaces between the columns. Lyros had been right. This place was a firetrap for Hesperines.

They swept upward. The temple's frieze flew by, carved scenes of the Mage King's victorious battle playing out as they passed. Lio landed lightly on the rooftop. He had crafted his veils so well that he couldn't hear the others' feet touch the stone around him.

In a crouch, Lyros darted along the roof, and they followed. When they were only a few paces away from the back edge of the temple, he halted and pointed down.

Cassia crouched on the peak of the roof, her fingertips splayed on the stone.

What do you sense? Lio asked. *Is this a Lustra site?*

I've never felt anything like this. It's so much more complex than the tower. Can you feel the spell weavings?

All I can sense is magefire. Will you show me?

She pressed her lips together. But her mind opened to him, and he sank into her again.

Their heartbeats blurred together, and the backs of his eyes pulled.

The world shifted to the left. Suddenly he could see their surroundings from Cassia's position.

Gazing out of her eyes, he beheld the magic. It held the temple together, glowing from between the stones. It drew him down, deep down, until he tapped a lush chasm somewhere in the earth. He thought he might go spinning into that darkness, not knowing if it were a grave or the place where all seeds were born.

Cassia pulled him back, centering him in her. *It's another letting site.*

Lio sucked in a breath, pulling his awareness back into his own body. *Goddess. It's as if the Lustra itself is nourishing those magefires.*

Ebah and Lucian's magics are completely unified here. The tower feels like an early experiment. This temple feels like the result.

Lyros gave Cassia a questioning look, and she nodded. So their plan would work.

She wet her lips, her pulse pattering faster. She adjusted her hold on her dagger. *I only have one chance to get this right.*

Now is not the time to hold back, no matter what path you take with your magic tomorrow.

Her head fell forward, her face hidden behind her hair. The night wind caught his braid.

Tiny green tendrils slipped from between the roof stones, gleaming with the temple's power.

All at once, the green shoots thickened into thorned vines. Stone cracked, and tiles shattered. Cassia's roses tore open the roof. In a rain of debris and black petals, the four of them leapt down into the temple's inner chamber.

THE MAGE KING'S FIRES

LIO CAUGHT ONE GLIMPSE of the mages. The war circle of Aithourians dodged flying stones while Skleros leapt away from the table, where roses had cleaved his game board and shattered his wine.

Then gouts of flame shot up from the war mages' hands, filling Lio's vision with fire.

He levitated backward as Cassia, Mak, and Lyros all shot away in different directions. Lio flattened his back against the wall.

The fire spells sailed into empty air between the four of them, sending hot prickles over his skin. In the wake of the flames came seven revelatory spells that shredded his veils.

The instant the fire sank, the Black Roses moved. Using Final Word for leverage, Lio pushed off from the wall and sped toward the other side of the room. Staying in one position would be certain death.

The mages now surrounded an altar where the temple's sacred sickle rested before a bronze brazier. In unison, they thumped their chest with their fists and held out their palms. The altar flame rose from the brazier in seven tendrils that whorled around each other.

Lio's Union Stone flashed from the top of his staff. Now.

Mak and Lyros's wards thickened the air, an invisible darkness. Cassia's roses broke through the floor and grew over every door and window.

Lio focused on the Aithourians' mental defenses. Seven clean strikes, and they would no longer be a threat. He reached into himself for his power.

But there was more than mind magic welling up within him. The ghosts of Castra Augusta were always just behind his eyes. Every suffering animal. Every crying child. Every parent and grandparent and spouse who had watched someone they loved die, knowing they were next.

Lio finally let out the cry of despair that had been building in him night after night. The echoes of their final moments overflowed from him and poured into the fire mages' minds. Still the seven men were not enough to hold so much pain.

Their mental defenses crumbled as easily as the castle had. They screamed like the dying villagers.

These men weren't helpless and harmless like Miranda's victims at Castra Augusta. Lio bared his fangs and flooded them with another wave of the pain their Order had caused.

One by one, they fell to their knees below him, clawing at their heads. Their fire spells spun out of control, finding anything they could to feed on. Every banner on the walls and offering at the altar caught fire.

Through the visions of slaughter in Lio's mind's eye, he saw Cassia's face before him. She clutched his shoulders.

Lio, what are you doing?

He gritted his teeth. *Following the plan.*

Lyros said to stop the fire mages with your mind magic, not this!

He didn't specify how I should break their minds.

"Cassia!" Lyros barked from somewhere beyond a wall of flames.

She glanced over her shoulder. Lio didn't take his eyes off the mages, but at the corner of his vision, Skleros raced toward a door, the sacred sickle in hand.

Lio dug into the corners of the war mage's minds and filled their every thought with the image of Neana's face. Then he drove Azad's despair into their hearts.

The men crumpled to the floor, weeping pitifully. "Neana," her enemies sobbed.

More roses sprouted to reinforce the tangle over the door in front of Skleros. But Cassia turned back to Lio.

She framed his face in her small, strong hands. Her strokes on his cheeks threatened to pull him back to himself. He couldn't come back. Not until justice was done.

Don't do this, his Grace pleaded.

They deserve it.

That doesn't matter. Don't make yourself their judge.

Lio sailed up, out of her hold. *I've seen your day terrors about Azad and Neana. How can you deny you want justice for them?*

Not like this!

The war mages' sweat and offal spoiled the air. Their heartbeats pounded faster and faster. Another moment, and they would beat their last.

Stop! Cassia shouted in Lio's heart.

Her magic slammed into their Grace Union. Her power twined through his every thought and tangled around his soul. There was nothing in him but her. His link with the mages shattered, and his staff flew from his grasp.

He hovered there, blind in the thrall of her beautiful, wild power.

When she released him, he fell. Her levitation caught him and set him on his feet.

The mages lay around him, their heads at unnatural angles. Broken necks. Swift deaths at the Stewards' hands. Mak and Lyros stared at Lio over the bodies.

Cassia landed in front of the door, where her roses lay in tatters, chopped away by a sickle.

THE DEAD SCREAMED IN Cassia's veins. Villagers? Mages? She didn't know anymore.

She couldn't afford to lose her focus on the pendant. It moved through the temple, a whisper of Lustra magic. The letting site murmured back, urging her forward.

Cassia beckoned. "I can track Skleros with the pendant. This way!"

Lyros gave Lio's shoulders a shake. "Focus on Skleros's dream wards now. Nothing else. Do you understand me?"

Lio yanked himself free, snatching up his staff. "I understood you when you said to do what I must to protect us from the fire mages!"

Mak shoved them both toward the door. Cassia plunged through the hole in the roses, the others close behind her. With a crash, more roof beams collapsed behind them in the burning chamber.

The hallway was so narrow that Lio's body pressed against hers. At the physical touch, their pain blended.

She poured it into a spell, ripping roses up out of the floor along the length of the hallway. A line of fire traps exploded, leaving her flowers in piles of ash.

"Good move." Mak's ward rose in front of her.

Cassia looked back at Lyros. "You predicted Skleros might escape. We fall back on your next plan?"

"Can you do it?" he asked.

She fingered the web of Lustra magic that glimmered throughout the temple. "I'll have to, won't I?"

Their success or failure, survival or death, depended on her magic now.

Skleros was a moving target, racing along a twisted path through the temple complex. She closed her eyes, trying to anticipate his destination.

The others followed her down the hall to a library. She flew across the room toward an alcove. With a silent apology to the Mage King, she knocked scrolls out of her way with a blast of levitation, then grabbed the solid oak shelves and physically hurled them aside. "Skleros is on the other side of this wall. He's probably warned the rest of the mages."

"Follow the plan." There was no more anger in Lyros's voice. "Please. Stay alive tonight."

Cassia gave him a quick, tight hug. Pulling from the letting site itself, she let her roses devour the wall of the library. The vines opened up the adjacent room, setting off half a dozen fire traps as they grew.

Cassia levitated out first with her Trial brothers covering her and Lio at her back. The mages' first volley of flames collided with Mak and Lyros's wards.

So many braziers. So little cover. They were in the main chamber of the temple, and another war circle of Aithourians was waiting for them with more than a dozen apprentices.

As fire and lightning burned through Mak and Lyros's wards, the Black Roses shot toward the ceiling again. War magic chased them to the rafters of the vast room.

The lights of the battle reflected off the bronze sun disk at the head of the chamber. Behind it towered a painted statue of her ancestor with sword held high and magefire hovering over his open palm.

Cassia dodged another tongue of fire and found herself face-to-face with the Mage King. There was no judgment in his noble blue gaze. The war mage's spell singed the seven-pointed crown resting on his blond hair, but missed her.

A bolt of lightning arced toward Lio, and he dropped behind the sun disk just as the war magic struck the bronze. Cassia flung out a hand, carpeting the floor below him with roses. No fire traps exploded. He landed safely on his feet, sending her his thanks in their Grace Union.

Then his eyes slid shut. As his thelemancy swept out of him, her gut clenched. But he didn't aim for the Aithourians. His power honed in on only one target: the Gift Collector.

Skleros stood in the center of the columned chamber, grasping Cassia's pendant. "Trying to take back your token of good faith, little witch? That's against your agreement with the Master. He may demand your head after all."

Lio's magic struck. Skleros's mouth twisted in a snarl, and he hurled a dagger at Cassia.

She whipped behind the statue to avoid the blade and tried to focus on the patterns of Lucian and Ebah's magic. Here in the main chamber, they were strongest of all.

The core of the letting site was right beneath the statue, as if Lucian were the eternal guardian of his queen's power. Her theory had been right. Ebah had wanted him to build this temple here.

Over the statue's shoulder, she could see Mak and Lyros blurring through the room, evading fireballs and repelling bolts of lightning with their wards. Blood sprayed where they landed blows with their weapons. Skleros wove among them to toss blades at Mak and Lyros, but his aim was not so deadly with Lio raking through his thoughts.

Mak grabbed one lightning mage by the throat and levitated with him. Bright forks of magic snaked over Mak, but didn't burn his warded skin. The mage struggled in his hold, then went still. Mak spun, using his dead opponent as a shield, and hurled the man's body into another mage's fire spell.

But there was always more fire. The Aithourians were drawing from the temple braziers. Anger filled Cassia at the sight of them exploiting the Mage King's power.

Lio, Mak, and Lyros were buying her time, but they couldn't hold out long when they were this outnumbered and the mages had an endless source of fire magic. And any time he wished, the Collector could decide he tired of this and end the round.

There was only one power in this room that would give the Black Roses the upper hand. The temple's. And she had only minutes to learn to harness it.

She'd healed Paradum with her blood magic and earned the tower's recognition. She could do this.

She had to.

Dagger in hand, she let her magic take root in the letting site. Energy rushed through her body. But the mages' spells were like invasive weeds, sucking life out of the Lustra. She had to make them stop.

The battle played out before her eyes while her mind was deep below the earth. Lyros's spear arced through a rush of flame and struck the caster in the chest. The apprentice beside him caught him as he fell back. While the young mage was distracted, Mak swooped down, aiming the Star of Orthros at the apprentice's head.

Cassia shut her eyes. She focused her Will on each point where the Aithourians were draining the Lustra.

This power was *hers*. She pulled the magic back to her with all her might.

Pain seared her veins. Dozens of fire spells scorched the arcane paths inside her.

She was screaming, falling. Then Lio's arms were around her. A bed of roses was under her back.

What happened? her Grace said in her mind.

She forced her eyes open and tried to sit up. *I have to try again. Keep fighting Skleros.*

Lio pulled her to him and covered her mouth with his wrist.

She growled in frustration at her thirst, but she couldn't deny she needed blood. She gave in and bit him hard. His hand tightened in her hair as she dragged a fast drink out of him and into her parched veins.

She lifted her head with a wet gasp. Lio hesitated an instant, as if he might not let her go, but then released her. Meeting his eyes, she gazed into a dark sky of mind magic. He had never looked farther away.

She dragged her hand across her lips and got to her feet. Wards now bracketed the space behind the sun disk. On the other side, fire roared. Flesh tore, and blood spattered. Their Trial brothers were fighting to keep the mages away from her and Lio so they could cast.

She was running out of time.

She braced her hands on the disk and reached into the letting site again. The mages were still using the Lustra-fed fires as they pleased. Her plant magic had done nothing to stop them.

Goddess help them. What if her plant magic wasn't enough?

Lyros had a plan for this, too. If her spell didn't work, it was Cassia's responsibility to find a Lustra portal and signal retreat. Was it time to surrender?

She stood paralyzed for an instant of indecision they couldn't afford.

Then she shot upward again to look over the disk. The Gift Collector was still on his feet, but his skin was sallow, his knuckles white as he drew yet another knife. The surviving war mages and their apprentices surrounded him in a battle formation. Mak and Lyros held their own in a desperate dance of stepping and levitation, weapons and wards.

There was no hope of fighting their way through to Skleros. If they tried to step, no doubt the mages would trammel them and drag them right into a fire trap.

She was the one who had lost the pendant. This was her crisis to solve.

A fork of lightning sent her ducking back behind the disk.

Are you all right? Lio's mind voice was strained.

Yes. How close are his dream wards to breaking?

Lio wrapped both hands around Final Word and stood the staff in front of him. Blood leaked from his fists. *Not as close as I should be.*

We have to escape.

His frustration roared through their bond, but he didn't argue.

Cassia opened one of Lio's hands and pressed her own bleeding palm to his. As their libation dripped to the ground, she sought the Lustra's guidance.

The portal was right behind them at the Mage King's feet. A doorway directly to the letting site. Goddess only knew what secrets Lucian and Ebah had hidden down there.

Cassia touched the portal with her magic. It answered her with angry whispers. From the center of the chamber, her pendant murmured back.

No, no, no. That was why Skleros was here. Why he needed the pendant. This portal required soothsaying to open.

She had failed. They were trapped.

There was only one way out—fighting. She touched a bloody finger to her Union Stone and flashed the signal to retreat.

"I'm sorry," she whispered, only for Hesperine ears to hear.

Raising her dagger, she demolished the floor in front of her with her vines. Hespera's Roses crawled over Anthros's sun disk, vines snapping and thorns scratching. Mak and Lyros's auras slid out of the way.

She gave her roses a push. The enormous bronze shield toppled forward. The Aithourians fled, some traversing to the other side of the chamber. But the two nearest and their apprentices disappeared under the sun disk's weight. She was grateful the roar of magic in her ears drowned out the sounds.

She stood in front of her Grace and faced the war mages with Mak and Lyros beside her.

Every single Aithourian fell to their knees at once. Their mouths fell open, screaming, but no sound emerged from their throats.

She reached for Lio's magic, but the thelemancy pouring out of him was flooding into Skleros. The Gift Collector's eyes were locked on Lio's as they stood frozen in their mental battle. It wasn't Lio causing the war mages' suffering.

Every Aithourian writhed on the ground, clawing at their chests. Tongues of flame and sparks of lightning writhed in the air as currents of magic tore out of their bodies. With sickening recognition, Cassia followed the flow of power with her gaze.

In the gallery above them stood Miranda.

THE SURVIVORS

MIRANDA'S HEART WAS THE first that had awakened Cassia's Hesperine empathy. Now that girl from her Gifting visions was here in the flesh. The full force of her emotions assaulted Cassia in the Blood Union.

Her sense of betrayal cut into Cassia, and she stood blind and dumb from Miranda's hatred. She thought she might vomit from so much bitterness. It was so familiar. She had lived for years with that same poison inside her.

Miranda let her head fall back. Fire cascaded into her mouth. The mages went still, empty of magic, devoid of life. She licked her lips.

Suddenly Lyros's spear flew toward her, a brilliant streak as fast as a lightning spell.

Her hand shot out. A gust of wind howled through the room and knocked Night's Aim off course.

Lyros's spear slammed into the floor. He raised his own hand and levitated the weapon back toward him. But a ring of fire sprang up around the Black Roses, and the spear rebounded off the flame ward to fall out of reach.

Phantom pain split Cassia's skull just before Lio cried out and staggered backward. She caught her Grace as he slid to the floor. *What happened?*

He groaned, lifting a hand to his brow. *She expelled me from Skleros's mind.*

Cassia cradled his head. *How can she do that?*

Mind magic...so much.

Mak stood over them, maintaining a ward, while Lyros dropped to his knees beside Lio. "Is he all right?"

Cassia took a breath to stave off her panic. "Miranda may not have the Collector's favor, but she's stolen more than enough power. Including mind magic."

"I can fight." With a snarl of effort, Lio levitated to his feet.

Cassia had fight left in her, too. As she had done on the roof, she called roses out of the magic in the temple's seams, this time in the gallery behind Miranda.

"I will not let you ruin this for me," Miranda spat. "Not again."

Cassia's vines had barely sprouted when Miranda swept fire around her, burning the plants before they could grow. How could she react so quickly to Cassia's spells?

Miranda smiled. "I took your magic. The same magic you still have inside you. I can always predict your spells. I can always find you."

Cassia's skin crawled. She pressed a hand to her belly.

She was bound to Miranda, as long as the Collector's Overseer possessed the plant magic she had ripped out of Cassia all those years ago.

Lio wrapped his arms around Cassia as she swayed on her feet. All the horror of the night she had lost her magic came back to him. He had relived that moment with her, but he had not been there to save her.

He wanted to shout his fury at Miranda. But all he could do was reaffirm his oath in Cassia's mind. *I will make this right. I swear in Hespera's name and by our Grace bond.*

I can't bear this. I need her out of my veins.

I will free you from Miranda once and for all.

Skleros backed toward the wall, his gaze darting between Miranda and the Hesperines. "So you're in the mood for a challenge, are you?"

"No. I'm here to kill you." Miranda pulled a weapon off her back. The digging fork's long iron handle was scorched, and its tines were sharpened to wicked points.

Skleros wheezed a laugh. "Descending to Cassia's level with gardening tools now, are you?"

Miranda traversed down to stand in front of him without breaking a sweat. Skleros pulled his executioner's axe from his back.

Lyros caught Lio's eye. "Plan four."

Lio nodded in agreement, then Cassia, then Mak.

Shadow wards slammed down around them. Still holding Cassia, Lio stepped through the ring of fire with their Trial brothers. Lending all the power they had to each other, they drove through Miranda's flame wards. Their opposing element seared his senses, but together, the Black Roses pushed through.

Lio landed behind Skleros with Cassia. Mak and Lyros appeared on either side of him, flanking the Gift Collector. Between them and Miranda, there was no way out for him.

Miranda's smile was more like a snarl. She swept her digging fork back and forth in the space in front of her, holding them all at bay. "Why not make it a melee, then? I can take four Hesperines and this spurred carcass, too. I'll teach all of you what I'm made of."

Everyone moved at once. Miranda lunged at Skleros, a manic gleam in her eyes. Lyros snatched up his spear and threw it in a single motion just as Mak swung his morning star high. Lio went low with his staff, aiming for knees.

Cassia ripped roses out of the ground to bind Skleros's legs so he couldn't dodge the four weapons striking at him.

Miranda screamed in fury and pivoted mid-attack to block the Star of Orthros. Skleros crouched, and Lyros's spear sailed over his head instead of into his heart. Final Word was about to make contact with the back of his skull when magefire nipped at Lio's feet. He cursed and levitated, missing his target.

"How dare you fight at my side!" Miranda shouted. "I won't let you steal my kill."

Shock rolled through Lyros's aura. Even he hadn't calculated for this. The Black Roses weren't the kill, and Skleros wasn't the thief.

Magic slammed into Lio's chest, propelling him upward. His back struck a pillar, and his head slammed back against the stone. Miranda's spell held him there, a weight on his chest, a burn in his lungs. Another deadly mix of warding and fire magic.

She released him. Stunned, he couldn't manage to levitate. He hit the ground. Pain blasted through his knees, and his teeth sank into his tongue.

Gingerly, he touched the back of his head, and his fingers came away bloody. Trying to focus his double vision, he looked for the others. Miranda had hurled all four of them to opposite corners of the chamber and encircled them with flame wards again. Cassia yelled his name and sent roses slithering around the confines of the spell. With the four of them separated, none of them had a hope of breaking out on their own.

Skleros circled Miranda. "You should let them help you. You'll last longer."

"Not a chance. I'll kill you with my own hands, and I'll enjoy it."

Skleros laughed. "You should know better than to try."

"You should know better than to harm my people." She spun her digging fork. "Do you know what this is?"

He sneered. "A weapon for a pawn like you."

"It's one of the few things that survived the fire at Mederi Village. Did you think I wouldn't find out you chose that target for Lucis's army? That you told the army from Cordium where the refugees were hiding?"

"I was counting on it. Learn your place, bitch."

"I'll show you our places in the game."

Skleros and Miranda drove each other back and forth across the length of the room in a fast, ugly fight. Every time Skleros's axe blade came at Miranda, Lio feared she would be destroyed, and her secrets with her.

Lio could find no way into the maze of dream wards over their minds. Miranda rebuffed him with the power of six mind mages. All he could do was watch through the wavering flames that trapped him, helpless to protect the one Gift Collector they needed alive.

CASSIA STRUGGLED TO RISE from the rose vines that had broken her fall. She saw Mak and Lyros on their feet. But her legs wouldn't hold her weight, screaming with the pain of Lio's shattered knees.

His gaze found hers from the other side of the chamber. *I'll survive.*

All her Grace instincts screamed that Miranda had hurt him. Again. Raw power blasted out of her and battered the flame ward around her. But that accomplished nothing except to make her arcane senses burn.

Miranda leapt onto the fallen sun disk to evade another swing from

Skleros's axe. He pursued her, his spurs clanking on the bronze. Their weapons clashed, and the grinding of steel against iron made Cassia's teeth ache. Then Miranda's digging fork fell, banging across the disk.

"No!" The word shocked Cassia even as it came from her mouth. She didn't want to care if Miranda lived or died. But she did.

Miranda whipped out a stone dagger. The ancient artifact she had used in her necromantic experiments on Lio and Cassia.

Skleros stood over her, his axe blade aimed downward. "Well, you are desperate if you dare show your relic blade in a fight with another Overseer."

"I'm not afraid of you," Miranda panted.

"You have spent your short existence showing mortals how afraid they should be of the game. Haven't you learned proper fear by now?"

Through the mix of betrayal and fury and pain Cassia shared with Miranda, she found one shard of clarity.

She couldn't let Miranda's life end like this.

Cassia took her dagger in both hands and slammed it into the temple floor. Stone chips flew at her, nicking her face. She didn't even feel them.

The unbound power of the letting site rushed up through her dagger. Endless cords of life and fire were right at her fingertips. If only she could reach a little farther, she could take hold of them. On her own terms, just as the Black Roses had triumphed in the tower's trials.

Cassia pulled. Her vision hazed under the onslaught of Lustra magic from below. But the fire fought her.

Skleros brought the axe down.

The blade rang on bronze. Miranda, rolling to the side with a hair's breadth to spare, sprang up with her dagger. Skleros doubled over. She pulled her arm back, her blade now bloodied.

Skleros took one step back, clutching his abdomen. "Your blade isn't enough to strike me off the board, little girl."

Her empty hand moved. From her sleeve, she drew Skleros's stone dagger. "No, but yours is."

Emotion seeped from behind Skleros's dream wards. His horror crept over Cassia as the color drained from his face. Miranda smiled.

Skleros drew a long, curved butcher's knife and was upon Miranda in an instant. She had already sheathed her own relic dagger somewhere

Cassia couldn't see. Snatching up her digging fork, Miranda disarmed Skleros with one move.

She fought with more strength than any human her size should possess. Cassia understood the power that came to your body when you were fighting to save—or avenge—the people you loved.

Miranda stabbed the digging fork into Skleros's chest and drove him onto his back. The smell of melting bronze filled the air, and he hissed, arching on the tines. Then frost skittered across the sun disk, and Miranda released the digging fork. Skleros lay pinned, his breath rattling.

Miranda dawdled his relic dagger in one hand. "Now who is learning his place?"

"You're a child!" For the first time Cassia had ever heard, Skleros sounded afraid. "You can never defeat a champion from the first game."

"My youth is my advantage. You're so ancient, you've forgotten what it's like to fear for your own survival. To be weak. Fear and weakness make me powerful."

"The Master only has use for the fearless and strong."

"Wrong. The Master values the survivors above all."

Two stilettos appeared in her free hand, and she flung them in quick succession. They landed in Skleros's hands, and the bronze glowed hot again, then cooled around her blades.

Miranda knelt over him and pressed his relic dagger to his gut. "Tonight, I will survive, and you will die slowly. No running back to the Master for a new body this time. You've played your last game, and I won."

Cassia turned her head away as Skleros began to scream.

While Miranda was focused on her revenge, the Black Roses might have a chance to escape.

Fire was death. Fire was life. Life—survival—was what awakened beast magic. If the portal in this temple obeyed soothsaying, then the fire must demand beast magic. Cassia had none, but she did have a Will to survive that had brought her though every trial. She could only hope the temple would respond to that.

She pulled harder on the temple's magic. The web of spells shivered.

Skleros's wails turned to deep, pleased laughter. Cassia didn't want to look, but she did.

"Miranda." Kallikrates spoke with Skleros's bloody mouth. "How I missed you."

She cupped Skleros's cheek. "Master."

"My clever girl. He never should have underestimated you. While he grew arrogant, you kept your eyes on the endgame."

"Always."

"You have proved yourself more powerful than he. You shall take his place in my games for all time."

An unnatural current of magic rose from Skleros's corpse and swirled into Miranda's mouth. A shudder went through her, and she bowed her head.

"Yes…" She sighed the word in two voices, her own and the Collector's.

Miranda didn't need saving from Skleros. Cassia had to save the Black Roses from her.

Cassia twined her rose vines up her arms, letting their thorns draw her blood. As her libation permeated the letting site, she flowed into the temple's spells, and them into her. Everlasting embers tasted hot and bright in her mouth, and her blood ran through the earth with water. She opened herself, a conduit for life and fire.

One current of magic surged through her body and out of her dagger, shattering the floor with a forest of black roses. But two more currents of the spell ran wild like a flood seeking a riverbed. There was nowhere inside her for them to go.

The unbound magic flowed into the only path there was: the spell patterns of the temple itself. The ground shook, and with a rumble, the walls began to fall.

She raced along the tearing threads of Ebah and Lucian's spells. Beyond the temple and across the miles of their kingdom. To the ruin of a lighthouse. To the center of a broken circle of stones. Round and round a burning tower.

At last, Cassia saw it. The pattern the Black Roses had been seeking in every ruin.

Six monuments. And at their center, three doors.

Nine nodes in all. But a Silvictultrix with only one power.

As the ancient magic in the temple unraveled, Cassia watched the second door open to reveal the third and final portal.

THREE TIMES THREE

PAIN PRESSED INTO CASSIA'S wrist. Her eyes focused on her physical surroundings again. A petite boot ground her arm against the floor.

Miranda stood over her. The pendant dangling from her gore-stained hand at the end of Cassia's torn ambassador cords.

The flame ward was gone, but Cassia was trapped in the rending web of the temple's magic. Spells tore her in every direction. She couldn't fight back, even as Miranda knelt and pried open her hand.

She lay helpless as Miranda tore her dagger from her grasp. Rosethorn. Her first and last focus. Stolen, just like her magic, while she lay helpless to stop it.

Mak and Lyros's shouts echoed. Miranda strode away from her through a haze of fire. Toward Lio. His fangs were out, his face twisted with fury. He slammed the end of Final Word against the flame ward that bound him.

The ring of fire shrank, coiling tighter around him. Miranda stalked closer. There was nowhere for him to run.

Agony drilled into Cassia's mind again, and she knew her Grace's pain was greater. He collapsed, his head snapping back, the tendons in his neck straining as he writhed on the ground.

She screamed with rage, even as she tried to whisper comfort in his tortured mind. *Lio, I'm here. I'll make it stop. I won't let her do this to you.*

The look of suffering on his face would haunt her day terrors. He gripped his head, fisting his hand in his hair. He held on to her braid as a groan escaped his gritted teeth.

Miranda pulled back Rosethorn and took aim at Lio's heart.

"No!" Mak yelled over the boom of another wall breaking.

Some force inside Cassia pulled her free of the crumbling temple's spells. Natural laws bent to her Will, and the world parted for her. She stepped to her Grace.

Cassia threw her body over Lio's and hurled black roses between them and the oncoming dagger. Rosethorn stabbed into her vines. She felt that wound all the way to the depths of the letting site.

The roses shot toward Miranda's throat, and she leapt backward. A rafter crashed to the floor behind her, halting her retreat. Her gaze darted from the roses to the collapsing roof.

She was cornered, and yet she smiled with certainty. "You may have spared him for one more night, but he'll never see eternity. He's my kill."

A traversal spell snapped in the hot, wavering air. She was gone.

The flame wards collapsed, only to leave them surrounded by magefire. The temple was destroying itself.

Lyros struggled toward her through the smoke. "Move!"

She followed his gaze upward. The roof above her and Lio caved in. Stones and burning timbers hurtling down toward them.

With her protective instincts still in command of her every thought, she wrapped her arms around her Grace. As she stepped Lio to safety, the last thing she saw was the Mage King's own fire engulf his statue.

CASSIA'S BLOOD BROUGHT LIO out of oblivion. He came to with his head on her shoulder and her wrist against his mouth. Mak and Lyros stood over them in the copse of cypresses. Beyond the trees, the temple was a burning ruin in the twilight.

Lio raised his pounding head. "You stepped to me."

The fires of the temple glowed in her green-gold eyes. "No one can keep me from your side."

He rested his face against her and shut his eyes. He was alive, his Will intact. He had never been so grateful to feel his Grace in his thoughts. Cassia was a balm everywhere Miranda had unleashed her fire in his mind.

Mak pulled his hands down his ashen face. "If she hadn't learned to step just now… Oh my Goddess. Miranda almost killed you with a weapon I made."

"I'm all right, Mak." Lio tried to stand. It would take more than one drink to heal the beating he'd just taken. The pain in his head and knees made his stomach churn, but with help from Cassia's levitation, he made it to his feet.

She supported him with his arm around her shoulders. "Are you well enough to step again?"

Mak didn't seem to hear them. "Miranda will make people suffer with that dagger. With my creation."

"We can't go after her now," Cassia said. "We have to get back to the tower."

Mak looked at Lyros, stricken. "I never meant for this to happen. I'm so sorry."

Lyros tugged Mak into his arms and held on, fisting his hand in the back of Mak's battle robe. "We can't do this any longer."

"I know," Cassia began. "We—I—can't afford any more mistakes, but if we don't make it back to the tower in time—"

Lyros let Mak go and threw down his spear. "We weren't ready. We still aren't. We never should have tried this as fugitives without the Charge's support. This is suicide."

Mak tried to pull his Grace close again, but Lyros backed away. Suddenly Mak's face went even paler.

Lio said in a warning tone, "What in Hespera's name has Mak seen in your thoughts that could put that look on his face?"

"I'm going to Rudhira," Lyros announced.

Cassia's eyes widened in horror. "You can't—"

He cut her off. "I'm turning us in. I'll submit us to the Queens' justice before I watch you all die around me."

"Lyros, no," Mak pleaded.

"You can come with me now, and we can face arrest together. Or you can all stay out here and run until I show the Charge how to find you. But we're going home."

Lio held up his hands. "Let's not make any rash decisions. None of us are thinking clearly, not after we just survived our worst battle—"

"By the skin of our teeth," Lyros retorted. "Now is exactly the time to make decisions. My thoughts are crystal clear. I only wish I'd stopped us before things were so far gone."

Surely Lio could reason with him. "Surrendering now won't make anyone safer. Think about this from a strategic perspective—"

"Now you try to be the diplomat?" Lyros scoffed. "I don't want to hear it, 'Glasstongue.' If you want to stop me, you'll have to do it with your fists."

"Mak," Lio said in desperation, "can't you cast the Blood Shackles on him?"

Mak hesitated, staring at his Grace, his aura bereft.

Even as Lio picked up his staff, he felt helpless. What could he do? Lyros would best him in any fight. If he used his mind magic to stop his Trial brother, his two best friends would never forgive him. And he would never forgive himself.

Cassia's gaze flicked between each of them, her thoughts racing in a calculation too fast for Lio to follow. *Listen to me, if you don't want the last door to fall. Try to stop them. Then meet me at the tower with whoever is left.*

Before Lio's eyes, she disappeared.

His mind went blank, and terror blinded him. She had stepped away without him. His Grace was alone in enemy territory.

Cassia! he called to her over the distance.

Trust me, she said through their bond.

Lio moved in front of Mak, facing Lyros. "How can you do this to your Grace? To mine?"

"Don't you dare lecture me on what's best for Mak."

"What happened to the promise you and I made the night we watched them get arrested? We swore we would do anything to keep them free. Now you want to turn them in?"

Lyros's voice rose. "I also swore to keep them safe!"

"You told me you had my back," Lio shouted. "I thought we were in this together. You can't decide this is over for the rest of us."

The weight of Mak's hand settled on Lio's shoulder. "Let him go."

Lio turned to his cousin. "This isn't fair to you. To any of us."

"You should go with him. If you and Lyros turn Cassia and me in, you'll get a lighter sentence."

"Never," Lio said. "I will not abandon my Grace or our quest."

"Our quest is already over." Lyros stepped, and his words hung in the empty air.

Mak's gaze traveled over Night's Aim in the grass, past the Star of Orthros in his hand, then to Final Word in Lio's grip. "I never should have made them. All I can do now is unmake them."

Lio closed both hands around his staff. "What are you talking about?"

"I have to make it to the forge before Rudhira finds me. Hand over your staff."

"No! We need the weapons now more than ever."

Mak held out his hand. "Don't make me fight you for it."

Lio planted the staff. "I will fight you over this."

His cousin barreled into him. With three moves Lio didn't know, Mak left him on the ground, disarmed and rubbing his head where Miranda had battered him. But the loss of his staff was more painful still. His connection to the artifact throbbed as if he'd lost a limb.

With their three remaining weapons in hand, Mak disappeared, too. Their Trial brothers were gone. Their errant circle was broken.

THE CONTINGENCY PLAN

His Trial brothers had abandoned him and his Grace. Lio had never felt so betrayed.

He was Cassia's only protector now. He pulled himself to his feet, and the world spun around him. But she was his sense of direction. He had to get to his Grace.

He stepped to her across the length of the kingdom and plunged into a cloud of smoke. More of it billowed from the open door of the tower. Flames were licking out of the high windows.

Cassia!

I'm coming. Stay outside.

Once again, she expected him to stand here and watch her throw herself into danger. And she called it protecting him. Had she learned nothing the night he had helped break her out of that cell?

Lio plunged through the doorway, slamming his senses open in search of living auras. Magic writhed all around him. The tower's spells were dying.

Following the cord of their Grace Union, he levitated across the hazy ground floor. His eyes burned as he flew up the stairs. The dining hall roiled with orange light and dark smoke. Hot, dry air scoured his skin.

"Cassia?" he called, coughing.

"Get out of here!" she bellowed over the roar of the flames.

He followed her voice toward the Mage King's fire and made out her silhouette before the roaring flames. She threw a blanket over the hounds. They were alive.

Lio picked up the other side of the blanket. "The stairs are still clear. This way."

Bright tears streaming from her eyes, and her anger snapped at him. "I told you to stay outside where it's safe."

"Stop asking me to break our vows!"

The fire overflowed the hearth. They levitated out of reach as the rug caught. The chairs were next. They passed over the table, where flames turned their research to ashes.

"No, no, no." Lio fixed on the magic emanating from his scroll case and summoned it to him. He caught the hot metal with his cloak and wrapped it close against his chest.

They fled the tower and sank to the cold, damp ground of the bailey. Lio dropped everything he held to run his hands over Cassia's head and shoulders and arms. "Are you all right?"

She nodded and turned to pull the blanket off the hounds. Knight was wheezing, but he sat up, licking her with anxious whines. Lio rested a hand on Dame's side. Still unconscious, but she was breathing.

Magic swelled inside the tower, a terrible pressure on Lio's senses. He threw himself over Cassia, covering as much of her and the dogs as he could. A boom split his ears, and the ground shook as heat blasted across his back.

The everything was silent. They lifted their heads and looked back at the ruin where the tower had stood.

Lio held Cassia tightly. She was shaking.

Then she scrambled out of his arms, fists at her sides, and faced the rubble. Black roses sprang up at her feet, then withered.

"I'm so sorry." In the wake of the explosion, his words sounded too quiet to his ears. Too insufficient for what she had just lost.

All that magic. All that knowledge. Gone before they'd had a chance to understand it.

He dragged himself to his feet. "Miranda did this."

Cassia wouldn't look at him. "Lyros is gone, isn't he?"

Lio hung his head. "I couldn't change his mind."

"And Mak?"

Lio looked away for a moment, then back at her. "He went to destroy the rest of the weapons."

She wrapped her arms around herself. Eternal braziers and the Collector's laughter haunted her thoughts. "All of this is my fault."

He took a step closer. "Cassia, what happened to you in the temple?"

Shame and despair welled out of her. Such feelings had no place in his proud, beautiful Grace. He couldn't bear this.

The next time he held Miranda's mind in his hands, he would kill her.

"What did she do to you?" he demanded.

"It wasn't Miranda." Cassia's voice was toneless. "It was me."

"What?" His ears were still healing from the explosion, his mind still scoured by Miranda's attack. He must have misunderstood.

Cassia finally turned to face him. "I tried to gain the temple's recognition, as I did with the tower…but I failed."

He closed his eyes for a moment. "Like the experiments we tried here that put the spell patterns under strain."

"I pushed the temple too hard. I felt the break through the entire spell the Changing Queen and the Mage King left behind across their kingdom. I saw the lighthouse and stone circle in ruins. The tower burning. And I finally understood. Six Lustra sites are bound to the three doors."

Cold spread through Lio. "Three times three. Nine nodes."

"Ebah and Lucian's monuments are keeping the doors sealed. The Lustra has been guiding us to them all along, trying to help me save the doors, but…"

"Miranda must have been the one following us," Lio realized. "She was tracking your shared magic and letting us lead her to the right Lustra sites. This must have been Kallikrates's contingency plan all this time."

"And we've been playing along. Since he couldn't open the doors with my magics, he's breaking them down by destroying the nodes."

"Leveling the monuments wouldn't be enough to break spells that powerful," Lio protested.

Cassia shook her head. "He has to destroy the magic."

Understanding hit Lio like a blow to the gut. "That's why he wants your artifacts. He must need a completed triune focus to tap into the spells and destabilize them."

Lio had no doubt the Collector could wield them through his Overseers, because he still possessed the key to all of this.

Cassia's first magic.

Her shoulders hunched. "He'll hardly need to use the foci at this point.

I just destroyed four of the nodes for him in one night. I saw the second door open."

"No." Lio took hold of her arms. "You cannot blame yourself for this. You were thrown headfirst into powerful magic none of us understand. And every step of the way, you've fought so hard to learn. To do the right thing."

She shook her head. "I should have known better. I reached for too much power in the temple. If only I'd been more careful…if only I'd accepted my limits and what I don't know…"

"Ignorance never kept anyone safe. If we'd known more—"

She held up her hands. "I don't want to know any more secrets. They're better left buried, where Kallikrates can't use them."

"Those secrets are yours by right. That power should be yours."

"That's what every arrogant mage and conquering warlord in the history of the shadowlands has said to justify their games! I won't become one of them, greedy for what I think I should have, leaving destruction in my wake to get it."

The injustice of it made Lio's magic pound inside him. "It broke my heart when he took your magic. But this, I can bear least of all—that you would stop trying to get it back because of him. If you give up, you'll lose a piece of yourself even more important than your magic. Don't let him take that from you."

"It isn't your choice to make." She backed away.

"Cassia, what are you planning?"

"Rudhira was right. Arrest in Orthros is the safest place for me. As long as I'm there, Kallikrates can't use me to destroy anything else."

"You can't really believe this world is better off without you fighting for it."

Lio reached for her through their bond, drawing her deep into his mind and heart. She fought his pull, her regrets washing through him.

"Get somewhere safe before dawn," she said. "Go as far as you can. I won't let the Charge take you easily."

For the second time, his Grace stepped away and left him behind.

Cassia slipped through the fabric of the world. In that instant, suspended between flesh and spirit in a current of her blood magic, she was out of the Lustra's reach. There was only Hespera.

Goddess, I'm sorry.

She had failed in her duty to protect the innocent with her immortal power. But what hurt most of all was that she had failed her eternal vows to her Grace.

The letting site at Paradum pulled her and Knight back to earth. True to her aim, she had landed them in the middle of her garden. She ran her hands over him to make sure he was all right, and he licked her chin in reassurance. She had managed to step him without making him ill or losing him somewhere along the way.

The strength of the restored letting site welled out of the soil and filled her, its undeserving Silvicultrix. Her one triumph here had not been enough to save them. She had failed the Lustra itself.

Casting her senses through the castle, she found it deserted. There were no patrols in the surrounding hills, either, ally or enemy.

Lio wasn't here. He hadn't followed her.

She didn't want him to chase her and fight her decision every step of the way. She didn't want him to martyr himself at her side, either. But some part of her had never expected he would simply let her go.

What was *he* planning?

Her only comfort was the light creeping over the horizon. He wouldn't have time to do anything reckless before the Dawn Slumber hit him.

But Lyros would. He might have already reached Rudhira. Cassia had lost the advantage of turning herself in first. So she would have to strike a more compelling bargain than what her Trial brother offered.

The one thing she had to bargain with was her.

The Lustra would never let the Charge take her. She was sure she could disappear into the wilds, and not even Kalos would be able to track her.

If they wanted her surrender, they would have to meet her terms about protections for Lio.

Keeping Knight close, Cassia slipped through Paradum to her old bedroom. The place where she had lost her magic and chosen the Gift.

She sealed the broken wall with a tangle of roses to block out the oncoming day. No Hesperine or mortal would find her here until she was ready.

Except for one. Miranda always knew where she was.

Cassia curled up on the floor and succumbed to the Slumber, praying her roses were protection enough.

Lio was alone in the silence.

Without his Trial brothers and his Grace, the Blood Union now felt empty, too. The specters rose behind his eyes, and he tried to push them away.

He had to think. Act. As long as he could avoid arrest, there was hope of breaking Cassia out again. But he would have to convince her to escape with him a second time.

He would find Miranda himself, and he would take Cassia's foci from her. Once he put them back in Cassia's hands, she would have to see how important her power was.

But right now, he had to find shelter for himself and Dame before dawn. Their Lustra refuges were gone, and so was Cassia's pendant, the key to the portals.

His hand went to his own medallion. The only Lustra artifact Miranda had overlooked.

He made a libation on the three wooden leaves and picked his way through the wreckage of the tower. He'd known his chances were slim, but he still felt devastated when no light sparked to guide him to a portal. The Changing Queen's spells truly had been destroyed here.

He wouldn't be satisfied until he checked the other Lustra sites to see for himself if Cassia's vision was true. Kneeling with a hand on Dame, he stepped them to the lighthouse.

They landed near the brazier, which was now cold and half-buried in stones so broken and worn that they looked like part of the bluff. He levitated down to the portal in the hillside only to find it already open. The underground ritual site was lost beneath a cave-in.

He took them to the ancient Lustra circle last. The standing stones had toppled and cracked. His day terrors had become reality. The magic here had been ravaged yet again by the conflicts of Tenebra.

But it was older than those wars. Older even than the spell Ebah and Lucian had built on it. Could hulaic magic still survive here? With a worried glance at the horizon, he bled on his pendant again.

Suddenly, he knew what to do. He didn't know what sense guided him—a rustle under his feet, a scent on the air, his heart pounding a warning through his body that predators lay in wait for him. Driven by instinct, he lifted his familiar in his arms and walked into the broken circle.

The winter fields of Tenebra disappeared. Beyond the stones, he saw land drenched in the burning light of sunset with fire raging on the horizon. Impossible. And yet somehow real in the Lustra's mysterious paradigm.

Lio found a narrow shelter where one stone had fallen across another. He worked himself and Dame into the patch of shade just as twilight gave way to dawn.

45

nights after

WINTER SOLSTICE

A HESPERINE HEART

Cassia survived the Slumber, and when she lowered her rose defenses, no enemies were lurking beyond. She would live to turn herself in to the Charge.

Her control slipped, and her Craving drove her to reach for Lio's presence. His thoughts and emotions eluded her behind his mind magic. Her hunger spiked, her heart pounding faster with instinctual fear.

He was hiding from her. That could mean only one thing. As she had feared, he was doing something dangerous.

Before he carried out whatever his plan was, she had to get the Charge's attention. But she would surrender on her own terms. She wouldn't go meekly to the elders. To keep what little negotiating power remained to her, she would have to remind them what she was capable of.

Could she even do that without her foci? Perhaps she was doomed to fail at this, too.

She stood in the spot where her magic had first awoken. Knight waited on the edge of the garden, as he had once done while she worked in her rows of peas.

Each of Cassia's choices since that night had brought her to this moment. She had survived all of that. For what? Hespera had saved her, remade her in this place in her Gifting visions. Only for her to fail.

Cassia *was* like Phaedros. She hadn't been worthy of the Gift.

But if she surrendered now, at least she would never become like Kallikrates.

The game was over for her.

She knelt and dug her fingers into the soil. She let her Will flow into the Lustra, showing it what she required. A magical explosion, just like last time, which would bring the elders down on her.

The letting site didn't pull. It gave. Magic, her magic, rushed into her. It was so beautiful and so familiar that tears pricked her eyes.

Dark blood and verdant earth filled her being. No explosion, but a quiet sustenance. Her dual magic overran the letting site through her and carried her mind beyond Paradum.

What was the Lustra doing? This was not what she had asked for.

In her mind's eye, she flowed through the Lustra passages under Patria. Deep into the heart of Solorum. She washed up before the final portal.

A sound came from within the third door. The rush of liquid. She put her hands to the rune-inscribed panel. The vibration in the stone matched her heartbeat.

She looked down at herself. Blood flowed along her arms and into the door. Its runes drank of her.

Cassia opened her eyes to see soil and her own hands. No red trails marked her arms. But she could still feel the current that ran between her and this garden and the final door.

When she had healed this letting site, she had repaired more than she'd known.

"This is a node," she breathed.

Surely the first one Kallikrates had ever destroyed in his quest to open the portals. The same night he had destroyed her. Or so he had believed.

She had restored the third door. She had broken the first two. So much healing and destruction existed in her, side by side.

"I don't know how to do this. Hespera help me, I don't know how to be both at once."

There was no Hesperine here to give Cassia answers except herself.

She covered her face, smearing soil on her cheeks. "Goddess, help me."

Would Hespera lend her ear, when Cassia had so much blood on her hands?

Cassia still believed the Goddess would answer. Somewhere deep in her, she even believed Hespera would open her arms to a Gift Collector.

Cassia didn't know if she and Miranda could ever forgive each other. But she couldn't bear for Miranda to have no hope of forgiveness. Because that meant Cassia might run out of chances, too.

Hespera never gave up on anyone. In her name, neither did Cassia. That meant not giving up on Miranda. Or herself.

Cassia lifted her face to the moons. She sat there and bared her soul to herself and the Goddess, with the grace immortals had always given her.

With honesty and without judgment, she re-examined every moment of the battle in her mind. She turned her thoughts over and sifted through every emotion she had felt as she had reached for more and more power.

She hadn't wanted Miranda to die, humiliated and afraid, at Skleros's hand. She couldn't let Kallikrates destroy one more woman who had been forged by fear and weakness and love.

All those years ago, when Miranda had cried out for help, only Kallikrates had answered. There had been no Hesperines to save her. Until now.

Cassia had broken the temple trying to protect the people she loved. And even the person she hated.

Cassia was Miranda's Hesperine.

"Lio was right," Cassia said to the moons. She pressed her dirty hand to her chest. "I do have a Hesperine heart."

She faced the room where she had made her choice, first before the Collector and again before Hespera.

"I will never be like Kallikrates." Her declaration filled the silence of Paradum. "I will never become a New Master in this game. Hespera, you already made me into the playing piece I will be through every round. A Hesperine errant."

A Hesperine errant didn't belong in a cell. She belonged in the field, fighting for lost causes until they weren't lost anymore. That's what the Black Roses did.

It might already be too late to stop Mak, but Cassia had to try.

Lio hovered over the circle of mages. Prostrate at his feet, they begged for Mercy.

"Where was your Mercy for the families of Tenebra?" he demanded.

He poured another wave of the villagers' suffering into their murderers. The Aithourians' screams echoed through the ruins of the temple. Finally, there was no more silence in Lio's head.

The two mages nearest him lifted their faces toward him.

Chrysanthos reached out a hand to Lio. "I don't care what you do to me. Just send me home alive to my nephew."

"Please," Eudias begged. "I never chose this. They made me an Aithourian."

Lio recoiled, but it was too late. Their hearts stopped beating, and the silence returned.

There was no sound in the circle but the distant crackle of the unnatural fires. No screams. No heartbeats except his own.

Lio fought his way out of Slumber, knowing, fearing what he would find. When he could finally move, he reached for Dame's lifeless body.

His hand met grass. She wasn't dead. She wasn't here at all.

Pulling himself out of their shelter, he looked around the circle and across the bizarre plain. He couldn't see her anywhere. "Dame? *Dockk!*"

He kept calling her, but she didn't reappear. Was she lost in this otherworld somewhere? Had she somehow slipped back into the natural world? Was she strong enough to find food? Would she get picked off by an enemy?

Slumping to the ground, he shoved his hands into his hair. He couldn't even keep a dog safe.

He was alone in this place the Lustra had brought him. Except for Cassia's worry, hovering at the edges of his awareness. He tightened his veils around his mind. His thoughts were not fit for her right now.

He shut his eyes. A mistake. He saw the victims at Castra Augusta again. Then the mages' bodies in the temple.

Lio had tortured seven human beings.

Finally, the reality of what he had done sank in. He had desecrated the sanctity of their minds. He had made them suffer and taken satisfaction in it. He, a Hesperine, a diplomat, had violated everything he believed in.

And what had that accomplished? It hadn't given their victims or him peace. It had only added more suffering to the world.

He would have killed the mages if his Grace hadn't stopped him. Cassia, who thought she could not be trusted with power.

Lio looked down at his hands. He hadn't even needed a weapon to break Hespera's tenets. Just the mind magic inside him.

He thought of the way Mak and Lyros had looked at him after they had given those men the Mercy he would not. He had placed the burden of violence on his brothers after he had promised to shoulder it with them.

Lio stared at his hands until his vision burned. Finally he closed his eyes and made himself look at the faces of his own victims.

A soft sound disturbed the dreadful quiet. Paws padding through the grass.

Lio's eyes flew open. Dame was trotting toward him across the circle. He had never been so glad to see a living creature.

"Hello, girl," he said softly. "You had me worried. Where did you go?"

She halted and dropped a dead rabbit in front of him.

Lio covered his nose with his hand. "Did you get hungry?"

She nudged the rabbit toward him, then sat down on her furry backside, her ears perked and eyes bright.

Lio laughed. He had no right to, not after what he'd done. He hadn't thought he could. But looking at Dame, so eager to please with her present, that laugh came out of him, her real gift.

"Is this your way of saying thank you for saving you?" With a smile tugging at his mouth, he lowered his hand from his nose and extended his fingers toward her.

She didn't bite them off, only flared her nostrils and sniffed him. Her jaws parted, and her tongue lolled out. It looked like she was smiling back.

He reached a little farther. She didn't move. Gently, he petted her fluffy ears, and she began to wag her tail. For the first time in many hours, peace came over him.

"Thank you."

Dame stretched out beside him.

He stroked her back next. "Dogs love unconditionally. That's what Cassia says. You don't decide if someone deserves it, do you? You just love."

Lio stopped wondering what he or the mages deserved and accepted the moment of calm. After a while, Dame began to gaze at the rabbit with longing.

"This is an impressive kill," Lio made himself say. "*Oedann*. You're such a good dog. So good, in fact, that I won't even ask you to share the rabbit with me. You can eat every bite yourself. Yes, truly you can."

He scooted away from her. She tensed, as if ready to spring up and follow him. He tried to remember what word might put her at ease.

"*Soor.* Relax and enjoy your rabbit."

He didn't go far, but he cast a veil over her so he wouldn't hear the crunching. Leaning on one stub of a stone, he looked out at the dreamlike landscape.

Where were Cassia and Mak and Lyros now?

He had thought he was protecting them. And yet his decisions on this journey had only made everything harder for them.

He had pushed Mak to use his weapons and pushed Lyros to fight instead of retreat. Worst of all, he had pushed his Grace harder and harder to wield her magic. He had only wanted to show them how much he believed in them when Orthros would not. But he'd driven them so hard that he'd driven them apart.

He had been so focused on the warpath that he had failed to be what they needed most. The cousin who talked Mak down when he was angry. The friend who understood Lyros when he was overthinking everything. The lover who comforted Cassia when she was fighting with herself.

He could hardly call himself a diplomat any longer. But even at war, he could be their peacemaker. He still believed in the Black Roses.

When Dame finished her rabbit, she approached him again, almost hesitant. She looked to him as if for guidance. Her whole life must have been so disciplined. Did she feel as adrift as he did right now?

His determination to hunt down Miranda was gone. Only one thing mattered now.

It would take a great deal of apologies and might end in a prison cell. But if that was what it took to bring their circle back together, then he would do it. Starting with the person he had hurt the most: Lyros.

He rubbed Dame's ears again. "Let's go find our pack."

AS A CIRCLE

THE RUINS OF MEDERI Village were not where Lio had expected Lyros's aura to lead him. Lio stood still by the village gate, keeping himself and Dame shrouded in thelemantic veils. She gave herself a vigorous scratch, as if his blood magic itched.

Lyros was the only Hesperine he sensed. The war truly had left Patria behind. Lio might be able to reach him before he reached the Charge.

Lio bit his hand and pressed it to the pendant. The portal that had been their escape the night of the attack opened for him again. He levitated down, but Dame paused on the threshold.

He held out a hand to her. "*Docck docck.* It's safe down here, I promise."

She picked her way down the stairs and pressed close to him. As he hurried along the passageway, she had no trouble keeping pace.

He huffed a laugh. "A liegehound might be the only creature fast enough to join me on my nightly runs. I suppose it's for the best that I didn't end up with a feline familiar, after all."

He caught the scent of blood, and his humor died. Lio tightened his veils and ran.

Around the next twist in the passage, Lyros sat against the wall, tightening a bandage around his thigh. The odor of burned flesh mingled with the blood.

Dame froze, sniffing in Lyros's direction. Lio rested a hand on her and swallowed. "Now isn't the time to have a relapse of anti-Hesperine sentiment. He's my Trial brother. Our pack."

She trotted a little closer to Lyros, then back to Lio, looking up at him. This must be so confusing to her.

He held out his blood-streaked hand to her and said firmly, "*Barda acklii.*"

There was still puzzlement in her aura, but she relaxed. Lio let out a breath. Lifting his hands, he approached Lyros and dropped his veils.

Lyros jumped, then grimaced. "Hypnos's nails."

"Don't run, please. I'm not here to fight."

"Do I look like I'm in any condition to outrun you?"

Dame peered around Lio, then prowled forward.

Lyros backed closer against the wall, averting his gaze. "She's alive. That's nice. But are you the only Hesperine she doesn't see as food?"

"No." Lio dropped down and put an arm around Dame. "It turns out she has a sweet temperament."

"I'll take your word for it."

Dame leaned forward, nearly nose to nose with Lyros. He sat very still. Then she began to lick his chin.

Lyros grimaced. "Aw, thorns. Her breath smells like dead rabbit."

"Er, yes, that is what she had for breakfast. Sorry."

"Where's Cassia?"

"She left me to turn herself in. What happened to you?"

"A raiding party interrupted me on my way to find Rudhira."

"You defeated an entire raiding party alone?" Lio didn't want to think about what could have happened to Lyros tonight.

"More or less. Came down here to Slumber and heal. The deserted passages seemed my best bet."

Lio examined his bandage. "This is magefire wound. How bad is it?"

"Not particularly good. It hit the deep vein in my thigh."

"Hespera's Mercy, you need healing. Now."

"I've got another couple of hours before the magefire permeates vital organs."

"That's not enough time to fight your way to Rudhira."

Lyros's gaze dropped to his wound. "It's enough time to re-examine my decisions."

"You can do that after you get some healing." Lio pulled Lyros's arm around his shoulders. "Come on. I'll get you there in one piece."

Lyros made no attempt to stand. "You've decided to follow Cassia and me into Charge custody, have you?"

"No. I'll take you to Mak if you'd prefer his blood over the healers. You tell me where we're going. Wherever it is, I have your back."

Lyros swallowed. "You don't have to take me anywhere, Lio."

Lio sat back down. "I would rather have this conversation when you don't have magefire seeping toward your heart, but if you need me to make amends now, I will. I owe you an apology, and I know words aren't enough. I'll try to make things right between us with my actions."

"What are you apologizing for?"

Lio wouldn't shy away from it anymore. He looked Lyros in the eye. "I'm ashamed of what I did in the temple. I feel such remorse for causing those mortals unnecessary pain, and for subjecting you and Mak and Cassia to that."

Lyros gripped Lio's shoulder. "It's all right."

"It is not, in any way, all right. Neither are the times when I failed to listen to you in battle. I went my own way, instead of fighting with you as one of a circle. I will endeavor to earn your forgiveness."

"None of us judge you for what you did to those mages. Of course our empathy made Castra Augusta torture for all of us, but none of us are thelemancers. We didn't walk through the minds of the dead like you did. All that pain has to go somewhere."

"That wasn't the right thing to do with it."

"No, it wasn't. That's why we were so horrified on your behalf. We knew how you would feel after you realized what you'd done, how you would torture yourself. Just as you're doing now."

"Oh," Lio said.

His circle had forgiven him before he had forgiven himself.

He tried to clear the lump in his throat. "I'm grateful for you."

Lyros gave his shoulder a squeeze before letting his hand drop. "Surviving a raiding party on my own made me more grateful than ever for you, too. That battle certainly showed me what I'm capable of. And what I'm not. So did the temple."

"Your strategies in the temple were faultless," Lio reassured him. "You planned for everything."

"Yes, I did. We still lost." Lyros sighed. "So I gave up."

"I can't blame you."

"I was an idiot." Lyros gestured to his leg. "While I was fighting this mage alone, there were so many moments when I remembered decisions each of you made in battle. That's what saved me."

"I can't imagine how any of my fumbling with my staff and throwing my magic about helped you tonight."

"Your faith in me helped."

Lio slid his hand into Dame's ruff. She lay down between him and his Trial brother. After a moment, Lyros ran a hand down her back.

"Mak and Cassia and I have been mired in self-doubt on this entire journey," Lyros went on. "You're the only person who had any confidence in us all. All along, you've been telling us to have faith in our power and use it to the fullest. You encouraged us to be our greatest selves. I wish I had trusted us as much as you did."

Lio frowned at him. "You've been the most confident of all. Your leadership has kept us going."

Lyros shook his head. "That wasn't confidence. That was fear. I've been terrified that a surprise I didn't plan for would get one of you killed out here. So I tied you all up in so much strategy you could barely move."

"We know you were trying to keep us safe."

"But I'm only one of the people keeping us safe. I shouldn't have fought like a general, but as one of a circle, just as you said. I'm equally sorry I didn't listen to you."

Lio clasped Lyros's wrist and held it. This journey had destroyed so much, but it hadn't cost him and Lyros their brotherhood. "Let's decide together if this ends in a prison cell or on the battlefield."

"All four of us."

Lio nodded. "I'm with you."

"We may have to start by breaking our Graces out of prison—again."

CASSIA CONCENTRATED ON MAK'S aura. Since they had a close bond, it shouldn't be difficult to step to him, but she would have to aim just right. She didn't know what she and Knight were heading into this time.

She stepped, landing in knee deep in snow on a narrow ledge. Knight's broad paws didn't sink so far, but his back legs slid down the snow bank toward the edge of the precipice.

Cassia threw her arms around him and levitated them both away from the long drop. They tumbled to the ground in a pile of slush and rocks. She looked up into the mouth of a cave.

"Cassia?" Mak hissed from the darkness inside.

At the sound of her Grace-cousin's voice, Knight began to wag his tail.

"I found you," she said with relief. She hadn't even bruised her head on his wards.

"Get in here before a Stand patrol sees you!"

He hauled her deeper into the crevasse in the rock, and Knight squeezed in after. Her eyes instantly adjusted, revealing the weapons in an undignified heap in the back of the cave.

She rubbed her bruised hip while it healed. "Are we in the Umbral Mountains?"

"Yes." Mak peered out, then rolled a heavy rock over the entrance. His veil spells sealed their hiding place. "You can't be here. I have to reach Nike's forge, and now it will be twice as hard not to get caught."

"You're trying to sneak back to her forge?"

"It's the only place you can melt down adamas," he said, as if she were dense. "But I can't seem to step there anymore—the elders must have locked it up. You can't talk me out of this, and I don't have time for you to try. Alkaios and Nephalea's patrol of this area ends in half an hour, and then I have to move."

So that was all the time she had to change his mind. She held up her hands. "Hear me out. That's all I ask. In half an hour, if you still feel that destroying the weapons is the right thing to do, then I'll let you go."

"I'm too tired for diplomatic games, Cassia." He sat down and leaned back against the wall. "But I know you're going to say your bit anyway, so get it over with."

"It's not a game, Mak!"

He sobered. "I'm sorry. Poor choice of words."

"We aren't playing with people's lives. We're trying to save them. That's what I'm trying to make you see." She propped her back next to him. "I know how you feel right now. If you're giving yourself a beating for your mistakes, wait till you hear mine."

One side of his mouth lifted. "Is that actually why you came out here? So we could moan together about how we've ruined everything for our Graces again?"

"And to commiserate about our terrible Craving and how our suffering is our own fault."

"Well, I won't say no to some sympathy."

She leaned her shoulder against his. "Would you like to know why the temple went up in flames?"

He raised his eyebrows.

"I mucked up the spells in it," Cassia admitted.

Mak let out a low whistle.

"And while I was blowing it to pieces in my own face, I saw all the other spells it's connected to. The lighthouse, the stone circle, and the tower are all leveled, too. All Lio and I could save were the dogs."

Mak's face fell. "Oh, Cassia. I'm so sorry."

"Oh, that's not the worst part."

"How could it possibly get any worse?"

She wrapped her arms around her knees. "All of those sites were nodes in the spell that's keeping the doors shut. There's only one portal left."

He stared at her, his eyes wide. Then he said a curse that was illegal in ten sister states of the Empire.

"Agreed," Cassia replied. "But it's all right."

His voice cracked as he laughed. "How is any of this all right?"

"Think about what happened at Paradum."

He paused for a moment. "It's a node, too, isn't it?"

Cassia nodded.

"Kallikrates broke it already. So that should mean there's only one site left out there somewhere, holding the third door closed. Except…"

She smiled at him.

Slowly, he smiled back. "You healed Paradum."

"With the dagger you forged for me."

Mak rubbed the back of his head and blew out a breath. "Well, it's good to know untold destruction won't come pouring out of the door in the next hour. But that doesn't change anything about the weapons. I could have reforged yours as an innocent garden spade instead, and it would have worked to heal the letting site."

"Miranda would still have it right now, and you already know how much damage she can do with innocent gardening tools."

He shuddered.

"It's not about the weapons, Mak. It's about what we do with them."

"Thorns, you're going to get as philosophical as Lio now, aren't you?"

"No. I don't have answers for any of the great questions about violence that we're wrestling with. But I know this. Hesperines are the heretics who always keep questioning."

He didn't reply. She thought he was listening, now.

"As a Steward, you've been carrying those questions for our people your entire life. You keep fighting, even though we don't have answers. You still believe in Mercy on a merciless path."

"Fighting without answers. Good description of us blundering around Tenebra in the dark."

She pointed to his heart. "Lyros, Lio, and I certainly got our heart wounds from blundering, but you didn't. Why do you think the Lustra gave this to you?"

He rubbed his chest where his scar lay hidden under his battle robes. "They're your ancestors. You translate for me. Was Lio right when he said it's a mark of honor?"

"Yes. I think they gave you a sign that you did the right thing."

He looked thoughtful. "The Lustra does seem to have some wisdom about bloodshed that eludes us immortals. Wolves don't commit violence for pleasure or cruelty. Only survival. And somehow, rebirth."

Cassia thought of the reborn letting site at Paradum. The magic was now more powerful than it had been before its wounds. Just like her. "Now who's getting philosophical?"

"Sunbind it, you scrollworms are rubbing off on me."

"And you warriors have certainly rubbed off on us." She pulled Lio's staff across her lap. "What do you say we liberate Rosethorn from Miranda so my blade can once again serve the side of right? I have an idea."

Mak ruffled her hair. "Then let's give one more Cassia scheme a try."

THE HEART OF THE LUSTRA

L IO LET THE VEILS in his mind fall slowly. The specters stirred.
Cassia's presence rushed into their bond, drowning out all else. *Don't ever shut me out like that again.*
Her anger was so beautiful. Even her worry was comforting.

Lyros snickered. "You have that newly-avowed look on your face."

"I've been such a fool." Lio shut his eyes and tilted his head back against the wall, savoring Cassia's emotions. He shouldn't enjoy the burn of her Craving, but a base part of him did. Her hunger for him felt so good.

Where are you? she demanded.

With Lyros.

Now her surprise flashed through their bond. *You turned yourself in?*

No. Neither did he. We want to talk with you and Mak about what we should do next. That's all we ask. That we decide as a circle.

Her relief warmed him from head to toe. *I found Mak, and we have your weapons for you.*

Lio opened his eyes, a smile spreading across his face. "It sounds like Mak and Cassia reexamined a few decisions, too."

"He's with her?" Now Lyros sounded like the one who was starving.

Lio frowned in concern. "Mak didn't tell you?"

Lyros looked away. "He may not be a mind mage, but he can be more stubborn than anyone about keeping his thoughts blocked. I hurt him."

"He hurt you, too."

"That doesn't matter now. Where are they?"

No sooner had Lio thought the question than Cassia envisioned where she was.

Lio hesitated. *Are you sure that's a good idea?*

I can keep us safe here.

"They want us to meet them at Paradum." Lio offered Lyros a hand and a levitation spell.

His face strained, Lyros let Lio help him up. "Let's hope this goes better than last time."

Focusing on their Graces' auras, Lio stepped them both with his magic.

The Blood Moon shone on Cassia's garden. The scene of their nightmares had become a dream. Her black roses had taken over the ground and walls, and the earth was full of her blood magic. She was waiting for him, his newgift, who had transformed here in his arms.

Beside her, Mak started toward Lyros.

Lyros held up a hand. "I'm all right."

"He's not," Lio said. "He has magefire in his veins."

Cassia gasped. "How bad is it?"

Lio didn't have an answer. Mak didn't wait for one before he scooped Lyros up in his arms. He gave his Grace one look, and Lyros didn't protest the bridal carry. Instead, he wrapped his arms around Mak's neck.

Cassia motioned for them to follow her. "Bring him inside."

Lio would have followed that freckled hand anywhere. Her magic pulsed, and the ground at her feet parted to reveal a stairway. Mak hurried down with Lyros.

"There are portals here?" Realization sent gooseflesh across Lio's skin. "This is a node."

Cassia nodded, and there was hope in her aura.

Lio hesitated in front of her. He gripped his scroll case to keep from touching her.

Her gaze dropped to Dame. "You saved her."

"You might say she saved me."

Hesitating behind Lio, Dame cocked her head at Knight, her ears perked. He sniffed in her direction and wagged his tail.

Cassia led them inside the portal, where steps spiraled around the wall of a deep, narrow cavern. They walked down with the dogs and joined Mak and Lyros by an underground stream. Spell-lit torches lined the bank, casting their shadows across the ferns that grew by the water. Archways inscribed with runes led away into darkness.

Mak laid Lyros down on the thick carpet of plants. Lio had never seen his cousin like this, silent and pale. He gave Lyros's wound a rapid examination before holding out his wrist.

Lyros struggled to a sitting position. "I won't drink until we talk."

"Bleeding thorns, Lyros!" Mak finally spoke. "You're an hour away from dying and you want to *talk*?"

"I want to apologize."

Mak shook his wrist at his Grace. "You think apologies matter to me right now? Drink!"

"Lyros," Lio broke in, "now isn't the time!"

Cassia glared at their wounded Trial brother. "What happened to 'no abstinence over foolish differences of opinion'?"

"I need Mak to know I'm not angry about the weapons."

Mak curled his hand into a fist. "You have every right to be. You told me not to do it, and when I was an idiot and didn't listen, you supported me anyway. No one could ask more of his Grace than that."

"Yes," Lyros said. "You can. You can ask me to trust your decisions. Even about this."

"I know you trust me. You always tell me I have the best intuition. But you're the one with sense."

"I'm wrong just as often as you are."

Mak sat back. "That's why you changed your mind about turning us in? You actually think I was right about the weapons?"

"I came back for the same reason I left. I was trying to do what would cause you the least pain."

Mak's face got ruddy, and his veils started to slip over his emotions. "Why in the Goddess's name did you think I would hurt less if you got arrested for my crimes?"

"I felt your guilt at the temple. I saw everything you imagined that Miranda would do with the dagger you forged. You were torturing yourself. I would have done anything to make it stop. And the only way I could think of to put an end to this was to turn us in."

Mak swallowed. "That was the stupidest strategy you've ever come up with. Watching you leave…*that* hurt."

"Then why did you tell me to go? Twice?" The words seemed to jump out of Lyros, and then he rubbed his face, as if he regretted them.

By silent agreement, Lio and Cassia said nothing. If talking this through would get Lyros to accept the healing he needed, they didn't dare interrupt.

Mak reached out and touched Lyros's tangled hair. "You know I was just trying to protect you from the consequences of my actions. You've done everything the right way. You never wanted to revolutionize anything, and you didn't need to in order to leave your mark on Orthros. Goddess, you're the finest warrior the Stand has ever seen. After how hard you worked for your speires, I ruined everything for you by trying to prove something."

"You think you have something to prove?" Lyros gave his head a shake. "Mak…you're a natural. You were made for the Stand. All I ever wanted was to be as worthy of these speires as you."

Mak's mouth hung open. "That's what you think?"

"I've felt that way since the first time you showed me how to throw a punch."

"You're always the one making me a better warrior. A better person."

"'The good influence who keeps Mak out of trouble.'" Lyros let out a humorless laugh. "I embraced that label from your parents. It made me feel…needed, I suppose. Like I brought something useful to the family."

Mak stared at him. "You thought you had to be *useful*?"

"More useful than a thieving urchin and a delinquent artist. So I influenced you right out of your bravest ideas and kept you from breaking rules that needed to be broken. Because I was trying to prove something, too."

Mak shoved his hands through his hair again. "You're my Grace, and I didn't know you felt this way. Goddess. It never occurred to me. It's always been so obvious to me that you're the best of us."

"You're hardly objective."

Mak made a strangled noise of frustration. "Why do you think I keep that lump of clay in our residence?"

Lyros huffed. "So you can tease me about it."

"Why do you think I love to tease you? It makes me happy every time

I look at your horrible attempts at art. If you'd been a master artist, you wouldn't have become a Steward with me."

"I would have."

"And then I'd feel guilty for pulling you away from something you were good at. But I didn't. You were meant to become a warrior."

Lyros smiled. "You were the good influence on me."

"Then listen to me. You don't have to prove anything. You're worthy of your speires in your own right. But if you need another reason, you're my Grace. You belong with me."

Lyros pulled Mak closer. "Let me back into your hard head, and I think I'll finally believe that."

The tension in Mak eased. Lyros's eyes unfocused, and he let out a sigh. His fangs unsheathed.

Over his shoulder, Mak motioned to Lio and Cassia and mouthed, *I've got him.*

Lyros would be all right. What he needed now was time with his Grace. As Mak's veil spells fell over the cavern, Lio and Cassia slipped through one of the archways.

They followed the stream along a lengthy passageway. Now that they were alone, her Craving seemed to fill the space. But he didn't reach for her yet. Dame stayed close to him, while Knight trotted ahead of Cassia.

They hadn't gone far when Cassia halted. She turned to Lio, unsaid words rising and falling in her thoughts. This time, he didn't push. He would wait as long as she needed him to.

Dame closed the distance between them, tiptoeing toward Cassia.

"Oh, hello, lovely lady," Cassia crooned, extending a hand. "How glad I am to see you on your feet."

After sniffing her for a moment, Dame licked her hand.

"Well, aren't you a sweetheart?" Cassia held out her other hand to Knight. "Come meet Dame properly, darling. *Barda acklii.*"

Dame stayed where she was, cautious, But Knight trotted over to her, and soon they were circling each other, sniffing one another's tails.

No aggressive posturing for pack dominance? Lio rubbed his temple. Either his blood had ruined Dame's liegehound instincts, or she was the friendliest dog ever forced into war.

Knight bounded away, then halted, looking back over his shoulder at Dame. She took a step toward him, but didn't leave Lio's reach.

"How do I tell her she's off duty?" he asked.

Cassia smiled. "*Soor obett.*"

Dame didn't move. Lio patted her. "Go be a dog. *Soor obett.*"

When he said the words, his familiar dashed off for a game of chase with Knight. They raced and tussled along the side of the stream. A little bubble of light seemed to fill Lio's chest, . His guilt snuffed it out.

Cassia held out her hand to him, a question in her eyes. His hand felt dirty. But if she wanted his touch, he would give it. He slid his hand in hers, and she held on tight.

She led him onward, moving with purpose. They wandered far, the dogs' happy yips echoing after them. The deeper they went, the thicker her magic grew around them. When the passage opened into another cavern, Lio looked around them in astonishment.

"This is the heart of the letting site." Cassia's voice was hushed.

The stream ended in a pool that glittered under starry spell lights. The Lustra magic was so thick here that he felt like they were swimming in it. Every current that flowed around him pulsed with Cassia's blood magic, immersing him in her dual power.

Some ancient hand had carved the inside of the cave into curving walls, graceful arches, and pillars like standing stones. Cracks marred the runes carved on every surface, and chunks of the megaliths had fallen to the ground. But everywhere this sacred place had almost collapsed, black roses now grew, filling and bracing the damage.

The sconces were blackened, as if they had once burned with magefire. Lio ran his fingers through the nearest spell light and started. "This is my magic."

"You're a part of this place now, too. Let me show you."

Borne on the currents of magic and emotion swirling between them, Lio sank into their Union. Spells ran out from this place in countless veins, and Cassia was their heart. She guided his mind through the patterns to the threshold of the only door that still stood. Her blood and his light traced the runes on the portal.

He opened his eyes to find his arms around her, her mouth a hair's breadth from his. He gazed down at her, more in awe of his Grace than ever. "You did it, Cassia. You healed the third door."

She traced his brow, then his cheek. "My power can save us, just as you always believed. I'm the only one who has a hope of stopping Kallikrates. But I can't do it without you."

"Everything I have to give is yours, now and always. But I won't push you ever again. I'm sorry I made this harder for you."

She shook her head. "You weren't pushing me. You were fighting for me. That's what I needed."

The weight of his sins lightened. He had made so many mistakes, but not this. He had still understood what his Grace needed.

She rested her face on his chest. "You were right. My fear almost cost me something even more important than my magic. My power. I spent my whole mortal life afraid to act because of what the king might do. It would be so much worse to sacrifice my power for eternity because of Kallikrates."

"Then I will keep fighting for eternity."

"Please. If it's not too much to ask of you, keep fighting. Even when I stop fighting for myself. I was losing a part of myself because of my fear. Hold onto that part of me when it's slipping from my grasp."

He held her more tightly. "I'll never let go, my Grace."

She wrapped her arms around him. Despite his promise, he felt as if she were holding the pieces of him together.

"In the temple…" He had to take another breath to go on. "Thank you for stopping me."

She stroked his back, saying nothing. He was glad she simply let him get his words out.

"You saved those men from what I would have done to them."

"I did it to save you."

"I know." He pressed his face to her hair.

When she spoke again, her voice was thick. "I didn't stop you soon enough to spare you this guilt. I'm so sorry."

"The consequences are mine to carry."

"No." Her hands tightened on his back. "We carry everything together now. Promise me."

When he didn't reply, she looked up at him, her gaze fierce. "I will never judge you or be ashamed of you. Not after how you've accepted me. I'm here to bear your burdens with you and hold you while you heal."

A sigh slipped out of him. "Goddess, what did I do to be blessed with you?"

"You loved me. Now let me love you. Promise me."

He drew back from her just enough to reach his scroll case. He pried the dented lid off and pulled out what he'd been keeping inside the warded cylinder.

He presented their avowal cup to her for the second time.

She gasped. "You brought it with us?"

"I could leave everything else behind but this." He wrapped both their hands around the cup. "You have all my promises."

She bit her hand and squeezed her blood into the cup, then pressed it to his lips. He swallowed the fresh libation before it could cool. An echo of her power moved through him, and at the thirst that taste awoke, he groaned.

He opened his wrist for her over their chalice. She watched, her fangs unsheathing. Burying one hand in her hair, he poured his offering onto her tongue. She swallowed hard, his blood trailing from the side of her mouth.

A tremble in the ground made them grab each other for support. The pool roiled, and her roses trailed up their legs.

She cried out, her knees buckling. He caught her against him and held her up. Before he could ask her what was happening, power flooded their Union, showing him the patterns of her channeling.

Magic was churning up from the letting site, through her, and overflowing from their avowal cup in a pure, powerful flood.

The current pulled him in, washing through every part of him. Arousal slammed through him, and he groaned, pressing their bodies together.

She rose up to meet him and crushed her mouth to his. Their blended blood tasted of dark places and shining light.

Cassia, does this mean what I think it does? Our avowal cup is…

My third focus. Oh, Lio. It was here all along. You made it for me.

I crafted it from us.

Let me love you, she said again, trailing rough kisses down his throat.

He tilted his head back. *Yes.*

She stripped his battle-stained robes off him. Finally the smell of fire cleared from his head, and the heavy sweetness of her roses reached him. Pulling her robes down off her shoulders, he licked her skin. The sharp, rich flavor of her hunger brought his fangs down. She tugged her clothes lower, and he chased her bare skin with his hands, running his palms over her breasts.

Fabric and leaves rustled as she slipped from his hold to kneel amid the roses. She reached a hand up to him. He let her pull him down to her.

She laid him back in the black flowers, running her hands over him. His eyes slid shut as he listened to her pulse. He'd had enough of death. All he wanted was the life inside her.

She took their avowal cup from his lax grip. He opened his eyes to see her biting her wrist. Her blood splashed into the clear chalice, filling it with red once more. The current of her magic swelled inside him, and his mouth watered.

As she slid her leg over him, he caressed the splash of freckles on the inside of her thigh. Straddling him, she tilted the cup, spilling her blood down her chest and over her breasts. The crimson flow parted around her pebbled nipples.

She put her hand to her breast and traced slow circles in the blood. Rising up on his elbows, he followed her motions with his gaze, his fangs throbbing. He flared his nostrils. As she played with her bloodstained nipple, he scented her pleasure.

She leaned down, letting him take her breast in his mouth. He groaned, licking her blood from the soft curve and sucking another taste from the taut peak. Thirsty for more, he caught the droplets falling from her other breast.

When she pulled back, he reached up to touch her, but she caught his hand. She sank her fangs into his wrist, and he grunted with satisfaction. Her eyelids grew heavy, and her throat worked, but she soon pulled her mouth back to add his blood to the chalice.

She poured the whole cup down her body. Now she traced her fingers between her breasts, down her torso, to paint her skin with his blood just above the apex of her thighs.

The sight unleashed his deepest instinct. *Mine.*

She opened his wrist to refill the cup again. He could bleed for her like this all night. This time, she splashed his blood across his bare chest and torso. Warm flecks spattered his face and hers.

Her eyes gleaming, she lowered her mouth to his heart. She made little moans in her throat as she licked her feast from his skin. The graze of her teeth around his nipple made him hiss.

She devoured him slowly, one mouthful at a time. Her tongue laved him into a daze of pleasure. There was no silence here, where her racing pulse defined the rhythms of magic itself.

Her heart beat faster, and her Craving pounded inside his chest. Her rising magic tingled across his skin, driving his desire higher and higher. This bloody worship only stoked their appetites. His body ached to give his goddess her fill.

In answer to his unspoke desire, she moved up his body. He kissed their feast from her lips, and she opened to him hungrily. When he rolled her onto her back, she arched beneath him, their bodies rubbing wet and warm against each other. While she was lost in his kiss, he untangled her fingers from the cup.

He let her up for air, and she gasped. He moved back to kiss his way along the inside of her thigh. When he sensed the flow of the powerful vein here, he sank his fangs in deep, relishing her husky outcry.

He pressed the cup to his bite. It was full before her Gift sealed her vein again. He swirled the chalice, savoring the bouquet that wafted up to him from her blood and body.

Hooking her other leg over his arm, he tipped the cup and let its contents trickle down the inside of her thigh. A shiver went through her. He caught the trail of blood on his tongue.

He emptied the chalice slowly, taking his drink from her knee to the groove of her thigh. Her sighs, her scent, the swell in their Union all told him she was on the verge of climax.

Suddenly, he was holding empty air. He turned toward her aura to see her at the side of the pool with their avowal cup in her hand. She gave him a saucy look over her shoulder and dove into the water.

He stepped after her, and despite the lust befuddling his thoughts, his aim was true. He appeared in front of her under the water and grabbed her.

As they surfaced together, water cascaded off her, slicking his braid against her head. Their blood swirled in the water around them. She looked into his eyes.

Her magic rippled through the water and down his spine. Arousal gripped him harder, and he gasped. Then her spell sank away into the pond, and she swam away from him.

He chased her, his longer arms bringing him close to her in a heartbeat. Just as he was about to grab her waist, levitation stirred the water, and she sank out of reach.

He dove after her. She was a shimmering shape below, a whorl of dark hair. The deeper they went into the letting site's heart, the thicker their magic flowed. Power cascaded over his skin with every stroke. Immersed, he was parched for her, desperate to sink into her body.

At last, the bottom came into sight, covered in black petals. She was there, floating on her back with her fangs bared.

Before she could escape him again, he caught her wrist, pinning her hand and the cup to the floor of the pool. With her other hand, she pulled him to her.

He thrust inside her in measures, pumping his hips with the currents of magic. She undulated beneath him like part of the spell. Nothing had felt like this since they had left their own letting site behind.

When he was as deep in her as he could reach, she wrapped her legs around him tightly, grasping his hair. Her climax shuddered through her. Her magic surged into him, and his body shook on the edge of control. He went still, clenching his teeth, and held her against the floor of the pond while she writhed under him.

Her peak faded, but she still rocked her hips in little hungry motions. Her fangs were straining for him.

He sank his fangs into her throat, anchoring her. She found her way to his vein and fastened on. As their blood flowed into each other, the cycle pulled the magic in and through them. It poured out of him in wave after wave of pleasure as he spent himself in the grip of her power.

When the cycle released them, they floated to the surface in each other's arms. She wiped blood and water from his chin with her thumb. Her eyes were still dilated, and her fangs showed no sign of retracting.

"Love me," he said.

She sank her fangs into his throat again. Floating, he savored the pleasure she pulled out of him with every suck. His back came up against one of the pillars that descended into the pool. Magic feathered across his skin.

Her wet heat came down over his shaft. He gripped her hips and thrust to give her more. Pushing him against the pillar for leverage, she rode him hard.

Her moans echoed through the cavern. Their night apart had cost her more than she had wanted to admit. He held her close, stroking her hair as she took her fill of him.

She devoured him until he lost himself in her again and his body served up his pleasure to her. His shout rang in his ears as she suckled his climax from his veins, her own body spasming with vicarious release.

When he could move again, he gathered her in his arms and carried her onto the bank. They lay together, dripping and fulfilled, while the pond lapped at their toes. He reached up and pulled a black rose petal from her hair.

"I will never leave you again," she whispered. "Not even for a night."

"I will never watch you go," he said. "I'll follow you until you let me catch you."

She rested her head on his chest. "You won't have to. Just hold me right here."

46
nights after
WINTER SOLSTICE

THE FINAL SANCTUARY

"Now that no one is dying and everyone's fangs are polished," Lyros said, "I think we can make some decisions."

Cassia thought it far too soon for such a jest, but before she knew it, all four of them were laughing.

They had gathered around a carved stone table in another chamber they'd discovered off the main cavern. Knight lounged under the table with Dame while she gnawed on a stick he had found for her.

She bent to check on the dogs and covered her smile with her hand.

"What?" Standing beside her, Lio gave her a bemused look.

"They're getting along even better than I hoped. I can tell when a champion is besotted with his lady."

Lio grinned, and she was sure he had already glimpsed her mental images of puppies. She knew she was getting ahead of herself, but she simply couldn't help envisioning a fuzzy, wiggling hoard of little liegehounds.

Cassia straightened, and the sight of their weapons sobered her. The bronze chandelier overhead glowed with Lio's spell lights, shining on the three remaining adamas artifacts Mak had set on the table.

Lio pulled their battered map from his scroll case and spread it out. "Where to, Black Roses?"

Cassia looked across at their Trial brothers. "None of us have to bear our doubts in silence anymore. If anyone has hesitations about continuing our quest, tell us."

Lyros gave an emphatic shake of his head. "Lio and I have faith in us all."

Mak smiled, his arm around Lyros's waist. "That's good, because Cassia and I have some ideas."

"You first, Mak," she said.

He thumped his mace with a finger. "I thought these were finished, but I've realized they need one more enchantment. A spell to limit how our enemies—or even we—can use them."

Lio leaned forward, aura bright with interest. "I've never heard of a spell like that."

"There isn't one." Lyros's pride shone through his aura. "Mak is inventing it."

Mak blushed. "It's just a ward. A modified version of the Blood Shackles that will effect anyone who attempts to wield one of our weapons."

"An enchantment that complex is far more than 'just a ward,'" Lio said. "When you're done making incredible arcane innovations, don't forget that your revolutionary proposal is intact in my scroll case."

"All right, one thing at a time." Mak waved him off, but his aura was pleased. "For the spell to work properly, I'll need to enchant all four weapons at once, since they're bound together by our Union Stones. So we'll need to rescue Rosethorn from Miranda first."

Cassia nodded. "To do that, we have to stop letting her lead us by the nose through Kallikrates's traps. I think we should lure her to us this time. We now know that's possible because she can track me just as easily as I can track her."

She was prepared for the dark cloud that gathered in Lio's aura. But the ferocious look on his face still took her breath away. "We will not use you as bait. I will never go along with any plan that relies on such a tactic."

She smoothed the front of his robe. "I am not the bait, my darling. I'm the trap."

He took her hands in both of his, holding them against his chest. "She has Kallikrates's favor now. It will take more magic than you have ever wielded to defeat them."

"I will channel the entire Lustra if that's what it takes."

A fierce smile came to his face. "That is a plan I can agree to."

"Us, too," Mak spoke up.

"Now this is good strategy," Lyros agreed. "How will we convince Miranda to show herself?"

"We have something she wants." This was the part of her plan that Cassia hated the most.

Lio swore.

"I know," she said. "If you don't have the heart to do it, my Grace, we'll think of something else."

"No. It's a good plan."

Lyros glanced between them. "Whatever it is, Mak and I may not be willing to risk it, either. What bait do you have in mind?"

Lio pulled their avowal cup out of his scroll case and stood it on the table. "Cassia's third focus."

Mak shook his head. "You've had your avowal cup with you all this time? Romantic idiot."

"Guilty." Lio smiled.

Lyros blew out an incredulous breath. "When did you realize it's one of your foci, Cassia?"

"Last night. It reacted to the letting site." Were her cheeks as flushed as they felt?

Lio rested his hand low on her back, and the possessive magic inside her hummed at her mate's touch.

Mak snickered. "Well, it's a good thing you two take your duties to the Lustra so seriously."

Lyros's eyes narrowed with amusement. "And a very good thing Lio didn't ruin that cup."

Lio cleared his throat. "In any case, if Cassia casts with it to reveal it as her focus, Miranda is sure to make her move."

Cassia nodded. "With my pendant and dagger already in her possession, she'll be rabid to complete the triune focus so she can use it to destroy the remaining node."

"This will work." Lyros rotated the map toward him. "We can choose our battleground, a location that will give us the advantage. Any thoughts on where?"

"Not a Lustra site we would risk endangering," Cassia said. "We have to keep her away from the remaining node, wherever it might be."

Lio's gaze sharpened on something no one else could see. She knew that look.

She brushed her fingers across his temple. "You have an idea, Sir Scholar."

"It has to be a place that will strengthen your magic as much as possible. But not a Lustra site. That means we need a Hesperine site."

"Oh," Cassia breathed. "Yes."

They would defeat Miranda with the Lustra, but on Hesperine terms.

Lio yanked all the documents out of his scroll case and scattered them across the table. "Think about how your roses responded to the Queens' ward. And in the Ritual hall at House Komnena."

Lyros stood back and let Lio have at the papers. "This could give us a real chance. If we fight where Sanctuary magic survives, Mak and I can cast stronger wards."

Mak chewed his lip. "That might help with the enchantment I want to put on the weapons, too."

"Your spell will be brilliant," Lyros said. "We'll simply have to accept the risk we face at any Hesperine Sanctuary. The Charge is likelier to discover us there."

Lio gave his head a shake, her braid falling in his eyes as he rifled through his notes and charts. "We aren't going to a Sanctuary."

Finally he seized on what he must have been looking for. He flattened out the small scroll in front of Cassia. It was another map, meticulously labeled in Lio's handwriting. She recognized the coastline and rivers, mountains and forests as Tenebra and Cordium. But none of the place names were familiar to her.

"Lio... is this the shadowlands in another time?"

"This map dates from the Great Temple Epoch. I copied it from one of my father's years ago. I thought this might help us on our journey... give us clues about the past."

Four stars drew her eye, each one at a different location on the map—north, south, east, and west. "Are those the Great Temples of Hespera?"

"They may have been razed, but that doesn't mean their magic is gone." Lio rested his finger on the star in the north. It hovered in the gap between two peaks, where a river flowed out of the Umbral Mountains.

"Hagia Boreia," Cassia said with reverence.

"Where our foregiver Anastasios sacrificed himself to keep our last

Sanctuary mage alive. His blood anointed that ground during one of Annassa Alea's greatest castings. There is nowhere in Tenebra we will stand a better chance."

Lyros's eyes shone. "Brilliant."

"It will be an honor to fight there," Mak said.

Cassia took Lio's hand. They had faced Kallikrates upon the graves of his victims at Tenebra's fortresses. Now, if they fought him on the sacred ground of Hespera's martyrs, they might prove to him that no matter how much he destroyed, the Hesperines were still standing.

With the Black Roses of one mind, it took less time than Lio expected to settle on their plan. When they stood ready in Cassia's garden with the hounds, a hush of anticipation came over everyone.

Lio took Cassia's hands. "After sixteen hundred years, using our foregiver's blood as a stepping focus is an uncertain experiment. But with both of us, it might just work."

Mak clapped Lio on the shoulder. "As long as you two don't drop us in the middle of a heart hunter camp, we'll be fine."

"Or too far east, into Rudhira's courtyard," Lyros added.

"Have some confidence." Cassia drew herself up. "I managed to step to Mak without falling off a cliff, didn't I?"

"Barely," Mak said.

Lio gave her hands a squeeze. "Our bond will make it easier."

He held all their auras in focus, closing his eyes, and recalled visions he'd seen in the elders' minds when they talked of the lost past. Cassia held the remembrance with him, and the glimpses sharpened. Their hearts pounded in unison, pulling Anastasios's power through their veins.

They stepped in Union. Their joined Wills carried them and those they loved through the world.

His feet hit frozen ground on a riverbank. The white-capped water churned past, pummeling jagged rocks that protruded from its surface. Just before Cassia tumbled into the raging current, he caught her and pulled her to safety.

She looked up at him, breathing hard, her fingers curled in the front of his robe. "Thank you. We don't have time for me to break my neck."

He kissed her forehead.

Mak levitated out of a nearby pile of snow and shook himself. "Could have been worse."

"Did it work?" Lyros called, climbing a short way to join them. The dogs clambered alongside him, looking none the worse for wear.

Lio cast his senses out and tried to recognize anything. They were at the bottom of a ravine with steep slopes rising on either side. Not far upriver, a waterfall crashed down into the gorge.

He caught something on the icy wind, like a song of comfort or of mourning. All four of them turned toward the falls and looked up to where the water cascaded from between two peaks.

There it stood. The Great Temple of Hespera in the North was now nothing more than a time-worn fall of stones above the flowing water. But a deep sense of recognition rang inside him. Cassia pressed a hand to her heart.

"One of the Great Temples." Mak sounded reverent. "Not many Hesperines can say they've set eyes on it."

"To think," Lyros said, "our parents found refuge here when they fled the destruction of the Last War."

"I didn't know your parents were here, Lyros," said Cassia. "I thought your mother and Nodora's father Kitharos came from Hagia Zephyra, the Great Temple in the West."

He nodded. "They did."

Lio knew this painful story well and wondered if Lyros would choose now to share it with Cassia. But it seemed here at the foot of one of the Great Temples was the right time to speak of it.

Lyros continued, "When the Mage Orders came for Hagia Zephyra, the mortals in the temple turned on their Hesperine leaders. They called their immortality hubris and believed the discovery of the Gift was what had incited the war mages' wrath against all Hespera worshipers."

Cassia touched his arm. "I had no idea. That betrayal must have been horrific."

"The mortals agreed to surrender the Hesperines to the Order of

Anthros to spare themselves. Our elder firstbloods, Daedala and Thelxinos, went willingly to buy time for those they'd Gifted. My mother and Kitharos led the escape, and my father was one of the few humans who helped them."

"I thought none of the temples were spared," Cassia said.

Lyros shook his head. "The Order never intended to keep their bargain. They slaughtered the mortal Hespera worshipers, too. But my parents and Kitharos made it here to Hagia Boreia with a small group of Hesperines and loyal humans."

"I'm so sorry."

His brow creased, as if something new had occurred to him. "My parents know what it's like to be abandoned by the people who should have defended you."

Mak ruffled his Grace's hair. "You didn't really think your 'artistic' hands were the reason they chose you for their son, did you?"

Lyros put an arm around Mak, and they started the hike toward the temple together. Lio took Cassia's hand and started after their Trial brothers.

As they approached, he gestured to the steep cliffs. "Before the Last War, two great stairways led to the gate. Light mages and warders escorted those seeking safety on the long climb. When the Aithourians laid siege to the temple, my father demolished the stairs."

The waterfall soon drowned out their voices and sprayed them with cool mist. Lio ran his hand over a pile of stones that might still hold pieces of the fallen stairways. He and Cassia put the hounds safely in a stay at the foot of the cliffs before beginning the treacherous ascent.

The Black Roses levitated over the footsteps of generations of Sanctuary seekers. Their immortal power carried them up to the place where the first Hesperines had walked when they were alive.

They landed on a broad ledge to one side of the waterfall. There had once been a bridge across to the opposite ledge, Lio recalled. Now, just a precipice of white water. He helped Cassia step the hounds carefully up to the ledge.

"Dame isn't nervous around the Hesperine magic here," Cassia observed. "She adjusted much faster than Knight."

Lio gave his familiar a pat. "Giving her my blood seems to have only positive effects thus far."

Cassia ran her hand through Knight's ruff. Lio knew she was wondering, hoping, that this could change her liegehound's future, too.

Lyros hefted his spear. "Let's keep an eye out in case any heart hunters choose tonight to vandalize the ruins. They would love to pick off some Hesperine pilgrims while they're at it."

"I'll vandalize their faces." Mak's belt-chain chimed as he drew the Star of Orthros.

"*Ckuundat*," Cassia said, and Knight came to attention.

Lio tried the command with Dame. Suddenly his sweet, timid familiar was standing alert, the fur rising on her back. She positioned herself in front of him.

He used Final Word for a walking stick as they half levitated, half scrambled up to level ground above the mouth of the waterfall. "The gate would have been here."

He started forward. Magic washed over him, as if a libation still dripped in the air. The others froze beside him, not even breathing.

"This was the boundary of the Sanctuary ward," Mak said.

Together, they crossed the threshold where Anastasios and Alea had made their last stand.

They walked out over the floor of the courtyard where Sanctuary Roses had once grown and the mages of Hespera had welcomed all who sought refuge here. Smooth white stones, begrimed with ash, still paved the ground. No snow touched the perfect circle, as if the fire that had razed the temple had marked it forever.

They ventured further into the ruins, where bas reliefs lay defaced. Heart hunters had scrawled obscenities on every pillar stub and scrap of wall. Mak blasted each one with a cleaning spell as they passed.

The temple complex ran deep between the two peaks, in some places carved right out of the surrounding stone. Cassia paused below a rocky overhang where a long wing cut into the mountainside. "I think there's some sort of magic this way. Does anyone else feel it?"

Mak and Lyros shook their heads.

Lio reached with his senses again. Something familiar tugged at his chest. "You're right."

As they followed her, the impression grew stronger. Pain. Decision.

Survival. By the time she halted, Lio was choked with emotion he didn't understand. There was nothing here but a window, tunneling through the thick walls to grant a glimpse of the stars beyond.

"Why does this place feel so important?" Cassia's voice was thick.

Mak exchanged a glance with Lyros. "We can feel the emotion here too, but it's not affecting us as much."

"Do we have any idea what part of the temple this was?" Lyros asked.

Lio knelt and ran the dust of the ages through his fingers, and the power that stirred brought to mind a familiar hand. "My father's magic lingers in this stone."

"Do you think…" Cassia hesitated. "Could this have been the Healing Sanctuary?"

"Yes." Lio's throat was tight. "Where they brought him when he was dying."

She rested her hand on his shoulder. "Where Anastasios Gifted him."

Lio ran a hand down his face. This was the place where his father had become the first Hesperine to receive the Gift. Where their bloodline had begun. The reason he and Cassia stood here tonight, immortal.

"Goddess bless," Lyros said.

Mak let out a low whistle. "I see what Uncle Apollon meant when he said his magic was destructive during his Gifting. Do you think all this stone magic is from when he demolished the room, or when he rebuilt it afterward?"

Cassia laughed, wiping her eyes. "I don't know. But perhaps I should cast my own destructive spells here."

Lio stood and pulled her to him for a moment. "Not yet. There's one more place we should try to find."

They wandered past rows of pillars that still stood, broken but defiant, and under pale archways blackened by fire. Their persecutors had not been able to erase this monument of Sanctuary magic from the face of the earth.

Walking among the ghosts of emotion that still soaked this ground, Lio had expected to feel horror. But this place was haunted by a more powerful spirit.

"I feel hope here," Cassia said.

Deep in the cup between the two mountains, they found what Lio had sought. The temple dome lay where it had collapsed, a wide ring of black rubble. They levitated to the rim and looked down through what had been a round opening at the top of the dome.

For thousands of years, the moons had shone through this skylight into the Ritual Sanctuary. For generations, the temple leaders had led blood rites here, ending with Anastasios and Alea. The great statue of Hespera that had looked on was long gone. All that remained of the most sacred place in the temple was this crater.

Aithouros had burned a glyph of Anthros on the floor in the statue's place. But Hesperines had survived, and his violation had not. A Rose of Hespera was now etched deep in the floor, glimmering with light magic and stained with royal blood. A ward lay over it like a seal.

Mak let out a breath. "It's just like the Blood Errant said. They came here and made a Ritual circle."

"Here," Lio said. "This is the most powerful place for your spell, my Grace."

She leapt down and landed in the center of the Goddess's petals and thorns. "I will make roses grow here again."

CASSIA HELD THEIR AVOWAL cup tightly to still her trembling hands. The countless libations made here resonated in her blood, and beneath Hespera's sacred ground, the Lustra endured. All the magic in this place felt poised in the chalice, ready to overflow when Cassia chose. She could only hope what she unleashed would not destroy what was left of Hagia Boreia.

Lyros appeared above her on the rim of the skylight and gave her an encouraging smile. "My wards are fortified for any and all chaos."

Mak took his position across the dome from his Grace, composed in a warrior's stance, but his aura jittered with nerves. "My spell is as ready as it will ever be. All it should take is getting Rosethorn back from Miranda. If it works."

"It will work." Lio gave Mak and encouraging clap on the shoulder before levitating down to join Cassia inside the Ritual circle. Dame peered uncertainly over the edge.

"*Het*," Lio called up to her. "You don't want to be in here when the magic starts. Stay up there and fight with Lyros and Mak. Ah, *barda acklii*?"

With obvious reluctance, Dame stayed by Lyros. He gave her a rueful look, then reached out gingerly to stroke her fur. She wagged her tail.

"See there?" Lio said. "You're friend, not food."

"Fine, as long as she doesn't lick me with dead rabbit slobber."

A smile tugging at her mouth, Cassia snapped her fingers and motioned her hound over to Mak. "Knight, *barda!*"

As he took up his guard stance, Mak scratched under his chin. "Hullo, Knight. Let's make some teeth marks on the Gift Collector, shall we?"

Lio rested his hands on Cassia's shoulders. *What do you need me to do for you, my Grace?*

She knew their chances of survival against the kind of power Kallikrates could wield through Miranda. *Stay alive. Let us protect you while you attack Miranda's mind.*

He pulled her into his arms. *You won't lose me.*

You can't promise me that, just as Azad couldn't promise it to Neana.

We can promise each other that we will go down together.

She clung to him, tears burning at the back of her eyes. *Yes. I swear to you. I will be at your side and never let you fight your last battle alone.*

And I will never leave you to waste away without me.

He stepped back. Somehow, he was smiling, and the sight made her heart ache.

She lifted the chalice, and he bit his wrist, making a generous libation into the cup. Cassia braced herself and opened her own vein to add her blood to his.

The petals and thorns of Hespera's Rose glowed with crimson light, and magic swelled inexorably up from the stones. Down from the stars. Cassia drew in a deep breath, and she tasted blood and roses in the back of her mouth.

"Hespera's Sanctuary," Lio breathed.

Cassia let her magic run through the temple, digging deep roots and drawing in blood spells long-untended. As potential stirred to life beneath the ruins, she gasped. "It's working."

She eased her spell out of the ground. Seedlings lifted their little green faces from between the broken stones around the Ritual circle. Magic throbbed through their veins and hers as they grew into mighty vines and flowered.

The spell felt so right. Two powers, wound into one whole. This was her magic, a perfect Union.

Yes, her Grace affirmed. *Your power...it's so beautiful, Cassia.*

She swept her spell out from the Ritual circle, and everywhere it touched, black roses bloomed. She let them twine around the pillars and fill the breaches in the walls. Following them in her mind, she stretched all the way to the gate and conjured a barrier of thorns where the Sanctuary ward had once stood.

The vines grew together, closing the final gap in her defenses, just as an aura loomed before the temple. Familiar, yet far more powerful than ever before.

Cassia gripped Lio's hand. "She's here."

LIO'S VOW

A SPELL BOOMED FROM THE direction of the gate, and the impact made the ground tremble under Lio's feet. Standing behind Cassia, he wrapped one arm around her and planted Final Word to steady them against the next barrage.

She raised their avowal cup in both hands, and black rose petals swirled around them on an arcane current. "It will take more than a few lightning spells to demolish my roses this time."

Mak let out a whoop. "I can feel the blood magic they're pulling out of the temple. It's almost as if the Sanctuary wards have come back to life."

"That will give even Kallikrates a challenge." Lyros raised his voice triumphantly over the crash of war magic.

"I'll make her pay for every step she takes toward us." Cassia leaned back against Lio. "Will this buy you enough time?"

"Yes." He honed in on Miranda's tainted mind.

While she fought her way through the fortifications, he would break down her mental defenses. And he would not stop until he knew what lay within the doors under Solorum Palace.

Standing in the whorl of Cassia's magic, Lio drew his own power out of himself. His surroundings faded from his awareness as he turned inward. A distant crack of lightning reached his ears, but all he could smell was the death that shrouded Miranda's thoughts.

The structure of her dream wards was forever imprinted on his thoughts, an arcane memory forged the night the Lustra had helped him defeat her. He had no letting site to empower him tonight, but he had his knowledge of her mind.

Calling on the pure blood magic in his veins, he navigated through the poisonous outer layers of her thoughts. Her resistance burned cold through his head, weighing on his chest, and a shudder wracked him.

He knew better than to force his way through. He must find his way through the befuddling shapes of her dream wards to her innermost weaknesses.

He wove through clouds of smoke, evading deceptive mirrors. Reflections of Miranda's past flashed at him. A crow coming to life in her hands. A human dying on her blade.

Then he saw Cassia's face, twisted with pain, her mouth open in a scream of despair. Rage hardened his power. He struck, and the smoke shattered, slicing through his mind.

He stood bleeding in the orchard at Paradum. In this mindscape, the trees were not dead, but heavy with apples. A crow winged between the branches overhead.

"You won't find this duel as easy as the last one," Miranda said.

Lio spun to face her. He tightened his hands around Final Word, unsure if he clutched his real staff or a vision of it that embodied their mental battle.

Miranda held the digging fork on which Skleros had met his end. "Every time you break me, I become stronger. That's the choice *I* made here, while Cassia chose the wrong side."

Lio stood his ground. "I'm not here to break you."

"You'll have to, if you want to know what's behind the doors."

Let her think that was all he had in store for her. She didn't suspect there was something he wanted even more than her secrets, and she couldn't imagine how long and hard he would fight to get it.

He made a mighty swing with his staff. Beyond the vision of the orchard, her mind strained against the force of his blow.

She blocked him with the digging fork. Lio felt the impact through every inch of his ephemeral shape, as if his body might dissolve into the pain in his mind.

Miranda turned and raced through the orchard toward the castle.

"You can't run any longer!" Lio shouted. "This ends here."

He tried to levitate after her, but the very air held him down. By sheer force of Will, he broke through the resistance and managed to run toward her.

He swept Final Word out before him, catching her in the ankles. She went down, and he aimed the butt of his staff at her head.

She rolled, springing to her feet. With a parry, she shoved his staff away from her. Her counterattack was as fast as thought. The tines of her fork slashed Lio's side as he dodged.

Gasping, he hunched over and pressed a hand to his bleeding abdomen. Through a haze of red over his sight, he saw Miranda flee again.

Lio! came Cassia's worried mind voice. *Are you all right?*

Is my physical form bleeding?

No. She hasn't reached the dome yet. Your body is safe behind my roses.

Then I'm better than all right. Gritting his teeth, he pushed through the pain of the mental wound and ran ahead.

He caught up to Miranda in the shadow of the inner wall. She disappeared through solid stone, leaving him outside her defenses.

Lio glanced left and right along the wall. No thorns grew on it, as they did in reality.

And yet, Cassia's stolen magic was here, too. He had to believe that her power, even held captive by Miranda, would know him. The Silvicultrix's mate.

Cassia.

Even as he thought her name, their Grace Union drew her nearer, in defiance of any dream wards. Her presence filled his mind, and he felt an echo in Miranda's. Could that be Cassia's lost magic responding to her nearness?

What do you need, my Grace? Cassia asked.

Just stay in Union with me. Can you do that and cast your spell?

Yes. Our nearness only seems to make my spell stronger.

Lio turned a savage smile on the walls of Paradum. His theory was correct.

Holding his connection to Cassia, he tore his hand with his fangs and spread his blood on the ground. Everywhere the drops fell, black roses sprang up, scaling the wall. With Final Word on his back, he took hold of one vine and climbed. Thorns tore at his hands, but his blood only strengthened the roses.

He made it over the top of the wall and leapt down into Cassia's garden to find Miranda standing guard. Shock crossed her face. She hurled her fork at him, and it shot toward his heart like a spear.

He blocked the gardening tool midair with his staff and sent it spinning away into the grasp of the roses. As he advanced on Miranda, she drew her relic blade. She was getting desperate.

Lio swung again. She disappeared, and his staff passed through empty air. She popped back into sight at close range, stabbing upward.

Before her dagger could slide under his breastbone, he fell backward, pulling his staff back with him. He drove the end of Final Word toward her gut, forcing her to retreat. Lio sprang to his feet again.

He battled his way forward, the shape of her mind bending around him with every blow from his staff. The walls crumbled and rebuilt, and each time, thorned vines grew thicker over the stone. Where his feet disrupted the soil, plants grew, then withered, then grew again, roses fighting with poisonous weeds. Miranda fought him tooth and nail with a deadly aim and agile dodges. But he was gaining ground.

He rammed Final Word into her breastplate, right upon the Eye of Hypnos written in his Grace's blood. The blow hurled Miranda backward through the broken wall into Cassia's sickroom.

The Overseer landed on her back on the table where she had tortured his Grace. The black roses grew eagerly over her wrists and ankles, tying her down. She fisted her hand around the hilt of her dagger and screamed a curse at Lio.

He came to stand over her. "Did you think Cassia's magic would choose your side, now that I'm here to rescue her power?"

"That's what you're really after?" Miranda laughed. "You're even more of a fool that I thought. Hesperines can't cast essential displacement anymore than you can be subjected to it. You'll never reclaim what I took from her."

"I just scaled your defenses with the help of her magic. Her power has turned traitor to you."

"That magic isn't hers anymore. It's *mine*."

He circled the table. "Then why haven't we seen you use it in battle? You throw fire, lightning, warding, even thelemancy at us. But no Lustra magic."

"I have more than enough mind magic to defeat you."

"Cassia's power barely obeys you, doesn't it? You're holding it back as you wait to push it through her foci, hoping it doesn't escape you before you can use it to destroy the last node."

"Her roses are falling to my war magic while we play this game. When I seize her third focus, it will be the end of the world as you know it."

"Kallikrates himself said it took him centuries to learn how to displace Lustra magic. He admitted he holds onto Cassia's by a thread. If he so much as touches her mind, her power will return to her." Lio leaned closer, his fangs sliding down. "I am the only one who will ever touch her mind again."

He watched as realization dawned in Miranda's eyes, and she understood what he was about to try. After the miles and the bloodshed and the regret it had taken to get to this moment, he savored it.

"This is the flaw in your plan," he said. "Me."

"It won't work," Miranda spat. "Whatever mental link you think you can forge between Cassia and me, it's not enough. You understand nothing of essential displacement."

He was educated enough in the arcane to know she was right. But he had more than thelemancy to draw upon. What Kallikrates and his Overseers would never understand was Grace Union.

"Watch me," Lio said.

Miranda's gaze hardened into another's, and she said in the Collector's voice, "If you try to take her power from me, you will pay my price."

Lio gathered the full force of his mind magic. "I won't have to try."

THE LUSTRA FED CASSIA and her roses more magic ripe with the temple's spells. As the channeling raged through her, Lio's grip around her waist anchored her to earth. She laid her arm over his and wound their fingers together.

Her strongest wall of thorns still stood before the dome, but beyond it, another line of her defenses succumbed to Miranda's fire spells. The odor of burning roses took her back to the shrine where she and Lio had fallen in love, which was now scorched earth. The night Hagia Boreia had been razed, the air must have been so thick with that stench that no one could breathe.

"You will not destroy another Sanctuary as long as I stand!" Cassia screamed at the unseen enemy. She sent out another blast of her power, regrowing the thorns that had just fallen. Above her, Mak and Lyros cheered.

But the necromancer's aura loomed, far too close to the final bastion and more powerful than she had been at the gates.

"Can you feel that?" Cassia shouted to Mak and Lyros.

"Kallikrates's presence," Mak confirmed.

Lio, Cassia warned. *Kallikrates is here.*

I know.

Miranda is about to break through the roses with him. Was it enough time?

His knuckles were white where he held his staff. *Yes. I have her right where I want her.*

They were so close. Cassia steadied their avowal cup in her hand. "Lio is ready!"

"Our wards are braced for the breach," Lyros called back.

She sensed her regrown barrier wither. No more time to shore it up now. She channeled all her determination into her final thorn wall, fortifying their last line of defense.

I will need you. Lio said. *Just like when we fought Kallikrates together at Rose House, and again at Paradum.*

I'm with you, my Grace.

Are you willing to channel more magic than you ever have before?

No holding back now. She opened herself to another wave of power and let it shudder through her. Somehow, she also felt stronger than at the start of the battle. How could that be?

She felt Lio smile.

Searing heat ate at her arcane senses, and she gritted her teeth. Smoke drifted between the tight weave of her vines. Then a glimmer of light.

She flooded the thorns with her dual magic. War magic fired back. She felt the breach grow, inch by agonizing inch, although she couldn't see it from her and Lio's position inside the dome. Mak and Lyros's wards enfolded them, an unseen darkness gathering against the glare of fire magic.

The power of a dozen fire mages exploded through Cassia's thorn wall. Hot air gusted in. Stone cracked. A hole exploded in the dome in front of her, spraying her and Lio with fragments of stone.

Miranda faced them through the smoke, a weed hook in one hand and a long mattock in the other.

Did she think turning Cassia's tools against her would frighten her? It didn't. But the sight of her pendant around Miranda's neck, resting over her own blood on the Gift Collector's leather breastplate, filled Cassia with a deep, instinctual rage.

Hold onto that beautiful anger, Lio said. *It has always been part of your power.*

Her fury took shape as rose vines that clawed out of the ground at Miranda's feet and bound her ankles. Mak and Lyros stepped, flanking her. The hounds descended from the dome in a single leap.

Rooted the spot, Miranda couldn't evade them. She twisted where she stood to hook her blade around Lyros's spearhead and parry Night's Aim. With her mattock, she blocked the Star of Orthros. Lightning sizzled at her feet, destroying the roses and forcing the hounds back.

Cassia snapped more roses around Miranda's limbs. They burned to ash the instant they touched her.

She dipped her fingers into her and Lio's blood, ready to pour more power from their avowal cup.

Mak and Lyros's Union Stones carved red paths in the air as they attacked again in tandem. Lio's staff pulsed slowly with the same signal. Wait.

Cassia held the wild power inside herself. Time to trust her Trial brothers. They had to engage Miranda at close range, if Mak had any hope of wresting Rosethorn from her.

Without warning, another wave of fire rolled toward Cassia. She raised thickets of black roses to fill the gap in the dome, like stakes on the field of a siege. The fire burned through two of them, but fell to embers before the third. She had to focus on defending their mind mage now.

Her thorn walls rose and fell before the fire and lightning that rained down. She stopped breathing the choking air. The dark shapes of the hounds leapt and circled in the chaos, harrying her into the reach of Mak and Lyros's weapons. More fire spells rolled off the shadows on their skin as bright adamas cut at Miranda.

A crack of lightning split the ground and forced Mak into the air. As he levitated, Miranda sliced her weed hook toward Lyros's neck.

He leaned backward with Hesperine balance. The curved blade swept past his face. Then he lunged forward and drove his spear into the weak point between Miranda's breastplate and shoulder armor.

Her blood scented the air, but she didn't even scream. With his spear buried in her armpit, Lyros wrenched a blade out of a scabbard at her belt.

Merely an ordinary knife. He used it to slice off her belt. It fell to the ground, scattering weapons. An awl rolled away, and a billhook landed at Cassia's feet.

"You think I would make it so easy for you?" the Collector asked.

Cassia's heart picked up pace. What if Miranda hadn't brought the dagger with her at all?

We can still defeat her. Lio's reassurance filled their Union. He was the calm in the center of the storm. Somehow, he was utterly confident in this moment. That certainty took root in Cassia's heart and became her own.

Mak descended in a blur. His morning star struck Miranda's arm. Adamas thumped on flesh and leather, and bone snapped. He tore off the scabbard under her sleeve, and his hand came away bloody. He hurled another mundane dagger to the ground.

Miranda popped out of sight, then reappeared, no longer surrounded by the warriors and dogs. Before Cassia's eyes, the bone protruding from the necromancer's arm righted itself, and her flesh knit back together.

Cassia swore. Miranda was still abusing Pakhne's healing power for her own gain.

The dogs raced toward her. Mak and Lyros took to the air and lunged down on her from above. The air around Miranda rippled, as if with heat.

A louder boom deafened Cassia. In silence, the warped air blasted out from Miranda. Mak, Lyros, and the hounds went flying, propelled in different directions. Then the spell rolled over the dome.

No heat touched Cassia's skin, but a tremor suddenly made it through the wards. Her quick levitation spell wasn't enough to keep her from toppling to the ground with Lio.

Their libation spilled from the chalice across Hespera's Rose. Lio lifted his head, a trail of blood sliding from his ear. His eyes focused on Cassia for an instant, and the ferocity in his gaze stole her breath.

Blood filled the lines of the petals and thorns. More magic spilled up from the Lustra, from the temple, a flood of growth and darkness. It seemed limitless.

But as another explosion rocked the dome, Cassia feared even this much power would not be enough.

LIO DREW CASSIA STILL deeper into their Grace Union. The roses snaked farther over Miranda's body, binding her more securely to the table. Thorns pricked her skin and drew blood.

But the cry that came from her lips was the Collector's. That one small betrayal of pain told Lio that he and Cassia had just defied history. For the first time, they had hurt an Old Master. But not for the last time.

Lio would cause him so much more pain before this was over. "You never should have touched my queen."

At that word, Cassia appeared, standing across the table from him. "Lio, what are you doing?"

"Taking something even more important than secrets."

Miranda strained against the roses. Flipping her relic blade in her hand, she tried to saw at the vines around her wrist. But neither she nor the Collector gave any sign they had heard Cassia. Just as in their past duels with Kallikrates, Grace Union was beyond his power.

The roses sprouted new branches and reached toward Cassia. She stared at them, and a hint of wonder dawned through her fear. "You're challenging him for my plant magic? Here? *Now?*"

"I told you I would make you as powerful as you were meant to be. Tonight is another step toward fulfilling that promise."

"I begged you not to put yourself in any more danger in Miranda's mind!"

"Look me in the eye and tell me you don't ache to feel your magic inside you. All of your magic. If you can do that, I will let it go."

The longing was stark on her face. All her protests and defenses, gone. When she spoke, it was not a timid whisper. It was the declaration he wanted to hear from her, again and again, as long as they both lived.

"I want it."

He held out his hand to her. "Then I will fight for it."

She gripped his hand. A current of magic opened between them, flowing from his heart to travel along his arm.

"Your foolish experiments will destroy you," the Collector warned.

"Not before we destroy you," Lio said.

As he unleashed all the thelemancy he possessed upon Miranda's mind, he tapped into the depths of his Grace Union with Cassia. A conduit opened between them with him as the gate.

Her plant magic knew him. He gasped as it spread into the arcane paths inside him. All her wildness. All her yearning to be free. This was the true extent of his Grace's power.

The sickroom stretched toward Miranda, as if a great mouth were sucking at the entire world. Emptiness split the seams of her mindscape. Pain sank deep into Lio's chest and pulled. He leaned on Final Word to keep from falling to his knees.

For the second time in his life, he teetered on the edge of Kallikrates's maw. But Grace Union kept him from being consumed.

Cassia's magic reached for her through him. He gave himself over to it, the living link to its Silvicultrix.

Miranda screamed. Vines snaked out of her mouth, coated in blood. Her body bowed with the force of the magic that poured out of her. The Collector's pull slammed her back onto the table and tore from Lio's spine out the front of his chest. He staggered toward Miranda as she choked.

His heart labored, and his chest felt like it was splitting in two. But he would forget the pain. What he would remember forever was Cassia in this moment.

She held out her arms and watched her black roses wind lovingly around her body. The thorned vines bloomed with more impossible colors. Bright moonflowers and brilliant yellow cassia. Pure Sanctuary Roses and rich purple betony. At last, soft, crimson Roses of Hespera. Their roses caressed her throat and spun into her hair, growing around his braid.

She looked into his eyes, hers blazing green with magic. Her lips parted, and she drew a deep gasp. On that breath, rose petals spun into her.

Joy unfurled in their bond. Pure. Untouched. An empty place inside her filled. As he felt that reunion, a piece of himself fitted into place, too.

Tears streamed down her face. "Thank you."

"I love you," he said.

"I know."

Miranda fell silent. The blood on her breastplate faded, line by line, until the Eye of Hypnos was gone. Her head rolled to the side, her lips moving in wordless horror. At last she rasped, "What have you done?"

Kallikrates's rage echoed out of the void, aiming for Lio.

Cassia's fangs flashed and held up her palms. They were covered in blood. Crimson tendrils flowed from her hands and spiraled around Lio, then splashed to the ground in a ring at his feet. The Collector's pull on his chest snapped.

She was suddenly beside him, and he sagged in her arms, clutching his staff for support.

"You have to get out of here," she cried. "He wants his revenge."

"Not until we learn what's locked inside the doors."

Thunder rumbled outside the castle, and a flash of lightning lit the room.

"Go," Lio said. "Defend our temple."

"My magic isn't inside Miranda now. It won't come to your aid. I can't abandon you here."

"We won't survive her war magic unless you wield all your power against her. We need you to fight with Mak and Lyros."

"Call me," Cassia demanded. "If you need me, pull me into our Union again."

He pressed a hand to his chest. "I will hold you right here."

The vision of her vanished, but her presence was still with him. And her magic was with her, where it had always belonged.

Lio grasped his medallion and struck the ground with his staff. The Lustra portal opened for him, and he and Miranda fell deeper into her mind.

THE BARROW

Cassia blinked the tears from her eyes. She lay entwined with Lio in a pool of blood inside the Ritual circle. Flowering vines wound around them, tying them to each other.

Petals of every color floated in their blood. This was real.

She reached inside herself and sank into familiar magic. The power she had once known flowed into her Gift and became Hesperine, and she knew it again.

With a thought, Cassia calmed the vines that clung to her. They fell away to cradle her Grace. She sat up and smoothed Lio's bloody hair back from his face. His eyes moved rapidly under his closed lids. She put Final Word back in his hand, and his fingers closed around the staff.

She lifted her head. Mak and Lyros were on their feet, battling Miranda across the cracked, scorched Ritual ground. She blocked the Star of Orthros once more, but her arm shook. As she spun to evade Night's Aim, her bare breastplate came into view. Cassia's blood really was gone.

They could win this battle. And if they could do that, they might win the war.

Cassia picked up the empty chalice and levitated blood from the Ritual circle to fill it. She rose to her feet and stood over her Grace. She didn't know what her power would do now, but she trusted it.

At her feet, Lio's Union Stone glowed once more. Hold.

Miranda traversed out of Mak and Lyros's reach, stumbling where she landed. Knight was on her in an instant and closed his jaws on her bloody sleeve. Her weakened arm broke a second time, and the weed hook fell from her hand.

"*Loma hoor!*" Before the command to retreat had left Cassia's mouth, Knight leapt clear. Miranda's fork of lightning struck the ground behind him as he raced toward Dame, the handle of the weed hook between his teeth. A smile came to Cassia's face. "*Oedann!*"

Miranda tossed tongues of flame to keep Mak and Lyros at bay while she healed. She was rationing her fire spells, and it took longer for her bleeding to stop this time.

Cassia lost sight of Mak in the smoke. Only the brush of a veil spell reassured her he was all right. Lyros faced Miranda head-on.

His whole body tensed. Cassia's heart lodged in her throat. Surely he wasn't about to try what she thought.

Lyros charged straight for the Overseer. She held out her empty hand and blew a gout of fire toward him.

He dropped low and rolled, a blur. For a terrible instant, Cassia couldn't see him. Had the fire hit him?

Then Lyros shot to his feet, untouched by Miranda's fire spell, in a flawless Martyr's Heart. He slid his spear up under her breastplate with Hesperine speed. Bracing the spearhead on her collarbone, he levered the leather armor off of her, snapping straps and her clavicle. Her breastplate fell away, leaving her in nothing but a necromancer's robe. Red light emanated from the scabbard across her chest.

She hacked at Lyros with her mattock. But it halted midair, then was hurled away. Eyes wide, she made to dodge, but an invisible force stopped her, too. Her arms were pinned to her sides, as if held by an invisible vice.

Mak's veils fell as he reached around her from behind and slipped Rosethorn out of the scabbard.

"Cassia, catch!" he called.

He tossed the blade, and it spun toward her. Her immortal reflexes took over. She caught the hilt midair.

The magic overflowing her chalice flowed into the dagger, honing to a focused current.

The Union Stones flashed. Now.

Cassia drove her power into all four of their weapons. Black roses sprouted from Rosethorn to twine around her hand. But from Final Word came moonflowers, while the Star of Orthros and Night's Aim sent blackthorn crawling over Miranda.

Mak's magic met Cassia's through the adamas. His new enchantment rang though their artifacts, and a resounding echo moved through the temple.

Kallikrates's voice disturbed the sacred air of Hagia Boreia. "Do you think this instant of victory matters? It is the blink of an eye, to be forgotten in my endless reign."

Heated air hurled Mak and Lyros away from him again. The dome exploded around Cassia.

Black chunks of stone hung suspended, as if the Collector had stopped the flow of time. Then they hurtled into the Ritual circle, closing in on her and Lio.

The pieces of the dome struck Mak and Lyros's wards and broke into smaller fragments. But they kept coming. Her Trial brothers shouted her name.

Cassia tilted her head. Something glimmered at her senses from inside each sliver of stone. Rock that could become soil. Blood that could become life. She touched the thousand fragments with her power, and shoots of green ate the stone, falling to her feet in a shower of leaves.

Kallikrates hurled more lightning through Miranda's hands. Cassia twitched her dagger, envisioning the proud cedars in the city of Haima. Saplings sprang up, lining the path to the Ritual Circle, and soared into mighty trees that drew the lightning. With a twirl of her wrist, she poured life back into their blackened branches, and they greened again.

Miranda stalked forward, and as she came, she hefted Lyros's fallen spear. Cassia held her power, letting her enemy come. Closer.

Miranda raised her arm to throw the spear. Blackthorn sprouted from the handle and turned on her, tearing into her flesh and shooting toward her eyes. With a yell, she dropped Night's Aim to claw the spiny branches off herself.

Mak rolled to his feet from a pile of rubble, the Star of Orthros in his grasp and a triumphant smile on his face. On the other side of the battleground, Lyros laughed and lifted his hand. His spear levitated back to him.

Rosethorn's Union Stone pulsed with a slow signal of concern from her Trial brothers. How was she holding up?

Cassia laughed. With this much magic, she could keep Kallikrates occupied until the next epoch. She shot power in the Union Stones, and they glowed like four red stars. No surrender.

Mak and Lyros let out a battle cry and closed in on Miranda again. The hounds took up the call and resumed their hunt.

The Black Roses wouldn't stand down until Lio won his battle.

Cassia lifted her cup high and splashed blood onto the ground at her feet. Vines of black roses tangled around Miranda once more. She shot lightning along their branches, but Cassia poured the life within her into the roses, and they did not burn.

At her command, the vines yanked the Overseer off her feet and dragged her forward. Cassia halted Miranda at her feet.

Looking into the Collector's eyes, Cassia yanked the pendant from around Miranda's neck.

"You have broken our bargain," he said.

"Save your breath. I don't negotiate with Old Masters."

With a dab of blood from within the chalice, she sealed her battered ambassador cords around her neck. Her medallion came to rest where it belonged.

The power in the cup and the dagger throbbed in her chest. All of the arcane felt perfectly in balance and ripe with endless potential. The whispers caressed her ears, and although she could not understand, she thought they spoke a blessing.

Her triune focus was complete.

The vines around Miranda tore suddenly. Her bloody hand emerged from her bonds, holding her relic blade. She lunged at Lio's prone form.

Dame cleared the rubble in one powerful leap and barreled into the necromancer. They rolled, landing with Dame's weight crushing Miranda. Spittle flew from the hound's jaws as she went for Miranda's face.

She scrabbled for the relic blade a hand's breadth away. Cassia shot a vine out and pulled the dagger toward her. A scream grated out of Miranda.

Then a blast of magic hurled Dame off her, and the hound fell heavily near Lio. Cassia's fresh fury and grief made her roses tighten around

Miranda's blade. But the dagger spun, cutting through the vine that bound it, and flew back to Miranda's hand.

The necromancer got to her feet, the mauled half of her face obscured with blood, and Kallikrates gazed at Cassia over Lio's body. "You remember how this game works. If he breaks the rules, I punish you. Now you have erred. I will punish him."

Lio landed in a crouch at the foot of the third door. He was closer than ever now.

Miranda lay where she had fallen, crumpled on the ground between him and the portal. She erupted into hoarse coughs, and her hand came away from her mouth covered in blood. As Lio approached her, she struggled to rise.

"Drunk on your victory?" The taunt wavered between her voice and the Collector's. "I'll humble you."

Lio planted the end of his staff on her clean breastplate and pushed her back down with little effort. Stealing Cassia's power had been Miranda's initiation as an Overseer. Had losing it also weakened her bond with Kallikrates?

"Is he worth this, Miranda?"

"You'll see the answer to that for yourself when he rules the world with me at his right hand and enjoys revenge on you as his eternal entertainment."

"Is that what you want? To spend the ages at his beck and call? There was a time when you wanted freedom."

"Power is the only real freedom."

"You could have power without him. Your power. Do you remember what that felt like?"

She laughed at him. "Little girls with necromancy don't have the luxury of power, Hesperine. My affinity was nothing but a prison sentence. Until it drew my master's interest and he showed me what I could become."

"I'm sorry no one else was there for you." He meant the words, although he doubted she would believe him. "You deserved better than

Kallikrates. A Hesperine wasn't there to rescue you then, but I am here now. I've freed people from him before, and I will do it again for you."

She spat blood at his feet. "I would rather die for the game than accept help from you, Deukalion. But I intend to survive to enjoy my reward from the Master. He has promised me the pleasure of killing you in front of him, slowly."

"You think you've chosen your side. But what kind of choice did you have? You turned to him out of desperation. You deserve to know what having a choice truly feels like. I will fight for you to have one, even if you won't fight for yourself."

"You can never break my bond with him." Her words were bold, but her fear ran down the walls of the passage and made pebbles skitter across the ground.

"It's not a bond. It's a chain. I will break it, no matter how this ends. Knowing that, will you tell me what lies behind the door? I don't want to cause you any more pain for his secrets."

"I'll fight you…with everything I have left."

She hurled her relic dagger at Lio. The attack scratched through his mind. He caught the hilt midair.

Your thirst for knowledge will be your undoing. The Collector's voice in Miranda's mind seemed to infiltrate Lio's own. *There is nothing more destructive than secrets. Why do you think they are my weapon of choice?*

Lio felt sick. He was holding Miranda's chain in the palm of his hand. But he knew what he had to do.

He drove the dagger into the door. Stone split stone. The door cracked open for the relic blade, and the final barrier in Miranda's mind fell to Lio's Will.

LIO STOOD IN A field that had been green, but now the tender crops lay trampled, and the mud ran with blood. He stared at the hues of orange and red that drenched the sky as a glowing ball descended toward the horizon. It was sunset on a battlefield in Tenebra.

A lone warrior stood with his boot propped on a corpse, the gore drying on his armor. In the distance, other men in his colors patrolled the field, piling bodies to be burned. But this man held himself apart. Waiting.

He reached up and pulled off his helmet. His blond hair was plastered to his head with sweat. When Lio saw the burn scar on the man's jaw, a shock of recognition hit him.

He was witnessing a moment from Lucis's past.

Lio found himself walking forward. He had no control over his own body. Panic stirred in his mind. He looked down at himself.

A black robe. A long beard. A quicksilver pendant in the shape of an Eye of Hypnos. He was experiencing this memory through the eyes of an undertaker.

A shiver moved through Lio's own consciousness. This was no remembrance of Miranda's. It had happened before Lucis's hair had turned white, when she and Cassia had not yet been born.

Lio opened his mouth and spoke. The Collector's voice came from his own lips, and he wanted to retch.

"I see that the last free lord who would oppose you lies dead under your heel. There is still the formality of the Full Council, of course, but allow me to be the first to address you as King Lucis. Congratulations."

Lucis pulled his sword out of the corpse and stepped forward. "My part is done. Are you here to uphold your end of the bargain?"

"I have already been generous." There was a faint warning in Kallikrates's tone. "The Orders would have discovered your magic long ago, had I not aided you in concealing your power all these years."

"And I've carved my way through every fucking swine who wants a crown, just as you asked."

"Don't pretend you didn't enjoy it."

Lucis's abrupt laughter mocked the dead men around them. "My reign has begun well enough. But I won't have it end like that of every other man who has called himself king—in the royal crypt. Or worse, with my head on a spike in the court of my successor. I need the power you promised me to become the next Mage King. I've seized the palace for us; now tell me what magic lies in the barrow under it."

The barrow. Was that what the doors had been guarding all along? A burial site?

"I will raise you above the so-called Mage King." Lio could taste the malice in the Collector's words. "But the only way to do that, my friend, is to destroy him."

Lucis barked another laugh. "Will you have me deface his statues and replace them with my own?"

"Oh, yes. I will take great pleasure in watching you erase his legacy. But better still, you will help me kill him."

Lucis's hand tightened on the hilt of his sword. "What necromancy is this?"

"Not necromancy. A spell by the witch he took to wife. Through her power, he has made a bid for immortality. He lies sleeping in the barrow she sealed around him. I have waited sixteen hundred years to remind him he is mortal."

Lio's own heart pounded somewhere in his distant body. His carefully thought-out theories had all been nonsense. A mythical tale was the truth.

The Mage King was still alive.

Lucis's face flushed, and heat wafted off him. "I've given half my life to our bargain, and all this time, you've been chasing an old wives' tale?"

"Calm yourself. The songs of the slumbering king are all true, I assure you. Haven't you seen enough impossible things in my company to take me at my word?"

Lucis's hard blue eyes glinted with wariness, but the heat faded to warmth. "Explain."

"You know I am ancient. It should not surprise you to learn that I was alive during the reign of King Lucian and the witch Ebah, who became Queen Hedera when they wed. In all my centuries of existence, I have seldom come to hate a pair of mortals so much."

Lucis scoffed. "What did he do, then? Steal her out of your bed?"

Kallikrates made a noise of disgust. "I would never go to such lengths for mere lust. I have greater concerns than the base desires of mortals. But these two thwarted my plans at every turn. Even in death, she deprived me of my revenge by leaving him alive, out of my reach, for their heirs to call upon for aid against me."

Lucis eyed him. "Well, well. Someone in history got the better of you. I'll keep that in mind."

Lio took a step toward Lucis. The warlord didn't draw back.

"His reign will end in a glorified royal crypt," Kallikrates said coolly. "Keep that in mind, as well."

"I've given my blood to claiming the throne of Tenebra, only to be told my predecessor from sixteen centuries ago isn't dead. If I must put the Mage King himself properly in his grave to get what should be mine, so be it. But I do hope there is more in it for me than another battle, or I may grow tired of our bargain."

"I suggest you adhere to our agreement to the letter, if you wish to get inside that barrow at all."

"Give me one reason I shouldn't leave him down there to rot, where he has been all along."

"Immortality."

Now Kallikrates had Lucis's attention.

"Your reign will not end at all," the Collector promised. "I will bestow his fire magic and his everlasting life upon you. Tenebra will be yours forever. And why stop your conquest here?"

"This witch's spell will work on me?"

"Yes. I have spent all this time becoming an expert on her magic."

"If you're willing to let me walk away with such a prize, there must be an even greater one for you."

"Of course."

Lucis waited.

"I assure you," Kallikrates said, "it would be of no interest to a pragmatic man such as yourself. But for me, a collector of arcane secrets, it is the endgame."

"You'll have no help from me unless I know the whole truth," Lucis said.

"Immortality isn't reason enough?"

"I must know what I'm fighting my way into."

"Ah, Lucis. Never one to hack blindly toward your goals, like the man at your feet. Fair enough. The witch queen left her husband behind not only as a champion for their descendants, but as the eternal protector of her legacy. He is guarding the source of her power." Lio felt the Collector's face twist in a smile. "You cannot imagine how long I have been chasing what she tried to keep from me."

Lio's mind reeled. Whatever he had imagined, it had not been this. He was certain of only one thing.

The power source Lucian was guarding belonged to Cassia.

Lucis crossed his arms. "So be it," he said at last, as if he had the choice to agree or disagree. But he was more tangled in the Collector's web than any of them. A covetous light in his eyes, he asked, "How do we open the barrow?"

"First, you must sire the witch's heir."

THE RELIC BLADE

THE BATTLEFIELD FLICKERED AROUND Lio. He sat in Agata's kitchen over a tray of apple tarts. Then across from Lucis in the solar while the king poured him a glass of wine.

Miranda's life and the Collector's secrets shuddered past each other until Lio fell through the cracks of her suffering mind. He landed on his hands and knees on a stone floor.

First, you must sire the witch's heir.

Lio could still taste those words on his tongue. The command that had ruled his Grace's mortal life. His belly heaved, and he emptied it, as if he could purge the Collector's evil from his mind.

"And you think you have the stomach to challenge me," Kallikrates mused.

Lio wiped his mouth and dragged himself to his feet to face the Collector. They were in the main hall of Paradum. At the head of the chamber, in Miranda's father's chair, sat Kallikrates.

Or at least a manifestation of him that he wanted Lio to see. He wore the black robe and pendant of the undertaker. Confident, elegant, he lounged there with his hooded face lost in shadow.

Miranda lay at his feet, insensate and bleeding. She had given him her love, her loyalty, her very Will. And this was all she was to him. Not a person. Merely another tool to be used until it broke.

Lio tested the fabric of the room. This was Kallikrates' final foothold in her mind, but he held on here with an iron grasp. Lio would not be able to free her without a fight.

He would have to fight even harder to free himself.

"You are too deep in the game now, Deukalion. You will never be free." Kallikrates stroked the crow that was eating out of his hand.

The bird had no heartbeat. Miranda's familiar? Or something more? Lio had seen it flying free in the ripe orchard. Coming to life in her hands when she had discovered her power.

He looked down at the dagger in his hand. If this was Miranda's chain, could the bird be her Will?

"Be careful," the Collector said. "You will hurt yourself on that blade."

"Your taunts no longer frighten me. You cannot make me doubt myself. You have suffered nothing but losses tonight, and I am not finished."

"I have known many like you who were consumed by the craving for knowledge. Few can look into the sun without burning their eyes. We all know how weak Hesperines are to the sun."

"Enough riddles. There is no genius in your plots. You have shaped and destroyed so many lives, and for what? Revenge. You are no better than any other petty man ruled by his rage."

Kallikrates chuckled. "You should know better. I will indulge in some revenge, yes, but that is not enough to satisfy me. I want the same thing you do. The power of the Silvicultrix."

Lio stalked forward. "You want her power for yourself. I want it for her."

"I would have made her more powerful than you ever can. Miranda has such sincere faith in my game. She is a knight who imagines herself a queen. But Cassia…I would have built her a throne. She believed in nothing. A superbly selfish being. She would have become my perfect, ruthless diamond if you had not ruined her with your weak-minded Hesperine principles."

"Those principles gave her the Will to refuse you. Ask yourself whose mind is weak."

"There is one pair in all of history I hate more than Lucian and Ebah. You and Cassia have that distinction."

"Lucian and Ebah were the complication in the previous round of the game, weren't they? They stood against you during the Last War, when you destroyed civilization to begin another cycle of suffering for the shadowlands."

Kallikrates laughed softly. "How innocent you are, to think the Last War was the destruction of civilization."

He kept using words as weapons to make Lio feel small. But Lio had now glimpsed one of Kallikrates's own memories, and that was the key for drawing the truth out of his lies.

Lio fortified his mental defenses and did the very thing he had been so angry at Cassia for doing. He kept Kallikrates talking. "How can this be? We're living in the same round as the last epoch?"

Kallikrates fed the crow another bit of apple. "At the true end of a round, we only preserve sufficient survivors to repopulate the board. We burn their scrolls and destroy all evidence of what they built. We take away their memories of their own families and the names of their gods."

"That was what you tried to do during the Last War," Lio realized, "but you failed. It was supposed to be the end, but the shadowlands survived. Lucian and Ebah helped save them."

"There is no saving the shadowlands. They belong to us, and so too will the Empire one day."

Lio took another step forward, going closer and closer to the shadow itself. "Ebah preserved her power in that barrow, where it will survive for future generations. You can't end this round unless you get inside to destroy the evidence."

"One more brittle door. Then the legacy of Cassia's ancestors will survive only in my mind. With that power, I will win the next round, too. This is already set in motion, and by the time you understand my strategy, there will be nowhere left on the board for you to move."

Lio laughed at Kallikrates. "This is why you hate us so much. Cassia's legacy will survive as long as she does, and I have made her immortal."

"Hesperines die a little more slowly than humans, but you still die."

"We didn't. We survived. As bravely as Lucian and Ebah resisted you, they alone could not have stopped you from finishing the round. There was another, even greater obstacle, wasn't there? Hesperines. We escaped and gathered the best of this epoch behind our Sanctuary wards. As long as Orthros stands, this round will never end."

"We can afford to be patient."

"You are not patient. All six of you are furious at being robbed of the conclusion of your game. And you most of all, Kallikrates. You relish this round, when the rules dictate you play with subtlety and secrecy. You were winning, weren't you? Until your playing pieces took their fates into their own hands and robbed you of victory."

There was a smile in Kallikrates's voice. "I am still winning."

"Not this time. This will be the last round. We will make sure of that."

Lio was only a pace away from Miranda now. He paused, holding so much latent thelemancy ready that his thought-form wavered. But the Collector made no move to stop him.

This was a trap. But Lio didn't know what would spring it, or what the consequences would be.

Miranda stirred, groaning. "Master?"

Kallikrates said nothing. She opened her eyes, and her gaze fixed on Lio standing over here with her relic dagger. Her chest rose and fell with a panicked breath.

For the first time, Miranda begged. "Please, Master. Any fate but this. Break me a thousand times more and let me earn my way back to you. Let me pay with my flesh. My magic. My pain. But don't let *him* destroy me."

"Stand and fight him, my champion. Show me you are still my greatest Overseer."

Miranda pushed herself up on her trembling arms. Blood still dripped down her chin. She got her legs under her, only for her knees to buckle. Her strength was gone.

Kallikrates had to know that. He was manipulating her. This was as much a trap for her as it was for Lio. But why?

"Stand!" Kallikrates's command echoed through the hall. "Defeat him, and you will have your reward. I will let you torture Cassia in front of him before you kill him for me, just as you have dreamed."

The crow fluttered as Miranda tried again to stand.

"My power is still with you, Miranda," the Collector crooned. "You are greater than Cassia will ever be. One night soon, she will be broken and humiliated before you and finally understand how powerful you truly are. I will listen with pleasure while she begs you for mercy, just as she did the night you took her magic. The way she wept as we hollowed her…I want to hear that again, don't you?"

Those taunts were designed to goad both Miranda and Lio into a rage. Why was Kallikrates pitting them against each other, when he could throw all his power at Lio through his Overseer?

There was only one explanation: he couldn't. Their bond was failing. Miranda was burning out. She had turned from a weapon into a weakness, one Lio had already exploited to steal Cassia's magic and the Collector's secrets.

Kallikrates wanted Lio to kill her for him and destroy his own link to the Collector's memories. And he believed Lio would do it.

Lio had tortured seven mages for the sake of slaughtered strangers, and the Collector knew it. He expected Lio to do even worse to Miranda because of how she had hurt Cassia. There were long nights when Lio had wanted to.

But once again, a Hesperine was about to defy the Collector's expectations.

Miranda lifted her head, glaring up at Lio through her ragged hair. Behind her, Kallikrates tightened his hand around the flapping crow. Lio adjusted his hold on her relic blade.

Miranda let out the battle cry and threw herself at Lio. The colors leached from the room as she drew on the last of her strength, aiming for the dagger.

Lio threw the blade, putting all the force of his mind magic behind the attack.

Miranda barreled into him. He caught her, holding her despite her feeble struggles. The relic blade flew true and landed in the Collector's heart.

His howl became a wind that blew the stone walls into smoke. The bird sprang free of his hand with a cry.

Miranda sagged against Lio. He scooped her up in his arms as the floor dissolved, and they fell together into the void.

Lio gathered the fragments of her thoughts into another mindscape. He dropped lightly to his feet before the Ritual Sanctuary of Hagia Boreia. The dome rose above them, whole and beautiful against the starry sky. Through the open doors, the great statue of Hespera smiled at them from among incense and shadows.

Lio laid Miranda's still form down on the threshold of the Goddess's

Sanctuary. There was no blood on her now, and her armor was gone. In the simple dress of an impoverished lady, she looked so young. So vulnerable.

The crow swooped down to nestle on her chest. She woke gently this time with a soft sound of question. She reached up to stroke the bird, so carefully, as if she feared it would fly away.

"Hespera gives us as many chances as we need," Lio said. "Here is your next one. Use it well."

And then he released her mind. She faded before his eyes in a swirl of black feathers.

As Miranda advanced on Lio's body, Cassia stepped in front of him. Blood ran fresh inside Hespera's Rose, circling his still form. She fed the libations of past heretics to the Lustra and conjured black roses around her Grace.

"I will—" Kallikrates declared again. But his deep, commanding tone faded into Miranda's own voice.

"I will—" she said. "I…will…"

Her relic dagger fell from her hand. The ancient stone artifact struck the floor and shattered into pieces.

The strength seemed to drain from her limbs. She stumbled forward into the Ritual circle and fell against Cassia.

Stunned, Cassia caught Miranda in her arms and eased her to the ground. Hoarse gasps wracked Miranda's body. She looked up at Cassia with fear and wonder and a question in her eyes. Just as on the day her necromancy had awoken and she had turned to Cassia to help her understand.

Her aura was pure. In that moment, she felt like the friend Cassia had once cherished. Cassia unclenched her hands from around her foci.

Lio had saved them both.

"What"—Miranda panted—"is happening—to me?"

Mak and Lyros drew near, their weapons at the ready, the hounds growling at their sides.

"It's all right," Cassia told them all. She stroked Miranda's hair. "You're going to be all right."

Cassia didn't know if that was true. Miranda's mortal body was covered in wounds only an Overseer could withstand. Had Lio restored her mind, only for the injuries of their physical battle to end her?

But if that was to be Miranda's fate, she would die free.

Cassia rocked her friend in her arms. She hoped her words would finally reach Miranda's heart, now that the Collector no longer ruled it. "I'm so sorry I betrayed you. I want you to know how much remorse I feel. I wish I could change our past. But I'm here for you now. I won't leave you."

Miranda clung to her. "Cassia…?"

She hadn't heard Miranda say her name like that in ten years.

The blood in the Ritual circle stirred. Mak sucked in a breath.

Lyros took a step back. "Cassia, is that your magic?"

"No. Could it be…?"

The circle pulsed with a myriad of magic left behind by all who had cast spells in defense of Hagia Boreia. Lio's thelemancy. Apollon's stone magic. And the healing affinity of Anastasios, their martyred foregiver.

As blood soaked into Miranda's necromancer robes, her wounds eased away. She drew one last deep breath, like a drowning girl breaking the surface at last.

Then a shock passed through her. Her gaze darted between Cassia, Mak, and Lyros. Recognition lit Miranda's eyes, then fear. She began to struggle.

Cassia released her, holding up her hands in a reassuring gesture. "You're free. Go somewhere safe where you can heal. Please, Miranda. Stay safe. Be well."

Miranda backed away, a lifetime of emotions reanimating her aura. A caw sounded from the sky, and her crow swooped down into her arms. With her familiar nestled against her chest, she disappeared.

"She traversed," Lyros said in astonishment. "She still has her magic."

Lio didn't merely save people. He made them whole. Cassia leaned over her Grace and took his face in her hands.

Lio? It's over. You won. It's safe to come back to us now.

Cassia! His arcane call sent a chill through her blood and pulled her in the depths of his mind.

The temple of Lio's mind shook. A pillar came crashing down, sending pain reverberating through his being. No. This shouldn't be happening.

Fire crackled behind him. He spun to see smoke billowing through the complex. The flames of the Last War flickered closer to him. He had to get out.

When a hooded figure in a black robe strode up the steps toward him, he knew who was taking control of the vision.

There was a tear in the chest of Kallikrates's robe. The relic blade hung from his hand. "You should have heeded my warnings about the dagger."

Cassia! Lio called.

I'm here.

Pull me back to you. Open our Grace Union with all your might.

Cassia's presence filled the Sanctuary behind Lio. Roses of every color flowed up from the ground and caught the falling pieces of the temple in their branches. Her vines embraced him and pulled him toward safety.

Lio hurled thelemancy at Kallikrates. The floor at his feet split open, and the air around him tore to reveal an endless sky. Lio looked into the seams of his own mind.

No. How was this possible? They were not in Miranda's thoughts anymore. Somehow, the Collector had exploited their link and followed Lio back into his own mind.

I'm holding you. Cassia echoed his own vow back to him. *No one touches your mind but me.*

Her power swept him back into the Ritual Sanctuary. The double doors slammed shut. Her roses twined up the Goddess's statue to close the skylight in the dome overhead.

The relic blade sliced through the vines above, and they both screamed. Lio clutched his head, crumpling to the floor, and met the Collector's unblunted power.

The agony of Miranda's attack in Hierax Temple had been nothing. Now Kallikrates cut through Lio's mental defenses with his own hands. His limbs seized, and his back arched off the floor. The mindscape around them wavered, flickering to blackness, then burning bright as fire.

Stay with me. Cassia filled his mind, and everywhere she touched, her presence dulled the pain of the Collector's attack. *You're not alone. We can defeat him together.*

Lio dragged himself to his feet. Smoke was pouring down through the skylight to fill the Sanctuary. From the billowing clouds before Lio, the Collector appeared.

Lio hurled another blast of his power at Kallikrates. The spell buffeted the Old Master's robes, and for an instant, his grimace was visible inside his hood. His gray lips stretched around his bared teeth, an image from the death throes of everyone he had sent to their graves.

His hand shot out, shrouded in black with long, sharp nails. Lio tried to dodge, but his own mind and body warped, throwing him into the Collector's grasp. Kallikrates grasped him by the hair and dug claws into Lio's skull.

Cassia's roses lashed out at Kallikrates. A spiral of vines closed around him like a shroud. But her thorns passed through his spectral form.

He forced Lio to his knees at Hespera's feet. "I am here to collect my price."

Lio's mind, his greatest strength, was fragmenting. The immutable pieces of himself shuddered and broke and rearranged. He reached for each certainty inside himself, only to find new voids where parts of him had been torn away.

He had never been so afraid.

Cassia! he called out to his Grace in desperation.

She was right there inside him, where she always was. He hadn't lost her yet.

He confessed the horror creeping into his every remaining thought. *I'm not sure I can stop him.*

Her love was in the void, filling the chasms in his fracturing mind. *I will stop him.*

I don't want you to go through this with me.

I know. But I will never leave you.

His Grace appeared before Hespera, her fangs bared in a snarl of fury. Her white avowal robes fluttered around her, untouched by the smoke. She held Rosethorn, dripping with blood over their chalice, and her pendant glowed on her chest.

She hurled her dagger at Kallikrates. Her power sailed through the landscape of Lio's mind toward the Collector's heart.

Kallikrates, faster than thought, drove the relic blade into Lio's throat. The statue of Hespera shattered into countless shards as Lio watched his own mind break.

LIO'S CRY OF PAIN died on the Collector's blade, but Cassia screamed for him. His jaw hung open. He lifted his hands to his neck, catching his own blood.

Words, thoughts, everything Cassia was ceased. She became her Grace's pain.

The Collector staggered away from Lio, his hands around the hilt of Rosethorn. He tried uselessly to pull her blade from his heart. A hole was growing from the wound, eating away his form to reveal a starry sky.

"You are no thelemancer, Cassia," Kallikrates hissed. "You have no power in his mind."

"I am the power in his mind."

The walls, the air, the sky above were a part of him and of her. Fractures were spreading across these manifestations of his tortured mind, and the dome above cracked a warning. But she was present in his every thought, and she would not let his innermost Sanctuary fall.

At her summons, the fragments of the Goddess's body spun around her. She hurled them all at Kallikrates.

A flurry of sacred stone shredded him. More bright stars shone through his wounds. His groan of shock echoed to the dome of the Sanctuary.

He had finally met a magic he could never collect. Grace Union was more powerful than him.

Cassia moved in front of Lio, pouring the strength of their bond into her dagger. Her black roses snaked out from the blade embedded in the Collector's chest. This time, they took hold of him.

As he opened his mouth to speak more poison, she wrapped her vines around his neck and squeezed. The voice from their nightmares halted in his throat.

Cassia raised a whorl of blood from the chalice. "I will cast you out. I will hunt you down, and when I find you, the price I collect will make you wish for the fleeting existence of a forgotten mortal."

She flung the blood at him. It splattered across his thelemantic form. Tiny cracks sounded, like frost eating at glass.

The Collector shattered. Shards of frozen blood scattered across the Sanctuary. As the smoke began to clear, the moons shone down through the skylight, making the crimson slivers glitter.

Cassia fell to her knees beside Lio and eased him onto his back. The relic blade was gone, banished with is creator. She pressed one hand to her Grace's bleeding wound and held her wrist to his mouth.

"Stay with me!"

His eyes slid shut. The walls of the Sanctuary disappeared, and they were kneeling in a vast expanse of stars.

"No! Hold on!"

She wrapped him in their bond. His heart beat with hers. But his mind faded beyond her reach.

THE WOUND

REALITY RETURNED IN PIECES. Her hand, covering Lio's unblemished throat. His lips, cold upon her wrist. Mak was holding him for her, massaging Lio's jaw. Lyros had his arm around her.

"I can't get him to bite." Mak's voice, angry, urgent.

Lyros pressed a strong hand to her forehead. "Cassia? Are you back with us?"

"I'm here," she said, dazed.

But Lio wasn't. Her heart raced, and she felt his matching pulse under her fingers. How could his mind be so far away?

"I—I can't reach him. Not even in Grace Union."

Thank the Goddess for Lyros's steady voice. "Try to describe how your Union feels. Does he seem asleep, unconscious? Or is his presence weakening?"

Cassia took a deep breath through her fear and focused on Lio's aura. "I can feel his mental wounds. His magic has never been like this. As if he actually exhausted it."

"Is it getting worse?" Lyros asked.

She caressed Lio's neck, listening, waiting. "No. He's not slipping away. But he's not coming back to me."

Mak swore and closed his hand around Lio's chin, pushing. Lio's fangs sank into Cassia's wrist. Mak took her other hand and showed her how to work Lio's throat.

Drink, she begged in their Union. *Please, Lio. Drink from me.*

Her Grace lay there, pale and still, while her blood trickled out of his mouth.

Dame nudged Lio with her nose, then licked his face. When he didn't respond, she let out a devastated whine. Knight leaned his bulk against Cassia. If not for him and Lyros, she thought she would collapse.

She fisted her hand, squeezing more blood onto Lio's tongue. "Why won't he swallow?"

"Cassia." Mak looked stricken. "What happened in there?"

She struggled for words while Lyros rubbed her back. She had to explain to them. For Lio's sake. "Kallikrates somehow followed him out of Miranda's mind and invaded his. The Collector made a mental attack on Lio that appeared in his mind's eye as a relic dagger in his throat."

Horror passed through Lyros's aura. "How did Lio break free?"

Cassia swallowed. "He couldn't."

Her Trial brothers said nothing, and the Blood Union was heavy with their dread.

"I banished Kallikrates," Cassia said. "I shut him out of our Grace Union."

Mak's eyes widened. "That's our Cassia."

She shook her head, her lips trembling. "I wasn't fast enough. Kallikrates still managed to strike a blow before I pulled Lio to safety."

She stroked his throat desperately, Willing him to swallow. Why wasn't her blood enough? Why had the Ritual circle healed Miranda, while it did nothing for Lio?

Mak slammed his fist down in the pool of blood. "Goddess above, where are our foregivers now?"

Cassia rested Lio's head on her lap, calling into their Union again and again, hoping to catch a whisper of his voice in her mind. "We have to find him a healer."

Lyros didn't hesitate. "Any chance of reaching Solia's forces in Hadria?"

"They Kyrian mages won't know what to do with this." Mak shoved a hand in his hair. "He needs a mind healer."

"Ukocha's village? Tuura could help, if we can avoid extradition."

"Is he stable enough to step that far?"

With calm words, Mak and Lyros fought for Lio. Cassia was so grateful for that. But listening to them try, she knew there was only one answer. "He needs Rudhira."

They fell silent. Lyros gripped her shoulder. "Yes. He does."

"You two can escape," Cassia said. "I will surrender and plead with them to put Lio in a bed, not a cell."

"We're coming with you," Mak told her.

Cassia's throat tightened. "Half of us should stay free for whatever comes."

"Not a chance," Lyros said. "We started this together. We finish it together."

She blinked hard. "You haven't even asked if Lio got the information we came for."

"Doesn't matter," Mak said. "No secrets are worth his life."

Lyros gave her a smile. "He got your magic. He would say that's what matters."

And this was the price he had paid to restore her power to her. She would save him, if she had to march into Kallikrates's own mind to do it.

"So, Black Roses," Mak said. "All agreed? Our quest ends at Castra Justa."

Lyros nodded gravely. "Victory or defeat, we face it as a circle."

"You have my gratitude," Cassia said.

"We'll be with you every step of the way, tonight and always," Lyros promised.

Mak eased Cassia's wrist off of Lio's fangs. "Let us step you."

Cassia picked up her dagger and avowal cup. "I don't want to move him. I'll bring the Charge to us."

Mak and Lyros exchanged a glance, but neither questioned her.

As she tapped into her power, the murmurs from her pendant grew louder. She sent out a lone wolf's call through the Lustra. Her heart beat. Again. A third time.

Kalos appeared at the edge of the Ritual circle. His gaze swept over them all and settled on her. "By Hespera's Cup and Habuch's Wings, do you know how glad I am you finally let me find you? I've spent every waking moment tracking you across the kingdom, fearing what had become of you. All we had to reassure us were tales. The Lustra itself hid your trail from me until I heard your call."

Kalos had seldom said so many words at once. She held out a hand to him. "I'm glad to see you, too."

He knelt beside her. "Silvicultrix, what can I do?"

"Bring Rudhira. He can do as he wishes with me, if only he will heal Lio."

"And we won't leave Lio and Cassia's side," Mak said. "Those are our terms of surrender."

Kalos shook his head. "Our prince doesn't want you to surrender."

"Ha," Mak replied bitterly. "What do you call his attempt to arrest us Paradum, then?"

"Soothsaying," Kalos said.

Lyros frowned. "What?"

A suspicion came over Cassia. "Kalos, please explain."

Kalos leaned forward, his hands on his knees. "Whatever words you thought you heard come from Rudhira's mouth, that's not what he truly said. It was because of the letting site's wounds. You saw how it affected the animals and plants, didn't you?"

Mak still looked wary. "Yes. The damaged beast magic scared them off."

"And the loss of Cassia's plant magic made the land barren," Lyros supplied.

Kalos nodded. "The third power of the Silvicultrix was running amok there, too. The corrupted soothsaying twisted Rudhira's words to you—and yours to him."

"I knew it," Cassia said. "I couldn't believe Rudhira would say such things. I sensed that something wasn't right. If only I'd trusted my instincts….my magic."

"What did he think we said?" Mak asked.

"I explained all of this to him," Kalos answered. "He knows you didn't mean what he thought you said, either. Please, hear him out when he comes."

"We'd appreciate a warning about Rudhira's frame of mind," Lyros said grimly.

Kalos rubbed the back of his neck. "He could explain it better. But Goddess forbid he talk about feelings. So I'll try." The scout gestured helplessly at them. "You're warriors. And Hesperines. You know how easy it is to blame yourself for things that aren't your fault. But he's also a healer, and our prince. He always fears he'll fail those of us who need him. Meeting you at Paradum rubbed that wound raw. He doesn't deserve to feel as guilty as he does."

Cassia had never thought of her Ritual father as someone who needed to be handled with care. But after everything the Black Roses had seen, she thought she understood what lay under Rudhira's eternal strength. And that gave her hope of clemency for Lio.

"We'll be gentle," she promised.

Relief crossed Kalos's face. "Hold on."

He stepped away. Mak and Lyros waited with her through the longest minutes of her eternal life.

At last, royal Hesperine power rolled through Hagia Boreia, a cleansing storm. Despair lifted from the Blood Union, and Cassia couldn't help but feel that deliverance was nigh.

The First Prince appeared before his mother Alea's Sanctuary with Thorn on his back and a red healer's satchel in hand. Cassia could read nothing on his pale, grim face, nor through his veil spells. But his magic wrapped around the Ritual circle and held all of them.

Before she could speak, Rudhira knelt beside Lio and tore open his satchel. "All of you are alive. Nothing else matters, do you understand me?"

She couldn't afford to feel weak with relief yet, but she did. She nodded.

Rudhira pressed his fingers to Lio's temples. "Can you tell me what happened?"

Mak and Lyros repeated what she had described to them, and she sent them her gratitude through their Union. She feared if she had to relive the duel again, she would lose what grasp on herself she had left.

She held onto Lio's hand in both of hers. Blood soaked into Rudhira's scarlet battle robe as he poured more theramancy into Lio's mind. The prince's magic washed over her Grace's wounds and filled his diminished aura. But their Union remained silent.

"Can you heal him?" Cassia finally asked, although she feared the answer.

JUSTICE

RUDHIRA MOVED HIS HAND to Lio's throat, and Cassia shuddered. The prince's eyes slid shut, and his fangs lengthened.

His magic blasted out from the center of the rose, and the blood in the thorns and petals overflowed the Ritual circle to spread across the ground. The prince's power rocked Hagia Boreia to its foundations, as cleansing as the enemy's attacks had been destructive.

Lio jerked awake and rose up, his mouth open in a soundless scream. He reached toward his throat, but Rudhira caught his hand and held on tight. "I've got you. It's over. Drink from your Grace."

Lio's lips moved. No words came. But he cried out for her in their Union, a wordless plea.

She wrapped him in her presence. *You're here with me. Everything will be all right now.*

His arm closed around her. She pulled his face to her throat. When he sank his fangs in and swallowed hard, everyone around them let out the breaths they'd been holding.

Cassia stroked his hair as he pulled desperately on her vein. The sweet ache of his bite made her feel the truth. *You're back with me.*

She looked at Rudhira over Lio's shoulder. "Thank you."

He touched her head, his eyes overbright. "I am so sorry I wasn't here."

"None of this is your fault," Mak burst out.

Rudhira put an arm around him and Lyros, pulling them to him. "I never meant for you to fight our battles for us. Alone. Not in Nike's forge and not in this war."

"They were our battles," said Lyros, "and we weren't alone."

Rudhira looked around them at the temple, then ran his hand through a cluster of Hespera's Roses. "I can see that. You'll have to forgive me if it takes me some time to accept it."

"There's nothing to forgive," Cassia said.

Rudhira sat back and ran a hand down his face. "Kalos told you about Paradum."

"Yes." Mak hesitated. "But I wouldn't mind hearing what you actually said."

"I wasn't searching for you," Rudhira said. "I was hunting Miranda."

"Yourself?" Lyros sounded as astonished as Cassia felt. "When there's a war and the Charge needs you in command? You could have sent someone…"

"I do not send my dependents to correct royal errors. The first time Lio and Cassia captured Miranda at Paradum, she escaped on my watch. If I hadn't allowed that to happen, the four of you wouldn't have needed to go on this suicidal quest at all. I was trying to apprehend her so you could interrogate her somewhere safe. That was all I wanted. To keep you safe."

"We couldn't have accepted safety in exchange for our freedom," Lyros said quietly.

"I would never arrest you." The Blood-Red Prince's anger vibrated through the temple. "We Blood Errant have so many bolt holes from here to Cordium that you could have evaded arrest—and your enemies—for however long it takes the Firstblood Circle to rise from their silken asses and recognize you for the heroes you are."

Lyros's eyes widened. "You were planning to help us escape?"

"Bleeding *thorns*, of course I was!"

"But Neana told us you gave her orders to arrest us," Mak said in confusion.

"The Charge had to believe I was upholding the law. And I had to make sure no Hesperines discovered where I was planning to hide you. I didn't tell anyone except Nike."

Mak looked at Rudhira with his most stubborn expression. "Cassia and I got ourselves arrested to protect my sister, and Xandra risked everything to help us avoid implicating you. We weren't about to let you aid us as fugitives."

Rudhira shoved a hand at the sword on his back. "I've been implicating myself with this blade for eight hundred years. And I have never suffered half the consequences that befell you in one night. I could not bear to live in my own skin for the next eight hundred if I didn't stand with you in this."

Cassia couldn't speak, but she reached out and squeezed Rudhira's hand.

"I tried to enlist your sister's aid." He looked chagrined. "Understandably, she is not in a charitable mood toward Hesperines after how we treated you. She informed me in no uncertain terms that even if she could get word to you from the warfront, she would sooner have me spend the Dawn Slumber in Cordium than trust your safety to me ever again."

Cassia bit her lip. Had that been a lovers' quarrel or a sign her sister didn't think of Rudhira that way? She had so many things to ask Solia when they could finally see each other again.

Lyros shook his head. "I'm sorry we thought we had to run from you all this time, but even if you'd offered us Sanctuary, we couldn't have accepted. We had to follow Cassia's magic to the Lustra sites. And, with all due respect, you could never have lured out Miranda as she did. We did what we had to do."

"I know," Rudhira rasped, "and I question the stars for it. Why couldn't I have at least made it easier for you?"

Mak rubbed his eyes. "Knowing you're on our side is enough."

"It's nothing like enough," Rudhira said. "I will not rest until you can walk through the streets of Selas, celebrated and not condemned. But for now, the best I can do is offer you refuge at Castra Justa."

Mak shook his head. "The firstbloods—even your own sister—question the Charge's mission enough without you also harboring criminals. That would implicate all our Hesperines errant, who are already making sacrifices for us."

Rudhira's red brows descended, and his fangs flashed. "Everywhere Hesperines walk outside the Queen' ward, I rule. Black Roses, as of tonight, you have an official pardon from the Prince Regent, and no one can question my decree."

Nights of fear drained out of Cassia's limbs. She held Lio closer, stroking his back. *Did you hear that?*

His muddled thoughts formed into a certainty of refuge.

Rudhira closed his satchel with a loud snap. "I would have issued the pardon sooner, but my hands were tied by my own sunbound Charge law. I had to wait for my sister's legal scroll on the matter to arrive on my desk at Castra Justa."

Cassia doubted her ears. "Master Kona helped you pardon us?"

"She has been scouring her own laws for some way to grant you clemency. When Neana returned to me with her Grace braid and word of the children you rescued, Kona finally had the basis she needed. Under the Law of Atonement, you served justice by delivering lives to safety, which earns forgiveness for your crimes. Since it happened on this side of the border, it's not enough to get you pardoned at home, but we will not give up on that, either."

Cassia couldn't quite take in the legal technicalities, but the result was clear. Lio would have a safe place to heal.

His jaw relaxed, and his eyes slipped shut again.

Cassia tightened her arms around him. "Rudhira—"

He eased Lio onto his back again. "He has enough of your blood in him for now. Let his mind rest. We'll know more about his condition when I get him to the Castra."

Cassia tried to brace herself for harsh truths, but she was out of armor. "What should we expect when he wakes?"

Rudhira's voice was gentle now. "I don't know. I have never seen an attack like Kallikrates is capable of. What I can say for certain is this: the only reason Lio is alive and sane right now is because of how you fought for him."

She wanted to believe that. But she kept seeing the dagger plunge into Lio's throat. Was there something she could have done to protect him from that blow?

"Look at me, Cassia." It was a command from her prince, and yet an offer of comfort from her Ritual father.

She lifted her gaze.

"You saved him," Rudhira said. "That is all you need to remember about this night."

She knew she would see the battle in her dreams. "I'll try to remember that."

Mak put his arm around her. "We'll be here to remind you."

"You all fought well." Rudhira's gaze swept over the carpet of Hespera's Roses that covered the ground, the Sanctuary Roses that shored up the ruins, and the thorned vines with their black blooms that stood guard. "Our Goddess's flower, growing in Hagia Boreia again."

"The destruction we brought here grieves me, though," Cassia said.

"Don't grieve," Rudhira replied. "Anastasios would rather have a garden like this as his memorial than a cairn. When my mother Alea hears of it, she will say our youngbloods have brought her temple back to life."

Cassia had spent so many nights despairing over what the Queens must think of her now. She drew hope from Rudhira's prediction that the Annassa would think kindly on tonight's events.

Rudhira beckoned to her, Mak, and Lyros. "Now come away from reminders of our martyrs. There is a living fortress of our Goddess, and I promise it will feel like home. Your horses are in my stables, and we've been making the fortress ready for you while we waited on the pardon."

As they gathered their belongings, Cassia hesitated over the pieces of the relic dagger. "What should we do with this?"

"Miranda left an artifact behind?" Rudhira asked sharply.

"Do you want it for study?" Lyros asked.

"It should go in the vault at Castra Justa," the prince answered. "There's a warded bag in my satchel. Be careful."

Mak and Lyros collected the dagger for him while Cassia retrieved her foci and took charge of Lio's scroll case and Final Word.

"What will we do for a stretcher?" she asked.

"Nonsense. I will carry him myself." Rudhira rose to his feet, lifting Lio in his arms. A bloodborn was no small burden to carry, but their prince appeared deeply grateful to have this one safely in his arms.

Cassia kept hold of her Grace's hand as Mak and Lyros gathered around them. The hounds came obediently, quiet in response to their pack's somber mood.

Rudhira quirked an eyebrow at Dame. "I am stepping *two* liegehounds into my fortress?"

"She isn't a liegehound anymore." Lyros put a defensive hand on Dame. "She's a Hesperine's familiar."

Rudhira shook his head. "That is a tale all of the Charge will want to hear."

"Lio can tell it to you when he wakes up again," Mak said staunchly.

Cassia was grateful for his encouraging words, but a chill of unease slid down her throat.

Rudhira's power bolstered them and carried them away from the fields of their battles. Cool, moist air enveloped them, and a river rushed in the near distance. Cassia stepped foot on green earth, and the vibrant Lustra murmured with interest.

They stood at the top of a cliff, with a long drop behind them and the gates of Castra Justa before them. The portcullis began to rise.

Mak craned his neck to look up at the massive fortifications. "The Fortress of Justice, in the flesh."

Lyros took Mak's hand. "From the night you forged your first adamas, I should have known you would lead us somewhere glorious."

The fortress dominated the bluff, built of the sharp gray stone of Tenebra's eastern wilds. The tall towers and layers of walls might have passed for a Tenebran castle, if not for the shining auras of the Hesperines within.

A banner flew over the keep, emblazoned with a lion, a star, a red crown, and a midnight-blue moon. Another was rising below it. Chill mountain wind caught at their robes, and the banner unfurled to display four black roses. Cassia pressed a hand to her mouth.

"I can't give you a victory parade to House Annassa—yet—but I can give you this." Rudhira led them into his stronghold.

Two crowds of Chargers packed the courtyard beneath black banners, and the aisle between them was scattered with black rose petals. The cheer that went up among the Hesperines errant split Cassia's immortal ears, and she had never heard anything more wonderful.

As Rudhira led their procession, carrying Lio between the onlookers, they reached out their hands to touch Cassia's slumbering Grace in benediction. Blessings in Divine and all the languages of the Empire wrapped her up and filled the Blood Union.

The prayers gave way to cheers as she, Mak, and Lyros passed. Orthros's bravest shouted their names. The epithet of their errant circle roared across every courtyard they passed through on their way deeper into the fortifications. Kalos cheered loudest of all, calling out the dogs' names. At his instigation, an entire fortress of Hesperines was soon celebrating liegehounds as if they had never been enemies.

Mak and Lyros lifted their joined fists over their heads, and a fresh wave of cheers erupted. Cassia levitated and raised her and Lio's avowal cup for all to see. As the emotions of her people rolled through her, she let them out in a spell that conjured black roses to line their way to the heart of the fortress.

The enormous oak doors of the keep stood wide open in welcome. Before Cassia saw who waited in the doorway, their love and pride swelled in her chest.

Apollon and Nike stood shoulder to shoulder, him in a golden battle robe, her in full Stand regalia of black and silver. Cassia had never seen the artifact her Grace-father held, but there was no mistaking the heavy adamas hammer. She had never imagined she would see Apollon's famous Hammer of the Sun in his hand. But after nearly a century, he had taken it up tonight in their honor.

Cassia's Ritual mother stood at attention with her round shield on her arm. The Chalice of Stars was black as the sky, glittering with celestial symbols as bright as the stars. But at Nike's waist hung a sword that sent a thrill down Cassia's spine. The curved blade with a golden filigreed hilt was one of the Fangs, Methu's long-lost pair of swords. The first bloodborn was with them in spirit.

When Rudhira reached the doors, Nike thumped a bleeding fist on her shield. The Blood Errant's Union Stones flared bright in the signal for victory. Mak lifted the Star of Orthros, and his sister's sign flashed through the Black Roses' weapons.

Borne on the voices and feelings of the crowd, they followed Rudhira into the Sanctuary of his keep. Apollon and Nike, like an honor guard, closed the doors behind them.

Then they were alone with the Blood Errant in a great hall. Here, the illusion of a Tenebran hold lord's castle ended. Peaked arches and vaulted ceilings made Cassia feel as if she had walked into Orthros. Beneath a blood-red stained glass window at the head of the room stood an intricately carved wooden throne.

They were in the First Prince's domain now.

Cassia went into Apollon's outstretched arms. He said nothing, only held her in his familiar, ancient strength. She felt safe for the first time since she had picked up her blade.

She drew deep, steadying breaths to keep from sobbing. "You're in Tenebra. Oh, Goddess, I'm so glad you're here."

He patted his chest. "And Komnena is only a thought away."

Nike had collared Mak and Lyros and showed no sign of letting them go. She hid her face against her brother's hair. "Nothing—nothing—has ever been as hard as not coming after you. I would have followed you to Cordium and back and fought at your side, my quest be sunbound. You know that, don't you?"

Mak grinned.

Nike sniffed. "But I thought you wouldn't want that. You protected our borders and our family while I was errant. This time, you needed me to stay, so you could go. Didn't you?"

"You understand," Mak said.

"Better than anyone." She drew back, running her hand over Lyros's hair as if to reassure herself he was in one piece. Then she met Mak's gaze. "I'm proud of your weapons. Don't ever doubt it."

This time when Cassia took Lio's cold hand, her Grace-father was at her side. Apollon held out his arms. "Let me take him."

Rudhira lifted his head, his magic ebbing, and handed Lio to his father. As Apollon cradled his son in his arms, Cassia felt the grief that passed through his blood.

"Come," Rudhira said. "I have a room for him upstairs."

He showed them to a modest chamber high in the keep, where an arched window looked out on untamed wilderness. There was a weapon rack for Final Word and Rosethorn, and a shelf held a small treasure trove of scrolls. Empty pots covered every surface, ready for plants. Cassia suspected Kalos had taken up a collection. Her gardening satchel hung from a hook on the wall, safe and sound.

The most luxurious residence could not have made her feel more welcome. For the foreseeable future, this was home.

A bed was waiting for Lio with clean, Imperial cotton sheets and the soft wool blankets pulled back. She adjusted the pillows as his father carried him over.

There was a century of sadness in Nike's aura. "Why is history so cruel to the bloodborn?"

Rudhira put an arm around her shoulders and shook his head.

She beckoned Mak and Lyros toward an adjoining door. "I'll show you your bunks, Stewards."

Mak hugged Cassia one more time before he and Lyros left with Nike. "We're right through that door if you need us."

Apollon laid Lio in the sheets, and Cassia sat on the edge of the bed. Even in sleep, tension lingered around his eyes and mouth. She pressed a hand to his chest just to feel his heart beating with hers.

Rudhira sank into a chair by the bed. "Now we wait."

54

nights after

WINTER SOLSTICE

THE MOST POWERFUL MAGE OF THIS EPOCH

H E HAD NEVER KNOWN such silence. But she broke it, calling. Or was she a dream?

He drifted. She kept trying to show him the way back. At last, his mind followed her.

He opened his eyes, and they came gradually into focus. There were flowers everywhere. What were they called? He only knew they meant he was somewhere safe. The furred beast beside him meant protection, too.

Familiar faces surrounded him. Their auras inundated him, but he couldn't put a name to the shades of power flowing across his senses.

They were everything to him. Where were their names?

He dug into the depths of his memory. Pain shocked through his throat, and his mind went numb.

She brought him back again. She stroked his face with a freckled hand. She was real. His other heart.

His life depended on her name. He dug deeper, gritting his teeth.

There was nothing but the pain.

He had once known words. He knew they should come easily to him. Why couldn't he find them?

She flowed into his mind. The emptiness filled with her voice. *Lio.*

That was his name?

He groped desperately for her thoughts. Her lips parted, and she rested her forehead against his.

Words rushed into his mind. All his words were still inside her, safe, true. She had guarded them for him.

Cassia, he cried in relief. *My Grace.*

She heaved a sigh. *You know me.*

I always knew you. But I... Shame halted his confession.

No, Lio. You have nothing to be ashamed of. Someone did this terrible thing to you, and it isn't your fault.

She had kept this memory for him too, protecting him from it. The Collector's shrouded face, his clawed hand. The inevitable blade. Pain so unimaginable, no words for it had ever existed in his mind.

He squeezed his eyes shut. *I lost your name. Until you gave it back to me. I will give everything back to you.*

The words in her thoughts took shape in the air, and he relearned the sound of speech. "He knows me. He was so confused at first, but he's speaking in our Grace Union now."

Lio looked around him again, letting their names run through his mind. Mak and Lyros, his Trial brothers. The great, drooling lump on the bed was Dame, watching over Lio in his sleep as surely as he had done for her. Knight sat just as faithfully beside Cassia.

A strong hand squeezed his shoulder. "Son?"

There were many names for the blond lion sitting beside his bed, but the one he cherished most was *Father.*

The Blood Errant were here. Nike stood sentinel by the window, and in another chair next to Lio's bed sat Rudhira.

When he saw his Ritual father, more memories came flooding back. *Did I dream it...or did he bring us to Castra Justa?*

You remember.

He gripped her hand. They had turned themselves in while he lay helpless to defend them. *I won't let you pay this price for my healing. As soon as I have the strength, I will fight our way out of the First Prince's own fortress, if that's what it takes.*

Amusement glinted in Rudhira's eyes. "You can stop staring daggers at me. Stand down, Hesperine errant. No one is under arrest."

Cassia smiled and shook her head. *We are pardoned in all of Orthros Abroad because of the children.*

The tension drained out of Lio. They could stop running. All because of the young mortals she had saved. She had saved everyone. But she had fought hardest of all for him.

He opened his mouth to say her name aloud, but no words came from his throat. He sucked in a breath, then let it out in a shout that made no sound, only sent his frustration blasting through the Blood Union.

Cassia put her hands on his shoulders to keep him from sitting up. "Easy. Be gentle with yourself, my love. You need time to heal."

He didn't need words to understand the fear creeping into her heart. *How long was I unconscious?* he asked.

You've been in and out for eight nights.

Shock jolted through him. *Cassia, your Craving—*

Whenever we woke you to give you my blood, Rudhira drew some of yours to keep me well and cycle your healing faster.

Lio grimaced in disgust. His Grace, drinking out of a tube for a week.

Cassia straightened his blankets. *Rudhira has barely left your side. Nike and your father visit every night and take news of your progress back to Orthros.*

Eight nights of his Grace's blood and the First Prince's healing, and Lio still couldn't speak. What had Kallikrates done to him?

Lio took another deep breath, drawing in Cassia's scent. He had to calm himself for her sake.

No you don't, she replied to his unspoken thoughts. *Be as angry and frustrated and sad as you wish. I'm here for you. Anything you need.*

I need to understand what's happening to me. Can Rudhira tell us what's wrong with me and how long it will last?

"Rudhira, he's asking for you to explain his wound and give him a prognosis."

Mak quirked a smile at Lio. "Such a scrollworm, even after getting your brain turned to jelly by a necromancer having a tantrum about his broken toys."

Lyros crossed his arms. "You should hear the other fellow's voice. Kallikrates is screaming into his own void after that defeat."

Lio cracked a smile.

Rudhira exchanged a glance with Lio's father, who nodded. Rudhira pulled his chair closer to Lio's bedside. When his father clasped his wrist, bracing, Lio realized he was not about to hear good news.

This couldn't be right. There was nothing the Gift couldn't heal.

Rudhira leaned his arms on his knees, knitting his fingers. "First, what we know. Your body is in perfect health. Nothing physical is causing your inability to speak. This is a purely thelemantic wound, and the mind is more far more intricate and challenging to heal, even for Hesperines."

But Hesperines are immune to essential displacement, Lio protested to Cassia. *Kallikrates shouldn't have been able to take anything from me.*

"He didn't possess you or try to take your magic," she reassured him. "We believe this spell was something entirely different."

Nike finally spoke. "Essential displacement is only one of the arcane techniques the Old Masters use. They have many more secrets that the people of this epoch have unlearned."

Rudhira's jaw tightened. "Which brings us to what we don't know. I've consulted with my mother Soteira, as well as Tuura and her theramancer colleagues. Argyros has convened a circle of mind mages to investigate. Your wound is new to all of us."

Impossible. The greatest minds of Orthros and the Empire had to come up with an answer. *How long long is this research going to take?*

Cassia passed Lio's question on to Rudhira.

"As long as it takes," his Ritual father said. "This is what I want you to know with absolute certainty. We are all fighting for you. I will make Orthros regret that you and your circle were abandoned in the field, in fear of your own people. I will make this right."

Lio looked up at the ceiling. This couldn't be happening. No matter how much of a warrior he had become, his words had always been his greatest strength.

And Kallikrates had known that.

Lio sought Cassia's gaze. *Did you see what I learned in Miranda's mind?*

Yes. But I haven't talked with everyone else about it yet. We've all been focused on you.

Bitterness rose up in Lio. *You'll have to tell them for me.*

I don't care about my inconveniently alive ancestor or Kallikrates's ill mood about his precious game. My Grace is wounded, and I would tie the whole world up in thorns to make them wait while you heal.

He tugged on his Grace braid in her hair and tried to smile for her. *I don't doubt you would. But can I ask you to do something else for me?*

Of course. Don't you dare try to be self-sacrificing right now. Always tell me what you need.

It's important to me that you tell them what I learned. He gestured at his throat. *So this doesn't feel like it was for nothing.*

Her expression softened. *Of course.*

Their Trial brothers and the Blood Errant listened as Cassia related the long-sought secrets he had finally managed to pry from Kallikrates. A stunned silence followed.

Only Lio's father let out a bemused huff. "So Lucian managed to outlive the Last War like the rest of us. Good for him."

Rudhira raised his ginger brows. "Solia won't be pleased to hear there's another contender for the throne."

"He's a reasonable man," Apollon said. "He swore the Equinox Oath with us, after all."

"That's what we've been fighting for this entire time?" Mak was flushed with anger. "That's why Lucis made Cassia's life a misery and Kallikrates wounded Lio? For one sleeping mortal?"

"Yes and no," Cassia said. "The Mage King isn't the prize in the barrow. What he's guarding is."

Lyros put a hand to his chin. "Yes. This has always been about the Changing Queen's magic."

Cassia nodded. "Kallikrates called the barrow the 'source of the Silvicultrix's power,' and he told me that his ultimate goal is unlimited magic. We also know one of Kallikrates's greatest limitations is that the people he possesses will die if he uses too much magic through them."

Lio hadn't had time to analyze the details. But Cassia had clearly been thinking through them all, and the implications sent dread creeping over him.

"He wants what we Silvicultrixes have always had," Cassia said. "The ability to channel unlimited power from the Lustra without burning out."

Despite all the things Nike had seen, the color drained from her face. "If an Old Master achieves that, there will be no hope for any of us."

Cassia straightened, sitting on the edge of Lio's sickbed with dignity, her aura shining far beyond the small room. "This is why Kallikrates has demeaned and destroyed women like me. He is jealous of us—and terrified of our power. He should be afraid, because I will gain my other two affinities and use them to beat him to that door. When I open the barrow, a Hesperine will become the most powerful mage of this epoch."

Threefold power pulsed gently in the pendant around Cassia's neck, the dagger in the nearby weapon rack, and their avowal cup on the table beside his bed. Her magic bled into the roses in the room, and their buds unfurled.

Lio realized why she had surrounded him with her flowers, the evidence of her power. Everywhere he looked, he saw not what they had lost, but what they had gained.

Lio had told her he would get her magic back, no matter the cost. Now he knew what the cost had been.

He wouldn't trade those roses for his voice. He may have come away wounded, but he had won his duel with the Collector.

Three words were so clear in his mind, and he said them to Cassia in their Union. *I love you.*

I love you so much, my Grace. I'll show you how grateful I am that you gave me back my power. I swear I will give you back your voice.

Lio reached out to touch their avowal cup. If anyone could keep that promise, his Grace could. He believed she could do anything.

You will do more than win the game, my rose. You will end it.

Join Cassia on her quest to restore Lio's voice in
Blood Grace Book 9, *Blood Ritual*.
Get notified when the next book is available:
vroth.co/ritual

GLOSSARY

Abroad: Hesperine term for lands outside of Orthros where Hesperines errant roam, meaning Tenebra and Cordium. See **Orthros Abroad**

adamas: strongest metal in the world, so heavy only Hesperines can wield it. Invented in secret by Nike.

affinity: the type of magic for which a person has an aptitude, such as light magic, warding, or healing.

Agata: the cook at Paradum, who took Cassia and Miranda under her wing when they were girls. After Miranda's essential displacement of Cassia's magic cost the lives of everyone in the castle, Miranda reanimated Agata as a greater bloodless.

Aithourian Circle: the war mages of the Order of Anthros, sworn enemies of the Hesperines, who have specialized spells for finding and destroying Hespera worshipers. Founded by Aithouros in ancient times, this circle was responsible for most of the destruction of Hespera's temples during the Last War. Oversees the training of all war mages from Tenebra and Cordium to ensure their lifelong loyalty to the Order.

Aithouros: fire mage of the Order of Anthros who personally led the persecution of Hespera worshipers during the Last War. Founder and namesake of the Aithourian Circle, who continue his teachings. Killed by Hippolyta.

Akanthia: the world comprising Tenebra, Cordium, Orthros, and the Empire.

Alea: one of the two Queens of Orthros, who has ruled the Hesperines for nearly sixteen hundred years with her Grace, Queen Soteira. A mage of Hespera in her mortal life, she is the only Prisma of a temple of Hespera who survived the Ordering.

Alexandra: royal firstblood and Eighth Princess of Orthros, the youngest of the Queens' family. Solaced from Tenebra as a child, the only Hesperine with an affinity for fire. A youngblood of the Eighth Circle who raises silkworms for her craft.

Alkaios: one of the three Hesperines errant who saved Cassia as a child. He retrieved the ivy pendant from Solia's body for her. He and his Grace, Nephalea, recently settled in Orthros after years as Hesperines errant with his Gifter, Nike.

Anastasios: Ritual Firstblood who Gifted Apollon, founder of Lio's bloodline. He was a powerful healer and Prismos of Hagia Boreia, who sacrificed his life to help Alea protect their Great Temple from the Order of Anthros's onslaught.

ancestors: forebears who have passed into the spirit phase. Imperial mages can commune with them to channel their power into spells and rituals. Hesperines cannot contact the ancestors or wield ancestral magic because their immortality prevents them from entering the spirit phase.

Andragathos: god of male virtue and righteous warfare in the Tenebran and Cordian pantheon. The seventh scion and youngest son of Kyria and Anthros. A lesser deity alongside his brothers and sisters, the Fourteen Scions. See **Knightly Order of Andragathos**

Annassa: honorific for the Queens of Orthros.

Anthros: god of war, order, and fire. Supreme deity of the Tenebran and Cordian pantheon and ruler of summer. The sun is said to be Anthros riding his chariot across the sky. According to myth, he is the husband of Kyria and brother of Hypnos and Hespera.

Apollon: Lio's father, an elder firstblood and founder of Orthros. In his mortal life before the Ordering, he was a mage of Demergos. Transformed by Anastasios, he was the first Hesperine ever to receive the Gift from one of the Ritual firstbloods. Renowned for his powerful stone magic and prowess in battle, he once roamed Abroad as one of the Blood Errant. Known as the Lion of Orthros. Now retired to live peacefully in Orthros with his Grace, Komnena.

apostate: rogue mage who illegally practices magic outside of the Orders.

arcane: of or related to magic, as opposed to mundane.

Archipelagos: land to the west of the Empire comprising a series of islands, which maintains strict isolation from the rest of the world. See **Menodora**

Argyros: Lio's uncle and mentor in diplomacy and mind magic. Elder firstblood and founder of Orthros from Hagia Anatela, Gifted by Eidon. Graced to Lyta, father of Nike, Kadi, and Mak. An elder firstblood and founder of Orthros like Apollon, his brother by mortal birth. Attended the first Equinox Summit and every one since as the Queens' Master Ambassador. One of the three most powerful thelemancers in history, known as Silvertongue for his legendary abilities as a negotiator.

Ariadne: an apprentice mage of Kyria who helped the Hesperine embassy take Zoe and the other Eriphite children to safety. Traveled to Orthros for the Solstice Summit and supported Solia's bid for the throne at Castra Patria. Eudias's secret love.

Arkadia: Lio's cousin, daughter of Argyros and Lyta. Solaced from Tenebra as a child. With her mother's affinity for warding and aptitude for the battle arts, she serves as a Master Steward in Hippolyta's Stand.

Armory of Akofo: armory on an island off the coast of Haima, named for Prometheus's human father. Hesperines and Imperials visiting Orthros Notou must secure their armaments here before entering the city.

Ashes: band of mercenaries renowned for their great deeds in the Empire. Hoyefe, Karege, and Tuura are the current members under Kella's command. Retired members include Solia, Tendeso, and Ukocha, their former leader.

Astrapas: Timarete's Grace and Lyros's father.

Athena: three-year-old Eriphite child Solaced by Javed and Kadi. Younger sister of Boskos by birth and blood. The severe case of frost fever she suffered as a mortal damaged her brain. While the Gift has healed her, she is still recovering lost development.

Autumn Greeting: ancient courtship festival of Tenebra. When a woman shares this dance with a man, it is considered a promise of betrothal, after which their fathers will arrange their marriage.

avowal: Hesperine ceremony in which Graces profess their bond before their people. Legally binding and an occasion of great celebration.

Ayur: Azarqi goddess of the moons.

Azad: a Ritual tributary of Blood Komnena, Gifted by Apollon, who became a warder in the Prince's Charge. Avowed to Neana.

Azarqi: nomads of the Maaqul Desert who control trade routes between Vardara and the rest of the Empire. Known for their complex politics, the Azarqi were the original negotiators of the Desert Accord with the jinn.

Baruti *or* **Baru**: Hesperine scholar and Fortress Master in the Prince's Charge; a theramancer and the librarian of Castra Justa, responsible for dangerous magical tomes and artifacts Chargers discover in the field. Began his mortal life in the Empire and chose to become a Hesperine at the First Prince's invitation; alumnus of Capital University.

Basir: Hesperine thelemancer and one of the two spymasters of Orthros alongside his Grace, Kumeta. From the Empire in his mortal life. His official title is "Queens' Master Envoy" to conceal the nature of their work.

beast magic: type of Lustra magic that gives those with this affinity the power to influence animals and, if very powerful, to change into animal forms. See **changer**

Bellator: Tenebran free lord who kidnapped Solia and held her for ransom inside Castra Roborra. Led the short-lived rebellion that ended there with the Siege of Sovereigns. Father of Benedict.

Benedict: First Knight of Segetia, Flavian's best friend, who harbors unrequited love for Genie. Traveled to Orthros as Lord Titus's representative during the Solstice Summit. The son of Bellator, he carries guilt over his father's treason and seeks to atone by supporting Queen Solia.

Blood Errant: group of four ancient and powerful Hesperine warriors who went errant together for eight centuries. See **Apollon, Ioustinianos, Pherenike, Prometheus**

blood magic: type of magic practiced by worshipers of Hespera, from which the power of the Gift stems. All Hesperines possess innate blood magic.

Blood Moon: Hesperine name for one of the two moons, which appears red with a liquid texture to the naked eye. Believed to be an eye of the Goddess Hespera, potent with her blood magic.

Blood Shackles: warding spell cast with blood magic, which compels a person to not take a particular action. Persists until they are released by a key, a magical condition determined by the caster.

Blood Union: magical empathic connection that allows Hesperines to sense the emotions of any living thing that has blood.

Blood-Red Prince: see **Ioustinianos**

bloodborn: Hesperine born with the Gift because their mother was transformed during pregnancy.

bloodless: undead, a corpse reanimated by a necromancer, so called because blood no longer flows through its veins, although it has a semblance of life. Often used as an insult by Hesperines.

Bosko *or* **Boskos**: eleven-year-old Eriphite child Solaced by Javed and Kadi. Elder brother of Athena by birth and blood. Zoe's best friend. Harbors anger over what the children suffered. Training to become a Steward is helping him adjust to life in Orthros.

Btana Ayal: "Shattered Hope," the ruins of an ancient city that flourished in the Maaqul Desert during the Hulaic Epochs. Under the leadership of the Diviner Queen, the people of Btana Ayal traveled to Tenebra via a spirit gate. Their encounter with the other continent ended in tragedy when the Diviner Queen had to collapse the gate to prevent the Old Masters from invading the Empire. The resulting magical cataclysm destroyed the city.

Callen: Perita's loving husband, once Cassia's bodyguard who escorted her to the Solstice Summit. Now a decorated soldier in Lord Hadrian's army who fights for Queen Solia's cause.

Cassia: new Hesperine recently transformed by her Grace, Lio. One of the only Lustra mages ever to become immortal, she has a rare unified duality of plant magic and blood magic. Serves Orthros as one of the Ambassadors for Tenebran Affairs in partnership with Lio. As a mortal, she was born the illegitimate daughter of King Lucis and his concubine, Thalia. She worked secretly with Lio to secure peace with Hesperines and now supports her beloved sister Solia's effort to overthrow their sire.

Castra Augusta: fortress in Segetia belonging to one of Flavian's allies, a Knight Commander in the Order of Andragathos. A key stronghold in defending Segetia and Tenebra as a whole from invasion from the south.

Castra Justa: the stronghold of the First Prince and base of operations for the Prince's Charge.

Castra Patria: the ancient fortress at Patria that dates from the Mage King's time, where the Council of Free Lords convenes.

Castra Roborra: fortress in Tenebra belonging to Lord Bellator where he held Solia captive. Site of the Siege of Sovereigns.

Chalice of Stars: Nike's legendary round shield, which she uses along with the Stand's hand-to-hand combat techniques.

changer: practitioner of Lustra magic with the power to take on animal form.

Changing Queen: Queen Hedera of Tenebra, the Mage King's wife and co-ruler during the Last War. A powerful Silvicultrix known as Ebah among her own people, the Lustri. Also called the Hawk of the Lustra and associated with her plant symbol, ivy. Cassia's ancestor through her mother, Thalia.

channeling: when a mage draws power from a source greater than themselves, instead of from an innate store of magical power. Progonaia and hulaia rely on channeling.

the Charge: see **Prince's Charge**

Charge Law: legal code of Orthros Abroad, named for the Prince's Charge. An evolving body of laws established and enforced by the First Prince, based on the Equinox Oath and Hespera's sacred tenets.

charm: physical object imbued with a mage's spell, usually crafted of botanicals or other materials with their own magical properties. Offers a mild beneficial effect to an area or the holder of the charm, even if that person is not a mage.

Chrysanthos: war mage from Cordium with an affinity for fire. As the Dexion of the Aithourian Circle, he is one of the elites in the Order of Anthros. During the Solstice Summit, he tried to sabotage peace talks with hostage negotiations. Now a hostage himself in Solia's custody.

Chuma: daughter of Ukocha and Mumba, beloved and protected by all the Ashes.

the Collector: one of the Old Masters known as the Master of Dreams. Both a necromancer and thelemancer, he possesses his victims and forces them to do his bidding. Using essential displacement, he amasses unnatural amounts of magic of various affinities. The Gift Collectors are his Overseers, willing followers who serve his far-reaching conspiracy to achieve his mysterious ends. His current objective, in alliance with former King Lucis, is to gain entry to the Lustra portal under Solorum Palace.

Cordium: land to the south of Tenebra where the Mage Orders hold sway. Its once-mighty principalities and city-states have now lost power to the magical and religious authorities. Wealthy and cultured, but prone to deadly politics. Also known as the Magelands.

Corona: capital city of Cordium and holy seat of the Mage Orders, where the main temples of each god are located. Also known as the Divine City.

Council of Free Lords: a body of Tenebran lords who have the hereditary authority to convey or revoke the nobility's mandate upon a reigning monarch. Their rights and privileges were established in the Free Charter.

the Craving: a Hesperine's addiction to their Grace's blood. When deprived of each other, Graces suffer agonizing withdrawal symptoms and fatal illness.

Daedala: Prisma of Hagia Zephyra. Ritual firstblood and Gifter of Timarete.

Dalos: Aithourian war mage who disguised himself as a Tenebran and, while possessed by Kallikrates, conspired with King Lucis to assassinate the attendees of the Equinox Summit. When the Hesperines' ward stopped him, the Collector's spells rebounded and killed him.

Dawn Slumber: deep sleep Hesperines fall into when the sun rises. Although the sunlight causes them no harm, they're unable to awaken until nightfall, leaving them vulnerable during daylight hours.

Deukalion: bloodborn firstgift of Apollon and Komnena with a dual affinity for mind magic and light magic. Among the three most powerful Hesperine thelemancers in history. Mentored by Argyros in both magic and diplomacy, his is now one of Orthros's Ambassadors for Tenebran affairs in partnership with his Grace, Cassia. Together, they have revolutionized relations between Orthros, Tenebra, and the Empire, but must now protect their hard-won treaties in a time of war.

Dexion: second highest ranking mage in the Aithourian Circle. See **Chrysanthos**

displacement gate: destructive portal that can be opened by necromancers skilled in essential displacement.

Divine City: see **Corona**

Divine Tongue: language spoken by Hesperines and mages, used for spells, rituals, and magical texts. The common tongue of Orthros, spoken freely by all Hesperines. In Tenebra and Cordium, the mages keep it a secret and disallow non-mages from learning it.

diviner: Imperial theramancer trained in ancient traditions who protects their people from necromancy and communicates with the ancestors. Their ancestral magic enables them to open passages through the spirit phase.

Diviner Queen: theramancer who founded Btana Ayal and the surrounding civilization in the Hulaic Epochs. When she led her followers to the shadowlands through a spirit gate, they taught the people of what would later become Tenebra and Cordium how to use magic. When the Old Masters began to abuse the power they had learned from her, she made the ultimate sacrifice and destroyed everything she had built to contain their evil.

the Drink: when a Hesperine drinks blood from a human or animal. A non-sexual act, considered sacred, which should be carried out with respect for the donor. It's forbidden to take the Drink from an unwilling person. *Or* Hesperine sacred tenet, the commitment to thriving without the death of other living things.

eastern Tenebrae: wilderness east of the settled regions of Tenebra, sparsely populated by homesteads under the leadership of hold lords. Officially under the king's rule, but prone to lawlessness. Hesperines roam freely here.

Ebah: see **Changing Queen**

Eidon: Prismos of Hagia Anatela. Ritual firstblood and Gifter of Argyros.

Eighth Circle: Lio and Cassia's Trial circle. See **Alexandra, Eudokia, Lysandros, Menodora, Telemakhos**

elder firstbloods: the ancient Hesperine founders of Orthros. Gifted by the Ritual firstbloods. See **Apollon, Argyros, Hypatia, Kassandra, Kitharos, Timarete**

the Empire: vast and prosperous human lands located far to the west, across an ocean from Tenebra. Comprises many different languages and cultures united under the Empress. Allied with Orthros and welcoming to Hesperines, many of whom began their mortal lives as Imperial citizens. Historically maintained a strict policy of isolation from Tenebra and Cordium to guard against the Mage Orders, but the Empress now seeks contact on her terms by supporting Solia, her chosen candidate for the Tenebran throne.

the Empress: the ruler of the Empire, admired by her citizens. The Imperial throne has passed down through the female line for many generations.

the Empress's privateers: pirates who sail with the sanction of the Empress, granted by a letter of marque, which authorizes them to rob her enemies. They make voyages to Cordium to secretly pillage the Mage Orders' ships.

enchantment: a spell anchored to a power source, which can last over time with only periodic maintenance from a mage.

envoy: according to common knowledge, a messenger attached to the Hesperine diplomatic service. In fact, envoys are the Queens' spies who gather information from the mortal world to protect Orthros and Hesperines errant. See **Basir, Kumeta**

Equinox Oath: ancient treaty between Orthros and Tenebra, which prescribes the conduct of Hesperines errant and grants them protection from humans. Now modified and expanded by the Solstice Oath and Orthros's alliance with Queen Solia.

Equinox Summit: peace talks in which the Hesperines send ambassadors from Orthros to meet with the King of Tenebra and renew the Equinox Oath. Each mortal king is expected to convene it once upon his accession to the throne.

errant: a Hesperine who has left Orthros to travel through Tenebra doing good deeds for mortals

errant circle: a group of Hesperines who go errant together, forming a strong bond through their adventures.

essential affinities: the four types of magic used by the Ritual firstbloods during the spell that transformed them into Hesperines.

essential displacement: ritual through which necromancers can transfer one person's magic into another or steal it for themselves. This process is one of the the Collector's secrets and the specialty of his Gift Collectors.

Eudias: young war mage from Cordium with an affinity for weather, including lightning. Compelled to join the Aithourian circle due to his magic, he defected during the Solstice Summit to ally with the Hesperines and Tenebrans resisting King Lucis. He and Lio faced the Collector in a mage duel, in which Lio helped him free himself from the Old Master's possession. Now turns his war magic against Queen Solia's enemies. Ariadne's secret love.

Eudokia: Hesperine youngblood, one of Lio's Trial sisters. Solaced from Tenebra as a child. An initiate mathematician, calligrapher, and accomplished scholar with expertise in methodological deconstruction. Daughter of Hypatia.

Eugenia: young Tenebran lady, believed to be Flavian's cousin and heir of his late uncle, Lord Eugenius. She is actually his sister, the daughter of Titus and his concubine Risara. Now a member of Queen Solia's retinue. Secretly returns Benedict's unrequited love.

Eukairia: Prisma of Hagia Notia. Ritual firstblood and Gifter of Ereba.

Eye of Blood: see **Blood Moon**

Eye of Light: see **Light Moon**

familiar: the animal companion of a Hesperine, bound to them by blood. They can assist during spellcasting and remain immortal as long as the Hesperine continues to give them blood.

the Fangs: Prometheus's famous twin swords.

the Feast: Hesperine term for drinking blood while making love.

feuds: bitter conflicts that have raged between the free lords of Tenebra for centuries, which cause widespread destruction and suffering.

First Circle: Rudhira, Nike, and Methu's Trial circle. They were the first Hesperines to go through the Trial of Initiation together and founded the tradition of Trial circles.

First Prince: see **Ioustinianos**

firstblood: the first Hesperine in a bloodline, who founds the family and passes the Gift to their children.

Firstblood Circle: the governing body of Orthros. Every firstblood has a vote on behalf of their bloodline, while non-voting Hesperines can attempt to influence policy by displays of partisanship. The Queens retain veto power, but use it sparingly.

firstgift: the eldest child of a Hesperine bloodline, first to receive the gift from their parents.

Flavian: Tenebran lord, son of Free Lord Titus and heir to Segetia's seat on the Council. Despite his family's feud with Hadria, he is admired by both sides and is a unifying figure for the fractured nobility. After his unsuccessful bid for the throne, he has sworn fealty to Queen Solia and fights alongside Lord Hadrian for her cause.

Florian: see **Chrysanthos**

foregiver: a Hesperine's ancestor who gave the Gift to their bloodline in the past.

fortune name: name given to an Imperial mercenary by which they are professionally known. Traditionally, they take the name of something they wish to avoid in order to ward off that evil.

free lord: highest noble rank in Tenebra. Has a seat on the Council of Free Lords and hereditary authority to vote on whether a king should receive the nobility's mandate.

Genie: see **Eugenia**

geomagical warming plate: a magical device created by a Hesperine with an affinity for geological forces. Emanates heat and can be used for brewing coffee.

get one's fangs polished: Hesperine slang for the Feast.

the Gift: Hesperines' immortality and magical abilities, which they regard as a blessing from the goddess Hespera. The practice of offering the Gift to all is a Hesperine sacred tenet.

Gift Collector: mage-assassin and bounty hunter who hunts down Hesperines for the Order of Hypnos using necromancy, alchemy, and fighting tactics. Known for adapting common items into weapons to skirt the Orders' religious laws against mages arming themselves. They secretly have a higher loyalty to the Collector, the founder of their profession, who calls them his Overseers.

Gift Night: the night of a person's transformation into a Hesperine, usually marked by great celebration.

Gifter: the Hesperine who transforms another, conveying Hespera's Gift to the new immortal. For Hesperines transformed as children, their Gifters are their parents. An adult, if not Gifted by a lover, becomes the Ritual child or Ritual tributary of their Gifter, who remains a lifelong mentor.
Gifting: the transformation from human into Hesperine.
Glasstongue: see **Deukalion**
glyph: sacred symbol of a deity. Each god or goddess in the pantheon has a unique glyph. Often carved on shrines and temples or used as a pattern in spell casting.
glyph stone: the capstone of the doorway of a shrine, inscribed with the glyph of the deity worshiped there, where any spells over the structure are usually seated.
the Goddess's Eyes: the two moons, the red Blood Moon and the white Light Moon. Associated with Hespera and regarded as her gaze by Hesperines.
Grace: Hesperine sacred tenet, a magical bond between two Hesperine lovers. Frees them from the need for human blood and enables them to sustain each other, but comes at the cost of the Craving. A fated bond that happens when their love is true. It is believed every Hesperine has a Grace just waiting to be found. See **Craving**
Grace braids: thin braids of one another's hair that Graces exchange. They wear them privately after professing their bond to one another, then exchange them publicly at their avowal and thereafter wear them for all to see to signify their commitment.
Grace Union: the particularly powerful and intimate Blood Union between two Hesperines who are Graced. Enables them to communicate telepathically and empathically.
Grace-family (Grace-son, Grace-father, Grace-sister, etc.): the family members of a Hesperine's Grace. Compare with human in-laws.
Great Temple Epoch: the historical period when the Great Temples of every cult flourished across Tenebra and Cordium, and all mages cooperated. Came to a cataclysmic end due to the Ordering and the Last War.
Great Temples of Hespera: powerful, thriving temples where mages of Hespera worshiped and worked their magic in peace before they were branded heretics. Razed during the Last War. See **Hagia Anatela**, **Hagia Boreia**, **Hagia Notia**, **Hagia Zephyra**
greater sand cat: species of large predator with special adaptations for surviving the Maaqul Desert. With specialized magic and great effort, they can be bonded to humans and ridden as mounts. See **Tilili**
Guardian of Orthros: see **Hippolyta**
Hadria: domain of Free Lord Hadrian, located on Tenebra's rocky western coast, where the seas are treacherous. Their military might makes them a necessary ally for any monarch hoping to hold the throne of Tenebra.
Lord Hadrian: one of the two most powerful free lords in Tenebra, who commands the fealty of many other free lords and lesser nobles. His family has been feuding with Segetia for generations. Although he served King Lucis

for the greater good of the kingdom, his loyalty was always to Solia, whom he now supports and protects as his rightful queen.

Hagia Anatela: one of the four Great Temples of Hespera that flourished during the Great Temple Epoch, located in the eastern part of the continent. When the Orders attacked it during the Last War, Argyros held off their forces with thelemancy, enabling Hypatia to evacuate the residents and save the library. See **Eidon, Ourania**

Hagia Boreia: one of the four Great Temples of Hespera that flourished during the Great Temple Epoch, located in the northern part of the continent, where Apollon became the first Hesperine to receive the Gift from a Ritual firstblood. The final temple to fall during the Ordering, where the surviving Hespera worshipers made their last stand. See **Alea, Anastatios**

Hagia Notia: the southernmost of the four Great Temples of Hespera that flourished during the Great Temple Epoch, located in Corona, where the mages of Hespera once co-existed with the mages of other gods. The first temple to be razed during the Last War in an unprovoked, surprise attack by the Order of Anthros. Only Phaedros survived. See **Khariton, Eukairia**

Hagia Zephyra: one of the four Great Temples of Hespera that flourished during the Great Temple Epoch, located in the western part of the continent. During the Ordering, the mortals in the temple turned on their Hesperine leaders and agreed to surrender them to the Aithourian Circle, but the war mages spared neither humans nor immortals. Kitharos, Timarete, and Astrapas were among the small group of Hesperines and loyal mortals who escaped. See **Daedala, Thelxinos**

Haima: capital city of Orthros Notou.

haima: blood magic. It is a subject of debate whether it is its own paradigm of magic or a blend of mageia and manteia.

Hammer of the Sun: Apollon's famous battle hammer, which he wielded while Abroad with the Blood Errant. He left it in Tenebra when he brought Komnena to Orthros, and Rudhira now keeps it at Castra Justa.

harlot's kiss: Tenebran and Cordian name for roses which, as Hespera's sacred flower, are forbidden to be grown there.

Healing Sanctuary: infirmary in Orthros founded and run by Queen Soteira, where humans are given care and Hesperines are trained in the healing arts.

heart bow: traditional gesture of devotion to the Queens of Orthros, a deep bow with one hand over the heart.

heart hunters: warbands of Tenebrans who hunt down Hesperines, regarded by their countrymen as protectors of humanity. They patrol the northern border of Tenebra with packs of liegehounds, waiting to attack Hesperines who leave Orthros.

Hedera: see **Changing Queen**

hedge warlocks, hedge witch: practitioner of Tenebran nature arts, including herbalism and remnants of Lustra magic.

Hespera: goddess of night cast from the Tenebran and Cordian pantheon. The Mage Orders have declared her worship heresy punishable by death.

Hesperines keep her cult alive and continue to revere her as the goddess of the moons, Sanctuary, and Mercy. Associated with roses, thorns, and fanged creatures. According to myth, she is the sister of Anthros and Hypnos.

Hespera's Gift: Hesperines' immortality and magical abilities, which they regard as a blessing from the goddess Hespera. The practice of offering the Gift to all is a Hesperine sacred tenet.

Hespera's Rose: the most sacred symbol of the Hesperines, a rose with five petals and five thorns representing Hespera's sacred tenets. Frequently embroidered on clothing or represented in stained glass windows. Based on real roses, which are the Goddess's sacred flower and beloved by Hesperines. The mages uproot them wherever they're found in Tenebra or Cordium and punish those who grow them for heresy.

Hesperine: nocturnal immortal being with fangs who gains nourishment from drinking blood. Tenebrans and Cordians believe them to be monsters bent on humanity's destruction. In truth, they follow a strict moral code in the name of their goddess, Hespera, and wish only to ease humankind's suffering.

Hesperite: human worshiper of Hespera, persecuted as a heretic by the Orders.

hex: a circle of six necromancers who exchange magical secrets and punish any who betray them.

Hierax Temple: temple built by the Mage King on the site of his decisive battle that halted Cordium's invasion of Tenebra during the Last War. Long before his reign, Lustri worshiped there.

Hippolyta: Lio's aunt, Graced to Argyros, mother of Nike, Kadi, and Mak. The greatest of Hesperine warriors, a founder of Orthros and powerful warder. Known as the Guardian of Orthros for her deeds during the Last War and for establishing the Stand.

Hippolyta's Stand: Orthros's standing army, founded by Hippolyta. Under her leadership, they patrol the border with Tenebra as Stewards of the Queens' ward. So few of the peaceful Hesperines take up the battle arts that the only Stewards are Nike, Kadi, Alkaios, Nephalea, Mak, and Lyros.

hold lord: Tenebran lord who holds a homestead in the eastern Tenebrae.

House Annassa: the residence of the Queens of Orthros, the Hesperine counterpart to a royal palace.

House Komnena: Lio's family home in Orthros, seat of his bloodline, named for his mother.

Hoyete: mercenary illusionist and master fencer, member of the Ashes. Of Owia descent, he is an alumnus of Imperial University's School of Fine Arts and a playwright favored by the Empress.

hulaia: lustra magic, the paradigm of magic that channels from nature. Includes affinities such as plant magic, beast magic, and soothsaying.

Hulaic Epochs: eras of pre-history before the Great Temple Epoch, known only through oral traditions.

the Hunger: a combination of sexual desire and the need for blood, which Hesperines experience with their lovers.

Huru: Ziara's first mate and lover, a knife expert and theramancer.

Hypatia: an elder firstblood and founder of Orthros from Hagia Anatela, mother of Kia. Orthros's greatest astronomer, who invented the Hesperine calendar.

Hypnos: god of death and dreams in the Tenebran and Cordian pantheon. Winter is considered his season. Humans unworthy of going to Anthros's Hall are believed to spend the afterlife in Hypnos's realm of the dead. According to myth, he is the brother of Anthros and Hespera.

Imperial University: illustrious university in the Empire. Only students with wealth and the best references gain entry, usually those of noble or royal blood. Known for traditionalism and conservative approaches to research.

In Sanctuary: Hesperine term for the current historical era, marked from the date of Orthros's founding.

initiate: Hesperine who has achieved initiate rank in their craft or service, more advanced than a student but not yet of full rank. Attained after the young Hesperine completes a significant crafting project or research treatise that meets with their mentor's approval.

Ioustin *or* **Ioustinianos**: First Prince of the Hesperines, eldest child of the Queens of Orthros. Lio's Ritual father. Solaced from Tenebra as a child. Once a warrior in the Blood Errant known as the Blood-Red Prince, he now leads the Charge. Young Hesperines call him Rudhira, an affectionate name given to him by Methu.

Iris: Tenebran lady, Solia's handmaiden and closest companion, who sacrificed her life for Solia at the Siege of Sovereigns.

Iulios: royal firstblood and seventh prince of Orthros, the seventh child and youngest son of the Queens. An accomplished historian who founded a museum with his Grace, a former Imperial prince.

ivy pendant: wooden pendant carved with a triquetra of ivy. An artifact of the Changing Queen secretly passed down by the women of her line. Thalia entrusted it to Solia so she could give it to Cassia.

Javed: Lio's Grace-cousin, avowed to Kadi, father of Bosko and Thenie. From the Empire in his mortal life. Has an affinity for healing and now serves in Orthros's Healing Sanctuary.

jinn: immortal beings that dwell in the Maaqul Desert. Unlike Hesperines, they were never human. Endowed with powerful magic drawn from elements of nature, they also have a connection with the spirit phase. A long history of conflict between jinn and Imperial humans culminated in the Thousand Fires War and ended with the Desert Accord.

Justinian: see **Ioustinianos**

Kadi: see **Arkadia**

kaetlii: word in the tongue used by Tenebrans to train liegehounds, meaning the person the dog is bonded to and will protect until death.

Kalos: the Charge's best scout, who uses his beast magic to track Hesperines errant who are missing in action. A heart hunter in his mortal life, he tried to mitigate his warband's cruelty. When they turned on him, Rudhira saved his life and gave him the Gift. He was the only Hesperine Lustra mage until Cassia's Gifting.

kalux: Hesperine word in the Divine Tongue for clitoris.

Karege: Hesperine warrior and member of the Ashes. Offered Sanctuary by Princess Konstantina five centuries ago, he prefers to spend his immortality adventuring and earning gold in the Empire, rather than fulfilling his duties as an elder in Orthros.

Kassandra: Lio's Ritual mother, an elder firstblood and founder of Orthros. Ritual sister to the Queens, who Gifted her, and mother of Prometheus. A princess in her mortal life, she abdicated during a dynastic dispute and became the first Hesperine from the Empire, securing her homeland's alliance with Orthros. Now the Queens' Master Economist who oversees Orthros's trade. Has the gift of foresight and, as Orthros's oracle, guides the Hesperines with her prophecies.

Kella: Azarqi princess, daughter of Hinan, and Ukocha's successor as first blade of the Ashes. A fierce warrior with a preference for daggers, as well as a water mage skilled at desert survival. Bonded to her greater sand cat mount, Tilili, after her legs were amputated above the knee due to a combat injury.

Khariton: Prismos of Hagia Notia. Ritual firstblood and Gifter of Phaedros.

Kia: see **Eudokia**

King of Tenebra: see **Lucis**

Kings and Mages: Tenebran and Cordian name for the game Hesperines call Prince and Diplomat.

Kitharos: elder firstblood and founder of Orthros from Hagia Zephyra, Gifted by Thelxinos. Father of Nodora and one of the Hesperines' greatest musicians.

Knight: Cassia's beloved liegehound. Solia gave him to Cassia as a puppy so Cassia would have protection and companionship.

Knightly Order of Andragathos: holy warriors who adhere to a strict moral code and persecute Hesperines in the name of their patron god. See **Andragathos**

Komnena: Lio's mother, still young by Hesperines standards. Fled a life of squalor as a Tenebran farmwife and ran away to Orthros with Apollon, who Gifted her while she was pregnant and raised her son as his own. Now a respected mind healer. As the Queens' Chamberlain, she is responsible for helping newcomers to Orthros settle and adjust.

Kona *or* **Konstantina**: royal firstblood, Second Princess of Orthros, the second child and eldest daughter of the Queens. From the Empire in her mortal life. As the Royal Master Magistrate, she is the author of Orthros's legal code and an influential politician who oversees the proceedings of the Firstblood Circle. Also the leading rose gardener in the Circle of Rosarians.

krana: Hesperine term in the Divine Tongue for vagina.

Kumeta: Hesperine light mage and one of the two spymasters of Orthros, alongside her Grace, Basir. From the Empire in her mortal life. Her official title is "Queens' Master Envoy" to conceal the nature of their work.

Kyria: goddess of weaving and the harvest in the Tenebran and Cordian pantheon, known as the Mother Goddess or the Wife. Her season is autumn. According to myth, she is married to Anthros.

the Last War: the cataclysmic violence sparked by the Ordering sixteen hundred years ago. When the Order of Anthros sought to suppress all resistance to their authority, magical and armed conflict ravaged Tenebra and Cordium, destroying the civilization of the Great Temple Epoch. Peace came at the cost of the Hesperines' exile and the Order of Anthros's victory, while the Mage King secured his rule in Tenebra.

letting site: a location where Lustra mages can channel the most power from the wilds. These ritual sites were created by the Silvicultrixes in ancient times to release magic from nature for their use.

liegehound: war dogs bred and trained by Tenebrans to track, hunt, and slay Hesperines. Veil spells do not throw them off the scent, and they can leap high enough to pull a levitating Hesperine from the air. The only animals that do not trust Hesperines. They live longer than other canines and can withstand poison and disease.

Light Moon: Hesperine name for one of the two moons, which appears white with a smooth texture. Believed to be an eye of the Goddess Hespera, shining with her light.

Lio: see **Deukalion**

Lion of Orthros: see **Apollon**

Lonesome: Hoyefe's fortune name.

Lucian: see **Mage King**

Lucis: former King of Tenebra, who reigned with ruthlessness and brutality. Born a lord, he secured the crown by might and political schemes, and he upheld his authority by any means necessary. Cassia has never forgiven him for his cruelty to her, Solia, and Thalia. Deposed when Solia secured the mandate of the free lords, he refuses to acknowledge her rule and makes war on her and her Hesperine allies with support from the Mage Orders.

the Lustra: the wilds of Tenebra, source of Lustra magic.

Lustra magic: The old nature magic of Tenebra practiced in ancient times by the Changing Queen. The Orders have never been able to understand or control it, and most knowledge of it is now lost. See **hulaia**

Lustri: the ancient peoples of Tenebra who practiced Lustra magic, led by priestess-queens known as Silvictulrixes, such as the Changing Queen.

Lyros *or* **Lysandros**: Lio's Trial brother and Grace-cousin, avowed to Mak, with whom he serves in the Stand as a warder and warrior. Spent his mortal childhood as a pickpocket on the streets of Namenti. Although Solaced by Timarete and Astrapas, he proved more suited to the battle arts than the fine arts.

Lyta: see **Hippolyta**

Maaqul Desert: a vast and treacherous desert the size of several states in the Empire. Few besides the jinn and the Azarqi nomads can survive here.

Mage King: King Lucian of Tenebra, who reigned sixteen hundred years ago, widely considered by Hesperines and mortals to have been a great monarch. He and his wife, the Changing Queen, made the original Equinox Oath with the Queens of Orthros. A fire mage and warrior, he resisted the Mage Orders' mandate that men must choose between wielding spells or weapons.

Mage Orders: the magical and religious authorities in Cordium, which also dictate sacred law to Tenebran temples. Responsible for training and governing mages and punishing heretics.

mageia: magery, the paradigm of magic that affects the physical world. Includes elemental affinities such as fire, water, and stone magic.

Magelands: see **Cordium**

Mak: see **Telemakhos**

manteia: sorcery, the paradigm of magic that affects thought, emotion, and life force. Includes affinities such as mind magic and necromancy.

Martyrs' Pass: the only known passage to Orthros through the Umbral Mountains. When an army of heart hunters possessed by the Collector ambushed the Tenebran embassy here, Lio defeated them with his mind magic and rescued Cassia.

Matsu: Nodora's Ritual mother and the only other Hesperine from the Archipelagos. A beloved thespian and fashion leader in Orthros.

Mederi Village: a small farming village near Patria, known for its loyalty to Solia's memory.

Menodora: Hesperine youngblood, one of Lio's Trial sisters. Daughter of Kitharos and Dakarai. An initiate musician, admired vocalist, and crafter of musical instruments. She is one of only two Hesperines from the Archipelagos and the immortal expert on the music of her mortal homeland.

Mercy: Hesperine sacred tenet, the practice of caring for dead or dying humans.

methodological deconstruction: an application of magic by which a scholar can use observation and deduction to reverse charms and spells by mages of other affinities.

Methu: see **Prometheus**

mind healer: see **theramancer**

mind mage: see **thelemancer**

mind ward: mental defense cast by a thelemancer, which protects a person's mind from mages seeking to invade their thoughts or subdue their Will.

Miranda: the Collector's youngest but most fanatical Overseer, formerly a lady of Paradum and Cassia's best friend. When Cassia betrayed Miranda, she became a Gift Collector and stole Cassia's magic for Kallikrates.

Monsoon: Tendeso's fortune name.

moon hours: by the Hesperine clock, the hours corresponding to night, when Hesperines pursue public activities.

moskos: Hesperine term in the Divine Tongue meaning testicles.

Mumba: Cifwani farmer, husband of Ukocha and father of Chuma.

mundane: unmagical, as opposed to arcane.

Muse of Orthros: Hesperine whose service is music, dancing, or poetry.

Namenti: Tenebran coastal city on the southern border, near Cordium.

natural phase: the physical world where living creatures exist, as opposed to the afterlife. See **spirit phase**

Neana: Azad's Grace, Gifted by him and now serving as a Hesperine errant in the Prince's Charge.

Nephalea: one of the three Hesperines errant who saved Cassia as a child. She and her Grace, Alkaios, recently settled in Orthros after years as Hesperines errant with his Gifter, Nike.

newgift: a newly transformed Hesperine or a person who has decided to become immortal and awaits their Gifting.

Night Call: magical summons a Hesperine elder can perform on a younger immortal to prematurely break them out of the Dawn Slumber.

Nike: see **Pherenike**

Nodora: see **Menodora**

Noon Watch: Karege's fortune name.

nyakimbi: means "little sister" in Sandira

the Old Masters: the oldest known hex of necromancers in Tenebran and Cordian record. Little is known about them from legends and surviving ancient texts, but their influence is linked to catastrophic events and suffering throughout history. They extend their lives and hoard power using abusive magic such as essential displacement. See **the Collector**

ora: strong Sandira liquor.

the Oracle: see **Kassandra**

Order of Anthros: Mage Order dedicated to the god Anthros, which holds the ultimate religious and magical authority over all other Orders and temples. Bent on destroying Hesperines. War mages, light mages, and warders serve in this Order, as do agricultural and stone mages.

Order of Hypnos: Mage Order devoted to Hypnos, which holds authority over necromancers, mind mages, and illusionists. Oversees rites for the dead, purportedly to prevent Hesperine grave robbing, but in practice to stop rogue necromancers from raising the dead. The Order of Anthros's closest ally in their effort to destroy Hesperines.

the Ordering: historical event over sixteen hundred years ago, when the Order of Anthros came to prominence and enforced its doctrines upon all other cults, who had previously worshiped and practiced magic freely. New mandates forbade warriors from practicing magic and required all mages to enter temples and remain celibate. The war mages also branded all Hespera worshipers heretics and destroyed their temples. The Ordering caused the Last War and the end of the Great Temple Epoch.

the Orders: see **Mage Orders**

Orthros: homeland of the Hesperines, ruled by the Queens. The Mage Orders describe it as a horrific place where no human can survive, but in reality, it is a land of peace, prosperity, and culture.

Orthros Abroad: the population of Hesperines who are errant in Tenebra at any given time. Under the jurisdiction of the First Prince, who is the Queens' regent outside their ward.

Orthros Boreou: Hesperine homeland in the northern hemisphere, located north of and sharing a border with Tenebra.

Orthros Notou: Hesperine homeland in the southern hemisphere, located across the sea to the southeast of the Empire.

Orthros Warmbloods: unique horse breed developed by Hippolyta. Hesperine blood magic gives them intelligence, strength, and longevity superior to mundane horses.

Ourania: Prisma of Hagia Anatela. Ritual firstblood and Gifter of Hypatia.

Overseer: see **Gift Collector**

Owia: the dynasty that currently holds the throne of the Empire.

Pakhne: a mage of Kyria who traveled to Orthros for the Solstice Summit along with Ariadne. Miranda later possessed Pakhne so Kallikrates could use her against Cassia and Lio. When Lio freed Pakhne's mind, the Collector stole her magic, leaving her powerless and suffering.

paradigm: a major pattern of magic, consisting of a set of affinities that follow the same rules and affect related aspects of reality. See **haima**, **hulaia**, **mageia**, **manteia**, **progonaia**.

Paradum: a hunting estate of the King of Tenebra, located near Patria. When Cassia was fourteen, the king sent her to live there with Miranda's family. Kallikrates stole her magic there, damaging the letting site beneath the castle.

Patria: a domain in Tenebra, the traditional location for the Council of Free Lords to gather each time they must grant their mandate to a new monarch.

Peanut: Tuura's fortune name.

Perita: Cassia's handmaiden and dearest friend who accompanied her to Orthros for the Solstice Summit and assisted with all her schemes. Now the handmaiden of Lady Sabina, Lord Hadrian's daughter, and involved in Solia's cause.

Phaedros: brilliant scholar from ancient times, among the first mages of Hespera to receive the Gift. The only survivor of Hagia Notia's destruction by the Aithourian Circle. When he took revenge against the mortals, he forfeited his status as an elder firstblood. Now lives in eternal exile under the midnight sun.

Pherenike: Lio's cousin, a warder and warrior like her mother, Lyta, and one of the three most powerful Hesperine thelemancers like her father, Argyros. Solaced from Tenebra as a child. Known as the Victory Star, one of the Blood Errant alongside her uncle, Apollon, and her Trial brothers Rudhira and Methu. After the surviving Blood Errant's campaign to avenge Methu, she remained Abroad alone, missing in action for over ninety years. Recently returned to Orthros to once again serve in the Stand.

plant magic: type of Lustra magic that grants the power to make plants grow.

Prince and Diplomat: board game and beloved Hesperine pastime; requires strategy and practice to master.

Prince's Charge: the force of Hesperines errant who serve under the First Prince.

Prisma: highest ranking female mage in a temple.

privateers: see **Empress's Privateers**

progonaia: ancestral magic, the paradigm of magic that is channeled from the spirit phase. Includes Imperial affinities such as divination.

Prometheus: legendary Hesperine warrior and martyr. Bloodborn to Kassandra and descendant of Imperial royalty. Known as the Midnight Champion, he was a member of the Blood Errant with his comrades Nike, Rudhira, and Apollon. Captured by the Aithourian Circle before Lio's birth. Orthros mourns his death, although his mother has prophesied of his return.

Pup: Solia's childhood nickname for Cassia.

pyromagus: mage with an affinity for fire.

Queen Mothers: matriarchs from each sister state within the Empire who possess the sacred artifacts that symbolize power to their particular people. Each Imperial dynasty must secure their blessings in order to reign.

the Queens: the Hesperine monarchs of Orthros. See **Alea**, **Soteira**

the Queens' ward: the powerful Sanctuary ward cast by the Queens, which spans the borders of Orthros, protecting Hesperines from human threats.

Redblood: in an avowal ceremony, the Hesperine welcoming their Grace into their bloodline and granting their partner a new blood name.

resonance: when a mage draws power from magical reserves within themselves, which resonate with certain aspects of the spiritual or physical, such as the mind or fire. Manteia and mageia rely on resonance.

revelatory spell: one of the Anthrian mages' specialized spells for revealing hidden Hesperines.

rhabdos: Hesperine term in the Divine Tongue meaning penis.

rimelace: flowering herb that requires extremely cold conditions. Difficult to grow in Tenebra, even with the aid of magic, but thrives in Orthros. The only known treatment for frost fever.

Ritual: Hesperine sacred tenet. A ceremony in which Hesperines share blood, but in a broader sense, the whole of their religious beliefs.

Ritual circle: area where Hesperines gather to perform Ritual, usually marked with sacred symbols on the floor.

Ritual firstbloods: the eight blood mages who performed the Ritual that created Hesperines. As the leaders of the Great Temples of Hespera, all except Alea were martyred during the Ordering. See **Alea**, **Anastasios**, **Daedala**, **Eidon**, **Eukairia**, **Khariton**, **Ourania**, **Thelxinos**

Ritual hall: central chamber in Hesperine homes where the bloodline's Ritual circle is located.

Ritual parents: Hesperines who attend a new immortal's first Ritual and remain their mentors for eternity. Comparable to Tenebran temple parents.

Ritual Sanctuary: innermost chamber of a shrine or temple of Hespera, where sacred rituals were performed by mages.

Ritual separation: eight nights that Hesperine Graces must spend apart to demonstrate their Craving symptoms and prove their bond to their people; required before avowal.

Ritual tapestry: tapestry crafted by Kassandra for a new Hesperine to commemorate their Gifting, into which she weaves prophecies about their immortal destiny.

Ritual tributary: Hesperine who establishes their own bloodline rather than joining their Gifter's family.

royal firstbloods: the Queens' children, who are to establish their own bloodlines in order to share the Annassa's power with their people.

Rudhira: see **Ioustinianos**
Sanctuary: Hesperine sacred tenet, the practice of offering refuge to anyone in need. *Or* Hesperine refuge in hostile territory, concealed and protected from humans by Sanctuary magic.
Sanctuary mage: a mage with a rare dual affinity for warding and light magic, who can create powerful protections that also conceal. Queen Alea of Orthros is the only mage with this affinity who survived the Orders' persecution of Hespera worshipers.
Sanctuary Rose: a variety of white rose that originated in the Great Temples of Hespera. The only vine that survived the Last War now grows in Princess Konstantina's greenhouse, and she has propagated it throughout Orthros. Traditionally, each person who requests Sanctuary is given one of these blooms in welcome.
Sanctuary ward: ward created by a Sanctuary mage, which can both protect and hide those within it. Strong Sanctuary wards require the caster to remain inside the boundaries of the spell. Should the mage die there, their sacrifice will increase the ward's power and sustain it indefinitely.
Sandira Kingdom: powerful sister state that controls the flow of gold, ivory, and copper between the Kwatzi City-States and the Empire's interior. Ruled by hereditary shifters whose animal forms signify their status within the hierarchy of warriors, nobility, or royalty.
Sea of Komne: the sea that separates mainland Orthros from the landmass where Tenebra and Cordium are located.
Segetia: domain of Free Lord Titus, landlocked and known for its fertile hills.
Selas: capital city of Orthros Boreou.
Severin *or* **Severinus the Younger**: son and heir of Severinus the Elder, a free lord known for persecuting Hesperines. Severin persuaded his father to support Solia and her Hesperine allies in spite of his prejudice. Hoyefe's lover.
shadowlands: Imperial term for Tenebra and Cordium, sometimes used with pity or disdain.
shifter: a person of Sandira descent who is blessed by their ancestors with the ability to shapeshift. Sandira shifters take on the form of a particular animal with which their clan has cultivated a sacred bond over many generations.
Siege of Sovereigns: King Lucis's assault on Castra Roborra, where rebel free lords held Solia for ransom. Ended the rebellion and resulted in the death of every living thing in the fortress.
Silvertongue: see **Argyros**
Silvicultrix: a Lustra sorceress with the triune affinity for beast magic, plant magic, and soothsaying. They ruled the Lustri as priestess-queens in ancient times, and one ascended to the throne of Tenebra as the Changing Queen. They have nearly died out, and Silvicultrixes like Thalia and Cassia are extraordinarily rare in the present day.
sister states: independent lands within the Empire ruled by their own monarchs, all owing allegiance to the Empress. She is seen as their eldest sister, and they are symbolically members of her clan.

Skleros: master necromancer and Gift Collector who holds the Order of Hypnos's record for completing the most bounties on Hesperines. Expert in essential displacement who helped the Collector cause devastation during the Solstice Summit. After Cassia and Lio's escape from Miranda at Paradum, he tried to apprehend them, but Rudhira beheaded him.

Slumber: see **Dawn Slumber**

Solace: Hesperine sacred tenet, the practice of rescuing and Gifting abandoned children.

Solia: the new Queen of Tenebra, former King Lucis's legitimate daughter, who wrested the free lords' mandate from him and now seeks to defeat him in a civil war. When she was princess, Lucis left her for dead at the Siege of Sovereigns, but she escaped to the Empire with the help of the privateers. After fighting with the Ashes for several years, she won the Battle of Souls tournament, earning the Empress's support for her overthrow of King Lucis. The love of Tendeso's life, Solia broke his heart when she chose to return to Tenebra.

Solorum: ancestral capital of Tenebra, royal seat of the king.

Solorum Palace: oldest palace in Tenebra, built by the Mage King, still the most important royal residence for the King of Tenebra.

Solstice Summit: diplomatic negotiations between Tenebra and Orthros that marked the first time a mortal embassy from Tenebra ever entered Hesperine lands. An unprecedented event proposed by Lio in an effort to prevent war and make it possible for Cassia to stay with him.

soothsayer: Lustra mage with the affinity for soothsaying, which gives them the power to influence others' thoughts and choices with their words.

Soteira: one of the two Queens of Orthros, who has ruled the Hesperines for nearly sixteen hundred years with her Grace, Alea. Originally from the Empire, she was a powerful mortal mage with an affinity for healing and theramancy before leaving to found Orthros alongside Alea.

speires: symbolic hair ties Lyta gives to trainees when they begin learning the battle arts. Stewards wear them as part of their Stand regalia.

spirit gate: a portal that allows magical travel by opening a passage through the spirit phase. Imperial diviners maintain regulated spirit gates throughout the Empire and Orthros Notou.

spirit phase: the spiritual plane of existence where the ancestors dwell, where living souls originate and to which they return in the afterlife. See **natural phase**

the Stand: see **Hippolyta's Stand**

Standstill: Kella's fortune name

stepping: innate Hesperine ability to teleport instantly from one place to another with little magical effort.

Steward: see **Hippolyta's Stand**

suckling: Hesperine child.

Sun Market: bazaar on the island of Marijani in the Empire, renowned for its wonders.

Sun Temple: see **Temple of Anthros at Solorum**

sunbound: mild Hesperine curse word.
Sunburn: Solia's fortune name.
Telemakhos: Lio's cousin, best friend, and Trial brother. Exposed as a child in Tenebra due to a club foot, Solaced by Argyros and Lyta. A warrior by profession and warder by affinity, he serves in the Stand. He and his Grace, Lyros, are newly avowed.
Temple of Kyria at Solorum: most influential and respected temple of Kyria in Tenebra, located near the royal palace. The Prisma was a friend and ally of Cassia's when she was in Tenebra.
Temple of Anthros at Solorum: temple in Tenebra's capital, once an ancient site of outdoor Anthros worship that was later walled and roofed by kings. The temple of the royal mage, where the king and his court attend rites.
Tendeso: Prince of the Sandira Kingdom and brother of King Anesu. After the ancestors passed over him and gave his brother the throne, he fought with the Ashes under the name Monsoon. Solia's lover for eight years until she defeated him in the Battle of Souls and chose her duty to Tenebra over him.
Tenebra: human kingdom south of Orthros and north of Cordium. Agrarian, feudal society, prone to instability due to rivalries between lords. Land of the Hesperines' origin, where they are now persecuted. Civil war has recently broken out as Tenebra's new Queen Solia fights to defeat Lucis, the former tyrant king.
Thalia: Cassia's mother, believed to be merely Lucis's concubine. In truth, a Silvicultrix descended from the Changing Queen. Born in Cordium, where she became a powerful mage of Kyria, she was forced out of her temple when her triune affinity manifested. She chose to join Lucis in Tenebra to escape the Mage Orders and make her own secret bid for the throne.
thelemancer: a mage with an affinity for thelemancy, or mind magic, which gives them the power to manipulate others' thoughts and control their Wills.
Thelxinos: Prismos of Hagia Zephyra. Ritual firstblood and Gifter of Kitharos.
Thenie: see **Athena**
theramancer: a person with an affinity for theramancy, or mind healing, who can use magic to treat mental illness.
the Thirst: a Hesperine's need to drink blood, a non-sexual urge like a human's need to drink water or eat food.
Thorn: Rudhira's two-handed sword, which he carried as one of the Blood Errant and now wields as he leads the Charge.
Tilili: greater sand cat bonded to Kella who serves as her mount and partner in combat.
Timarete: elder firstblood and founder of Orthros from Hagia Zephyra, Gifted by Daedala. Mother of Lyros and one of the Hesperines' greatest painters.
traversal: teleportation ability of Tenebran and Cordian mages. Requires a great expense of magic and usually leaves the mortal mage seriously ill.
Trial circle: age set of Hesperines who go through the Trial of Initiation together. They consider each other Trial sisters and brothers for the rest of their immortal lives. Although not related by birth or blood, they maintain strong

bonds of loyalty and friendship for eternity.

Trial *or* **Trial of Initiation**: Hesperine rite of passage marking an immortal's transition into adulthood.

triune affinity: the combination of three powerful types of Lustra magic: plant magic, beast magic, and soothsaying. See **Silvicultrix**

triune focus: a set of three artifacts required by a Silvicultrix to control the vast amount of magic she channels from the Lustra. Ancient Silvicultrixes used their foci to create letting sites.

Tuura: mercenary theramancer, the Ashes' diviner and alchemist.

Ukocha: retired leader of the Ashes, a swordswoman and fire mage who inspires awe among mercenaries. Mother of Chuma and wife of Mumba.

Umbral Mountains: mountain range spanning the border between Tenebra and Orthros.

unified duality: a rare type of affinity in which a mage's two magical abilities combine to form an even more powerful hybrid. Compare with a dual affinity, in which the mage's two abilities remain distinct.

Union: Hesperine sacred tenet, the principle of living with empathy and compassion for all. See **Blood Union**

veil hours: by the Hesperine clock, the hours corresponding to day, when Hesperines Slumber or devote their private time to friends, family, and lovers.

veil hours robe: Hesperine garment worn during veil hours, only in the presence of those with whom a Hesperine has a close relationship.

veil spell: innate Hesperine ability to cast magical concealments that hide their presence and activities from humans or fellow immortals.

Victory Star: see **Pherenike**

Vigil of Thorns: five nights of meditation during the Hesperine Winter Solstice observances. Each vigil is dedicated to a thorn of Hespera's Rose, representing the Hesperines' sacred duties. See **Mercy**, **Solace**, **Will**, **Union**, **Gift**

war mage: person with an affinity for fire, lightning, or other type of magic that can be weaponized. The Order of Anthros requires them to dedicate their lives to the Aithourian Circle.

warder: mage with an affinity for warding, the power to create magical protections that block spells or physical attacks.

Waystar: Hesperine fortress, Orthros's first refuge for those crossing the border from Tenebra. Hesperines errant who use weapons must leave their armaments here before crossing the Sea of Komne to Selas.

Whiteblood: in an avowal ceremony, the Hesperine joining their Grace's bloodline and taking a new blood name.

Will: free will, willpower. *Or* Hesperine sacred tenet, the principle of guarding the sanctity of each person's freedom of choice.

Winter Solstice: the most sacred time of the Hesperine year, when they celebrate Hespera with the sacred Festival of the Rose and Vigil of Thorns.

Wisdom's Precipice: a tall cliff in Orthros with a treacherous drop to the rocky sea below. When Mak, Lyros, and Lio were newbloods, they jumped off in the hopes of awakening their power of levitation, only to fall and suffer painful injuries.

Xandra: see **Alexandra**

youngblood: young adult Hesperine who has recently reached their majority by passing the Trial of Initiation.

Ziara: one of the most accomplished of the Empress's Privateers, famed for her powerful wind magic and daring voyages to Cordium. Captain of the Wanted, which she sails with her first mate and lover, Huru, and their all-woman crew.

Zoe *or* **Zosime**: Lio's little sister, an eight-year-old Eriphite child Solaced by Apollon and Komnena. Loves her new family and idolizes Lio and Cassia for their roles in saving her from Tenebra. Still healing from the emotional wounds she suffered as a mortal.

Blood Ritual
Blood Grace Book IX

Join Cassia on her quest to restore Lio's voice in Blood Grace Book 9, *Blood Ritual*. Book description and pre-orders coming soon!

Sign up here to receive an email when the next book is available. You will only get notified about the Book 9 pre-order and release. No newsletter subscription required.

vroth.co/ritual

Get free books about characters from the world of Blood Grace!

Are you excited to read more books about the Hesperines - for free? Get bonus stories about Cassia and Lio as well as other characters from their world when you sign up for Vela's newsletter!

From dangerous adventures with Hesperines errant to cozy coffee dates on the docks of Orthros, new and familiar couples find Grace or fall deeper in love in these spicy reads.

Some stories are only available for a limited time, so be sure to check out the current selection of freebies before they're gone.

Read the free books here:
vroth.co/free

Immersive Fantasy ✦ Eternal Romance

VELA ROTH manifested unstable writing powers at a young age, and many of her early experiments had unintended results. As she grew, a curriculum of fantasy novels with strong heroines helped her learn to control and wield her abilities.

Eventually she dared pursue the knowledge inside the most forbidden tomes: romance novels. She's been practicing the dark arts of fantasy romance ever since, but strives to use her noveling powers only for good.

She lives in a solar-powered writer's garret at the foot of the mountains with her familiar, a rescue cat with a missing fang and a huge heart.

Vela loves hearing from readers and hopes you'll visit her at velaroth.com, where you can find her social media links or get signed books and swag at her shop, the Moon Market.